Cynthia Harrod-Eagles was born and educated in Shepherd's Bush, and had a variety of jobs in the commercial world, starting as a junior cashier at Woolworth's and working her way down to Pensions Officer at the BBC. She won the Young Writers' Award in 1973, and became a full-time writer in 1978. She is the author of over sixty successful novels to date, including twenty-nine volumes of the *Morland Dynasty* series.

Visit the author's website at www.cynthiaharrodeagles.com

CYNTHIA HARROD-EAGLES

The Third Bill Slider Omnibus

Shallow Grave
Blood Sinister

sphere

SPHERE

This omnibus edition first published in Great Britain
by Sphere in 2007

The Third Bill Slider Omnibus Copyright ©
Cynthia Harrod-Eagles 2007

Shallow Grave Copyright © 1998 Cynthia Harrod-Eagles
Blood Sinister Copyright © 1999 Cynthia Harrod-Eagles

The moral right of the author has been asserted.

A CIP catalogue record for this book
is available from the British Library.

ISBN-13: 978-0-7515-3948-6

Typeset in Amasis by Palimpsest Book Production Limited,
Grangemouth, Stirlingshire
Printed and bound in Great Britain by
Mackays of Chatham Ltd, Chatham, Kent

Sphere
An imprint of
Little, Brown Book Group
Brettenham House
Lancaster Place
London WC2E 7EN

A Member of the Hachette Livre Group of Companies

www.littlebrown.co.uk

Contents

Shallow Grave

For Tony, my accessory before and after

CHAPTER ONE

Eheu Fugaces, Postume

The Old Rectory, St Michael Square, on the Mimpriss Estate, was the sort of house Slider would have given anything to own.

'On a copper's pay? Your anything wouldn't even make a down payment,' Atherton said.

Slider shrugged. 'What's a man without a dream?'

'Solvent,' said Atherton.

It was a long house, built of stone, whose façade reflected three different periods. The middle section had the perfect proportions of classical Georgian domestic, with a fanlighted door and small-paned sash windows disposed harmoniously about it. To the right was an early-Victorian addition, very plain, with tall, large-paned sashes. The section to the left seemed much older: the stone was undressed and uneven, the windows casements, and at the far end were two pairs of double wooden doors like those of an old-fashioned garage. But despite, or even because of, its oddities, Slider coveted it. Whoever had altered and added to it over the ages, they had had a sense of proportion. As with a beautiful woman, he thought, the character in its face only made it more beautiful.

The Mimpriss Estate was itself an oddity. In the middle of the west London sprawl of Victorian–Edwardian terraces, it was a small area of large and desirable houses, built in the Arts-and-Crafts style at the turn of the century by a wealthy man with a bee in his bonnet. Given the proximity to central London, houses on the estate were now worth small fortunes. For the Old Rectory you were talking a three-quarter-million touch, minimum, Slider reckoned. Atherton was perfectly right, though it was unnecessarily cruel of him to have pointed it out.

The estate comprised half a dozen streets, with St Michael Square in the middle and the railway running along the back. The church in the centre of the square was dedicated with nice inclusiveness to St Michael and All Angels. Slider turned to look at it as Atherton locked the car, and was mildly surprised. This was no painstaking 1890s copy. It stood in its own small, railed churchyard with all the grave, reserved beauty of the fifteenth century, its grey stone tower rising serenely above the tombstones to dwell among the clouds. 'There should be rooks,' Slider said. 'Or jackdaws.'

'Settle for magpies,' Atherton said, as one of them went off like a football rattle in a tree overhead. He turned to look at the church as well. 'It's old, isn't it? Not just Victorian?'

'Early Perp,' Slider said. So, there must have been a village here once. 'He built the estate round it.'

'He who?'

'Sir Henry Mimpriss. Industrialist and amateur architect.'

'The things you know!'

'I read,' Slider said with dignity.

'*Si monumentum requiris*,' Atherton remarked admiringly. 'Wren only had a cathedral, and even that had some other bloke's name on it.'

It was one of the nice things about London, Slider thought, looking round, that you never knew when you would come across the good bones of an ancient settlement visible under the accumulated flesh of urban development. In this square, as well as the church and the Old Rectory, there was a row of cottages whose Victorian tidying-up couldn't fool the trained eye, and a pub called the the Goat In Boots whose wavy roof and muddle of rear buildings dated it along with the church. Inn, church, rectory and a few houses: all you needed for a country village – set, in those days, amid the rolling hayfields and market gardens of Middlesex. And then the railway came, and life was never the same again.

Atherton was reading the church noticeboard. 'Rev. Alan Tennyson. Tennyson's a nice sonorous name, but I think the Alan's a mistake. Lacks gravitas.'

'Make a note to tell his mother.'

'And they only get a service every second Sunday,' Atherton said. They started across the road towards the house. 'If this is the Old Rectory, where's the new one? Or does "old" just mean "former"?'

'Pass,' said Slider.

'It looks like three houses in a motorway shunt.'

'Don't be rude. It's just very old and altered,' Slider said defensively. 'The left-hand bit shows the real age. The Georgian face is only skin deep, and the Victorian wing's been added, by the look of the roof.'

'I'm glad I brought you along,' Atherton said. 'And now they've got a body. Careless of them. Gin a body meet a body lying down a hole . . .'

'That's "doon", surely?'

'If you insist. But don't call me Shirley. Shall we knock or go round the side?'

'Side,' said Slider. To the right of the house – between it and the next house, from which it was divided by a fifteen-foot hedge of that omnipresent British Leyland spruce that someone was soon going to regret not keeping cut down to a manageable height – was a gravelled parking area on which stood a very dirty, light blue Ford pickup with various items of builder's equipment in the back. Parked at the roadside and blocking it in were a patrol car and the Department wheels – a maroon Orion, which had brought DC McLaren, who had been on duty when the shout came in. At the back of the gravel area was a low wall that gave straight onto the terrace behind the house.

Slider and Atherton crunched over the gravel, stepped through a gap in the wall, and then stopped.

'Now that's what I call a patio,' Atherton said, with a soundless whistle.

'And I thought I was the Philistine,' Slider replied. 'That's not a patio, that's a terrace.'

It ran the whole length of the house, a broad and glorious terrace paved with York stone in slabs so wide and worn and ancient they might have been nicked from a monastery, and who knew but they were? Beyond it there was a steep drop to the lawn, which sloped down to a belt of trees, behind which, but hidden at this leafy time of year, was the railway. It should have been a river, Slider thought, for perfection. Still he coveted, country boy though he was at heart. Sitting on this terrace and gazing at the trees, you could almost believe . . .

Presumably the forces of nature were exacting a toll on the structure, for there was all the evidence of building work going on: a heap of earth and rubble, another of sharp sand, a pile of bricks, three bags of cement, a bright orange cement mixer, a wheelbarrow with two spades and a pick resting across it, and a blue plastic tarpaulin the colour of the inside of a lottery-winner's swimming-pool, with frayed nylon rope through the eyelet holes at the corners.

The tarpaulin was folded back on itself, half covering a long trench dug in the terrace, parallel with its front edge, about three feet wide and two feet deep. The paving stones which had been levered up were neatly stacked away to one side, and an opportunist black cat was sitting on top of them in the sun, its paws tucked fatly under itself and its eyes half closed.

The builder himself was sitting on the low wall with his hands and his lips wrapped around a mug of tea: a stocky, powerfully built man in his thirties, with untidy thick blond hair, bloodshot blue eyes, weather-roughened cheeks and an unshaven chin. He was wearing mud-streaked work trousers and boots, and a ragged blue sweater over a check shirt. His strong hands, grained white with cement, were shaking so that the mug chattered against his teeth; he stared at nothing over the rim, past the blue-black legs of PC Willans, who was standing guard over him with an air of gentle sternness. It was a demeanour, Slider noted, often adopted by coppers towards remorseful domestic murderers.

McLaren came across to report. He was eating a cold Cornish pastie straight from the Cellophane wrapper and his lips were flecked with pastry and whatever the pallid glop was that passed for filling. 'Breakfast, guv,' he justified himself, seeing the direction of Slider's gaze. 'The body's down the hole.' With his free thumb he indicated the builder. 'That's Edward Andrews – Eddie Andrews. It's his wife.'

'And presumably his hole,' Atherton suggested.

'That's right,' McLaren said, with a world of significance. 'He got here very early this morning – earlier than usual – but, bad luck for him, the lady of the house was up even earlier and found the body before he could concrete her in. The plastic sheet was apparently pulled right over, bar a corner that'd blown back, when she found it. It was like it is now when I got here.'

'Householder's name?'

'Mrs Hammond. Lives here with her old dad. Norma's inside with 'em – I picked her up on my way here.' He gestured towards the uniformed constable, Defreitas, guarding the body. 'Daffy's got all the gen about Andrews. He lives round here.'

'On a PC's salary?' Atherton said disbelievingly.

'Well, not on the estate *as such*,' McLaren admitted, 'but only just round the corner. Woodbridge Road. Anyway, he knows this geezer Andrews.'

'All right, let's have a look,' Slider said. He went over to the hole and hunkered down. The victim was lying on her back. She had not been tumbled in, but laid out carefully as though in a coffin, decently composed, her clothes straight, feet together, hands folded one on the other. She was a slim woman in her thirties with well-cut blonde hair (helped, to judge from the roots, but not by all that much), wearing a short-sleeved, fitted dress of navy cotton with a red leather belt, bare legs and strappy leather sandals. She had full make-up on, rather on the heavy side, Slider would have thought, for a woman as attractive as she must have been; and her finger- and toe-nails were painted red to match the belt. Her eyes were closed, and there were no obvious marks of violence on her. She might have been fresh from the mortician's parlour.

'Expensive scent,' he said. Even after however long it was lying out in a trench, it had lasted well enough for Slider's sensitive nose to catch it. He felt her hand: it was cold and stiff.

'Expensive jewellery,' Atherton said, looking over his shoulder. She was wearing a wedding-ring and an engagement hoop with five large diamonds, a sapphire and diamond dress ring of more expense than taste, a rather nice gold watch and three gold chains of varying thickness around her neck. 'I wonder why he didn't take them off? The rings and the watch at least. Shame to bury them in concrete.'

'He says he didn't do it,' Defreitas offered.

'Well, he would say that, wouldn't he?' Atherton said.

Slider stood up. 'Things must be on the up in the building trade.'

'It's a good area for it,' Defreitas said. 'Lots of work – quality stuff, and no trouble about payment.' Something about his voice made Slider look up, and he noted that Defreitas seemed upset.

He was pale, and there was a rigidity about his expression that suggested he was holding himself firmly in check. His cheek muscles trembled with the effort of control, but he went on steadily, 'Eddie's been doing all right for himself. Just built himself a big new house, down the end of Woodbridge Road. Corner of the main road. Fourways, it's called.'

'Yes, I know it,' Slider said. He had passed it often over the months while it was being built in what had been the back garden of a big Edwardian house: the Curse of Infill. He had noticed it because it had irritated him that it was called Fourways when it was on a T-junction, not a crossroads.

'Supposed to be really smashing inside,' Defreitas said. 'Built it for her.' He moved his head slightly towards the body, but without looking at it. 'Her name's Jennifer.' He stopped and swallowed a couple of times. Some men couldn't bear a corpse, even such a seemly and undamaged one as this.

'Take it easy, lad,' Slider said. 'You'll see worse in a long life.'

Defreitas swivelled his eyes towards Slider and then away again. He was a good-looking youngster, with brown eyes and a lean face and the sort of vigorous, slightly fuzzy tight brown curls that look like pubic hair. 'I know, sir. But it's different when it's someone you know, isn't it?'

'What do you know about Jennifer Andrews?' Slider asked.

'She works – worked – part time for David Meacher – you know, the estate agent? – and she did part time at the pub, too. The Goat In Boots, I mean,' he added conscientiously, 'not the Mimpriss Arms.' That was the estate's own pub, built at the same time as the houses: draughty and uncomfortable, an overblown, over-quaint thing of pitch-pine and vaulted ceilings, like the fruit of an illicit union between a village hall and a tithe barn. 'The Mimpriss is a bit rough sometimes. The Goat's where the nobby people go. It's got a restaurant and everything. You know, a posh one – *nouveau cuisine* and all that.'

'How well do you know Andrews?' Slider asked.

'Just to say hello to,' Defreitas said. 'I've seen him in the Goat sometimes. He seems a nice bloke. I've heard people say he's a good builder.'

'You drink in the Goat?'

He seemed embarrassed by the implication. 'Well, I used

to mostly go to the First And Last in Woodbridge Road, but they've got music there now and a lot of young kids come in. The Goat's nice and quiet, more like a village pub. Local people like it quiet. They don't like the Mimpriss – lets the tone of the estate down, they say.'

'They're not going to like having a murder here, then,' Atherton observed.

'Oh, I don't know,' Defreitas said. 'A murder like this—' He swallowed again. 'It's quite a toney crime, really. They'll all want to be in on it.'

'No trouble getting them to talk, then?' Slider said.

'Getting 'em to stop, more like,' Defreitas said succinctly.

'Doc's here, guv,' McLaren called.

Out in the road Slider could see reinforcements arriving and the photographer's van drawing up too. A group of onlookers was gathering on the pavement. 'Get some crowd control going,' he told McLaren. 'And we'd better get Andrews back to the shop before the press arrives.'

'When murder comes, can the *Gazette* be far behind?' Atherton enquired rhetorically. 'D'you want me to take him? I can have a crack at him while he's still warm. He's obviously number one suspect.'

Slider turned to look at him.

The morning sun shone on Atherton's face, illuminating the fine, deep lines, that looked as though they'd been grooved with an etching tool, and the indefinable bruised look that Slider associated with people who have been gravely ill. Atherton had not long been back at work, after an extended leave during which there had been doubt as to whether he would come back at all. His knife wound had been slow to heal; and there was the psychological wound as well. But Atherton was not the only one affected by the incident. For some weeks Slider had been obliged to consider the prospect of carrying on in the Job without Atherton, and to face the unwelcome realisation that he didn't want to.

That touched more than vanity. It was dangerous to be dependent on someone else in that way, and Slider had always thought of himself as self-sufficient. In a long career as a policeman he had made many working alliances and had had some very good partnerships, but he had never allowed himself to become attached to any colleague as he had to Atherton in the past few years. Atherton's wounding and long sick-leave had forced him to realise how strong that attachment had become, and it scared him a little. He had coped with losing his wife and children to Ernie Newman, a man who could have bored for England; had coped – just – with losing his new love, Joanna, before he got her back again. But those traumas were in the social side of his life, and early in his career he had learned to keep the two sides separate. The Job was much the larger part of his existence.

It was not just that Atherton was a good bagman – anyone competent could learn his ways and fill those shoes; it was that he helped him to keep a sense of proportion about it all, something that got harder as time went on. Oh, he could do the job without Atherton, of course he could; it was just that, when he thought about it, really got down to it and looked it in the face, he felt an enormous disinclination to bother. Perhaps he was war-weary; or perhaps it was just the fleeting years. They were none of them, the Boy Wonder included, what they had been. But he had felt that if Atherton didn't come back, it would be time to empty his Post Office savings book and go for that chicken-farm in Norfolk.

Well, the boy was back; but looking fragile. Only yesterday Porson, the new detective superintendent who had taken over from Little Eric Honeyman, had stopped him on the stairs and asked him how Atherton was 'shaking out'. It was one of those maddening Porsonisms: it was obvious what he meant, but how did he get there? Did he think he was saying shaping up, shaking down, or working out? Or had he in mind even some more obscure metaphor for settling down, like Atherton shaking dusters out of the window, or shaking a pebble out of his shoe? Porson used language with the neatness and efficiency of a one-armed blind man eating spaghetti.

Slider had answered him optimistically; things were quiet and there was nothing even a fragile Atherton, given his gargantuan intellect, couldn't cope with. But now here they were with a murder shout, and who knew where that might lead? If there was any likelihood of rough stuff, Slider had already determined, he would make sure Atherton was kept well away from it. But the trouble was, these days, you couldn't necessarily predict the

direction the rough stuff would come from. You might knock
on any ordinary door and meet Mr G. Reaper in the shape of
some crazed crack-head with half a Sabatier set clutched in his
germans. And that was the worry, of course, that would wear
you down. It was one thing to go into a known dangerous
situation, with your body-armour, back-up and adrenaline all in
place. But the creeping anxiety that any closed door and street
corner, any routine roust, sus or enquiry, could suddenly turn
bad and go for your throat, was unmanning. Slider wished he
knew how Atherton was feeling about that; but Atherton had
not brought up the subject, and Slider would not touch on it
uninvited.

Atherton had noted his hesitation, and now said, with dangerous patience, 'I don't think he'll turn nasty, but if he does,
I'm sure Willans will protect me.'

Now the pressure was on Slider not to seem to be coddling
Atherton, so he agreed. And then, of course, because Atherton
had put the thought in his head, he started wondering whether
Andrews would turn violent after all. This friendship business
was a minefield, he thought resentfully, and went to meet
the doc.

It was not, however, the duty police surgeon, but Freddie
Cameron, the forensic pathologist, in all his splendour.

'What's this – short of work?' Slider asked.

'I'm actually nearer than Dr Prawalha,' Cameron explained.
'I don't mind, anyway: if I'm going to be doing the doings, I'd
just as soon see everything for myself while it's untouched.'

'You don't need to apologise to me,' Slider said, 'except for
looking so disgustingly brown.'

'It was only Dorset,' Cameron protested. 'The Madam's got
a sister in Cerne Abbas. Lovely place, as long as you don't
suffer from an inferiority complex. What have you got for
me?'

Slider took him to the trench. In accordance with procedure
Cameron pronounced life extinct, but offered no suggestion as
to the cause of death. 'There's nothing at all to see. Could
be drugs of some sort, or even natural causes – heart, or a
stroke. Can't tell until I get her on the table. Presumably she
died elsewhere and was transported here?'

'Unless it was suicide and she took the precaution of lying

down neatly in her grave first. And then covered herself with the tarpaulin.'

'Those questions I leave to you, old dear,' Freddie said, and shook his head. 'Don't like this sort of case. Too much room for error.'

'Dead men don't sue,' Slider comforted him. 'Can you give me an approximate time to be working on?'

'Well, she's cold to the touch and stiff, but there's still some warmth in the axilla. It was a warm night, wasn't it? And she's been sheltered down this hole. Could be six to eight hours. Could be more. Probably not less than six.'

'Late last night, early this morning, then?' Slider said.

'Is that enough to be going on with? I'll have a better idea from the temperature, but I don't want to do a stick here when I've no idea of the cause of death. You never know what evidence you might be destroying. Do you know who she is?'

'She's Jennifer Andrews, wife of local builder Edward Andrews.'

'He the one who dug the hole?' Freddie asked. 'Ah, well, there you are, then.'

'Here I am then where?' Slider asked, resisting the obvious.

'Whoever put her in here took the trouble to lay her out nicely,' Freddie said. 'So presumably it was someone who cared about her.'

'Could be remorse,' Slider pointed out.

'Comes out the same.' Freddie shrugged.

'Get on with your own job, Sawbones, and leave the brainy stuff to me.'

Cameron chuckled. 'You're welcome to it.'

A small door from the terrace let Slider into a coats lobby sporting an array of wax jackets, waterproofs, overcoats, shapeless hats, walking sticks, a gardening trug, a fishing basket, rods in a canvas carrying sheath, green wellies, muddy shoes and an extra long canvas-webbing dog-lead. A narrow door with opaque glazed panels gave onto a loo, an old-fashioned one with a high seat and a stout pipe going up the wall behind it to the overhead cistern. That would give you a healthy flush, he thought. A third door passed him into the house. Here was proof that the Georgian elevation was only skin deep: he was in the beamed hall of a fifteenth-century house, going right up into the roof-space. Some Victorian, during the Gothic revival, had added a massive oak staircase going round three sides of it, and an open gallery on the fourth providing access to the rooms on the upper floor, giving it a sort of baronial-hall look; but the wood of the beams was silvery and lovely, and it worked all right.

He could hear a dog barking somewhere. On his left, the Victorian extension to the house, there were two doors. The first he tried revealed a large, high-ceilinged room, empty of life and smelling pungently of damp. It was furnished with massive, heavy pieces, partly as a dining room and partly as a study or office: a vast mahogany desk with a typewriter and books and papers stacked untidily on it, and a rank of ugly steel filing cabinets occupied the far end. There were two tall windows overlooking the terrace, and one to the side of the house, looking onto the gravel parking space.

The second door opened on the room at the front of the house, a drawing-room, equally huge, with a Turkish carpet over the fitted oatmeal Berber, one whole wall covered floor to ceiling with books, and the sort of heavy, dark furniture usually associated with gentlemen's clubs. Here and there about the room were framed black-and-white photographs. Slider noted amongst them one of a man in climbing gear against a background of mountain peaks, a group of men ditto, the front row crouching like footballers, and another of a climber with his arm across the shoulder of a well muffled-up sherpa, both grinning snow-smiles at the camera.

The room also contained WDC Swilley, an old man in a wheel-chair, and a large woman struggling with a dog. The dog was one of those big, heavy-coated, dark Alsatians, and it was barking with a deep resonance that was making the chandelier vibrate.

'Oh, for God's sake, woman, let her go!' the old man said irritably. 'Why must you always make such a fuss? Stand quite still,' he commanded Slider, 'and she won't hurt you.'

The dog, released, sprang unnervingly forward, but stopped short of Slider, sniffed his shoes and his trousers, then looked up into his face and barked again, just once, its eyes wary and suspicious.

'Good girl, Sheba,' the woman said nervously. 'Good girl, then. She won't hurt you.'

Slider had known a good many dogs in his time, and wouldn't have wagered the hole in his trousers' pocket on the temper of this one. He offered his hand to be sniffed, but the dog flinched away from it, and then he saw that its ears were bald and red and scabbed with some skin complaint, which made him both wince and itch in instant sympathy.

'Poor girl,' he said quietly, 'poor old girl,' and the dog waved her tail uncertainly.

But the old man snapped, 'Sheba, come *here*!' and the bitch turned away, padded over to the wheelchair, and flopped down, near but just out of reach.

'I'm so sorry,' the woman fluffed, blushing awkwardly. 'She's a bit upset, you see. She wouldn't hurt a soul, really.'

'Oh, for God's sake, Frances, shut up!' the old man snapped. 'You don't need to apologise to him. And what's the point of having a guard dog if you tell everyone she's harmless?' He looked at Slider with a kind of weary disgust. 'I despair of women's intellect. They have no capacity for logical thought. The Germans had the right idea: confine them to *kinder*, *küche*, and *kirche*. Trouble is, *this* one's no bloody use for the first two, and the last is no bloody use to me. Who are you, anyway? Another of these damned policemen, I suppose.'

Slider passed from Swilley's rigid expression – was she suppressing fury or laughter? – to look at the old man. He had a tartan rug over his legs, and his upper half was clad in a black roll-neck sweater and a crimson velvet smoking jacket: very sprauncy, but that jacket, with the scarlet of the Royal Stuart plaid, was an act of sartorial vandalism. He sat very upright, and Slider thought he would have been tall once; now he was thin, cadaverously so, with that greyish sheen to his skin and the bluish tint to his lips that spoke of extreme illness. He had a full head of white hair, though that, too, had thinned until the pink of the scalp showed through, like the canvas on a threadbare carpet. His hands, all knuckles and veins, were clenched in his lap, and he stared at Slider with eyes that were surprisingly, almost shockingly dark in that corpse-white face, eyes that burned with some desperate rage, though the thin, petunia lips were turned down in mere, sheer contempt. Some poem or other, about a caged eagle, nagged at the back of Slider's mind. There was nothing really aquiline about this old man's appearance. A caged something, though. If he was the climber in the photographs, it must be a bitter thing to be confined to a wheelchair now.

'I'm Detective Inspector Slider, Shepherd's Bush CID,' he said, showing his brief. 'May I know your name, sir?'

The old man straightened a fraction more. 'I am Cyril Dacre,' he said superbly.

The woman shot a swift, nervous look first at the old man and then at Slider. That, combined with the annunciatory tone of voice gave Slider the hint, and he was saying in suitably impressed tones, '*The* Cyril Dacre?' even while his brain was still searching the old mental card index to see why the name sounded familiar.

'You've heard of me?' the old man said suspiciously.

The woman crackled with apprehension, and Swilley, trying to help, swivelled her eyes semaphore-style towards the bookcase and back, and, concealed from Dacre by her body, made the unfolding gesture with her hands that in charades signifies 'book'. But – and fortunately – Slider really had heard of him and remembered just in time why, so he was able to say with obvious sincerity, 'Not the Cyril Dacre who wrote all those history books I learned from in school?' How many times had he opened one of those fat green tomes and seen that name on the title page? *A Cambridge History of England* by Cyril Dacre. *Volume VII, The Early Tudors, 1485–1558.* A name so well known it had become generic, like Fowler or Roget: 'All right, settle down now, and open your Dacres at chapter seven ...'

'I am indeed Cyril Dacre the historian,' Dacre said, and there was no mistaking the pleasure in his voice. 'Why does it surprise you?'

'Your name was such a part of my schooldays, it's like meeting – oh, I don't know – a legend,' Slider said. For some reason, when he was at school he had always assumed that the authors of all textbooks were long dead, so it was even more unexpected to come across a live one all these years later. But Dacre didn't look as if he had too tight a grip on life, so Slider didn't think that it would be tactful to put it that way.

Dacre waved a skeletal hand towards the bookcase. 'Of course, my Cambridge History series is only a small part of my oeuvre.' In his head, Slider heard a ghostly Atherton voice saying, '*An oeuvre's enough,*' and resisted it. 'Though perhaps when the account is totted up, it may prove to have been the most influential part.'

'It's an honour to meet you, sir,' Slider said, and looked pointedly at the woman, so that Dacre was obliged to introduce her.

'My daughter Frances. Frances Hammond.' The woman made a little woolly movement, as though unsure whether to step forward and shake hands or not, caught her toe in the carpet and stumbled. Dacre glared at her and made a sound of exasperation. 'Clumsy!' he said, not quite under his breath.

Slider stepped in to rescue her. 'And there are just the two of you living here?'

'Yes, that's all – now,' she said, in a failing voice. 'Now the boys are gone. Left. Grown up, I mean. My two sons, who used to live here.'

Slider sensed another *for God's sake, woman* just under the horizon and turned to the glowering historian to say, 'I should like to talk to you later, sir, but I'd like to take your daughter's statement first, if you'll excuse me.'

Dacre's eyebrows snapped down. 'Excuse you? Where are you going?'

'I'd like to speak to Mrs Hammond alone.'

'Oh? And what do you think she'll have to say that I mayn't hear?'

'We have rules of procedure which we have to follow, sir,' Slider said smoothly, 'and one of them is that witnesses must make their statements alone and unprompted.'

He snorted. 'Statement? The woman can't string two words together without prompting. You'd better talk to her here where I can help her.'

'I'm sorry, Mr Dacre, but I must stick to the rules,' Slider said firmly. 'Mrs Hammond, if you'd be so kind?'

She fluttered again and started towards the door, hesitated, and glanced uncertainly back towards her father. Dacre looked irritated. 'Yes, go, go! I don't need you. Take the dog with you – and for God's sake try to look as though you remember how to walk. Why I wasted all that money on ballet and deportment lessons when you were a child I don't know—'

While he carped, Mrs Hammond called the dog, but it didn't

move, only looked up at Dacre, which seemed to please the old man, but made Mrs Hammond blush again. She had to go back and take hold of the dog's collar. Slider held the door open for her, but Mrs Hammond, bent over to tow the dog – for she was a tall woman – misjudged the opening and hit her head on the edge of the door.

Dacre roared, 'You are the clumsiest moron of a female it has ever been my misfortune to—'

She passed Slider in an agony of confusion, and he shut the door on the dragon, feeling desperately sorry for her. She had a red mark on her forehead, and her eyes were bright and moist. 'I'm sorry,' she muttered disjointedly. 'My father – all this is so upsetting. He's in a lot of pain, you see. He has pain-killers, but they don't stop it completely, of course. It makes him rather – cross.'

The childish, inadequate word was somehow the more effective for that. 'Is he ill?' Slider asked.

'Cancer,' she said. She met his eyes starkly. 'He's dying.'

'I'm sorry,' Slider said. She looked away. She had let go of Sheba's collar: the dog was trotting rapidly round the enormous hall, tracking the smell of police feet back and forth across the carpet. 'Is there somewhere we can go to talk?' Slider asked.

She gestured limply across the hall. 'The kitchen – we could – if that's all right?' she said. 'It's where I usually . . .' Slider had to stand aside and make a courtly gesture to get her to lead the way. He could see how her constant ineffectual wobbling would get on Dacre's nerves; on the other hand, maybe Dacre's roaring and snapping was what had made her that way. If tyrants proverbially make liars, surely bullies make faffers?

CHAPTER TWO

It Takes Two To Hombre

The kitchen was on the far side of the hall, in the third section of the house. Mrs Hammond opened the door onto a room as different as could be from the drawing-room – about twenty feet square, low-ceilinged and stone-floored. Its long casement window facing onto the road was set deep into a wall two feet thick, and there were beams overhead and a stunning arched stone fireplace with a delicately carved surround, which now housed a rather beat-up looking cream Rayburn. Judging by the quality of its stonework, this must have been one of the main rooms of the original house, Slider thought, reduced to the status of kitchen when the house was enlarged.

Slider turned to his hostess. Frances Hammond, *née* Dacre, was a big woman – not fat, but tall, and with that unindented solidness that comes with a certain age. Slider put her in her middle fifties, but it was not altogether easy to tell, for her clothes and hair and general style made her look older, while her face, if one could take it in isolation, looked younger. It was a soft, creaseless face, pink and somehow blurred, with uncertain eyes and a vulnerable mouth. She made Slider think of a child of about ten finding itself trapped by sorcery in someone else's body. Perhaps that accounted for her lack of co-ordination: she moved like someone coping with an alien planet's gravity. But she might have been pretty once, and could have been handsome even now had anyone taken the trouble to encourage her. Her hair, in the dull, too-old-for-her style, was light brown and softly curling, and her eyes were large and brown and rather fawn-like.

'What a splendid room,' he said to her, to prime the conversation.

She looked pleased, but nervous. 'Oh, yes,' she said, moving her hands vaguely. 'I like it. I tend to sit here mostly.' There was a saggy old sofa, stuffed with a variety of cushions, standing endways on to one side of the Rayburn, and an old-fashioned high-backed oak settle facing it on the other side. 'It's warm and quiet, and Father – well, he finds – he likes to be alone for reading and working and . . .' She seemed to run out of steam at that point. Her voice had a faded, failing sound to it, so that she started her sentences feebly and lost impetus as she went along.

'You don't worry about his being alone, in his condition?'

'He rings if he wants me. The servants' bells are still . . .' She glanced towards the indicator above the door, one of those boards with little handbells on brass springs. 'And he has Sheba with him most of the time, though sometimes she gets on his nerves. And then he . . .'

'What's wrong with her ears?' he asked, turning to look at the dog; it seemed restless, tracking round the kitchen with its nose to the floor, ears flicking with irritation.

'Oh, it's nothing catching,' Mrs Hammond said at once, as though she had been accused of it many times. 'It's a nervous complaint, the vet says. Or maybe hormonal. It makes it difficult to . . .' Fade-out again. It was like listening to Classic FM in a poor reception area. 'She's a bit upset, poor thing, with all this . . . I'll just shut her out.'

Mrs Hammond opened a door on the far side of the kitchen, giving Slider a glimpse of a stone passageway with doors on either side – storerooms, he supposed – and called the dog. It did not obey, and she was obliged to catch it by the collar and drag it out, nails protesting on the stone floor, and shut the door quickly. Coming back, Mrs Hammond said, 'Would you like a cup of tea? Or coffee. Or anything.'

It would probably soothe her to have something to do with her hands, Slider calculated. 'Yes, please, if it's no trouble. Tea, please.' He waited until she had drawn the water and set the kettle on the hob, and then said, 'It must have been a terrible shock to you this morning to find Mrs Andrews like that.'

Instantly her eyes filled with tears and her mouth trembled; it was as though she had forgotten the dreadful events in the business of taking care of Slider. He was almost sorry to remind her. 'Oh! It was awful. Poor Jennifer!' She put her hands to her mouth. 'Who would do a terrible thing like that?'

'A terrible thing like what?'

Her cervine eyes lifted, puzzled. 'Well – you know – murder her.'

'We don't know that she was murdered,' he said, leaving an opening for her; but she only looked at him in utter dumbfoundedness.

'But—' she said at last. 'But she couldn't have – I mean – how did she get into the hole? With the tarpaulin pulled over her. Someone must have put her there – mustn't they?' She added the last in a kind of horrified meekness, as though expecting him to produce some ghastly official knowledge of bodies and holes beyond the range of the ordinary citizen.

'Someone must have put her there,' he agreed, 'but it doesn't follow they killed her. She might have died naturally, and this person for some reason didn't want to get involved.'

Mrs Hammond stared a moment longer, working it through, and then looked hugely relieved. 'Oh! Yes, I see. That must be it! Oh, I'm so glad it wasn't . . . I didn't want anyone to . . .' She sat down awkwardly on the edge of the sofa. 'Of course, he might think no-one would believe him. They were always quarrelling.'

'They?'

'Eddie and Jennifer.' She looked up at him anxiously, as if she had done something wrong. 'Oh, but I don't mean to suggest . . . It doesn't follow that . . .'

'Most married couples quarrel,' he said.

She looked relieved again. 'Yes, of course. I didn't want you to think . . .'

'That's all right,' he said, in general reassurance. 'What work is it that Eddie's doing on your terrace?'

'Subsidence,' she said. 'All these dry summers. We're clay here, you see, and it shrinks. There was a section of the terrace where the paving stones were sinking, and cracks appeared in the terrace wall.' She paused, thinking.

'So you called him in?' Slider prompted.

'I mentioned it to him, just in passing, and he said he'd come and have a look. And then he said it was subsidence and it was very serious. We'd have to have it done or the whole terrace might collapse.'

'So it was he who suggested you have the work done?'

'Oh! Yes. I suppose so, if you put it like that. But he would know: he's a very good builder. Everyone says so. And he's done lots of little things for us over the years. He's very reliable.'

Slider nodded. 'When did he start work on the terrace?'

'On Monday.'

'And what time did he finish work last night?'

'I'm not really sure. I think it was – perhaps some time after six.'

'Didn't he usually come and tell you he was leaving?'

'Oh! No, you see, he could come and go as he liked, round the side. He didn't need to be let in, so he . . .' He waited sturdily and she went on, 'I didn't go out there much while he was working. I didn't want to get in the way.'

'You can't see the terrace from here,' he observed. The only window looked onto the road. 'You say you usually sit in here?'

'My father likes to be alone. He has his end of the house, the two big rooms for his study and sitting room, and his bedroom and bathroom above. I stay at this end. My bedroom's above here, and my sewing-room, and I generally sit here in the kitchen – unless he asks for me, to read to him. Or play chess.' She blushed. 'I'm not very good, so he doesn't often ask me.'

'So it's almost like being in two separate houses?'

'It was the arrangement we had when the boys were little, so that they wouldn't disturb him. Mummy was alive then, of course. She and Father had their end, and the boys and I had ours. Their bedrooms and our bathroom are next to my bedroom, and my sewing-room used to be their playroom. Of course, they're gone now, the boys. Left home. They've got their own lives,' she added with unconscious pathos. 'But Father – we just kept the arrangement the same.'

Slider felt almost shivery, thinking of these two people alone at opposite ends of the house, isolated by the great no man's land of the baronial hall. He thought he had never come across a woman so sad – in all senses – as Mrs Hammond.

He resumed questioning. 'So how do you know that Andrews left after six yesterday?'

'I took Sheba out at about half past six, and he wasn't there then.'

'But he could have left earlier than six?'

'Oh, he wouldn't do that,' she said earnestly. 'Whenever he's worked here for us, he's always started at half past eight and worked till six or later – at least, in the summer. He liked to get the job done, you see.'

Slider accepted this for now. 'How did he leave things? Was the tarpaulin covering the hole completely last night?'

She fluffed. 'Oh! I think so. I didn't really notice. I'm so sorry! I mean, I didn't have any reason to look. I think it was, though.'

Slider made a calming gesture. 'Would you like to tell me what happened this morning?'

'I – I went to take Sheba out. I was earlier than usual. I didn't sleep well last night. I don't sleep much as a rule; Father sometimes needs me in the night, and it's made me something of an insomniac.'

'Were you disturbed in the night – last night, I mean?'

She looked confused. 'Oh! No – nothing like that. It was very quiet, actually. But I didn't sleep well all the same, so I got up early. I took Sheba out, and – and the corner of the tarpaulin was turned back. I suppose it must have blown like that in the night. As I went past I just glanced at it and – and saw – saw the legs.' Her lips began to tremble. 'It was so terrible.'

'Yes, it must have been a dreadful shock for you,' Slider said encouragingly. 'What did you do next?'

'I couldn't think. I didn't know what to do. I thought I'd better make sure. So I pulled the tarpaulin right back. Then I saw it was Jennifer. Then I – I suppose I was frozen to the spot for a while. And then Eddie arrived.'

'In his pickup?'

'Yes. He pulled onto the gravel and jumped out and came towards me and – and I – I screamed, I'm afraid. I was frightened. And he said something like, "What are you doing here?" and I said, "It's Jennifer," and he said, "You've found her!" or something like that. And then he looked at her, and he seemed very shocked and sat down on the wall and handed me his telephone and said, "You'd better call the police." So I did.'

'Why were you frightened when he arrived?'

She paused at the question, as though surprised, and then

oaid nervously, 'Well – because I thought he'd killed her. So I was afraid he might – attack me.'

'What made you think that?'

'I don't know. I suppose it was silly. It just seemed obvious at the time.'

'You were quite sure she was dead?'

'She looked dead,' she said faintly. 'You don't mean—?'

He had no desire to add to her mental burdens. 'No, I'm sure she was. I just wondered why you were so sure. And Andrews seems to have been sure, too. He told you to call the police, not an ambulance?'

She nodded. 'But she looked dead,' she said again. The kettle boiled and she got up and lifted it off with hands that were trembling badly again. Prudently, he waited until she had poured the boiling water and put the kettle down before asking the next question.

'So after you had telephoned the police, what did you do?'

'I went indoors to get Father up.'

Slider raised his eyebrows. 'You just left Andrews there on his own?'

She coloured. 'Was that wrong? But I had to see to Father. He gets so cross if his routine is interrupted.' Her hands moved about feebly as if trying to escape. 'Eddie – he wasn't doing anything, just sitting on the wall. But Father—'

She was obviously much afraid, or in awe, of her father; the thought that Andrews might destroy evidence probably never occurred to her. And if she really did think he had killed his wife, she might not want to remain alone with him. Slider could hardly carp about that, but it was inconvenient: Andrews must have been alone out there for a quarter of an hour or so. 'I believe you told one of the other policemen that Eddie Andrews arrived earlier than usual this morning?'

She handed him a mug of tea. 'Yes. He always started at half past eight, but it was before seven o'clock this morning.'

'Did you usually see him arrive?'

'Well, I see his truck go past the window if I'm in here. Half past eight was his usual time. I didn't expect . . .'

'No, I'm sure you didn't,' Slider said.

There was a scratching, rattling noise at the far kitchen door, and it swung open to admit the Alsatian, which glanced sidelong at Mrs Hammond and then resumed its restless padding around the kitchen, nose to the floor. Mrs Hammond looked guiltily at Slider. 'She can get the door open now, the bad girl. She pushes the latch up. She doesn't like being shut out.' She turned to the dog. 'Basket! Go to your basket.' For a wonder, the dog obeyed. The basket was in the corner, a big wicker one, lined with blanket. The dog turned round three times and flopped down, and then nosed out what looked like a bit of red rag from under the blanket and began chewing it in an obsessive kind of way.

'Good girl,' said Mrs Hammond, with a hint of relief. It must be nice for her, Slider thought, to get her own way in something for once.

Andrews looked up as Atherton came in with the tea. He was more haggard than ever, though his hands had stopped shaking; and despite his burliness of shoulder he looked small sitting at the table with the great solid bulk of PC Willans standing in the corner behind him.

'I didn't do it,' he said, without preamble.

'He denies it: write that down,' Atherton said to the wall.

'I want to go home. You can't keep me here.'

'No-one's keeping you here, sir,' Atherton said blandly. 'You're helping us with our enquiries, that's all. It's purely voluntary.' He pushed a cup across the table to Andrews, and raised the other to his lips in a relaxed, social manner. 'You do want to help us, don't you?'

Andrews' defiance deflated. 'I don't know anything,' he said pathetically. 'I don't know what happened. I would never have hurt her. Aren't I supposed to have a solicitor?'

Atherton, absorbing the sequence of words, said in tones of pleasant interest, 'You can have one if you want, of course. Do you think you need one, then?'

Andrews shook his head slightly, which Atherton took as an answer, though it might just as easily not have been. Andrews was drinking the tea now, staring blankly through the steam. He looked as if he hadn't slept for a week, and he certainly hadn't shaved for twenty-four hours. The shock was genuine enough, Atherton decided. He had seen before how a murderer didn't really take in the enormity of his actions until he was found out, and saw them, so to speak, through someone else's eyes. Only then did he let all the normal human feelings out of the locked room where they'd been kept out of the way while the deed was done.

Start with the easy stuff, Atherton thought, from chapter one of the *Bill Slider Book of Getting People To Blurt It All Out*. 'So, tell me about this work you're doing for Mrs Hammond.'

Andrews blinked, having expected a worse question, and took a moment to recalibrate. 'She was worried about subsidence. Well, some of the pavings had sunk a bit, and there were some cracks in the retaining wall, but I told her it was nothing to worry about. They move about a bit, those old buildings, but they'll stand up for ever. But she insisted I do something about it, so I did.' He looked at Atherton and shrugged slightly. 'I've got a living to make.'

'Cheating her out of her savings, eh?'

He looked nettled. 'I *told* her it was all right. Anyway, the money's all Mr Dacre's. She hasn't got a penny of her own. It was for Mr Dacre to say if he wanted the job done, so he must've agreed.'

Atherton smiled smoothly. 'I see. Of course, you didn't mind taking the money from an old man in a wheelchair?'

Andrews flared up. 'What're you trying to say? I'm an honest builder, anyone will tell you that.'

'Just trying to get an insight into your character.'

'Mr Dacre's a bad-tempered old bastard, and he treats her like dirt, so you needn't take up for him! What's all this got to do with it anyway?'

'Well, you see,' Atherton said, 'here was this handy hole in the terrace and, lo and behold, your wife's body turns up in it. Naturally I wondered whose idea it was to dig the hole in the first place.'

Surprisingly, Andrews crumpled and a couple of convulsive sobs broke out before he covered his face with his hands and sat making choking noises into them, his shoulders shaking. 'I didn't kill her!' he cried, muffled. 'I wouldn't! I loved her! You've got to believe me!'

Atherton waited implacably until the noises stopped. Then he said, 'All right, tell me about you and Jennifer. How long have you been married?'

'Ten years,' Andrews said pallidly. 'We have our ups and downs like any couple – you know how it is – but . . .' It was one of those sentences not designed to be finished.

'How did you meet her?'

'I was doing a job in St Albans. That's where she comes from. I went to the pub after work one evening and there she was.'

'Working behind the bar?'

Andrews didn't like that. A little point of colour came to his cheeks. 'She was a customer, same as me. She was there with some friends. It's only recently she's started working at the Goat – and anyway, she's a waitress in the restaurant there, not a barmaid.'

'You've got something against barmaids?'

'Not as such. It's just – not something you want your wife doing, is it? She helps out sometimes in the restaurant at the Goat, that's all, because Linda asked her to, as a friend.'

'Linda?'

'Jack's wife. Jack Potter, the landlord. Linda runs the restaurant. It was her idea to start it – she reckoned there was lots of money round here for a posh restaurant. Sharp as a packet of needles is Linda.'

'And your wife also worked for an estate agent, I understand?'

'That's her proper job,' Andrews said. He seemed eager, Atherton thought, to distance the Andrews name from the taint of licensed victualling. 'That's what she was doing in St Albans when I first met her. She does four mornings in the office for David and the occasional Saturday and Sunday, if there's a lot of people wanting to see over houses.'

'And David is?'

'David Meacher. It's his own business. He's got two offices, one in Chiswick High Road, and the other out where he lives, out Denham way. But that's not open all the time. The Chiswick one's the main branch.'

'And that's where your wife worked?'

He hesitated, and Atherton saw his hands, resting on the table, clench slightly. 'Mostly. Sometimes David would ask her to man the other office, when he couldn't get anyone else. But not often.'

'She was working at the Chiswick office yesterday?'

'In the morning.'

'You saw her off to work, did you?'

'We left at the same time. Half past eight – just before. I was only going round the corner, to St Michael Square. She had to get to the office for nine. Nine to one, she did.'

Atherton nodded encouragingly. 'And you got to work at the Old Rectory at about half past eight? And stayed there all day?'

'Yes.'

'Where did you go for lunch?'

'I—' He stopped himself, looking at Atherton suspiciously. 'I didn't go anywhere. I don't stop for lunch. I just worked through.'

'All alone all day? Did Mrs Hammond come out and chat to you?'

'No, why should she? Anyway, I like to get on when I'm working.'

'And what time did you finish?'

'Six. I started packing up when the church clock struck six.'

'And then you went—?'

Andrews paused, his eyes still but his mind apparently busy. 'I went for a drink.'

'At the Goat?'

'Not in working clothes. They don't like it. I went for one at the Mimpriss. Then I went home.'

'What time did you get home?'

'It would be – about half past seven, I suppose.'

'Your wife was there?'

'No. It was her night on at the Goat.'

'Ah, I see. So what did you do?'

'Got some supper. Watched telly. Went to bed.'

'And what time did your wife come home?'

Andrews looked away. 'She didn't come home,' he said sullenly.

Atherton laid his hands slowly on the table in front of him. They were large, open, relaxed, handsome hands; strong contrast to Andrews' battered and whited fists, bunched and wary opposite them. 'Now that's interesting. She didn't come home at all, and yet you weren't worried about her?'

'Course I was worried!' Andrews flashed. 'Who says I wasn't?'

'But you didn't call the police and report her missing.'

'You don't report someone missing when they've not come home just one night.'

'She'd done it before, had she, stayed out all night?'

'No! But – well, a person might go and see a friend and get talking and so forth, and, you know, forget the time. You know what women are like, yackety-yack all day and all night when they get together.' He appealed weakly to Atherton, *hombre à hombre*.

Atherton remained stony, *hombre*-proof. 'But she didn't telephone to say where she was, and you didn't phone around to check? I find that very remarkable.'

'How do you know I didn't?'

'Because you'd have said so. No, you just said you watched television and went to bed.'

'Well, I did phone round,' Andrews said defiantly.

'Who?'

'Lots of people. I don't remember,' Andrews muttered.

'Give me some names.' Atherton cocked his pen at dictation angle.

'I can't remember them all.'

'Give me just one name, then, that I can check.' No answer. 'Well, it doesn't matter, we can get the numbers from BT,' Atherton said cheerfully. 'They're all recorded by computer now, did you know that? Every phone call you make, it's all logged.'

Andrews looked at him resentfully. 'Oh, leave me alone!' he cried. 'Why are you going on at me? I didn't do anything!'

'That was rather the point,' Atherton said, with a sinuous smile. 'Your wife, whom you loved, didn't come home as expected and you didn't do anything. It just struck me as strange.' Andrews said nothing. 'Well, let's move on, shall we? You got up the next morning and went to work again – rather early, I understand. Why was that?'

'Why was what?' Andrews seemed confused by the question.

'Why did you go to work so early?'

'I – I hadn't slept well. Worried about Jen, you see,' he added, on a happy thought.

'Do you usually wash and shave when you get up in the morning?'

'Course I do. What d'you mean?' He caught the purport of the question. 'Well, I usually do, but I was upset this morning. Worried.'

'Of course you were. You tossed and turned all night, woke up early, and thought as you were up you might as well go and make a start at Mrs Hammond's?'

'That's right,' Andrews said. 'Get on with the job, get it finished.'

'Get on with the job of mixing up the concrete to pour into the nice hole you'd dug, perhaps? Filling it in before anyone could discover what was lying in the bottom?'

'No!'

'Only, bad luck for you, Mrs Hammond got there first, eh? Pity you didn't start a bit earlier. But I suppose the sound of a concrete mixer at dawn would have been a bit much, wouldn't it? A bit suspicious. Wake up the neighbours, bring them round to complain. And then they'd see what you were up to—'

'No! I tell you, no!' Andrews was on his feet, his face congested with emotion – fear, anger, what? 'It wasn't like that! I didn't kill her! It wasn't me!'

'*Sit down,*' Atherton said icily, and Andrews subsided, trembling. Atherton stared at him impassively for long enough to get him really nervous, and then said, 'It wasn't you that murdered her, eh? Well, you see, when I came in here, I didn't even know she'd been murdered. I thought it might possibly have been death from natural causes, or even an accident. But you seem to know more than me, Mr Andrews. So suppose you tell me how you did it? What did you use? And where did it happen? You know, if you get it off your chest, you'll feel a lot better.'

But Andrews laid his head down on his arms, moaning, and seeing it was not going to stop soon, Atherton decided to leave him to stew for a bit.

Emerging again into the great hall of the Old Rectory, Slider bumped into a bit of a frackarse. PC Renker, newly arrived, was standing at the open door of the drawing-room, from within which Cyril Dacre was concluding a long and fluent tirade.

'—outrageous overreaction! Coming in here mob-handed – bursting into a private residence like a gang of storm troopers! And don't think I can't see you smirk,' he added furiously, as

Renker made a face at Swilley. 'Opening doors without knocking – are we living in a fascist state? Yes, you look like a Hun! Pure Nordic type. Love the uniform, too, don't you? What did you say your name was – Reinke? I knew a Reinke in Berlin before the war, ended up as a top-echelon SS man. Complete fanatic. Well, you can get out of here! I insist on my privacy. Yes, and you can take this nursemaid away, too,' he added furiously, gesturing towards Swilley. 'I don't need watching in case I fall out of my chair. I may be old but I'm not senile!'

Slider jerked Swilley out with his head, apologised tersely, and shoved Renker gently out of Dacre's line of vision. Renker, tall, broad-shouldered, fair-haired and blue-eyed, looked at Slider with a hurt quirk of the mouth. 'I just opened the door looking for you, sir,' he murmured. 'Didn't get a chance to say more than my name, and he was off.'

'He's had a trying morning,' Slider said. 'Go outside and help McLaren. Swilley, wait here in case I need you.' He inserted himself politely into the doorway and faced the smouldering historian. 'I'm sorry to have to disturb you, sir, but I would like to talk to you about what's happened here,' he said firmly.

Dacre looked out from under his eyebrows. 'Well, if you must, you must. I shall have to do my civic duty, I suppose. You're not quite such a fool as some of the others, at any rate.' Slider accepted the compliment gracefully and came in. 'Shut the door,' Dacre commanded. 'I see you've left the Rhinemaiden on guard. I called her a nursemaid, but I rather guessed she was meant as a gaoler.'

'WDC Swilley was just making sure you weren't disturbed,' Slider said smoothly.

'Didn't work, did it? That bloody Hun still came bursting in.'

'There are quite a few reporters outside, sir,' Slider mentioned.

'Ha! The vultures gather. Where there's a corpse . . .'

'We'll try to keep them away from you.'

Dacre shrugged. 'I've nothing to tell them – or you. I slept rather soundly last night, for a change, so I knew nothing about it until Frances came in this morning with her incoherent babble about Andrews having murdered his wife. My daughter,' he added severely, 'falls into a flap at the sight of a spider, so you can imagine the state of what serves her for a mind when she came across a real human corpse on the premises. It is rather hard, by the way,' he pursued, 'to be cooped up in here with your Amazon looming over me – to make sure I don't destroy any evidence, no doubt – when I wanted to see the body.'

Slider, seeing a gleam in the dark eyes, began to suspect he was being teased, and relaxed cautiously. 'It's gone now,' he said.

'Yes, I saw the undertaker's vehicle go past. "Meat wagon" – isn't that what you fellows call it? But if one is to be embroiled in a sordid case of murder, it's hard not to be allowed any of the fun.'

'Why do you think it's a case of murder?' Slider asked mildly.

'I hardly think Jennifer Andrews lay down in the hole of her own accord, quietly died, and then covered herself up with a tarpaulin. Please, Inspector, don't patronise my intelligence.'

'Someone put the body there, of course,' Slider said, 'but she may have died by accident.'

'No, no, my money's on murder. She was a vulgar, unpleasant woman, ripe for the plucking,' he said largely.

'Someone is dead, sir,' Slider reminded him.

Dacre threw a sharp glance under his eyebrows. 'At my age, and in my situation, death loses its semi-religious glamour. You can't expect me to feign a pious reverence for a mere biological process, and one, moreover, that I am already in the early stages of.'

Slider made no comment on that. Instead he said, 'Tell me what you know about Jennifer Andrews. You said she was unpleasant. In what way?'

'Loud-mouthed, brash and vulgar. The sort of woman who always has to be the centre of attention and doesn't mind how she achieves it. She liked to organise everything that happened around here so that she could manipulate people and situations to her own advantage. She hadn't a scintilla of proper feeling or sensitivity. She flirted with every man over the age of sixteen and even treated *me* with an appalling kind of coy roguishness.' His wrath mounted to a peak as the final, horrible revelation burst from his lips. 'She called me a "dear old boy" and referred to

me as her "sweetheart"! If ever a woman deserved to die it
was her!'

'Yes, I see.'

'Oh, well . . .' Dacre looked a little shaken by his own vehe-
mence. 'I don't suffer fools gladly.'

Or at all, Slider thought. 'How well did she know your
daughter? Did she call here often?'

'She called here from time to time in the course of organising
things. And she and Frances were both involved in activities
at the church. She's a neighbour: not quite of us, but with
aspirations. There is a species of, if I may call it so, village
life on the Mimpriss Estate, of which Mrs Andrews longed to
be part. Whatever activity there was, she wormed her way into
it. Socially ambitious, you see – the worst type. I think she
viewed this house as the local manor, and myself as lord of
it, so she was always eager to ingratiate herself. She couldn't
get anywhere with me, so she attached herself to Frances.'

'Would you say she and your daughter were friends?'

His lip curled. 'Frances hasn't the knack of making *friends*.
Never had. She and Jennifer Andrews had acquaintances in
common and sat on the same committees. And, of course, the
husband did quite a few jobs for us. You took him away, I see.'
He nodded towards the windows that looked out on the street.
'Poor devil. Driven to it by that frightful woman. The man should
be decorated for performing a public service, not hanged.'

'We're not allowed to hang anyone nowadays,' Slider reminded
him.

'More's the pity.'

'You seem to be very sure it was Andrews who killed her.'

'Oh, please, Inspector, play your parlour games with someone
else! The body turns up in a hole in my terrace, which by
complete chance was dug by the victim's husband – with whom
she was on famously bad terms! It's hardly a challenge to the
intellect!'

'Why were they on bad terms?'

Dacre seemed to lose interest quite abruptly. 'I have no idea,'
he said, and turned his face away with a stony expression. 'I
don't interest myself in other people's domestic affairs.'

'Do you remember when you last saw Mrs Andrews?'

He seemed to consider not answering, and then said, 'On

Sunday morning. She called on Frances briefly. Something about arranging the flowers for the church, I believe. I didn't see her – Frances went out to her, in the hall. She didn't stay long.'

'Did she come to see her husband here, while he was working?'

'I sincerely doubt it. But how would I know? I can't see the terrace from here.'

'Do you always sit in this room, then? I noticed there is a desk and typewriter in the other room, which looks out on the terrace and garden. Is that where you write?'

'I don't write any more,' he said irritably. 'In case it has escaped your notice, I am a dying man.'

'I'm sorry, sir. I do have to ask questions—'

'About the protagonists in this sordid affair, perhaps. You do not have the right to interrogate me about my own activities!' He put a hand rather theatrically to his forehead. 'I must ask you to leave me now. I tire easily these days.'

Slider stood up patiently. 'I shall probably want to ask you some more questions later.'

Dacre snorted. 'If you insist on wasting my time in this way, you must take the consequences. However, since Jennifer Andrews was obviously *not* killed on these premises, you would be better advised to find out where she died and how she was brought here. Why don't you try to find out who put her body into the hole?'

Slider felt his hackles rising. 'Thank you for the valuable advice. I would never have thought of that for myself.'

Dacre's face darkened. 'How dare you display your insolence to me! You are a public servant! I pay your wages!'

'And my parents paid yours!' Slider went cold all over as he heard himself say it. In the brief silence that followed Dacre's eyes opened very wide; and then, surprisingly, his face cleared and he began to chuckle.

'Yes, I dare say they did! I am justly rebuked. You must forgive me my occasional self-indulgence, Inspector. At my time of life, being rude to people is the only kind of bad behaviour one is still capable of.'

CHAPTER THREE

Char Grilled

To the right of the Old Rectory, beyond the gravel parking space and hard by the overweening hedge, was St Michael House, which had presumably been named by someone who had never shopped at Marks and Spencer. It was one of those 1920s joke Tudor houses, stucco above and herringbone brick below, with so many pitch-covered beams, horizontal and vertical, it looked as though it had been scribbled out by a child in a temper. It had an oak front door studded and bedecked with extraneous pieces of iron, hysterically quaint diamond-pane casements, and cylindrical chimneys so tall and elaborate they looked like confectionery. If you could have snapped them off, they would undoubtedly have been lettered *Merrie Englande* all through.

Not that WDC Kathleen 'Norma' Swilley, owner of the most fantasised-about legs in the Met, thought in those terms. Walking up the brick front path to start the house-to-house, her verdict was, 'What a junky old dump!' She lived in a brand new flat in a brand new block in West Kensington, and had no use for things antique, false or genuine. The newer the better, was her motto; and if whatever it was could function on its own by means of electricity, so much the better. She'd have had electric food that ate itself if she could.

When she reached the front door, there were so many bits of old iron attached to it that it took her a while to work out that the bell was operated by a pull-down handle on a shaft. The instant it rang, however, the door was opened by the householders, who must have been crouched behind it waiting, and she was glad-handed and whisked into the lounge with the avidity of an Amway induction. Defreitas had been right about that, it seemed: the Mimpriss residents were aching to be in on the act.

The inside of the house was at one with its exterior. The lounge had cast-iron wall lights in the shape of flaming torches, a wheel-shaped iron chandelier supporting electric candles, and a vast herringbone-brick inglenook containing a very small gas log fire. Perhaps to foster illusion, a log basket sat on the brick hearth, filled with real logs and pine-cones: Norma bet the old dame dusted them daily, probably with the Hoover attachment. The furniture was all fumed oak and chintz-covered; there were display cabinets full of the sort of limited-edition figurines that are advertised in the *Sunday Times* magazine, Vernon Ward framed prints on the walls, dried flower arrangements everywhere, and a row of royal-commemorative plates around the picture rail.

Mr and Mrs Vanhurst Bright – Desmond and Mavis, they assured Swilley eagerly and watched until she wrote it down – were in their sixties and gave the same impression of careful prosperity as the house. His face had the over-soft look of a man who has been thin all his life and only put on fat in retirement, and he wore the willing but slightly tense expression of a very intelligent dog trying to understand human speech. She was thin, brittle and ramrod straight, and looked as though her whole life had been a battle against importunate door-to-door salesmen. She had evidently gone to the same hairdresser as Mrs Hammond, though her arrangement was tinted a fetching shade of mauve; with her chalky-pink face-powder and rather bluish shade of lipstick it made her look as though she were slightly dead. She was dressed in a pink cashmere twinset and heather tweed kilt complete with grouse-claw kilt-pin, pearl earrings, two rows of pearls round her neck, more diamond hoop rings than perhaps the strictest of good taste would think necessary, lisle stockings, and well-polished brogues as brown and shiny as a racehorse's bum. He was wearing a lovat tweed jacket over a cad's yellow waistcoat, khaki shirt and green knitted tie, grey flannel trousers, and a beautiful pair of expensive brown Oxfords, which were so unexpectedly large compared with the rest of him that he looked as though he had been inserted into them as a preliminary to being tied up and dropped into the harbour.

Swilley wondered at their immaculate appearance so early in the day. Did they always dress like this, or had they made a special effort in anticipation of a police visit? The house was immaculate too: perhaps they were the sort that would still change for dinner on a desert island. She bet they had twin beds with satin quilts and his 'n' hers library books on the bedside cabinets. Well, good luck to them.

'I'm sorry to have to disturb you—' Norma began routinely, but they jumped in eagerly.

'Oh, no, not at all. Our pleasure,' said Mr Bright, with a social smile.

'Naturally we were expecting to be called upon,' said Mrs Bright, 'and of course we are eager to do anything we can to help in these dreadful circumstances.'

'It's our duty,' Mr Bright added.

'We've never held back when it was a question of duty,' said Mrs Bright, 'however inconvenient.'

'Well, I hope I shan't have to inconvenience you for long,' Norma said.

'Oh, please, not at all, it's no trouble,' Mr Bright waffled happily. 'Won't you sit down, Miss – er?'

Norma sat on a slippery chintz sofa. Mr Bright looked at her legs with a slightly stunned air and sat down opposite her. Mrs Bright arranged herself carefully in an armchair between them and looked to see what Mr Bright was looking at. A spot of colour appeared in her cheeks. 'Would you like a cup of coffee, Miss – er?' she asked, rather sharply. 'Desmond, shall we have coffee?'

He snapped out of it and began elaborately rising and enquiring about the nature of preferred beverage and Norma saw herself reaching retirement in this mock-Tudor embrace and said quickly, 'No, thank you very much, no coffee. I'd just like to ask you a few questions and then I can take myself out of your hair.'

He sat again, trying to keep his eyes from her legs and not succeeding very well. 'Ask away, then,' he said heartily. 'It's no trouble. We're glad to help.'

'Not that we have much we can tell you,' Mrs Bright put in, in a bid for attention. 'We didn't know Mrs Andrews well.'

'She seemed a nice sort of gel,' Mr Bright rumbled gallantly, and Mrs Bright gave him a sharp look.

'I wouldn't say that. I'm afraid my husband is rather susceptible to a pretty face. Mrs Andrews wasn't really One of Us.

She worked at the pub, you know, the Goat In Boots.' She gave Norma a significant nod, as though this explained everything. 'She was rather a *forward* young woman. One might almost say *pushy*. She's quite taken over the church social committee, *and* the flower arrangements, and I have to say that some of her ideas of what's fitting for a religious building are—'

'My dear,' Mr Bright interrupted anxiously, 'she is dead.'

'That doesn't change the facts,' Mrs Bright went on relentlessly. 'She didn't understand our ways, and she never seemed to realise where her interference wasn't welcome.'

'Oh, come, I wouldn't say "interference".' Mr Bright seemed anxious for his wife not to expose herself. 'Someone has to organise things and she had so much energy—'

'Well, I have to say I didn't like her,' Mrs Bright said, giving him a nasty look, 'energy or no energy. She attached herself to poor Frances Hammond, who hasn't the sense of a day-old chick, poor creature, and *forced* her way into our circle, and then tried to impose her vulgar ideas on us. There's a time and a place for everything, and *our* church fête is not the time and place for a bouncing castle, or whatever they like to call it.'

Mr Bright appealed to Norma. 'I always found her very polite. Quite a nicely spoken girl. She was always cheerful and pleasant to me.'

'Yes, well she would be, wouldn't she?' Mrs Bright said sharply.

Mr Bright went a little pink. 'I don't know what you mean, Mavis.'

'Work it out for yourself,' Mrs Bright snapped, with an appalling lapse from British Empire standards, and clamped her thin lips shut.

Norma, fascinated by this glimpse under the carpet, reflected how odd it was that the more determinedly a couple kept up their shop front, the more eager they were to trot out old grievances before a 'safe' audience like a policeman, priest or doctor. She looked at Mr Bright. 'Tell me what you know about Mr Andrews.'

He got as far as 'Well,' when his wife interrupted.

'We didn't know him. I've heard he's a good builder, but we have our own people that we've used for twenty years.'

'Kept himself to himself,' Mr Bright said approvingly.

'He's done one or two jobs next door. I can't say whether he did them well or not,' Mrs Bright went on, finding another grievance, 'but I wouldn't use anyone who wasn't more careful about leaving things clean and tidy. Only a few months ago I had to speak to him quite sharply about parking his lorry outside our house. Quite apart from spoiling the view, it leaked oil all over the road. There's still a stain there.'

Swilley tried another pass over the subject. 'So you have no idea how things stood between Mr Andrews and his wife?'

'I don't interest myself in other people's private business,' Mrs Bright said loftily. 'It's poor Cyril Dacre I'm sorry for. It's a dreadful thing to have happen on one's own premises.'

'All those people tramping about,' Mr Bright joined in, now the topic was safe again. 'Journalists everywhere. And in his state of health—'

'He's very ill, you know. *Cancer.*' She lowered her voice and almost mouthed the word, as if it were indelicate. 'It's dreadful that he should be upset at a time like this.'

'You know him well?'

'Oh, of course. Margery Dacre was one of my *dearest* friends,' Mrs Bright said eagerly. 'She's been dead – oh, ten years now?'

'Ten, it must be,' he confirmed.

'Of course, Cyril Dacre is a *very distinguished* man. We're proud to have him as a neighbour. His mother was a Spennimore before she married – very old Hampshire family.'

'Wonderful brainy chap,' Mr Bright said admiringly, and added with faint puzzlement, 'Odd sense of humour sometimes, but I suppose that comes with being so clever. He writes books, you know.'

'The parties they used to give, before Margery died! She was fond of music. They had a grand piano in the hall, and they had wonderful musical soirées. Quite famous musicians came to play, friends of Cyril's. He had friends in every circle – artists, actors, scholars—'

'That athletic chap, the one who broke the Olympic record, what's his name? Became an MP—' Mr Bright shorted out, frowning with the effort of remembering.

'Dinner parties, garden parties,' she went on, ignoring him, 'intellectual conversation.'

'It was like *The Brains Trust* in there some evenings.'

'Of course, one had to make allowances for Cyril. He could be quite devastatingly rude, but he is a genius after all. And there was that terrible tragedy – his son dying so young. I think that made him a little strange.' She nodded to Swilley as if she ought to know. 'After Margery died Frances took over as hostess; and I must say,' she added, with a hint of surprise at discovering it for herself, 'that one never noticed the difference. Of course, Margery never did say much.'

'Nice woman, but quiet,' Mr Bright agreed. 'Left all the talking to Cyril.'

'And Frances hasn't two words to say for herself,' Mrs Bright concluded. 'But, of course, since Cyril's become so ill all that's stopped. They haven't entertained in – oh, two years. He keeps himself completely to himself now. I suppose,' she added with a sigh, 'that when he goes it will be the end of an era. One can't see Frances keeping up the old traditions. She hasn't many friends. That's why she fell a prey to Mrs Andrews.'

'There's that chap who visits,' Mr Bright said. 'What's his name? Married to the horsy woman – what's her name?'

So far Norma had nothing down in her little book. 'Mrs Bright, if I could just—'

'*Vanhurst* Bright,' she corrected with sharp affront. 'No hyphen.'

'Mrs Vanhurst Bright,' Norma said obediently, 'if I could just come to the events of last night: did you notice what time Mr Andrews left work?'

'Just after six,' she said promptly. 'We were watching the six o'clock news when the lorry started up. The engine makes a dreadful noise – and the tyres crunching over that gravel. We could hardly hear what was being said.'

'I suppose it went past your window?'

'No, he went the other way.'

'And did you hear him arrive this morning?'

'We certainly did!' Mrs Bright said, with tight annoyance.

'Well, people have to work,' Mr Bright said, making all possible allowances.

'But not at that time of the morning. It's inconsiderate to be making noise at half past six in the morning—'

'It was a quarter to seven, dear,' said Mr Bright. 'I looked at the clock,' he added to Swilley.

'It's still much too early,' his wife said, annoyed at being corrected. 'Half past eight is quite early enough; a quarter to seven is beyond reason. I said to Desmond, "I suppose we'll have the cement mixer starting up next, and have to close the windows." People shouldn't have noisy jobs done in the summer when people have their windows open.'

'So you heard the truck arrive and pull onto the gravel? What else?'

Mrs Bright considered. 'Well, I thought I heard someone shout, and then some voices talking – I suppose that was Frances and Mr Andrews – and then nothing until the police arrived and all the fuss started.'

'You didn't look out of the window when you heard the shout?'

'No. It wasn't loud. More a sort of – exclamation.'

'I didn't hear it,' Mr Bright said.

'In any case, you can't see the terrace from any of our windows because of the hedge.'

'That's why it's there,' he pointed out.

'And what about during the night?' Swilley asked. 'Were you woken by any disturbance?'

'No, not that I remember,' Mrs Bright said. 'Why? Did something happen?'

Mr Bright, surprisingly, proved more on the ball than his wife. 'Well, dear, poor Mrs Andrews must have been put into the hole during the night, or someone would have seen.'

'Oh,' she said, evidently not following.

'Under cover of darkness,' he elaborated. 'If Frances found her there before Mr Andrews arrived—'

'Oh. I suppose so.'

'But you didn't hear anything during the night?' Norma pressed.

'No,' she said, with a world of regret. 'Did you, Desmond?'

'Nothing,' he said, shaking his head.

'Do you sleep with the windows open?'

'Always,' he said.

'That was why we heard the lorry arrive in the morning,' she said. 'I'm sure if he'd driven up in the night and stopped outside we'd have heard. It's very quiet round here at night.'

Swilley extracted herself with difficulty, and went to try the neighbour on the other side of the Old Rectory, but knocking and ringing elicited no reply, and the place had a shut-up, empty look. Out at work or away? she wondered. They would have to try again later. She saw Mackay emerge from three doors down and called out to him. 'Hoi, Andy!' He turned. 'Have you done this one?'

'No-one in,' he called back. 'I've done the next two. I'll do the rest of this row if you like.'

'Okay, I'll start at the corner, then,' she said, and trudged off. Breakfast seemed a distant dream. If the next house was decent, she decided, she'd accept a cup of coffee. With a bit of luck they might break out the biccies, too.

Atherton came back with the keen-eyed look of a police dog entering a vagrants' hostel. 'Open and shut case,' he said.

'Oh, really?' said Slider, leaning on the car roof and addressing him across it. It was going to be another hot day. The earth smelt warm and the sunshine on the pale stones of the churchyard wall made them hard to look at.

Atherton leaned too. 'Andrews says he went home from work last night, watched telly and went to bed. His wife was out at work so he was all alone. His wife didn't come home all night, but he didn't do anything about it, just got up and went to work this morning as usual – having forgotten to wash and shave – and blow me, there she was, down the hole! Well, you can't help being convinced by a story like that, can you?'

Slider assumed a judicious frown. 'I don't know. Cyril Dacre, the owner of the house and thus the hole, was extremely anxious to lay the crime in Andrews' lap, despite accidentally giving away the fact that he – Dacre – loathed the deceased with a deep and deadly loathing, and rejoices that she's dead.'

Atherton slapped a hand to his cheek, wide-eyed. 'Of course, I see it all now! It must have been Dacre. He pursued her up and down the terrace in his wheelchair until she fell into the hole and died of exhaustion. And, come to think of it, Andrews did say that the work on the terrace was Dacre's idea. He says he told Mrs H there was no need to do anything, but she – i.e. her father, since his was the final authority – insisted.'

Slider shook his head. 'Pity he said that, because Mrs Hammond says it was Andrews who told her that the work needed to be done, or the whole terrace would collapse.'

'So he was trying to distance himself from authorship of the hole?'

'It was a silly lie to tell – too easy to expose,' Slider said.

'Perhaps he hasn't had much practice. This could be the first time he's murdered his wife.'

'We don't know she was murdered,' Slider said, for the third time that day. 'She might have dropped dead of a heart-attack, during a quarrel, for instance, and Andrews – or whoever – panicked and tried to get rid of the body.'

'"Might" is right,' Atherton said.

'Well, we'd better try to expose a few more of Andrews' lies, hadn't we?' Slider said. 'If it was a domestic murder, the most likely place for him to do it was at home: private, convenient, and a thorough knowledge of the tools to hand to boot. The forensic team's going over there when they've finished here, but we might as well have a look first.'

Woodbridge Road was the long road that led from the other side of St Michael Square to the main road. Fourways was at the far end, on the corner with the main thoroughfare. There was a red sports car parked on the hard standing, with the registration number JEN 111.

'Hers, I bet you,' Atherton said.

'Give that man a coconut. Well, if she was working at the Goat In Boots last night, she must have come back here afterwards.'

'Or she might have walked to work.'

'So she might.'

'Or he could have driven it back himself from wherever he killed her.'

'So he could. Not much help, is it? Shall we go in?'

Fourways was a large, modern, well-appointed house, smelling strongly of new plaster, and full of large, modern, well-appointed furnishings of the sort that were obviously expensive without being in any way luxurious or even particularly pleasing. It was the sort of house to which you might invite people you didn't know very well so that they could marvel at how well you were doing for yourself.

It had Atherton gaping. 'Gloriosky, what a gin palace!'

'Every mod con,' Slider agreed. 'Sunken whirlpool bath, electrically operated curtains—'

'The expense of spirit in a waste of shame,' Atherton said.

There was no sign of any struggle anywhere – no sign of life at all. Everything was clean and tidy, the beds made, the bathrooms spotless. There was no dirty crockery in the kitchen: if Andrews had eaten supper on Tuesday night and breakfast on Wednesday morning, he had not only washed up after himself but dried up and put away too.

'As if!' Atherton snorted. 'No man on this planet puts away after he's washed up. It's against nature.'

The kitchen waste-bin contained a fresh bin-liner and nothing else; the toothbrushes in the *en suite* bathroom were both dry, as was the wash-basin, the bath and the floor of the shower. The towels were clean and folded and looked as if they had just been put out.

'It doesn't look as if he's been home at all,' Atherton said.

'He said he was watching television all evening, but the TV listings are folded open at Monday,' Slider observed. 'Not that that proves anything. He could have known what was on, or just put it on at random when he got home.'

'There was football on last night,' Atherton blinked, feigning astonishment. 'Blimey, even I know that! An international – England versus Italy. If he'd been in, he'd've been bound to look and see what time it started.'

'Maybe he doesn't like football.'

'And the Pope's a Jew.'

'Just trying not to jump to conclusions, that's all. One of us doing it is quite enough. Well, I think we've seen all we'll see here. How was Andrews when you left him?' Slider asked, as they headed for the front door.

'He's gone sulky,' Atherton said. 'Decided his best policy is to say nothing – but he's not agitating to go home.'

'Oh?' Slider asked significantly.

'I dunno,' Atherton answered elliptically. 'I don't think I'd read anything into it necessarily. He seems to be in a state of lethargy.'

They opened the front door, and found a woman outside arguing with the guardian policeman. She was a small, fair woman in her fifties, with a neat face and figure, wearing a raincoat which hung open over a pink nylon overall, and she was carrying a raffia shopping-bag. She turned to them, her expression a mixture of belligerence and fear, and her sharp eyes effortlessly singled out Slider as the present peak of authority.

'What's going on?' she demanded. 'What's happened? Only I was going past and I see all this kerfuffle. There's not been a burglary?'

'No, I'm afraid it's more serious than that,' Slider said. 'Would you tell me who you are, please?'

'I'm Pat, their cleaner. Pat Attlebury – Mrs,' she added, as though they might already know several Pat Attleburys from whom she wished to be distinguished. 'Tuesday and Friday mornings I do for them, two hours, though there's not a lot to do, really, between you and I. Except for the dust. You always get a lot of dust in a new house,' she explained, still scanning their faces. 'What's going on, then, if it's not a burglary?'

'How about a cup of tea?' Slider invited, recognising a bunny champion when he saw one. 'I expect you know your way around the kitchen?'

Over the requisite cuppa, Mrs Attlebury was perfectly willing to chat. She expressed a properly hushed shock at the news, but she seemed less than grief-stricken about Mrs Andrews' fate.

'It's *him* I'm sorry for. He'll take it hard. Besotted about her. Such a nice man, too – though I'm always having to speak to him about his boots. I mean, all right, the building trade's a good business, and *he's* done all right out of it – look at this place! But building sites mean dirt, you can't get away from that. I think that's what *she* didn't like – always down on him, sneering, you know – as though she thought she was too good for him. Didn't mind spending the money, oh, no! But it was beneath her to be married to a builder, even though he had got his own business. I mean, that's where it is, isn't it? He's like the company chairman if you want to look at it that way. But he wasn't good enough for Mrs Lady Docker Andrews! She didn't like him coming home mucky, if you ask me. Though she had a point. It was bad enough when I used to do for them where they used to live before, but a new place like this shows up every mark, and she would have these pale carpets – madness, I call it. It made it hard for me, and he wasn't careful where he put his

feet. Well, men never are, are they? Take off your boots at the
door, I said to him over and over, that's all I ask. Well, even
this dry weather there's still earth and cement and everything,
isn't there? But I couldn't get it through his head. But apart from
that, I've no complaints. There's hardly anything to do, really.
To tell you the truth, I don't think they're ever in much. He's
down the pub often as not, and she's gallivanting God knows
where. Which, when you think of it, is a waste, this lovely new
house built specially for her and everything. But she wasn't a
bit grateful.' She sipped her tea. 'How did she die, then?'

'We don't know yet,' Slider said. 'Did she have heart trouble,
do you know, or any chronic condition like that?'

'Heart? Strong as an ox, her,' Mrs Attlebury said. 'Far as I
know, anyway. But you'd want to ask him, really.'

'Oh, we will. But it's nice to get these things confirmed. Was
she on any medication, that you knew about? Did she ever take
sleeping pills?'

'I never heard that she did. There was never any on the
bedside table, anyway – or in the medicine cabinet. Her doctor'd
be the one to know, I expect. Dr Lands, same as me, she went
to, in Dalling Road.'

Slider noted down the name, and she watched him, her mind
working. 'So it wasn't a road accident, then, or anything like a
shooting or a stabbing? I mean, you wouldn't be asking about
pills if it was,' she said ruminatively, and then seemed to feel
this comment lacked proper feeling, for she looked at them
defiantly and said, 'I hadn't any time for her, if you want to
know. She wasn't a nice person, in my view.'

'In what way, not nice?' Slider prompted.

'Fast,' said Mrs Attlebury decisively, and made a face. 'I don't
know how he stood her, to tell you the truth. He had a hell of a
life with her, poor soul. All right, she kept herself nice, and I don't
say she wasn't a smart-looking woman, but it was his money she
spent dolling herself up, and she should have been doing it for
him, not showing herself off to every Tom, Dick and Harry. I
mean, he's out working every hour God sends to make money
for her to spend, and she's off gallivanting around and flirting
with anything in trousers. Oh,' she said, with a significant look, 'it
wasn't a secret. I mean, she didn't bother to hide it. Flirted openly
– if it wasn't worse than flirting. I wouldn't put it past her.'

'How did Mr Andrews take that?'

'Well, he didn't like it, of course,' she said. 'What man would?'

'Did they quarrel about it?' Slider asked.

'What do you think?'

'Were the quarrels violent?'

'Shocking! I've heard them going at it hammer and tongs in another room when I've been cleaning. Heard them over the Hoover more than once – well, she was a loud-mouthed woman, you know, voice like a foghorn. And bossy? Always telling you how to do your job. Had to organise everything – you know the sort. She'd organise a pig into having puppies, that one. Well, it's not nice for a man, being taken down by his wife like that, in front of other people, like she did. It's no wonder he got mad.'

'Did he hit her?'

She seemed to realise at last where this was going. 'We-ell,' she said cautiously. 'I can't say I've ever seen him lift his hand to her. He's not that type, to my mind. And, like I say, he worshipped the ground she walked on. Except when she got him riled and he lost his temper. But he's the quiet sort, really.'

'Those are sometimes the worst,' Atherton said wisely. 'Quiet till you push 'em too far, and then – bang.'

'He could be shocking when he was provoked,' she acknowledged, 'but that's the same as any man. But he's never hit her that I know of. He's a nice man. It's her I couldn't stand.'

'Did they have any children?'

'No, and it's a pity if you ask me, because he'd have made a lovely dad, and it might have kept her at home a bit more, clipped her wings. But they didn't, and why I couldn't tell you, though I expect it was her that said no. Selfish, she was. Spiteful, too,' she added, looking towards Slider with an old grievance plainly bursting to get out. 'She changed the flower rota at the church so that I lost my turn, because the week she changed me to I was on holiday. She *knew* that. She just wanted another turn herself; thinks she's God's gift – her with her dead sticks and dandelions and runner beans! Load of rubbish! I mean, who wants to look at that ugly stuff instead of proper flowers? I do a nice arrangement, roses and pinks and pretty things like that.

But she says, Oh, Pat, she says, that's so old-fashioned! Nobody does that sort of thing any more! Never mind if they don't, I said, it's what people want to look at that matters, and they don't want to look at your rubbish, modern or not. It's like that modern art, dead cows in fish tanks and all that stuff. It's just plain ugly, I said to her. But you might as well talk to the cat. And, of course, Mr Tennyson backs her up. That's why he gave her the rota – thinks the sun shines out of her eyes, and no wonder, the way she makes up to him. Making up to a reverent! It's disgusting to my mind. But she'd flirt with anything in trousers, that one.'

She stopped abruptly, remembering the occasion, and what was required of it. She sipped her tea again, and then said, 'Oh, well, they say you shouldn't speak ill of the dead, but I speak as I find, and it has to be said, she was a right cow.'

Outside in the sunshine, having seen her off, Slider turned to Atherton. *'De mortuis?'*

'At least.'

'I've heard things can get pretty fierce at those flower-arranging classes.'

Atherton snorted. 'And this from the man who thinks oasis is a band!'

'At least we've got a motive now,' Slider said.

'The old green-eyed monster: an oldie, but a goodie. And we've bust Andrews' story wide open. Mrs Prattlebury left the house clean yesterday morning, and there's not so much as a builder's footmark to be seen, so he couldn't have gone home after work last night.'

'Unless he cleaned up after himself.'

'Hoover ye lightly while ye may? But he wouldn't, would he? If that's his alibi, he'd want it to look as if he'd been there. He wouldn't cover his tracks. It's not as if there were oceans of gore to clean up.'

'No, you're right, of course. I have to admit that it looks as if he didn't go home.'

'Crikey, if Mr D. Thomas is convinced, it must be so! Where next, guv?'

'I think we should pay a little visit to the Goat In Boots.'

'Ah, *nunc est bibendum.*'

'Come again?'

'I said, it's a fruity notion. Lay on, McDuff. I'm right behind you.'

CHAPTER FOUR

Shorts And Whine

The pub was not open yet, and Slider and Atherton walked in on an argument about whether it should be. Jack Potter, the landlord, was in favour of staying closed for the day, out of respect for the dead.

'It's not as if we've got the brewery to please,' he said. He was a wiry, flexible-looking man with a slight and incongruous paunch. He looked in his late forties, with thick black hair brushed back and slightly too long, bulging eyes, and a loose mouth. They came upon him bottling up behind the bar, shifting plastic crates of light ale about with the absent, practised strength of a circus juggler. He was wearing denim shorts, because of the heat, and a dark red polo shirt, which left his stringy, muscled arms bare. They were obviously strangers to the sun, for they were gleamingly white, and so generously veined and tattooed they looked like Stilton.

'It doesn't seem right to me to open up when Jen's – you know,' Potter went on, with syrupy tact.

'She's not "you-know",' his wife Linda said irritably. 'She's dead. It's not an indecent word.'

He glanced at her, hurt, and then appealed to Slider. 'Well, it doesn't seem respectful, anyway. What do you think?'

'I can't advise you on that,' Slider said.

'It's not as if she died in here,' Linda objected. She was fortyish, professionally smart, so well turned-out that you would never remember after meeting her whether she was attractive or not. Her appearance was designed, like waterproofing, to repel. She was in full fig even this early in the morning, right down to her earrings, with her hair lacquered to immobility in one of those ageless styles only suburban hairdressers can achieve. She had eyes hard enough to have etched glass, and a chain-smoker's voice rough enough to have sandblasted it afterwards; but a determined inspection revealed that under her makeup she looked pale and shaken, and her eyes were ringed. She clutched a packet of Rothmans and a throw-away lighter in one hand, and a man-sized Kleenex crumpled up in the other. 'I mean, no-one could be more sorry than me that she's dead, but when it comes right down to it, she wasn't family. Family you shut for,' she decreed. 'Not friends.'

'But she worked here, Lin,' Jack protested. His eyes were red and watery, and moistened further even as he spoke. 'I think people would expect it. I mean,' he appealed to Slider again, 'they're classy people round here. It's all lounge trade – you know, shorts and wine. You don't want to go offending them. And there won't be a soul on the estate doesn't know about it by lunchtime.'

Linda's voice hardened. 'I've got a full restaurant tonight, and five tables booked for lunch already, and I'm not giving all that away. Besides, they'll all want to talk about it,' she added, with an acidulous knowledge of human nature, 'and where are they going to go and do that, if not here? We'll have sales like you never saw for a Wednesday. Call it a public service, if you like, if it makes you feel better, but the long and the short is I'm not closing up for the sake of an empty gesture. It won't bring Jen back.'

Jack looked cowed. 'All right, love, if you think so. I just want to do what's right, that's all. I mean, Jen was—' His lips trembled and his eyes seemed in danger of overflowing. He took out a handkerchief and honked briskly into it, and then emerged, looking almost shyly at Slider and Atherton, to say, 'Can I offer you gents a drink, atawl?'

Linda shot him a hard look, and Slider said, 'It's a bit early for me, thanks all the same.'

'Cuppa coffee, then?'

'Jack, they want to ask questions,' Linda said impatiently. 'You get on with your bottling up, or you'll have the twirlies in before you're ready. If you'd like to come through to the snug where it's quiet . . .' she said to Slider and Atherton.

Slider fielded her smoothly, 'I know how busy you must both be, so to save time I'll talk to you while my colleague has a word with your husband, if that's all right.'

Linda Potter looked as though no-one had ever conned her in her life, but she nodded briskly, and walked away before him into the private bar.

The pub had obviously been a number of separate rooms, before most of the walls had been knocked out to make one large irregularly shaped one, low-ceilinged, beamed, the upright timbers showing where the walls had once been. The bar was three sides of a rectangle, and the snug was behind the wall on the fourth side, with a wooden serving-hatch through to the bar, and a little brass bell hung on a bracket beside it for service. The snug had one casement window of diamond panes too small and old to see through, though the sunshine streamed in strongly and illuminated the eternally falling dust. The air was heavy with the smell of furniture polish. The cherry-red carpet was tuftily new. There were three small round imitation antique oak tables, and banquettes and Windsor chairs upholstered in a chintz-patterned material. A beam running the length of the wall opposite the bar supported a range of the kind of junk pubs display to make them look homey: leather-bound books, pewter mugs and plates, a copper kettle, a crow-scarer, a set of donkey-boots, wooden butter-pats, wicker baskets. Since the real-ale, real-pub revolution there was a whole new vocabulary of clutter, and presumably merchants who combed the antique shops of the realm and supplied it by the yard.

Mrs Potter slapped the hatch shut, sat down on a banquette, crossed her legs, and extracted a cigarette one-handed from the packet. It was such a dextrous, professional action that it reminded Slider of a prostitute he had once seen up an alley near King's Cross extracting a condom from its wrapper without looking, using only her left hand. He shook the thought away.

'Smoke?' said Mrs Potter.

'I don't, thanks,' said Slider, pulling out a chair and sitting opposite her, sideways on to the table.

'I don't usually in here. Get a lot of non-smokers in our class of trade, and I like to keep the snug smoke-free. But this morning – sod it! I'm not going to get through today without my fags. You watch 'em come in later, all the ghouls, to pick over the body.'

She put the cigarette into the dead centre of her crimson lips, and Slider reached across to take up her lighter and strike the flame for her. She looked at him over the cigarette with her eyebrows raised, and then leaned forward, sucking the flame onto the tobacco with little popping puffs. Then she leaned back again, dragged deep, blew long and ceilingwards, and said, 'Ta,' with just enough surprise in her voice to convey the words, 'It's nice to meet a gentleman with manners. You don't get too many of them these days.' She folded her free arm, the one holding the Kleenex, across her chest, and propped the other elbow on it so that the cigarette was in the operative position just in front of her face. 'Well,' she said. 'So how did it happen? Everyone's talking about it, but nobody seems to know anything. Not that that stops them talking,' she added viciously. 'But they say – well, if she was found where they say she was – it looks like she must've been done in.'

Her eyes behind the mascara were frightened, and she looked at him with flinching courage, waiting to hear the worst; dreading it, but facing up to it all the same. The spirit of the Blitz. He liked her a little better. He put the lighter down neatly on top of the cigarette pack and said, 'We don't know yet what the cause of death was.' And because of the fear in her eyes, he added, 'There were no obvious signs of violence on her.'

'Oh.' Linda relaxed slightly. 'Well, I suppose that's something. But you do think it was murder?'

'We're keeping an open mind about it. But however she died, someone must have put her body where it was found.'

Her mouth hardened. 'Well, you don't have to look far for him, do you? Eddie Bloody Andrews. Is that right you've arrested him?'

'He's helping us with our enquiries.'

'Same thing.' She dismissed the distinction. 'He's the one all right, take my word for it. Bastard! I don't know how Jen put up with him.'

'Womaniser, was he?' Slider suggested.

'It wouldn't surprise me. But that's not what I meant. No, he was a jealous swine, always following her around and spying on her. But men are all the same.' She brought the Kleenex into play, dabbing her eyes and blowing her nose carefully so as not to smear her makeup.

'You don't have much of an opinion of men,' Slider observed.

'I've seen too many freeloaders. I've been in the trade all my life, you see. My dad had a pub. My grandad, too. I grew up in a pub – served behind the bar as soon as I was old enough. Then I married Jack. He's not from the trade – he was a merchant seaman till he married me, then he gave it up and we started off managing a tied house in Watford. Then we got a tenancy in Chiswick, and then we bought this place.'

'How did you meet Jennifer?'

'I met her at the birth-control clinic when we moved to Chiswick. We sort of hit it off. She didn't have much good to say about men either, and no wonder. Worst thing she ever did was marry that Eddie.'

'You don't like him? Why is that?'

'Oh, what, apart from the fact that he's murdered her, you mean?' she said sarcastically, and then took a puff at her cigarette to compose herself. 'No, I'll tell you. He's one of those men who has to own a woman. Thinks if you put a ring on a woman's finger she's your property, at your beck and call every minute of the day. Jen couldn't have any life of her own. And jealous? He's mad. I mean literally – unbalanced, if you ask me. Always following her about and spying on her, accusing her of this, that and the other.' Mostly the other, Slider gathered. 'Terrible rows they had, because of course she wouldn't take it lying down. You can't, can you? Let 'em start walking all over you and you might as well be dead. But it didn't matter what she said. He wouldn't have been happy unless he had her under lock and key twenty-four hours a day.'

'Did they have money problems?'

She looked surprised. 'Why? Did someone say they did?'

'I was wondering why she took the job with you.'

'Oh, it wasn't for the money, it was just to get away from him for a bit. He's got plenty of money – doing very well for himself.'

'Generous with it?'

She seemed unwilling to grant Eddie Andrews any mitigating features. 'She never wanted for anything. But then she never asked him to keep her. She had her own career.'

'Working for the estate agent?'

'That's right.' She nodded. 'She was earning her own living before she met him, and if you ask me she made a big mistake ever giving it up, because it just gave him ideas. She couldn't stand being stuck at home doing nothing all day, so she took it up again part time.'

'Why part time?'

'Because *he* made such a fuss about her going out to work! That's why he built her that house – thought it would keep her home. It was a cage, that's what that was. But Jen was wise to it. She came to me and asked me for a job, to give her a reason to get out.'

'Why didn't she do the other thing full time?'

'Meacher's didn't want her full time. Anyway, it was evenings she wanted to get away from him. Of course, he was furious. He couldn't stand any wife of his working in a pub.'

'I thought she worked in the restaurant?'

She looked at him shrewdly. 'Is that what *he* said? God, he's a snob! He makes my blood boil! He's not the bloody Duke of Westminster, he's only a bloody builder, but he thinks himself so-o superior! Can't have his wife being a barmaid, oh no! Can't have her consorting with people like Jack and me! Publicans? The way he talked to me, you'd think I was a common prostitute! I said to him, you want to change your attitude, mate, I said, 'cause if you're not careful they'll stuff you and stick you in a museum, and good bloody riddance!'

'They didn't have any children, I understand.'

'Jen didn't want any, and who can blame her? *He* wanted 'em, but then it wouldn't be him had to go through it all, would it? Jack's the same way – all sentimental about "kiddies". Never mind morning sickness and backache, losing your figure, to say nothing of childbirth, and then being stuck in a house for the best years of your life changing nappies and wiping noses. No, she wasn't having any of that, thank you very much. Of course, it was another thing he held against me – as if I made her mind up for her!'

'You say he accused her of having affairs,' Slider said. 'Was there any truth in the accusations?'

She coloured angrily. 'Of course there wasn't! What are you trying to say?'

He made a small open gesture with his hand. 'Mrs Potter, I don't *know* the people involved. I'm not saying anything – I'm asking.'

She calmed a little. 'Well, there wasn't, that's all. It's just his morbid imagination. He wanted her locked up like some Arab woman, you know, and he couldn't stand it that she wanted a life of her own. I mean, Jen's smart, pretty, full of life, always into everything; all he ever wants to do is sit slumped in a chair watching football on the telly. Never wants to go out anywhere or do anything, just wants to go home and lock the door with Jen inside. Well, she doesn't want to spend her life doing housework, which is all he'd've let her do if he had his way. And then he accuses her of things she hasn't done, the nasty-minded, jealous little snob.'

- 'Did he hit her?'

'Oh, yes, he's done that too. When they've rowed. I don't know why she stayed with him. I mean, he was earning the money, and Jen always liked the good life, but I would never have to do with a man that'd hit a woman.'

She stubbed out her cigarette with shaking fingers and immediately racked the packet for another. Slider, with a reputation now to maintain, lit it for her. Then he said, 'I understand Jennifer was working here last night. Was that her regular evening?'

She looked sidelong at him. 'She didn't have regular times here. I just asked her, or Jack asked her, when we were busy. But yesterday – well, it was a bit different.' She sighed out a mouthful of smoke. 'I can't believe it was only yesterday. My God, I still can't believe she's dead.' She took a few more serious drags to steady herself. Slider waited in sympathetic silence, and at last she went on, 'I'll tell you how it was. Jen was at work at Meacher's in the morning – till one o'clock, she did – and about, oh, quarter, twenty past one she came here, came round the back to the kitchen to talk to me. Well, we were standing chatting when suddenly Eddie turns up—'

'Eddie Andrews came to the pub yesterday lunchtime? From his work at Mrs Hammond's house?'

She glanced an enquiry at him. 'That's right.'

'He said you didn't allow working clothes in the pub.'

'That's right, we don't. Well, it's all lounge trade here. But we don't mind in the garden. Not that you really get working clothes coming in very often – people like that go to the Mimpriss, where they've got a public bar. But, of course, working at the Rectory, this is closer, so I suppose he just popped across for a drink. Anyway, the first I know about it is he comes into the garden with a pint in his hand, and sees Jen standing at the kitchen door talking to me. So he comes over and says, "What are you doing here?" and Jen says, "Talking to my friend, do you mind?" And he says, "Yes, I do mind, I don't want my wife hanging around pubs."'

She looked at Slider to see if he appreciated the insult, and he nodded encouragingly.

'So I can see Jen's really fed up with him, and she says, "I don't care what you want. As it happens, Linda's asked me to work tonight and I've said yes," which I hadn't, but of course I had to back her up, so I said that was right, and he gets mad and says he won't have it and there's a bit of a barney, and at the end of it Jen says she'll do as she likes and if he don't like it he can do the other thing, and she walks off. So then Eddie starts mouthing off at me, how I'm a bad influence on Jen and all that old toffee, but I'm not taking it so I tell him to clear off. I said I've had enough of you, I said, and you're barred from now on. So he says I wouldn't drink here if you paid me, and he tips his beer out all over my clean kitchen step and walks off.'

'Weren't you afraid?'

'What, of him? If he'd tried to hit me, I'd've decked him first – and he knew it. He's all mouth and trousers, that one. A bully, like most men: if you stand up to them they cave in. You get to know who's dangerous in my trade and who isn't. But then I wasn't married to him.'

'Go on,' Slider said. 'Did Mrs Andrews come in to work that evening?'

'Well, she phones me up in the afternoon, about ha'pass three. She sounded upset, and I said what's up, and she just says, oh, men, I hate 'em all. So I told her I'd barred Eddie, and she said thank God for that, at least there was one place she could go to get away from him, and I said do you really want to come in tonight, because of course Tuesday isn't a busy night in the bar, and she said, yes, is that a problem, so I said did she fancy helping out in the restaurant instead because I had an office birthday party, twelve covers, coming in, and you know what those parties are like, it takes for ever to get the order down with 'em all talking and changing their minds. But she said no, she'd do the bar, and Karen – that's our bar girl – could do the restaurant. So that's how we left it, and she was to come in at seven.'

'And did she in fact come in at seven?'

'Oh, yes. Well, I didn't see her, but Karen came through and said Jen had just arrived. As it turned out the restaurant was really busy – we had a lot of casuals in as well as the bookings – so I never got a chance to go through to the bar, and by the time I'd finished Jen was gone.' Her eyes moistened abruptly. 'So I never got to say goodbye. I mean, not that I'd have known it was the last time – but – you know.'

'Yes, of course, I understand,' Slider said, and she nodded and retired into the tissue again, and then emerged for a therapeutic puff. 'And you didn't see her or speak to her again?' She shook her head. 'And what about Eddie? Did you see him at all last night?'

'Oh, he came in that evening, all right, but I didn't see him. Jack'll tell you all about that. Of course, if we'd known what was going to happen, we'd have got the police on to him, but we didn't know,' she said harshly. 'No-one could have known, that's what I say. I mean, he led that poor woman a hell of a life, but I'd never have thought he had it in him to do what he did, the evil bastard.'

Atherton sat on one of the bar stools as Slider was led away by the female of the species, and said to her mate, 'You carry on with what you're doing. What are twirlies, by the way?'

'Eh?' Jack seemed distracted. He was watching his wife's departure with what looked like perplexity, and came back to attention with difficulty. 'Oh – they're the ones who turn up every day on the dot of opening, if not before – pensioners, usually, with nowhere else to go. They dodder into the bar the minute you unlock and say, "Am I too early?" Too early – twirly. See?'

'You perform a social service, really, don't you?' Atherton said. 'Like the public library.'

Jack Potter took him seriously. 'Well, yes, we do. The public house has a unique place in the social fabric of this country. There's nothing like it anywhere else in the world, did you know that? And this was a village pub once – back in history.'

'Really?' Atherton marvelled.

'Oh, yes. It's any age, this place. All these beams are genuine, you know.' He slapped the nearest in a horsemanlike way. 'There was a village here goes back to Doomsday, before they built all this lot on top of it.'

'It's an unusual place to find in this part of London,' Atherton said.

'Oh, there's a lot of old stuff about, if you know where to look,' Potter said. 'Trouble is, most of it got messed up before anyone started caring about that sort of thing. The First And Last – in Woodbridge Road, you know it? – that was an old coaching inn, stage coaches and all that, though you'd never know to look at it now. But this one, being out of the way, it got missed out when all the modernising was going on. And now it's listed, so the outside's protected at any rate. But it's a nice place, and we get a very nice sort of clientele round here. Shorts and wine trade, like I said—'

'And the occasional murderer,' Atherton remarked.

Jack looked upset. He leaned on his hands on the bar, pulling the bar-towel taut between them. 'Don't say that! I can't bear to think of it. That poor woman! It *was* murder, then? Nobody seemed to know, but people were saying . . .'

'What do you think?'

'I don't know. I don't like to. I mean, Eddie and her were always having rows, but I never would have thought he'd go so far as to . . .' He filled in with a shake of the head. 'How did he do it, anyway?'

Atherton said, 'I don't want to go into that. Tell me about yesterday.'

'Well, he was here yesterday lunchtime, and they had a bit of a barney out in the garden, but I didn't actually see that. Linda will tell you all about it. She ended up barring Eddie, and I wasn't sorry. He had it coming. I mean, he was a nice enough bloke most of the time, but it made it awkward, with Jen and Lin being friendly, and her working here. I mean, you never want to get in between a husband and wife rowing, see what I mean? I'd've stayed out of it, kept neutral, if I could've. But with the situation what it was – and I didn't like the way he behaved to my wife. Very rude to her he was. So I'd've ended up barring him myself sooner or later.' He looked at Atherton to see if he believed him. Atherton already had a fair idea who was the Lord Warden of the Trousers in this family.

'And Jennifer Andrews was working here last night, was she?'

'That's right,' he said, though his eyes moved about a bit.

'She was here all evening?'

'That's right,' he said again.

'In the restaurant or in the bar?'

'Well, she came on to help me in here, so that Karen – that's our girl – could help the wife out in the restaurant. Had a big party in, Lin did. Jen came on about seven, or a bit after, and then Karen went through to help Lin.'

'And what time did she leave?'

'What, Karen?'

Atherton curbed his impatience. 'No, Jennifer.'

Jack Potter stared at him, and his face congealed with guilt. 'Look,' he said. Atherton looked, but he seemed not to be able to go on. His eyes shifted sideways and back. 'Look,' he said again, pleadingly now, 'I want to tell you the truth, but you've got to keep it from the wife. I mean, it's nothing bad,' he added hastily, 'but I don't want Lin coming down on me for it. She's got a sharp tongue, my wife, and – well, married life's hard enough, d'you know what I mean?'

Atherton smiled, inviting confidence, persuasive as the Serpent on commission. 'Every marriage has its little secrets,' he said.

'You're not wrong!' Jack said gladly. 'Women? I tell you, it's a juggling act, keeping 'em sweet. Well, look, strictly between you and me – the thing was, Jen wasn't really working here last night. She'd arranged it with the wife lunchtime, and all I knew was what they'd arranged between them, about Karen going in the restaurant and everything. So Jen comes in at about seven, like I said, or a bit after, and Karen goes through, and Jen and me chats a bit, because there's no-one in the bar yet; and then she says, Jen says, "Look, you don't really need me here tonight, do you?" Well, Tuesdays are quiet – in the bar at any rate. So she says, "You can manage without me," and I says yes, and she says, "Good, because I've got to go somewhere, to see someone." And she gives me a wink, just like that, you know.'

'Did she say where she was going?'

'No,' he said, and seemed to find it a naïve question. 'Well, the thing was, she wanted me to cover for her. Now Eddie was barred, it meant he couldn't come in and check up on her, so he'd think she was in here, and—' He shrugged.

'What time did she leave?'

'About half seven, it must have been. She went out through the back, down the passage past the ladies' and out through the garden, and that was the last I saw of her. She said she'd be back later but she never. Luckily Lin never came through until after ten, so I just told her Jen had finished and gone home.'

'Why didn't she want Linda to know where she was?'

'Well, Lin's a bit – careful with the money. It's not that she's not generous, I don't say that, but she's the one that keeps the books and everything and she's – careful. She wouldn't've liked if it I'd paid Jen for the evening and she wasn't here.'

'But then why did you have to pay her, if all you were doing was providing cover for her?'

'Well, if I hadn't paid her, Lin would've known she wasn't here.'

'Why shouldn't your wife know Jennifer wasn't here?' Atherton asked, patiently trotting another circle.

'Well, Lin's a bit, you know, strait-laced,' Jack said, with what seemed like sudden inspiration. 'She would never tell a lie, my wife, which is why Jen never asked her to cover for her.'

'Did you think Jennifer was going to meet another man?'

Jack looked defensive. 'I don't know, I don't know where she was going. It was probably all innocent, but Eddie wouldn't've thought so, which is why she needed me to cover for her. I'm sure it was all innocent. She just wanted to get away from Eddie.'

As yarn went, Atherton thought, this was multi-coloured lurex thread. He went on unravelling. 'So what would you have done if your wife had come through during the evening and found Jennifer not there?' Atherton asked.

'Well, she wasn't likely to, with a big party in, but Jen said if she did I was just to say she'd felt a bit iffy and gone home; but as it was, Lin was really pushed and never come through till closing, so she never found out, and I never said.'

'And what about Karen? Didn't she come through at any point?'

'Oh, yes, she was fetching the drinks for the restaurant. But I just told her to keep schtumm. She's a good girl, she does what I tell her.'

'I see. But surely the customers would know Jennifer wasn't there, and let it out some time?'

'Well, they wouldn't expect her to be there anyway, so why should they mention it to Lin that she wasn't?' Atherton offered no reason. 'You won't tell her – Linda – will you?' Jack pleaded, and laughed unconvincingly. 'There's no harm in it. I just want a quiet life, that's all.'

Atherton let it go. 'What about Eddie Andrews? Did he come to check up on his wife at all?'

'Twice,' Jack said, seeming relieved to reach something more stable underfoot. 'First time he came it was around eight, eight thirty. He'd had a few by then, I could tell. He comes bursting in through the door over there, but I nipped out smartish and stopped him, and told him to get out. "You're barred," I said, "and besides which we don't allow work clothes in here."'

'He was in his work clothes?'

'Oh, yes, mucky boots and all. So I grabbed him by the shoulder and hustled him out, and he was, like, trying to look behind me and saying, "Where's my wife?" so I said she was in the storeroom and he wasn't going to annoy her, not on my premises, and I shoved him out. And he stood there a bit, arguing with me, but I just said I wasn't moving until he'd gone, so after a bit he got into his pickup and drove off.'

'And the second time?'

'That must have been near eleven o'clock. Not long before closing, anyway. He came in just like before, only I was serving someone and I wasn't quick enough to catch him before he got up to the bar. Anyway, he asks where Jen is and I told him she'd left and gone home, and he said I was lying, she'd gone off somewhere and I knew where. Well, in the end I told him if he didn't clear out I'd call the police – which he didn't want, because he was well over the limit and still driving about in that truck of his. So after a bit he goes, and that was the last I saw of him.'

'Where was your wife at the time?'

'She was in the kitchen clearing up and getting ready for the morning. She didn't see any of it, fortunately, but I told her afterwards, of course. I mean, I told her Eddie'd been in drunk looking for Jen after Jen'd gone home. She said, Lin said, I ought to phone Jen and warn her, but I said Jen could take care of herself and we shouldn't get involved, and she saw the sense of that.' He stopped and gazed at Atherton with fawning eyes. 'I didn't know how it would turn out. I mean, covering up for Jen, I was just doing a favour for a friend, that's all. I didn't do wrong, did I?'

'That's entirely your business, sir,' Atherton said, 'but as far as these timings go, we shall have to have a statement from you about it.'

'Yes, I do see that.' He bit his lip, frowning anxiously. 'But it wasn't my fault he killed her, was it? I mean, who'd have thought he'd do a thing like that? All right, he got drunk and mouthed off a bit, and he had hit her once or twice, according to what Lin says, but I'd never have thought he had the balls to really do it.'

Atherton thought of Eddie Andrews, drunk and looking for his wife, being fobbed off so easily by Jack Potter, and was inclined to agree with him.

CHAPTER FIVE

Eyes That Last I Saw In Tears

In the CID room, the sandwiches were out in force. 'I don't suppose anyone got me anything,' Slider said plaintively.

General mastication was arrested for a micro-second of guilty silence; then McLaren said, 'I got an egg and cress here you could have.'

'I don't want to deprive you.'

'No, it's all right, guv, I got plenty.'

That was true. He was already eating a sandwich, and Slider saw on his desk, besides, two jumbo sausage rolls (made with real jumbos, to judge from the grey colour of the filling), a Cellophane-wrapped Scotch egg, a Twix, a big bag of salt 'n' vinegar crisps, an apple turnover and, betrayed by its slippery stench, a Pot Noodle sweating it out from the microwave in the coffee-room next door. Slider accepted the sandwich. It was the depressing sort of low-grade egg and cress on white sliced, with margarine instead of butter, and the thin slices of hard-boiled egg which, given nothing to weld them together, fall out of the side of the sandwich when you lift it. But beggars, Slider reckoned, couldn't be critics, and he was famished.

'You can have my Kit Kat as well, boss,' Norma said, slinging it over, belatedly troubled by conscience.

'Thanks,' said Slider.

'Don't mensh.'

Hollis had already got the name and details up on the whiteboard, along with the photographs of the body and its position. 'My second murder since I've been here,' he said with satisfaction. 'And I thought it was going to be quiet.'

'We don't know that it's a murder,' Slider said patiently, but he still had no takers. Over the groans he said, 'She might have died of natural causes: pegged out in the middle of a naughty, for instance, leaving someone in an embarrassing position, or a blind panic, with a body on their hands. Don't let's get carried away. Remember Timothy Evans.'

'What, the Christie murders geezer?' Mackay asked thickly, through a cheese-and-pickle gag. 'What's he got to do with it?'

'He went to the police station to say he'd put his wife's body down a drain, but the officers assumed he was confessing to murder, and he never smiled again.'

'Careless talk costs lives,' Atherton remarked.

'And careless listening, too,' Slider warned. 'So let's wait for the post-mortem report before we go assuming anything.'

'My money's on murder anyway,' Mackay said, swallowing. 'And it doesn't take a genius to guess who.'

'Disappointed?' Hollis said.

'Oh, I like a challenge, me. But it's got to be the husband, hasn't it?'

'I met Murder on the way: he had a face like Eddie A.' Atherton said. He intercepted Slider's look and said defensively, 'You can *et tu* me all you like, but our Eddie's story's got more holes in it than the Labour Party manifesto.'

'All right,' Slider said, settling on the edge of a desk, 'I can see you're not going to heed my warnings, so let's have it out in the open.'

Atherton, stretching his elegant legs across a good part of the room, extended his thumb. 'Point one – to begin at the beginning: Andrews says that the work on the terrace was at Mrs Hammond's instigation, that she practically begged him to do it, though he told her it wasn't needed. But she says he told her it had to be done, the terrace would fall down otherwise. Why would he lie about that, except to cover up that the existence of the hole was all his idea? And what was the hole for, if not to conceal his wife's body?'

'He may just have wanted the work,' Norma said.

'Everyone says he's doing very well,' said Atherton. 'She was dripping jewellery, and he has just a stately pleasure dome decreed—'

'Eh?'

'Built himself a big new house, which, vile though it is in every detail, is someone's idea of luxury.'

'He might have put himself into debt satisfying her and building it,' Norma pointed out reasonably. 'We don't *know* he didn't have money troubles.'

'Good point.' Slider nodded. 'That's something to check up on.'

Norma went on, 'All the same, I can't see why he lied about whose idea the work was. It's nothing to us if he persuaded Mrs H. to part with unnecessary cash. It does look as if he's trying to dissociate himself from it, which looks guilty. So I'll give you half a point, Jim.'

'Ta very much,' he said, and extended his forefinger. 'Point two: he says he went home from work and stayed there all evening, had supper, watched telly and went to bed. But the house is as immaculate as if the cleaner had just left it – which I propose is the case. Mrs Chatterbury did for them on Tuesday morning after both Andrewses had gone to work, and she was the last person to set foot in the house before we arrived.'

'But hang on,' McLaren objected, 'surely Mrs Andrews would've gone home at some point? I mean, minimum, a smart-looking bint like her wouldn't've stayed in the same clobber all day, would she?'

'You'd expect her to've gone home to change before going to the pub for the evening,' Hollis seconded.

'According to Jack the Lad, she wasn't going to the pub for the evening,' Atherton pointed out. 'She was going on a date.'

'All the more reason, then,' said Norma.

'Check on that,' Slider said. 'What was she wearing at lunchtime? But I suppose she might have changed without leaving any trace in the house, though God knows why she should.'

Atherton sighed and extended his middle finger. 'Point three: Andrews says he worked through his lunchtime and stayed home all evening, whereas we already know he made three visits to the Goat In Boots. Why is he lying?'

'Because he's dead stupid,' McLaren said pityingly.

'Harsh words from a man who has to write L and R on the bottom of his shoes,' Swilley said.

'And point – whatever this finger is,' Atherton pursued patiently, 'we have from several sources that the Andrewses were on bad terms and given to quarrelling, and that he was a jealous beast and had been known to hit her. We know he was looking for her, and probably the worse for drink. *Ergo*, dear friends, we may postulate that he found her – somewhere – and had a row with her; killed her – somehow – and put the body in his nice handy hole, meaning to fill her in with concrete in the morning. Unfortunately for him, the early-rising Mrs H. got there first. Simple.'

'You are,' Swilley agreed. 'What's all this somewhere and somehow stuff? You sound like a chorus from *West Side Story*.'

'Well, obviously,' Atherton said kindly, 'there are a few minor details left to be filled in. That's just routine legwork, and since you are *numero uno* in the legs department, Norm, I feel I can safely leave that to you.'

Slider retrieved crumbs of hard-boiled egg-yolk from his chest and said, 'There's a great deal we still have to find out. Where the death took place and how the body was transported to the terrace of the Rectory are two that spring to mind, whether it was murder or not.' There was a general groan, and he raised his voice slightly. 'Whether it was murder or not, we are still dealing with a crime: not reporting a death is an offence, not to mention attempting to conceal a dead body, and our old friend obstruction. But to ease your turbulent minds, I will say that I am now much more inclined to think that it was Eddie—'

'Hallelujah! A conversion!' said Atherton.

'And the best way we can overcome his natural reserve is to apply some facts to his story.'

'Or electrodes to his *cojones*?' Atherton suggested hopefully.

'I thought that was Spanish for rabbits,' Norma objected.

'Comes out the same,' said Atherton.

Slider went on patiently over the top of them, 'We must find out exactly where he was all through the evening and last night and present him with it. When he knows we know nearly everything, I think he'll cough up the rest. If he did love her, he'll want to tell us – it's just a matter of helping him to get there. We also need to find out where Mrs Andrews was for the whole of the day—'

'And what she was wearing,' Norma added.

'Nothing like some nice, knobbly facts to trip up a liar,' Slider concluded. 'So how about garnering me some?'

Atherton stood up, sighing. 'Here we go. Another *crime passionelle*.'

'Sounds like an exotic fruit-flavoured blancmange,' said Norma.

'Blancmange?' McLaren pricked up his ears, like a dog hearing its name.

'Never fails,' Norma said witheringly. 'Mention food . . .'

'You what?'

'Confection is good for the soul,' Atherton explained kindly.

'Yeah, I read that,' McLaren said, starting on his apple turnover.

'An alimentary deduction,' Atherton concluded.

Slider was in his own room doing the preliminary paperwork when Hollis shoved his head round the door.

'Guv? Some good news.'

'I'm up for that.'

'They've found a handbag in the back of Eddie Andrews's pickup.'

'A handbag?'

Hollis followed his head in. 'Funny, everyone says that when I tell 'em. It's like being stuck in a lift with Edith Evans.'

'What do you mean, everyone? You mean I'm the last to know as usual?'

'Oh, not the last, guv. I thought *you*'d like to tell the Super.'

'Always grateful for crumbs. What sort of handbag?'

'It's Jennifer Andrews's all right. Got her driving licence and all sorts inside. I suppose he chucked it in there meaning to get rid of it later, and forgot. Or didn't have time.'

'We must have it tested for prints.'

'They're doing that,' Hollis nodded.

'Not that it will help to find Andrews' dabs all over it. There's no reason why they shouldn't be there.'

'No, guv. But there's every reason why the bag shouldn't be in the back of his pickup. I can't see someone like her riding on the sacks, can you?'

'Quite. If it had been in the cab, now—'

'Well, no-one can think of everything.'

'But where a woman is, there shall ye find her handbag also. Meaning—'

'Get Forensic to check the back of the motor for any traces of *madarm*,' Hollis said smartly, 'dead or alive.'

'You're quick. You'll go far.'

Hollis looked hopeful. 'Is it enough to arrest him on?'

'If he can't provide a decent explanation, I think it probably will be.'

Half an hour later Slider was back in the CID room with the good news.

'Andrews burst into tears at the sight of his wife's handbag, and offered no explanation as to how it got into the back of his pickup, so I'm here to tell you, ladies and germs, that with Mr Porson's blessing, Andrews is now officially nicked.'

'For murder?' Anderson asked.

'Hold your horses. We still don't know what she died of. Suspicion of interfering with the body is all we've got so far, but it means we can get stuck in.' There were murmurs of satisfaction around the room. 'Right, the house-to-house continues. Norma, you're going to look into Andrews' finances. Let's have the BT record for his home number – that will give us some corroboration as to whether he was home or not, and may help us with the whereabouts of Mrs. Find out if either or both had a mobile and get the call records on them – McLaren, you can do those. And someone had better call her GP and find out if she had a heart disease or was taking anything.'

'Guv, what's the SP on the post?' Anderson asked.

'Doc Cameron's doing it this afternoon, if we're lucky.'

'Blimey, that's quick,' said Hollis.

'Close personal of the guv'nor,' McLaren said. 'It pays to be popular in this game.'

'How would you know?' Norma asked cruelly.

Freddie Cameron telephoned very late. 'What are you doing still there?'

'What are you?' Slider countered.

'Struggling with this corpse of yours.'

'Metaphorically, I hope.'

'Thanks to you I'm now thoroughly behind with the rest of my work. It was an absolute stinker – *absit omen* – but I think I've cracked it at last. Would you like to guess?'

'Can't be anything obvious, if it took you so long.'

'Thanks for the vote of confidence. Mine in you to solve the crime, let me say, is as solid.'

'Crime? It is murder, then? I'm glad to hear it, because we've got the husband binned up.'

'You arrested him? That was bold of you.'

'We found her handbag in his truck, and Porson agreed that was enough to start with. But we'd sooner know what crime we're dealing with. So far all we've got is interfering with the body.'

'Ah, yes, now, we knew she must have been moved, but the hypostasis confirms it. The distribution suggests she was left at first in a sitting position for several hours. Sitting as if on a chair, with the legs bent at the knee. And she was tied to whatever it was to keep her in position.'

'Tied up?'

'With something broad and flat, like a luggage strap, for instance, passed around the upper body, but with the arms inside. Definitely post-mortem. No ante-mortem ligature marks. Tied quite loosely: her weight had fallen forward against the strap.'

Slider digested that. The being tied in position suggested it had been for purposes of hiding the body, presumably until it was late enough and quiet enough to take it to the trench. In the back of Eddie's truck, sitting on a sack under a tarpaulin? Something like that. 'So what did you decide in the end was the cause of death?'

Freddie hesitated. 'If it came to court, it's one of those cases where defence would probably bring in their own expert opinion to contest my findings, so you'd better try your utmost for a confession. But I'd say it was suffocation.'

'I've never known you so cautious,' Slider said. 'Suffocation? Surely that leaves definite signs? Petechiae, for instance? And cyanosis?'

Cameron chuckled. 'There's my educated copper!'

'It's a misspent youth hanging around morgues. Well, am I right?'

'You are,' Cameron agreed. 'But, you see, petechiae aren't caused by the lack of oxygen itself; it's the raised venous pressure that does it – due to; for instance, constriction of the throat or thorax. Cyanosis – and oedema, for that matter

– are congestive signs. Where asphyxia is not accompanied by any violence or struggle, the classic signs can be completely absent. Plastic-bag suicides, for instance, are often quite pale.'

'So what's the actual cause of death in those cases?' Slider asked.

'Probably a neurochemical reaction of the heart. The heart just stops; which, of course, leaves an appearance of natural death. Which is what makes it fun.'

'So you're saying she could have died naturally?'

'My personal belief is not, though it was a close decision, I have to tell you, even on my part; and my assistant – who likes to err on the safe side of not sticking his neck out – doesn't agree with me. But I would say she was smothered.'

'Smothered? You mean with a pillow, or something?'

'Little Princes in the Tower job,' Freddie agreed.

Slider laid this against the image of the drunken marital row and found it wanting. 'But how could you smother somebody without a violent struggle?'

'It happens – probably more often than we like to think – with the frail and bedridden. It's the front runner for easing your terminally ill relly out of life without having the State come down on you for the price.'

'Mrs Andrews was hardly frail and bedridden.'

'Quite,' Cameron said. 'But a healthy and active adult could be smothered without violent struggle if she was first rendered helpless or comatose.'

'Made drunk, you mean?'

'Possibly, or drugs. I'd put my money on sleepers – I've sent blood and stomach samples off to the lab, by the way, so we shall see what we shall see. But if she was slipped the appropriate mickey, and fell into a nice deep one à la Sleeping Beauty, the rest would be easy.'

The dirty little coward, Slider thought indignantly. His native caution asked, 'If there are no signs, what makes you think that's what happened?'

'This is where I triumphantly produce the pedigree angora from the depths of the old silk topper,' Cameron said, 'and announce that purely owing to my analytical genius and thoroughness of method, I have found some slight bruising on the inside of the mouth, consistent with the lips having been pressed against the teeth by the pressure of the killer's hands on the pillow – or whatever he used.'

'But you say your assistant doesn't agree with you?'

'It is *very* slight bruising,' Freddie admitted. 'It wouldn't be necessary to press very hard, you see, if she was comatose. If I hadn't been sure it wasn't natural death ... No signs of violence, but Freddie "The Bloodhound" Cameron wasn't satisfied. Don't you want to know why?' he prompted when Slider didn't speak.

'I was afraid to ask. I'm beginning to think you're after my job.'

'No, no, my dear old thing, I leave all that messy dealing-with-the-public to you. I prefer my Smiths and Joneses as mute and docile as possible. But look here,' he became serious suddenly, 'this woman was rather tarted up, wasn't she?'

'Yes, that's what I thought,' Slider agreed.

'And if you place a pillow over the face even of a sleeping victim, the other result, apart from death, is that the old maquillage gets smudged.'

'You mean—?'

'I think it was touched up after death.'

'Good God!'

'Yes,' said Freddie, 'it struck me as a bit macabre, too. I found smears of the coloured foundation cream *inside* the nostrils, where a woman would have to be very clumsy to get it when making up her own face; and even more telling, traces of mascara on the right eyeball and contact lens. No-one alive would leave that where it was. You'd have spots before the eyes – and that stuff smarts, too.'

Slider thought a moment. 'Of course, touching up the makeup doesn't in itself mean it was murder. But it must have been meant to conceal something. Why else would it have been done?'

'That I leave to you, dear boy,' Freddie said, 'and, frankly, you're welcome to it. I'd stand up in court and swear to the bruises, but the defence could easily put up someone else to say they didn't exist.'

'So we've got to hope for the lab to show something up?'

'You can hope,' Freddie said grimly, 'but if it was a sleeper, and if it shows up, and if it was a normal dose, what's to say she didn't take it herself, voluntarily? Then you're back to my

expert opinion on the bruises versus the defence expert opinion.'
Slider was silent. 'Oh, and by the way, talking of the lab, there
was a quantity of semen in the vagina. I sent a sample off to
be typed. No sign of forcible penetration, though.'

'From what we hear she didn't need to be forced.'

'But if you get a suspect, it might be a help to prove she was
with him.'

'If it's the husband's, it won't prove anything. Oh, well,' Slider
sighed, 'it's early days yet.'

'And you have miles to go before you sleep,' Freddie said.
'Talking of which, I should be long gone. I'm supposed to be
taking the Madam to the golf-club dinner tonight. Must go
home and get into the old soup-and-fish. And scrub off some
of the smell of offal – Martha says it's like a slaughtermen's
convention being in the car with me.'

'You? Never! You're a mountain breeze, Freddie.'

'Thanks, but best friends notoriously don't tell. Better to rely
on one's wife for brutal frankness. I'll be in touch when the lab
report comes back. Goodnight.'

'Goodnight.'

'Oh – and, Bill?'

'Hello?'

'Go home, there's a good chap. It's after seven.'

The flat was empty when he got back: Joanna was away
overnight, doing a concert in Swansea, from which it was
not practicable to drive home to sleep. Or, at least, Joanna
didn't think it was. Some musicians, he knew, drove back
and pocketed the 'overnight' allowance, but Joanna said, 'I'd
sooner relax, wind down and go for a drink after a concert
than hammer down the M4. And I should have thought as a
policeman you wouldn't want me to drive all that way when
I'm exhausted,' so after that there was nothing more he could
say. And she was right, of course. He'd got to the ridiculous
stage of worrying about her whenever she was out of his sight,
particularly when she had a long drive to do, which was often.
She was an excellent driver, he knew, but it wasn't the excellent
drivers who caused the accidents.

She was right to stay away; but still he felt rather pathetic
and hard-done-by, coming home to an empty house after a

hard day at work. Where was the warm greeting, the nicely adjusted bath-water, the 'supper in half an hour, darling' that a man ought to have the right to expect? Joanna wouldn't be alone this evening. After the concert she would go for a drink – or more likely several – at the hotel where they were all staying. He expected it would turn into quite a late session, since she was more inclined to hang around with the brass players than anyone in the string section, and everyone knew brass players were boozers. Joanna didn't much like other violinists – tea-drinkers, she called them – and he put it down to her having been corrupted early in her career by that trumpet player she used to go out with, Geoffrey whatever-his-name-was. Geoffrey! What kind of name was that for a grown man? he asked, with savage illogic. Then there was Martin Cutts, the man they called Measles, because every girl had to have him at some point. And that big trombone player with the beard who always put his arm round Joanna's waist when he was talking to her . . . Slider would not allow himself to think about what else brass players had the reputation for being besides boozers. As Joanna had said, in her limpid way, 'You either trust me or you don't'; and, of course, it wasn't that he didn't trust her. He did, completely. Absolutely. But you couldn't expect hormones to be logical, and his hormones had a vivid imagination and no sense of proportion whatsoever.

He stumped off to get himself a large malt – Aberfeldy, he decided, since he needed soothing – and went with it in his hand to look in the fridge. There was salady stuff, he saw with deep indifference: salad was not what he wanted, when he'd had nothing all day but McLaren's spare sandwich. Salad! Rabbit fodder! Well, what did he expect? Hot food didn't spring into existence, like Athene out of Zeus's head, just because he thought about it. For a moment he contemplated cooking himself something, but the silent emptiness of the flat was striking lethargy deep into his bones, and after a moment he took out the cheese box instead. Too far gone even to make himself a sandwich, he cut some thick wedges of Cheddar and put them on a plate with some oatcakes; hesitated, and added a chilly tomato (Dutch! In the middle of summer!) that he knew even then he would leave.

He was half-way to the sofa when he remembered he hadn't

turned off the answering-machine and, dumping his plate and glass, went back into the hall. The little red light was blinking away like a contact-lens wearer in a sandstorm. He pressed Replay. There were several messages about work for Joanna, one irritatingly casual, 'Hi Jojo, it's Ted Bundy, give me a ring, okay? Chiz!' (Jojo? Who the hell was Ted Bundy? And why did he assume she knew his number? He hated people who said cheers instead of goodbye.) And then a click and one for him.

'Hello, Mr Slider, it's Yvonne here from Ralph Easterman.'

That was the estate agent to whom he'd transferred the ex-marital home in Ruislip, after the original two had failed to shift it. She went on, sounding annoyed, 'You seem to have made some new arrangements. Um, it would have been helpful if you could have let me know, because actually I did take someone round there this afternoon, and it was a bit embarrassing. So, um, could you give me a ring, please, and confirm whether you are taking the house off the market or not? Thanks very much. 'Bye.'

That was all. Slider stood a moment, frowning, while his magnificent analytical brain went to work on it. Then he picked up the receiver and, with a peculiar sensation of unfamiliar familiarity, tapped in what for so many years had been his home number.

Irene answered. She had always been one of those annoying people who answer the phone properly, with the full number, as specified in the *GPO-Debrett Book of Telephone Etiquette*, 1965 edition; but this time she just said, 'Hello?' in the uncertain tone of someone who has arrived by appointment at night at a lonely house on the moors and found the windows dark and the front door standing open.

'It's me,' he said. 'What are you doing there?'

She didn't speak at once, and he heard in the background the sound of the television on loudly in the sitting room, with the peevishly upraised voices of some soap-opera characters being unpleasant to each other. Suddenly and painfully he was back there in the cramped little hall with its smell of incipient food, glimpsing through the open door the children sitting on the floor gaping at one of the early-evening banalities, in which there was always someone with their hands on their hips saying aggressively, 'What's that supposed to mean?' His children, his home, his wife: the encrusted habit of so many years which, however little pleasurable it had been at the time, was so very hard ever afterwards to scrape off the old hull.

Then Irene said tautly, 'Wait while I shut the door.' Clatter of the receiver being put down; click of the sitting room door being shut, and the soap stars were cut off in mid plaint. Then Irene was back, with an air of speaking without moving her lips. 'I didn't want the children to hear.'

Why? he wondered. Had he become an indecent secret? But he had a more urgent question. 'The estate agent left me a message on the answer-machine—'

'Yes, she was round here today. She wanted to show someone round. I told her the house wasn't for sale any more.'

'You did what? *Why?* What are you doing there, anyway?'

'Why shouldn't I be here if I want to?'

'Irene!' he said, exasperated. 'Are you saying you've moved back in?'

'Brain of Britain,' she said disparagingly.

It was a bit of a blow. 'You might at least have told me.'

'Why should I? It's my home, isn't it?'

'Is this permanent?'

'I don't know. Maybe. Any objections?'

'Well, yes, as it happens! It may be your home, but it's not his. I'm damned if I'm going to subsidise Ernie Newman. What's happened, anyway? Has he lost all his money on the horses or something?'

'Don't be ridiculous,' Irene said icily. 'Ernie isn't here. Do you really think I'd—?'

'What, d'you mean you've left him? You've split up?'

She paused, selecting her words. 'Ernie and I aren't living together any more.'

My God! What did he feel about that? Vindication – he'd always known it wouldn't work. Triumph – the smug, boring prick that his wife had preferred to him had lost after all. Dismay – Irene without Ernie became his responsibility again. Fear – what was she going to demand of him in these new circumstances, and how was he going to cope? And also – and not least – horrible, embarrassed sympathy for Irene herself, because whosever choice this was, it must be humiliating for her.

'So it didn't work out, then?' he heard himself say, and his voice sounded definitely peculiar.

'I didn't say that.' She sounded strange too. 'It's just that, for the time being, at least, we're going to have separate homes.'

'There's something going on here,' he said suspiciously. 'I know you. You've got that tone of voice when you've done something you know you shouldn't – like when you bought the conservatory furniture without asking me. Marilyn Cripps was behind that, as I remember. I bet you've been talking to her.'

'Oh, you love to play the great detective, don't you? You think you're so clever!' She was trying to sound scornful, but there was a quiver of defiance in it.

'What's that bossy bitch up to now? Why has she turned you against Ernie?'

'Don't you call my friend a bitch! She hasn't done anything of the sort. And what do you care about Ernie all of a sudden? You've never done anything but sneer at him, when he's never done anything to you—'

'Apart from waltz off with my wife, you mean?' He knew as he said it that it was a mistake but he couldn't stop himself in time. The trouble with these marital rows was that the script was all engraved on the brain from years of television, and lumps of it tended to come out of their own volition.

Irene was furious. '*Your* wife? Pity you didn't think a bit more about *your* wife when you started messing around with that dirty little cow you're shacked up with! I told you I'd make you damn well pay, and I will!'

'Marilyn is behind this,' he concluded.

'She gave me some good advice, simply because she has my welfare at heart – unlike some people!'

'She told you to move back in?'

'Yes. So that I can take you for every penny you've got!'

He tried to assemble the words so that she would hear them. 'Irene, it doesn't work like that any more. Divorce is all no-fault, these days – didn't your solicitor explain that to you?' A suspicion took hold of him. 'You have spoken to a solicitor, haven't you?'

There was a tell-tale pause. 'I don't need to. Marilyn knows all about it. She's got a friend who's a solicitor who deals with divorce all the time. She practically does nothing else but divorce, this friend. So Marilyn's quite well able to advise me, thank you.'

A huge tired sadness overwhelmed him, so that he couldn't even be angry. Irene was such a plonker when it came to people with big houses and Range Rovers. '*Please* listen to me,' he said. 'They don't take fault into account any more. Unless there are special circumstances, they always end up dividing everything fifty-fifty. Including the house – which means selling it, so that the proceeds can be split. The courts won't automatically give you the house, like in the old days, just because you're living in it. And they won't automatically expect me to go on paying the mortgage.'

'I don't believe you,' she said stonily. 'Why should I believe you?'

'You don't have to take my word for it,' he said. 'Any solicitor will tell you. But it would be so much better if you and I came to an amicable arrangement first. Look,' he said gently, 'do you really not want to live with Ernie?'

'I don't know,' she said. 'I don't know what I want.' Her voice broke, and she was obviously close to tears. Behind her he heard the television grow suddenly loud, and she said sharply, away from the receiver, 'Go back in and shut the door.'

'Is it Daddy?' he heard Matthew's voice ask wistfully, and his heart lurched painfully. 'Can I talk to him?'

'Go back in, Matthew, I want to be private. Go on! It isn't Daddy, it's – a friend.'

There was a pause, during which he could imagine Matthew accepting what he knew was a lie, and turning away, obedient but hurt. Then the sitting room door shut again.

Irene said, 'I must go. I can't talk about this now.'

'We must talk about it some time,' Slider said.

'Oh, that's big, coming from you, isn't it?' she said resentfully.

'Please, Irene, don't let's quarrel.'

'I can't talk now,' she said again. He could tell she was trying not to cry. 'Don't call me – not here. I don't want the children upset. I'll call you.' And she snapped the phone down.

Slider put his end down too, and stared at it unhappily for a moment, reflecting that it did things to a man to know that whenever he spoke to a woman he was going to leave her in tears. He went off in search of his whisky. What a time for Joanna not to be here! He needed more comfort than alcohol, even a glass of the good stuff, could give him.

CHAPTER SIX

Up To A Point

Nobody loves an estate agent, but David Meacher was a handsome, well-groomed man in his late forties. His suit was beautiful, his shirt and shoes exquisite, his silk tie daring without being vulgar, his hair thick and glossy, his face firm and alert and lightly tanned. He was on his way out of the Chiswick office door and held a poser-phone in one well-manicured hand, and in the other a car key whose leather fob bore the Aston Martin badge. Slider hated him instantly and effortlessly.

'Hello,' Meacher said, in a cultured, well-modulated voice, and smiled a professional smile. 'Do come in.' He stepped back into the shop again and held the door open for Slider, but with the poised look of a bird about to take to the air. 'Can I leave you in Caroline's capable hands?' he asked rhetorically, gesturing towards the very young, very fair, very nervous-looking girl behind one of the desks.

'I don't think so,' Slider said. 'Are you David Meacher? I'm Detective Inspector Slider of Shepherd's Bush CID. I'd like a word with you, if I may.'

Meacher's expression became grave and helpful, the look of a serious, responsible and well-intentioned citizen. 'Oh! Of course. About Jennifer Andrews, I suppose? I read the paragraph in the paper this morning. It's a terrible business. Well, do come in and sit down.' He retreated to the largest and handsomest of the desks and waved Slider to a deep-buttoned leather swivel chair on the supplicant side of it. 'Er – Caroline? Could you go and put the kettle on, there's a good girl.'

The fair girl departed through to the back of the shop, and Meacher took his place at the desk and rested his hands on it, leaning forward just a little, like the headmaster of a fee-paying school interviewing applicants. 'I suppose,' he enquired delicately, 'that it was murder?'

'Why should you suppose that?' Slider delicated back.

Meacher withdrew a fraction. 'It said very little in the paper, but when a body is found in those circumstances . . . You're not saying it was an accident?'

'My mind is completely open at the moment,' Slider said blandly. 'I'm still trying to establish exactly what happened.'

'Of course,' Meacher said, with just a touch of impatience. 'I supposed that was why you were here.'

'You were one of the last people to see her,' Slider suggested casually.

'I doubt that,' he jumped in sharply. 'She finished work here at one o'clock on Tuesday. There must have been lots of other people who saw her after me, in the afternoon and evening.'

Slider looked mildly puzzled. 'Why do you think she was still alive in the afternoon and evening? I didn't say what the time of death was.'

'Oh, but—' He frowned. 'I'm sure it was in the paper.'

'It wasn't.'

Meacher's frown cleared. 'Well, murders usually take place during the night, don't they? I just assumed. Are you telling me she was killed just after she left here, then?'

'No, I'm not telling you that,' Slider said. Unfortunately, there was truth in what Meacher said: it was natural to assume that murder took place at night. He had to give him that one. 'Would you tell me, please, about her last morning here?'

Meacher gave a faint shrug of his elegantly clad shoulders. 'There's nothing to tell. It was a normal day. She arrived at the usual time – nine o'clock – did the usual things, and left at one.'

'She was in this office the whole time?' He assented. 'And were there any unusual incidents? Did anyone come in to see her? Did she take any personal telephone calls?'

'Absolutely nothing happened that I know about, except what you'd expect from a normal working day.'

'And when she left, did she say where she was going?'

'I assume she was going home. I don't know whether she actually said she was.'

Slider was silent a moment. He felt there was something

here, something to be found out. But this was a very cautious witness: unless he could ask the right question he wasn't going to get at it. You didn't get to be a wealthy estate agent by giving things away. 'What was she wearing?' he asked abruptly.

'What?' It took Meacher by surprise.

'What was Mrs Andrews wearing at work on Tuesday? What clothes was she wearing?'

Meacher hesitated, his eyes watchful. 'I don't think I remember.'

'Try.'

'She was always smart. I really don't remember in detail.'

'Perhaps your assistant would remember.'

'Caroline wasn't here. She and Jennifer do different days.' Slider raised an eyebrow, and he said impatiently, 'That's the point of it. She and Jennifer and Liz, my other assistant, each do part time, covering the week between them. They're never on together.'

Slider nodded. Because of the employment laws, three part-timers cost less than one full-timer. All females, Slider noted. It was funny how ripely handsome businessmen like Meacher always had to assemble a harem about them. He continued to regard Meacher in silence, and finally the estate agent felt obliged to break it, and said, 'I think it was a navy dress. Yes, with a red belt. I remember now.'

Why had he pretended not to know? What was he afraid of? 'How well did you know Mrs Andrews?' Slider asked.

'She's worked for me for a couple of years. I wouldn't say I know her well,' he said indifferently.

At random Slider said, 'What sort of car do you drive, sir? An Aston Martin, is it?'

Meacher paused a fraction before answering. 'No, I sold the Aston last year. It cost too much to run. I have a black BMW now.'

'Registration number?'

'The same as my Aston – DM 1. I transfer it from car to car. Why do you ask?'

'Just routine,' Slider said. He was poking sticks down holes, that was all; but lo, he'd unearthed another saddo with a personalised number-plate. Any connection? 'What did you do on Tuesday afternoon? Were you here in the office?'

Another faint pause. 'No, I went over to my other office, in

Denham. I wasn't there all the time either, though. I was out looking at properties some of the time – empty properties.'

'And in the evening?'

'I had a meal with a friend and went home. Why? What have my movements to do with anything?'

'As I said, sir, it's just routine. We like to know where everyone was who was connected with the subject.' He was framing another question when Meacher changed the subject abruptly.

'It's poor Frances I feel most sorry for. It must have been a terribly upsetting thing for her, finding the body like that. I'm an old friend of the family, you know.'

'No, I didn't know that.'

'Oh, yes. I've known her for a very long time. I was a friend of Gerald's – her husband. He and I were at school together. Between you and me, he treated her rather badly over the divorce. She ended up without a roof over her head and the two boys to look after, while Gerry took off to South Africa with the girl and the loot.' He gave a half-roguish, half-apologetic smile. 'I have no brief for him. He behaved like a complete swine. Frances would have been out on the street if her father hadn't invited them to go and live with him. Not that that's been a bed of roses. I have the greatest admiration for Cyril, but he can't have been an easy man to live with. Though, of course, Frances's mother was still alive then, which helped.'

Slider listened with interest to this considerable slice of volunteering from what should have been a donation-free zone. It was a smokescreen, he thought, but meant to distract him from what? It offered, however, a fertile new field for consideration.

'You'll have telephoned Mrs Hammond, then, when you heard about it?' Slider suggested. 'Perhaps that's where you got the idea that it happened in the night.'

It was extraordinary to watch the thoughts flitting across Meacher's face as he wondered what to lay claim to, and what traps were being set for him. There's such a thing, Slider thought, as being too clever.

'No,' Meacher said at last, 'no, I haven't phoned her yet. Well, I only heard about it this morning – read it in the paper

– haven't really had time. I didn't want to intrude. People don't want endless enquiries after their well-being at a time like that, do they?'

Slider stood up to go. 'Well, thank you for your time, Mr Meacher. Oh, by the way, could you let me know where you went after you left here on Tuesday?'

He looked uncomfortable. 'I told you, I went to the Denham office, and then to look at some properties.'

'Yes, sir, but I need some addresses. Perhaps you'd be so kind as to make me out a list of the places you went, and the approximate times?'

Meacher reddened. 'I say, what is all this? Are you trying to accuse me of something? Why should I have to tell you where I was every minute?'

'No-one's accusing you of anything, sir,' Slider said soothingly. 'It's a matter of eliminating people from the picture. We get hundreds of reports in from witnesses, and it's just as important to eliminate the people we don't suspect, so that we can be left with the ones we do.'

Meacher seemed to accept this explanation without probing its structure, promised but without grace to see what he could do, and saw Slider off the premises with an air of wanting to be sure he'd really gone. Slider went back to his car with his mind whirring like a sewing-machine. Something was going on, but *what*? *Had* he telephoned Frances Hammond and got details of the finding of the body from her? If so, why had he denied it? Why had he mentioned her at all? And why the hesitation over what Jennifer Andrews had been wearing? And what *had* he been up to on Tuesday afternoon?

He telephoned the station and Mackay answered. 'Oh, guv, we got the word from Jennifer Andrews' doctor. She wasn't on sleepers or tranks or anything. And no heart disease. He says she was perfectly healthy as far as he knew. He hadn't seen her for eighteen months, and then it was only a holiday jab.'

'All right,' Slider said. 'Nothing from Forensic?'

'Not yet. But the Potters described what she was wearing, and it was the same at lunchtime and in the evening as what we found her in. So it looks as though she might not have gone home at all.'

Except that her car was there, Slider thought. Did she just leave it there without going into the house? It seemed unlikely she would have gone in and left no mark – no cup or glass used, no cushion dented, no towel crumpled. Unless, inexplicably, Andrews tidied up afterwards. Or perhaps her car was with her elsewhere when she was killed, and the murderer drove it back.

'Okay. Get on to this, will you? David Meacher, her employer, has a mobile phone – get a list of all the calls he made from it on Tuesday.'

'Okay,' McLaren said. 'But what's up, guv? What's he suspected of?'

'I don't know. All I know is he's keeping some little secrets from me, and I want to know what they are.'

The Crown and Sceptre was a Fuller's pub, so it was worth the extra distance from the station. Atherton came in singing a cheery little policeman's ditty. 'If I had to do it all over again, I'd do it all over you . . .'

Slider, waiting in their favoured corner, looked up. 'What are you so cheerful about?'

'Why not? I've been on a pub crawl,' Atherton reminded him. 'Is that for me?'

'Do I usually buy my pints in pairs?'

'I'll take that as a yes.' He sat down and took the top off the pint. 'Ah, that's better. First today.'

'I thought you'd been on a pub crawl.'

'I can't drink at a pub with no ambulance.'

'Did you say ambience or ambulance?'

'Yes. And I'm here to tell you that the First And Last is about as like unto a coaching inn as my dimpled arse is like a Moor Park apricot.'

'Who said it was a coaching inn?'

'Jack Potter of the Goat In Boots, that's who. The F and L, however, is a brewery's delight. The lounge is all plastic rusticity and elastic Muzak—'

'That's easy for you to say!'

'—and the public is stuffed with every electronic money-snatching device from bar pool to a Trivial Pursuit machine.'

'I gather you didn't like it.'

'The Mimpriss at least was ghastly in an honest, unenterprising way. A bit like the Dog and Scrotum – oversized and underprivileged. How was your estate agent?'

'Smooth, plausible and shifty.'

'So what's new?'

'He sold his Aston Martin and bought a BMW.'

'The man has no taste. No wonder you didn't like him.'

'Who says I didn't like him?'

'Shifty is generally deemed to be a pejorative term.'

'He had a personalised number-plate, too – DM 1.'

Atherton raised his brows. 'Now there's a coincidence. Is bad taste catching, I wonder?'

'I don't know, but there was something about him that didn't ring true. I don't know what, but I wonder whether he didn't know more about Jennifer Andrews than he was admitting to.'

'Ah, well, it wouldn't surprise me, after what I've heard this morning,' Atherton said, putting his hands on the table in preparation for a speech.

But Slider wasn't listening. He had seen a shadow outside the window, and now the door opened and Joanna appeared, brown, bare-shouldered, ruffle-haired, with her fiddle case in her hand and her sunglasses pushed up on the top of her head. His heart sat up and begged. 'Here she is,' he said.

Atherton looked, and then glanced sideways at his boss. 'I knew I didn't have your full attention.'

Joanna came over to them, wreathed in smiles. 'Ah, my two favourite policemen!'

Atherton made a wrong-answer buzz. 'That should have been "My favourite policeman and my second favourite policeman." Thank you for playing.'

Slider stood up and kissed her across the table. 'Pint?'

'You know the way to a girl's heart. God, the motorway was awful this morning! The queue for the Heathrow spur was backed up ten miles down the M4.' She chatted, as newly arrived drivers do, about the journey. Atherton listened, while Slider fetched her drink.

Putting the glass on the table in front of her, Slider said, 'Who's Ted Bundy?'

She looked up. 'How do you know Ted Bundy?'

'Why do you always answer a question with a question?' Atherton said to her.

'Why do you?' she countered.

Slider sat down. 'There was a message on the machine last night for "Jojo" to call Ted Bundy. He seemed to think you knew his number well enough for him not to have to leave it.'

'What it is to have a detective in the family,' Joanna said, licking the foam off her top lip in an unstudiedly sensuous way that made Slider's trousers quicken. 'He's a trumpet player.'

'Ha! I knew it! And why does he call you Jojo?'

'Because he's a nerk,' she said. 'Ted's all right, but you wouldn't want to get cornered by him at a party. And everyone knows his number, dear heart,' she assured her fidgety mate. 'He's a part-time fixer – organises small ensembles for private parties and catering gigs and the like. All right if you haven't got any other work: not much money, but usually plenty to drink. I once subbed in on a gig he fixed for a wedding reception at the Heathrow Hilton. I still can't remember much about it, but the bride flew off on the honeymoon alone while the groom was having his stomach pumped at Hillingdon Hospital.'

'Innocence itself. I hope you feel suitably chastened,' Atherton said to Slider.

'Oh, shut up,' Slider scowled, and to Joanna, 'I missed you.'

'I missed you too,' she said.

'Well, that's all right, then.'

'What have you been up to while I was away?' Joanna asked generally.

'A murder on the Mimpriss Estate,' Slider answered.

'Sounds like that Agatha Christie novel where everybody dunnit,' Joanna said. 'Anyway, you can't have a murder on the Mimpriss Estate. It's far too posh.'

'Well, up to a point, Lord Copper,' Atherton said, amused.

'To be fair,' said Slider, 'we can't be absolutely sure it was murder.' He outlined the case so far for her.

'If Freddie Cameron says it's murder, don't you have to take his word? He's never wrong, is he?'

'Hardly ever.'

'You've got the old man saying the victim was a bossy cow, the cleaner saying she was a multiple adulteress, and the friend saying she was an angel and the husband a jealous monster,' Joanna summarised. 'But whether she did rude things, or the husband only thought she did, it comes out the same, doesn't it? Obviously he's the best candidate.'

'Especially when I tell you my latest news,' Atherton said. 'Andrews was in and out of various local pubs all Tuesday evening, in his work clothes, drinking steadily, and at intervals telling anyone who would listen that he was looking for his wife, and when he found her he was going to kill her. And at ten forty-five or thereabouts he got chucked out of the Mimpriss for trying to get into a fight with the landlord. Don't you want to know what about?'

'Do tell,' Joanna invited daintily.

He told. Brian Folger, the landlord of the Mimpriss, was one of those leering, slippery customers whose every word and gesture is loaded with sexual innuendo. 'The way he thrust a cloth-shrouded hand inside a glass to dry it was positively gynaecological,' said Atherton. Folger was a thin, bald man with little, suggestive eyes, and a wet, carnivorous mouth like one of those meat-eating plants. All the time he spoke his fingers were straying as if of their own accord into various cavities, slipping into his mouth and up his nose and into his ears like an involuntary overspill of lubricity. Atherton had caught himself thinking that Folger's nose even looked like a penis – long, fleshy and flexible with a bulbous end. It gave a whole new significance to sneezing.

Folger made no bones about the quarrel with Eddie Andrews. 'Oh, he comes in here a lot. On his way home from work usually. Well, some pubs don't allow working clothes. I say the money's the same, and a working man's got a right to his pleasure, hasn't he? We've got nothing in here to get dirty. I don't mind what stains a man's got on his trousers, as long as he gets the right thing out of 'em. His money, I mean! Ha ha!' All his conversation was like that.

'I bet his customers love him,' Joanna remarked.

On the evening in question, Andrews had come in at about half past six and had a couple of pints, making them last an hour. 'He said there was nothing to go home for, because his wife was out working that evening,' Folger had said. 'I made a little joke about his wife being a working girl, see, but he never picked up on it. Anyway, he went about half past seven. Then he comes back middle of the evening.'

'What time?' Atherton had asked.

'It must have been about an hour later. Half eight, say. He has a pint. He's looking depressed, like, so I ask him, how's the lovely wife, still showing off her assets down the Goat? He says no, she's not there. He thought she was, but he's gone over there and just seen her drive off somewhere. He's driven past his house, but her car's not there either. So I say something about what she's up to, and he gets a bit shirty. I say, you want to learn to take a joke, mate, and he says how would I like it if everyone was after my wife. I says, my wife? I'd sell bloody tickets, I says, only who'd buy one? So he says if he knew where she'd gone he go after her and wring her neck. And he drinks up and he's off again. About ten to nine, by then.'

'Did he say where he was going?'

'Nah, he just storms out in a temper. Anyway, he's back again about ah pass ten. Getting to be a right little bar-fly, I says to him. He has a couple o' shorts in quick order, and I ask him if he's found his wife yet. He says no and mutters something about he's not gonna let her work at the Goat any more, so I says, little joke, like, if Jack Potter's finished with her, I wouldn't mind having her behind my counter. He says he doesn't want her to be a barmaid, I says, who said anything about being a barmaid?' Folger winked horribly. 'Then he starts getting nasty. I'm not having that. I tell him to get off his high horse, everybody knows why Jack Potter give her a job. If that's all he's giving her – because between you and I and the bedpost, Jack Potter never says no to it if it's free, and all the nice girls love a sailor, know what I mean? Anyway, I says to Eddie, when she gets sick of the nobs at the Goat, she can come over here and give me a turn – and I'll even pretend she's the barmaid if it makes everybody happy. So then he tries to start a fight with me, and I chuck him out. Must a' been about quart' to eleven then.'

At this point in the narrative, Joanna said, 'What a sweetheart. Do you think there's any truth in any of it?'

'Maybe,' Atherton said thoughtfully. 'Jack Potter was very nervous and very evasive when I spoke to him, and his story sounded like a load of Tottenham. He said Jennifer went off somewhere, which fits what Folger says Andrews told him, but he didn't seem to have a convincing reason for covering for her.'

'That'd stand a follow-up,' Slider said.

Atherton nodded, and went on, 'Andrews was also in the First And Last during the evening – after his first visit to the Goat, to go by the timings – and he was there again at around eleven, trying to get a drink, being refused, and telling the barman his wife was cheating on him and if he found her he'd kill her.'

'People say that sort of thing all the time,' Joanna said. 'Doesn't mean they'd really do it.'

'But in this case,' Slider said, 'the person he said it about is dead. I'm sorry, because I didn't want to think Andrews was guilty of murder – and such a cowardly murder, if Freddie's right – but it's certainly looking bad for him.'

Atherton lowered his pint to half mast with some satisfaction. 'I think I'd better have another little *parlare* with the guv'nor of the Goat, see if I can't make him come clean about the real nature of his relationship with Jennifer A.'

'All right, and when you've done that, I'll interview Andrews again. Now we can table his movements up till eleven o'clock, it may be enough to make him tell us the rest.'

'Especially when you apply the delicate sympathy over how badly you think he was provoked,' Atherton said.

'That's not cricket,' Joanna said sternly.

'I wonder where she did go, though,' Slider mused. 'And was it innocent or guilty?'

'If she was guilty with Jack, she was probably guilty else-where,' Atherton said. 'One thing, though – we now know she drove away from the Goat, so that means either she or the murderer brought the car back later in the evening or night. If anyone saw it arrive back, we might have something.'

'Talking of having something, are we going to nosh?' Joanna said. 'I'm starving.'

'I'll go,' Atherton said. 'What does anybody want?'

While he was up at the counter ordering their food, Joanna asked Slider, 'Were there any other messages for me?'

'A couple about work. I haven't cleared them off the tape.' He hesitated. 'I've had some news, though.'

'Oh?'

'Irene's moved back into the house.'

She stared, reading his face. 'With the children? Has she split with what's-his-name, then?'

'It's hard to tell. She was very evasive about it – all she'd say was that they've decided not to live together for the time being.'

'Oh, Bill, what now? It's not going to be more trouble for us, is it?'

'It needn't be for you.'

'If it is for you, then it is for me. What's going on? Is she trying to get you to go back to her?'

'I don't think so. It sounds,' he said slowly, 'as if her friend Marilyn has told her that if she moves back into the marital home she'll get a better settlement in the divorce.'

Joanna thought about that for a moment, sipping her pint. Slider watched her, knowing that she was choosing her words – perhaps her thoughts, too – carefully. She didn't want to say unkind or disparaging things about Irene, to seem petty, spiteful, grasping or demanding, to belittle anyone's pain or inflate her own. She wanted to come out of it all with her character intact – not to make herself look good, he knew, but because her own self-esteem rested on it. 'And will she?' was what she eventually said.

'Yes and no.'

She grinned at him. 'I used to be indecisive, but now I'm not so sure.'

'What I mean is that the courts decide these things on relative need. They don't take fault into account any more, which is what I can't get her to understand. Okay, while she was living with Ernie, her needs would have been assumed to be taken care of, though not the children's.'

'You mean you wouldn't have had to pay maintenance for her, only for them?'

'Right. But even without Ernie, the courts will expect her to get herself a job. They won't expect me to keep her for ever.'

She raised her eyebrows. 'I didn't know that.'

'Nor does she. The good old days of skinning the erring husband down to his socks are over – though it's all going to change again, apparently, when the new legislation goes through in 1999.'

'And what about the house?'

Atherton came back. 'Grub's on its way. What house?'

'Mine,' Slider said.

'Oh, sorry, private conversation?'

'I don't know what there is about my life that you don't already know.' Slider shrugged.

'Oddly enough, neither do I,' Atherton said. 'Shall I go away again, or hum loudly?'

'Don't be silly.' He turned to Joanna again. 'The house is pretty academic, really. It's not in negative equity, thank God, but what's left after the mortgage won't be enough to buy a greenhouse. But if she goes to court they could order it sold so that the proceeds can be split. And then where would she be?'

Joanna looked grave. 'Homeless?'

Slider rubbed his hair up the wrong way in anxiety. 'I can't let that happen.'

'Wouldn't she go back to Ernie?'

'But if she didn't? Or couldn't? I've told her if we agree to a settlement between us, the courts will uphold it. But with Marilyn needling her, she doesn't trust me.'

Joanna laid a hand briefly on his. 'She must be mad.' Atherton looked at her and away again. He didn't think she'd grasped the implications yet. Then she asked, 'What sort of settlement?'

'I couldn't let them be homeless,' Slider said again.

Now she saw. She removed her hand and put it back round her pint. 'You'd go on paying the mortgage.'

'Until the children leave school,' he said.

'Or university, or home, whichever is the latest,' she qualified. Her voice was as neutral as Bird's Instant Custard. 'You'd go on paying the mortgage, and the house insurance.' He nodded minimally. 'And the bills – gas and electricity and so on.'

'Yes.'

'And maintenance for the children, of course. And for Irene?'

He looked at her helplessly. 'She's never been out to work since we were married. She couldn't get a job now. What could she do?'

'Bill, that's your whole income accounted for. What are you supposed to live on? Something has to give.' She knew what. Living with her he didn't have rent to pay, but he had been contributing to household expenses. That's where the only slack was. Joanna would have to keep him, effectively, so that he could keep his family. She tried not to let her mouth harden, but she could never hide from him. 'Let her go to court,' she said at last.

'They're my responsibility,' he said.

She looked at him with enormous sadness. 'And I'm not.' It wasn't a question. They were back to where they had begun: Irene and the children were real life to him, and she was fun and magic and fantasy, but essentially separate, independent, outside him, the thing that, however little he would ever want to, he could jettison, because she could manage without him. He could put down his pleasures, but not his burdens.

Atherton felt the pain of both of them acutely, and wished to be anywhere but here. Any moment now she would nobly offer to leave him, and Bill would accept sadly and go back to prison with Irene because it made financial sense. Atherton didn't want to be here to witness it. He had been against Joanna and Bill getting together in the beginning, but he knew now it was the best thing for Bill, and it was too late by an extremely long chalk for him to go back. Atherton didn't want to see the two people he was fondest of in the world commit suicide.

Fortunately, at that poised moment, a figure loomed up to the table and said, 'One sausage, egg and chips and one chilliburger and chips, was it?' They all looked up, and after a blank instant Joanna said, 'That's right.'

The woman smiled and set the plates down. 'And there's a lasagne to come, and I'll bring your knives and forks. Any sauces, atawl? Salt and pepper? Vinegar for your chips?'

When the interruptions were over and they were alone again with their food, Joanna said, 'Isn't it strange how of all the spices in the world, the only one that's routinely offered is pepper? A weird sort of hangover from the Middle Ages.'

'There's spices in my chilli,' Slider said, with an effort.

'In it, not offered separately. Imagine her asking, "Salt and cinnamon?" or "Mace and nutmeg?"'

'But they're sweet spices.'

'All spices are sweet. Pepper's sweet.'

Atherton joined in helpfully, 'Have you tried black pepper on strawberries?'

They talked about anything but the cloud that hung over them.

Atherton could see how a man more stupid, more selfish, more violent in his passions than Bill – like Eddie Andrews, perhaps – might end up murdering the cloud because he could neither face up to it nor see any way out from under it. But facing up to things was Bill's forte, poor devil, and Joanna was not enough of a selfish bitch to force the issue. Too good for her own good, really.

CHAPTER SEVEN

Publican's Tail

Slider got back to the factory with a headache. He tried to sneak it up to his room to seduce it with aspirin, but as he tiptoed past the door to the shop, Paxman, who was duty sergeant, spotted him and called after him. 'Sir! Bill!'

Slider turned back resignedly. 'Thanks for the knighthood.'

'Eh?' Paxman's stationary eyes were troubled. He was a big man, solid as a bull, and he had never quite got to grips with Slider's humour.

Slider waived the flags. 'Did you want something?'

'There's someone waiting to see you.'

'I was born with someone waiting to see me,' Slider said sadly.

'Name of Potter. Mean anything? Looks like a cat on hot bricks. I put him in interview room two, but I can get rid of him for you if he's trouble.'

'No, I'll see him. Thanks.' Atherton had just gone off to the Goat to re-interview him. Slider rubbed his forehead. 'You haven't got any aspirin, have you, Ted?' he asked. Paxman had. Slider washed them down with a gulp from the water-cooler in the charge room. They lay sulkily on top of his chilliburger and chips, with which they were obviously not going to play nicely.

Jack Potter was pacing about the interview room, looking worse than Slider felt. He turned eagerly as Slider came in. 'I was just thinking of leaving,' he said.

'I'm sorry, I've only just got in,' Slider said. 'Have you been waiting long?'

He gave a short laugh. 'Cold feet,' he said. 'I don't want to say what I've come to say, but it's on my conscience. And if

I don't and you find out anyway, it'll look worse than it is. Besides, I don't want anyone coming round the Goat asking questions in front of the wife.' There was a question mark at the end of the last sentence, and a fawn in the eyes.

'If it's about you and Jennifer Andrews—' Slider began.

Potter's scalp shifted visibly backwards as his eyes widened. 'How the hell did you know?'

'Detective Sergeant Atherton's on his way round to interview you at this very minute,' Slider said.

'Oh, blimey! He won't go and—? I mean, Linda's there, my wife, that's why I came here. If Lin finds out she'll skin me alive. Your bloke won't blurt it out?'

'I'm sure he'll be discreet,' Slider said. 'He's a man of the world. Why don't you sit down and tell me about it?'

Potter sat automatically, his eyes flat with apprehension. 'I wanted to tell you when you came round that first time, but with Lin in the house – suppose she'd walked in and heard? You do see? I did feel bad, with Jen – with Jen—' His eyes filled abruptly with tears. 'I can't believe she's – you know. Did he do it? Did he kill her? Eddie?'

Slider avoided the question. 'Tell me about you and her,' he said, sitting down opposite him.

Potter took out a handkerchief and blew his nose. 'I never meant it to happen. I mean, with Jen being Linda's friend, it was a bit too close to home. You don't shit on your own doorstep, know what I mean? But she was always around, Jen was – *you* know,' he went on pleadingly. Nothing propinks like propinquity, Slider thought. 'I mean, she was a bit of all right. You never met her, but she was a real smasher. And when she started coming on to me – well—'

'What man could resist?' Slider said.

Potter looked relieved at his understanding. 'It's not that I was looking for it. I'm not the running-around sort. Oh, I've had my moments,' he added modestly. 'I mean, before I married Lin I was in the merchant. Well, it goes with the job, know what I mean? I've had women all over the world. Some of them eastern tarts, you wouldn't believe the things they can do! Oh, don't get me wrong, I love my wife. All right, since I been married there's been one or two occasions, but all very discreet. But, well, when it comes down to it, a man's a man, if you get my drift, and when it's offered him on a plate—'

'Jennifer Andrews offered herself on a plate?'

He shrugged. 'Let's face it, Jen was a sparky girl. I wasn't the first and I won't be the last.' He didn't seem to see the incongruity of those words. 'But Linda thought Jen was a snow-white lamb and Eddie was the coal-black villain, and no shades in between, get me? Though if you ask me that man had the patience of a Jonah, with what she put him through.'

'He knew about her – infidelities?'

'Yes and no.' Potter frowned a little. 'Funny thing, that. I mean he was jealous, and I don't say he didn't have cause, but I don't think he knew anything definitely. That was the ironic bit, really,' he said, with a mirthless laugh. 'I don't think he believed half of what he said he thought she'd got up to. I reckon he probably thought a lot of the time that he was probably being jealous about nothing, when all the time he was probably right.'

Slider felt disinclined to untangle that sentence. He got the general idea. 'So let's get this straight, you and Jennifer Andrews were having an affair? How long had it been going on?'

'Oh, best part of a year, but it was only occasional. I mean, it was tricky for both of us, both being married. We done it once or twice upstairs at the Goat, when Lin was out, but I didn't like leaving Karen on her own down the bar, and you never knew if she might come up for some reason. And it's always hard for the likes of me to get time off. You wouldn't believe the hours involved in running a pub! But, well, Linda likes to have a day's shopping up west every now and then, and I cover for her, so in return she sometimes tells me to have a day off. I'm a bit of a motor-racing fan, I like going down Silverstone or Brands Hatch once in a while. At least,' he dropped a ghostly wink, 'that's what I tell the wife.'

'But instead you met Mrs Andrews – where?'

He grinned. 'Well, that was the beauty of it, Jen being in the estate-agent business: she'd always have keys to houses they were selling, and we'd use one of them. It was a bit exciting sometimes, wondering if the owners were going to come back early and catch us.' He caught himself up abruptly, and appealed to Slider, 'It was just a bit of fun, and no-one ever knew about it, so where was the harm?'

Slider refused the wig and gown. 'So has this got something to do with Tuesday evening?' he asked.

'Well, yes, it has. You see, lately she hasn't been much interested – Jen. Got other fish to fry. She used to hint stuff, to get me going. She wasn't a nice person, you know. She was a bit of a prick-teaser, if you want the truth. She liked to brush past me when Lin was in the room, and say things that meant one thing to me and something else to Linda. For a couple of weeks she'd been winding me up, and then when I tried to do something about it, pushing me away and saying she had someone else and she didn't need me. Only when I got mad at her she'd threaten to tell Lin.'

'But two could play at that game, surely?'

He looked uncomfortable. 'Well, yes, and I said that to her, but she always said I'd never do it, because if I split on her to Eddie, he'd come straight round to me and then Linda would find out, and that would hurt me worse than it hurt her – Jen – because when it came down to it she didn't care if Eddie did find out, but I did care about Lin. Well, I love my wife, you see.' He slithered his eyes sidelong. 'And in any case, the pub's in her name. I couldn't get a licence 'cause of a little bit of trouble I had a long time ago. So everything belongs to Lin, officially. If she chucked me out, I'd get nothing. Jennifer knew that, of course. So she used to say to me, "You just be a good boy and do what I say and don't get any funny ideas. Because I shall be gone soon anyway," she said.'

'Gone? Where?'

'She never said. I s'pose she was just hinting she'd take off one day. She was always saying she was bored with Eddie. I mean, he's a nice enough bloke, but he's dull, and she's a bit of a bright spark, know what I mean? I never thought she'd stop with him for ever. Ambitious girl, was Jen.'

'So that's why you agreed to cover for her on Tuesday night?' Slider asked. 'She blackmailed you into it?'

'Well, yes, I suppose you could say that. And of course, once I'd covered for her, I couldn't let Lin find out. That's why I couldn't say anything when you came round the pub. But you won't let on, will you? I mean, I didn't do anything wrong, just told a little porkie or two, and what man doesn't do that to the missus?'

'Do you know where Jennifer went?'

Potter's look was eager now, willing to help. 'No, I don't, and that's straight up. She just said she had to see someone. Well, naturally I thought it was another man. She was – excited, see? All worked up and – sort of electric, like it was a bit dangerous. She liked a bit of danger, did our Jen. That's why she liked using clients' houses – give her a charge to think someone might walk in. I said to her, You'll go too far one day, I said. I s'pose,' he added dully, 'that's what happened in the end.'

'So she left at about seven thirty, and you've nothing more you can tell me?'

'That's right. Old Eddie only just missed her. When he came in the first time and I went to chuck him out, he said he'd just seen Jen drive away and he wanted to know where she was going. I said she'd gone home with a headache, and he said I was lying, because she'd gone in the other direction, so I said in that case I didn't know where she was because she'd told me she was going home. Well, I *didn't* know where she'd gone, did I? I s'pose he realised I was telling the truth – anyway he seemed to believe me and away he went. But the second time he come in he was pretty drunk, and he said, I know you know where she's gone, he said, and if you don't tell me I'll smash your face in. I said to him if there was any smashing of faces in, it'd be me that done it to him, and I told him to go home and sober up, because I didn't know where Jen was and that was all about it. Well, after a bit I managed to get rid of him, and that was that.'

'You don't think he knew about you and Jennifer?'

'No,' Potter said, with clear certainty. 'He'd have said if he did.' Interesting, Slider thought: evidently Eddie hadn't believed the guv'nor of the Mimpriss. It just went to prove that jealousy is all in the mind. 'No,' Jack said, 'he just thought I knew who she was with and wouldn't tell him, but I think he believed me in the end that I *didn't* know. Because I didn't, did I?' This accidental cleaving unto veracity seemed to give him some perilous comfort.

'Do you know who else Jennifer Andrews was – seeing?'

Potter shook his head. 'Well, no. I don't know for certain that she *was* seeing anyone else. I just wouldn't be surprised if she was. I mean, no-one found out about her and me, did they?'

It was possible, of course, that the landlord of the Mimpriss was merely making mischief and guessing right by accident; but the picture Slider was forming of Jennifer Andrews suggested that she liked to wield her power over people and enjoy the credit for her bad behaviour. If he read her right there would be at least one other person who knew about Jack Potter, but it would be someone who couldn't make use of the information, as Potter couldn't about the last mystery appointment.

He no longer wondered that someone had wanted to murder her. He only wondered there had not been a queue; he'd have taken a low number himself. But it was still obvious who was clutching ticket number one. It was time, Slider thought, to have another chat with Eddie. He must remember, if sympathy for this long-suffering man threatened to overcome him, that if Freddie Cameron were right, it had not been a murder of impulse, of the man driven to a hasty lashing out he instantly regretted. If she had been smothered while comatose, then a degree of premeditation had been present. He must have waited for her to fall asleep: plenty of time for temper to cool and better instincts to take over.

When he returned to his room, he found Hollis looking for him. Hollis, a scrawny man with failing hair, bulbous pale green eyes and a truly terrible moustache, was also cursed with a Mancunian accent and a sort of strangulated counter-tenor voice. He covered his aspects by cultivating an air of gentle self-mockery, as though he were weird by choice. 'Sitrep, guv,' he said, as Slider came along the corridor.

'You what?' Slider said absently.

'We've got the list of calls for the Andrews house from BT,' Hollis explained. 'None at all made on the Tuesday.'

'None?'

'Not a tinkle. So either they weren't fond of talking—'

'Or they weren't home,' Slider concluded. 'Well, it all helps.'

'We've got the list from Meacher's mobile, and we're putting names to numbers now. Andrews didn't have a mobile, but Mrs A. had a car phone, and we're waiting for that list. Oh, and Norma says the Andrews' finances check out. He had a loan to finance building the house, but the repayments have been met all right, and there's money coming in as well as going out.'

'Okay. Anything come yet from Forensic?'

'Not yet.'

'Oh, well, I don't suppose it'll be much help when it does. That's the trouble with domestics.'

'Send you clean round the bend,' Hollis agreed solemnly.

'I'm going to have another chat with our prime suspect,' Slider decided. 'You'd better come with me.'

Nicholls was custody sergeant, a lean, handsome Scot from the far north-west, with blue eyes and a voice like silk emulsion. 'Come to get a confession?' he asked, walking Slider and Hollis along to Andrews' cell.

'It'd be nice to get him to talk at all. Mostly he just stares at the wall. Interviews with him are as exciting as a Thomas Hardy novel,' Slider sighed.

'Well, I hope you bring it home before I go on my holidays,' Nicholls said. 'It'd be like missing the last episode of *Murder One*.'

'That gives me two weeks, doesn't it? Where are you off to, by the way?'

'Norway.'

'I've never seen the point of Norway. It's just Scotland on steroids.'

'Och, Mary fancied it for the kids. They love canoeing.'

'A sort of fjord fiesta, then?'

Nicholls grinned. 'Lots of healthy outdoor activities to wear the wee anes out, so that we get quiet evenings alone for once.'

'For once? That's how you got six kids in the first place.'

'Oh, aye, I forgot.'

'You'd better not forget again,' Hollis warned. 'You can't afford any more on a sergeant's pay.'

'Nae worries, old chum. Don't you remember, I've had the Snip?'

'How could anyone forget?' Slider winced. Nicholls adored his wife, and had wanted to curb his rampant fertility without having Mary risk the Pill. Now with the enthusiasm of the convert – or, as Slider thought of it, of the tail-less fox – he was a crusader for the operation. Pale, doubled-up young constables hurrying out of the canteen were a sure sign that Nutty was in there on his break, campaigning.

'You should try it, Bill,' he said seriously. 'No more worries, no more condoms. It makes a vas deferens to your sex-life, I can tell you.'

'The condommed man ate a hearty breakfast,' Slider murmured, as they reached the cell door. Nicholls brought the key up to the lock. 'Can I have a look at him first?' Slider asked. He slid back the wicket and applied his eye to the spy-hole. Eddie Andrews gave the impression of having settled into his cell, as if he neither expected nor hoped to be released. He was sitting on the edge of the bunk with his hands clasped loosely between his knees, and didn't move or look up at the sounds at the door. Slider stepped back.

'Is he like that all the time?'

Nicholls had a look too, and nodded his handsome head. 'Just sits quiet like a good wee boy. No trouble at all.'

'Eating all right?'

'Eats and drinks, says thank you—'

'Thank you?'

'I told ye it was bad. He asks no questions. Doesn't want a solicitor. Doesn't want anyone told he's here.' He met Slider's eyes gravely. 'I don't like it, Bill. The quiet, obliging ones are often the ones you lose. It can mean they've made up their minds to go. We've got his belt and shoelaces, but they'll always find a way if they're determined.'

'You think he's one of those?'

Nicholls hesitated. 'I'm not just sure. It could be he did it and wants to be punished. Or it could be shock, and he's just not connecting up. But he's not in a normal state of mind, and that's a fact.'

'All right, Nutty, thanks for the tip. Can I have him out?'

Slider signed for Andrews and they took him along to the tape room. Andrews was docile, almost dreamy, as Slider went through the preliminary procedures. He needed shaking out of it.

'Now then, Eddie, you told us that on Tuesday night you had one drink in the Mimpriss and then went home, and stayed home all evening watching television. Is that right?' Andrews nodded. 'For the tape, please.'

'Yes,' Andrews said, in a lacklustre voice. 'We've been through all this. Why can't you leave me alone? I've got nothing to say.'

'What programmes did you watch on the television?'

'I've told you before. I don't remember.'

'Just tell me one.' No answer. 'Did you watch the football?'

'Yes,' he said, after a hesitation.

'Who was playing?'

'I don't remember.'

Hollis intervened, in a voice of utter amazement, 'You don't remember the Man United–Aston Villa match? That wicked goal in extra time by Sheringham?' He mimed a header into the net.

'Oh – yes – I remember now,' Andrews said, blinking at him. 'That was it. The football.'

Hollis shook his head sadly. 'Man United didn't play that night. It was an international.'

'Come on, Eddie, don't waste my time!' Slider took the ball neatly on his toe. 'We know you weren't home watching television. You were out on a drunken pub crawl. You were in the Mimpriss three times. The guv'nor there's told us about the argument you had with him, over what your wife was up to.'

That got a reaction. His hands on the table tightened. 'My wife wasn't up to anything.'

'That's not what Mr Folger says,' Hollis said, with a knowing grin. 'He knew all about your wife and Jack Potter. Fruity stuff!'

'It's not true,' Andrews cried. 'Don't you talk like that about her! Brian Folger's a foul-mouthed liar!'

'And then later you were in the First And Last,' Slider picked up the pass, 'telling the barman there your wife was cheating on you—'

'She wasn't! It's not true.'

'—and that when you found her you'd wring her neck.'

'It's not true!'

Slider leaned forward a little. 'Eddie, you were there and you said those things. We know that. We've got witnesses to everything you did that evening, the pubs you went to and the times you were there and what you said. There's no point in going on lying when we've got witnesses. Why not give up and tell us the truth? You must have had reasons for what you did. I want to know what they are. I want to hear your side of the story.'

Andrews looked across the table at him, and the little spurt of energy that had been generated died away. He sighed. 'I've got nothing to say to you, except what I've already said.'

'You've got to tell me, Eddie,' Slider said gently but insistently. 'Because, you see, it's looking really bad for you. You left the First And Last at ten past eleven, vowing to murder your wife. And some time between then and one o'clock, she was murdered.' Andrews kept silent, looking down at his hands again.

'You said she didn't come home all night, but her car was there on the hard standing in the morning. How did it get there, if she didn't come home? Did you drive it back from the place where you murdered her?'

No answer.

'Her handbag with her car keys in it was found in your pickup. How did it get there if you didn't put it there?'

No answer.

'Eddie, we'll find out, just as we found out what you were doing the rest of the evening. We always find out. So why don't you tell me about it now, get it all out in the open? I promise you you'll feel better.' Andrews sighed. 'I want to hear your side,' Slider urged. 'You must have been under terrible pressure, to do what you did, because I know you loved her. You were driven mad by her behaviour. I understand that. I know what she was like.'

Now he looked up. 'You don't!' he said, and his red-rimmed eyes blazed briefly. 'You don't know anything about her – none of you!'

'All right, you tell me, then,' Slider said, settling back as if the story was just beginning.

'It was all my fault!' Andrews cried. 'She didn't do anything. It was all down to me.'

'Yes,' Slider nodded encouragingly, while Hollis almost held his breath, trying to turn himself into paint on the wall. 'Go on.'

'I was jealous. But I had no right to think those things. I loved her, and I thought bad things about her, and now she's dead!'

'I'm so sorry, Eddie,' Slider said tenderly. 'Tell me all about it. After you left the First And Last. Where did you meet her?' Andrews stared, haggard, bristly, flame-eyed, goaded. 'Tell me what you did to her.'

'I didn't kill her!' he cried.

'All right, but tell me what you did. Where did you go after the First And Last?'

'I don't know. I don't remember. I just wandered about all night. Every time I went past the house her car wasn't there, and it made me mad wondering where she was. So I just wandered. I fell asleep for a bit, sitting in the van. And then in the morning I went to work, straight to Mrs Hammond's. I didn't go home because I didn't want to find out she'd been out all night. I thought she was with another man. But I had no right, you see! I thought bad things about her, and they weren't true! If I'd only trusted her! And now she's dead, and it's my fault, all my fault.' He put his head down into his hands again, and made moaning noises.

Slider felt Hollis looking at him, waiting for him to pull the rabbit out of the hat, perform the *coup de grâce* – or what Atherton called the lawnmower. Oh, the responsibility of greatness! 'Tell me, then, Eddie. Get it off your conscience. Tell me how you killed her.'

Outside the tape room, Hollis shoved his hands deep in his pockets, hunching his spindly-looking shoulders like a depressed heron, and said, 'Oh, bollocks. He was *that* close, guv.'

'Tell me,' Slider sighed.

Nicholls came back. 'Any joy?' He read their faces. 'You couldn't crack him, even after I gave you a full psychiatric profile?'

Slider smiled unwillingly. 'Come off it, Nutty. You haven't got the figure to play Cracker.'

'Robbie Coltrane hasn't got my voice,' Nicholls countered modestly.

'There is that,' Slider agreed.

'Is that right you're playing the female lead in Mr Wetherspoon's opera?' Hollis asked.

'Operetta,' Nicholls corrected. He had famously once sung the Queen of the Night aria from *Zauberflöte* in a police charity concert, but Commander Wetherspoon's next production was to scale lesser heights. '*HMS Pinafore*. I'm the captain's daughter.'

'Well, everyone likes Gilbert and Sullivan,' Hollis said reasonably.

'That's his reasoning,' Nicholls said neutrally. 'He's sinking to the occasion.'

It was a new age, Wetherspoon had told the assembled troops during one of his recent descents on the Shepherd's Bush nick from the Valhalla of Area Headquarters. 'Caring is the watchword. Relating to the People. We are the People's police service.' There had been a distinct sound of retching at that point, but Wetherspoon was one of those elevated beings who didn't care whether he was popular or not, and he had carried on unmoved. 'It's not enough to Relate, we have to be Seen to Relate. It's all about Trust, boys and girls. Above all, we mustn't appear élitist.' So it was goodbye, Wolfgang Amadeus, hello, Ruler of the Queen's Nayvee.

'Never mind, you'll look lovely in a bonnet,' Slider said comfortingly. There was nothing in the least effeminate about Nicholls: it was just that his features were so classical, he looked equally good in a dress or trousers.

'It could be worse,' he said philosophically. 'At least it's still music. There was a moment when he was toying with *Aspects of Love.*'

'So what now?' Hollis asked, as he and Slider headed back upstairs.

'We'll have to do it the hard way.'

'Oh, that'll be a nice change.'

'Someone must have seen him,' Slider said. 'Someone always does. And we haven't had the forensic reports yet. If necessary we'll go over the whole of west London on our hands and knees.'

Hollis smiled behind his ghastly moustache. 'When you say "we", sir, I assume your own hands and knees will be otherwise engaged.'

'Naturally. I've got to go and see the Super.'

Detective Superintendent Fred 'the Syrup' Porson was in his room, pacing about dictating to a hand-held recorder. He was hardly ever seen sitting down – a man of constant, restless energy. When Slider appeared in the open doorway he raised his eyebrows in greeting as he finished his sentence, clicked the machine off and barked, 'Come in. Enter. I was just going to send for you.'

Slider came in and entered, almost simultaneously. Porson was a tall, bony man with a surprisingly generous nose, a chin like a worn nub of pumice-stone, and deep, cavernous eyes below craggy, jutting eyebrows that could have supported a small seagull colony. It was hard, however, to notice any of these things when looking at him: the eye was ineluctably drawn to the amazing rug which had given him his sobriquet. It wasn't just that it was ill-fitting, it was an entirely different colour from his remaining natural hair, which prompted the constant nagging question: *why?*

The thing that drove the language-sensitive Atherton mad, however, was that Porson talked like Peter Sellers playing a trade-union representative doing his first ever television interview. He chucked words about like a man with no arms, apparently on the principle that a near miss was as good as a milestone.

'Now then,' he said, as Slider closed the door behind him, 'the Andrews case: as regards the suspect, what is his current status at this present moment, *vis-à-vis* confession?'

'Hollis and I have just had another crack at him, sir,' Slider reported, concentrating on the portrait of the Queen on the wall behind the Syrup's left shoulder. 'But he still won't cough.'

Porson frowned. 'We are in an advanced state of the clock with regard to this one, if I'm not mistaken?'

'We've got six hours to go, before it has to go before the Muppets.' After thirty-six hours, a magistrate's authorisation was needed to detain an arrestee any longer.

'All we've got against him is the handbag?'

'And his refusal to tell us where he was and what he was doing. And the fact that he was heard threatening to kill her.'

Porson walked about a bit, deep in thought. 'I think we'll let him go,' he said at last.

Slider was surprised. 'Sir, I think the Muppets'd let us keep him. He's the obvious suspect, and his statement has been shown to be—'

'Oh, yes, yes, I'm quite well aware that his whole story has been a tinsel of lies. Nevertheless, if he's decided to dig his teeth in, then there's no point in banging our heads against a glass ceiling.'

'But if I carry on working on him—'

Porson shook his head. 'We can't afford to be giving free bread and board to every Tom, Dick and sundry. There's such a thing as budget restraints, you know. I've seen 'em like this one before, and believe you me, he's not going to come across until we present him with irreputable evidence. That's my judgement. Your job, Slider, is to get the evidence, and you'll concentrate on it all the better if you're not running up and down stairs waiting on him like a housemaid's knee!'

'Yes, sir,' Slider said blankly. The knee threw him somewhat.

'Besides, I'd just as sooner let him go while we've got some time left on the clock, in case we want to bring him back in again at some future eventuality.'

'Well, it's for you to decide, sir.'

'It is, laddie, it is, and I've decided.' Porson looked at him sharply. 'You think he'll make a skip for it, is that it?'

'No, sir, probably not, but—'

'Well, if he does, that's all grist to our mill, isn't it? No, my mind's made up: send him home, keep an eye on him, and meanwhile, let's see your team come up with some new evidence. Time to look in some fresh directions; get a new prospective on the case.'

'It's a long road that gathers no moss,' Slider concluded.

He didn't realise he'd said it aloud until Porson, terrifyingly, clapped him on the shoulder. 'That's the idea,' he said approvingly. 'Neil Desperado. Well, carry on. Keep me informed. And if you want any help, my door is always here. Knock, and ye shall find, as they say.'

Tufnell Arceneaux, the doyen of the forensic laboratory services, was a big man with a big voice. Slider always had to hold the receiver away from his ear when Tufty came on.

'Bill! How's she hanging, my old mackerel?'

'Limp as a three-legged dog.'

'That's terrible! Trouble at t'mill?'

'Trouble everywhere. I hope you've got good news for me.'

'Depends on how you feel about no news. I can't find anything in your victim's blood or stomach contents – nothing of significance, anyway.'

'Damn.'

'Hold fast, chum! That doesn't mean there isn't anything there to be found,' Tufty bellowed. 'I suppose you can't give me an idea of what I'm looking for?'

'I wish I could. Her doctor says she wasn't written up for any sleepers or tranks, and there was nothing in the house or in her handbag. But Freddie Cameron says—'

'Ah, the ineffable Freddie! Yes, I've read his report. Well, old hamster, I've been through all the normal prescription drugs from soup to nuts, and scored a big fat zero. Nix. *Nada.*'

'What about alcohol?'

'Oh, she'd been drinking, all right, but there's not enough alcohol there to account for coma or collapse.'

'There must be something,' Slider said in frustration.

'Very likely, old love, but I can't test for "something". Tell me what to look for, and I'll look for it.'

'I wish I could,' Slider said. 'It's one of the vast army of things I don't know yet. Anything interesting on the victim's clothes?'

'I'm just your bodily fluids man. I passed the clothing to a minion who is e'en now working on it for you.'

'What about the semen, then? Though with my luck it'll probably turn out to be the husband's.'

'I'm hoping to get round to the basic tests tomorrow. You know the problem: too much work and not enough assistants. They're always promising us more manpower tomorrow, but somehow tomorrow never comes. I've sent the semen off for DNA profiling, too, but as you know, dear, it's easier to lift a live eel with chopsticks than to get a quick result from the DNA lab.'

'Well, never mind, I dare say I shall still be in the same position when the results come back.'

'Dear boy,' Tufty boomed, 'you sound infinitely pathetic!'

'I'm up to my gills in pathos—'

'Not to mention bathos and Abednego. How are things on the domestic front? Got your love life sorted out at last? Getting it together with your lovely Euterpe?'

'My turkey?'

'Your lady musician,' Tufty translated kindly.

'Oh! She's a joy, but the other side is not so harmonious.' He told Tufty, who knew Irene of old, about the latest development.

'You do have all the luck,' Tufty acknowledged, in what were for him muted tones. 'My sympathy, old horse. And just when you thought you'd got her nicely bedded in with El Alternative! But you know what the old Jewish proverb says: life is like a cucumber – just when you think it's firmly in your grip, you find it's up your arse.'

'That's the most helpful thing anyone's said to me all day.'

'Go and see Irene face to face, that's my advice. You know you're at your most persuasive in the flesh. One look into your sad, doggy eyes, and she'll be putty.'

'You might have something,' Slider acknowledged.

'And meanwhile, go out and have yourself a good meal and bottle of decent wine. You've got to rejuvenate the manly juices.'

'That's already in the plans,' Slider said. 'Joanna and I have been invited to dinner tonight with what Fred Porson would call a Gordon Roux chef.'

Tufty chuckled. 'Ah, the dear old Syrup! What a character!'

'It takes one to know one,' said Slider, amused.

CHAPTER EIGHT

Apart From That, Mrs Lincoln . . .

Oedipus was sitting in one of his outrageous positions – this time balanced on the top of the chairback of the fireside Queen Anne.

'He can't be comfortable,' Joanna observed.

'He just does it to prove he can,' Atherton said. 'It's a form of intellectual intimidation. The less he appears to want to be noticed, the more he expresses his mental dominance over me.'

Oedipus had his paws tucked under and his eyes shut, but his ears moved like radar saucers, following every movement of Atherton in the kitchen, freezing with special alertness at the sound of the fridge door opening. Joanna leaned against the frame of the door between the sitting-room and the tiny kitchen, watching: she knew better than to offer to help. Slider had taken non-participation one step further and, nursing a G and T, was sitting in the other fireside chair reading the paper, something he hardly ever had time to do.

'You know who's missing from this gathering,' Joanna remarked, watching Atherton frying something.

'Who?' he said absently.

'I love the way you shoogle those things in the pan! Wonderfully professional wrist action.'

He glanced her way. 'White woman speak with forked tongue. Who?'

'Sue, of course. She loves your cooking.'

'Don't start that again,' he warned. 'If she wants to see me she's only got to ring.'

'She gave you all the encouragement a nicely brought-up girl can give. It's for *you* to ring *her*.'

'Why?' he said brutally, slinging the fry-ees onto plates.

'Because she's not going to make all the running. She's a womanly woman.'

'And why should you think I want a womanly woman? Move, please, you're in the way.'

Joanna rolled herself round the supporting jamb as he passed her in the doorway. 'What would be the point in any other sort?'

'Sit down,' he told her, and raised his voice slightly, 'Bill, are you joining us?'

Joanna regarded her starter of two miniature fishcakes in a puddle of pink sauce, decorated with a twig of watercress. The whole thing was like a bonsai garden: tiny tree, two pebbles and a sunset pool. 'The trouble with your food is that it looks so professional, it's discouraging for people like me. I cook things best eaten with the eyes shut.'

'It's no more difficult,' Atherton said, pouring wine.

'It is,' she said indignantly.

'I like your food,' Slider said stoutly. 'It's filling.'

'Oh, thank you! What's this sauce?'

'It's a sauce. Dill, mostly.'

'Why is it pink?'

'Why does Superman wear his knickers over his tights?' Atherton countered. 'Do you think I'm going to reveal all my secrets to you?'

Slider sampled cautiously; he wasn't fond of fishcakes. 'Delicious,' he discovered, with relief.

Atherton looked at him cannily. 'I expect you'd prefer a nice half-a-grapefruit with a dazed cherry in the middle, but, dear heart, you are not going to get it in this house.'

Slider smiled at him with perfect concord. 'This stuff,' he said, lifting the watercress with his fork, 'is just the Islington equivalent of a cherry tomato and two slices of cucumber.'

'Eat it, it's full of iron. You need iron at your age,' Atherton said.

They ate companionably, but the empty fourth side of the square table now seemed a rebuke. Atherton cursed Joanna for bringing the subject up again. He had 'dumped' Sue, according to his own script, because she was getting 'too heavy'. Any minute, he had complained, she was going to use the dreaded C-word.

He liked his carefree bachelor life, and there were thousands of women in the world that he hadn't had yet. But Joanna had said to him – only once, and casually, but it was enough – that she believed he had dropped Sue out of fear that Sue would drop him first.

The idea nagged at him; and alone and immobile in the hospital there'd been plenty of time to be nagged. Of his numerous previous girlfriends, only Sue had sent a card, only Sue had visited him. He had been half touched, half angry at her attentions. Getting her claws into him while he was vulnerable, he had told himself cynically; but even his angry half didn't really believe that. He had enjoyed her visits. She didn't seem to feel the need to be bright and cheery; hadn't even minded when he was too down to talk to her. On those occasions she had just sat and read the paper for half an hour, and it had been nice simply having her there. He had found himself looking forward to her visits, and had had to force himself not to ask as she left when she would be coming again.

Only as he grew stronger, and his ambivalence about going back to the Job had troubled him more, he had rejected what he saw as a despicable dependency. The idea of him, the randy young copper's role model, settling down to banal domesticity – Darby and Joan facing each other like Toby jugs across the fireplace – appalled him. Since he left the hospital he had not contacted her. A bit of him had been hurt that she had not contacted him, but mostly he told himself that he was relieved that he didn't have to go on being grateful to her for rallying round in his time of need.

But if he was honest – which he tried not to be too often – he had to admit that the house had seemed horribly cold and empty when he first returned to it; even since Oedipus had come back from his temporary stay with Bill and Joanna, he had felt lonely in it. Him, lonely! Logic told him that it was just the aftermath of shock. He hadn't felt up to going out on the pull yet: didn't want to have to show a stranger his scar. Besides, his nerve had taken a bashing: he had come face to face with his mortality. All those things, he told himself, only made him *feel* that he was lonely. He was still the same Jim Atherton underneath, the old tom-catting free spirit who depended on no-one.

All of which was both true and untrue in about equal proportions. He looked across the table at his boss, who wore an almost visible aura of sappy contentment whenever he was with Joanna, despite all his other troubles; and he wished he had Bill's courage simply to admit he needed to love and be loved. Bill could acknowledge not just to the world but to *himself* that he was not complete without Joanna; the idea terrified Atherton. If the integrity of his shell were once breached, what chaos might not come flooding in?

He cleared the plates and went out to the kitchen for the main course – chicken breasts with lime and bay on a bed of polenta, with mangetouts and baby carrots – and as he laid it all out he suffered a brief spasm of revulsion for the whole performance. Was not this dilettantism a denial of life? Who was he doing it all for? What was the point? But he took himself firmly in hand and dismissed such barbarous thoughts, marched the plates in by the scruff of their necks. When cast away on a desert island, *always* dress for dinner.

The other two – thank heaven – had changed the subject. 'So what's this committee meeting you've got to go to tomorrow?' Slider was asking Joanna.

'Just the usual shinola, I expect. In the old days it used to be all about not letting enough women into the orchestra. Now women are accepted, it's all about what they ought to wear. Long black or long coloured? Patterned or plain? The LSO is anti-sleeveless; the LPO won't allow tails.'

'Eh?' said Atherton.

'For women,' she explained. 'The arguments are endless.'

'So that's what concerns you all in the nineties? Do you want to finish up the Macon, Bill, or go on to the red?'

'Oh, red, thanks.'

'Joanna?'

'I'll have another splash of white, thanks. No, clothes are just on the surface. The deep concern is one none of us wants to look in the face.' She sipped and replaced her glass. 'I think there's a move afoot to get rid of some of the older players.'

'Because they're no good?' Slider asked.

'Good God, no! Because the marketing men think concert-goers only want to look at dewy youth. They think grey hair and glasses put the punters off. And for all I know they might be right,' she shrugged.

'Surely music-lovers can't be that shallow,' Slider protested.

Atherton looked at him with amusement. '*You* say that, with all your experience of human nature?'

'I've heard comments about Brian Harrop, our second trumpet,' Joanna went on. 'I think they're trying to get him out. He plays like an angel, but, hey, he's bald on top and white round the sides and wears half-moon glasses on the platform. Who wants an old giff like him?'

'Eat your nice din-dins,' Atherton said sympathetically.

She picked up her knife and fork, but passion drove her on. 'I know what it's really about. They want to bring in Dane Jackson, who was Young Musician of the Year last year, because he looks like Nigel Kennedy, and he can do all that fast-fingering, pyrotechnic stuff they teach in College now. Never mind that he can't actually make a nice *sound* on the thing. They don't teach that any more.'

'Careful, dear, you're sounding bitter,' Atherton said.

'Why shouldn't I? All these kids coming out of College have got technique to die for, they can play things most of us couldn't get near, but they're not orchestral players. They don't know how to fit in and, what's more, they don't want to. Brian knows every piece in the repertoire and a thousand that aren't, he knows how to get the right sound at the right moment, and he can adapt to any first trumpet's playing so that they sound like one. Dane Jackson loves himself first, the music a poor second, and the ensemble way down the list. If he plays in a Mozart symphony, he's going to make sure what you hear above all else is Dane Jackson.'

'But if it's what the audience wants,' Slider said doubtfully, 'I suppose it has to be. They're the ones buying the tickets.'

'I can't argue with that,' she said abruptly, and addressed herself to her chicken.

'You agree?' Slider said, surprised.

She grinned over a forkful. 'I didn't say I agreed, I said I couldn't argue with it.'

'Let's pick up the phone, here, and dial for Ronnie Real,' Atherton said expansively. 'We're talking what's Now. And Now is about Image. Youth is Cool, and Cool is where it's at. Okay?'

'You think you're joking,' Joanna snorted. 'You should hear them at the meetings!' She sighed. 'They're all so bloody earnest and humourless, that's the worst thing. When I think of some of the old characters who were around when I first started playing—'

'Here it comes,' Atherton said to Slider. 'Anecdote Alert!'

'Another Bob Preston story,' Slider agreed.

'Well, why not? I feel like a treat,' she said defiantly. 'We were doing a recording of the Capriccio Italienne, and of course there's that really fiendish cornet bit in it: fast, A-transposition and full of accidentals.' She da-da'd the phrase, and Atherton, at least, nodded. 'Anyway, every time we got to it, Bob fluffed it, and finally after about five takes the conductor looked across and said sarkily, "First cornet, would you like me to take it slower for you?" Bob says, "No, actually, could we do it a bit faster, please?" The conductor looks amazed. "But could you play it faster?" he says, and Bob says, "No, but it'd be a shorter fuck-up."' She sighed. 'I loved that man!'

Atherton fetched the pudding, and they got on to discussing the case.

'I think Porson's right to let him go,' Slider said. 'The old man may be a bit strange, but he knows his onions. Being held by us was probably just enough punishment to keep Andrews comfortable. Being all alone in the house – the house he built for her – may work on his guilt and bring him to the point of remorse where he has to confess.'

'But he didn't kill her at home, did he?' Joanna said.

'We didn't find anything to show that he did,' Slider said. 'The trouble is, if he didn't kill her in the privacy and comfort of his own home, where did he do it?'

'In the cab of his pickup is the next best bet,' Atherton said. 'But it could equally well have been in the long grass or round the back of the bike sheds. We just don't know.'

'Not on a hard surface,' Slider said, 'or the back of her head would have been bruised or abraded. Of course, since she was found lying in the earth, the presence of earth or grass on the back of her clothes and hair wouldn't tell us anything.'

'But wherever he killed her,' Joanna said, 'how did he transport the body? I suppose if the handbag was in the pickup, it suggests the body was too.'

'It could be. But that's another problem: why didn't the neighbours on that side of the house hear the pickup driving up?'

'Oh, come on,' Atherton objected. 'Who pays any attention to the sound of traffic? Your brain edits it out.'

'But the sound of crunching gravel—'

'Well, he'd be nuts to drive it over the gravel,' Atherton said impatiently. 'He'd park it on the road.'

'*He*'d still have to walk over the gravel – and with a body over his shoulder,' Slider said. 'Surely they'd hear that? It's the point of gravel – it's an alarm system.'

'Couldn't he have got to the terrace any other way?' Joanna asked.

'Up through the garden,' Slider said.

'But that would mean crossing someone else's garden first,' Atherton said. 'There's a footpath at the end of the row, but there's three houses between it and the Rectory. That's four fences to get the body over. Of course it's possible, but would anyone?'

'Where does the footpath go to?' Joanna asked.

Slider raised his eyebrows. 'To the railway footbridge. But of course, good point! From there he could have got onto the railway embankment, which runs parallel with the gardens: only two fences, and cover in between. Maybe we oughtn't to get too hung up on the pickup.'

Atherton cocked his head. 'Time for a general appeal for witnesses, do you think?'

'We haven't enough manpower to extend the house-to-house much further,' Slider said, 'and Porson's already burbling about budget restraints. Yes, maybe it's time to ask him to go public. But on a limited scale – local television, perhaps. We don't want sightings from Aberdeen and Abergavenny clogging up the system.'

'Why don't *you* ever do the TV appeals?' Joanna said, slipping a hand on his thigh under the table. 'It'd be a feather in my cap having a celeb for a lover. Your handsome face all over the silver screen—'

'Not in these trousers,' Slider said firmly. 'I'm a private man and I intend to stay private. Det sups get the big money – they can have the exposure as well.'

'Mr Modesty!'

Atherton was still musing. 'What I can't understand is why he retouched the makeup. It seems to me that, if Freddie's right about that, it's a point against its being Eddie. If he was going to bury her in concrete, it wouldn't matter what she looked like.'

'It is odd,' Slider acknowledged. 'Maybe the oddest thing about the whole business.'

'But, to my mind, it's only her husband who *would* do a thing like that,' Joanna said. 'Why would anybody else care what she looked like? It's a strange, obsessive kind of thing to do. I can imagine him plotting the murder, carrying it out, and then brooding over the body – you know, like those chimps that won't be separated from their dead babies and keep on licking and grooming them.'

'I see your reasoning,' Slider said. 'But is he obsessive in that way?'

'Don't ask me, I've never met the bloke,' Joanna said. 'But if he says he loved her, and she was a bad hat, maybe that was enough to make him obsessive.'

'How much of a bad hat we've still to discover,' Slider said, and looked towards Atherton. 'You know, I'm wondering if there wasn't something between her and Meacher. Given the way she was with Potter, her other boss – and the availability of empty houses to do it in.'

'Eddie says Meacher sometimes asked her to work at weekends, and he obviously didn't like it,' Atherton agreed cautiously.

'Maybe that was just an excuse. I got the feeling Meacher was keeping something back from me, and he's never come in with the list of where he was that afternoon. There's something about that man I don't like.'

'I thought it was everything about him you didn't like,' Atherton said. 'The ordinary bloke's hatred of the man of style and taste—'

'None of your sauce,' Slider countered. 'You forget I have it in my power to retaliate. There are jobs and jobs, and I'm the one who gives 'em out. For instance, Andrews' pickup had an oil leak – left stains on the ground where it was parked. Now that might give us a clue as to where it was on Tuesday night.'

Atherton rolled his eyes. 'No! Mercy! You want me to go and investigate every oil patch in west London? I don't have the stomach for it! I don't have the trousers for it!'

'Well, just watch your lip, then,' Slider warned. 'And go and get my coffee. Can't you see I've finished?'

Atherton jumped up, cowering, grabbed the plates and shuffled out, one shoulder hunched and his left leg dragging.

Joanna replaced her hand on Slider's thigh. 'I love it when you're masterful,' she said, batting her eyelids. 'Would you like to sleep with me tonight?'

'I'll think about it,' he said lordly-wise, but his smirk gave him away.

Morning streamed into Slider's office to fidget with his hangover and remind him that nothing worthwhile was ever had without payment. They had been drinking brandy late into the night, and he was beginning to think brandy didn't agree with him. Certainly morning had come too soon and was being far too loud about it. Still, at least the windows were decently grey again, now that the awful cleanliness of the Barrington era had worn off. Det Sup Porson had a proper respect for crud. Dirty windows saved on net curtains.

He was talking to Atherton when Mackay came in with the long-promised cup of tea.

'You took your time,' Slider grumped.

'Sorry, sir. I got sidetracked,' he said, putting the cup down without taking his eyes from the typesheet in his hand. Slider sighed and patiently poured the slops back into the cup and found a paper hanky to wipe the cup's bottom. 'I left yours on your desk, Jim,' Mackay said.

'Safest place,' Atherton said.

'The thing is, guv,' Mackay went on, 'it's these phone numbers. Mrs Andrews' car phone. On the Tuesday she made two calls to a number that turns out to be David Meacher's mobile. The first was a short one at one fifty-five – lasted only thirty-five seconds. The second was a long one – nineteen minutes. Cost her a small fortune – or would've,' he corrected succinctly. 'That was at eighteen thirty-one.'

'Half past six in people-time,' Atherton translated.

Slider reflected. 'Well, there's no reason she shouldn't phone her boss, I suppose. I wonder where she was, though, and why it couldn't wait until she got home? Any others?'

'Well, I dunno if it means anything, but about half past five she phoned a number that turns out to be the vicarage of the vicar that does the church in St Michael Square.'

'The Rev. Alan Tennyson,' Atherton said.

'That's right. Well, we know she was very inty at the church, so there's nothing funny about that, but I did wonder—'

'Whether she asked for spiritual advice?'

'It wasn't a long enough call for that – four minutes. But seeing as it was the day she died, she might have said something to him that would give us a hint.'

'Quite right,' Slider said. 'We'll look into it. Anything else?'

'She phoned the First And Last just before eleven o'clock. Ten fifty-five, to be exact, one minute fifty seconds. I wondered if she spoke to Eddie. Maybe that was when he arranged to meet her somewhere, wherever it was he killed her.'

'The barman said it was after eleven that Eddie came in,' Atherton reminded him. 'After closing-time, which was why he refused him a drink. But I suppose he could have got the time wrong.'

'Or the pub clock could be fast,' Slider said. 'It's a thought, anyway. What about Meacher's mobile?'

'Nothing that strikes the eye, guv,' Mackay said, 'except—' He hesitated. 'Well, I dunno if it's anything to do with anything, but he did make a call to the Target Motel that morning. At half past eleven.'

'Half past eleven? He was still in the office at that time, wasn't he?'

'Well, that's what I wondered. If he used his mobile instead of the office phone, maybe he didn't want anyone to hear what he was saying. And it being a motel, naturally I thought—'

'That his call had naughty purposes,' Atherton concluded. 'It's shocking the effect the word "motel" has on people.'

'Well, why don't you pop round there and find out?' Slider told Mackay. 'No, no, don't thank me. I like to reward virtue. Meanwhile,' he said to Atherton, 'I think you may pay a visit to the parish priest, and see if you can get any more information about Mrs Andrews and her little proclivities.'

'Pretty large ones, from what I've heard,' Atherton said,

unfolding his long body from the window-sill like a hydraulic arm. 'What about a Meacher follow-up?'

'I'll do that,' Slider said. 'I need the fresh air.'

Meacher's office was womanned by a very smart, well-preserved female in her forties who was very nearly pretty. Her hair was dyed blonde, but very nicely, and her makeup was perfect, except that she had eaten off her lipstick leaving only the outliner, which gave her rather a clownlike look. A lipstick-stained coffee cup on her desk completed the story, and the stale-laundry smell of instant coffee on the air suggested to the trained mind that she had only just finished it and hadn't yet had time to renew the lippy. It was easy when you knew how, Slider told himself, and asked her for the boss.

She replied, with a clipped smile and an authoritative voice, 'I'm sorry, he's at the other office today. Can I help you?'

'You must be—' Slider sought memory for the name. 'Liz – I'm sorry, I don't know your other name.'

'Liz Berryman,' she admitted, looking a query.

'Detective Inspector Slider, Shepherd's Bush CID.'

'Oh! Yes,' she said, and her face became grave. 'About Jennifer, I suppose. That was a terrible thing. I suppose it was murder?'

'We're treating the death as suspicious,' Slider said cautiously. The eyes behind the mascara were watchful and intelligent. 'I suppose you didn't know her very well?'

'Oh, I knew her all right,' she said bitterly. She looked down, and then up again as though coming to a decision. 'I suppose you know about her and David?'

Slider sat down in the chair on the other side of her desk with an air of settling in for the spill. 'Funnily enough, that's what I was going to ask him about when I came here.'

'If he'd tell you. It's supposed to be a big secret. But *I* 'll tell you if he won't.' She translated his waiting expression as an enquiry into her motives. 'I don't owe him any loyalty on that score. What loyalty did he ever show me, or anyone? And they were both married people. Besides, it's everyone's duty to help the police, isn't it?'

'I wish everyone thought so,' Slider said. 'So Jennifer and David Meacher were having an affair, were they?'

'If that's what you want to call it,' she said sourly. '*He* tried to keep it a secret at the office, but *she* was always brushing up against him, and saying things no-one else was supposed to understand. She was always calling him, too, when it wasn't her day on. She'd disguise her voice sometimes and pretend to be a client if it was me answered the phone, but I knew it was her, all right. I expect she did the same thing at his home. Her sort always do. I pity his poor wife.'

'But Mr Meacher said that you and she were never here at the same time,' Slider queried.

'That was the basic principle, but our times overlapped, so as to make sure the office was always covered. And she did extra hours when we were busy. And, of course,' she added harshly, 'she liked to hang around after I arrived talking to David and looking sideways at me to see if I'd noticed.'

'Why would she do that?' Slider asked mildly.

She glowered at him. 'Why don't you just come right out and ask me? I've got nothing to hide, though David seems to think I have. But I wasn't the one who was married. I was perfectly entitled to do whatever I wanted, especially given—' She stopped, biting her lips angrily.

Slider was there at last. 'It used to be you,' he said. 'He dropped you for Jennifer?'

She coloured. 'There was no dropping about it! He wanted to go on seeing me as well, but when I found out about Jennifer I told him there was no way I was going to share, let alone with that vulgar, brassy – well, tart's too good a word for her. He wanted to have both of us. That's when I got out – and I was right to.'

'But you were already sharing with his wife,' Slider said, though he had guessed what came next. Oh, Lord, what fools we mortals be!

'He promised to marry me. I would never have started it otherwise. He said he was going to leave her, that he was only waiting for the right time to tell her. But when he took up with Jennifer, I realised what a fool I'd been. He never meant it. It was just what he said to get me into bed.'

'Well, at least you've realised it now,' Slider said encouragingly. 'Some people never see the truth, even when it's under their noses.'

She didn't answer that, only stared broodingly at the computer screen, alone with her thoughts. And Slider thought, Yes, she's discovered the truth, but she's still here, working for him. Why is that? Just to be near him? Still in love with him, in spite of everything? What *was* it about some men?

'So when did it start between him and Jennifer?' he asked.

Miss Berryman's attention snapped back into place. 'Oh, right from the time she first came to work here. In fact, I wouldn't be surprised if that wasn't *why* he gave her the job – so as to have more opportunities for it.' She looked into Slider's eyes as one coming to the worst and barely credible thing. 'They used to do it in the clients' houses, you know. The ones we had keys for. On their beds. God knows what would have happened if they'd got caught.'

Slider wondered for a moment whether the two-timing Meacher had known he was being two-timed by Jennifer. What a pair they were! 'And yet,' he said aloud, 'you wouldn't have thought she was his type. I wonder what he saw in her.'

'Oh, I understand she was fabulous in the sack,' Miss Berryman said, in a hard voice. 'As for her, she thought David was worth a mint, and she couldn't wait to get her claws into him. She'd have found out!'

'Found out what?'

She looked at him with narrowed eyes. 'I do the invoices, and I know how to get into his accounts on the computer. The business is on the rocks. If his wife doesn't bail him out again, he'll go bust. Well, serve him right, I say. I know I'll lose my job if he folds, but it'd be worth it just to see that smug look wiped off his face.'

'His wife has money, has she?'

'Oh, she's rich as Croesus. That's why he'll never leave her. I learned *that* the hard way.'

Instructive, Slider thought, out in the street, though it didn't get him much further forward. So Jennifer was making the beast with two backs with Meacher, who had previously been bonking Liz Berryman. And what price now the little fluffy one he'd seen the other day – what was her name? – Caroline? Meanwhile, Jennifer was Doctor Dolittling with Jack Potter on the side, and who else? Oh, brave new world, that had such people in it. He should have known Meacher was a villain. Any man who'd sell an Aston to buy a BMW couldn't be all good.

In his car, he dialled the number of Meacher's Denham office, but all he got was an answering-machine in Meacher's voice.

'I'm sorry we can't come to the phone right now, but if you'll leave your telephone number and any short message, we'll get back to you.'

Slider put down the receiver with irritation. Why 'right now'? Was there some other, less immediate sort of now during which the telephone might possibly be answered? And why 'get back to you'? The phrase had such overtones of hardship dauntlessly overcome, conjuring images of the faithful family dog, accidentally left behind, struggling mile after mile over unfamiliar terrain to find its way home to the masters it adored. Get back to you, indeed! Slider knew perfectly well that his dislike of David Meacher was in essence irrational; but the mark of maturity, he always felt, was the ability to sustain irrational prejudices with grace and dignity. He made a few more telephone calls, and then rang Joanna.

'Fancy a trip out into the countryside?'

'You mean now? As opposed to finishing the pile of ironing I've just started, hoovering the sitting room, cleaning the bath and putting in a solid hour's practice? That's a hard one to call.'

'I've got to go out to Denham to interview a bloke, and there's a really nice pub in Denham village – the Kestrel – where they do toasted bacon and tomato sandwiches. I thought we could meet there for lunch.'

'What beer do they do?'

'Marston's and Brakspear's, if memory serves.'

'You're on.'

'You're not working today, are you?'

'Just that committee meeting at six.'

'Hedonist!' he said.

The Denham office of David Meacher Estate Agents turned out to be a wooden hut standing all alone beside the bypass between a garden centre and a timber yard. Traffic thundered past, bypassing for all it was worth, and four lanes and a central reservation divided the hut from the pavement on the other side where there was a row of shops, a pillar-box, houses, and pedestrians. However cheap the hut was in terms of rent and rates, it was unlikely to pay its way in walk-in trade, Slider thought, as he parked in the lay-by. The hut had two shop windows and a door in between. The windows were filled with cards advertising houses for sale, but half of them had 'sold' stickers across them, and they all looked very yellow. A hecatomb of dead flies lay inside on the window-sill, and the door had its blind pulled down and a 'closed' notice hanging from a suction hook. There was a hand-written notice stuck to the inside of the glass of the door, instructing interested parties to contact the Chiswick office; but this, too, Slider noticed, was yellowed with age and exposure to sunlight. Without any hope, he banged on the door, but there was, as he expected, no answer.

He returned to his car. The lay-by was tenanted by a flower-seller, a young man in cut-offs and teeshirt perched on a camp stool reading a paperback, guarding a green-painted barrow displaying the indestructible flowers of the roadside: long-stemmed rosebuds that would never open, multi-headed chrysanthemums whose petals would fall off in one shattering lump ten minutes after you bought them, and the sort of scentless carnations that looked exactly the same whether they were alive or dead. The lad looked up as Slider approached, but not with any expectation of making a sale. Slider wondered how he – or whoever employed him – could possibly make a living. Who bought these joyless objects, which could not merit so exuberant a title as 'blooms'? Someone going to the funeral of an office colleague, perhaps, cramming it into a working day between meetings? A businessman with sweat rings under the arms of his striped shirt and fear of discovery in his heart, hurrying to a clandestine lunch with his mistress in one of those tomb-like exurban Italian restaurants, where the food is frozen in individual dishes for ease of microwaving, and the coffee is reheated from day to day?

'Know anything about the estate agents there?' Slider asked. The young man shook his head. 'Has anyone been in there this morning?'

'Never seen anyone go in there,' he said.

'You here every day?'

'Mostly.'

'What time is it usually open?'

He shook his head again. 'Never seen it open.' He eyed Slider keenly. 'Police?'

Am I that obvious? Slider thought. 'I'm looking for the owner,' he said.

'I think they've closed down,' the young man said. 'It's been shut up like that since I been coming here. Never seen anyone go near it. You only got to look at the weeds.'

Slider looked back, and noticed, sure enough, the ragwort and dandelions growing up between the cracks in the pavement and between the pavement and the hut's wall. This was a pavement that never knew the touch of human foot. People drove into the garden centre and the woodyard, or parked briefly in the lay-by for the flower-seller's wares and then drove off again.

'Thanks,' Slider said. It was all Hatton Garden to a hatful of mice that this man had no trader's licence, but Slider had no wish to appear ungrateful, and besides, he reckoned the lad had already devised his own punishment. He got into his car, thought for a moment, looked at his watch, and then in his notebook for Meacher's home address. If he wasn't there, at least there might be someone who knew where he was.

CHAPTER NINE

Babes and Suckers

Meacher's house was as irritating as the man: a large and lovely 1930s mansion, built in the Lutyens-Jekyll vernacular, with cottage casements, elaborate tile-hanging, mossy paths, and a garden of full-blown, tangled beauty whose natural, untended look was the ultimate in artifice and must have taken endless work to achieve. It was down a quiet lane on the outskirts of Denham, and when Slider climbed out of his car, only the distant waterfall-roar of the M40 spoiled the rural idyll.

Slider had more than half expected to find no-one home, but after a long delay, the door was flung open to reveal a woman holding a black Labrador by the collar. 'Can you just come inside,' she said, without waiting for him to speak, 'so I can shut the door? Bessie's on heat and I don't want her to get out.'

Slider obeyed and stepped into a large vestibule full of beautiful old furniture covered in clutter, terracotta walls covered in watercolours and prints, the woodblock floor covered in an old Turkish carpet and muddy paw-marks. A tall Chinese vase of obvious antiquity was filled with blue and white delphiniums spitting their petals everywhere. Coats hung over the newel post of the stairs, a heap of books and papers sat on the third step waiting to go up, a George III side table was littered with opened and unopened mail, dog-leads and a tin of saddle-soap, and the air smelt of furniture polish, dogs, earth and damp. Slider soaked it all in. He was in the presence, he knew, of genuine Old Money. None of your Chiswick-and-Islington, upper-middle-class, fresh-painted spotlessness here: this was how the real nobs lived, the sort of country gentry his father had worked for and whose houses Slider as a child had occasionally entered. There had always seemed to him an effortlessness about everything they did, which he as a struggling mediocrity to whom nothing came easily had deeply admired; but with later wisdom he supposed that, like the garden, it looked effortless because someone behind the scenes had put in a great deal of hard work – in the case of his childhood icons, probably a grim-faced, uniformed nanny.

The present example released the dog, which instantly danced smiling up to Slider to bash his legs with its black rudder of a tail and invite him to play. He stroked the big, domed head and the dog instantly reared up and placed huge paws on his stomach to make the stroking easier. Over its head, he looked at the woman.

She was tall and thin, probably in her late fifties, tanned, with a mane of streaked grey hair, which seemed to grow naturally back from her face like Tenniel's illustrations of Alice. She was dressed in black leggings and a body-hugging sleeveless pink top, something like a leotard, over which she wore a loose, baggy white shirt, hanging open and with the sleeves rolled up. Her feet were bare and her toe-nails were painted. Her large-featured face must once have been staggeringly beautiful, and even now, though her skin was tired, her neck crêpy, and the veins on her hands like jungle creepers, she was still stunning.

'Mrs Meacher?' he asked.

'Lady Diana Meacher,' she corrected, though not as if it mattered very much.

'I beg your pardon, ma'am. Detective Inspector Slider of Shepherd's Bush CID.' He removed one hand from the dog's head to reach for his ID, but she waved the formality away.

'I suppose you've come about this wretched Andrews woman? You'd better come through. Do you mind the kitchen? I was potting some fuchsia cuttings. You won't mind if I carry on?'

He followed her down the passage beside the stairs, glimpsing through open doors rooms that were larger performances of what the hall had rehearsed. The dog trotted after them, nails clicking on the parquet, but when they reached the kitchen it turned and went away again, back the way they had come. The kitchen had an Aga under the mantelpiece instead of a range, and fitted cabinets round two walls, but otherwise was pretty much unchanged from the 1930s, with the original tiles, quarry floor, wooden dresser and shelves. A huge deal table stood in the middle of the room covered in newspaper on which stood a potting tray full of earth, ranks of small plastic flower-pots and jam-jars full of rooted cuttings. An ancient yellow Labrador with filmy eyes and a nose the colour of milk chocolate lay in a basket by the Aga and did not get up, and there were three vast dozing cats, two sitting on the top of the Aga and the other on the window-sill by the open window onto the garden. Out on the lawn another three Labradors, two black and a yellow, were racing about, ears flapping, having a glorious game with a stick. Slider felt sorry for poor Bessie, gynaecologically excluded from the fun. Wasn't that just a woman's lot?

Lady Diana followed the direction of his eyes. 'Rusty, Leo and Bob. The chap in the basket's Billie, who's too old to bother with miscegenation. Bessie's the only girl, poor bitch. I'll take her out later for a run round the garden, but she has to stay on the lead when she's in purdah, and I just haven't time now.'

'I don't want to disturb you,' Slider said. 'I was really looking for your husband.'

She looked at him with large, intelligent, beautiful eyes, whose tired orbits had been delicately shaded with grey eyeshadow, the lashes darkened with violet mascara: even when not expecting to be seen, he noted, she tended her garden. 'He's not here,' she said abruptly. 'I don't know where he is. Probably looking at some property. Or he may be at his health club, or propping up a bar somewhere, who knows? Look here, I suspect this is going to turn into a long session. Why don't you make us some coffee, while I carry on with these cuttings? I've promised two hundred for the church bazaar tomorrow, and they're still in water. I don't know why I do these things. The coffee machine's over there, and the coffee's in the blue tin on the shelf above it. Can you manage that?'

'I can manage that,' he said. While he was managing, the black Labrador reappeared with a small, much-chewed rag doll in her mouth, which she laid at his feet, smiling and waving her tail. He thanked her gravely, and she trotted off again.

'That's Lucy, her baby,' Lady Diana explained. 'Bessie's frightfully maternal and won't be parted from the thing, except when she's on heat, and then she gives it away to all and sundry. So, you were looking for David?'

'I tried his Chiswick office, and they said he was at the Denham office, but when I went there—'

She snorted. 'Oh, that! David's alibi. Some men have a potting shed, some men have the club. David has a hut on the A40. They all serve the same purpose. What do *you* do when you don't want anyone to be able to contact you?'

'I'm a police officer. We don't need any other excuse,' Slider said, smiling. 'So the Denham office doesn't actually do any business?'

'It did once, back in the eighties when estate agency was flourishing. David opened branches – the hut and another office in Chalfont St Peter – took on extra staff, planned to conquer the world. But the recession and the property crash ended all that. He closed the branches and sold the building at Chalfont, but he kept the hut.'

Bessie reappeared with a dog-lead in her mouth. She ran up to Slider but when he put his hand out she jumped away and carried the lead to her mistress. Lady Diana took it absently and put it on the table. The bitch gazed at her hopefully for a while, and then pattered away again.

'Why did he keep the hut?' Slider asked.

She filled a pot with compost and shook a cutting free of its companions. 'Male pride, partly. He couldn't bear to think that his days as a business mogul were over. He loved having three branches and six employees, driving from one to the other and being paged in between. He doesn't really like business, you see, just the trappings of it. For instance, I thought it would break his heart to part with the Aston, but I think he actually likes the BMW better because it's got more gadgets.'

Slider nodded, watching her long fingers dive into the soil like fish getting back into the water. 'What was the other reason?'

'For keeping the hut? Oh, for his affairs, of course,' she said brutally. 'He has a sofa in there that turns into a bed. There's nothing else in there now, except for the answering-machine – equally useful for genuine enquiries or messages from his tarts. He changes the call-in code all the time so that I can't collect them before he does. As if,' she gave him a burning look, 'I care any longer what he does.'

Slider nodded. The machine was making a noise now like an advert for instant coffee. 'You cared once, then?'

'I married him for love, strange though that seems now,' she said. 'My family were against it. They saw him for what he was – a hollow man. But to me he seemed so sophisticated, charming, urbane. And he told me he loved me. Women are fools where words are concerned. A man can behave as badly as he likes, as long as he tells you he loves you.'

'Perhaps he did love you,' Slider said. 'Why wouldn't he?'

'I was beautiful when I was a girl,' she said, reaching for another cutting.

'You're beautiful now.'

She paused, and then looked up, and gave a puzzled laugh. 'You're a strange sort of policeman.'

'Are policemen all the same, then? Like women are all the same?'

She shook her head wonderingly. 'You can't go round saying that sort of thing, you know. Talking to people as if they were human beings. As if you knew them.'

Bessie came trotting in at that delicate moment with another gift for Slider. When he disengaged it from her jaws it proved to be a pair of white cotton knickers. Slider held them up to Lady Diana with a look of innocent enquiry, and she blushed.

'That wretched dog! She's been in my chest of drawers again. She's worked out how to open a drawer by gripping the knob in her teeth, but she can only open the small ones, so it's always something embarrassing she brings out.'

'Perfectly decent, respectable knickers,' Slider said blandly. 'Nothing to be ashamed of. Marks and Sparks finest.'

'Oh, throw the wretched things away!' she protested, laughing. 'Bessie, you bad bitch, I shall have to lock you out of the bedrooms next. Go and lie down. Lie down! Is the coffee ready? You're very handy about the kitchen, I must say.'

By the time Slider had poured two mugs, and drawn up a high stool to perch on at the other side of the table, his hostess seemed to have accepted him completely. Bessie was lying down with the old dog, rolling about and play-biting its ears and paws; the cats were fast in sleep, a clock ticked peacefully somewhere deep in the house, and the coffee aroma mingled with the smell of warm compost. Everything was set for confidences.

'Would you like to hear the whole story?' Lady Diana asked. 'I suppose you only came to enquire about David and the Andrews woman, but it might help to place it in context.'

Slider exuded comfort and being settled here for the morning. 'I want to hear everything you want to tell me,' he said, with perfect truth.

She sighed just discernibly. 'You have a wonderful – what's the police equivalent of a bedside manner? Do people always end up by telling you absolutely everything?'

'I wish I knew,' said Slider.

She was born Lady Diana Seldon, youngest daughter of an old family with a new earldom. 'Grandpa was created by Edward VII, but we'd been at Old Warden for five hundred years. I think that's what attracted David in the first place. Property – real estate – is his passion.'

'I'm interested in architecture myself,' Slider mentioned.

'Architecture!' She gave him a humorous look. 'Oh, David hasn't any artistic sense. What he loves about houses is their size, age, extent and value. Their saleability. It's a purely commercial passion. He may have the body of a demi-god, but he has the heart and mind of a grocer.'

'Cruel,' Slider said.

'Not at all. Praise where praise is due. David has the uncanny ability to put a price on any property after the briefest inspection. He can balance location, bedrooms, condition and come up with exactly the figure the market will bear. And he has an incredible memory for what's on his books: he can match a client to a house without even looking in his filing system. He just loves selling houses. He was born to be an estate agent.'

It sounded like the ultimate insult. 'They also serve?' Slider suggested.

'Oh, don't worry, he doesn't need defending. He loves his calling. His other ambition was to be an MP, so you see popularity doesn't figure in his calculations.'

Slider smiled at the jest, but not too much. There was a great deal of pain here somewhere and he had no wish to press on a bruise. 'How did you meet him in the first place?'

She took another seedling and slipped it into the ready earth like a Norland nanny slipping a baby into its cot. 'Daddy was selling some property – a couple of Victorian houses in the village. He contacted Jackson Stops, and they sent round David.'

Her fingers stopped firming the earth for a moment and she stared at nothing. 'He was very handsome, and so fresh and eager. Nothing like the men I'd been used to seeing who were bored with everything, or pretended to be. He was rapturous about the house – it was rather touching. I thought he was loving it, the way I'd always loved it, almost as a person—' She glanced at him to see if he understood, and he nodded. 'Of course, I didn't realise until a long time later that all he wanted to do was to sell it.' She gave a little snorting sigh. 'That's what turned Daddy against him in the end – David kept urging him to sell up and move somewhere more convenient. Daddy had never liked him, but he put up with him for my sake, and he thought it was rather touching that David should worry so much about his health and welfare, even if he did show it in an inappropriate way. But he finally understood that David wasn't concerned for him at all: he just wanted to handle the sale.'

There, in the peaceful kitchen, Slider heard the whole story. Lady Diana had fallen in love with David Meacher more or less at first sight. As the youngest of the family and everyone's pet, she had remained at home long after the others had married and/or moved away. Even her eldest brother, the heir, was living in a flat in Chelsea and running an interior-design shop jointly with a schoolfriend from Eton.

'I suppose I'd never really grown up,' she mused. 'I was happy just going on doing what I'd always done at home – dogs, horses, parties, the family. I had lots of friends, and I'd always had plenty of boyfriends, but I'd never been serious about any of them. I suppose I thought I might marry one day, but I wasn't in any hurry. When you're pretty and popular,' she said frankly, 'you don't feel the same pressure as other girls. I was approaching my thirtieth birthday, but I was still the baby of the family and Daddy's pet.'

Bessie, who had fallen asleep with her head pillowed on the old dog, groaned in her sleep, rolled over and stretched out, exposing her swollen nipples to the cooler air from the window.

'But David was so different. I suppose I fell in love with him because he was different. And he seemed determined from the beginning that he was going to have me. He was always single-minded like that about anything he really wanted.'

He courted her hard, and she was flattered and fascinated. She had started seeing him regularly, but it was not until she announced that she meant to marry him that her family had become alarmed. 'They simply never imagined I could be doing more than amusing myself with him, because – as Bob, my brother, said – he just wasn't one of us. I was furious. I was desperately anti-snobbery in those days and, in any case, as I was always pointing out, David had been to a decent school and everything. It wasn't as if he ate peas with a knife or wiped his nose on his sleeve. The more the family argued, the more I was determined to have him. And in the end Daddy said I was old enough to make my own mistakes, and made everyone else shut up.' She shrugged. 'Of course I found out they were right about David and I was wrong, but it was too late by then. I was married to him and that was that.'

'You never thought about divorce?'

She shook her head. 'Pride, at first. I couldn't have admitted my wonderful love affair was a fish story. And, of course, I did love him. Later I suppose it was just stubbornness. I wouldn't be beaten by him. And fear, too.' She looked at him sidelong. 'I'm not used to being on my own. I don't think I'd like to have to go out there again as a single person.'

'I don't suppose you'd stay single for long,' Slider said.

'Very gallant of you.'

'No, just the truth.'

She moved away from the compliment. 'But to have to start again, go out and meet people, all that dreadful who-are-you and what-do-you-do business – ghastly enough at sixteen, but at fifty-eight? No, I don't think I could go through that again. So we go on as we are. A *modus vivendi* has been reached. I ignore his infidelities and pay his bills. He plays the dutiful husband on public occasions for the sake of my cheque book.'

'But doesn't he make a living? Didn't you say he was a good estate agent?'

'He is, but he's a lousy businessman. He'd have done better to stay with a firm like Jackson, but of course he was ambitious and wanted his own company. What man doesn't? And I was ambitious for him. I set him up, and I bailed him out whenever he made a bad decision, which was often. I suppose that was part of the trouble.'

'How's that?'

'All the money in the marriage is mine. Daddy made a large settlement on me when I married – fortunately, very well invested. David knew that. He married me at least partly for my money – no, please, don't protest.' She stopped Slider with a lift of a muddy hand. 'The trouble is that he's an old-fashioned creature underneath and thinks a man ought to wear the trousers and bring home the bacon. He has affairs to put me in my place, and the worse his business does, the more women he flaunts in front of me. It's his way of asserting his masculinity.'

'It must have been very hard for you,' Slider said gently.

She looked at him nakedly. 'I'm crazy to put up with it. That's what my family says. But I married him. You can't just shrug off responsibility because it's inconvenient, can you?'

'No,' said Slider uncomfortably.

'And they don't really mean it, anyway,' she went on. 'Bob's wife drinks, for instance, and sometimes she steals things, but he'll never leave her. Not just *noblesse oblige*. Either you're that sort of person, or you aren't – don't you think?'

'I used to,' Slider said. 'Lately I've wondered whether everything isn't changing.'

'I know what you mean.' She nodded rather glumly, and then said, 'Is there any more coffee?'

He took her mug and went to refill it, and her voice followed him across the room in a puzzled way. 'I was right, you are a strange sort of policeman. Dangerous, too.'

'Dangerous?' he said, amused.

'Look how much I'm telling you. Why should I do that?'

'Because I'm interested.'

'Exactly.' She tried for a lighter tone. 'I imagine all the young policewomen are nuts about you.'

He came back with the coffee. 'They don't even notice me. They think I'm dull and safe.'

'I bet they don't.'

'Tell me what Jennifer Andrews was like,' he said firmly.

'Haven't you seen her?' She seemed surprised.

'I never met her alive,' he pointed out. 'What was she like as a person?'

'Pretty, smart, lively. Rather obvious. Vulgar, of course. And she was man mad.'

'What did your husband see in her?'

'She was a conquest,' she said. 'I don't know if you know women like her, but she was very mannish in some ways – brassy, confident, at home in pubs, handled her drinks and cigarettes like a man, liked to drive fast, took the lead in conversation. Women like that are a challenge to some men.'

He nodded. 'And what did she see in him?'

She shrugged. 'Another scalp on her belt.'

'Is that all?'

She hesitated. 'I have a theory that women like that are really not interested in men at all. What they are trying to do is get their own back on women. She wasn't taking David *for* her, she was taking him *from* me.' He stirred a little restlessly at this advance into the psycho-Saharan dunes without a water-bottle, and she noticed it. 'They always go after married men, you notice,' she justified her argument. 'What they're really trying to do is to take their father away from their mother. They're scoring off Mummy.'

'You knew her quite well?' he suggested noncommittally.

'Not well, but better than I wanted to.'

'How did David meet her?'

'Oh, that was through Frances Hammond. I suppose you know David was friendly with her husband?'

'I understand they were at school together.'

'Yes, though not in the same year. Gerald was three years older than David, but I suppose he saw a kindred spirit in him. They became great chums after they left school, at any rate. The four of us spent quite a lot of time together – David, Gerald, Frances and I – though really it was more for David's sake than mine, because they weren't really my sort of people. Then after Gerald left, David set himself up in a sort of avuncular role to Frances, listening to her problems and offering advice. One of the things he advised her to do was to get herself involved in local affairs, as a way of taking her out of herself. Be more like Diana, he told her: I don't suppose she liked that any more than I did. But she joined the parish council, any-way, and met Jennifer Andrews, and at some point introduced David to her. I expect he bumped into her at the Rectory.

Then Jennifer said she wanted a part-time job, and David took her on.'

'Was it a genuine job?'

'Oh, yes, I think so. At first, anyway. She'd done that sort of work before. I expect she wangled the meeting so that she could ask him for a job; and David, of course, always liked taking on more staff. That was why his business failed. But at least Jennifer knew what to do, unlike some of them.'

'But then at some point they began to . . . ?'

'What a delicate pause. Yes, they "began to". I don't know exactly when – he did *try* to be discreet, though not very hard – but I don't suppose they lost much time about it, when there was so much goodwill on both sides.'

'I'm sorry, this must be very painful for you.'

'I don't care any more.' She eyed him with a hard, defiant look. 'No, really. I used to, but there comes a point when it all just stops. He can do as he pleases, as long as I don't have to know about it.'

'But you did know about Jennifer Andrews.'

'Yes, and now that she's dead, I suppose it will all be dragged out into the open for people to paw over.' She sighed. 'I must say you were a pleasant surprise compared with what I'd expected.'

'A uniformed constable with big boots who licked his pencil?'

'Come, I'm not as out of touch as all that! I thought it would be a callow youth with a moustache and an attitude, who'd look around this house with a serves-you-right expression.'

'What would he think served you right?'

She looked at him slightly askance for a moment, and then said, 'No, don't play games with me. It doesn't suit you. You know she came here that evening, so why not ask me about it straight out?'

Long experience kept Slider's face impassive. 'Fair enough,' he said. 'What time did Jennifer Andrews arrive here on Tuesday night?'

'It must have been about nine o'clock. I heard the car drive up and the dogs started barking. I thought it was David coming back. I was upstairs, in my bedroom – I'd just gone up to look for my reading glasses. I went and looked out of the window and saw her getting out of the car. She has a red sports car with a personalised number-plate.'

He noted the incipient scorn in her voice on the last words, and said diffidently, 'Your husband has one, too, hasn't he?'

'I imagine that's where she got the idea. I suppose they were alike in some things – a taste for the meretricious and showy. Perhaps that's what they saw in each other.'

'What was she wearing?'

'Wearing?' The question seemed to surprise her. She thought a moment. 'A navy dress, sleeveless, with a red belt. And a red silk scarf over her hair. She pulled it off as she got out of the car and it hung round her neck.' She looked to see if that was enough and then went on with the story. 'I went downstairs and opened the door to her. She was in a temper and she'd been drinking – I could smell it on her breath. She demanded to know where David was. I said I had no idea, and she screamed, "Liar!" at me. I saw no reason to put up with that sort of thing so I started to close the door. She shoved her foot in the way of it. The dogs were barking their heads off and I told her she'd better move it before it got bitten, and she laughed in a sneering sort of way and said she knew all about the dogs and how they wouldn't hurt a fly.' Her eyes filled suddenly, shockingly with tears. 'That was the moment when it really came home to me. This dreadful woman knew all about my dogs. She probably knew everything about me and my home and family. He'd *told* her. She and David had discussed me and my private affairs together. It made me feel – quite *sick* for a moment.'

Slider nodded with painful sympathy. 'It must have been a dreadful shock. What did you do?'

'I told her David wasn't there, and that if she was so desperate to see the inside of my house she could come in and search for him if she liked. She said she'd already seen the inside of my house. She said that she and David had – had made love here once when I was out.' Her hands were trembling slightly, he noticed. She saw him looking at them, and put down the cutting she was holding and folded them together to keep them still. 'I said she was an unprincipled slut and told her to go away. She said she'd go all right when I'd told her where David was, because he'd stood her up. She'd been waiting for him for nearly an hour in Romano's – the Italian restaurant at Baker's Wood, just up the road from here, do you know it?'

'I know the one.'

'It's a dreadful place.' She met his eyes. 'It was the first glimmer of light for me, thinking of her sitting in there alone all that time waiting for him. David and I went there once in desperation when there was a power cut at home. There was mould on the salad and the lasagne felt like rubber and smelt like sweat.'

'God, yes, I know what you mean.' Slider remembered his earlier thoughts about the flowers and the businessman's assignation. Out of the mouths of babes and sucklings? 'And where was David, in fact?'

'I said I didn't know, and I didn't. Do you think I would stoop to lie to a woman like that?' He looked at her steadily. 'He went out to the office that morning and I hadn't seen him or heard from him since; but that was quite usual. We lead our own separate lives for most of the time.'

'Had you been in all day?'

'No, I was out several times, shopping in the morning, to the bank early in the afternoon and to take the dogs out later. He could have been home while I was out, if that's what you mean.'

He nodded. 'What happened next with Mrs Andrews?'

'Nothing happened. She talked for a bit, told me more than I wanted to know about her relationship with David. She asked me several more times where he was, and then left.'

'At what time?'

'She couldn't have been here more than ten minutes or so.'

'Did she say where she was going?'

'No, and I certainly didn't ask. I was simply glad to be left in peace – though it wasn't for long, of course, because at about half past nine her wretched husband arrived.'

Now Slider did jump. 'Eddie Andrews came here?'

She raised an eyebrow. 'Didn't you know that?'

'No. You've filled in a gap for me.' Allowing for the drive here and back, it probably accounted for the missing time between his leaving the Mimpriss at ten to nine and returning there at ten thirty.

'He came looking for his wife, of course. He, at least, had the grace to apologise for disturbing me.'

'Was he drunk?'

'He'd been drinking. I think he was more upset than drunk. I felt rather sorry for him, really. He couldn't manage to come straight out with the question at first. He was beating around the bush, and I supposed he didn't know whether I knew about David and Jennifer, so I put him out of his misery and said I knew all about it, and that she had been here looking for David. Then his face—' she paused, thinking '—it *collapsed* with misery. He hadn't been sure, and now he was. I felt as though I'd kicked a puppy. He was such a pathetic little man.'

'How long was he here?'

'About a quarter of an hour. He was rather shaken and I felt sorry for him so I took him into the kitchen and gave him a cup of coffee – I had some already brewed. He asked where David was and I said I didn't know but that he obviously wasn't with Jennifer, since she was looking for him, and that I was pretty sure that he had finished with her.' Slider looked the question and she shrugged. 'I thought it would be better for him to think so – and it rather looked that way, to judge by Jennifer's desperation.'

'And what did he say to that?'

'He said, "But has she finished with him?"' she said glumly.

'Ah,' said Slider.

'Yes, it was rather horribly perceptive. Anyway, he drank the coffee, thanked me very courteously, and left – that would be about a quarter to ten.'

'Did he say where he was going?'

'He said he was going to look for her, and when he found her, he'd wring her neck.' She met his eyes with a clear look. 'People say that sort of thing.'

'I know,' Slider said.

'Yes, I suppose you do. Well, he drove away and that was that.'

'And what time did your husband come home?'

The clear eyes moved away. 'I don't know. Not exactly. I went to bed at about eleven, and read for a bit before putting out the light. I was probably asleep by about half past. I didn't hear him come in. I was up early the next day and took the dogs out for a long run. By the time I got back he'd left for work.'

'He didn't wake you when he came in?'

'We have separate rooms,' she said, her voice as neutral as wall-to-wall beige Wilton.

'And you didn't see him when you got up? Did you see his car?'

'He keeps it in the garage. I didn't go and check whether it was there or not.'

'So you don't actually know whether he came home at all that night?'

'I just assume that he did. But, no, if you put it that way, I couldn't say for certain.'

'Do you take sleeping pills?' Slider slipped the question in, and it was sequitur enough not to bother her.

'I didn't that night, though I do have diazepam for when I need it.'

Slider noted it mentally, though Tufty would surely have tested for that. He went on, 'What did your husband say when you told him about your visitors the evening before?'

'I didn't see him to speak to until Wednesday evening. And by the time he came home, I'd heard about Jennifer being dead, so I didn't mention it. I wasn't sure how he felt about her death, and I didn't want to know. The whole subject was too fraught to open up.'

'So you've never spoken to him at all about both the Andrewses coming here on Tuesday evening?'

She eyed him defensively. 'You seem to find that remarkable, but I don't go seeking out unpleasantness. It's a subject I would far rather not raise with anyone, and especially not with my husband. Why should I? It's not my business.'

'If Andrews killed his wife, and it was because she was having an affair with your husband—'

'If?'

'It's all supposition at the moment. We don't know that Andrews did it.'

She looked at him for a moment, but her eyes were focused through and beyond him. 'I suppose as a loyal wife I ought to be providing David with an alibi, but I'm a hopeless liar, and it's always safer to stick to the truth, isn't it? And the truth is that I don't know what time he came in on Tuesday night. But it doesn't matter, does it? Wherever he was, he wasn't with her.'

CHAPTER TEN

Fresh Words And Bastards New

'She thinks he did it,' Slider said to Joanna as they sat thigh to thigh in a quiet corner of the Kestrel. 'Or at least, not to put it too strongly, she's afraid he might have.'

Joanna lowered the level of her pint of Marston's by a quarter and put the glass down in the beam of sunshine that came in through the crooked, ancient casement window for the express purpose of turning it to liquid gold. 'But if she did, wouldn't she be sure to give him an alibi? Or do you think she's so friendishly cunning she's trying a double bluff on you?'

'Good God, no! That sort of thing only happens in books. But there are people who just tell the truth, you know, because it's the right thing to do. Not many of them, granted.'

'She really impressed you, didn't she?' Joanna looked at him curiously. 'The way you've described her to me, stunningly beautiful, intelligent, noble, good – it's enough to make a person chuck.'

'Don't be silly,' he said comfortably, nudging her knee. 'But if Meacher was out all night—'

'If. She didn't say he was.'

'Quite. But he didn't tell me he had an assignation with the Andrews woman that evening. He didn't tell me he'd been having an affair with her—'

'Would you, in his position? It doesn't mean he bumped her off.'

'Why are you so keen on him?' he asked resentfully.

'My darling dingbat, you've just had a thorough job done on you by a master – or should one say mistress? – of the art. You loathed Meacher on sight and you adored Mrs ditto, so it hasn't occurred to you that if he was out all night, *she* hasn't got an alibi either. Why shouldn't she have killed this ghastly woman?'

'Ridiculous!'

'Is it? Maybe she didn't know before that the affair was going on. Bleach-bag comes to her door and spills the beans, demands where Meacher is as if she's got a right to know, *and* brags that she's done it on the marital premises. Who has a better motive now?'

'I hate it when you're reasonable.'

'Maybe Jennifer never left the house again. Maybe Mrs M. did her right there and then on the doorstep in a fit of righteous, wifely rage.'

'Lady Diana, not Mrs M. And anyway, Jennifer wasn't killed violently, remember. Freddie thinks she was drugged to help-lessness.'

'Even better. Lady Diana got her inside, gave her a drink, and drugged her.'

'With?'

'*I* don't know. I can't do everything for you.'

'She says she does have sleeping pills,' he said reluctantly.

'There you are then! She did her, bunged her in the pantry, then late at night drove her to the Rectory and shoved her down the hole, knowing that everyone would suspect Eddie Andrews, and that there was nothing to connect the deed with her.'

'It holds together—'

'Of course it does. I'm brilliant!'

'—so far, I was going to say. But why didn't Eddie see Jennifer's car when he arrived? And how did it get back to Fourways?'

'Lady D. hid the car temporarily, and took Jennifer home in it so as not to leave any traces in her own, of course.'

'And got back home—?'

'Somehow. Bus, train, taxi, shanks's pony. Aeroplane.'

'I see. And if she did it, why did she tell me about the visits of the Andrewses at all?'

'She didn't know how much you knew. The fact that you were there was a worry. She had to think fast.'

'She did?'

'Notice,' Joanna pursued, 'how she cunningly deflected sus-picion away from Eddie Andrews, by telling you she felt sorry for him and gave him a cup of coffee. That was so that she could plant the seed about her husband in your mind.'

'Why should she do that?'

'Because hubby is a much better smokescreen. If *he*'s guilty, she's innocent. You have to be innocent to be someone's alibi.'

'But she *wasn't* his alibi.'

'Which makes her even more innocent – too good even to lie for her own husband.'

'I love it when you're unreasonable,' he grinned, glad to discover she wasn't serious. They stopped talking while their toasted sandwiches were put in front of them. When they were alone again, he said, 'Joking apart, what we've got now is a much better motive for Eddie. If Jack Potter was right, Eddie didn't really believe, deep down, that Jennifer was straying; after his visit to Lady Di, he knew for certain that his worst fears were founded. I'm afraid he's still the front runner. We'll have to check up on Meacher, though.'

Joanna said, 'Poor thing, you so wanted it to be him instead of Eddie, didn't you?'

'It still might be. The thing that puzzles me about him is, why didn't he call Mrs Hammond when he heard about the body being found on her premises? If he was such an old friend, and was sorry for her . . . It's as if he's trying to distance himself from the whole thing.'

'Could be any number of reasons,' Joanna shrugged. 'People don't phone each other like anything, every day of the week. Especially when they ought to.'

'True,' he sighed. 'Well, it looks as though we know where Jennifer was going, anyway, when she left the Goat and told Jack Potter she was going to meet someone. But why didn't he keep the appointment?'

'Probably he was finished with her and that was his noble way of letting her know.'

'Unnecessarily cruel. I know restaurants like that. Lady Di said she went there once and had rubber lasagne that smelt like sweat.'

'Very graphic. I can see why you liked her.' Joanna grinned suddenly. 'It reminds me of the story of the man who went to a very bad Chinese restaurant. When he'd eaten his main dish the waiter came and asked him if everything was all right. He said, "Well, the duck was rubbery," and the waiter said, "Thank you, sir. We have bery nice rychees, too."'

When they emerged into the sunlight and walked towards their cars, he said, 'What time do you think your meeting will be finished?'

'I expect it'll last a couple of hours. Why?'

'I thought if I could get away early enough I ought to go and see Irene and try and sort things out.'

'I thought she said don't ring us, we'll ring you?'

'Yes, well she can't expect to make all the rules,' he said irritably. 'Besides, it's my house as much as it's hers, and if I can't stop her going there, she can't stop me.'

'It's rather more yours than hers, I would have thought, since you pay the mortgage and everything.'

'What do you mean by that?'

Joanna blinked. 'Sorry, which bit of the sentence are you having difficulty with?'

'I thought the subject would come up sooner or later. It all comes down to money, doesn't it?' he said angrily. 'These things always do.'

'What things?'

'Divorce, first wives versus second wives, the whole palaver! Mortgages and maintenance and who gets the pension! The next thing you'll be complaining that we live in penury while she swans about in a big house, and that I never spend any money on you.'

She whipped round on him like a cobra striking. 'Hold it right there! In the first place I'm not your wife, second or any other sort. In the second place I haven't the slightest interest in your money or what you do with it. All I want is for this business to be sorted out so that people can stop hurting each other, and you and I can have a little life together, and I can stop having to watch you turn grey and wrinkled as you wonder what the next ghastly cock-up will be. And in the third place,' she went on, forestalling his attempt to break in, 'if you ever speak to me like that again I shall smack you round the ear with a wet fish.'

'You'd assault a police officer?' he said feebly.

'In a second.'

They looked at each other for a moment. 'I'm sorry,' he said. 'Abject grovel. I get so strung up about it all.'

'I know. Just don't take it out on me.'

'I'm really sorry.' He kissed her contritely and she kissed him back. 'I don't deserve you.'

'I know,' she said.

'I miss my children.' It burst out of him without his meaning it to.

'I know,' she said again, in a different voice.

'Matthew sounded so sad on the phone the other night. And if I can't get her to agree to a settlement and the lawyers come between us, there'll be a contentious divorce and she'll get custody, and I'll be just another weekend father. I'll have to spend every Saturday of my life in McDonald's.'

She stepped close. 'Don't cry outside a pub, it looks bad.' He put his arms round her. 'It will come out all right,' she said. 'Go and see her, talk to her. Who could resist you? You'll work it out.'

'I love you,' he said.

'I know,' she said for the third time, and he felt her smile against his chest.

Atherton suspected Slider had sent him off to interview the priest on the assumption that it would keep him safe, and resented it. Of course, he mused, many priests through the ages had been seriously bonkers, so it didn't mean a thing – which Slider must know as well as he did, so it rather spoilt his argument, but he went on feeling resentful for as long as it suited him anyway.

The priest's house was across the road from the church with which St Michael and All Angels shared him. Atherton needed Slider to tell him the vintage of the church – St Melitus – though he put it down tentatively as (?) late Victorian, or at least not very old (?); but his own eye was enough to tell him that St Melitus Church House and Community Hall had been built, if that was the right word, within the last twenty years. To judge from its neighbours, a large Edwardian house had been knocked down to accommodate it, and it stuck out like a baboon's bottom: a flat-faced, ugly building of pale yellow brick with a roof too shallow and metal-framed windows too large for it. It had a porch, which was just a square slab of concrete meanly supported on two metal poles, and some unnecessary panels of barge-boarding by way of ornament, from which the paint was peeling like an unmentionable skin disease. The Community Hall was a single-storey extension to the side, with a flat roof and wire-cast windows. Bountiful Nature was represented by a plant-pot in the shape of a giant boot made of something grey, which looked almost entirely but not quite unlike stone. It stood beside the Church House porch and contained the leggy ghosts of some dead pansies and a flourishing crop of chickweed. The whole complex was surrounded by a liberally stained concrete apron for parking, and had all the warm invitation and spiritually uplifting charm of one of the less popular stalags.

Atherton thought of the aspiring beauty of St Michael's and the solid harmony of the Old Rectory, and wondered when it was that the church had completely lost its marbles; and what God thought of an organisation that so passionately promoted ugliness. He rang the Church House doorbell, and it was answered by a tall man in khaki chinos, and a black teeshirt inscribed in white letters *If Jesus is your Saviour CLAP YOUR HANDS!*.

'Mr Tennyson?' Atherton enquired politely.

'Yes – are you from the police?'

'Detective Sergeant Atherton. I spoke to you earlier.'

'Yes, that's right. Come in.'

Inside, the house smelt like a school, Atherton discovered: dusty, with a faint combined odour of socks and disinfectant. 'Come through,' Tennyson said, leading the way to the back of the house. Here there was an open door labelled 'Waiting Room', a narrow room facing onto what would have been the garden if it hadn't been concreted over. It had french doors and two large picture windows – metal framed with wired glass – and since it was on the sunny side of the house it was as hot and dry as the cactus house at Kew. The low window-sills were of chipped quarry tile – as if the room had once been meant to be a conservatory – and along them lay a weary row of dead flies and wasps, desiccated corpses that Atherton could almost hear crackle in the sunshine beating in. The room contained a beat-up sofa and two 'office' armchairs, a coffee-table bearing a sordid array of ancient, coverless magazines and a tin ashtray, the whole underpinned by a cherry-red cut-pile carpet pocked with cigarette burns, and spillings of something that had turned into that strange black toffee you find on carpeted pub floors.

'Nice place,' Atherton said. 'It must cut down on time-wasters.' Five minutes alone with your troubles in this room, he thought, and you'd slit your wrists – except, of course, that the window glass was unbreakable. On the whole, he'd sooner spend a night in the pokey.

Fortunately, Tennyson didn't understand his comment. 'It's a bit warm, but I'm afraid the windows don't open. They've warped, I think. Probably just as well,' he added, with unexpected bluntness. 'Nobody thinks twice these days about stealing from the Church.'

Tennyson was an interestingly gaunt man in his forties, with thick, bushy grey hair and deep-set brown eyes, hand-some except that his skin had the dull pallor of the lifelong costive. He had a good, resonant voice, with a faint trace of an accent Atherton couldn't pin down – somewhere north of Watford Gap, anyway. Tennyson sat in one of the chairs and Atherton, after one dilating glance at the sofa, perched gingerly on the other. Somewhere in the room was a smell of babies, and he was rather fond of the trousers he had on.

He couldn't resist asking, 'Don't you sometimes long to exchange this for the Old Rectory?'

Tennyson shook his head. 'Couldn't afford it. I dread to think what their heating bills are like with those high ceilings. And the rooms here are better suited for our purposes. Besides,' he added, 'it just wouldn't be secure. Anyone could break in with those old windows, leave alone the fact that the garage doors don't lock.'

'How do you know that?' Atherton asked with interest.

'Frances Hammond's one of our stalwarts. I know the house very well. The oil man delivers through the end doors, and our sexton uses the tap in there, to get water for the flowers on the graves. Mrs Hammond doesn't mind. She's only too eager to help. Our best helpers are usually lonely women,' he added, not entirely as if he were glad about it.

'And talking of lonely women,' Atherton suggested.

'You want to know about Jennifer Andrews,' Tennyson picked

him up. 'I wouldn't have said "lonely" was the best adjective in her case.'

'No? What would you have said, then?'

'Predatory.' Tennyson clasped his hands between his knees and stared broodingly at the carpet. Don't do that, Atherton wanted to warn him, you'll go blind. 'She was one of my flock, a member of the PC, she was on the flower rota, the bazaar committee, the coffee rota, the Happy Club, the Refugees Aid – she was into everything that was going. A valuable helper – but I didn't like her.'

'Are you allowed to say that?'

He glanced up with a bitter look. 'I'm a clergyman, not a saint. I'd sooner have Mrs Hammond's wool-gathering than Jennifer Andrews' help, for all her energy. Frances Hammond has the same urges, but at least she knows how to behave herself.'

'Urges?'

He paused, as if selecting the appropriate words, but when he spoke, it came out with the fluency of an old and oft-rehearsed complaint. 'There is a certain type of woman who is just attracted to priests. Altar babes, we call them. Something about the dog-collar turns them on – it doesn't matter who's wearing it. Young, old, married or single. Sometimes they just gaze at you from afar and sublimate it by helping; but sometimes they make a nuisance of themselves. The worst sort throw themselves at you, always hanging around, trying to touch you, wangling ways of being alone with you.'

'Jennifer Andrews was one of those?'

'The worst. The sort that, when they finally get the message that you don't want them, make trouble out of spite. You're damned if you do and damned if you don't with women like that. Have you ever wondered why there are so many stories about priests messing around with parishioners? Sometimes the only way to avoid being falsely accused is to go ahead and do it.'

'It happens to coppers too,' Atherton said. 'The glamour of the uniform. Are you married?'

'No,' said Tennyson, 'but don't think that would stop them. My married colleagues get pestered to death just the same.'

'Did Jennifer Andrews falsely accuse you?'

Tennyson gave him a horrible look. 'What are you imply-ing?'

Atherton spread his hands. 'I wasn't implying anything. It was a straight question.'

'What you're really asking,' Tennyson contradicted, 'is whether I slept with her. And the answer's no.'

'But she wanted you to?'

'What do you think?' Tennyson said morosely, staring at the floor again.

Atherton summoned reserves of patience. This interview was not without peril after all. If the hideous surroundings didn't drive him to suicide, he could be bored to death, or choke on the smog of the vicar's gloom. He decided to try a direct question of fact.

'When did you last see Jennifer?'

'Tuesday afternoon,' he said promptly. 'I thought you knew that. Isn't that why you're here?'

Atherton adjusted smoothly. 'I want to hear it in your own words. Where did you see her?'

'She came here, of course. It was about six o'clock, or just before. She rang up earlier to ask if she could come and see me and I said no, it wasn't convenient, but she came anyway. She knew I'd be here, preparing for the mid-week service at seven. The woman knows my schedule better than I do. If there was any justice in law, clergy could get these women taken up as stalkers. Anyway,' he responding to Atherton's prompting expression, 'she turned up here, smelling of drink, and said she needed to talk to me. I brought her in here.'

Atherton glanced around him eloquently. 'That ought to have cooled her ardour a bit.'

'That's why I did it. She made a fuss about it, said why couldn't we go to my sitting room or the kitchen. Said why didn't I offer her a drink and why was I being so unfriendly. I told her I hadn't much time before service and if she had anything serious to say she'd better get on with it. So she dropped the smarm and took the hint, and it all came out. Her – lover, boyfriend, what you will – had dumped her.'

'Did she say who it was?'

'Oh, she made no secret about it. It was her boss. She'd been telling me all about it for weeks, trying to make me jealous – though she'd pretend it was a religious or a moral problem she had, so that she could tell me all the details. Thought it would get me excited. That's the trouble with these altar babes, they're cunning. And you've got to listen to them, or they're straight off telling everyone you don't care.'

Atherton tried a curve ball. 'So this was her boss at the pub, was it?'

The bushy eyebrows rose. 'Good Lord, no. The estate agent, David Meacher.'

'Have you ever met him?'

'Once or twice, at St Michael's events. Just to recognise him. He's chummy with Mrs Hammond. What he saw in Jennifer, I don't know.'

'I should have thought it was pretty obvious,' Atherton said mildly.

'I suppose you're right,' Tennyson said glumly. 'Anyway, she said she'd met him that day at a motel somewhere – one of their usual places. They'd spent the afternoon in bed, and then he'd calmly told her it was to be the last time.'

'Should you be telling me all this?' Atherton asked in wonder.

He scowled. 'You asked. I'm co-operating. Isn't that what you want?'

'I'm delighted,' Atherton said hastily. 'I just wondered whether—'

'It wasn't a secret. And she's dead now anyway, so what does it matter? I've told you, she just liked telling me these things as part of her game of seduction. I had to pretend to give her advice, tell her to give up her activities and be faithful to her husband, but that was part of it too, for her. Gave her a thrill.'

This bloke was definitely in the wrong profession, Atherton thought. With his misogyny he should have been a fashion designer. 'When she told you this about being dumped, how was she? What was her mood like?'

'She was furious. She thought he had some other woman lined up, and she wasn't going to be dumped for anyone else. She said, "He's got some game going, and I'm going to scotch it." She even asked me if I knew what he was up to – as if I would! I said, "I hardly know the man," and she said, "All you men like to stick together." Then she said she was going to get him back, whatever it cost. I told her she ought to be satisfied with her husband, and stop running around with all these men.'

'There was more than one, then?'

'*You* ought to know,' Tennyson said, shortly and obscurely. 'But she seemed particularly keen on David Meacher – or that's what I'd thought. But when I said that about not running around, she said, "I'd drop them all in a moment if you made it worth my while."'

'What did she mean by that?'

'Use your imagination! She meant if I'd go to bed with her. Not that she would have given up the others even if I did. She collected men like badges. It was quantity she liked, not quality.' He stopped abruptly, as if he thought that was a bit too uncharitable even for him. 'Well, anyway,' he went on, in a milder voice, 'I told her that was out of the question, and got rid of her. I said she knew what she ought to do, and that I had to go and get ready for service.'

'And what did she say to that?' Atherton was fascinated by this glimpse behind the scenes of an English vicarage.

'She said she knew what to do all right, that she was going to make Meacher see her again that night, and when she got him alone, he'd come back to her. And then she went.'

'What time was that?'

'About half past six, I suppose. I went to the window to make sure she'd gone, and she was sitting in her car outside. I thought she was lying in wait for me, but then I saw she was talking on the phone. And after a bit she drove off, still talking.'

Ringing David Meacher, Atherton thought, to make an assignation. That accounted for two of her mystery phone calls. Almost twenty minutes, that had been: he must have been hard to persuade. 'How well did you know her husband?' he asked next.

'Not at all. He wasn't a church-goer, and she didn't tend to have him with her at social things. I only knew what she told me about him, which wasn't much. It was mostly the things he'd bought her. Like her car – a Mazda RX5. Red.'

Atherton nodded. 'Dashing. And expensive.'

'He bought her a personal number-plate, too. Cost him thousands.'

Poor sucker, thought Atherton. It didn't sound as if he got

much of a return on his investment. But it was all beginning to shape up nicely now. Motive was not everything, but it was a lot, and Eddie Andrews was coming out more of a martyr every minute.

The department was seething like a hedge full of sparrows when Slider got back. The extra help which had been drafted in crowded the confined space, no-one was at his own desk, phones were ringing, and there was a cluster round the whiteboard like dealers expecting a stockmarket crash. Files and papers migrated across the room majestically as continents, and McLaren sneezed sloppily whenever anyone got within spraying distance.

'I'm not feeling well,' he said plaintively, as Hollis went past.

'Maybe it's everything you ate,' Hollis said heartlessly.

Atherton was perched on a desk, looking as elegant and pleased with himself as a particularly fashion-conscious gazelle with a Harvey Nichols card. 'Talking of eating,' he said, 'what *was* that meat in the canteen today?'

'What d'you think I am? A pathologist?' Hollis retorted.

'And the lemon sponge,' Atherton's voice descended to a tomb of horror, 'was made with synthetic flavouring.'

'Dear God!' Hollis responded like a poor man's Christopher Lee. 'I can't believe it!'

'Contrary to what you may think,' Norma said witheringly, 'your stomach is not the focal point of the universe. Some of us manage to raise our minds a fraction higher.'

'I shall treat your contempt with the remark it deserves,' Atherton retorted.

Slider felt the moment had come. 'If I can interrupt your lemon harangue for a moment,' he said. Sadly, no-one noticed. Ain't it always the way? he thought. He tried something else. '*Ten-hut!*'

That got them. All eyes turned his way. 'Ten hut?' Norma said wonderingly.

'He never forgets a phrase,' Atherton said kindly.

'Gather round, children, and let's see where we are,' Slider said. 'Atherton, how was your priest?'

'Turbulent,' Atherton replied, and gave his report. Then Slider recounted his morning's discoveries.

'So where does that leave us?' Norma asked, at the end of it. 'Are we still after Eddie, guv, or are you putting Meacher in the frame?'

'Eddie's still got to be favourite,' Hollis said. 'Closest to the victim, won't say where he was, and everything we find out about the woman gives him a better and better motive. Trying to knock off a priest—' He shook his head in wonder at the depravity of humankind, and blew reproachfully through his moustache. 'And if Andrews didn't know until Lady Di told him that Jennifer was knocking off Meacher, that could have been the last straw. A night of ghastly revelation, all his fears confirmed, then – bang.'

'I agree,' Atherton said. 'Meacher's got no motive. If he'd already chucked her, why should he want to kill her?'

'Because she wouldn't be chucked,' Norma suggested. 'And maybe she was planning to make trouble.'

'Who with?' Slider said. 'Meacher's wife already knew about her.'

McLaren made a nasal contribution. 'With the new bint, whoever she was, that he was chucking her for, that probably didn't know about her, but she might chuck him if she did, the new one might, if she told her about her – about herself, I mean, Jennifer.'

'What did Horace say, Winnie?' Slider asked the air.

'You don't know for sure that there *was* another woman,' Atherton said. 'It might be just what Meacher told her to get rid of her.'

'All right, but Meacher hasn't got an alibi,' Norma continued doggedly.

'We don't know that he hasn't,' Slider said. 'We'll have to check – when we can find him.'

'Why don't you ring him on his mobile, sir?' Swilley urged. 'Ask him where he is?'

'Thank you, Wonderbread, I did think of that. It's switched off.'

'That's suspicious for a start,' Atherton said. 'For a man like him, turning off your mobile is like voluntary castration.'

'We know his reg number. Shouldn't we put out an "all cars", guv?' Anderson asked, with the eagerness of a former Scalextric owner.

'He's not a suspect yet,' Slider said. 'I can't gear up an

expensive pursuit just because he's turned his mobile off. He'll answer eventually, or turn up somewhere. Meanwhile, let's hear what else we've got.'

'Forensic report on the house is negative,' Hollis said. 'No sign of a struggle anywhere, nothing that looks as if it'd been used for smothering.'

'What about the handbag?'

'We might have something there, guv. There's a set of marks on the handbag that don't belong to Andrews or the victim. A good, clear set.'

'Interesting,' Slider said. 'But, of course, she could have said to anyone at any point, "Chuck my bag over, will you?"'

'We've put 'em through the system, and they come up negative. Whoever it was, they had no previous.'

'That's what you'd expect in this case,' Slider said. 'It might be an idea to eliminate the staff at the pub, anyway.'

'What about at the estate agent's?' Anderson said.

'Yes, if nothing else, it'll be a way to get hold of Meacher's for the record,' Slider said.

'If the prints proved to be Meacher's, it wouldn't help either way,' Norma said. 'He could have handled her bag quite legitimately at work.'

'Yes, I know. I don't think the prints are going to be useful, except maybe as supporting evidence,' Slider said. 'What else?'

'We've had the report back from Mr Arceneaux about the semen sample,' Hollis said, 'and it seems there are two different types present.'

There was a crash as someone at the back of the room knocked something off a desk. 'All right, don't get excited,' Slider said. 'So she had sex with two men that day? Assuming for the moment that Meacher was one—'

'The priest could have been the other,' Atherton said. 'He could have been lying about not succumbing to her charms.'

'Or it could have been Eddie in the morning before going to work,' Anderson said.

'Or Potter in the storeroom before she left on her date,' Mackay said.

'Or person or persons unknown,' Atherton concluded impatiently. 'Are we going to start looking for an entirely new and unconnected suspect?'

'Why not?' Norma said, at least partly to annoy Atherton. Slider had noticed a slight friction between them of late. For some reason, Swilley had disapproved of Atherton's dating WDC Hart, the loaner who had come as his temporary replacement and stayed on for a few weeks after his return. Hart had gone back to her home station, and as far as Slider knew the affair was off; but something about the situation had annoyed Norma, and the banter that she and Atherton had always exchanged now sometimes had an edge to it. 'If she was stock-taking, she could have met another lover that night that we don't know about yet, who turned nasty – which would put Eddie telling the truth all along.'

Atherton looked lofty. 'What makes it Eddie for me is the car. If anyone else had killed her, I can't see they would have risked taking her car back. Only Eddie knew that Eddie wasn't home: anyone else risked having him come out to look as they parked it. And there again, the car keys were in her handbag, which was in his pickup. I can't see how you can get round that one.'

'She must have had a spare set,' Anderson said,

'Yes, but who would have had access to them, except Eddie? People keep their spare keys at home,' Atherton pointed out.

There was a silence of general consent to that. Slider moved on. 'All right, how's the welly brigade getting on?'

'The back garden's a blank, guv,' Hollis reported. 'Trouble is, it's been so dry there's nothing to take footmarks. They've done an inch by inch search of the Rectory garden from the bottom up and found nothing. Nothing on the wall at the bottom, either, to show anyone going over with a heavy object. Plenty of evidence of people walking along the railway embankment, but there's a broken fence-panel at the bottom of the footbridge, and apparently kids get through onto the embankment there, so it needn't have been Eddie. And there is an oil patch on the road not far from the footpath entrance, which could be where Eddie's van was parked. But lots of people have leaky cars.'

'Get a sample and have it tested,' Slider said. 'It should be possible to match it to the pickup.'

'Or otherwise,' Hollis concluded. 'And, of course, he could have parked there any time.'

'Well, that's a fine upstanding body of negatives,' Slider said. 'Unless we get some eye witnesses—'

'When's the public appeal going out, guv?' someone called from the back.

'Tonight on the regional news at six thirty. So you'll all be drawing overtime tomorrow. I hope you're pleased.' A general response of mixed yesses and noes. 'And we shall need a team for tonight. Any volunteers?'

'I don't mind, sir,' said Defreitas, who was amongst the uniformed men drafted in.

'By golly, I hate a volunteer,' Hollis said. 'What's up with you, Daffy? Ain't you got no home to go to?'

Defreitas looked embarrassed. 'As a matter of fact, no. The wife and me are not getting on. I'd just as soon stop out, and earn a bit extra while I'm at it.'

'As the actress said to the bishop,' Atherton concluded for him.

'What about you, Jim?' Hollis said. 'With your lifestyle, the extra wad must come in useful.'

'Count me out,' Atherton said. 'I've got a date tonight.'

Norma glanced at him sharply, and he gave her a defiant look in return.

'I'll leave you to sort out the rota,' Slider said to Hollis. 'Meanwhile, let's get back on the street, boy and girls, and ask those questions. I want you to ask about vehicles: Eddie's, Jennifer's, and let's include Meacher's this time. I'd like to end up with a complete log of where they were every minute. Re-interview the householders in St Michael Square. Any luck with the neighbour on the other side, by the way?' he asked Norma.

'No, boss, still no answer. I think they must be away.'

'Well, it's probably not important. They wouldn't be likely to have heard anything from that end, anyway. But keep trying. And let's extend the house-to-house to the surrounding streets. Any nocturnal comings and goings. Any sightings of our three vehicles. What time did Jennifer's car get back home? Talk to the householders on the other side of the railway, whose windows look onto the embankment: did they see Eddie, or anyone else, humping a suspicious-looking bundle along there late at night? And let's have a team at the footbridge to find who are the regular users, and whether they saw anything. The back garden's still the best way to the terrace. Swilley, keep chasing Forensic for the report on her clothes. She was somewhere before she was down that hole.'

CHAPTER ELEVEN

Do You Remember An Inn, Miranda?

When patient telephoning eventually located Meacher, he was back at his office in Chiswick. Having clapped a metaphorical hand over the jam-jar, Slider and Atherton hurried round while he was still buzzing with irritation.

'I've been looking at properties, if you must know. I wasn't aware I had to account for my whereabouts to you, or anyone.'

'You've been out on business with your mobile turned off?' Atherton said.

'I turned it off to save the battery. I forgot to recharge it last night – if it's any of your business. Really, this is too much!'

'Do you think we might talk to you privately for a moment?' Slider asked emolliently. Meacher's assistant – a different one, Jennifer's replacement, he assumed, a flat-faced young woman of obviously high breeding and presumably correspondingly low pay – averted her gaze abruptly at his words and concentrated on her computer screen, cheeks aglow.

Meacher also looked, and then, with a theatrical sigh, said, 'Oh, very well, if it will get you to go away and leave me in peace. Come through to the back. Victoria, I shall be five minutes. No calls until I come back.'

'Right-oh,' Victoria said, with false cheerfulness; her eyes followed them anxiously as Atherton and Slider trooped after Meacher into the small back office and shut the door. The room contained a sink with a hot-water geyser and a table with tea- and coffee-making equipment on it, four filing cabinets, and boxes of stationery stacked against the unoccupied wall. Another door, ajar, revealed a lavatory and washbasin. There was nowhere to sit and barely room to stand, and this seemed to please Meacher, who almost smiled as he leaned against the sink and folded his arms across his enviably suited chest with an exaggerated air of relaxation. He looked guilty as hell to Atherton, who was almost ready to give up the Eddie theory in favour of nailing this sartorial rival.

'Right, make it quick,' Meacher said. 'I have a business to run.'

'It can be as quick as you care to make it,' Slider said evenly. 'Just tell me where you were on Tuesday night, and we'll be off.'

'It's none of your damn' business where I was. I don't have to answer to you,' Meacher said impatiently.

Slider sighed. 'This is just time-wasting. I thought you were in a hurry?'

'I'm not in a hurry to tell you my private business.'

'Not as private as all that,' Atherton said, in a tone calculated to annoy. 'The Target Motel hardly counts as private property within the meaning of the act. Rather a hackneyed choice for a man of your sophistication, I thought, by the way. Or did you think that was all she merited?' Meacher stared. Atherton added kindly, 'The "she" I'm referring to is Jennifer Andrews, just in case you were going to waste more time by asking.'

'I don't know what you're talking about,' Meacher said, while his mind worked frantically behind his fixed eyes.

'Yes, you do,' Slider said. 'You and Jennifer Andrews spent Tuesday afternoon together at the Target Motel.' Meacher's confidence had been such that he hadn't even bothered to use a false name. 'The registration clerk has identified Jennifer from her photograph, and he says you've been there several times before and he's quite willing to pick you out from a line-up if necessary. And,' he added a body blow to the reeling Meacher, 'the post-mortem found semen in Mrs Andrews' vagina. Fortunately the sample is good enough to get a DNA fingerprint from.'

Slider was punting on this last, since until they had a sample from Meacher to compare with, they couldn't know the semen was his; but it was a fair guess that they hadn't gone to the motel to play bridge. Meacher seemed to sag as the confidence trickled out of him into a little heap of sawdust at his feet.

'What intrigues us most, you see,' Atherton followed up with a smart left hook, 'is that you didn't tell us this before. You spent the afternoon engaging in social intercourse with Mrs Andrews – the last afternoon of her life – and didn't think to mention it. Does that seem like the behaviour of an innocent man to you?'

Meacher rallied enough to get his gloves up. 'Why should I mention it? I didn't want my private life pawed over by a pack of prurient policemen.' That wasn't easy to say, and Atherton gave him grudging admiration. Meacher even looked surprised at himself, but followed up his advantage quickly. 'Anyone could guess that as soon as you knew about *that* you'd start imagining all sorts of other things – just as you are doing, it seems. Yes, I saw her in the afternoon, but that's the last time I saw her, and I know nothing about her death. *Now* are you satisfied?'

Slider pulled his chin judiciously. 'Well,' he said slowly, 'there is just one other little matter. You agreed to meet her in Romano's restaurant at eight fifteen that evening, but you didn't show up. After waiting for three-quarters of an hour she went round to your house in a state of agitation, looking for you. She spoke to your wife, and told her all about it.'

Meacher started at that. So, Slider thought, Lady Diana still hasn't told him. Now, was that odd of her, or not?

'After leaving your house, Mrs Andrews disappears from view – and so do you,' Slider went on. 'So when I discover you've concealed information from me about your relationship with her, I can't help wondering if she didn't find you after all, when she went looking for you. If perhaps you and she were together for those vital hours. You do see my problem, don't you?'

Meacher made a few silent passes before he managed to strike speech. 'It's preposterous. You can't march in here accusing me of murder—'

'I didn't hear you say murder,' Atherton said quickly, looking at Slider. 'Did you say murder, sir?'

'No, it was Mr Meacher who said murder.'

'Don't play your infantile games with me!' Meacher spluttered. 'I know a great many influential people. If you think you can come in here making these ridiculous accusations—'

'Not so ridiculous from where I'm standing,' Slider said. 'If you were innocently engaged all night, the night she died, tell me all about it, and then I can cross you off the list. You won't get rid of me otherwise.'

Silence fell in the little room. Beyond the door to the shop, the gentle murmur of Victoria's voice could be heard answering a telephone enquiry, interspersed with the flat clacking of the keyboard as she typed in information. The tap behind Meacher dripped softly into the stainless-steel sink, heartbeat slow, clock steady. Beside him, Slider felt Atherton almost quivering with eagerness restrained, like a sheepdog at the beginning of the trials who has just seen the ewes released at the far end of the field.

'Very well,' Meacher said at last, trying to sound stern and condescending and not quite managing it. 'I'll tell you about it, but only so that I don't have you hanging around here ruining my business day after day. I had been seeing Jennifer, but it was all over. She'd been seeing someone else – she didn't tell me who – and she was obviously more interested in him than me. I told her when we met at the Target that I didn't care to share her favours. She said very well, in that case we had better call it a day.'

'Did this genial conversation take place before or after sex?' Atherton asked.

Meacher's face darkened. 'How dare you? It's none of your damned business whether—'

'We've been over this already,' Slider said patiently. 'The only way out of this situation is to tell me the truth. If Jennifer was happy to split up with you, why did she arrange another meeting with you later that night? And why didn't you turn up?'

'Oh, all *right*!' Meacher cried petulantly, and then remembered Victoria and lowered his voice. 'All right, if you must know I was getting tired of her. She was getting more and more demanding, wanting to see me every day, being ridiculously possessive. It was becoming unpleasant – and dangerous: she was starting to get careless, and I was afraid any minute her husband was going to find out about it. I didn't fancy having him after me. He didn't strike me as the understanding sort. So I told her when we met at the Target that it had to end. She didn't like it. In fact, she got quite hysterical. I had to take her to bed to calm her down.' He intercepted an expression of distaste on Atherton's face and said angrily, 'Do you want the facts or don't you? Because if you're going to stand in judgement over me like some—'

'Go on,' Slider said. 'What time did she leave the motel?'

'About half past three, I suppose. I didn't notice exactly.'

'And where was she going?'

He shrugged. 'She didn't say. Home, I imagine.'

'How was she when she left? What was her mood?'

'She was all right – quite calm. She seemed to have accepted the situation: I was surprised when she rang me again.'

'This was at half past six?' Atherton put in.

'That's right.' He didn't question how they knew. 'She said she must talk to me. I said couldn't it wait? She said no, there were important things we had to sort out. Then she started crying and begging. The last thing I wanted was to see her again, but I had to promise to, to stop her crying. So I said Romano's at eight fifteen.'

'But you weren't intending to keep the appointment?'

He hesitated. 'I hadn't decided. I thought I would. But as the time approached I couldn't bear the thought of sitting in a restaurant with her making a scene. So I didn't go.' He looked from Slider to Atherton and back. 'You say she went to my house?' he asked thoughtfully.

'Your wife told her she didn't know where you were. Quite an elusive character, aren't you?' Meacher said nothing. 'Would you like to tell us where you were between nine p.m. Tuesday night and nine a.m. Wednesday morning?'

'I was with someone.' They both waited, looking at him. 'I was with a woman,' he said impatiently.

'All night?' Slider asked.

'All evening and all night. I went to her flat at around eight thirty, and I stayed with her until I left to come to the office in the morning.'

'Name and address?'

'I'm certainly not going to tell you that,' Meacher said, loftily as a gentleman whose honour has been impugned. 'What do you take me for?'

At the moment, I wouldn't take you on a bet, Slider thought, but he said patiently, 'Mr Meacher, unless we can speak to this person and ask her to verify your whereabouts, you remain unaccounted for. I can't cross you off the list.' He stopped there, and maintained an insistent silence, while Meacher stared at the floor, apparently weighing things up.

'All right,' he said eventually, and with a show of reluctance.

'I was with Caroline Barnes – my assistant, whom you saw last time you came harassing me here. But I don't want her upset. Her relationship with me is our private business. If you have to ask her questions, for God's sake be tactful. She's very young and very sensitive.'

Slider took down her name, address and telephone number, with weariness at his heart. This was going to be nothing but an added complication. Neither Meacher's reluctance nor his capitulation rang true.

'Oh, there is just one other thing, sir,' he said, as they were turning to go. 'We have a set of fingermarks on Mrs Andrews' handbag which don't belong to her or her husband, and we would like to eliminate anyone who might have touched it during the last day. Would you be so kind as to come along to the station and give us your fingerprints for comparison purposes?'

Meacher stared long and hard, trying to work out if it was a trap, but Slider looked steadily and blandly back, and eventually he agreed. 'I can't come right away – I have some things to clear up here first.'

'Very well, sir, but as soon as you can, if you wouldn't mind.'

'Things to clear up!' Atherton said, when they were out on the street again. 'You can bet your last banana he's ringing up his alibi. He'll write the script and she'll read it out when we come asking.'

Slider didn't disagree. 'We'll have to go through the motions, but it'll be one of those alibis you can't prove or disprove. It just leaves us with the same questions. Why should he want to kill Jennifer? If it was him, how did he do it, and where, and how did he transport the body? And if he didn't kill her, where was he, and why all the subterfuge?'

'You really did hope to cross him off,' Atherton discovered.

'Of course. One suspect at a time is enough for me.'

'But you quite like Eddie and don't like Meacher,' Atherton pointed out.

'Right. I hoped if he wasn't cross-offable, he'd be definitely suspect. One or the other. Look, why don't you get over to this Caroline sort right away, and get her story? Even if you can't get to her before he does, you might unsettle her by turning up so soon. Or wear her down with your charm and finesse.'

'Or warn her she's next in line, after Jennifer, when he's tired of her,' Atherton suggested.

'You're devious!'

'Maybe I am, and maybe I'm not,' Atherton said mysteriously. 'Where are you off to?'

Slider looked at his watch. Just after half past four: at that moment, someone somewhere in the country was saying, 'I think she's really clever, that Carol Vorderman.'

'I think I'll go and have another look at the Old Rectory,' he said. 'I'd like to see if what Mr Tennyson told you about the garage doors is right.'

As Slider had remarked before, there were two sets of wooden double doors in the left-hand third of the Old Rectory's façade. The far left pair were older, of tongue-and-groove with a simple brown Bakelite doorknob, the wood uneven, shrunk with age and split at the bottom, the black paint generations thick, so that it was cracking down the grooves where it was unsupported. There was an old-fashioned keyhole, heavily bunged up with paint. The other pair of doors had a Yale lock and a newish brass mortice-type keyhole below, so it was easy to tell which pair the vicar had meant. Slider tried the Bakelite handle, and it turned, the door opening towards him effortlessly: Tennyson was right. But the moment he opened the door a fusillade of barking smote his ear and made him jump, and he closed it hastily and stepped back. A moment later the open kitchen window was pushed wider and Mrs Hammond looked out, her soft face creased with anxious enquiry. From the simultaneous boost in volume, Slider guessed that Sheba was in the kitchen with her.

'It's all right, it was only me,' Slider said. 'Detective Inspector Slider,' he added, in case she had forgotten him.

'Oh! I see,' she said, like a willing-to-please child asked an incomprehensibly difficult question.

'I wonder if I could have a look at your garage and storerooms? Would that be all right? May I?'

Mrs Hammond bit her lip, thinking it through. 'You'd better come in,' she said. Yes, Slider thought, that would be a good start. She withdrew her head, and he walked down to the front door. She had some difficulty in opening it, and when eventually she confronted him, she said, 'It's a bit stiff,' and gave a placatory laugh, not with amusement but as a threatened cat purrs. 'Warped, I'm afraid. Mostly people go round the back – those who know.'

She looked at him anxiously, neat in her middle-aged print frock with matching fabric belt. Marks and Sparks: he recognised the one-size-fits-all style of it. Apart from the anxious expression, her face was a smooth indeterminacy framed by her amorphous, middle-aged waved hair. There were thousands of women like her, millions, he thought, up and down the country, going about their dull, useful routines: women who defined themselves by their men, as daughters, wives, mothers; whose time had been used up with cooking, washing-up, fetching, listening, agreeing. Their lives had been lived always at one remove, on the dry shore above the high-tide mark of passions, in a sheltered place out of the stinging wind, out of the swing of the sea. Great events did not happen to women like her. They did not rub shoulders with murder. How bewildering it must all be to her.

'I'm sorry to disturb you,' he began politely, and she jumped in with, 'Oh, it's all right, Father's having his physiotherapy at the moment.' Her being disturbed was not in question with her, it was her father who mattered. 'That's why Sheba's in with me, to keep her out of the way. She's been rather upset since all this ...' She led the way back to the kitchen. The dog barked once behind the door at their approach, and as Mrs Hammond opened it, backed away, looking at Slider and growling, but with the tail swinging hesitantly, just in case. 'It's all right, Sheba. Be quiet, there's a good girl,' Mrs Hammond said, catching hold of the collar. 'Just let her sniff your hand, and she'll be all right.' The dog sniffed his offered hand briefly, and then, released, smelt his shoes extensively, with embarrassing canine frankness. Then, apparently satisfied, she went back to her basket in the corner and curled down. Slider noted she was chewing the piece of rag again. Obsessive behaviour. That dog must be an animal psychiatrist's dream.

Mrs Hammond asked. 'Can I get you a cup of tea?'

'No, no tea, thank you. I'd just like to see what's beyond the kitchen door, here, if I may. You have storerooms, I believe?'

'Yes, and the boiler-room, and the garage. Is there something wrong?'

'No, not at all. Nothing to worry about,' he said, with his most reassuring smile. 'I'd just like to get the geography straight in my head, if you wouldn't mind.'

She looked unreassured, but opened the further door and stepped back to let him through. He found himself in a stone-floored passage about four feet wide, the whitewashed walls of rough stone, like the outside of the house. There were two doors on either side, of solid tongue and groove, painted dark green, and the only light came through the glass panel of the door at the far end.

'This is the oldest part of the house,' Mrs Hammond said. 'This and the kitchen. It probably goes back to the fourteenth century, or even earlier. A friend of ours who knows about houses told us.'

'Is that Mr Meacher?' Slider hazarded.

She flushed. 'Oh! Yes – yes, it is. Do you know him?'

'Yes, I've met him,' Slider said. 'What's in these rooms?'

'Nothing in particular,' she said. 'They're just storerooms.'

'May I have a look?'

'Oh. Well, if you want. They're not locked.'

He could see that. They had only country latches, and no keyholes, though the doors to the left – the street side of the house – had bolts on the outside. When Slider opened the first left-hand door he found that the room was quite empty except for a bundle of torn hessian sacks in the corner. It was about eight feet long by six wide, and windowless. The walls were whitewashed, and the door was rather battered and splintery at the bottom, with grooves down to the pale wood under the paint as if it had been gouged with a garden fork.

'We used to keep the gardener's tools in here,' Mrs Hammond said, 'but there's a shed outside now, which is more convenient. So we don't use it for anything, really.'

Slider thought of his house at Ruislip, which assumed no-one had more belongings than could dance on the head of a pin, and wondered at having so much storage space you could leave a whole room empty. Glorious waste!

The first room on the right was the same size, but had a small, high window, and smelt strongly of apples. There were boxes of them stacked around the walls, a sack of carrots, strings of onions on hooks on the walls, and jars of jams and fruit on a long shelf along one wall. There were other boxes too, of tins of dog food and tomatoes and so on, and various bits of junk lying around – a jumble of empty flower-pots, a child's cot mattress, a set of pram wheels with the handle still attached, an ancient vacuum cleaner, a stack of books. 'The dry store,' she said, waving a nervous hand round it. 'Nothing here, you see. Nothing important, anyway.'

The second door on the left gave onto another windowless room, which was furnished with self-assembly wine racks, about a quarter full with bottles of wine, some looking authentically dusty. The second room on the right housed nothing but the smell of oil and a massive boiler, its tin chimney bending precariously before disappearing through the wall, with the fine carelessness of earlier, uninspected days.

The door at the end of the corridor was locked, but the key was in it. It gave onto a garage in which the Range Rover now stood. On the far side again was another half-glass door, unlocked, beyond which was the empty garage whose doors he had tried earlier. There was a cold-water tap in the middle of the far wall, and in the wall at the back of the garage was another door. Slider opened it, and found a tiny yard, walled in all round, containing what was obviously the filling-cock to an underground oil tank.

Slider closed the door again and turned to Mrs Hammond, who was waiting at his elbow nervously, as if expecting to be ticked off about something.

'When I tried those doors just now,' Slider said, nodding to the pair, whose cracks and chips and missing chunks were cruelly revealed by the bright sunshine outside, 'they weren't locked.'

She moved her hands anxiously. 'Oh, well, no, they don't lock, you see. At least, I think there was a key once, but I don't know where it is now.'

'So those doors are always unlocked?'

'Well, yes.' She searched his face for clues as to where the rebuke would come from. 'You see, the oil man brings his pipe in through here and out to the back yard.' She gestured towards the rear door. 'For the central heating. It means I don't have to be in for him. He can just come when he likes.'

'Aren't you worried about people breaking in?' Slider asked.

She looked mildly surprised. 'But why should they? There's nothing here they could steal.'

'The Range Rover?'

'Oh, but they couldn't get it out, could they? I *never* leave the keys in it. And the doors to that garage *are* locked.'

'Someone might go through into the passage – there's all your father's wine, for instance. That must be valuable. And they could get through the kitchen to the rest of the house.'

She shook her head. 'I lock the door at night – I mean the door from the garage into the passage. And Sheba's in the kitchen at night. She'd bark if anyone broke in.'

'And on the night in question, the Tuesday night, she didn't bark?'

'Oh, no. I'd have heard her. I always wake if she barks.' She seemed to falter. 'Is there something wrong? Did you – were you—?'

'It occurred to me to wonder,' he said, 'whether Mrs Andrews was left in your garage during that night, the Tuesday night. Or perhaps in one of your storerooms. I don't like to upset you by the thought, but—'

She still seemed puzzled. 'Oh, no, she couldn't have been,' she said. 'I'm sure she was never in any of the storerooms, or the garage, except when I was there. Why should you think so?'

He tried to find a gentle way of making her understand. 'You see, we know that she was moved at some point – that she wasn't laid straight in the hole where you found her. She was put somewhere else first, for some hours and then moved later.' Mrs Hammond seemed to pale, and put her fingers to her mouth as she understood him at last. 'And it occurred to me that perhaps whoever killed her used your garage at first—'

'That's horrible!' she said, through her fingers. 'No, I don't believe it. I'm sure she never was – not there! Oh dear, I can't—' She turned away, and with her back to him, fumbled a handkerchief out of her pocket and blew her nose. 'No, it's not possible,' she said, muffled but for once definite. 'Sheba would have barked.'

They returned to the kitchen. The dog looked up briefly at them and then down again, resting her nose on her paws, her sore red ears twitching.

'Your bedroom is above here?' Slider asked.

Mrs Hammond turned to him. Her eyes looked a little pink and frightened. He had upset her by talk of the body, he saw, but how could it be helped?

'My bedroom and the boys' rooms and our bathroom. Do you want to see?'

'No, thank you, not now. Your father's bedroom is at the other end of the house?'

'Over the dining-room; and Mother's was over the drawing-room, with their bathroom in between.' She searched his face again. 'But he has a bell by his bedside to call me, if he wants me. I'm a light sleeper.'

It was sad how anxious she was to avoid blame, he thought. 'And in fact your father didn't call you on Tuesday night?'

'No, he had a good night. He slept through.'

'Yes, so he told me. Does he take sleeping pills?'

'No, but he does have pain-killers. He was offered sleeping pills, but he wouldn't have them. He doesn't like the idea.'

Slider left no further on than when he had arrived. All the same questions remained to be answered. It had to be Eddie, didn't it? But if he did it, *where* did he do it? And where did Meacher come in? There was a hole in the story somewhere, and he was running out of leads. He had to hope that Porson's appeal to the Great British Public would turn something up.

He was on his way back to his car when something that Lady Diana had said came back to him, and he diverted to the Goat In Boots. Mrs Potter was 'upstairs, resting', according to her husband. 'This business with Jennifer has knocked her bandy,' he confided. 'Well, it's got to all of us, really. One minute someone's with you, and the next—' He shook his head dolefully. 'I could go and wake her for you,' he offered doubtfully.

'No, it's all right, I've just got one question, and you can answer it just as well. You've told me that when Jennifer left for her meeting on Tuesday night, she was wearing a navy dress with a red belt?'

'That's right.'

'Can you remember whether she had a red scarf as well?'

'What, on her head, you mean?'

'On her head, round her neck – anywhere.'

Jack pondered weightily. 'I dunno,' he said at last. 'I can't say I remember really. She could have had, but—'

Karen, the barmaid, who was polishing glasses nearby with her ears on stalks, interrupted these musings impatiently. 'But she did, don't you remember? A red silk scarf. It was tied to the strap of her handbag.'

Oh, very seventies, Slider thought. 'You're sure about that?' he asked Karen.

'Yes, course I am,' she said. '*You* remember, Jack?'

'Can't say I do. But she could have. I wouldn't swear one way or the other.'

'That's all right,' Slider said. 'Thank you,' to Karen. 'It's just a small point, but I wanted to clear it up.' So the scarf was real, he thought as he walked across the square; and sometime during the evening she had lost it. Somewhere between the Meacher house and the grave. It was something to file away at the back of the mind. Probably it wasn't important – not important unless it turned up in an interesting place, that is.

The CID room was crowded again: the troops, together with various hangers-on who had nothing better to do, were waiting around the television for the appeal to come on. It would be Porson's first television appearance since he came to Shepherd's Bush, and the excitement was as palpable, and probably of the same kind, as among spectators at a Grand Prix hoping for an accident.

Anderson and Mackay were playing the Porson game. 'What's the Syrup's favourite part of north London?' Mackay asked.

'Barnet, of course. Too easy.'

'What's his favourite place in Leicestershire?'

Anderson looked blank. '*I* don't know. I've never been to Leicestershire.'

'Wigston,' Mackay said triumphantly.

'Never heard of it. You can't have that one.'

'All right, how does he like to travel, then?'

'Dunno,' Anderson said, after some thought.

'By hairyplane,' Mackay said triumphantly.

'*Hairyplane?*'

'For God's sake, shut up, you two imbeciles,' Swilley said impatiently. 'Here's the boss.'

Slider squeezed through to the front. 'Where's McLaren?'

'Gone home, guv. Sick as a parrot,' Mackay said.

'About time, after he's infected all of us,' Anderson put in.

'Atherton back yet?'

'He's just coming in,' Swilley said, gesturing towards the door.

Atherton slithered through to them, looking glum but resigned. 'Caroline Barnes confirms the alibi,' he told Slider, without preamble. 'I tried to shake her, but she stuck to it, though she looks nervous as hell. She says he came round, they had supper and went to bed.'

'A simple story.'

'And none the less incredible for that. So there we are.'

'Yes, there we are,' Slider said. He pondered. 'It could be true.'

'But then again . . .' Atherton sighed.

'Maybe someone will have seen Meacher's car parked outside,' Slider suggested.

'Yes, that would be handy. But of course if no-one remembers seeing it, that doesn't prove it wasn't there. And knowing our luck—'

'Shh, here it comes,' Swilley said. There was a chorus of hoots and wolf-whistles, which Slider silenced in the interests of discipline. However odd Porson was in his mannerisms, he was still the boss, and Slider could not let them mock him in front of him. But in fact, Porson was surprisingly good on the screen. The portentous, trade-unionist delivery did very well on television, and under the unnatural lighting everyone looked as if he could be wearing a wig; the regional news presenter, indeed, looked as if he was breaking in a face for a friend. And the Super only slipped in one Porsonism, when he affirmed that anyone calling with information would have their unanimity respected – and even then you had to be alert to catch it.

When it was over there was a storm of applause, not entirely ironic. Then the hangers-on drifted away, and the night team went to their desks to wait for the first telephone calls. Atherton stood up and stretched, brushed down his trousers, and said, 'Well, I'm off.'

'Oh, yes, you've got a date, haven't you?' Slider said absently.

'Yup. How do I look?'

Slider examined him. 'Too excited.'

'Somewhere at this moment a woman is preparing for an evening of bliss with me,' Atherton said, 'and there isn't a thing she can do to me that I don't deserve. If she plays her cards right, she could be staring at my bedroom ceiling till dawn.'

'Who is this thrice-blessed female?'

But Atherton only smiled enigmatically and sloped out like a cat on the prowl. And the first phone rang.

CHAPTER TWELVE

Lettuce, With A Gladsome Mind

He half thought that Irene would be out on a Friday night, but when he had called her to suggest the meeting she had grudgingly agreed.

'Matthew won't be here, you know,' she said. 'Friday's Scouts night.'

Slider tried not to sound disappointed. 'It's you I want to see.'

Perhaps his choice of words touched her, for she became defensive. 'What time d'you expect to get here? Though knowing you that's a silly question.'

'I'll try and get away by seven, so I should be with you before half past.'

'Half past seven? You don't expect me to cook for you?'

'I can pick up a sandwich or something and eat it in the car,' he said, already resigned.

But she said, 'Oh, I can make you a sandwich. I can do *that*,' as if some other and outrageous personal attention had been in question.

So when the Syrup's broadcast was over he detached himself from the tentacles of the department and hurried down to the car before anyone could think up any more urgent questions for him.

It was a fine summer evening; the air was heavy with the baleful stench of barbecue. Everywhere flesh was being scorched by flames, and a pall of oily smoke hung over London. It was like living in the sixteenth century, he thought. Funny how willing people were to eat burnt sausages and limp lettuce, provided you put them on a paper plate and made them do it in discomfort out of doors. At least he could be sure Irene wouldn't do that to him. Barbecuing was men's work: she was a very traditional woman.

When he reached the house he thought for a minute there was someone else there: he'd forgotten she'd changed her car since she'd been with Ernie. She had a Toyota Celica – what Porson would call a Cecilia, of course. A bit posh for Irene. He assumed Ernie had put some money towards it, if he hadn't bought it entirely, and wasn't sure how he felt about that; then told himself it was damn well time he stopped feeling like anything about Irene and Ernie, if he really intended her to be his wife *quondam* but not *futurus*.

He had a key, but tactfully rang the bell, and stood on the doorstep of what he had called home with many painful feelings, which were only sharpened when she opened the door to him and stood looking at him nervously and with an inadequately hidden expectancy.

'Hello,' he said, since she didn't seem to be going to.

'I thought you'd be late.' She didn't move to let him in.

'Shall I go away again?'

'Don't be silly,' she said, and stepped back at last. She was nervous, and she had too much scent on: it hung in the hall like a cloud of insecticide and made his eyes burn. She closed the front door, and he suddenly felt nervous too, trapped in this small space with her, not knowing what she was feeling or what she might say. It was absurd not to know how to behave with his own wife of so many years; and he looked at her back as she shut the door and thought, *She's been to bed with Ernie Newman*, and it completely threw him. Horrid images flashed up in his mind without his volition: her with Ernie; her with Ernie in the nude; her doing with someone else what she had only ever done with him before. Sex was such an absurd stroke revolting thing when it was someone other than oneself doing it.

'Are you all right?' Her voice brought him back to reality.

'What? Yes – yes, of course.'

'You looked as if you had a pain, or something.'

'No, I'm all right. You look very nice,' he said almost at random, but found that, indeed, she did. She had always been neat and pretty; tonight her smooth short dark hair was curling slightly with the heat, so that it looked like duckling feathers, and the descent from severity suited her. Her makeup was carefully done, and her pale mauve cotton dress left bare her slender arms, which were lightly tanned. 'Is that a new frock?'

'This old thing? I've had it years.' But she seemed pleased, almost fluttered. 'No-one says "frock" any more,' she went on, her eyes scanning his face on a mission of their own.

'Bishops do.'

'Don't be silly,' she said again, automatically; and then grew brisk. 'Well, don't stand about in the hall like a visitor. Come into the lounge.'

Everything was perilously the same: the three-piece suite, the carpet, the television tuned to some appalling sitcom which, to judge from the *Beano* jokes and weirdly 1950s stereotypes, had been written as a school project by a team of bright fifth-formers.

No, one thing was different. There was no little button nose pressed against the screen. 'No Kate?' he asked.

Irene's eyes slid away. 'I arranged for her to go to Flora's for the night.'

'Oh.' Slider wondered why she was embarrassed. Did she feel guilty for depriving him of his daughter? Or was it something else? What? Her guilt made him feel wary. Was there trouble here for him?

'I thought it would be better for us,' she went on with elaborate casualness, 'to be on our own so we could – talk freely.'

'Oh,' said Slider again. A horrid thought was struggling to be born, and he was reluctant to be its mother.

'Well, sit down, then. Would you like a drink?'

'Have you got any beer?' he asked – a *num* question if ever there was one. But she was full of surprises tonight.

'I've got a can of lager in the fridge. I thought you might like one.'

He smiled. 'Just one?'

'Well, it's a four-pack, actually. They don't sell single cans in Sainsbury's. No, stay there, I'll get it.'

She went out, and he got up and turned off the television, having lost his immunity to it since living with Joanna. Into the sudden quiet, sounds jumped from the open french windows: children's voices – next door's, playing in the garden – and a clatter of cutlery from somewhere, a distant lawnmower, a car in the street accelerating past and changing up a gear, a dog barking with the monotonous rhythm of one who knows no-one's coming. He walked to the window to look out. The square of garden was neglected: the grass needed cutting, and the borders between the dull shrubs had gone all Isadora Duncan with gracefully unfettered weeds, where once there would have been a Coldstream Guard of annuals. Neither of them had been here to do anything, of course.

Burnt-sausage smoke rose up from the garden to the left, spiced with a whiff of paraffin; the sky was hazy and quivering with it. As he stood brooding, there was a characteristic thump-and-scrabble sound as a black cat came over the fence from next door and trotted by fast with its ears out sideways and the cunning-gormless look of a cat with prey. It had a barbecued spare rib clenched in its teeth, and only glanced at Slider as it passed, intent on escape. It reached the opposite fence, crouched and sprang up, and disappeared to crunch in peace in the empty garden beyond.

'Oh, there you are.' He turned back at Irene's voice, and seeing her with a tray in her hands hurried to relieve her of it; but she said, 'No, it's all right, just take the *Radio Times* off the table, will you?'

She put the tray down on the coffee table, which was drawn up to the sofa, and sat, evidently expecting him to sit beside her. On the tray was a tumbler of lager with the can beside it – the glass was too small to take the whole fifteen ounces – and another tumbler of what looked like gin and tonic. There was a plate on which stood a pork pie flanked with lettuce, cherry tomatoes, slices of cucumber and a teaspoonful of Branston pickle, a knife and fork, a paper napkin, and a jar of mustard.

'I thought you'd prefer it to a sandwich,' she said.

His heart hurt him. Cans of lager, and now a pork pie. She didn't approve of pork pies, she thought them common, but she knew he liked them, and there was a little tremor in her voice when she said, 'I thought you'd prefer it,' which told him she had deliberately arranged this treat for him and was waiting to feed off his pleasure and surprise. And she'd laid it out so nicely, with traditional pub garnish; and remembered the mustard. He wanted to howl and bite the furniture. 'This all looks very nice. Thank you,' he heard himself say. It sounded falsely avuncular to him, but she seemed satisfied.

'Dig in, then. I know you must be hungry. I had something with Matthew before he went out.'

He cut the pie and loaded his fork with Dead Sea fruit – or was it coals of fire? She waited until his mouth was full and then asked him brightly, 'How is your case going?'

He chewed and swallowed with painful haste. 'I didn't know you knew about my case.'

'I didn't. I don't. But you've always got one on, haven't you?'

'It's a murder, actually – a domestic. Bit of a puzzler,' he said telegraphically.

'Oh, then I'm surprised you've got time to come and see me,' she said. 'When you've had a murder before you've hardly had time to come home to sleep.'

Ah, a hint of acid: this was more like the old days. But he couldn't afford to revel in comforts like that.

'I wanted to talk to you properly,' he said evenly. 'Can we be civilised and talk without recriminations on either side? I think this is too important for quarrelling.'

She looked away from him for a moment at the blank television screen. He was close enough to see the fine lines around her eyes under the makeup, the sad, tired droop of her mouth. He knew her so well, and discovered now that he didn't know her at all, as though she were a character in a new drama played by a very familiar actor. He felt no *attachment* to her. At some point all his belonging feelings had redirected themselves towards Joanna. It made things easier; but harder, too, in a way, because it meant he didn't know what Irene was thinking. His domestic thoughts moved to Joanna's rhythm now; framed themselves in her idiom.

'Yes,' she said. 'You're right. I'm sorry I blew up at you on the phone the other day. I was a bit tense.'

'I know. Nothing about this is easy, for any of us. But we've got to sort it out, and it's better that we do it between us, just you and I, without any third parties getting in on the act.'

'What does your *mistress* think of that?' she said, with a flash of the old spirit.

'What's decided between you and me has nothing to do with her,' he said steadily.

She said nothing, reaching out for her glass, drinking at it straight, like a poker-player, without looking at him.

'Irene,' he said gently, 'what's happening between you and Ernie? Don't you really want to live with him any more?'

'I don't know,' she said, and put her glass down. She didn't look at him. 'I don't know what I want any more. It all seemed clear once. I was fed up with you never being home, being stuck here alone with the kids all the time, no proper social life. I used to think sometimes, what was the point of being married at all? And then Ernie was so kind to me, and – everything,' she concluded, hopeless of defining her former bridge-partner's charms. Slider thought he knew – some of it, at least. Irene had always been a sucker for the trappings of middle-class advancement. It was what she had always thought she wanted. And everyone wanted attention. God, he knew that! It was the origin of so much crime.

She seemed to have got stuck, and he tried to help her along. 'So when he asked you to come and live with him . . .'

She made a strange little noise, like a snort of amusement, except that she didn't look very amused. 'Oh, *he* didn't ask *me*. He's much too shy. Well, not shy exactly, but he doesn't value himself highly enough. He'd never have thought he was good enough for me. No, I had to ask him.' She flicked a glance at him. 'I suppose you think that's funny?'

Oh, far, far from it, he thought. 'I never had anything against Ernie,' he said.

'You could have fooled me. You've always been so rude about him.'

'Defence mechanism. I was jealous,' he said thoughtlessly.

'Were you?' she said, turning to him fully as though she had only been waiting for that. The fearful eagerness in her eyes warned him, too late, to look where he was treading. He *had* been jealous of Ernie, but it was mostly on account of his children, and a bit of atavistic resentment of another man taking his possessions. It was not the sexual jealousy that Irene was wanting him to mean. But how could he explain that to her? While he was not explaining, she carried on, stupidly brave, 'Ernie's been good to me, but it hasn't all been roses. The children haven't really taken to him, and it's strange living in his house. You'd laugh, but I miss this house in a way, and now I'm back here – well . . .' She paused, gathering her words. 'I only told him I wanted to think things out for a bit, but what I think is – what it seems to me—' She swallowed. 'I think I'm still a bit in love with you.'

He couldn't say what she wanted him to say. He sat there, stupidly silent. She died, like someone in variety with the wrong act before the wrong house, but could only carry on, stranded there in the middle of his unreceptiveness with her hopelessly inappropriate script.

'What I mean is – it would make so much more sense for us just to go back to where we were. There's the children to think about. The house – you can't afford two places, can you? It makes no sense to be paying rent and housekeeping for this place, and not living here. Oh, Bill,' she rose up like a surfer on a wave of urgency, 'we could be comfortable! I know it wasn't ideal before, but I understand more now. I'd be more patient about your job – and you could try and be home more, so we could have more of a life together.'

'Irene—' he began helplessly.

'I'm your wife!' she cried desperately. 'Doesn't that count for anything?' He was silent. She turned her face away. 'I don't want to live here alone,' she concluded.

He had to speak. 'I can't go back to the way it was. I can't come back here.'

'You don't want to.'

It took courage for her to ask that, and courage for him to answer with the truth. 'I don't want to.'

'Well,' she said after a moment, in a flat voice, 'that's that.' She drank some more of her gin and tonic. 'I suppose you're really in love with her, then – this woman?'

'*Please* don't let's quarrel about it.'

'I'm not going to quarrel. Just give me a straight answer to a straight question.'

It seemed best to, now. 'Yes, I'm in love with her. I love her.'

'Are you going to marry her?'

'We haven't talked about it. One day, maybe.'

She looked at him starkly. 'I spoke to a solicitor, after you told me all that on the phone the other night. I went to see one yesterday. She confirmed what you said about no fault.

And she says I can't stop the divorce, that it's automatic after a time, whether I want it or not.'

He nodded, very gently. 'That's the law now.'

'Do you want a divorce?'

The house seemed to hold its breath. Even the barbecue smoke beyond the window paused, and the distant cutlery ceased to cuttle. He'd have given anything not to answer, but this was another case where his anything wouldn't even buy the handles. He had to speak. 'Yes,' he said.

Her shoulders went down in an exhalation, and Ruislip started up again. She finished her drink, pulled out her handkerchief and blew her nose, and then said in a different voice, quite briskly, 'Well, thanks for telling me. I needed to hear it from you straight.'

'I'm sorry,' he said.

'No, it's all right. Things come to an end. I just didn't want to face it, I think, that's all.'

'What do you want to do?' he asked her cautiously.

She hardly paused. 'I suppose I'll go back to Ernie,' she said.

Her courage was staggering. He had never admired her so much. 'You don't have to, you know. You can stay here. I won't let you want.'

She shook her head. 'I don't like living without a man; and the children need someone.'

'I thought you said they didn't get on with him?'

'It's early days. Everything's strange, still. They'll get used to him. He's a good man.' She looked at him. 'My mother would have liked me to marry someone like him. She was never sure about you being a policeman.'

'Nor was I,' he said, wanting to laugh, God knew why. It was just the thought of Mrs Carter weighing him up and finding him wanting. It was so beautifully Victorian. A policeman is not a *gentleman*, dear, however nice he may be. 'I get less sure all the time.'

'Does she mind it?' she asked curiously. 'The hours and everything?'

'She's a musician, you see,' he said. 'She has hours herself.'

'Oh. Well, that's different, then. She'll understand.'

'Yes,' he said. 'It's different.'

*   *   *

He didn't go straight home. He drove around a bit, not really aware of where he was going; just going, with that instinct to escape the emotional scene that throughout history had made men leave home, fleeing their mother's pain, their wife's, their children's, going to the Crusades, to war, to the Colonies, the Antarctic, the Moon, the pub; hopelessly fleeing the eyes that always went with them, followed them for ever and all the way to death's dream kingdom. He wanted to be tired enough to sleep: that other escape. He thought suddenly of Eddie Andrews, and his story that he had driven about all night and didn't remember where. Well, it was plausible. Hard put to it, Slider could probably have dredged up some kind of memory of his own itinerary, but then Slider's emotional turmoil was kindergarten stuff compared with Eddie's.

When he got back to Turnham Green, Joanna was just parking, and waited for him outside the front gate while he eased his car into a space further up the road, the last roadside gap in all west London. The time would soon come when they'd have to build cars with retractable stilts so that you could park above one another.

'You'll never guess what!' she called to him as he approached.

With an effort, he remembered her meeting. 'They're going to allow you to wear trousers?'

'Phooey! I'm talking sensational news here.'

'Sensational good or sensational bad?'

'Good. Well, I think so.' He reached her and she slid her arms round his waist. 'Jim Atherton had a date tonight.'

'I know, he told me.' His brain caught up belatedly. 'How do you know?'

'Because I know who it was with!'

'You don't mean Sue?'

'Yes! Isn't that terrific? Our subtle campaigning the other night must have worked. Aren't you pleased?'

'Oh, yes, I like Sue.'

'I think she'll be good for him.' She realised at last that he was elsewhere, and scanned his face anxiously. 'What is it? Did you see Irene? Did it go badly?'

'Yes and no. She's agreed to a divorce, and she's going back to Ernie.'

'What's the "no", then?'

'She's agreed to a divorce, and she's going back to Ernie. Do we have to discuss this in the street?'

'Yes. I want to know why you're upset.'

He drew a deep, long sigh that came all the way up from his boots. 'It's easier to fight with her than admire her. She was so brave.'

'Oh,' said Joanna, and turned to walk up the path with him. She had her key out ready, and let them in, and once the door was closed put down her bag and put both arms round him again. Some of his muscles took the opportunity to slump into her familiar curves, and he closed his eyes a moment and rested his face against her. It was a thingummy devoutly to be wished, to consummate and then to sleep.

'Is it all settled now?' she asked carefully.

'Yes, all settled. We've agreed maintenance and everything. Provided she doesn't go back on it.'

'Which is always a possibility, if lawyers get involved.'

'Or her friend Marilyn. But for now . . .' For now the arrangement was the best that could be hoped for. She would have a home with Ernie Newman, and Slider could sell the Ruislip house – which, with the market picking up, now looked possible – relieving him of having to pay the mortgage, insurance and other associated bills, which had been a huge chunk out of his wages. So he wouldn't be stony broke and utterly dependent on Joanna after all. He'd be able to pay for his food and petrol, at least. So everything was peachy, wasn't it?

'Did you see the children?' Joanna asked, going instinctively to the heart of it.

'No, they were out,' he said.

She detached herself enough to look up, saw the closed eyes and the tired lines beside the mouth. 'Bill?'

He opened his eyes then, and she saw he was almost spent. 'Can we go to bed?' he asked. 'Right now?'

She squeezed him hard and reached up to kiss him. 'Come on, then.' They walked interlinked towards the bedroom and the haven of her bed where he was king and emperor, all-powerful, always wanted; safe. 'You big, dumb, strong ones are always the first to go,' she said, unbuttoning his shirt. 'You should learn to let it all out.' But he never would do that, couldn't, and she knew it.

The public appeal was getting results. Atherton greeted Slider with the news when he came in.

'It's the best response we've had since Hunt missed a typing error on a flyer, and we invited the whole of F Division on a sponsored wank.'

'I've just been to see Mr Porson and congratulate him on his performance,' Slider said. Porson had been as happy as a randy dog in a Miss Lovely Legs competition. It was touching, really. 'He said his wife recorded him on video as a momentum of the occasion.'

'He didn't!' Atherton said admiringly.

'He did. Had a good time last night?'

Atherton grew inscrutable. 'Yes, thank you,' he said, with grammar-school politeness. 'I've got some good news and some bad news.'

'Bad news first.'

'McLaren hasn't called in sick. The good news is that the fingermarks on the handbag are not Meacher's – official.'

'That's good news?'

'Well, it wouldn't have helped us if they had been, would it? We know he was with her. At least this way there's a chance they may be useful.'

'True, O king. What about the staff at the Goat?'

'Haven't done them yet. Mackay's seeing to it.' Atherton eyed his guv'nor, wondering how events went with Irene last night and trying to gauge the answer from his expression. But Slider's mild worried frown was practically permanent and told him nothing, and he could hardly ask for intimate confidences if he wasn't prepared to offer them himself, so he went away unsatisfied and got on with his work.

The trouble with public appeals was that they generated so much work, panning the rubbish for the real information, which occurred with about the same frequency as gold nuggets. It was mid-morning before McLaren tapped on Slider's open door and said nasally, 'Guv, I think we got one.' Slider beckoned him in. 'It's a Mr Tarrant, lives in Hamlet Gardens, says he was walking his dog Tuesday night, saw a man and a woman talking at the end of the footpath down to the footbridge. Quarter past eleven, give or take.'

'What does he sound like?'

'Posh-ish voice. Not young. Sounds normal.'

'Right then, send someone round to get his story.'

'Can't I go, guv?' Slider hesitated about inflicting biological warfare on the general public. 'Everyone else is busy. I could get you a sandwich on my way back,' he added guilefully. 'From that new place, where they do the nice bread and everything.'

'Trying to bribe a senior officer?' Slider said sternly.

'No point in bribing a junior,' McLaren pointed out logically. He dragged out a handkerchief and blew into it.

'Yes, go,' Slider said hastily. Anything to get rid of him.

Mr Tarrant turned out to be older than his voice, a well-preserved man in his sixties, a retired chartered accountant. He had the ground floor of an Edwardian terraced house converted into a one-bedroom flat, with no room to swing an environmental health inspector, but at least with the tiny square of garden. 'I wouldn't think of having a dog if I didn't have a garden,' he told McLaren, as he made tea in the galley kitchen, so small that McLaren had to stand in the hall and watch him through the door, 'but even so, I take Tosca out twice a day. Dogs need a lot of exercise. People rarely understand how much they do need. A five-minute stroll to the nearest tree isn't enough, you know. Tosca has a brisk walk for an hour, twice a day. That's what keeps me fit.'

'Yes, sir,' McLaren said encouragingly. 'You do look fit.'

'Man was made to walk. Best exercise in the world. We do all too little of it these days. Children especially. Taken everywhere by car – driven to school, even! When I was a boy everyone walked to school. Most people walked to work, as well. It's no wonder there's so much obesity. And ill health,' he added as McLaren blew again. 'Now *I* never get colds.'

McLaren was resigned to having hobby-horses aired in front of him. It was funny how many people saw a policeman as a captive audience. He let Mr Tarrant ramble on until the tea was made, and then, sitting down in the tiny living-room with the big yellow Labrador watching him doubtfully from uncomfortably close quarters, he eased the old boy round to the topic of Tuesday night.

'I often take my walk around St Michael Square because it's quiet and away from the traffic. On that particular evening I had just come round the end of the churchyard and I was intending to go over the railway footbridge and back down Wenhaston Road, but I saw there was a young couple standing on the pavement just where the footpath to the bridge comes out.'

'Yes, I know.' McLaren answered the slight query at the end of the sentence.

'Tosca was investigating the railings so I just waited for a moment to see if they would move away, but when they didn't, I walked on along the side of the church and made the circuit round it and went home via Woodbridge Road.'

'So why didn't you go over the footbridge, then?'

Mr Tarrant frowned slightly. 'Well, they looked as if they were having an argument. I didn't want to interrupt them.' He eyed McLaren, and gave a self-conscious cough. 'If you want the truth, I'm a little nervous of young people in general; and I've once or twice received abusive language and even threats from couples when I've interrupted them, quite innocently. I'd always sooner avoid trouble of that sort, and it didn't matter to me which way I took my walk.'

'So this couple were having a barney, were they?'

He nodded. 'That's what it looked like. Of course, I couldn't hear what they were saying, being across the road from them. At one point he looked as if he was threatening her. He leaned very close, poking his face at her – you know – like this.' He demonstrated the aggressive tortoise position of the head. 'And another time he grabbed her by the shoulder, and she sort of pulled herself away angrily, like this.'

This bloke should be on telly, McLaren thought. 'Can you describe what they looked like?'

'Well, she was blonde, I could see that. Short hair. She was wearing a dark dress of some sort – with bare arms.'

McLaren got out the photo they were using of Jennifer. 'Is this her?'

Mr Tarrant looked at it carefully, turning it to catch the light from the window. 'It might be. I couldn't say for sure. She had her back to me, you see, so I didn't see her face. But the hair looks all right.'

'What about the bloke?'

'Oh, just ordinary. Tall. Youngish – not teenage, you know, but a young man. In his twenties or thirties, I'd say.'

'Beard? Moustache? Glasses?'

'No, nothing like that.'

'What colour hair?'

'Just ordinary, really. Brown, I suppose. Light brown. Short. Curly, I think.'

McLaren jotted things down in his notebook. 'Do you remember what he was wearing?'

Mr Tarrant looked apologetic. 'Well, you see, most of his body was hidden from me by the woman. They were standing face to face, quite close to each other, so I could only see her back, and his head over the top of hers. I really wouldn't like to say what he was wearing, no.'

'But you saw his face, all right? Do you think you'd recognise him again?'

'I might do,' he said doubtfully.

'Do you wear glasses at all, Mr Tarrant?'

'For reading. I can see distances quite well. I'm long-sighted, you see.'

'All right. Now, you say this man was tall? How tall?'

'As tall as you, or taller, I should think,' Mr Tarrant said. 'He was quite a bit taller than the woman.'

McLaren considered. Jennifer's height in life had been five-six, and Eddie was five-eight, a difference of only two inches. McLaren himself was five-ten – nearly five-eleven in his thick-soled shoes. 'But of course it was dark, wasn't it?' he said aloud. 'And you were across the road.'

'Yes, that's true,' the old man said, not quite sure where McLaren was going.

'And what with the whatjercallit – you know, like when you're drawing pictures?' He waved his hands expressively.

'Perspective?' Mr Tarrant suggested.

'That's it. The perspective could make him look taller than he was.'

'It might,' Mr Tarrant said hesitantly.

'He might only have been an inch or two taller than her?'

'Yes, I suppose it's possible.'

'And can you say what time this was?'

'A quarter past eleven. The church clock struck the quarter just as I was coming round the corner.'

Back at the factory, McLaren sought out Slider with Mr Tarrant's statement in his hand and a song in his heart.

'The time's perfect, guv. A quarter past eleven. Eddie left the First And Last just after eleven, where he'd been swearing to find Jennifer and kill her. It's five minutes from there to the footpath. This Mr Tarrant ID'd Jennifer from her picture, and he reckons he could pick out the bloke from a line-up. The description fits as far as it goes – clean-shaven, a bit taller than her, with short, light-coloured hair. I questioned him about vehicles and he thinks there could have been a pickup parked just along from the footpath, where the oil stain was found.'

'What's your idea, then?' Slider asked, always ready for fresh input.

'He's looking for Jennifer, he finds her. End of story.'

'You call that an idea? That'd be a low output for a glass of water.'

'Well, guv,' McLaren said, thinking on his feet, 'he's got his motor nearby. Maybe he gets her into that, pretends to've swallowed her story, whatever it was. She thinks they're driving home. Instead he drives to some quiet place, parks the motor, and kills her.'

'With?'

'Oh, something he'd got in the cab. His jacket, or a bit of cloth or something. Afterwards, when he calms down, he realises what he's done. Doesn't know what to do. When everything's quiet he drives back, lays her out nicely in the trench, does her makeup and hair to make her look nice. Remorse and all that. He spends the rest of the night in his cab somewhere, sleeping. Means to come early the next day to fill her in. But Mrs Hammond gets there first.'

'Hmm,' said Slider, a sound McLaren had come to know.

'You don't like it?'

'It's not a theory, it's a sieve,' Slider said. 'For instance, if he's going to kill her, why not take her home and do it there, in real privacy?'

'The way I play it, he's never thought it out. He's just acting off impulse.'

'And how come she was waiting for him by the footpath? What was she doing there?'

'Maybe she was on her way home in her car and he saw her pass and flagged her down.'

'No prizes,' Slider said.

'Well, guv,' McLaren said, 'at least we've got Mr Tarrant's evidence that he saw them quarrelling not long before she died. You can't get over that.'

'I'll try not to,' Slider said. 'All right, d'you want to go and take over a phone, now, give someone a break?'

'Okay, guv,' McLaren said philosophically. He had worked long and hard on that statement, but time would prove its worth. He turned to go.

'Oh – and where's my sandwich?' Slider called after him.

McLaren looked blank. 'Blimey, I forgot all about it.'

CHAPTER THIRTEEN

Bridesmaids Revisited

By the time Detective Superintendent Porson came to see how
they were getting on, a few more pieces had been added. The
most interesting, and one that perhaps helped McLaren's theory
along, was that a man leaving the First And Last just before
eleven on Tuesday night had seen Jennifer's car parked on the
hard standing in front of the Andrewses' house as he walked
past. He had noticed it because he had recently been looking
to buy a new car and had fancied the Mazda RX5 himself,
but was going to have to go for something more practical
because of the kids. He had noticed it was red and that it had
a personalised number-plate, something like a name with an
interesting number. He had added that he thought the engine
was still ticking.

'That gets rid of one of our problems,' Atherton remarked,
'that of the murderer getting her car back home. It looks as
if either she met him on foot, and was killed close to the Old
Rectory, or was taken away and brought back in the killer's
motor.'

Other sultanas in the pud were 'a van of some sort' parked
down the end of St Michael Square, not far from the footpath,
at about half past eleven, according to a woman driving past
on her way home; this more or less accorded with the oil stain
on the road. Then there was a man on the railway embankment
'between half past eleven and midnight', according to a woman
drawing her bedroom curtains in a house on the other side of
the tracks. The man had been 'messing about in the bushes',
said the woman, and when invited to expand her information
thought he had been 'covering something up' with his coat or
a blanket or something.

A further piece fell into place when an anonymous caller said he had been crossing the footbridge at about half past eleven on his way home from the station and had seen a man and a woman making their way along the embankment. He had assumed they were heading for the bushes for a bit of how's-your-father. No, she wasn't struggling or anything; they were holding hands. She was just walking along behind him like he was leading her. No, he didn't want to leave his name, thank you, but they could bank on his story. He was quite sure it was Tuesday because that's the only night he'd been out that way.

McLaren had his faults, but you had to grant he wasn't dogmatic. 'All right, he didn't do her in the cab, then. Maybe he invited her for a walk along the embankment, and did her there, hid her in the bushes, and carried her up through the garden later. It's better that way, 'cause of not having to drive up in the middle of the night and have the neighbours hear the engine.'

'But why would she *go* for a walk with him on the embankment?' Slider asked.

'Why wouldn't she?' McLaren said simply. 'She was his wife.'

'Overcome with passion,' Atherton suggested ironically.

'Five minutes from home and a comfortable bed?' Slider objected.

'You're showing your age,' Atherton grinned. 'Younger people like adventure and thrills, acting on the impulse of the moment.'

Slider frowned. 'There is Jack Potter's evidence that she liked doing it in dangerous places; but hidden in the bushes on the railway embankment is not particularly dangerous, especially with her own husband.'

'Dangerous? It turned out to be fatal,' Atherton pointed out.

The reasoning went down all right with the Syrup. 'I don't think you want to get too bogged up as regards the whys and wheretofores, when dealing with people of this calliper. In my experience they frequently do things that to you and I would seem quite irrationable. Let's just stick to the established facts as we know them, and let the CPS worry about the presentational angle.'

'We haven't got many established facts,' Slider said. 'Only semi-established possibilities.'

'Well, pickers can't be choosers,' the Syrup said comfortably. He swivelled a finger in his ear thoughtfully. 'Let's see, Eddie Andrews – he's had two days to think about it now, hasn't he, since we let him go?'

'Yes, sir.'

'Hmm. Two days. I should think the onermous silence at home ought to be getting on his nerves a bit by now, don't you? Remorse and ecksetera eating away at him, not to mention the investigation hanging over him like the Sword of Damascus. He knows that we know his entire statement was a virago of lies. And he knows we're watching him. With a uniform parked more or less outside his door, he'll have read the handwriting in the wind, all right.'

'You want me to go and talk to him again, sir?' Slider suggested.

'Yes, do that. Have a little chat. Shake the kettle and see if it boils. You might just persuade him to put his hand up like a good boy, and save us all a sackload of trouble.'

'Yes, sir.'

Porson looked at him sharply. 'And take Atherton with you. If anyone can scare Andrews—'

'Atherton?' Slider said, in surprise.

'He's highly articulated – got all the la-di-da chat and the posh grammar. That sort of thing can throw a simple man like Eddie Andrews right off balance.'

'Do you think so, sir?' It was an unexpected insight.

Porson met his eyes with a gleam of humour. 'He scares the shit out of me,' he said frankly.

'Porson called you articulated,' Slider told Atherton, when he passed on the message afterwards.

'Like a lorry,' Atherton said in delight. 'But I've always said I'm in the van when it comes to vocab.'

'I'll have no truck with puns,' Slider told him curtly. 'Let's get going.'

Andrews looked terrible: unshaven, dirty, with matted hair and red-rimmed eyes. He let Slider and Atherton in without question or comment, and wandered before them into the sitting room, where he slumped down in a chair without looking at them. The room was untidy, with glasses and crockery on the floor, an empty baked-beans can with a spoon standing in it perched on the television, newspapers strewn about, a duvet and pillows falling off the sofa.

'I've been sleeping down here,' he said, when Slider asked about them. 'I can't stand it upstairs. I can't stand it anywhere, if you want to know.' He looked round the room as if noticing the untidiness for the first time. 'Pat didn't come Friday. She sent a note. She says she's not coming any more. I don't blame her.' He put his head in his hands and rubbed and rubbed at his eyes. 'This house – I built it for her. Everything she wanted – whirlpool bath, automatic oven. She chose everything – carpets, furniture, wallpaper, everything. Fitted wardrobes, I put in, with a light that comes on when you open the door. Her dream home. Anything she asked for I gave her. Self-defrosting fridge. Automatic washer-dryer. Digital microwave. But it wasn't enough. I couldn't keep her.'

'Woman is fickle,' Atherton commented.

Eddie lifted his head, his eyes unfocused. 'She cheated on me. I didn't want to believe it. I told myself they were all lying. I don't know. Maybe they were. No, she cheated on me. But she loved me, really. You got to understand. Underneath, it was me she loved.'

'That last night, Eddie,' Slider said gently. 'We know you met her after you left the pub at closing time. Down by the footpath that leads to the railway bridge. Someone saw you there talking to her. Did you have a quarrel?'

He stared as if Slider were talking a foreign language. 'Quarrel? What about?'

'You tell me. You met her by the footpath, didn't you?'

'Later you were seen on the railway embankment,' Atherton added.

'The embankment,' he said. 'Yes, I remember. I did go there. When I was walking about.'

'You were hiding something in the bushes. Covering it with something,' Slider suggested.

'It was Jennifer, wasn't it?' Atherton said. 'Jennifer's body.'

'Jennifer's body,' he repeated. He looked exhausted, run to the end of his strength. The Kindly Ones, Atherton thought, had bayed him at last.

'You were seen walking with her along the embankment to

the bushes. But she never came back, did she?' Slider said. 'What did you do, Eddie? Tell me.'

'Her body.' Eddie looked at him in agony, his eyes focused now. 'She's dead.' He quivered all over, as a frightened dog shivers. 'I'll never see her again. Oh, what have I done?'

'Tell me about it,' Slider urged, and to Atherton, his gentleness was a terrible thing, as a sword is terrible; and yet to a man fleeing the Erinnyes perhaps a welcome thing. Andrews looked at him with the hope with which such a man might look at his executioner: the hope only of an end to it all.

'Yes,' he said at last. 'I want to tell you.'

Porson read the statement aloud as he hoofed restlessly about the room.

'I found out she had been cheating on me. I swore I would kill her. I was looking for her all evening. I had been drinking a lot. I met her by the path that leads down to the footbridge over the railway and we quarrelled. I led her onto the embankment and killed her in the bushes and covered her with my jacket. Later when it was quiet I carried her up the garden and put her in the hole I'd dug on Mrs Hammond's terrace. I was going to fill the hole in in the morning, but Mrs Hammond found her first. Now I'm sorry she's dead and want to get it off my chest.'

Porson paused in his peregrination and tapped the paper with his finger-nail. 'Good work,' he said. 'And within the week, too. An expertitious result like this will bring us a lot of kewdos with the Powers That Be, I can tell you, Slider. Especially as it's a nice, clean, straightforward case: confession plus corroboration, obvious suspect, comprehensive motive, creditable witnesses – nothing to tax the imagination of the twelve men and true. I think there's no doubt the CPS will prosecute on this one, and a conviction will do us no end of bon.'

For a rare moment he was still, away in some pleasurable place of plaudit. His big hands twitched as he received a commendation and shook the hand of the Assistant Commissioner, as a dreaming dog's paws twitch at that special rabbit moment.

Slider stirred a little, unhappily. Confession is as confession does, he thought, and there was something unsatisfyingly blood-less about this one. The show without the substance. Someone somewhere wasn't inhaling. But he must try to be specific for Porson: he didn't know him well enough to play the old instinct card, as he could have done with Dickson in the dear dead days of long ago.

'He doesn't say how he killed her,' Slider said. 'Or how he met her there. And what became of the jacket?'

'Eh?' Porson said, dragged unwillingly back to cold reality.

'The jacket, sir. He wasn't wearing one in the morning, and we've been over every inch of the embankment and the garden. There was no jacket in his pickup, either.'

'Well, he could have dumped it anywhere,' Porson said.

'But why would he? It wasn't as if there was any blood.'

Porson looked kindly. 'Well, obviously this statement is only a preliminary starting place. There's plenty more work to be done; d'you think I don't know that? But you don't need to lose any sleep. He's put his hand up, that's the main thing. This is not the moment to go picking hairs and getting bogged down in the fine print. Cut yourself a bit of cake, Slider: you've done a good job.'

'Sir,' Slider said, unconvinced.

'Come on, you don't need me to tell you how the thing works: he feels relief after confessing, and out comes all the rest – if he's handled the right way up. That's down to you – asking the right questions is your providence.'

'Yes, sir.'

'I've every confidence in your interrogatory technique.'

'Thank you, sir.'

Porson was on the move again. 'As he's here voluntarily, we're not on the clock, that's one good thing. We won't arrest him unless he looks like taking a wander – that'll give us a chance to get all the witnesses taped up and labelled. Get the old chap who saw them – Tarrant, is it? – get him in and we'll do a line-up. And get the motor witnesses to come and look at the book and pick out the van they saw in the square. Tomorrow will do for that.'

'Yes, sir.'

'Meanwhile, give Andrews half an hour, spot of grub and a cup of tea, and then have another go at him. Take him through the timetable, and run him gently up to the murder so he doesn't even see it coming, get my drift?'

Slider got it. Excitement was making the Syrup unusually direct. Quite comprehensive, in fact.

Slider was late home, after the failure of the Porson Plan Mark I: Eddie Andrews cantered gently up to the fence, had not precisely refused, but had jumped carelessly, scattering brushwood. He was willing to co-operate – too willing, in Slider's view: he followed wherever he was led, like a bloodhound on an aniseed trail, and the result was a less than compelling narrative. He didn't deny anything, but he didn't offer any explanations for the things that bothered Slider, either; he seemed to want the answers laid out for him as well as the questions. It left Slider restless. Everything added up to Eddie Andrews, and yet nothing added up. It was like eating without swallowing, making love with gloves on.

Talking of which, Joanna was home, and miffed that she had had a rare Saturday evening free and he had not been there to share it with her. 'I know it's not your fault. I'm not blaming you. I'm just saying it's a pity, that's all.'

'What did you do?'

'Had something to eat. Watched that film we taped the other day. The Clint Eastwood thing.'

'Oh, I wanted to see that,' he protested.

'Don't worry, by the time you get the leisure to sit down and watch it, it will be far enough in the past for me to watch it again.'

He was mollified. 'I don't suppose there's anything to eat in the house?'

'Didn't you get anything?'

'Not since . . .' He pondered. 'Breakfast, actually.'

'They let you starve all day? You ought to stand up for yourself.'

'Like Narcissus?'

'What an educated quip. You sound like Atherton.'

'Never mind all that. Your mind should be on me. Food, woman, food!'

Obligingly, she looked in the fridge. 'Well, there's salady stuff.'

'I hate salad. I wish it was winter.'

'That was practically a pout. Actually, when I say salad, it's just a sort of honeymoon salad – lettuce alone. There's some cheese and a bit of pâté left, but the bread's a bit old.' She looked at her lover's suffering face and said, 'Tell you what, there's some bacon in the freezer compartment. I could whack that into the microwave to defrost it, and make you a toasted bacon sandwich. How would that do?'

'I love you,' Slider confessed.

'So you say. It's just my cuisine you fancy, really.'

'You have a beautiful and curvaceous cuisine, but I love you for your mind, as well.'

One bacon sandwich thing led to another, so Saturday night was not a total flop after all; but Sunday started badly. He overslept and woke feeling doomed and heavy in the legs, and Joanna rushed in in a panic and said her car wouldn't start.

'I'll have to take yours.'

Slider hated to be without a car. And he hated anyone else driving his. Irene wouldn't have asked; but with a new relationship you have to tread gently. He gave his objection mildly. 'Can't you go by public transport?'

'Not possibly. I've got a rehearsal in Milton Keynes this morning, then that blasted dedication service or whatever it's called at Eton, and then back to Milton Keynes for the concert in the evening. I can only just do it *with* a car. Why do I take on these ghastly economy-class dates?'

'Because you need the money.'

'You've only got to get to Shepherd's Bush, haven't you?'

He couldn't refuse against such reason, little as he liked it, and heaved himself out of bed. 'You ought to get rid of that old wreck and get yourself something reliable,' he grumbled, searching his jacket pocket for his keys.

'Are you talking about my car or my man?' she asked, eyeing his gummy state.

'And how am I supposed to get to work?'

'You could cycle up the avenue, but you haven't got a bike. Or you could call out the AA and take mine when they've fixed it.'

'I haven't got time for that.'

'You'd better have, or I'll have to take your car tomorrow as well,' she said, taking the keys from his nerveless fingers and kissing him hard on the lips in the same movement. ''Bye. Love you. Good luck with your murderer.'

'See you tomorrow,' he said glumly, knowing she would not be back before midnight.

Things didn't get better. Eddie Andrews was still in pliant mood, and willing, not to say eager to make a further, expanded statement. But the details he added were vague in the extreme, and when pressed to be specific about times, places and materials he fell back on, 'I can't remember,' and 'It's all confused – just a blur in my mind.' He seemed more cheerful, and was eating well. Now he had confessed, the responsibility had been taken from his shoulders: it was a syndrome Slider had seen before – indeed, it was the basis of the Catholic Church's success – but in this case he didn't find it comforting.

Andrews readily agreed to an identity parade, but Sunday was not a good day for organising a line-up, and Slider had to rummage through the staff to make up the numbers.

'I'll do it,' Swilley said kindly, when Slider asked for volunteers.

'I don't think his heart could stand it. McLaren – no, of course he knows you. Anderson, then. For me, laddie.' Anderson got up, grumbling. Slider surveyed the room. The uniform loaners were in plain clothes today. 'What about you, Defreitas?'

'Not me, sir. I'm allergic to line-ups.' Defreitas said hastily. 'Take Renker. He wants a break.'

Renker stood up. 'I don't mind, sir.'

There was a chorus from around the room.

'Don't do it, Eric!'

'Never volunteer, son!'

'I wouldn't touch it with a ten-foot pole, mate!'

'Yeah, whatever happened to him?' Renker enquired. '"Stretch" Polanski, the ten-foot Pole?'

'That's it!' Slider exclaimed. 'Not another word! Anderson, Renker, Willans – front and centre. You've volunteered. And when all this is over, I'm going to run away and join the circus.'

The three men filed out from their desks with a show of reluctance. 'I thought this *was* the circus,' Renker protested. 'Otherwise, how come all the clowns?'

Slider rolled his eyes. 'Everyone's a comedian. Get downstairs, you three. And for God's sake, try not to look like policemen.'

*   *   *

Tosca waited in the front shop, where she and Nicholls fell instantly and deeply in love, while Mr Tarrant did his duty. He did not pick out Eddie Andrews.

'No,' he said regretfully after a long and careful scrutiny of the line, 'it isn't any of those. The one at the end – number eight,' this was Renker, 'he's about the right height. But he's too fair. Number two's hair is more like it.' This was Anderson. 'But he looks too heavy and broad. And I don't think he's quite tall enough. And three, four and five are much too short.' Number four was Andrews.

Slider took Mr Tarrant out. 'I'm sorry,' the old man said. 'I wanted to help. But none of them looked right to me, and I couldn't say they did if they didn't.'

'Of course not,' Slider said. He hovered over a delicate area. 'Regarding the height of the man you saw, sir, in your statement, you did say he was only "a bit taller than the woman"?'

'No,' Tarrant said anxiously, 'I said he was *quite* a bit taller than the lady. I did tell the other officer, the one who came to my house, that I thought he was a very tall man, but your officer talked about perspective and about it being dark, and he pointed out – well, he persuaded me I was mistaken. But I *did* think at the time that he was very tall. Tall and slim.'

'And with fair, wavy hair?'

'Brown,' Mr Tarrant said firmly. 'A lightish brown, perhaps, but not fair or blond. And definitely curly. Quite tight curls.'

McLaren was unrepentant. 'He wasn't all that sure what he'd seen, guv. I had to help him out a bit. I didn't twist anything, just talked him through it, so as to get it down clearly.'

'Clearly?' Slider was keeping a tight hold on himself, but it wasn't easy. 'He says brown hair and you write fair? He says curly and you write wavy?'

'Well, guv, I mean, how's he going to tell the difference anyway between light brown and fair? I mean, he's across the road, and it's quite wide there. And it's dark, and he's an old bloke, and his eyes are probably not up to much.'

'McLaren, you are a waste of space!' Slider raved. 'You have the intellect of a brick! If he couldn't see across the road, what's the bloody point of having him as a witness?'

McLaren shifted uncomfortably. 'I don't mean to say he

can't see, but – you know – I was just, sort of, guiding him a bit.'

Slider put his head in his hands. 'All you had to do was to take down what he said. Just let him tell you, and write it down.'

'But, guv, we've got a confession,' McLaren pointed out. 'You can't get over that.'

'A paraplegic terrapin could get over that! Mr Tarrant says Andrews was nothing like the man he saw. He also picked out a Transit van from the cards, not a pickup, as the motor he saw parked on the square – an identification, incidentally, confirmed by the other motor witness we had. The phone-in who saw a man and a woman on the embankment didn't leave his name. And the woman across the railway lines was too far away to identify the man she saw in the bushes. How long do you think it would take defence counsel to knock that house of cards down, balloon-brain?'

'But Andrews still confessed. We know it was him. He knows it was him. We'll get other evidence – bound to.'

'Andrews is in a highly suggestible state of mind, and his confession is extremely suspect. And now you've contaminated the field. How are we supposed to know now what he really remembers and what's been suggested to him? You were given a simple task to do, basic police work, and you made a complete Horlicks of it. I'm disgusted with you.'

'Sorry, guv,' McLaren said, with a stubborn lack of contrition.

'Oh, go away,' Slider said. He still had to go and tell Mr Porson his prince was a frog.

Porson, annoyingly, was inclined to side with McLaren. 'It's a nuisance, of course, but I don't think the situation is irredeemable. It's not as if we've got *no* corroboration. We know he was drinking all evening and threatening to kill her, and we know she was having affairs. And her handbag was found in his pickup. We've got enough to be going on with, and other witnesses will come forward in time. Andrews isn't asking to go home, is he?'

'No, sir, but—'

Porson held up his hand calmly. 'There you are, then. Andrews is here completely gratuitously. And if he wants to make a voluntary statement of his guilt, then it's his perjorative to do so.'

Slider stumped up to the canteen for a cup of tea and a quiet fume. He found Atherton there at a table on his own, resting his elbow on the table and his chin in his hand like a Scott Fitzgerald débutante, dunking his teabag delicately with the other hand.

'Your problem is, you always want to know everything,' he said languidly, when Slider had unpocketed his troubles. 'You want all the teas dotted and the eyes crossed. Porson's probably right. And Eddie probably is guilty.'

'Probably? Where's your intellectual curiosity?'

'Oh, I can't be bothered with all that on a Sunday.'

Slider took a few deep breaths and drank some tea. 'And to have to stand there while Mr Porson mangles language at me,' he grumbled, diminuendo.

'You don't really mind that,' Atherton told him. 'That's just psychosemantic.'

Somewhat restored, Slider went downstairs again and found Swilley looking for him. 'I think we may have got something here, boss. A woman's phoned, who says she was Jennifer's best friend. And she says she saw Jennifer on the Tuesday evening.'

Janice Byrt lived, worked and generally had her being in that strange and lost part of Hounslow that lay under the flightpath of Heathrow. Once there had been only little villages, tile-hung farmhouses and rustic churches. Then arterial roads had linked them with ribbons of mock-Tudor semis, traffic lights and neat set-back arcades of shops. But the placid life still went on, in a world where people wore hats, and walked to the shops pushing babies in prams; for few had cars, and their sound was but as the trickle of a stream, and you could hear the birds when you went out of doors.

And then the airport came. Now the great white bellies of arriving and departing jumbos flashed like monstrous fish above them, crushing down the sky and leaving a shimmering wake of hot kerosene like a snail's trail over the frail roofs. Roaring cars and bellowing lorries sucked up whatever air was left, and, to prevent any pocket of peace taking root, satellite dishes on every house probed the sky for new sources of bedlam, while shops and pubs vomited endless loops of strident pop.

In this insanity of noise and stink, a race of people clung to existence, like those bizarre microbes that manage to live inside volcanoes. The thirties semis had been armoured with triple-glazing and wall insulation, and a cheerful, and to all appearances normal, life went on, monument to man's astonishing adapt-ability. Janice Byrt had a little hairdressing establishment on one of the traffic-lit corners where one arterial road crossed another, and the music of the day was regularly informed with the screaming brakes and tinkling glass of yet another driver's belief that red lights were optional. Her shop front was painted pink, with pink ruched curtains in the windows and the name of the salon hand-painted in curly magenta writing on a pink background over the top: *Hair You Are*. It was an especially good joke, Slider discovered, because Janice came from Lowestoft, where they pronounce 'here' as 'hair'.

She lived in the flat above the shop. Slider parked in the service road in front of the parade, and then found the archway several shops down that led to the granite stairs, which led to the balconies at the back, which gave access to the flats. Inside, the traffic noise was several degrees lower, and when a plane came over it was still possible to carry on talking, though the whole flat trembled like a vibrating bed in a motel, so that Janice's collection of china figurines tinkled together as though they were chatting in tiny china voices.

'You get used to it,' she assured Slider when he asked about the noise. 'I hardly hear it any more. And those new jumbos are ever so much quieter.'

Slider felt as though his brains were being scrambled by a master chef with an extra large whisk, but there certainly could be no more pleasant, normal and relaxed person than Janice Byrt seemed. He supposed it was natural selection. Those who went bonkers were carried off screaming to a suite at the Latex Hilton, and the rest just got on with their lives.

She had been shocked to learn of Jennifer's death. 'I didn't know a thing about it,' she said. 'Well, I don't have time for newspapers, and I never watch the news on telly – too depressing, all that war and MPs and stuff. It wasn't till a friend of mine rung up this morning – she'd seen it on the news last night, and of course the name made her jump. She said she wasn't really watching, but when she heard the name she looked up, and there was Jen's picture all over the screen! That give her such a fright! So she rang me up this morning, and she say to me, "What d'you think about our Jen getting killed like that?" and there, I say to her, "I don't know what you're talking about, girl." ' Her accent became stronger as she grew agitated, Slider noticed.

The friend who had rung her lived in St Albans. 'Val and me were Jen's bridesmaids when she married Eddie. Would you like to see the photo?'

Slider accepted with interest, and was handed a framed photograph from its place of honour on one of the crowded shelves of the chimney alcove. It was a typical wedding-photographer's line-up: bride and groom flanked by two bridesmaids and best man, grass under foot and grey stones of the church out of focus behind. There was Jennifer with a glittering smile and meringue hair, scarlet lips and nails, all in white grosgrain, tight bodice and puffed sleeves that Princess Di had made fashionable up and down the land back in another age. She held red roses and white lilies wired into one of those bizarre flat-fronted sheaths designed by florists purely for holding in wedding-photos, and a silver cardboard horseshoe dangled on white ribbon from her wrist. Her other hand rested on the sleeve of a younger, blonder Eddie, bundled into a blue suit patently not his own, and looking, from his expression of bewildered euphoria, as if he'd just had his brains beaten out with a lump of pure pleasure in a silk sock.

To Eddie's other side stood the best man, a scrawny, raw-faced, crop-haired youth who looked as if he'd only just learned to walk upright. To Jennifer's other side stood a plump, dark-haired bridesmaid, and Janice.

'That's me,' she said helpfully, pointing. The bridesmaids were in matching Princess Di jobs in bright pink taffeta with circlets on their heads, and small, flat, round bouquets of Valentine-pink roses that looked like Las Vegas wedding-parlour pizzas. 'They were lovely frocks,' she said wistfully, 'only Val had the figure for it and I didn't. My sleeves kept slipping down.' Slider remembered being told just recently that no-one said 'frocks' any more. Who was that? Yes, poor Janice was small and weedy and flat in every dimension and looked as if her frock was independently rigged like a bell-tent, and she merely standing inside it, looking meekly out of the hole at the top. In a pneumatic-bust competition with Val, she was definitely the twin who didn't have the Toni.

Janice took the picture back from him and caressed it with a thumb. 'It was a lovely wedding. Val's married now, got two children. I'm the only one not married. That's the only time I was ever a bridesmaid, too.' She put the picture back in its special place, probably unaware that she had just told her whole life's philosophy in four sentences.

'You've known Jennifer for a long time?'

'We went to the same school. She was Jennifer Harris then.'

'In St Albans?'

She nodded. 'She was my best friend. I was ever so shy, and then, well, my mum and dad moved from Lowestoft when I was fourteen, so I didn't know anybody, and I felt really awkward and, sort of, out of it. I was never much good at making friends. But Jen just came over to me on the first day and started talking to me, and after that she sort of looked after me, and let me go about with her. She was lovely! I mean, she was pretty and everything, and so lively, too, always into everything, always laughing and teasing the boys. She was never scared of anything. And popular! I never did know what she saw in me.'

Slider nodded encouragingly. Every Dame Edna needs a Madge, he thought; and often the wildest extroverts were the most insecure underneath. They needed one quiet, loyal, reliable lieutenant who loved them blindly and uncritically – and also, who would never be a rival. 'Did you wear glasses at school?' he asked unwarily, out of his thoughts.

'Yes,' she said, surprised. 'I wear contacts now. How ever did you know?'

He waved it away. 'Doesn't matter. Please go on. You kept up with Jennifer when you left school?'

Jennifer went to work in an estate agent's office, and Janice became a hairdressing apprentice, and was still permitted to hang about with Jennifer's gang, and play buffer and straight man in Jennifer's games of seduction with the boys. 'Of course, it wasn't the same after she married Eddie, but we still kept in touch, and after she came to London, I decided to come too, to be nearer.'

Though quiet, plain, and shy with boys, Janice was no duffer. She had worked her way up the hairdressing hierarchy and finally opened her own salon which, though not in a fashionable place – or perhaps because of that – had a large and loyal clientele. It was making her a nice little pot of money. 'I don't really have anything to spend it on,' she said to Slider, but without self-pity. 'I don't go out much, and I bought the flat cheap from the council years ago so there's no mortgage. I like to buy things for my nephews – my brother's boys – and I like nice holidays. But it still builds up. I suppose,' she laughed deprecatingly, 'it's for my retirement, really.'

Over the years, too, Jennifer had come to value the quiet friend more, and had increasingly entrusted her with her confidences. 'People think not being married I must be really sheltered. But that's funny what women will tell you when their hair's wet. I think they feel vulnerable – well, no-one looks their best like that, do they?' She laughed the little laugh again. 'I think it's a bit like being a priest – you know, the confessional? I bet I've heard things that would make your hair stand on end. Well, not yours,' she amended humbly, 'you being a policeman, but most people. And you don't have to do everything to know about it, do you?'

'I should hope not,' Slider said. 'So tell me what happened on Tuesday.'

'Well, Tuesday's my half-day closing. Of course, Jen knew that. She turns up, oh, about ha' past four, it must have been. I could see right away she was upset. She comes right in and says, "Give me a drink, Jan, before I start crying and make a fool of myself." So I made her a gin and tonic, a big one. That was her drink, gin and tonic. I always kept some in for when she dropped in. I like a Cinzano, myself, or a sherry.'

'Had she already been drinking, do you think?'

'She wasn't drunk, if that's what you mean. But I could tell she'd had a couple. But she was too upset and angry to get drunk. She was burning it up, sort of.'

Slider nodded. He knew that mood. 'What was she upset about?'

'She'd been with one of her men that afternoon – David.' She looked at Slider to see if he knew about him, and he nodded again. 'She said, "He's dropped me, Jan, the bastard's dropped me. Now what am I going to do?" You see, it was different with David. She was always having affairs, but they never meant much. But she had high hopes of David.'

'High hopes?'

'Well, he was posh – you know, educated and upper class. Went to a public school and everything. And he was rich, too. Jen had always wanted someone like that. Eddie – he was a mistake, really. She married him too young. If she'd stayed single a bit longer she never would have married him at all, because they weren't suited. He was dull, you know? No ambition. Jen wanted to go up in life. And she thought with David she'd really found the right man.'

'Didn't she know he was married?'

'What, David? Yes, of course, but he didn't love his wife. She was much older than him, and it was never a love match in the beginning. That wasn't a problem. Jen was crazy about David, and what with everything he said she thought he felt the same. She was just waiting for him to say the word, and then she was going to leave Eddie and he was going to leave Diana – that's David's wife's name – and everything would be all right. You see, Eddie's ever so jealous, but he'd never start anything with a person like David. He's very polite with people like that – scared of them, almost.' She sounded faintly puzzled by the idea; Slider thought of the Syrup saying that Atherton would scare Eddie with his grammar. Was this his day for having insights thrust upon him from unlikely sources?

'So what had happened between her and David?'

'Well, apparently they'd met as usual that afternoon – at a motel somewhere, I think.' Slider nodded. 'And they were laying in bed afterwards and he suddenly says that was to be the last time, he didn't want to see her any more. Jen was absolutely flabbergasted.'

'Did he say why?'

'She said he had some other woman on the go, and things were getting serious with her, and he was thinking of marrying this woman, and he couldn't afford to have his affair with Jennifer messing things up, because this other woman was very proper and if she found out she'd have nothing more to do with David, and he didn't want to lose her. Well, Jen said, "I thought you loved me," and he said, "It's got nothing to do with love." Well, you can imagine how Jen felt when he said that! It turns out this woman's going to come into a lot of money, you see. So Jen said to him, "What do you need money for? You're rich enough." And then he sort of laughs and says that he hasn't got a penny, all the money is Diana's, and what's more she's fed up with him, Diana is, and threatening to cut him off. So he's got to make sure of this other woman right away. So he says, "I'm sorry, my dear, but it's curtains for you and me."'

She stopped with a fine dramatic sense, and looked at him, large-eyed, for his response.

'Jennifer must have been very upset.'

'She was. She was crying fit to break her heart at first, because she really thought he was going to marry her, and now it turns out he was just toying with her.' Lovely phrase, Slider thought. 'So I say to her, Jen, I say, if he ha'n't got any money, you don't want to marry him anyway, and she say, I do, Jan, I love him. I don't care if he's rich or poor. And besides, she say, I can't stay with Eddie no more. I don't care what happens, she say, but I'm getting out of that.'

'Did she say why she couldn't stay with Eddie?'

'No. Just the usual, I suppose.'

'What's the usual?'

'Well, he was terribly jealous, was Eddie, and never wanted to let her out of his sight. He'd've locked her up if he could have, literally. They were always having rows. And, then, he used to hit her as well.' She looked at him sidelong to see what he thought about that. 'That's another reason she ought never to've married him, but there, she didn't know at the beginning. It was only when he lost his temper with her, when they had their rows, not, like, all the time. But still, I think it'd been getting worse lately. Anyway, she said she'd got to get out.'

'Yes, I see. What happened next?'

'Well, after a bit, she calms down, and she says, "I'm not giving up. I'm going to see him again and make him take me back." David, she meant. She reckons if she can just get him to meet her, she can talk him round. She was a great talker, was Jen.' Her eyes filled with tears and her lips trembled at her own use of the past tense.

'Did she say when she would see him?'

'She was going to ring him and make him meet her that

evening. She cheered up once she thought of that, and she went to my bathroom and washed her face and did her makeup again, and then she went off. That would be about ha' past five. And that's the last time I saw her.' She blew her nose carefully. 'I can't believe I'll never see her again. She was my best friend in the world. I don't know what I'll do without her,' she said bleakly. She looked towards the net-curtained window as another full-bellied jet, pregnant with tourists, battered the air over her roof. The romance and glamour had gone out of her life. Now there was just Hounslow, and other people's hair, for ever and ever.

Slider suppressed his pity. She wouldn't want it, in any case, who had none for herself. 'When she left here, do you know where she was going?'

'What, you mean right away? Well, I can guess. It was what she said about, if it didn't work with David, she was getting out anyway. She said to me, "I've got a couple of other irons in the fire," she said, "and I might as well make sure they're still hot, just in case." She couldn't just leave Eddie, you see, unless she had someone to go to, because he'd've come after her and knocked her about and made her go back. I mean, she knew she could always come here, but I couldn't have helped against Eddie. And she wouldn't want to live with me, anyway. She wasn't someone that would want to be without a man.' Janice seemed to accept this practical attitude to the heart's obligations without offence; indeed, with approval.

'So you mean, if David wouldn't marry her, she was going to get one of these other men to?' He was fascinated and appalled by Jennifer's philosophy as it was revealed by her friend. Suppose other women thought like this, seeing men as a commodity, like meat with an income attached?

Janice nodded. 'Though, really, it was just one. I don't think she ever had any chance with Alan, because he was a reverend, you know, a vicar, and she wasn't really cut out to be a vicar's wife.'

Understatement of the decade, Slider thought. He wondered, though, how hot the turbulent priest's iron had been. Had he protested too much to Atherton about his resistance to Jennifer's charms? Had he, in fact, been her lover?

'Yes, we knew she'd been to see the vicar,' Slider said. 'That fits in. But who was the other man, do you know?'

'He was a policeman, as it happens,' she said, with a nod and a shy smile to Slider. 'She was quite excited about him, though he was married too; but she said he was very passionate. I think she half wished he had David's class, because she fancied him a lot more. She didn't tell me his name, though. She had a nickname for him. Duffy, I think it was. No, Daffy. That's right, Daffy.'

Bloody Nora, Slider thought, as a lot of little pieces tumbled into place. And then he remembered Steve Mills, one of his firm who had become a suspect in a murder case he had investigated; and, like the famous petunia, he thought, Oh, no, not again!

CHAPTER FOURTEEN

Stalling Between Two Fuels

Defreitas was as white as paper. 'I didn't kill her, sir. You've got to believe me. I didn't. I wouldn't.'

Slider's anger was cold. 'Then why the hell didn't you tell me about your involvement? What am I supposed to think when you conceal important evidence like this?'

'I thought it wouldn't come out,' Defreitas said miserably. 'You see, things are difficult at home. Me and my wife aren't getting on. I hoped—'

Now Slider remembered how Defreitas had got out of the identity parade; and further back, the crash from the back of the CID room when he had mentioned that there were two types of sperm in the victim's vagina. 'My God,' he breathed, 'it was you she met on the footpath! It was you who was seen with her on the embankment!'

Defreitas looked as though he might cry. 'I couldn't tell you, sir. I was afraid if it came out no-one would believe me, they'd think I did it. But I didn't, I swear it!'

Slider's mouth turned down. 'You swear it? What use is your word to me now? My God, I don't think you begin to see what you've done!'

'I'm sorry, sir. But I didn't destroy any evidence, or lie about anything. I just—'

'You just let us bring Eddie Andrews in on the basis that it was him who met his wife by the footpath. Don't you understand? The heaviest evidence against him was that he was seen arguing with her shortly before her death, near where her body was discovered – near a place where he might have killed and concealed her. Now it turns out that person was you! Where do you think that leaves you?'

Defreitas saw now. He shook his head slowly from side to side, not so much in negation but like someone in pain. 'No, sir. No, sir. You don't believe that. She was all right when I left her. I would never have done a thing like that.'

Slider wanted to believe him. He seemed a nice lad. But images were chasing across his brain. The witness who saw Jennifer being led along the embankment towards the bushes. The witness who saw a man covering something with his jacket. In his mind Slider saw it: kisses, panting, a quick, practised coupling in the bushes – two people who'd done it before and knew how to get it done. Then something wrong was said, sharp words, a quarrel: Jennifer threatening to tell his wife; Defreitas, still kneeling over her, losing control. Then a quick movement and his jacket over her face, smothering her . . .

Thus far it played like panto. But after that, questions arose. Why would Defreitas go back to move her body from a place where it might lie concealed for days to a place where it would certainly be immediately discovered, by the householder or the builder? To implicate Eddie, was the only answer to that – and if it were so, it was a foul and despicable act; but risky, stupidly so. Defreitas had not previously impressed him as stupid; though people in unprecedented situations did do silly things.

But why had she not struggled? If she had, there would have to have been more bruising about the face, at least. Why – and how? – had he restored her makeup? And how had her handbag got into Eddie's pickup? No, it didn't make sense as it stood; but he could see how easily it would make sense to someone less particular – or someone who had an anti-police agenda, like the tabloids, and their readers, if it got that far. Exposure of that sort would cause great embarrassment to the Department; and even if they eventually charged someone else with the murder, there would always be those who believed Defreitas had 'got off'. His future would be blighted.

But his career was blighted now, anyway – perhaps over. Slider came back from long thoughts to find pleading eyes on him. 'You'd better have a bloody good alibi,' he said. 'And now you'd better tell me what happened.'

Defreitas had been drinking in the Goat on Tuesday evening. 'I only had the one pint. I was making it last. I didn't want to go home. I'd had a row with the wife earlier, you see, so I'd been out since about half past nine, just walking about. I got to the Goat about a quarter past ten and just went in for a pee, but by then I was fed up with walking the streets so I decided to have a pint.'

Just before closing time Jennifer had telephoned there asking to speak to him. 'Karen took the call. Jen didn't give her name, just asked to speak to me, and Karen passed it over. She was busy – I don't think she really noticed. Jen said she'd been phoning round trying to find me – tried the First And Last and a couple of other places she knew I used. She said she wanted to see me right away. I said, where are you? and she just said, meet me at the footpath to the railway bridge in five minutes. So I went.'

When he met her she had come straight out with it, and said it was time he put his money where his mouth was and married her.

'I was thrown – I mean, we'd never talked about that. As far as I was concerned we were just having a bit of fun, and I thought she felt the same way. But when I said that she got angry and started to create. Said a lot of things, about, you know, leading her on and taking advantage of her and so on. The usual old Tottenham. I said no-one had deceived anyone and she was old enough to know what was what, and if anyone had been doing any leading on it was her. Which was the truth,' he added, seeing Slider's frown. 'I mean, it was her come on to me in the first place.'

'And you were the helpless victim, forced to have sex with her against your will,' Slider said with distaste. Defreitas reddened. 'Go on.'

'Well,' he continued, 'she said it wasn't like that for her, that it was serious – though I swear she'd never even hinted anything like that before. I mean, if she had, I can tell you I'd've never have – well,' he checked himself, 'anyway, she said now she couldn't stand living with Eddie any more and she'd got to get out. Well, I said what went on between her and Eddie was her business, and I couldn't help her. Then she said if I didn't agree to marry her, she'd go straight round and see Becky – my wife – and spill the beans. Well, then I got mad with her and said if she dared go anywhere near my house I'd—'

'You'd kill her?'

Defreitas swallowed. 'I don't think I said that, sir. But I was angry. It's the last thing I wanted then, her going round my house, with things like they are between Becky and me.'

They had argued heatedly for a while, and then suddenly Jennifer had back-pedalled, apologised for the threat, said she didn't mean it, and started sweet-talking him instead.

'It was all lovey-dovey then. She was very persuasive when she wanted. I couldn't resist her,' Defreitas admitted. 'She started sort of rubbing herself against me, and then she suggested us going down on the embankment and – and doing it.'

He hadn't taken much persuading. After the argument his blood was up, and much else besides. They went down the footpath and climbed over the fence onto the embankment. There was no-one around – Defreitas didn't think they'd been seen. They went into the bushes: 'We'd done it there before.' He took off his leather jacket and spread it on the ground and they had sex.

'We weren't there long. I mean, it was a quick job. Truth to tell, I think she had her mind on other things. I think she was just . . .' he hesitated '. . . making sure of me. She'd got me mad, and now she was softening me up again.'

An echo in Slider's mind: stock-taking. Who had said that of Jennifer?

'And as soon as it was over,' Defreitas went on, 'she was up and off.' She had straightened her clothes and her hair, and they had walked back to the footbridge. 'She told me to go the other way – over the footbridge and down Wenhaston Road – in case anyone saw us. She went the other way, back to the square. She said she had someone else to see. I said at that time of night? Because it was about twenty to twelve by then. She just laughed and turned away. And that's the last time I saw her, until—'

Defreitas had gone straight home, arriving at about five to midnight. His wife was already in bed. He had washed, cleaned his teeth, and got in beside her and slept. His wife was not speaking to him the next morning, and he had got into work late for the early shift, which started at six; and so on his arrival had been sent straight round to the Old Rectory to discover the cold body of the woman he had inseminated warm only hours earlier.

Slider, furious as he was with the man, could sympathise with Defreitas in that ghastly situation.

In his rage, Porson towered like a demiglot. 'I find it totally incredulous that an officer of your experience could behave in such a way! Do you think you're some kind of special case, that you can just flaunt the rules whenever you feel like it?'

'No, sir.'

'No, sir? Is that all you've got to say? I don't think you realise the trouble you're in, Defreitas. Your lamentacious conduct has put this whole case in jeopardy. As to your career—'

Defreitas tried a few feeble words of defence. 'Sir, as far as my relationship with Jennifer Andrews is concerned—'

Porson, walking fast back and forth across the office, turned at the end of a width with such a jerk his hair visibly swivelled before his face caught up with it. 'Yes, and if this was twenty years ago, I'd have had something to say about that score, as well! It's incomprehensive to me that you could even contemplate an affair of that sort. When I joined the Job, a policeman had to be beyond repute, in his private life as well as on duty. The public demanded impeachable behaviour at all times, and for a married officer to have carnival knowledge of a woman other than his own wife would have been a disciplinary offence of the severest consequence, I can tell you!'

When the mute and miserable Defreitas had eventually been sent on his way, Porson signalled to Slider to shut the door, and, on a last little spurt of anger, walked another width and muttered, 'These young officers don't seem to learn anything! Think they can just carry on any way they please, as if the Job was just a job. That kind of attitude is a milestone round our necks. It's no wonder the public don't trust us!'

'What about disciplinary action, sir?'

'That's for Uniform to decide. Suspended pending investigation certainly. After that, I don't know. Not my providence, thank God. But I shall have to report, and I shall make a strong recommendation that he gets more than his knuckles rapped for concealing information. What's more to the impact, how does this affect the case?'

'It removes quite a bit of the evidence, or rather the suppositions, against Andrews. And of course it blows a hole through his confession – which was already a bit flimsy to my mind.'

'Yes, you never were happy with it, were you?' Porson stood still and looked straight at Slider. 'Do you think Defreitas did it?'

Slider looked straight back. 'No, sir.' He explained the questions which Defreitas as suspect would leave unanswered. 'We ought to be able to substantiate his story. They know him at the Goat, so they ought to be able to say when he arrived and left, and Karen, the barmaid, will probably remember the phone call.'

'That doesn't clear him of the murder.'

'No, sir. But even if Mrs Defreitas doesn't know exactly what time he came in, I think it's unlikely he could have got out of bed again in the middle of the night to go and move the body without her knowing. I think we can clear Defreitas all right. The infuriating thing is that we'll have to waste manpower doing it.'

Porson nodded. 'I'll see he gets his come-uppance, don't worry.'

'To my reasoning, Eddie Andrews is still our best suspect,' Slider went on. 'For one thing, putting the body in the trench – that only made sense for Andrews, who would be the one to fill the hole with concrete the next morning. For anyone else, putting her there wasn't hiding her, it just hastened discovery. And for another, there's this thing about making her face up again. It doesn't make sense. As an action, it's just bonkers. And who but Andrews would have been bonkers in that particular way about killing her?'

'But still, you don't think it was Andrews?' Porson asked cannily.

'It isn't that, sir,' Slider said. 'I don't see who else it could have been; but we just don't have enough evidence against him.'

'Well, there's still plenty of phone calls coming in.' Porson said philosophically. 'We'll have to let him go again, but if he did it, you'll find the evidence all right. And if it wasn't him, something will break sooner or later. Don't worry about it. You'll get there. I've got every confidence in you.'

Just when you think you've heard it all, Slider thought, the old man comes down all sensible and kind and touches your heart.

*   *   *

Back in his own room he found Atherton waiting for him. 'News?' Slider asked, reading his lieutenant's eye.

'Two of them,' Atherton said. 'The owner of the Transit that was parked just down from the footpath has come forward. Renker's checking him out, just to be absolutely sure, but it all looks perfectly innocent.'

'Oh, well, that clears up a point,' Slider said. 'What's the other?'

Atherton eyed him. 'I don't know if you'll like it. We've had a call from a long-distance lorry driver – bloke called Pat McAteer. He was driving an artic on Tuesday night – well, he'd been driving all day Tuesday, tacho notwithstanding, but we'd better not go into that if we want his co-operation. Anyway, he was heading for a ferry crossing on Wednesday morning and he'd got a bit ahead of his schedule so he pulled off the motorway to catch a couple of hours' sleep in his cab in a safe lay-by he knows on the A40. When he pulls into the lay-by he's not pleased to see someone else is there before him.'

'Don't tell me!'

'A light-coloured Ford pickup – light blue, he thinks. He's going to move on when he sees the driver's sleeping in the cab, so he reckons he's safe enough. He sets his alarm to wake himself in good time and gets into his bunk and goes to sleep. When he pulls out in the morning, the pickup's still there, and the bloke's still asleep.'

'Does he remember the number?'

'Enough of it. I suppose we'll have to check the other possible combinations through the PNC, but I'm willing to bet it was Eddie's all right.'

'Well, we knew he must have gone somewhere for the rest of the night,' Slider said. 'Get someone out there to check if there's an oil stain, and try and get a sample. Forensic may be able to match the oil from the pickup, to give us a bit of corroboration.' He read Atherton's face. 'All right, what's the catch? What time did McAteer arrive and what time did he leave?'

'He pulled into the lay-by at one o'clock, and he pulled out again at five. So you see the problem? We've got Eddie missing from just after eleven, when he left the First and Last, to about six forty-five when he turns up at the Rectory. Even driving like the clappers, it's going to take Eddie half an hour to get to the lay-by – three-quarters, really, in a pickup – and the same to get back.'

'So the alibi doesn't cover him for the actual time of the murder – supposed actual time.'

'Yes, but when would he have had time to lay out the body? Suppose he fell upon her the instant she left Defreitas, at eleven forty-five; give him fifteen minutes to do the murdering, he's only got an hour to conceal the body and get back to the lay-by.'

'And we know she wasn't put straight into the trench,' Slider said. 'She was left sitting up somewhere for a couple of hours. Of course, she could have been sitting up in the back of the pickup.'

'So we've got two possibilities,' Atherton said. 'Either Eddie slept in the cab until, say, two a.m., drove back to the Rectory – quarter to three – shifted the body, laid it out, did the makeup – got to allow an hour for that – quarter to four – and then drove back—'

'To the *same* lay-by—'

'Arriving at half past four in order to be seen by the lorry driver at five, and then slept, or pretended to sleep, until six when he left to go back to work in order to fill in the trench – which is physically possible—'

'And which is pure Vaudeville.'

'Or he was there and asleep in his cab between one and five—'

'Which means he wasn't the murderer, and we've got to start all over again from nothing,' Slider said glumly.

'Even William Hill wouldn't give you odds on that,' Atherton said. 'As Mr Porson would say, it's back to the drawing-pin.'

Atherton volunteered to give Slider a lift home.

'Haven't you got a date, or anything?' Slider asked.

'Not even anything. But you shouldn't have to ask that. Don't you know Sue's doing Milton Keynes as well as Joanna?'

'Oh,' said Slider, unsure whether that was a snub or not. He sat quietly for a bit, watching Atherton from the corner of his eye as he drove. Atherton drove well and stylishly, as he did most things – perhaps a little on the generous side when it came to accelerating and braking, but that was the way of youth. As a long-term married man Slider had got used to thinking of Atherton as younger than he actually was. But his age was showing in his face now, after the trauma of his wounding. The portrait had been brought down from the attic: he would probably never get back that fine careless rapture.

Slider wondered what the score was between him and Sue. His last answer might have been a snub, or an irony, or a revelation of the truth; but Slider was naturally delicate of enquiring into a colleague's personal life. Then he thought, What the hell? He can always tell me to mind my own business.

'So is it on again between you and Sue?' he asked, as unprovocatively as he could.

Atherton swivelled an eye briefly. 'What do you care?' It was said flippantly, not with rancour.

'Self-defence. She's Joanna's friend. If you upset her, she'll complain to Jo, and Jo will come down on me for damages.'

'Bollocks. Just admit you're nosy.'

'Don't tell me,' Slider said, looking ostentatiously out of the window. 'I wouldn't listen now if you begged me.'

After a moment, Atherton said, 'We're going out again. How serious it is I don't know yet.' All the flippancy had dropped from his delivery, and the sudden stripping away of defences made Slider nervous. There was a balance and a distance that had to be maintained between working colleagues. Once he and Atherton had kept it effortlessly, but since Joanna, and particularly since the wounding, it had been shifting about like a sand dune on fast forward. Unsure of its present position, Slider didn't say anything; and into the silence, like any victim of interview-technique, Atherton gave more. 'I missed her. Even before I got wounded. God knows why. I mean, she's not glamorous or exciting—' Slider glanced at him, and he interpreted it easily enough. 'That's always been a minimum requirement. After all, I have a reputation to keep up,' he protested.

'You're not that shallow,' said Slider.

'Don't over-estimate me,' Atherton said with a touch of bitterness. 'I have been just that shallow. And don't forget you can drown in an inch of water.'

That sounded so profound they both had to think about it for a moment.

Then Atherton resumed. 'All those weeks in hospital gave me time to think. I'd always been so terrified of getting involved, but I remembered you saying to me once that there was no alternative, that if you weren't involved you weren't anything.'

'Did I? I'm hardly one to dish out advice.'

'No, you're right. Whatever you get wrong,' and his tone suggested it was legion, 'you're in there, facing the balls.'

'Eh?'

'At the crease. Batting. I thought you'd like a cricketing analogy.'

'This conversation is getting weird,' Slider said. 'Just tell me how come you got in touch with Sue again.'

'I wanted to see her,' Atherton said simply, and then added with deeper honesty, 'I was peeved. I thought she ought to have been more attentive, considering my plight. And I thought, considering what a fabulous catch I was, she ought to chase me a bit. That's what I'm used to. When Joanna said that with Sue I had to make the running, I thought, Dream on, Phyllis! But when I managed to disengage the ego for a bit, I decided I might just give it a try.' He grimaced. 'Anything for a new experience.'

'She's a nice person,' Slider said, ignoring the self-mockery. This was serious, he could see.

'She is,' Atherton agreed. 'And she's seen me at my worst. That's a comfort.'

'And since she's not glamorous and exciting, you don't have to be on your mettle all the time,' Slider suggested.

Atherton looked hurt. 'That was a bit blunt. You really do think I'm shallow.'

'Spot of irony,' Slider said. 'As it happens, I think she probably is exciting. I mean, look at Joanna.'

'Yes,' Atherton said, accepting the shorthand. There was a silence while he eased round a right-turner who wanted to occupy the whole road, and then he went on. 'When I was wounded, I lost a sort of – integrity. That maniac made a hole in me – literally and figuratively. My shell wasn't whole and perfect any more.'

'Yes,' Slider said. He couldn't have put it into words, but he knew what he meant.

'I'm afraid,' Atherton admitted starkly, 'and I hate it. *Hate* it!

I feel as if something's been taken away from me, and I resent it like hell.' He paused, and went on in a different voice, 'And then, I missed her, and I can't afford to cope with that as well as everything else.' He glanced sideways again. 'These days I see you looking at me, wondering if I'm going to make it.'

'I don't—' Slider began, but Atherton stopped him.

'You do, but it's all right; I wonder too.'

'You'll make it,' Slider said, with a great deal more certainty than he felt. He wasn't always sure about himself, let alone his damaged companion.

'But I don't think I can do it on my own. Not any more.'

'Well,' Slider said again, 'she's a nice person.'

Atherton smiled privately at this concluding benediction. His boss might just as well have said, 'You have my blessing to proceed.' Bill had never had much facility in expressing emotions, and with Joanna was having painfully to learn a whole new language. Atherton, on the other hand, had always had all the words, an easy, sparkling stream of them; now he was going to have to learn to put his money where his mouth was.

'But nothing worth having was ever achieved without effort,' he concluded aloud. Slider grunted agreement without questioning of what the comment was apropos.

When they reached the flat, Slider invited Atherton in for a drink, and finding that they were both hungry, rummaged through the kitchen and offered the old standby bread and cheese. Atherton looked at the bread and the cheese and quickly offered to make them both Welsh rarebit, which he did the proper, painstaking way, melting the cheese in a pan and adding mustard and Worcestershire sauce before pouring it over the toast and grilling it. While all this was going on and Slider sat on the edge of the kitchen table watching, they both sipped a handsome-looking Glenmorangie with a beer chaser, and talked about the case.

'Now that Defreitas has made a complete Jackson Pollock of the evidence,' Atherton said, 'and Eddie's turned out to have an alibi, I suppose it puts Meacher up as prime suspect. There's this story about him chasing some other woman, a rich one. But if Jennifer was about to queer his pitch with some serious money, that's a good enough motive to kill her, if he's really the creep you think he is.'

'But he's got an alibi.'

'Not much of one. The girl would obviously say anything she was told to, but a little judicious – or even judicial – pressure might change that. Effectively, he's not accountable for most of the evening and all of the night.'

Slider shifted restlessly. 'But most of the same objections apply to Meacher as suspect as to anyone else. We're not just trying to find someone to nail this to, we're trying to find out what really happened.'

'Hey,' Atherton said, wounded, 'it's me.'

Slider made a gesture of acknowledgement, and went on thinking aloud. 'There's the problem of the makeup. How would the murderer do the retouching out of doors and in the dark?'

'Maybe that's why it was done clumsily,' Atherton said.

'It wasn't *that* clumsy. Most men couldn't do it that well in a barber's chair under a spotlight.'

'Well, what about in someone's car? You know that most drugs are bought, sold and ingested in cars: it's the new privacy. So why not murder? You'd have interior light to do the making-up by.'

'Well, it's a possibility,' Slider said.

'A bare one, by the tone of your voice,' Atherton complained. 'Here I am thinking my heart out for you—'

'Well, look, if she was smothered without a struggle, she must have been drugged in some way, and how was that to be done? You don't suddenly produce a pill when you're out for a walk in the country and say, "Here, swallow this." Or even,' he anticipated Atherton's rider, 'sitting in a car.'

'All right, then, maybe it was done indoors,' Atherton said. 'There are other houses in the world than Eddie's. And we don't actually *know* it wasn't at Eddie's. It's just that we've no evidence it was.'

'But then you've got the problem – which applies to any house – of hauling the body out and getting it across to the Rectory, and I can't believe no-one would notice.'

'People don't notice things like anything, all the time, every day of the week,' Atherton pointed out.

Slider shook his head. 'The thing that's really bugging me, I suppose, is that even if no-one noticed at the loading-up end, and even if the Rectory neighbours didn't notice the vehicle driving up and the crunching feet over the gravel, I can't believe all that activity went on on the terrace in the dead of night without the dog barking. That dog's on a hair-trigger.'

Atherton pulled out the grill pan to inspect progress, and pushed it back in to bubble some more. The kitchen was filling with the delicious aroma of roasting cheese, and he kept expecting to feel Oedipus's solid body pressing against his legs in the ritual food gyration. Oedipus was particularly fond of cheese: quite a Cheshire cat, he thought.

'And yet,' Slider continued with a frown, 'that's precisely what did happen. Whoever put the body into the hole, the dog didn't bark in the night.'

'Don't go all Sherlock Holmes on me,' Atherton said. 'Maybe they just didn't hear it. People with yappy dogs can learn to shut out the noise – like people living by a railway not hearing the trains.'

'It isn't exactly a yappy dog. And it's supposed to be a guard dog: would anyone ignore the barking of a guard dog, especially in the night?'

'It's possible they simply didn't hear it,' Atherton said reasonably. 'Mr Dacre said he slept well that night for a change, so presumably he needed the sleep. Maybe he even took something to help him.'

'Mrs Hammond says she's a light sleeper. And she said she didn't sleep well that night. If the dog had barked, surely she would have heard it?'

'People who say they don't sleep actually sleep a lot more than they think – it's a proven fact. It's a peculiar form of vanity, to claim not to sleep,' he diverged. 'As though sleeping were something rather gross and common. Like those nineteenth-century ladies who prided themselves on never eating, and fainted all the time to show how refined they were. In any case,' he reverted robustly, pulling out the grill pan again, '*que voulez vous*? There are only two possibilities, aren't there? Either the dog didn't bark, or they didn't hear it.'

'Some help you are,' Slider said.

They carried the supper through to the sitting room to eat. Atherton made free with Joanna's sound system and put on Brahms' fourth symphony, because that's what the women were playing at Milton Keynes that evening, and he thought it might give them sympathetic vibrations and improve his chances for later.

Slider said, 'If it was Meacher, or anybody else come to that, *why* would he put the body in the hole? It doesn't make sense for anyone other than Eddie Andrews. It's *got* to be Eddie, even if it can't be.'

Atherton sat with his plate and glass and stretched out his legs. 'Let it go, now. You've got to learn to switch off, or you'll burn yourself out.'

'That's what I've always told you, about women,' Slider said, with a slow smile.

'That's better,' Atherton said approvingly. 'Just forget about it for a few hours. We've probably missed something glaringly obvious, and the subconscious will chuck it out if we leave it alone. You'll wake up in the morning knowing everything from aardvark to zymosis.'

'Tomorrow,' Slider said. 'Oh, Nora, Joanna's going to take my car again.'

Atherton raised his eyebrows. 'Bad move,' he said. 'You know there's a tube strike tomorrow? And some of the buses are probably coming out in sympathy.'

'*Bloody* Nora.' Slider upped the stakes. Of course, that would be why she had to have the car. Why hadn't he remembered?

'There you are,' Atherton said, watching his face, 'counter-irritant. A nice go of toothache to take your mind off your headache.'

The solution to the transport problem turned out to be an early call to the AA while Joanna, having inspected the breadless kitchen cupboards, departed in Slider's car for Henry Wood Hall near enough to the crack of dawn to be able to stop for breakfast somewhere on the way. Slider made a few phone calls and tried to let his mind lie fallow so as to let the back-burner syndrome take effect. He had woken no closer to making sense of the senseless than he had gone to sleep.

The AA man arrived unexpectedly soon, and Slider hurried out to unlock the car for him. He was a young, burly and immensely cheerful man, who when Slider apologised for the early call, said, 'No worries, mate, I'd sooner this than the middle of the night trying to work in the dark.' But his demeanour suggested he'd have been just as cheerful at midnight in December. Slider envied him such a robust disposition.

He tried it first and checked the fuel gauge. 'Just in case,' he said. 'How are you for petrol? Quarter full, that's okay. You'd be surprised how often I get called out and all it is, there's no petrol in the tank. Not just women, either.'

He put up the bonnet of Joanna's Alfa and dived in with enthusiasm, while Slider hung about and looked over his shoulder like an auntie in the kitchen. They were watched through the window of the van by a large mongrel that plainly featured collie and Dobermann amongst its varied ancestors.

'The wife feels happier if I've got him with me, the lonely stretches of road we get called to sometimes,' the patrolman said, in answer to Slider's conversational query. 'He loves it, out and about all the time. I don't approve of leaving a dog shut up in the house all day. It's not fair on them.'

Slider agreed absently. 'Good guard dog, is he?'

'If anyone tried to mess with me or the motor,' the man said elliptically, looking back over his shoulder at the intent face at the window. 'One-man dog, that one,' he added proudly. 'I'm the only person who can do anything with him.'

'Oh?' Slider said, and grew very still, thought taking hold of him. Further conversation went over his head, and he barely even noticed when the engine jumped at last to life, following a delicate mechanical operation, involving a judicious whack on the starter-motor with a hammer.

The AA man slammed the bonnet down and said, 'Well, that'll tide you over for a bit, but I don't promise anything. It could go again any time. You really want to get that starter-motor replaced.'

'I will. Thanks. Thanks a lot. I've really got to dash now, but I'm very grateful to you.'

'S'all right. All part of the job, squire,' the AA man said easily.

CHAPTER FIFTEEN

Alf The Sacred

He drove to St Michael Square, deep in thought. The square was quiet, basking in the young sunshine at the innocent time of day when workers have departed, non-workers are still indoors, and intentions, good and bad, are only just waking up. He parked round at the end of the church and stepped out to stand leaning on the railings, hoping inspiration would strike. It was cool in the shadow of the tower, but across from the churchyard, the odd but mellow façade of the Old Rectory was warm with sunlight. Squint up a bit, he thought, and you could be in a village. A brisk dog, trotting on its rounds, smiled up at him as it passed; all that was wanted was the schoolmistress on a bicycle and the village bobby on his beat. Not that that was how he remembered his own village life as a child. Perhaps he had grown up through a rainy decade, but his images of childhood in Essex were chiefly of mud: lanes, yards, fields of it, as far as the eye could see; cows plastered with it, hens sodden with it, wellies clogged with it; football boots weighted with it, welding tired junior legs to a school pitch like the Somme; passing tractors on the road chucking great homicidal gouts of the stuff at your head from between the lugs of their tyres. His mother had waged a lifelong, losing battle to keep the tide of mud from invading the house. Her life, he thought, was the microcosm of the struggle of civilisation: an endless fight to keep out the forces of chaos. It was why he had become a policeman, really – that and the recruiting-sergeant's promise of all the women he could eat.

The evocative clang of a heavy wrought-iron gate was transmitted through the railings to his hand, and he roused himself to see an old man in a flat cap, collarless white shirt with the sleeves rolled up, elderly grey flannel trousers and stout army-surplus boots, just leaving the churchyard from the gate on the side that faced the old Rectory. He held a large metal ring on which a number and variety of keys were hung, and now fumbled for one with which to lock the churchyard gate. Slider went round and accosted him.

The old man turned sharply, but seemed reassured by the look of Slider, and said pleasantly, 'Hello! Where did you pop up from?' while he went on locking the gate.

'I've just parked over there. Detective Inspector Slider.' Slider showed his brief, and the old man inspected it with watery blue eyes, nodded, and then slowly dragged out a handkerchief and blew his nose thoroughly, ending up with several wipes, exploratory sniffs, and a general polishing of the end, before restoring the handkerchief to his trousers.

'I suppose you're looking into this business about Mrs Andrews,' he concluded. 'Shocking! Is that right she was done away with?'

'It seems that way,' Slider said. 'I see you have the keys to the church.'

'Who else should have 'em?' he said, straightening up as though coming to attention. 'Sexton, me. Alf Whitton's the name.' He inspected his palm to see if it was fit for the task, and then offered it to Slider. Slider usually avoided shaking hands with the public, but there was something beguiling about the man and the gesture, and he took the dry, horny palm and shook it briefly. 'Just been sweeping up,' Whitton added, jerking his head towards the church. 'She don't get so dirty this dry weather, but she do get get dusty. Mondays I sweep, even when there's not been a service the Sunday; Tuesdays I does the woodwork – dust and polish.'

'There must be a lot of work in keeping a church like this nice,' Slider said sympathetically.

'Oh, there is, there is,' he said eagerly, 'but I don't mind it. I learned all about spit an' polish in the army, and there's a kind of rhythm to cleaning, a knack, if you like. Satisfying, it is, seeing things come up. Brass and silver especially: it's 'ard work, but the results are lovely. There's a brass lectern in there, shape of an eagle. All feathers! Cuh!' He jerked his head and lifted his eyes to demonstrate the difficulties of cleaning brazen birds of prey. 'But it comes up a treat when it's done. I been looking after this 'ere church for forty years, give or take,' he went on, casting an affectionate eye over his shoulder at the grave, grey tower.

'I should think they're lucky to have you,' Slider said warmly.

He looked pleased. 'Sexton of her and St Melitus's, but it's her I like best. Otherwise I wouldn't've taken on the cleaning, not at my age. Used to have a cleaner, up till five year ago, then they said they couldn't afford to pay for one any more. Couldn't *justify* it, they said,' he added, as though it were a particularly nauseating weasel-word – which perhaps it was. 'Well, I couldn't stand to see her get grubby and sad, like I seen so many churches, so I said I'd do it. Keep her lovely, I do, though I says it as shouldn't. But I wouldn't do it for no-one else. I don't clean St Melitus's,' he said sternly, in case Slider got the wrong idea.

'You seem to keep very fit on it,' Slider said.

Whitton jutted his white-bristled chin and slapped himself in the chest. 'Eighty-two come September. How about that?'

'Marvellous!'

'And I still keep the graves, *and* stoke the boiler in winter. Not that that's a job I like. Messy stuff, coke, and I never did like being down the crypt. Reminds me too much of air-raid shelters. Don't like cellars and tunnels and such.'

Where Alf the sacred cleaner ran, through caverns measureless to man, thought Slider. Eighty-two and still shovelling it – they bred 'em tough before the war.

'Wouldn't mind someone younger taking over the boiler, but where you going to find one?' Alf went on. 'Young people today weren't brought up to service like you and me was. Never think of nothing but themselves.'

'If you've been sexton here all that time, you must know a lot of people hereabouts.'

'Course I do,' he said smartly. 'Know everyone in the square, and the church, all the congregation, the council. Seen 'em come and go. Eight vicars we've had here since I been sexton. It's the trufe! And everyone knows me, what's more. Knew Jennifer Andrews, if that's what you're working up to. Want to have a little chat with me about it, do you?'

'Yes, if you don't mind.'

He smacked his lips. 'Can't talk with a dry mouth. Want to come in and have a cup of tea?'

'In?' Slider queried. In the church, did he mean?

'My house,' Whitton said, gesturing across the road.

Slider looked blank. 'You live nearby, do you?'

'Church Cottage, next to the Rectory,' he said patiently, gesturing again.

Now Slider twigged. He meant the small cottage next door on the left of the Old Rectory. 'You're the missing householder!'

'How's that?'

'We tried to interview everyone in the square, but we never got a reply from your house, so we thought you were away, on holiday or something.'

'Away? I don't go away. Prob'ly wasn't in. I'm not in much – here and there, doing little jobs.'

'We tried in the evening, too.'

'I like to go to the pub of an evening. And even if I'm in, I don't answer the door. Not at night. Never know who it might be.'

'And you don't have a telephone.'

'Never have had,' Whitton said triumphantly. 'Never felt the need.'

'So how do people ever manage to get hold of you?' Slider asked in frustration. 'Suppose someone had an urgent message?'

'Oh, I'm here and there and round about. People know where to find me. You managed all right,' he pointed out.

Slider gave it up, and followed the old man across the road to the cottage. In contrast to the baking day outside, it was dark and cold inside Church Cottage, and smelt strongly of damp and faintly of dog. The door opened directly onto the sitting room, which was dominated by a large fireplace with a fire of logs and paper in it made up ready to light. There was a massive beam over the fireplace, which supported a mess of ornaments, knick-knacks, letters, bills, photographs and assorted small junk, and a door beside it which Slider guessed would conceal the stairs to the upper floor. The low ceiling was also beamed, the plaster between them stained richly ochre by years of smoke – an effect refurbished pubs paid decorators large sums to replicate. For the rest there was a thin and ancient carpet on the floor, two old armchairs covered in imitation leather from the fifties flanking the fire, and a portable television on an aspidistra stand. Under the window was a small table covered by a lace cloth on which stood a birdcage containing a blue budgie. It whistled as they came in, but then fell silent, looking rather depressed. The window was small and heavily draped in nets which kept out most of the light, so Slider was not surprised.

'That's Billy,' Whitton said, noting Slider's look. 'He's company for me, since my old dog died. I'd like another dog, but I haven't got the time to train a puppy, and I don't fancy someone else's leavings.' He chirruped at the bird, but it just sat there glumly, shoulders hunched, like someone waiting for a bus in the rain.

Whitton led the way through the open door on the other side of the fireplace to the kitchen, evidently the only other downstairs room. It was a narrow room, lino-floored and defiantly unreconstructed: an earthenware sink with an enamel drainer and a cold tap, a geyser on the wall above for hot water, one of those 1950s cupboards with the flap in the middle that lets down to make a work surface, and on a home-made shelf beside it an electric kettle and a double gas-ring.

There was also a wooden kitchen table and two chairs, drawn up under the window. Whitton gestured Slider towards it. 'Have a seat, while I put the kettle on. I mostly sit in here in the summer, when I don't have the fire going. It's brighter.'

It was. Slider sat as requested, and looked out through the window at a neat square of garden, gay with flowers. Where the Rectory's plot went all the way down to the railway, Whitton's extended a mere twenty feet, ending in a high fence over the top of which could be seen the walls and roofs of some natty new little one-size-fits-all houses. 'Your bedders look very nice. Are you a keen gardener?' Slider asked, convensationally.

Whitton turned from his kettle activities with a bitter look. 'Used to be. Nothing to be keen *with*, now. Used to go all the way down to the bottom, my garden. Fruit, vegetables, apple and pear trees. Lovely chrysanthemums, I used to grow. Potting shed down the bottom. Greenhouse. And a little bit of a wall I grew figs against. You like figs?'

'Yes.'

'All gone now. Sold the land, they did, for development. Cuh! Call that development? Rabbit hutches! I said to them, I seen that kind of development in a dead bird I found under a hedge. Developed into a maggot farm, it had.'

'They sold your garden without your permission?'

'Belongs to the Church, this cottage. They can do what they want. Oh, I got advice,' he added, seeing Slider's concern. 'I asked Mr Dacre what he thought, and he asked Mr Meacher, the estate-agent man, to look into it for me, but it turned out I didn't have any right to use the land. I didn't understand the ins and outs of it, but that was how it was in the Law. Mr Dacre's a proper gentleman. He wouldn't put me wrong.'

It had led very nicely to the subject. 'You've known him for a long time, I suppose?'

'Oh, yes. He's an important person around these parts – practically like the local squire, if you take my meaning. Lived here all his life. His dad bought the Old Rectory from the church when they built the new one in eighteen ninety or thereabouts – that's that big house on the other side of the square, with the bay windows. Course, they've sold that now, too. Vicar's got a new house opp'site St Melitus's. Sell everything in the end, the Church will,' he added gloomily.

'So Mr Dacre was born in the Old Rectory?'

'That's right,' he said, milking the tea. 'Only son, he was, and with his father dying when he was only a boy – died of the Spanish flu, just after the First World War – he come into the house then, so to speak, so he never needed to move away. Three older sisters, he had: they all married and went. Then it was just him and his mother. I remember her – she died in, what, 'thirty-six it must have been.' He put a cup down in front of Slider and sat with his own opposite. 'Real hatchet-faced woman she was! What I'd call a Victorian matron, if you get my drift. Tongue like a razor blade. And everything had to be just so. Even used to tell the rector off – it was a rector we had then. Used to criticise his sermons.' He chuckled at the memory. '"My husband was a literary figure," she used to say, "so I know what I'm talking about." He was in publishing, Mr Dacre's dad – had his own company. Mr Dacre's a writer, did you know that?'

'Yes, I did,' said Slider.

'I suppose that's why he went in for it. Went to university at Oxford, and then started writing books and everything, and got famous straight off.' He shook his head in wonder at such cleverness. 'Got married straight off, too, to a very pretty young lady, and they had a little boy. 'Thirty-two or -three, he was born. Gor, Mr Dacre doted on that kid! Frank, his name was.'

'So he's Mrs Hammond's brother?'

'Half-brother. I'll tell you how it was. Terrible sad thing. Mrs Dacre had this message that her dad had been took queer and took to hospital. Winter of nineteen forty, that must've been. Anyway, she went over to see him. They lived in South London,' he added, in the same tone of voice that he might have mentioned Zanzibar or Bogota. 'So she's on her way back when the air-raid siren goes off, and she goes down the tube to shelter. That was the night Balham tube station took a direct hit. A bomb goes right through to the tunnel. Sixty people killed. Terrible.'

'I've read something about it,' Slider said.

'And the worst thing, so Mr Dacre always said to me, was that her dad wasn't even really bad. They thought he was having 'eart-attack, but it turned out to be just his stomach turning him up. He had one of them drastic ulcers. By the time she got there, he was getting dressed to go home. So she needn't've gone.' He shook his head. 'Ironic, Mr Dacre always said it was. He said God must have a funny sense of humour. He used to talk to me a lot when he was on the council. Tell me all sorts of things. People like him think people like me are a safe pair of ears. Truth to tell, I think they think we don't understand half what's said to us.'

Another insight. Slider wondered whether that accounted for his own confidability. 'So Mr Dacre married a second time?'

'That's right. Near on right away it was. Well, he was always an impulsive one. Young Frank got that from him. Anyway, he married a nurse he met at the hospital where they took Mrs Dacre's body. Margery, her name was. Ever such a nice lady, but not glamorous – older than him – very quiet and shy. Not shy, but—' He groped for a word.

'Self-effacing?' Slider hazarded.

'That's it. Like that. I suppose he thought she'd be a good mother for young Frank. Anyway, she was Mrs Hammond's mother. Born in 'forty-two, Mrs Hammond was, so you can see Mr Dacre didn't waste any time.'

'And they called her Frances as well,' Slider mused.

'That's right. It was a bit of a rum do, that was. To tell the truth,' he leaned forward confidentially across the table, 'I think he regretted marrying the second Mrs Dacre because, nice as she was, she wasn't his class, and, like I said, not glamorous. But, well, when a man's in a state like that, it's easy to fall for a nurse. And the uniforms they used to wear in them days, with them big white head-things like nuns—'

'Hard to resist.'

'That's right. But then, of course, when he got her home and woke up, like, from the dream, he was stuck with her. A gentleman like him wouldn't go back on his word, and divorce just wasn't done in them days. And then when she has her baby, it turns out to be a girl – which Mr Dacre's got no use for daughters anyway. So *I* think he named her after young Frank, just to put the second Mrs Dacre in her place.'

Some gentleman, Slider thought. But it was throwing an interesting light on the domestic set-up at the Old Rectory. 'So he was never very fond of Mrs Hammond?'

'I don't think he knew she existed when she was a little kid. Well, her ma kept her quiet, and there was young Frank, you see. He came first in everything. Mind you, he was a smashing kid. Handsome lad, full of fun. Clever, too. Always up to something.' He looked across into Slider's eyes. 'Don't you think sometimes that youngsters like that are marked out to die young? Everything golden about them – too good to last. You know what I mean?'

'Like spring sunshine,' Slider said.

Whitton seemed struck by that. 'That's it. You said it. Just like that. Spring sunshine.' He dreamed a little.

'What happened to him?'

'Smashed himself up on a motorbike. His dad had just bought it for him – Frank wheedled him into it, because Mr Dacre didn't like the idea. Not because of the danger, but because he didn't want his lad mixing with all them rock-and-rollers and teddy-boys. Then the first time he takes it out – woof. Gone. He was only twenty. I don't think Mr Dacre ever really got over that.'

Another instance of God's funny sense of humour? 'It ought to have made him fonder of the child he had left,' Slider suggested.

'*Ought* to of,' Whitton agreed economically. 'Another cup?'

'If there is.'

'I can always add a bit more water. Well,' he said, heaving himself up, 'after that it was all downhill, as the saying goes. Mr Dacre buried himself in his writing, and Mrs Dacre, Mrs Hammond's mum, and Mrs Hammond, not that she was married then, of course, they looked after him. It was a queer set-up,' he mused, as the kettle came back to the boil. 'You'd have thought they were the housekeeper and the parlourmaid, rather than his wife and daughter. Oh, I never offered you a biscuit.'

'No, thanks, not for me. Tell me about Mrs Hammond getting married.'

'Wait'll I do the tea.' He brought back the refilled cups and sat down again, his face alight with the pleasure of having someone to tell the story to. 'Well,' he began with relish, 'that was a queer thing, too. How it happened was this: one of Mr Dacre's sisters died, and he was the whatjercallit for her will and that.'

'Executor?'

'That's right. Anyway, she had this big house, which Mr Dacre had to sell, and he put it with this posh estate agents, and the person they sent round to deal with it was David Meacher – you know him?'

'Yes, of course. Mrs Andrews worked for him. I've talked to him about her.'

'Course you have. Well, selling the house turns out to be a complicated business, and he's around a lot, and Mr Dacre seems to take a shine to him, and he becomes like a family friend. Wormed his way in, I shouldn't wonder,' Whitton added with disapproval.

'You don't like him?'

'Not for me to like or not like, but he strikes me as smarmy. Anyway, he introduces this friend, Gerald Hammond, that he was at school with, and before you know where you are this Mr Hammond's asking Mr Dacre for his daughter's hand in marriage, which Mr Dacre don't hesitate to say yes.'

'Why did he do that, I wonder?'

'Why? To get her off his hands, o' course. Well, she was pushing thirty by then.'

'I mean, why did Hammond want to marry her? Was he in love?'

'After her money, if you ask me. It must have been a big shock when he found she didn't have any. No, to be fair, she was pretty, but very, well, mousy. Well, you know what she's like now, and she was never any different. Wouldn't say boo. How could she, brought up like she was? Still, I expect Mr Hammond thought Mr Dacre would part with some money for his only daughter, not realising he couldn't care tuppence for her. I do know that later on he asked Mr Dacre to invest some money in his business – Mr Hammond did – and Mr Dacre said no. Quite a row there was about it, Mrs Hammond told me. And it was soon after that that Mr Hammond run off with this young girl to South Africa. Sold the business and took every bit of money, and even sold the house without telling Mrs Hammond. She'd have been homeless with her two little boys, if Mr Dacre hadn't invited her to come back home.'

'That was kind of him.'

'Well, it was really, I suppose. But he hasn't suffered by it, because Mrs Dacre was never a well woman and she was ailing by then, poor thing, so Mrs Hammond was able to take over running the house, and when her mother got really bad, she looked after her as well.'

'Living at the far end of the house,' Slider murmured.

'That's right,' Whitton nodded. 'Her and the boys in the servants' end of the house, and her ma and pa right the other end. And if ever the boys made a noise, or broke anything, or played ball in the garden, there was an almighty row, and poor Mrs Hammond in tears in the kitchen, which I've seen with my own eyes on more than one occasion. But still, she owed everything to her father, and there was nowhere else she could go, never having earned her living in her life. I mean, women like that, they can't get on without a man, can they?'

'No,' said Slider; and he thought briefly, painfully of Irene. Thank God for Ernie Newman – and who'd have thought he would ever say that? But if there were no Ernie in the case, he would have had to support Irene for the rest of her life, whatever the courts said, because she, like Mrs Hammond, had never earned her living. She had been promised as a child that if she was good, she would get married and never have to, and it wasn't her fault that history had overtaken her.

'It was different for her boys, of course. Harry and Jack

– nice youngsters, and clever. As soon as they could, they left home.'

'You'd have thought Mr Dacre would be fond of them. His only grandchildren – and they're boys, not girls.'

'Ah, but they're Hammonds, you see, not Dacres. They're not Frank's boys.' He drained his cup, wiped his lips, and sighed. 'You got to feel sorry for Mrs Hammond, really. Her husband gone and her mother gone and now her boys gone, stuck there looking after her father, and he's no company for her. And now he's on the way out, poor gentleman. It just shows you, money can't buy you happiness nor health.'

'I suppose he *is* well off?' Slider asked cautiously.

'Oh, yes, rich as treacle. Well, there's his books, and he had a share in his dad's company. And then there was money the first Mrs Dacre left him, and I heard tell his sister, that he was whatsisname for, she left him a lot. And there's the house, o' course. That must be worth a bit nowadays.'

'And will it all go to Mrs Hammond?'

He shook his head. 'I couldn't tell you on that score. He's never cared for her, and I've never heard she'd been promised anything. But when it comes right down to it, who else is there? I reckon she'll come in for it. For the house, at least, because he's always been keen for it to stay in the family. Hates the idea of selling it.'

'It is a lovely house.'

'D'you think so? Can't see it, myself. If I had that sort o' money, I'd buy a nice modern place. Mind you, some old places I can see the beauty of, though it's not what I'd want. But the Old Rectory – well, it's neither fish nor fowl to my mind. And it's not been a lucky house for Mr Dacre. You wouldn't think he'd be so attached to it. I mean, even his last days are going to be upset with all this business over Mrs Andrews.'

'I gather Mr Dacre didn't like her?'

'Well, he wouldn't. She was common, was Mrs Andrews – not Mr Dacre's sort at all. And thick-skinned. She never knew when she wasn't wanted. You couldn't freeze her out, or give her a hint. I've heard Mr Dacre at church give her a set-down, real cutting-like, and she's not even known it was one. Took it for a compliment. She thought everyone was mad for her company.'

'She went to the Rectory a lot?'

Whitton assented. 'Sucking up. She always wanted to be in with the nobs. They used to give parties, before Mr Dacre got ill, musical evenings in that big hall, and garden parties in the summer on the terrace, and his posh friends would come. She'd have died to get invited, would Mrs Andrews. That's why she got herself in at the church, because Mr Dacre and Mrs Hammond is both church people, and the vicar and some of the others on the council got invited to the house, and she thought she could get in on their back. And, of course, being Christians, the church couldn't refuse her when she said she wanted to help. Didn't get her invited to parties, but now she thinks she's so well in she just calls round when she likes anyway.'

'Or she did until last Tuesday,' Slider corrected.

He opened his faded eyes in comic alarm. 'Deary me, I was forgetting for a minute! Yes, and her visit there must have been nigh on the last she ever made anywhere.'

'Her visit there when?' Slider asked.

'Tuesday night. Quarter to midnight, just after, I see her go in. The quarter struck as I was coming up the steps from the crypt. I'd been—'

Slider leaned forward. 'Wait, wait, you're telling me you saw Jennifer Andrews going into the Old Rectory last Tuesday night?'

'The night she was murdered. Like I'm telling you. I was on my way home from the pub when I stopped off to check everything was locked up, which I always do, because you can't trust anyone these days. And then I went down the crypt to check how much coke we had, because I remembered vicar had give me a leaflet from the coal merchants saying there was a big discount if we ordered our winter fuel now, and he asked me to see if there was room to get any more in, and if there was, to order it, so I thought as I was there I'd have a look and then I could order it the next morning. So then I come up again and locked the crypt behind me, and as I turned round I saw Mrs Andrews just skipping across the parking place beside the house and round to the back door.'

'You're sure it was her?'

'Course it was. D'you think I don't know Mrs Andrews after all this time? And I remember thinking the next day when I

heard about her being found dead that I must have been one
of the last to see her, barring Mrs Hammond and Mr Dacre.
And her husband, of course.'

'Her husband?'

'Eddie Andrews, the murdering swine. Well, he must have
been the last, if he killed her, mustn't he? But I suppose you
don't count that. Poor creature. I didn't like her, but I don't
hold with that, not with murdering her.'

Slider thought of all the hours they'd spent trying to trace
the woman's footsteps that fatal evening. 'Why didn't you tell
us this before?' he asked, with strained patience.

'You never asked,' Whitton said indignantly. 'I thought someone would come and ask me questions, me having known all
the people in it, but no-one did until now.'

'No-one could catch you in.'

'Well, they could've come and found me, couldn't they? I'm
out and about all day, and anyone could've told you where I
was. Anyway,' he went on reasonably, 'I don't see it makes
any difference. Mr Dacre and Mrs Hammond will've told you
all about it already. I know you've been to see them.'

'Of course,' said Slider. 'There is that.'

Eileen Rogan, the physiotherapist, was an athletic-looking girl,
trim of figure, nicely tanned, and with such wonderfully clear
skin it looked like exceptionally delicate eggshell china with a
light behind it. Her hair, short and dark in a pageboy bob, shone
and bounced with health like one of those irritating shampoo
ads, and the whites of her eyes were so clean they looked blue.
At the sight of her all the late nights, bad food, excesses and
bodily neglects of Slider's life coagulated in his veins, rusted up
his joints, and withered his brain. He felt like a cross between the
Straw Man and the Tin Man. He could feel his face wrinkling
and his hair greying as they spoke, like She after the ill-advised
second bath.

'I understand you want to know something about Mr Dacre?'
Miss Rogan said, preceding Slider into the sitting-room of her
little flat in a small modern block in Ealing. She had a noticeable
but pleasant Australian accent, and Slider wondered, not for
the first time, why so many Antipodeans became physical
therapists of one sort or another, from doctors and dentists

through to masseurs and sports trainers. Maybe it was the climate: spending so much time out of doors and semi-nude must concentrate the thoughts on the body.

'If you don't mind,' Slider said politely, trying to keep his thoughts off her body. She was wearing a white uniform dress with a broad black elastic belt, like a nurse, but the skirt was short and the neckline low and when she bent to clear a heap of files off an armchair for him he discovered he wasn't as old as he'd thought after all.

'No, I don't mind,' she said, answering him literally, 'but I can't give you too long. I've got to get to a patient, and I expect the roads are terrible this morning, what with the strike and all.'

'They don't seem too bad,' Slider said, sitting. 'I got here from Turnham Green all right.'

Miss Rogan perched on the arm of the chair opposite and folded her arms, a compromise between staying and going which had the, no doubt unintentional, effect of enhancing Slider's view of her legs and her bosom. 'Righty-o, then. What did you want to know about Cyril? I hope you're not intending to upset him? He's a real cantankerous old divil, and he can be a pain in the nick sometimes, but I wouldn't want him disturbed at this late stage.'

'Late stage?'

'He hasn't got long to go,' she said bluntly. 'He's fighting gamely, but it's a losing fight. A few weeks – a couple of months at most.'

'I see,' Slider said. 'And what treatment do you give him?'

'Me personally? Well, I work for the Princess Elizabeth Clinic, which is a private health clinic specialising in the treatment of terminal illnesses, like cancer, which is what Cyril's got. The PEC's philosophy is to adopt a holistic approach to disease and pain management.' This part sounded like a quotation from the brochure. 'As part of that holistic approach I provide physiotherapy, massage and other hands-on treatment. Raising the physical and mental levels of well-being through physical contact can have a big effect on the immune system.' Her eyes widened a little and she dropped into normal speech. 'A lot of old people die, you know, because no one touches them any more. We live in our bodies, and we need to be kind to them.'

'So you give Mr Dacre physiotherapy and massage as part of his treatment?'

'That's right.'

'Always at home?'

'Sometimes at the clinic, when there's equipment there I want to use. He gets his drugs and radiotherapy there, of course, and he comes to see me at the same time. I encourage him to swim to improve his muscle tone – there's a pool at the clinic – and I give him heat treatment there. But I visit him at home twice a week – more, if he's having a bad spell.'

'All that must be pretty expensive,' Slider suggested.

'Not my province,' she said shortly. 'I don't send out the bills.'

'But it's not on the National Health?'

'Oh, no, it's private medicine. A lot of the patients have insurance, of course, but that hardly ever covers everything we do at the PEC.'

'So Mr Dacre must be pretty well off to afford it?'

She shrugged. 'He doesn't look as if he's short of a bob or two, does he, living in that big house? But if you want to know about his financial position, you'd have to speak to the PEC's secretary. She's the one who sends out the bills.'

Slider nodded to that, and said, 'What I wanted to know from you was, how disabled is he really?'

'Cyril? He's not disabled. I told you, he has inoperable cancer.' She looked puzzled, and then her brow cleared. 'Oh, you mean the wheelchair business?'

'Is he able to walk at all?'

'Oh, he can walk all right. I told you, he's not disabled; he's just weak. It's understandable at his age, even without the extra burden of his illness; but I'm sorry to have to say, in his case, he's also lazy. I have to bully him into doing things, or he'd just sit around all day feeling sorry for himself. Probably never get out of bed at all. And his daughter encourages him, I'm afraid. I gather she's always waited on him hand and foot, and that's the last thing he needs now.'

'So he can walk? Get out of his chair unaided?'

'Oh, yes, if he wants to. He can push himself up. He's surprisingly strong in the arms still – I suppose it was all that mountaineering when he was younger. Did you know he used to be a climber?'

'I've seen the photos in the drawing-room.'

'He went on well into his fifties, and even after that he still went hill-walking. He was very active right up until he got ill. He talks about it a lot. I think he resents not being able to do what he used to do, so in a contrary way he kind of revels in doing nothing at all – cutting off his nose to spite his face, you know?'

'Yes, it's understandable,' Slider nodded.

'And then, I think he likes to keep Mrs Hammond running about after him. It'd probably be better for him not to have her around, in some respects. But of course the stage will come – pretty soon, in fact – where he really can't help himself, and then he'll need her.' She eyed Slider with birdlike curiosity, trying to fathom his thoughts. 'This is something to do with that woman's death, right?'

'Did you ever meet her?'

'What, Jennifer Andrews? Not to say met her, really, but I passed her in the doorway once or twice. Cyril couldn't stand her. I always got an earful when she'd been round to the house. I think she was probably quite good for him in a way – got his circulation going, and took his mind off his troubles for a bit!' She smiled to show this was a joke, revealing even teeth of dazzling whiteness. Teeth, hair, skin, figure – and she did massage as well, Slider thought. She was like an updated version of a Stepford wife. He had always wondered why Ira Levin set such store by housework.

'Does he only use the wheelchair downstairs, or is it taken upstairs for him as well?'

'Oh, he has it by his bed, and comes down in it in the morning. He has a lift – haven't you seen it?' she said. 'Not a stair-lift, the real thing. They installed it years ago when Mrs Dacre was in her last illness. One of the spare bedrooms was turned into a sort of vestibule for it, and it comes out in that room between the front door and the kitchen. That used to be Cyril's study, until he had his desk moved into the dining-room. Well, he likes it better there anyway. He can see everyone go past his window. Nearly everyone comes in round the back, you see.'

'Yes, so I understand. The front door sticks.'

She dimpled at him. 'To tell you the truth, Cyril won't let Mrs Hammond have it fixed. He likes being able to keep an eye on who visits her. He teases her dreadfully, the naughty man.'

'Teases her? About what?'

'Oh, about her husband leaving her, and not being able to keep a man, that sort of thing. And now he's made this joke for himself about her having hundreds of men chasing her, and every time a man comes to the door – the postman, the milkman, anybody at all – he goes on about, "Here's another of your gentlemen followers." It makes her blush, poor thing, because of course she's well past the age for getting married, and she can't like having him keep reminding her that her husband ran off with a girl half his age.'

What a prince the man was, Slider thought.

She stood up, and looked at the smart watch that clasped her slim wrist. 'Well, look, I really do have to go, if that's all the questions you wanted to ask me?'

Slider stood too. 'Just one more,' he said. 'Does Mr Dacre have sleeping pills?'

'No, not as such. He doesn't like the idea. But he does have flunitrazepam for the pain, which has a sedative effect.'

Slider took out his notebook. 'What's the name again?'

'Flunitrazepam. The PEC's using it experimentally to control intractable pain, especially at night, so that the patients can get a good night's sleep. It's not available on the National Health, but some of our people are getting very good results with it.'

CHAPTER SIXTEEN

Sick Transport, Glorious Monday

When he got back into the car, he found the traffic had suddenly thickened, as though everyone who'd skived off work because of the strike had decided at the same moment to abandon their lie-in. At least the creeping and stopping gave him a chance to use his phone without violating moving-traffic regulations. He dialled Tufty's number, and tried him with the name of the drug Miss Rogan had mentioned.

'Oho!' Tufty bellowed with mighty interest. 'So that's how the milk got into the coconut!'

'Mean something to you?'

'Flunitrazepam, my old banana, is the chemical name for Rohypnol, or in other words, our old friend the Roofie.'

'Oh,' said Slider, enlightened. New friend rather than old friend; and no friend at all, come to that. 'That's not nice.'

'Do you think your victim might have been slipped one?'

'It's possible. The old man had them, who owns the house where she was found. He goes to a private cancer clinic that gives them out.'

'Well, flunitrazepam would certainly do the job.'

'Can you test for it?' Slider asked anxiously.

'Now I know what I'm looking for, I can try,' Tufty said. 'It leaves the bloodstream after thirty-six hours and the urine after seventy-two, but since she died within minutes, there's a good chance we'll be able to detect it. I'll do my best, anyway.'

'Thanks, Tufty,' Slider said. 'Let me know as soon as possible, will you?'

He rang off and sat staring at nothing, remembering what he knew about Rohypnol. It was a tranquilliser ten times stronger than Valium, which induced a trance-like state and mental blackout which could last for up to twelve hours. It had been used by some doctors to treat back pain and insomnia, and was in circulation on the black market in Scotland as a cheap substitute for heroin; but more notoriously, especially in America, had been implicated in date rape, and it was in this context that it had come to Met police attention. The small purple pill was colourless and odourless when dissolved in alcohol, and after about ten to fifteen minutes – or less if the drink was gulped down – the drinker would turn into a helpless zombie without ability to resist and without memory afterwards of what had happened. Memory of events usually returned some days later when the drug had passed out of the system, which made it difficult to prosecute, even if the victim came forward. Many didn't, unable to understand what had happened to them, thinking perhaps they were going mad or hallucinating.

He shivered a little, his mind working on, whether he liked it or not. It was his job to track down the killer, but he didn't like it – he never liked it – when he got close to the answer. He didn't ever want to have to realise about anyone that they were capable of such a monstrous act as murder. And this murder—! There was something of the hunt in it. He saw Jennifer Andrews on her last day, increasingly frantic, running from place to place – no, not stock-taking, seeking escape. But one by one the earths were stopped, until finally she had gone to ground. No matter that her character had been flawed, her conduct faulty, her motives less than pure; she had still been dug out and killed. How much had she known about her own death? But he didn't want to think about that.

He picked up his phone again and rang Atherton. 'I want you to meet me at the Old Rectory. Park on the other side of the square, though – I want to talk to you first.'

'Have you got something new?' Atherton asked, recognising the tone of voice.

'I'm not sure if it's nuts or not. That's why I want to talk.'

'He needs me! Thank you. Thank you. You've made a young man very happy,' Atherton said, in a tremulous voice.

'Shut up and get going,' said Slider.

*   *   *

Atherton drew up behind him and sprang from his car with something of his old eagerness. Slider pushed open the passenger-side door and he slipped in.

'Why are you driving this old wreck?'

'Because Joanna's got my old wreck. Don't breathe on anything: it's got to get me home tonight.'

'So what's cooking?'

Slider hesitated a moment longer before plunging in. 'It was the AA man who put me on to it.'

'What, Mr Milne?'

'For once—!' Slider pleaded. 'The dog was the key element. I didn't see it at first, not consciously, but it always bothered me, nagging at the back of my mind. There was something not *right* about it. Look, you said there are only two possibilities: either the dog didn't bark, or they didn't hear it.'

'Succinct, elegantly phrased: sounds like me,' said Atherton.

'But if the murderer was out on the terrace in the small hours, morrissing about with a corpse and a tarpaulin – which we know he must have been – *why* didn't it bark?' Atherton looked at him cannily, trying to read his thoughts. Slider continued, 'The AA man had a dog that he said no-one else could do anything with.'

'A common boast.'

'So here is your starter for ten: name the one person who could have stopped the dog barking during nocturnal corpse-shifting activities.'

Atherton got there. 'Isn't it this time of year your head goes in for servicing?' he said. And then, quizzically, 'You're not kidding me. You are seriously setting up old Professor Branestawm for murderer?'

'Why not?'

'Because he's about two hundred years old and wheelchair-bound. If he was a car, this car would give him points.'

'Ah, but he's not wheelchair-bound,' Slider said. 'Eileen Rogan, his physiotherapist, says he's weak, not crippled.'

'Oh, that's where you've been!'

'She says he can walk, and he's quite strong in the arms. She even hinted that he could probably do more than he lets on, but likes having his daughter wait on him. Suppose even Eileen Rogan isn't aware of how strong he really is?

Suppose in a good cause he's quite strong enough for a one-off operation?'

'But why suppose it?' Atherton countered.

'Because the private clinic he attends prescribes him flunitrazepam tablets for the pain at night. And flunitrazepam is the chemical name for Rohypnol.'

'Ah,' said Atherton. 'Roofies, or how to induce quietus in your date's bare bodkin.'

'Praise God for an intelligent bagman.'

'I do my homework, that's all. Okay, his possession of Roofies is one point to you. Walk me through it. You might start with motive.'

'Cyril Dacre is a clever man, embittered by personal tragedy. Several people have said, or hinted, that he has a warped sense of humour, and I got a little of that impression myself. He has no liking or respect for women, and he particularly hated Jennifer Andrews: a vulgar, attention-grabbing woman who patronised and embarrassed him. He told me she was ripe for the plucking. In the shadow of death himself, inflicting it on someone else may no longer be unthinkable to him; and his mind could well be unbalanced by pain and illness to the point of acting out his thoughts.'

'Could and might butter no parsnips.'

'True, but play the possibility through with me. You know that Jennifer told Defreitas she had one more person to visit?'

'At a quarter to twelve, yes.'

'I have a witness who saw her going into the Old Rectory at that time.'

'You have been busy this morning. Why did she go there?'

'I don't know. For some reason. The question is rather, why didn't Cyril Dacre mention it before?'

'Another point,' Atherton allowed. 'But maybe he didn't see her.'

'Being a regular visitor she goes to the back door rather than the front, knowing that the front door sticks, and in doing so must pass Cyril Dacre's window. Miss Rogan says he takes a keen interest in all comings and goings – suggested that's why he won't get the front door fixed. I think he saw her pass the window, and was suddenly overcome with the irresistible desire to get rid of this ghastly woman for good. Maybe he was in pain; maybe she waved cheerily as she passed, or blew him a kiss—'

'Whatever. You're winning so far,' Atherton said.

'Frances Hammond is in the kitchen,' Slider continued. 'Coming from the direction of the footpath, Jennifer doesn't pass the kitchen window, so Mrs Hammond doesn't know she's there. Dacre whizzes out in his chair and intercepts Jennifer at the back door. He invites her into the drawing-room, and offers her a drink.'

'Which she accepts because—?'

'Why wouldn't she? She knows him – why should she refuse? She's been drinking all evening. She likes drink. She likes men's company, even an old man like Cyril. He can be charming when he wants to, and he was celebrated in his heyday; and he's still, presumably, rich. We know she liked rich and eminent people. We also know she was always trying to get in with the Dacre set. She'd probably feel flattered if he showed her attention: I imagine he didn't usually.'

'All right,' Atherton said grudgingly. 'It plays.'

'Like Broadway,' Slider said sternly. He went on, 'It's late and Cyril was about to take a Rohypnol tablet to give himself a night's rest. He slips it instead into Jennifer's whisky or whatever, and chats charmingly until she suddenly goes blah. Now that she's helpless, even in his – putatively – weak state he has no difficulty in smothering her with a cushion.'

'I'll give you this,' Atherton said. 'It makes sense of the drug angle. In his weakened state, he'd need to drug her to be able to smother her, whereas if Eddie – or any other red-blooded male in the throes of sexual jealousy – killed her, you'd expect him to do it on impulse and overcome her with his physical strength. Drugging and smothering is much more like an old man's murder – a calculating, clever old man's murder.'

'That's what I thought,' Slider said unhappily.

'But what about the dog? If the dog's the key to your theory, do you think it's going to sit by quietly while the murdering goes on?'

'There would be no violence, no struggle. No sound, even. Unless the dog's tuned to alpha waves, it wouldn't even know she'd died. And Dacre's the one person who can shut it up with a glance or a word.'

'I suppose it might not even have been with him at that point. It might have been in the kitchen with Mrs Hammond. Although then you'd have expected it to bark when Jennifer arrived, and alert Mrs H.'

'Dacre usually kept the dog with him. But I'll come back to that. It's later that night that his influence over it becomes crucial,' Slider said, 'because he's got to move the body out to the terrace. That's what I keep coming back to. If the dog had barked in the night, Mrs Hammond would have heard it, because she sleeps over the kitchen and she's a light sleeper. If it didn't bark, it could only be because the person moving around was Cyril Dacre.'

'It's persuasive,' Atherton said. 'All right, retouching the makeup: what was all that about?'

'A ghastly joke, that's all I can think of.'

'I suppose whoever did that would have had to be either thick and earnest, or clever enough to have a diabolical sense of humour and a contempt for his fellow man. This seems to be going quite well, you know. But to go back a step: after the drugging and smothering, there he is with a body in the drawing-room. What's he going to do with it? Wouldn't he have to hide it temporarily in case Frances comes in?'

'I had a thought about that,' Slider said, even more unhappily.

'Tell.'

'When Rohypnol first starts to take effect, the victim becomes mentally helpless, but she still has some ability to move, though slowly and in an uncoordinated way. She can still walk, with assistance – like a drunk.'

'I don't like what you're thinking,' Atherton said.

'I don't like it more than you don't. But suppose Dacre makes her get up and walk to wherever he means to hide her, and smothers her there?'

'Where?'

'What about the dining-room – his study, whatever you want to call it? I doubt whether Mrs Hammond would go in there at that time of night – if at all, without reason. We know the body was left in a sitting position. Suppose he walked her to the next room, sat her on a chair, and smothered her there. That would avoid exciting the dog, which he left in the drawing-room. And then he tied the body to the chair as it was to stop it falling to the floor.'

'Why would he want to do that?'

'Because it would make her easier for him to pick her up later. He might not have the strength to get her up off the floor, but from a sitting position he could get her over his shoulder – or hoist her into his wheelchair and push her to the terrace.'

Atherton now looked unpleasantly disturbed. 'You're making this sound too reasonable. I don't like it. It's nasty.' He thought. 'Why did he put her in the trench, anyway?'

'Again, diabolical sense of humour plus contempt of fellow man. Or perhaps he felt Eddie ought to have controlled Jennifer better, and wanted to punish him too. I don't know. It's only a theory.' The last words had something of plea in them, as if he wanted Atherton to produce some serious flaw for him.

But Atherton only said, 'Yes, and what do you propose to do about it?'

Slider spread his hands helplessly. 'I can't think of anything *to* do, apart from putting it to Cyril Dacre and seeing how he reacts.'

'Phew! Sooner you than me.'

'That's what I wanted to talk to you about.'

Atherton's eyes widened. 'What – now? Me and you – go in there? But I'm a young man! I haven't lived!'

'If he were a younger man, or a well man, we might ask him to come into the factory, and work on him, soften him up over a period of time. But we can't do that. And I don't see that we can do nothing, now that we know she went there late that night. That's the last known sighting of her – and neither of them mentioned it.'

Atherton shrugged. 'Well, that's legit at least. Okay, guv, let's get it over with, then.'

Dacre was in his study, at his desk, which faced the side window, looking onto the gravelled area. Slider and Atherton stopped in front of the window. He seemed to be staring at them, but gave no reaction: so unmoving was his face that for a shaky moment Slider thought perhaps he had died with his eyes open and hadn't been discovered yet. But then Dacre's focus changed, and Slider realised he hadn't been staring at them, but at nothing. Now he registered their presence and made a resigned yes-all-right-come-in gesture to Slider's mimed request.

The back door and the lobby door were both open, and when they stepped through into the hall, Dacre was there, in his wheelchair, with the dog behind him in the dining-room doorway. She watched them warily, but didn't bark. One point to the theory.

'Well, what is it?' Dacre said coldly.

'I'd like to talk to you, sir, if I may,' Slider said. 'This is Detective Sergeant Atherton, by the way. May we come in?'

Dacre looked from him to Atherton, and something happened to his face. It was an almost frightening greying. *He knows we know*, Atherton thought, and for the first time he really believed his guv'nor was right about this. The old man turned his chair away without a word, wheeled himself briskly before them into the drawing-room with the dog padding after.

'Shut the door behind you,' Dacre snapped, turning to face them.

'Is Mrs Hammond in the house?' Slider asked.

'She's in the kitchen. She won't come unless I call her.'

How did he know this was private? Atherton thought. But a man so intelligent would know when the game was up, and wouldn't drag it out. He'd turn over his king – wouldn't he?

'Well? You've questions to ask, I suppose?'

Slider looked for the end of the string. 'What time did you go to bed on Tuesday night, sir?'

'I don't remember,' he said at once.

'What time do you normally go to bed?'

'I don't have a regular bedtime. I am not an infant. I go when I feel like it. You had better tell me why you want to know. It may jog my memory.'

There was nothing for it. Slider said, 'A witness has come forward to say that he saw Jennifer Andrews come to this house on Tuesday night, very late, at a quarter to midnight. He saw her cross the gravel and go round to the back door.'

Slider, who had removed his eyes from the old man's face as he asked the question, saw the phthisical hands tighten on the chair-arms. But Dacre sounded confident as he said, 'Witnesses are frequently mistaken.'

'It was someone who knew her – all of you – very well. I don't think he was mistaken. But I wondered, you see, why neither you nor Mrs Hammond had mentioned the visit. Of course, if she came to see Mrs Hammond, and you had already gone up to bed, you wouldn't have seen her pass the window.'

'If she had visited my daughter, she would have said so. Frances is incapable of lying. She hasn't the wit,' he said, his voice cold and dark as the Mindanao Trench. 'Your witness was mistaken, that's all.'

Move the question sideways. 'You have tranquillisers for the pain at night, I understand?' Slider said.

'What the devil business is it of yours?'

'A tranquilliser called Rohypnol, which has rather unusual properties,' Slider went on steadily, and now he looked up from the hands to the face. He saw Dacre draw a sharp, small breath, and in the silence that followed, the dark, intelligent eyes, caged with pain, were occupied with a chain of thought, rapid and unstoppable, like a nuclear reaction.

'Yes,' he said at last, very far away. 'I do.'

'Mrs Andrews didn't struggle when she was smothered to death, so it seems likely she was somehow rendered helpless beforehand. The interesting thing about Rohypnol is—'

'Thank you,' he said, raising his hand like a policeman stopping traffic, 'I know all about Rohypnol. I have read the sensational stories in the press. And do you think I would accept any drug without knowing its exact properties? But you have not found the drug in Mrs Andrews' body.'

'Why do you say that?'

'Because you would have said so if you had. That would be a piece of solid evidence, rather than mere wild conjecture.' He was getting his voice back now; he sounded confident again.

'We are testing for it,' Slider said. 'We haven't had the results yet. But as you say, if the tests are positive—'

'I understand that you are trying to suggest in your clumsy way that *I* killed Jennifer Andrews,' Dacre said impatiently, 'but I can't think of any reason why I should.'

'You told me yourself that you loathed her.'

'I loathe many people. I loathe most people, if it comes to that, but I do not kill them.'

'You haven't the means or opportunity to kill most of them;

and they don't thrust themselves on you, invading your very house, as Mrs Andrews did. She was an extreme irritant, I do see that,' Slider added sympathetically. 'I can understand how you might want to be rid of her.'

'In that case, you may as well suspect everyone she ever met. You might perhaps,' he went on, with withering irony, 'consider promoting to the head of your list someone not confined to a wheelchair.'

'Oh, but you aren't,' Slider said gently. 'Miss Rogan says that you are quite capable of standing and walking, and that you are surprisingly strong in the arms – a legacy from your mountaineering days, no doubt.'

His face darkened. 'How dare you discuss my condition with Miss Rogan? That is a private matter, and none of your business.'

'She suspects you may pretend to be weaker than you really are,' Slider went on as if he hadn't spoken. 'And it occurs to me that a mountaineer knows a great deal about how to move a body about in difficult conditions.'

Now Dacre laughed. 'This is most entertaining! Do go on with your work of fiction. I don't know when I've been more diverted.' But to Atherton, the laughter was forced, and there was a blank look about Mr Dacre, like that of someone who has had a bad shock and hasn't yet quite registered it. And if he really was innocent, why wasn't he angry? Atherton would have expected blistering rage. Why, indeed, was he even listening to all this, unless it was to find out how much they really knew?

Slider went on. 'What really started me wondering was the question of the dog.'

'Sheba?' Dacre said in surprise, and the Alsatian lifted her head briefly to look at him, triangular yellow eyes under worried black eyebrows. Then she sighed and lowered her nose again to her paws.

'You see, if Mrs Andrews had been killed elsewhere, as we first thought, and a stranger had carried her body to the terrace and laid it in the trench, the dog would surely have heard and started barking. You said yourself she's a guard dog, and I know from my own experience that when I tried your garage doors, it set her off – and that was in daylight. But if Sheba had barked, Mrs Hammond would have heard her. She's a light sleeper, and sleeps in the room above the kitchen where Sheba is shut at night. And Mrs Hammond says she didn't bark. One thing we know for certain is that the body was put into the trench on the terrace during the night. That leaves us with the question: who could have persuaded the dog to remain silent while all that was going on?'

There was no answer. For a moment there was silence; the bright day outside and the dusty air within equally still. Atherton glanced towards his guv'nor, and saw, with a strange chill, that Slider had thought of something, was pursing a train of thought which must have been triggered by something he had just said or noticed. He was preoccupied; he was no longer looking at Dacre. The urgency of his thoughts was almost palpable to Atherton, and he tried anxiously to work out what it was Bill had thought of, because he had a sense of being left behind in a cold place where he very much didn't want to be.

Then he looked at Dacre. The dying man was etched against the bright window, thin as a Byzantine martyr and with eyes as deep and dark and burning; failing hair making a fuzzy aureole around that thinker's skull. And then Dacre started shaking, his bunched hands, his knees under the tartan rug, his shoulders, his head. Slowly as a cinematic western shoot-out, he moved one hand to his lap, caught at the rug, pulled it away and threw it down, shoved away the foot-rests, put down his feet and stood up. It was terrible and unnatural, like seeing a tree uproot itself and walk. The dog looked up, startled, and then rose, backing away a step, tail and ears down, unsure what reaction was required. Dacre let go the chair-arms and reached equilibrium. Erect and burning, impressive and frightening as a forest fire, he said with quiet triumph, 'You're right, Inspector. I applaud your diligence and persistence. I killed Jennifer Andrews – or rather, I exterminated her! Don't look upon it as murder, if you please, but as a public service. I killed her, and I am ready to take my punishment.'

Slider rose as well, facing him, and the dog began to growl menacingly; and when Atherton, between them, stood up, she jumped at him, barking. Dacre turned his head and fixed her with a look. 'Quiet, Sheba! Lie down!' The dog subsided slowly; but in the moment Dacre was thus occupied, Atherton looked at Slider, and saw that his earlier expression had changed from the taut, preoccupied look of the man on the scent to a look of sadness and defeat.

'Please sit down, Mr Dacre,' Slider said quietly.

Dacre stared a moment, and then lowered himself back into his chair. He did not attempt to replace the rug; his legs inside his trousers were like broomsticks inside a Guy Fawkes effigy. 'Well,' he said, and Atherton could see it cost him an effort to speak, 'what happens now? Am I to be arrested and carted off to the police station?' He met Slider's eyes, and some message passed between them, something almost of pleading from the old man, out of a black depth beyond anything Atherton could imagine. Bottom of the trench, sea-bottom, colder and darker than death.

But Slider had no opportunity to answer, for the door opened and Mrs Hammond was there. She registered the scene and a look of alarm came over her vague, indeterminate face. 'What is it? What's happening? I didn't hear anyone come in.' She came forward, her hands moving nervously. 'Father, what is it? Are you all right?'

'Everything is quite all right, Frances,' Dacre said. 'Don't fuss.'

She went on scanning the room, trying to understand. 'Why is the rug on the floor?'

'I put it there. Be quiet. There is nothing for you to do here,' Dacre said. 'I was merely demonstrating a point to Inspector Slider. And now, having satisfied him on that point, I am going to make a statement, which he will take down to my dictation.' He looked at Slider, trying for hauteur and almost succeeding. 'I imagine that will obviate the need to take me to the cells? As you are aware, I am in no condition to flee the country – or, indeed, this house – and I should prefer not to be locked up for the short time that still remains to me.'

'A statement is all that's required at this stage,' Slider agreed neutrally, dividing his attention between Dacre and his daughter. 'You can make that here as well as anywhere.'

'What are you talking about?' Mrs Hammond was looking bewildered. 'Statement? Father, what's going on? Statement about what?'

Dacre held her eyes. 'A statement about how I killed Jennifer Andrews.'

She whitened. 'No!'

'I told you, Frances, there's nothing to make a fuss about.'

'No, you mustn't!'

'I understand it must be a shock to you, but you know I always disliked the woman. I am perfectly happy to confess to my crime and take what's coming to me. And at my age and in my condition, I have nothing to fear. What can they possibly do to me?'

'No, Father, no!' Her face was collapsing in distress, with the slow inevitability of a demolished factory chimney; almost tumbling in anguish. Her hands were twisting about as though they were trying to burrow into her stomach for shelter; her eyes held her father's pleadingly. 'Oh, no, please!'

'Be quiet, child,' he said, so gently it made Atherton shiver. 'Leave the room now. I wish to be alone with the officers. No! Not a word. Go!'

The command in the voice was so firm it even had the dog on her feet again. Mrs Hammond dragged out a handkerchief and applied it to her face, covered her trembling lips. She was making hoarse noises, a cross between sobs and gasps, and her eyes were everywhere, but she turned away, to obey as she had obeyed all her life.

And Slider said, 'Just a moment.'

His voice was quiet, but Mrs Hammond jerked as if she had been hit across the spine with a heavy stick. She stopped, turning only her face back towards him, so that her eyes showed white like those of a frightened horse.

'Go, Frances,' said Mr Dacre, but the command had gone out of his voice. It sounded much the same, but it was powerless; an empty firework case. 'Inspector, I forbid you to speak to my daughter. I forbid you to trouble her with this. I've told you, I'm ready to make a statement.'

But Slider only looked at the woman. 'Mrs Hammond,' he said, 'I can quite see how, when you realised the enormity of what you'd done, you wanted to cover your tracks, but how could you let us arrest poor Eddie Andrews? How could you let him take the blame for your crime? That was cruel.'

Atherton looked at Slider. *Her?* he thought.

She turned. 'Cruel?' Her face was working horribly, like something trying to escape from under a blanket, and her voice rose as she repeated, '*Cruel?* What do you know about *cruelty*?'

She flung herself at Slider. Atherton moved fast – the reaction of instinct, which later he would remember and be glad about – to try to interpose himself between them. The dog barked like machine-gun fire and jumped at him, teeth not quite making contact, but keeping him back. But as he tried to fend it off, and Mr Dacre shouted at it and him and Slider almost indiscriminately, Atherton saw that Slider was holding Mrs Hammond, not wrestling with her, that she was not trying to kill him, but weeping on his shoulder, in his arms; a big woman, almost as tall as Slider, too big and ungainly easily for him to comfort.

CHAPTER SEVENTEEN

Ethics Man

When sufficient back-up had arrived, Slider pulled Atherton out of the room, which saved Atherton from having to pull Slider out.

'Are you crazy, or am I?' Atherton asked urgently. 'I'd just like to know.'

Slider hardly noticed. 'Come with me. I need you to witness this.'

'What?' Atherton demanded, but he got no answer.

Slider led the way across the hall to the kitchen. The kitchen door was open, the room was empty, cool in shadow, the window a dazzling rectangle of white light. A cup of tea, half drunk, stood on the table, and a library book lay open and face down on the sagging sofa where Mrs Hammond must have abandoned it when she heard the dog bark. Under the scarred polythene protective, the dust jacket showed a passionate embrace, a woman in red, a man with dark hair and huge shoulders. Here it was: love – authentic, romantic, unfailing, marriage guaranteed; every woman's birthright. What Irene had been promised as a little girl. No, not Irene, this was not the time for that. Frances, woman turned monster, still feeding on the poison, the white refined sugar that warped and rotted.

He crossed the kitchen to the darkest corner and bent over the dog's basket, probing down amongst the hairy blankets. In a moment he straightened up, with the shredded strip of red silk dangling from his fingers, damp with dog saliva. He felt as though, with a very little encouragement, he would be able to cry.

He turned to Atherton. 'Jennifer's scarf,' he said, in a dead voice. 'The one she was wearing the last day, that got lost somewhere between the Meacher house and the grave. I saw the dog chewing it in its basket, but, God help me, I never made the connection until just now.'

Atherton came close and looked. 'Her scarf?'

Slider was looking round. 'Here. She did it here, on this sofa, where she always sits – where she was going to go on sitting, drinking tea and reading romances. My God, what a monster!'

'That pathetic nothing of a woman?'

'She didn't take the dog out that morning, as she said she did. I should have realised from the beginning. I did know something wasn't right about it, but I didn't know what, and of course I never suspected her – a pathetic nothing of a woman, as you say.'

'But what—?'

'Don't you see? If she'd taken the dog out with her on the terrace that morning, it would have found the body! It would have gone straight to it and barked its head off. But she never said a word about the dog's reaction to the corpse, and neither did Eddie. And the next-door neighbours, who heard her cry out or shout when Eddie arrived, heard no barking. Because the dog wasn't there.'

'But where does that get us? When you said the dog was the key, I thought you meant about the barking in the night.'

'Yes, I did. I was wrong there, too. My God, I made such a stupid, elementary mistake!' he said fretfully. 'And after I'd been warning everyone else – *and* referring to the Christie case. Timothy Evans hanged because no-one entertained for a moment the notion that he might be telling the truth and Christie lying. It was the same with Eddie Andrews and Mrs Hammond. I thought Andrews was trying to distance himself from the trench by saying the work was her idea, but in fact he was telling the truth and *she* was trying to distance *herself*. I should have known the corner of the tarpaulin couldn't have blown back. It was a still night, and the ropes on the corners showed that he was in the habit of tying it down. It was she who turned the tarpaulin back, because she knew what was under it. But from the very beginning I took her as the standard, and everything had to be measured by her truth. Stupid, stupid!'

'Don't beat yourself up. Who would have thought—?'

'I should have thought.' He looked at Atherton. 'There weren't two possibilities, but three. Either the dog didn't bark, or they didn't hear it – or it did bark, and she was lying.'

'Yes,' said Atherton.

'Mrs Hammond had the same access to the Rohypnol as her father. Jennifer went to see her that night. Mr Dacre must have been already tucked up asleep in his bed, and he slept soundly all night. She gave Jennifer a spiked drink here in the kitchen, and smothered her, probably with one of the cushions from this sofa. At some point in the – not exactly struggle, but let's say transaction – Jennifer's scarf came off and I suspect got lost amongst the cushions. In her distracted state, Mrs Hammond didn't notice it, or its absence; but later the dog nosed it out – she was wearing quite a lot of scent, you remember – and carried it to its basket, where I saw it chewing it. Saw, but didn't see.'

'But what did Mrs H. do about the dog? If Dacre was already in bed, it must have been in the kitchen with her while she was murdering.'

'Yes, of course. The dog was upset, and she couldn't deal with the corpse with it barking and growling, maybe even trying to attack her. She had to drag it out into the passage; but she knew it could get the kitchen door open by lifting the latch – I saw it do it – so she dragged it into the empty storeroom, the first on the left, which had a bolt on the outside. The dog went mad trying to get out – I saw the gouges on the inside of the door, and the empty sacks were ripped where it worried them in its frenzy. But no-one could hear it in there. The room has no window, and those walls are two feet thick.'

'My God, yes. It's the perfect cell.'

'And there the dog stayed all night. It was still in there in the morning when she went out on the terrace to do whatever she meant to do.'

'And what was that?'

'I don't know. There are some things I shall have to ask her, little as I want to. But I think I've worked most of it out.'

'You might let me in on it, then,' Atherton said. 'What did she do with the body? Leave it on the sofa?'

'No, I think she moved it straight away, started dragging or carrying it out as soon as she'd shut the dog in. I don't know what she meant to do with it in the long run, but I think she got it as far as the back lobby and then decided to hide it temporarily in the downstairs loo, perhaps because that was the one room she knew her father would never go in – the door's too narrow for his wheelchair.'

'Oh, my God, and she sat the body on the loo?'

'On the closed seat, and kept it in place by tying it to the down-pipe. Freddie said the ligature had a broad, flat section like a luggage strap, and I saw a long webbing dog-lead in the lobby she could have used.'

'I expect the dog was very much on her mind,' Atherton remarked.

'Later, when the Mimpriss Estate had gone to bed and there was less chance of anyone passing in the street, she took the body out to the terrace and laid it in the trench. Early in the morning she went back out to do something else with or to the body—'

'What?'

'God, I don't know. Maybe she didn't either. Eddie said she was just standing staring at it, didn't he? Maybe she was frozen with horror and simply couldn't think. But anyway, he interrupted her. He made her call the police, and then sat down with his head in his hands, desperately upset, and that was when she took the chance—'

'To throw Jennifer's bag into the pickup!' Atherton finished triumphantly.

'Yes. Then she had to hurry indoors, because she knew the police were coming and she didn't have long to cover her tracks. She had to let the dog out of the storeroom—'

'Sooner her than me. I don't suppose it was pleased.'

'It was probably exhausted by then. And she had to go and check on her father and make sure he hadn't heard anything.'

'Yes, and wait a minute,' Atherton said, frowning, 'what was all that with the old man? Why did he confess?'

'To save her, of course,' Slider said miserably. 'I think maybe he'd had a suspicion all along. He's an intelligent man, with a trained, academic mind and plenty of time to think; and I remember how quick he was from the beginning to suggest it must have been Eddie who did it, and to tell me Eddie and Jennifer were on bad terms.'

And Slider remembered, too, how he had abruptly stopped

himself on that same subject – not happy to be incriminating an innocent man, even though he felt he had to do it. But his suspecting must surely at that point have been only back-of-the-mind stuff, for how could he really, consciously have believed his daughter a murderess?

Atherton said, 'When Mrs Hammond came in, he said he'd been proving a point to you.'

'Yes, proving that he could stand, that he was capable of moving the body. But did you see his legs?'

'Like knitting needles,' Atherton agreed. 'It was a terrible effort for him to get upright.'

'He's got very little time to live. He wants to take the blame to save her, because it can't matter to him.'

'I thought he had nothing but contempt for her?'

'Perhaps he thought that too, until he saw her in danger. It's surprising how deep the instinct of fatherhood goes.'

He thought of Dacre's burning eyes, and the appeal in them at the end. Caged in his failing body, raging at life – and perhaps suddenly guilty at the way he had always treated his daughter, the one thing left to him that mattered, wealth and repute having proved no barrier to encroaching chaos. That last, furious, noble gesture saddened Slider immeasurably because it was futile. It would not save her, for truth was stronger than the devices of men, as Cyril Dacre, historian, ought above all to have known. The writers of history may lie for their own purposes or of their prejudice, but the truth has a life of its own, in stones and bricks, in the earth, in artefacts, in the marks it makes on the fabric of the world. An historian, if he is a scholar, and a detective, if he cares about his craft, are very much akin: both study the traces men leave behind them, in order to reveal their actions.

Atherton brought him back from his thoughts. 'So he struck the manly chest and said, I cannot tell a lie, I did it with my little hatchet. I wish you had taken his statement now. It would have been interesting to see exactly how much he had worked out.'

'He'll have to give a statement anyway. I want you to take that. Now that you know what to look out for, he can't lie to you. But I think probably he won't try, now.'

'No endgame,' Atherton said, remembering his earlier thought.

'Eh?'

'Never mind. What about you? Mrs Hammond?'

'Yes,' Slider sighed. 'I'll do a preliminary here, because we can't take her away until something's been arranged about her father. He can hardly stay here alone. And if he goes, something will have to be done about the dog. It's the devil of a mess,' he concluded gloomily.

'Not your fault, guv. People shouldn't murder people. I wonder why she did it, by the way?'

'Only she can tell us that. But I have an idea,' said Slider, turning back reluctantly towards the place where duty lay.

In Atherton's little bijou back yard – he called it a garden by virtue of a square of grass so small it didn't even merit a lawnmower and was cut with shears – Slider and Joanna sat on canvas folding chairs and looked at the jasmine climbing over the wall opposite, beyond which the upper windows of the next row of houses peeped Chad-like, only two ten-foot plots away. Everyone was out in their back gardens this evening, and a muted composite of conversation and cutlery noises rose into the air, along with the inevitable barbecue smoke, to mingle with the sound and smell of traffic to which they were so accustomed it was actually an effort to notice it.

'Did you read that bit in the paper,' Joanna said, on the thought, 'about the new research they've done in America on tinnitus? They reckon it's not physical damage that causes it but mental damage. There's background white noise all the time that our brains automatically filter out, but the brains of tinnitus sufferers have forgotten how to edit.'

'Makes sense,' Slider said. 'After all, every copper knows that what you see is not what goes into the eye but what the brain registers. It's the great forensic myth, the infallibility of the eye witness. And then there are the other forms of blindness – like blind prejudice.'

Joanna laid a hand on his knee. 'You got there in the end.'

'By machete-ing my way through Eddie Andrews' life.'

Along the A40 for quite a stretch, between Savoy Circus and Gypsy Corner, the houses had been pulled down to make way for road widening. But the widening had never happened – the scheme shelved, perhaps for ever – and the gardens of the houses remained, isolated, untended, the sad ghosts of a settlement which had come and gone and would soon be forgotten. Eddie Andrews reminded Slider of those gardens, when he had gone to tell him he was no longer suspected of the murder – unkempt and overgrown, not with any temporary absence of care, but with the desperate neglect of the ending of everything. No-one was ever coming back to prune the bare, ten-foot-high roses, trim the privet, pull up the rosebay willowherb flourishing impudently amongst the grasses of the lawn. Eddie's hollow cheeks were sprouting, his hair was a thicket, there were seeds in his eyes, and his clothes seemed ready to migrate from his hunched and shambling shoulders. His world had been destroyed and he would never be put back together again.

'Bill, you've got to stop picking at yourself,' Joanna said reasonably. 'You know you're always low at times like this. In the balance of things it probably didn't make any difference to the man. He might even have been glad of the counter-irritant.'

'You sound like Atherton,' he said, with a grudging smile.

Atherton came out at that moment with two tumblers. 'Nobody sounds like me. I'm unique. A little drinkie for the memsahib?' He handed a man-sized gin and tonic to Joanna. 'And one for my dear old guv'nor, what is covered with laurels.'

'Privet's the highest I rate on this one,' Slider said.

'Do I detect the chafe of sackcloth?' Atherton enquired.

'Are you coming out?' Joanna asked him. 'I want to hear all the details.'

'Not if you want to eat tonight. Bill can tell you. I've heard it.'

'What about Sue?'

'I'll tell her while we stir.'

'Oy!' came a bellow from the kitchen. 'Should it be boiling like this?'

'Coming, Mother!' Atherton trilled.

Joanna tried her drink. 'Crikey, this is strong!' she spluttered.

'Matches the strength of my character,' Atherton said modestly.

She dimpled at him. 'I think you're cute.'

He dimpled back. 'So do I, but what do we know?' And disappeared.

'Now,' said Joanna, turning to her lover. The westering sun lit up the tired lines in his face and the shadows under his eyes. He hadn't been home at all last night. The rest of Monday and the whole of Tuesday had been taken up with interviews, new forensic examinations, writing reports, and sorting out the Dacre-Hammond *équipe*. Joanna had had a call this afternoon to meet Slider and Atherton at the latter's house at around seven for a celebration meal. She had arrived to find Sue already there, but the men hadn't arrived until half past – in Atherton's car. Joanna's beloved wreck was still sitting in St Michael Square: when Atherton had driven Slider there to pick it up, it wouldn't start.

'So, tell me all,' Joanna invited. 'Why did she do it?'

'Love,' Slider said. 'Jealousy. Desperation. All the old candidates. I'd begun to suspect – not the detail, but the general direction. I knew David Meacher had to be involved in some way – he kept popping up everywhere I looked. Jennifer Andrews told her friend that Meacher was dropping her for another woman, a rich woman, who mustn't find out about his other affairs.'

'And that woman was Mrs Hammond?'

'Cyril Dacre's a wealthy man, and he's dying. A few months ago he told Mrs Hammond that he was going to leave her the house and half of everything else, the other half to be divided between her sons. She'd looked after him so long it was only justice – and maybe he'd begun to realise what a rotten life she'd always had. Anyway, at about the same time David Meacher, the good old family friend, started to take a more romantic interest in her.'

'She'd told him about the legacy?'

'It's conjecture. I doubt whether Dacre would have said anything, but Mrs Hammond might easily have let it out. Or Meacher might just have assumed: there was no-one else, after all. The house alone would have been enough to fill him with lust: he had a thing about beautiful real estate; but I gather Dacre was otherwise rich as well. But Mrs Hammond didn't make the connection. When the swine started making love to her, he told her that he'd always admired her and it just happened to be now that his admiration had ripened into love, and she believed him.'

'The need being father to the thought?' Joanna said.

'Perhaps. Probably. However difficult her father was to live with, she must have been frightened at the thought of being left all alone by his death. And Meacher is a smooth, plausible man, and *apparently*,' he put the word in with a large air, 'attractive to women. Anyway, when Meacher started to make delicate approaches to her, she responded with eagerness and gratitude.'

'And most things twinkled after that,' Atherton said, re-emerging. 'Something to soak up the alcohol, children, and stave off the pangs of thingummy.' He put down an ashet bearing slices of French bread toasted and spread with pâté. 'I suspect – though Bill doesn't agree with me – that she'd been in love with him for years, probably ever since her husband left her and Meacher was nice to her.'

'It was Meacher who introduced her rotten husband to her in the first place,' Slider reminded him.

'All the more reason to be grateful. She'd never have been married at all, otherwise.'

'And marriage is every woman's dream and salvation, is it?' Joanna said indignantly. 'Go away, you horrible, sexist, patronising beast. Get back in the kitchen where you belong.' Atherton smiled at his most sphingine and went away. 'Go on,' she said to Slider. 'More about Meacher.'

'His wife was finally getting fed up with him. All the money in the marriage was hers, and her father had sensibly tied it up so that Meacher couldn't touch it. If she was threatening to pull the plug on him – as she hinted to me – and divorce him, it was going to leave him right up a close.'

'Hence the urgency to woo Mrs Hammond, and shuffle off Mrs Andrews?'

'Quite. Of course, he might have been fed up with Jennifer anyway. I imagine a little of her went a long way. Jennifer, however, wasn't ready to be shuffled. She was desperate to get away from Eddie and wasn't going to be thwarted by a flabby middle-aged nonentity like Mrs Hammond. She tried desperately to get Meacher back, and when he proved adamant, and all her other options failed, she decided to tackle the problem from the other end and put Mrs Hammond off him.'

'That's stupid! Even if she succeeded, how was that going to make him marry her?'

'She was in a panic and a temper and she'd been drinking: I don't suppose she was thinking very clearly. And there was an element of revenge in it, I expect. "Other women" who tell wives usually do it in the hope that the wives will punish the men, since they can't make any impression on the men themselves.'

'Yes, that's true,' Joanna said thoughtfully. 'Have one of these.'

He took one without looking, his mind elsewhere. 'Mrs Hammond was devastated.' He stopped a moment, remembering how she had cried just telling him about it, torn with the desolation of loss and humiliation. 'She'd thought he loved her truly for herself alone.'

'And, of course, like every woman who finds out her man has been two-timing her, she turned her hatred on the other woman. She couldn't hate him, so she blamed Jennifer.'

He didn't want to think about that. It brought it too close to home. 'She'd just come down from settling her father in bed when Jennifer arrived. She'd given him his Rohypnol, and still had the box in her pocket, and she was crossing the hall when Jennifer came in at the back door. She said she had something important to talk about, so Mrs Hammond took her to the kitchen. Jennifer must have been getting cold feet about it, because she asked for a drink, and Mrs H. fetched her a whisky. Then she spilled the beans. She told Mrs H. that she and Meacher were lovers, that he loved her and had promised to marry her, and that he was only after Mrs H. for her money. She said Meacher had told her he meant to wheedle the money out of Mrs Hammond after her father's death while stringing her along with false promises, which, as Mrs Hammond was so desperate for a man, she would believe. She said she and David had often laughed together about it, and that he had called Mrs Hammond a sad old man-eater.'

'The poor creature,' Joanna said with feeling. 'That Andrews woman deserved—'

'Don't say it,' Slider stopped her. 'It's not true.'

'Metaphorically, I meant.'

'I know what you meant.'

'Go on, then. What happened next?'

'A murderous rage came over Mrs Hammond.' The temper her father had bequeathed her came into its own at last, and for once in her sorry existence she hit back at the forces that had bullied and mocked and subordinated her, taken from her everything pleasant and lovely and left her with nothing but the shucks and the labour. 'It was easy to slip a pill into Jennifer's second whisky. Jennifer went on talking. She was not entirely sober, of course, and I imagine Mrs Hammond's apparent lack of reaction threw her. She must have expected a flare-up of some kind, but of course Mrs H. had spent a lifetime being meek, patient and silent, and her responses were all bottled up inside. Eventually Jennifer went floppy, and Mrs Hammond got up, put one of the cushions over her face and smothered her.'

Just like that, Joanna thought. Slider had stopped, and she didn't prompt him, seeing he had gone away, probably back to the long, frequently interrupted, exhausting and harrowing interview he had conducted with Mrs Hammond. For Joanna, the whole story was just a story: she knew none of the protagonists and they meant nothing to her. But through his distress she could catch a glimpse of the reality behind the words; could feel through him the leading edge of the black, bitter cold of chaos and evil that lay under the surface crust of the world and every now and then broke through. He must be so much stronger than her, Joanna thought, to be able to bear such repeated contact with it and still stay on his feet and sane. At times like these she admired him almost painfully.

Sue stuck her head out of the door. 'Jim says to eat inside. We don't want your responses to the food confused by the smell of other people's barbecues.' They looked at her but didn't move. 'Well, shift then,' she commanded. 'We're just dishing up.'

'What's all this "we"?' Joanna said, getting up. 'From a woman who couldn't burn water . . .'

'We're a team,' she said with dignity. 'He cooks, I taste.'

'How did he ever manage without you?' Joanna marvelled. She held out a hand to Slider, and he took it and got up, and then drew her to him and held her a moment gratefully, resting his head against hers. It felt heavy to her, and she knew how much effort it took him not just to lay it on her shoulder and go to sleep.

A long time later, after a prolonged and mostly merry meal, when they were back at her place and in bed, Joanna was ready for sleep, but felt how the tide had gone out again for him, leaving him wakeful. The talk and the company as well as the food and drink had stimulated him, and she had been glad to see him shake off his sadness and respond. There had been plenty of chat and plenty of laughter to dilute the rest of Mrs Hammond's strange story, as Jim and Bill between them told it to her and Sue.

For all the rest had been Mrs Hammond's story, and Joanna, who had never even seen the house, saw with strange clarity, as though watching a film, her shock and fear at finding herself, as her rage dissolved, alone with the corpse, intruder in her familiar kitchen. She watched Mrs Hammond struggling with the hysterical dog, dragging it out to lock it in the storeroom, hurrying away from its muffled barking and scrabbling, to face that lolling dummy on the sofa, and wonder in spinning terror what she was going to do with it.

The downstairs loo was the immediate and desperate hiding place, just to get the thing out of her sight. Then she had returned to the kitchen and paced up and down for hours, trying to think what to do. She couldn't leave the body where it was for ever. She considered briefly throwing it onto the railway lines in the hope that a train would run over it and thereby advance a reason for the death. Then she thought of burying it in the garden; but the ground was rock hard after the long drought, and how could she dig a hole big enough and fill it in again, all before Eddie Andrews arrived?

And thinking of Eddie she thought of the hole in the terrace, which he had already dug. It was the right size and shape, and she was sure she could get the body that far. She went back to the cloakroom to look at it again, half fascinated, half horrified, and it was then that she noticed how smudged the makeup was. She fetched Jennifer's handbag and redid Jennifer's face with her own makeup.

'But *why*?' Sue had demanded at that point in the story. 'That was bonkers.'

'Guilt, shame; some confused idea of covering up her traces,' Atherton said. 'You have to realise she was bonkers by that time. But it had the benefit, from her point of view, of reminding her of something that had to be dealt with – Jennifer's handbag left behind on the sofa.'

She took the handbag with her out onto the terrace and put it down by the wall while she untied the tarpaulin and folded it back. Then she went back for the corpse, hoisted it over her shoulder, and staggered out with it: she was a strong woman, and having nursed her mother and her father, had some experience of handling inert bodies. She put it into the hole, but at the sight of it lying there was overcome with fear and guilt and remorse. As an act of atonement she had straightened the limbs and pulled down the skirt, laying it out decently. Then she had simply knelt there, frozen, unable to think or act.

'But what was she meaning to *do*?' Joanna had asked. 'I mean, Eddie was due to arrive next morning. How was she going to explain it to him?'

'Her idea was to fill the hole in with the stuff that had come out of it,' Atherton had explained, shaking his head in wonder, 'and when Eddie came, tell him they had changed their minds about having the work done and send him away. You see, Eddie had said all along that it wasn't really necessary; she'd insisted out of fear of the terrace falling down, after all the horror stories she'd heard from other people about subsidence. So if she now said she'd changed her mind, there was nothing he could do about it.'

'Now that is bonkers,' Joanna had said. 'Wasn't he supposed to wonder why she'd filled the hole in with her own hands in the middle of the night? Or why there was so much of the filling left when the hole was full?'

'You can't expect someone in her position to think straight,' Atherton said kindly. 'It was the best she could manage in the circumstances. But anyway, when it came to it, she couldn't do it. The thought of throwing earth and rubble into Jennifer's face might have been enticing in life, but was impossible in death. She was still standing there trying to bring herself to the point when Eddie arrived, much too early, and she realised the night was over and her chance had gone.'

The shock of seeing his wife dead, especially after his drunken ravings the night before, had gone to Eddie's legs. He told Mrs Hammond to phone the police, sat down on the wall and put his head in his hands. It was at that point Mrs Hammond had seen the handbag which she had left there, practically under Eddie's feet, and in a panic she had grabbed it and thrown it into his pickup, not to incriminate him, but simply to be rid of it. Eddie was in no state to notice. Mrs Hammond had gone into the house, leaving Eddie with time to think how bad things were going to look for him, and to decide on his feeble story of having been home all evening watching television. And so the stage was set, as Slider had said, 'for the rest of the farce'.

Joanna felt his chest move under her cheek in a sigh, and she pressed herself a little closer for comfort – his and hers, both.

'What will happen now?' she asked, knowing he would still be thinking about it.

'I don't know,' he said. Mrs Hammond was in custody; Dacre had been found a bed in the clinic where he had his treatment, and from his state of collapse it seemed unlikely that he would ever leave it. The problem of the dog had been solved by Alf Whitton, who had willingly taken it into his cottage next door. Sheba had gone with him without a struggle, and he had seemed happy to have a dog about the place again. 'She knows me, she'll be all right with me, poor old girl,' he had said, and Slider had thought it would be a good permanent home for the creature, should such a thing become necessary. The house – that lovely old house he had coveted – was empty. For centuries it had grown and changed, matured and mellowed harmoniously, sheltering generations of normal, happy families. Now in one short week its peace had been destroyed, perhaps – who could know? – for ever. It was such a terrible, pitiful waste, he thought.

But that was not what Joanna meant, of course. 'Porson thinks the CPS won't go for it,' he said.

'But you've got her confession.'

'They won't go on a confession these days, not after all those overturned sentences. There's got to be good material evidence as well.'

'But you've got – what, the scarf?'

'Can't prove that was Jennifer Andrews'.'

'The fingerprints on the handbag – didn't you say they matched Mrs Hammond's?'

'Yes, but they could have got there any time. Jennifer visited the Old Rectory frequently.'

'What about the traces of makeup on the cushion?'

'That's suggestive, but not enough on its own; and even with the Rohypnol in the bloodstream, we can't prove it was Mrs Hammond gave it to her. The trouble is, you see, that the CPS is judged on results. If they take a case and don't win it, it's a slap on the wrist for them; too many failures and bang goes their bonus. And they've got budgets – prosecutions are expensive, and Mrs Hammond is low priority, quite apart from the winnability factor. In the old days, when the police conducted their own prosecutions, we'd have a go if we were sure, and if we lost, well, *c'est la guerre*. Now we catch 'em, and the CPS shrugs and let's 'em go.'

'Is that why you're so down?' she enquired delicately.

'No. Not entirely,' he amended. He was silent a moment, and she waited for him. 'So many lives have been ruined. Jennifer, Eddie Andrews, Mrs Hammond; her sons – how will they live with it? Dacre's last days turned into horror. Janice Byrt. Lady Diana.'

'It's not your fault. It's Meacher's, for being a greedy, unprincipled tart. And Jennifer Andrews', for being a spiteful, heartless tart. And Mrs Hammond's—'

'For being what? A put-upon tart?'

'For being a murderess,' Joanna said robustly. 'Nobody made her do it. And it was her who let Eddie Andrews suffer by being wrongly accused, not you. She should have owned up. You don't need to feel sorry for her.'

'I don't – not for that. For the rest of her life, perhaps.' He thought about her reluctantly, and saw, quite separated from the meek and bullied woman of his first acquaintance, the monster in the kitchen – as if they were two different people. The monster had slipped Jennifer Andrews the drug, and then waited for it to take effect before killing her. Waited and watched. That was what horrified him. It had not been the action of an instant, it had been slow, calculated, deliberate; and he couldn't convince himself otherwise than that, at the moment Mrs Hammond had smothered her victim to death, *she had enjoyed it*.

He dragged his mind away from the image, which he knew from experience was going to dog him for a long time. 'Well, she's paying for it now, anyway.' Horror and shame and guilt were her portion. 'And even if it never comes to court, she'll have to live with it for the rest of her life. Her father's dying. Meacher will never speak to her again. Perhaps her sons won't either.

She'll never be able to serve on any more church committees. She'll be ostracised – all alone in that house for ever.'

'Well,' Joanna said, 'maybe after all it's really Gerald Hammond's fault, for leaving her in the first place for a younger woman.'

'Oy,' he protested.

'You asked for it. Listen to me, my darling dingbat, I think you are wonderful: clever, resourceful, thoroughly professional, honest, full of integrity; and kind and tender-hearted into the bargain. I am very proud of you – and very proud to be here in bed with you, too.'

'Really?' he said, almost shyly.

'One thing you can be absolutely sure of is that I'm here because I want to be.'

'It's your bed.'

'Don't nitpick. All right, you're here because I want you to be. I'm trying to tell you that I love you.'

'Tell me, then. Don't let me stop you.'

'I love you, Inspector.'

'I love you, too.' He kissed her, long and thoroughly, and then settled again with her head on his shoulder. 'Are we going to be all right, do you think?'

'What, you and me? It should be me asking you that. Have you really settled things with Irene?'

'I think so. I hope so. Of course, there will always be problems. And I'm going to be pretty tapped until the children leave school.'

She didn't say anything to that. Pretty tapped was putting it mildly, if the experience of various of her divorced musician friends was anything to go by. And that meant she would be tapped too. It wasn't that she had wanted him for his money – fat lot of use that would ever have been! – but her life as a self-employed musician was doubly precarious: she might fail, or the work might fail. Was it unreasonable or base of her to have hoped that if ever she did get together with a man, he would provide a little fall-back security for her? Setting aside accident and the various physical ills that attacked violinists, and provided she had no breakdown of nerves or temperament, she could go on playing the fiddle to orchestral standard until, and perhaps after, retirement age; but with new young musicians pouring out of the colleges every year, and rampant gerontophobia attacking promoters and managements alike, would anyone go on employing her? Just a little security in an insecure world was all she had hoped for; but it seemed that was not to be. She would have to provide the fall-back position for him instead, and try not to feel resentful of the wife and children she would be indirectly supporting.

Well, that was the way the bones had fallen. Ain't nothin' but weery loads, honey. He was here, that was the important thing, warm and alive and wrapped around her in her bed, and that was worth the price. She could feel he had relaxed now: his breathing had steadied, and she thought he was falling asleep. But then he said suddenly, diffidently, and in a perfectly wakeful voice, 'Should we get married, do you think?'

That was one out of left field, if you like! 'Are you in a position to ask me, sir?' she said, temporising.

'Well, I will be, one day. When I am, if I ask you, do you think you'll say yes?'

She started to smile, unseen in the darkness. 'That's a hypotheoretical question, as your Mr Porson would say.'

'I wasn't thinking of asking him,' Slider assured her.

Blood Sinister

For Bill's good friends, Marcia and Geoff,
and Sharon and Chris;
and of course, as always,
for my indispensible Tony, with love.

If the red slayer think he slays,
Or if the slain think he is slain,
They know not well the subtle ways
I keep, and pass, and turn again.

Ralph Waldo Emerson: *Brahma*

CHAPTER ONE

Big horse, God made you mine

'Have you noticed,' Joanna said as they sped along the M4 towards London, 'how the self-drive hire business has been completely taken over by that Dutch firm?'

'What Dutch firm?' Slider asked unwarily.

'Van Rentals.'

'How long have you been thinking that one out?'

'I resent the implication that my wit isn't spontaneous.'

'I resent your having been away,' he countered. 'It was daft going to Switzerland when it's cold enough here to freeze the balls off a brass tennis court.'

'Do you think I wanted to go?' Joanna said. 'Beethoven Eight six times in one week – and in a country where they still think fondue is cuisine.'

Despite the best efforts of that husband-and-wife circus act May Gurney and Cones Hotline, he had got to the airport in time to meet her. Though it was the umpteenth time he'd done it, there was still that thrill when she came out of the customs hall doors with her fiddle case in one hand and her battered old fits-under-the-seat-in-front travel bag over her shoulder. It had bothered him when she came through with the trumpet section, Peter White and Simon Angel. Put those two horny young bloods – only one of them married (and it was a well-known fact that blowing the trumpet had a direct effect on the production of testosterone) – together with a curvaceous love goddess like Joanna Marshall, and it spelled trouble with a capital Trub. But she had kissed him and pressed herself against him with an avidity that had had the lads whooping, so his pride was assuaged, and he led her off like a prize of war to find the car.

The Orchestra of the Age of the Renaissance, despite the handicap of a name that wouldn't fit across a poster unless it was in characters too small to read, had come in as a life-saver. Its fixer had called Joanna as a last-minute replacement for the pregnant deputy principal, whose blood pressure had gone over into the red zone. Post-Christmas was always a drought period for musicians, but this year was particularly bad. Her own orchestra had nothing for two months and freelance work was as rare as elephants' eggs.

Joanna's thoughts were evidently on the same track as she watched the chill, bare fields of Middlesex reel past the windows. 'Do you know what's in my diary between now and March?'

'Yes,' he said, but she told him again anyway.

'Two Milton Keynes dates and one Pro Arte of Oxford – and I'm lucky to get those.'

'Why are things so bad?' he ventured.

'They're just getting worse every year,' she said. 'Fewer people going to concerts or buying records, and more and more musicians pouring out of the colleges. And then,' she made a face, 'we all have to do this blasted "outreach" crapola, going into schools and encouraging more of the little beasts to take up music. If we had any sense we'd be breaking their arms, not telling them what a fulfilling life it is, ha ha.'

'Have you just come home to complain at me?' he asked, trying for a lighter note.

She didn't bite. 'Seriously, Bill, it's getting to be a hell of a problem. The Phil's in financial trouble and there's more amalgamation talk. That old chestnut, "Can London sustain four orchestras?" The Government's threatening to withdraw the grant from one of us, and everybody knows we're the likeliest.'

'But all this has been said before, and it never happens,' Slider comforted her.

'Even if it doesn't,' she said, sounding very low, 'we aren't getting enough dates to live on.'

'We'll manage somehow,' he said. 'Tighten our belts. We'll get through.'

'Hah!' she said. She didn't elaborate, for which he was grateful, but she meant, of course, how much belt-tightening can you do when your salary already has to go round an almost ex-wife and two school-age children?

But she wasn't a whiner, and a moment later she said, 'Peter and Simon were telling me on the plane about this wonderful scam for parking in the short-term car park while you're on tour. All you have to do is borrow a tuba.'

'A tuba?'

'Well, of course it only works if you're touring with a big orchestra. Anyway, apparently a tuba is a big enough mass of metal for the automatic barrier to mistake it for a car. So, when you get back from tour, you walk up to the entrance barrier holding the tuba in front of you, and it issues a ticket, which you then use to get out, throwing away the original one. You pay for ten minutes instead of two weeks. *Voilà*.'

'Should you be telling me this? I am a policeman.'

'That's what makes you so sexy.' Her warm hand crept gratefully over his upper thigh. 'I'm glad to be back,' she said. 'Have you missed me?'

'Does a one-legged duck swim in circles?'

'Nice hot bath and an early night tonight,' she said.

He'd just got to the bit where the motorway narrows to two lanes and his attention was distracted. 'I suppose you must be tired,' he said absently, keeping his eye on a BMW that didn't want to move in.

Her hand slid further up. 'Who said anything about sleeping?'

The office was its usual hive of activity when he got in. DS Jim Atherton, his bagman and friend, was sitting on a desk reading – of all things – *The Racing Post*.

'What do you reckon for the first race at Plumpton, Maurice?' he said.

'Shy Smile,' DC McLaren answered, without looking up from the sausage sandwich and *Daily Mail* that were occupying him. Atherton opined that McLaren read the tabloids only because the broadsheets needed two hands, which meant he couldn't eat and read at the same time.

'Are you sure?' Atherton probed. 'Everyone else gives Bally-doyle.'

'Not after that frost last night. Ballydoyle likes a bit of give in the ground.'

'Shy Smile?' Atherton pressed.

'She'll walk it,' said McLaren.

'How d'you know about horses anyway?' Anderson asked, clipping his nails into the waste-paper basket. 'I thought you grew up in Kennington.'

'Y'don't have to have a baby to be a gynaecologist,' McLaren answered mysteriously, sucking grease and newsprint off his fingers.

Slider, at the door, said, 'It would be nice if you could at least *pretend* to be usefully occupied when I come in. Give me an illusion of authority.'

'Didn't know you were there, guv,' McLaren said imperturbably, rolling a black tongue over his lips.

'That much is obvious.' Slider turned to Atherton. 'And why are you reading the racing pages? Since when did you have the slightest interest in the Sport of Kings?'

'Ah, it's a new investment ploy,' Atherton said, unhitching his behind from the desk. 'I'm thinking of buying a part share in a racehorse. I saw this ad in the paper and sent off for the details. I'm going to put my savings into it.'

'Have you been standing around under the power lines without your lead hat again?' Slider said mildly.

'Well, there's no point in leaving cash in deposit accounts, with interest rates at rock bottom,' Atherton said. 'And anyway, it's not a gamble, it's a scientific investment. Serious businessmen put big money into it. This Furlong Stud is a proper company: they've been putting together consortia for years. It's all in the information pack. It's no more risky than the stock market, really.'

'What's the name of the poor wreck of a horse they're trying to flog you?' Slider enquired.

'The one I'm looking at is called Two Left Feet,' Atherton announced, and when Slider groaned he said, 'No, it's a really cute name, don't you see? All horses have two left feet.'

'Mug punter,' said McLaren pityingly, turning a page. 'It's sad, really. Bet on the name, every time. Here,' he recalled suddenly, looking up, 'talk about names, did you see that story in the paper a bit since, about those two Irish owners who tried to register a colt, and Tattersalls wouldn't allow it? They wanted to call it Norfolk and Chance.'

'I'm worried about you,' Slider said, as Atherton followed him into his office. 'You didn't used to be irrational.'

'How do you know?' Atherton said cheerfully. 'Anyway, I need a bit of excitement in my life. I used to get it chasing women, but now I'm settled down in cosy domesticity, I have to look elsewhere for that thrill of danger.'

'I wish I thought you were joking,' Slider said, going round his desk. He shoved fretfully at the piles of files that burdened it. They bred during the night, he was sure of it. 'What's this steaming pile of Tottenham?'

'Case files. Ongoing. Mr Carver's firm passed them over, Mr Porson's orders. They're down four men again, with the 'flu.'

'Carver's firm are always catching things,' Slider complained. 'What do they do, sleep together?'

'I wouldn't be a bit surprised,' Atherton said. 'It's worse than it looks, anyway. Most of it's to do with that suspected fags-and-booze smuggling ring.'

'Take 'em away,' Slider decreed. 'I'm too frail for gang warfare at this stage of the week.'

WDC Swilley, who had answered the phone out in the office, came to the door now, her posture suddenly galvanised, which, since Swilley was built like a young lad's secret dream, was hardly fair on the two within. 'We've got a murder, boss!' she announced happily.

'Gordon Bennett, what next?' Slider said. 'It shouldn't be allowed on a Friday.'

'Phoebe Agnew!' Atherton enthused as he drove, with an air of doing it one-handed, through the end of the rush-hour traffic. How come so many people went to work so late? 'I mean, I know she's a bit of a thorn in the copper's side—'

'In spades,' Slider agreed.

'Yeah, but what a journalist! Took the Palgabria Prize in 1990, and winner of the John Perkins Award for '97 and '98 – the only person ever to win it two years running, incidentally. And she really can write, guv. Awesomely chilling prose.'

'Well, don't get so excited. You're not going to have a conversation with her,' Slider pointed out.

Atherton's face fell a fraction. 'No, you're right. What a wicked waste!'

As they turned off the main road they found their way blocked by a dustcart. It had a selection of grubby teddy bears and dolls tied to the radiator grille. Why did scaffies do that, Slider wondered. With their arms outstretched and their hopeless eyes staring ahead, they looked depressingly like a human shield.

Atherton backed fluidly, turned, and roared down another side street. 'Anyway, AMIP's bound to take the case from us,' he said.

The Area Major Incident Pool took all the serious or high-profile crimes and, these days, virtually all murders, unless they were straightforward domestics. Judson, the present head of 6 AMIP, was an empire-builder. He was that most hated of creatures, the career uniform man who had transferred to CID purely in pursuit of promotion.

'Judson's welcome to it,' Slider said. 'He'll probably enjoy being crawled over by the press.'

'You are in a doldrum,' Atherton said, turning into Eltham Road, which was parked right up both sides, like everywhere else in London these days.

'You can't have a single doldrum,' said Slider. 'They always hunt in packs. This is it. You'll have to double park.'

'It's the reason I became a policeman,' said Atherton.

The house was one of a terrace, built in the late nineteenth century, of two storeys, plus the semi-basement – which Londoners call 'the area' – over which a flight of wide, shallow steps led up to the front door. Eltham Road was in one of the borderline areas between the old, working-class Shepherd's Bush and the new yuppiedom, and a few years ago Slider would have said it might go either way. But rising incomes and outward pressure from the centre of London were making his familiar ground more and more desirable in real-estate terms, and there was no doubt in his mind now that the 'unimproved' properties in this street soon wouldn't recognise themselves. Anyone who had bought here ten years ago would be sitting on a handsome profit.

The house in question was divided into three flats, and it was the middle one which had been occupied by Phoebe Agnew, a freelance journalist whose name was enough to make any policeman shudder. An ex-*Guardian* hack with impeccable left-wing credentials, she had made a name for herself for investigating corruption, and had concentrated in recent years on the establishment and the legal system, exposing bad apples, and sniffing out miscarriages of justice with the zeal of perfect hindsight.

Slider was all for rooting out bent coppers; that was in everyone's interest. His biggest beef with Agnew was that she had been instrumental in the release of the Portland Two, attacking the evidence that had got a pair of exceedingly nasty child-murderers put away. Well, the law was the law, and you had to play by the rules: he accepted that. Still, it galled coppers who remembered the case to hear Heaton and Donaldson described as 'innocent', just because some harried DC at the time had got his paperwork in a muddle. And who was the better for it? The Two had been quietly doing their porridge, and would have been up for parole in a couple of years. Getting them out on a technicality had simply banged another nail into the coffin of public confidence. According to eager *Guardian* polls, half the population now believed the police went round picking up innocent people at random for the sheer joy of fitting them up.

Well, now Phoebe Agnew was dead. The biter bit, perhaps – and theirs to identify the guilty dentition.

At the front door PC Renker was keeping guard and the SOC record. With his helmet on and his big blond moustache, he looked like exotic grass growing under a cloche.

'Doc Cameron's inside, sir,' he reported, 'and the photographer, and forensic's on the way. Asher's upstairs with the female that found the body – lives in the top flat. Bottom tenant's a Peter Medmenham, but he's not in, apparently.'

'Probably at work,' Slider said. The front door let into a vestibule, which contained two further Yale-locked doors. They were built across what was obviously the original hall of the house, to judge by the black-and-white diamond floor tiles. One gave access to the stairs to the top flat; the other was standing open onto the rest of the hall and Phoebe Agnew's flat. It had been the main part of the original family house, and had the advantage of the fine cornices and ceiling roses, elaborate architraves and panelled doors; but it had been converted long enough ago to have had the fireplaces ripped out and plastered over.

There was a small kitchen at the front of the house, a tiny windowless bathroom next to it, and two other rooms. The smaller was furnished as an office, with a desk, filing cabinets, cupboards, bookshelves, personal computer and fax machine, and on every surface a mountain range of papers and files that made Slider's fade into foothills.

'Oh, what fun we'll have sorting through that lot!' Atherton enthused, clasping his hands.

'We?' Slider said cruelly.

The other room, which stretched right across the back of the house, was furnished as a bedsitting room.

'Odd decision,' said Atherton. 'Why not have the separate bedroom and the office in here?'

'Maybe she liked to get away from work once in a while,' Slider said.

'I suppose it saves time on seduction techniques,' Atherton said, always willing to learn something new. 'Shorter step from sofa to bed. I wonder what she spent all her money on? It wasn't home comforts, that's for sure.'

The furnishings were evidently old and didn't look as if they'd ever been expensive. There was a large and shabby high-backed sofa covered with cushions and a fringed crimson plush throw, which looked like an old-fashioned chenille tablecloth. In front of it was a massive coffee table, of dark wood with a glass inset top, on the other side of which were two elderly and unmatching armchairs. One had a dented cushion, and a bottle of White Horse and a glass stood on the floor by its right foreleg. The other was a real museum piece with metal hoop arms and 1950s 'contemp'ry' patterned fabric. There was a folded blanket concealing something on its seat. Slider lifted the edge and saw that it was a heap of papers, correspondence and files, topped off with some clean but unironed laundry. The quickest way to tidy up, perhaps.

Along one wall was a low 'unit' of imitation light oak veneer, early MFI by the look of it, on top of which stood a television and video, a hi-fi stack, a fruit bowl containing some rather wrinkled apples and two black bananas, a litre bottle of Courvoisier and a two-litre bottle of Gordon's, part empty, some used coffee cups and glasses, and a derelict spider plant in a white plastic pot. The hi-fi was still switched on, and several CDs were lying about – Vivaldi, Mozart and Bach – while the open case of the

CD presumably still in the machine was lying on the top of the stack: Schubert, Quintet in C.

Along another wall were bookshelves with cupboards below, the shelves tightly packed, mostly with paperbacks, but with a fair sprinkling of hardback political biographies. 'Review copies,' Atherton said. 'The great journalistic freebie.' Slider looked at a title or two. Hattersley, Enoch Powell, Dennis Healey. But Woodrow Wyatt? Wasn't he a builder?

The window was large and looked over the small, sooty garden, to which there was no access from up here. It was the original sash with the lever-lock, which was, he noted, in the locked position. Of course, someone breaking in that way could have locked it before departing by the door.

'But then, why should they?' said Atherton. 'The Yale on that door's so old and loose a child could slip it. You'd have thought someone in her position would have been a bit more security-minded.'

Slider shook his head. 'Obviously she was unworldly.'

'Other-worldly now, if you want to be precise.'

The right-hand end of the room was furnished with a wardrobe, a tallboy, a low chest of drawers doubling as bedside table, and a double bed, pushed up into the back corner and covered with a black cotton counterpane. The wardrobe was decorated with a variety of old stickers: CND; Nuclear Power – No Thanks; Stop the Bloody Whaling; Troops Out of Vietnam; and, fondly familiar to Slider, the round, yellow Keep Music Live sticker. Instead of pictures there were posters stuck up on the magnolia-painted walls, amongst them a very old one of Che, a couple of vintage film posters, some political flyers and rally leaflets, and some cartoon originals which were probably pretty valuable. The room, though tidy, was scruffy and full of statements, like a student bedsit from the early 1970s. Given the age and status of the occupant, it seemed a deliberate two fingers raised at conventional, middle-class expectations.

The body was on the bed.

Freddie Cameron, the forensic pathologist, straightened and looked up as Slider approached. He was as dapper as a sea lion, a smallish, quick-moving man in a neat grey suit, with a dark waistcoat and, today, a very cheery tartan bow-tie – the sort only a very self-confident man or an expensive teddy bear could have got away with. It was the kind of bow-tie that had to be sported, rather than merely worn, and Cameron sported it, jaunty as a good deed in a naughty world.

'Bill! Hello, old chum,' he warbled. 'Good way to end the week. How's tricks?'

'Trix? She's fine, but I've told you not to mention her in front of the boy,' Slider replied sternly.

Freddie blinked. 'Ha! I see they haven't knocked the cheek out of you, anyway. You know who we've got here?'

'I do indeed.'

'There won't be many tears shed for her in the Job, I suppose. Sad loss to journalism, all the same.'

Slider raised his eyebrows. 'I didn't think you read the *Grauniad.*'

'*Indy* man, me,' Cameron admitted. 'But she wrote for that occasionally, and the *Staggers*, which I read sometimes. Got to keep an open mind. I always liked her pieces, even when I didn't agree with her.'

'*Someone* didn't agree with her,' Slider said, and – there being no more excuse for ignoring it – for the first time looked directly at the corpse.

What had been Phoebe Agnew was sprawled on her back, one leg slipping off the edge of the bed, toes touching the carpet. Her arms were flung back above her head, and her wrists were tied together and to the bedhead with a pair of tights. Her auburn hair, long and thick and loosely curling, was spread out around her like a sunburst, vivid against the black cloth, seeming to draw all the life and colour out of the room. It was amazing hair in any circumstance, but if, as Atherton had told him, she was around fifty, it was doubly so, because the colour looked entirely natural.

She was wearing a large, loose, oatmeal-coloured knitted sweater and was naked from the waist down; a pair of grey wool trousers and scarlet bikini briefs lay on the floor at the foot of the bed. Slider flinched inwardly, and felt a stab of pity for the woman, so exposed in this helpless indignity. It was always the worst bit, the first moment of acknowledging the person whose life had been taken from them without their will. There she lay, mutely reproachful, beseeching justice. A body is just a body, of course, but still it wears the face of a person who lived, and was self-aware, and who didn't want to die.

The nakedness seemed worse because she was not young: there is an arrogance to the nakedness of youth which defies ridicule. In life she must have been good-looking, perhaps even beautiful, Slider thought, noting the classical nose, the wide mouth, the strong chin; but no-one looks their best after being strangled. The face was swollen and suffused, the open eyes horribly bloodshot; her lips were bluish, and there was blood on them, and in her left ear; and round her neck was the livid mark of the ligature. The ligature, however, had been removed.

After all these years, the first sight of a corpse still raised Slider's pulse and made him feel hot and prickly for a moment – almost like a kind of violent teenage embarrassment. He took a couple of deep breaths until it subsided.

Atherton looked away, shoving his hands into his pockets. Tall and elegant, gracefully drooping, he looked as out of place in this room as a borzoi in a scrapyard. 'Wonder why they took one ligature and left the other,' he said.

'Maybe the one round her neck was traceable in some way,' Slider said. 'Time of death, Freddie?'

'Well, she's cold and stiff, so that puts it between eight and thirty-six hours, according to the jolly old textbook. It's not over-warm in here, and though she looks reasonably fit she's no spring chicken, so I'd put it in the middle range, say twelve to twenty-four. Not less than twelve, anyway.'

'So we're looking at sometime yesterday, probably evening or afternoon,' Slider said. 'And I suppose the cause of death was strangulation?'

'I wouldn't like to commit myself until I've got her on the table. There are no other apparent injuries, but I'm not blessed with infra-red vision, and it's getting dark as Newgate Knocker in here. These hypoxia cases are notoriously tricky, anyway. But she certainly has been strangled.'

'There doesn't seem to have been a struggle,' Slider said. 'No furniture overturned or anything.'

'She may have been drugged, of course,' Cameron said. 'Which is why I reserve judgement on the cause of death. Have you seen enough? Well, let's get the photos done, then, and we can get her out of here.'

Slider left him to it and went to look at the kitchen. It must have been fitted in about 1982, with cheap units whose doors had slumped out of alignment, and daisy-patterned tiles, all in shades of brown: pure eighties chic. The cooker was old and flecked with encrusted spillings that hasty cleaning had missed. The fridge was also old, with leaking seals, and filled with a clutter of bowls containing leftovers: bits of food on plates, ends of cheese in crumpled wrappings, an expiring lettuce, and tomatoes that had gone wrinkly. A bottle of skimmed milk was past its sell-by date and there was a platoon of yoghurts, one of which had a crack down the side of its carton and was dribbling messily. The comparative tidiness of the bedsitting room was evidently only skin deep.

The sink, with draining boards and a washing machine under it, had been fitted into the bay window. There was a plastic washing-up bowl in the sink. In it, and on the draining boards, was a collection of dirty utensils: plates and bowls, knives, forks and spoons, saucepans and various serving vessels. It looked as though there had been a dinner, featuring some kind of casserole, vegetables and potatoes followed by tiramisu. The last wasn't hard to guess as the remaining half of it was still in its glass dish sitting on top of the grill hood of the gas stove. There were several empty bottles standing at the back of the work surface – three wine and one brandy – though there was no knowing how long they'd been there. They might not all appertain to the same meal.

The meal surprised him a little. Knowing Phoebe Agnew's politics, he would have bet on her being a vegetarian. And actually, given the state of the flat and the fridge, he would have expected her to be above cooking, just as she was apparently above home-making. The cookery books lying open amid the clutter of the work surface suggested a certain lack of practice in the art. *Casserole Cookery*, with the unconvincing, orange-toned food photographs of the seventies by way of illustration, was obviously old but had not, to judge from the lack of food splashes, been heavily used in its life. It was open at Italian-Style Chicken With Olives and had a fresh smear of tomato paste on one edge. The other book, *New Italian Cooking*, was brand new – so much so that the page had had to be weighted to stay open at Tiramisu.

So she had entertained someone to a home-cooked meal yesterday and gone to some trouble about it: in his experience women never got out the cookery books for a man they were sure of. But was it the murderer she had cooked for? Or had she been dozing off the effects of the grub and booze when someone else called to cancel her ticket?

'Guv, come and look at this,' Atherton called.

He was in the bathroom. Being windowless it had one of those fans that come on with the light. It was as ineffective as they usually are: the room had that sour smell of rancid water you get in towels that have been put away damp. It needed redecoration: the Crystal tiles staggered crazily over the uneven walls, the grouting on its last legs, and the paint on the woodwork was lumpy and peeling. There was a calcium crust around the taps, and the bath and basin were mottled white where the hard water had marked them, which looked particularly nasty since the suite was brown.

'My whole life just flashed before me,' Slider said. A brown bath had been the *dernier cri* when he first married.

There was a washing line strung over the bath, on which hung more undies from a well-known high street store. Naturally she would shop at Marks and Engels, Slider thought. He counted six used towels – on the rail, over the edge of the bath, stretched over the radiator, and 'hung up on the floor', as his mother used to say.

'And the plug hole's clogged with soapy hair,' he commented, looking, though not too closely, into the sink.

'Never mind that, see here,' Atherton said, and drew back for Slider to look into the lavatory bowl. The sad little rubber 'o' of a condom looked back at them.

'She definitely had company,' Atherton said.

'We already knew that,' said Slider. 'Better fish it out.'

'*Me?*'

'Don't whine. You've got gloves on.'

'It's the principle of the thing,' Atherton grumbled. 'I was fashioned for love, not labour.' As he reached fastidiously into the bowl, he was reminded of an anecdote. 'The plumber I use now and then told me about how this woman called him out one time because she wanted a new lav fitted. He asked her if she wanted a P-trap or an S-trap, and she went bright red with embarrassment and said, "Oh – well – it's for both, really."'

'Get on with it,' Slider said. Outside there was the sound of reinforcements arriving, and a voice he hadn't expected. 'Is that the Super? What the chuck's he doing here?'

'The voice of the turtle was heard in our land,' said Atherton. He secured the floating evidence and followed Slider out.

It seemed to have got even colder, and the sky was now featureless, low and grey, like the underside of a submarine. Detective Superintendent Fred 'The Syrup' Porson was on the doorstep, draped in a wonderful old Douglas Hurd coat of military green, voluminous and floor-length. What you might call army surplice, Slider thought. Behind Porson stood three of his DCs, presumably brought in the same car – the Department was short of wheels, as always.

'Ah, Bill,' Porson said. The cold air had given his skin a greyish tinge. With his big-nosed, granite face he looked remarkably like one of the Easter Island heads; the preposterous toupee was like a crop of vegetation growing on the top. 'What's the current situation, vis-à-vis deceased? Let's have a stasis report.'

Porson used language with the delicate touch of a man in boxing gloves playing the harpsichord. It was one of the endearing things about him – as long as you didn't suffer from perfect literary pitch.

'It looks as though it wasn't suicide, sir,' Slider said. He recapped briefly, while Porson tramped restlessly on the spot like a horse, using his hands thrust into his pockets to wrap the strange coat about him.

'Hm. Yes. Well. I see,' he said. He seemed in travail of a decision. 'You are aware, of course,' he said at last, 'that this 'flu epidemic has precipitated a crisis situation, Area-wide, with regard to personnel? It's a problem right across the broad, and as such, AMIP has asked if we'd be prepared to keep the case.'

Slider raised his eyebrows. 'It'll be high profile, sir.'

'The highest of the high, to coin a phrase,' Porson agreed. A few tiny pinpoints of snow were drifting down, settling on the eponymous rug. It looked as though it was developing dandruff. Slider dragged his eyes away – Porson didn't like the wig to be noticed. 'The papers will be full of it,' Porson went on. 'Our every movement will be scrutinised with a tooth-comb. I'm well aware

it'll be no picnic, believe you me. But the fly in the argument *is*',
he explained, 'that AMIP's even worse hit, absentee-wise, than
we are. Half their manpower's been decimated, *plus* they've
got three other major investigations on the go as well. So the
upshoot is, they've asked if we'll do the premilinary work, at
least to begin with.'

Slider shrugged. Upshoot or offshot, his was not to reason
why. 'I hope the budget will stand it, sir,' he said.

'Don't you worry about that.' Porson seemed relieved at his
docility. 'I'll sort all that out with AMIP. Well, now I'm here you'd
better show me round, recapitate what you've got so far.'

Slider obliged. Only as Porson was leaving did he think to
ask, 'By the way, sir, how did AMIP hear about it so soon?'

Porson gave a grim smile. 'They heard it from Commander
Wetherspoon. Some reporter rang him at ten this morning,
asking who was heading the investigation.'

'Good God,' said Slider.

'So you see the problem.'

He tramped off down the steps to the car, his coat brushing
regally behind him. Atherton, at Slider's shoulder, said, 'Given
who she was, I suppose there was never a cat in hell's chance
of keeping the press out of it.'

'Not a toupee's chance in a wind tunnel,' Slider agreed.

'That's not an original toupee, you know, it's an elaborate
postiche,' Atherton said. Another car pulling up further down the
road caught his attention. Two men got out and headed towards
them with an air of restraining themselves from running. 'I hope
the Super's sending us some more uniform – the vultures are
beginning to gather,' he said.

'If you stand around there you'll get your picture taken,' Slider
warned. 'Time to go and talk to the female that found the body,
I think.'

CHAPTER TWO

Many are cold, but few are frozen

In contrast to Phoebe Agnew's unreconstructed seventies pit, the upstairs flat had been through the sort of make-over that wouldn't have disgraced a *Changing Rooms* designer. Its tiny fragment of hall was made almost unbearably elegant by a bamboo plant stand bearing a vase of artificial roses, a large mirror in an elaborate gold plastic frame and, dangling from the ceiling, a Chinese lantern with tassels.

The Chinese theme continued up the stairs with red and gold wallpaper, vaguely willow-patterned. The carpet was crimson, and at the top was a small landing and a glimpse through an open door of a dark and sultry boudoir, with red flock wallpaper and velvet curtains, a double bed covered in a purple and gold brocade counterpane, a velvet chair stuffed with tasselled silk cushions, pierced-work incense burners, and a surprising number of mirrors, including a full-length cheval standing at the foot of the bed.

The sitting room, by contrast, was furnished in cheap, bright Ikea pine and jolly primary colours, chiefly yellow and lime. There was a window-seat occupied by a row of stuffed toys; the mantelpiece and various tables bore a collection of china animals, mostly pigs, frogs and mice; and on the walls were pictures of winsome puppies and kittens and other adorable fluffy baby animals in agonisingly lovable poses. There were enough moist eyes in that room, Slider reckoned, to have supplied an entire sultan's banquet.

'The occupant of this flat', Atherton concluded, 'is either seriously schizophrenic, or a working girl.'

'Oh dear, how will we ever tell which?' Slider wondered.

The occupant was sitting on the sofa before a gas fire, sniffling into a Kleenex. WPC Asher stood at hand with the box, and made an enigmatic face over her head as the two appeared in the doorway.

'Miss Jekyll, I presume?' Slider enquired.

She looked up. 'Eh?'

'What's your name, love?'

'Candi,' she said. 'With an "i". Candi Du Cane.'

'Real name?'

She looked a trifle sulky. 'Lorraine, if you must know. Lorraine Peabody.'

She had a chubby, snubbily pretty face which gave her an air of extreme youth, though closer examination suggested she was in her middle twenties. Her hair was straight and dyed blonde, pulled back carelessly in a wispy tail; her juicily plump figure was outlined by a black body, over which she wore a tracksuit bottom, and a vast knitted cardigan which looked as if it came from the same needles as Phoebe Agnew's sweater. It was so much too big for her that she'd had to roll the sleeves into thick sausage cuffs just to get her hands free. Her eyes and nose were red with weeping, and there was a black smudge under her eyes where the mascara had washed off with her tears.

'Lorraine's a nice name too,' Slider said, taking Asher's place on the sofa. Candi/Lorraine looked at him with the automatic alarm of the born victim. 'I want to ask you some questions – nothing to worry about,' Slider said. 'I'm Detective Inspector Slider. You're the one who found the body, aren't you?'

She shivered in automatic reaction, and then excused herself by saying, 'It's bleedin' taters in here. The central 'eating never works prop'ly, but old Sborski – the landlord – he won't never do nothing about it.'

'You don't own the flat, then?'

'No, s'only rented. I did talk to Phoebe once about buying a place, but she said for girls like us what was the point? She said you might as well spend your money on yourself an' enjoy it as tie it up in bricks an' mortar. But it's just you can never get nothing done.' She was talking rapidly, and her voice was tight and too high. 'I mean, Sborski's a real old bastard. Last year there was water coming through the roof right over my bed, and he wouldn't do nothing about it until Phoebe got on to him. She was brilliant. She jus' stood up to people, you know? If it wasn't for her—'

She shivered again and hunched further into her vast jumper, her eyes wide and strained.

'Shall I turn the fire up a bit?' Slider asked, eyeing it doubtfully. It was a vintage piece with brown and wonky ceramic panels and four flames of uneven height, one of which was yellow and popped rhythmically.

'Nah, it don't work on the other setting,' Lorraine said. 'I'll be all right. I jus' can't get it out me mind – you know, what I seen down there.' Her arms wrapped around herself, she began to rock a little.

Slider saw hysteria not too far off. 'Don't think about it for the moment,' he said in his cosiest voice. 'Tell me about you. You're – what? – a model?'

'Well, I've done modelling,' she allowed. 'I do escort work mostly. Hostessing. Promotional. That sort o' thing.' She met his eye and, as though goaded by an irresistible honesty, blurted, 'Well, *you* know.'

Slider nodded. He did indeed. 'Lived here long?'

'Two years, nearly.'

'You've done it up really nicely,' Slider said with his fatherly smile, the one that melted the golden hearts of tarts.

'Ju like it? My mum always said I got a flair for it – colour an' that. Said I shoulda gone in for it, for a living.'

'I bet you could have. And all these animals – quite a collection you've got.'

A little more of this and she had stopped shivering and staring and was beginning to unwrap her arms. Slider led her gently up to the fence again. 'So Phoebe only rented the flat below, then, like you?'

'Yeah. I don't think she cared much about stuff like that. Possessions an' stuff. She was always on about causes an' everything.'

'You knew her well?'

'Yeah. Well, she was always really nice to me, done things for me, like making old Sborski mend the roof an' that. I used to go down for a chat an' we used to sit an' have a drink an' a laugh an' everything. She was great. She always had time for you.'

'You obviously liked her.'

'Yeah, she was a great laugh. You'd never've fought she was as old as she was. I mean, I could never talk to my mum, but Phoebe was like as if she was the same age as me. Ever so modern and young in her attitudes an' everyfing. Except for abortion. Funny, she was really down on that. The only time she ever went for me was when I got up the duff an' said I was gettin' rid of it. She tried to talk me out of it – I mean,' she said in amazement, 'what'd I do wiv a kid? She wouldn't talk to me for ages after that. But it blew over. She was a real mate.'

'She lived there alone, did she? She wasn't married?'

'Nah, she never had time for all that. She said she had enough of dealing with men all day, without having to come home and look after one. She had *'ad* boyfriends – she was quite normal in that respect,' she assured him earnestly, her blue eyes wide. 'But she said, "You and me, L'raine," she said, "we know the trouble men cause in the world," she said, an' she said, "You and me know marriage ain't the answer to every problem." Not like some o' them daft girls you see on the telly, think gettin' a man's the most important thing in life.'

'Did Phoebe have men friends come to visit her?' Slider asked casually.

'She had friends all right,' Lorraine said cautiously. 'I've see people go in and out, but I couldn't tell you pacificly, not names or anythink. Up here, I wouldn't know if someone come unless I was looking out the window. But she did have someone in yesterday.' She looked at him hopefully, wanting to please.

'How do you know that?'

'Well, I went down to the hall about twelve o'clock time to see if there was any letters. I'd just got up. And as I open me door, Phoebe comes in wiv her arms full of shopping.'

'She came in from the street?'

'Yeah, wiv all bags of food an' that. So I says, how about a cup a coffee an' that, because we hadn't had a good old chat for ages, not since before Christmas, really. But she says no, she can't stop because she's got someone coming to dinner and she's got to get the place tidied up.'

'Did she say who was coming?'

'No, but she seemed sort of excited, so I reckoned it was a man. I mean, she wouldn't tidy up for a girlfriend, would she? I made a joke about it, because she never normally tidied anything. Me, I like things nice, but her place was always a tip. Tell the trufe, I couldn't see her cooking for a girlfriend either. I mean, she mostly eats out, or buys a Marks an' Sparks thing, from what I've seen.'

'Did she say what time this person was coming?'

'Nah, but when I was going back up I asked if she fancied coming down the pub later, an' she said no, she couldn't, because of this person coming, and she said she didn't want to be disturbed and not to knock on her door or ring her up for any reason whatever. So I just said pardon me for living, an' I went. And that was the last time I see her.' She sniffed. 'If I'd of knew it was the last time, I'd of never of said that. But she got up my nose.'

'Why did she? Was she bad-tempered about it?'

'Oh no, not really. Like I said, she seemed kind of pleased an' excited when she said about someone coming; but then when she said that – about not disturbing her – she went all strict and teachery, an' I just thought, well, I thought, excuse *me*! I know when I'm not wanted.'

Slider was accustomed to the habit of the ignorant of taking offence for no reason. She must have been a trying neighbour for the intellectual Agnew – probably forever 'popping down for a coffee'. A person who worked from home was always vulnerable to the dropper-in with an empty schedule and a vacant mind.

'I suppose you didn't see the visitor arrive?' he asked without hope.

'Not as such,' she admitted reluctantly, 'but I think I heard music playing down there later, so I reckon he must of come all right.'

'What time would that have been?'

'I dunno, really.' She thought for a moment. 'It must a' been about hapass six, summink like that, 'cos I had the radio on before that, but I turned it off when I went to have me bath, and then I heard the music downstairs, that classical shite she likes.' She made a face. No votes here for Vivaldi and Bach, then.

'What about during the evening? Did you hear any other noises from downstairs?'

'Well I wasn't in, was I? I went out about seven, down the club.'

'Which club?'

'The Shangri-la,' she said. 'D'you know it?'

He did indeed. It was a well-known pick-up place for prostitutes, and he had always wondered whether it was by design or accident that the illuminated sign over the door had lost its 'n'.

He was about to ask the next question when she evidently thought of something. 'Oh, wait! I dunno if it matters, but I did hear the door downstairs bang. That'd be about sevenish. I was just pulling the curtains in here, 'cos I was going out. So that could of been him going. And now I come to think of it, when I went past her door just after, there was no music playing inside, in her flat. So he must of went.'

'Didn't you look down and see, when you heard the door bang? You were standing at the window.'

'Well, no, 'cos I'd just pulled the curtains closed. And I wasn't that interested, tell you the trufe.'

Slider sighed inwardly. 'And what time did you come back from the club?'

'It was about – I dunno, going on ten o'clock.'

'Alone?'

She looked away. 'Maybe, maybe not. What's it matter?'

'Of course it matters. Look, Lorraine,' he explained carefully to her stubbornly averted profile, 'we're going to have to ask everyone if they saw anyone entering or leaving this house yesterday evening. We'll get hundreds of reports, and we'll have to go through them all. Now if we can cross out the ones we know came to see you, it'll help us find the right one. Do you see?' She didn't answer. 'Don't you want to help find out who killed Phoebe?'

She wavered, but said, 'I ain't gettin' meself into trouble. I ain't getting no-one into trouble.'

'There's no trouble in it, not for you or your visitors. I just want to eliminate them.'

She looked sidelong at him. 'What if I don't remember their names?'

'A description and the time they came and left will do, if that's all you've got. You'll have to write it all out for me.' She still looked far from convinced, and he left the subject for now and went on, 'Tell me what happened this morning.'

'Well,' she said cautiously, 'I just come down this morning to bum a bit of coffee off of her, 'cos I'd run out. I rung her bell and, like, shouted out through the door, "It's only me, Feeb," but there was no answer.'

'What time was that?'

''Bout quart' to ten, ten to ten maybe.'

'Go on.'

'Well,' she said, and paused. 'The thing is,' she went on, and paused again.

He thought he saw her difficulty. 'If the door was closed, how did you get in? Have you got a key?'

'Well, not *as such*,' she said reluctantly, 'although she has give me a key from time to time, when she wanted someone letting in, a workman or something, you know?'

'But you didn't, in fact, have a key this morning?' Slider pressed.

Now she looked defiant. 'All right, if you must know, I slipped the lock. Well, I knew Feeb wouldn't mind. She never minded me lending a bit o' coffee or whatever. And it was me what pointed it out to her in the first place, how rotten that lock was and how anybody could get in. I told her she ought to make Sborski get a new one fixed, but she never got round to it. I don't think she was that bothered. She trusted people too much, that was her problem.'

Slider nodded patiently. 'So you went in?'

'I called out, "Are you there, Feeb?", 'cos the front room door was open and I could see the curtains was still shut, so I thought she might be sleeping in.'

By 'the front room' she meant, of course, the living room. Slider was accustomed to this Londonism and was not confused. 'Was the light on or off?' he asked.

'Off. That's what I mean, it was dark in there, so she might have been still in bed. Well, so I went up to the door and just stuck me head round, and I see her laying there. I could see right away something was wrong, the way she was laying. So I went and pulled the curtains back.' Another pause. The chubby face was very pale now, and the hands gripping the handkerchief were shaking as she relived it. 'Then I see her face and everything.'

Slider prompted her gently. 'So what did you do?'

'I jus' dialled 999.'

'You used her phone? The one in the room?'

She nodded. So that ruled out last number redial, which might have been useful.

'It was awful, with her laying there, you know the way she was – and her eyes open an' everything. After I phoned they said to wait there but I couldn't stay in the room with her like that. So I went out in the hall and pulled the door to. It felt like hours, waiting. I thought they'd never come. And', the thought struck her, 'I've never even had me cup a coffee yet.'

'Well, I shall want you to come down to the station and make a statement,' Slider said, 'so we can give you a cup of coffee there.'

'What, I've got to say all this again?' she asked indignantly.

'For the record,' he said. 'And you've got to list all your visitors for me. But it's nice and warm there, and the coffee's not bad. You can have a bun as well. They do a nice Danish.' She shrugged and sighed, but had plainly resigned herself to her fate. 'By the way, did Phoebe ever mention to you anyone that she was afraid of,' he went on, 'or anyone that might want to do her harm?'

She shook her head slowly. 'No, I don't know about that. There was this bloke I seen hanging about sometimes – Wolsey, Woolley, some name like that. She got him off this charge. He was s'pose to've blagged some building society, but he reckoned he was fitted up, an' she found some evidence to get him off.'

'Michael Wordley?' Atherton suggested.

'Yeah, Wordley, that's him,' Lorraine said.

Slider nodded, remembering the case. It had been a sore point at the time: Miss Agnew hadn't hesitated to generalise from the particular. 'But why would he want to harm her? He'd be grateful to her, wouldn't he?'

'You haven't seen him. He's a right tasty bastard, built like a brick khasi, face like a bagful o' spanners. He's a nutter, and you never know what them sort'll do next. I tell you, I never liked having him come round here, I don't care what Phoebe said. I mean, you've only got to say one wrong word, or look at 'em a bit funny, and you've had it. If anyone coulda done – what they done to her,' she said with a shudder, 'it was him.'

Ungrammatical, but emphatic. 'When did you last see him round here?'

'I can't remember exactly. It would be – I dunno, maybe last week or the week before.'

'Well, we'll certainly look into him,' Slider said. 'Anyone else you can think of?'

'No, but she had been worried lately,' Lorraine said. 'She never said what about, but for weeks now she's been a bit—'

'Preoccupied?'

'Yeah. Yesterday was the first time I seen her smiling an' happy for, like, a couple o' months. Well, since Christmas, really. An' then some bastard goes an' does that to her! It's not fair,' she mourned. 'I bet it was that nutter.'

'One more thing,' Slider said, 'do you know who her next of kin was? Are her parents still alive?'

'I dunno. She never said.'

'Any brothers or sisters?'

'She never mentioned any to me,' Lorraine said slowly. 'We didn't talk about that sort o' thing much. Maybe Peter'd know – him what lives down the area. He's lived here longer'n me. He was always in there, chatting away. Real bunny merchant. Bored the pants off Phoebe, if you want my opinion, but she was too polite to say. Always too nice to everyone, that was her trouble.'

'He doesn't seem to be in at the moment. I expect he's at work, isn't he?'

'I 'spec' so. He's a reporter, works for the *Ham and Ful*,' said Lorraine.

The *Hammersmith and Fulham Chronicle* was a local paper, but with ambitions to be the next *Manchester Guardian* and go national. It took itself seriously, reported hard news, uncovered local council scandals, campaigned for the homeless and refugees, and hardly ever mentioned jumble sales or 'amdram' pantomimes.

'So,' said Atherton as they went downstairs again, 'another newshound. Maybe that accounts for the rapid response.'

'What, you think he was the reporter who rang the Commander? But how could he have known about it?'

'Maybe he did it.'

'Down, boy,' said Slider.

Back in the Agnew flat, the body had been taken away. The room was strangely lifeless, all colour gone with her. The tattiness was now merely depressing rather than defiant.

'There's a mess of stuff to be sorted through,' Atherton said gloomily. 'Why did she live in a place like this, anyway? I'd have thought she earned plenty.'

'You heard from L'raine what a saint she was. Maybe she gave it all away to charity.'

'And leapt tall buildings in a single bound,' Atherton said. 'No, I see her as one of those pathetic pseudo-intellectuals who leech on dimwits to give themselves a sense of superiority. Better to reign in hell, etcetera, etcetera.'

'I don't know,' Slider said. 'With Candi up-atop and Peter the Bunny down under, I'd have thought Phoebe Agnew was the one being leeched on.'

'Precisely my point,' Atherton groused. 'Why didn't she stop slumming it and move somewhere else?'

'Did you get a package of hostility through the post this morning? I thought you thought she was a brilliant writer.'

'She was obviously a slob,' Atherton said, watching the forensic team opening cupboards and drawers. The tidying had evidently been done student-style, by bundling up everything visible and stuffing it into hiding. 'Why can't we ever investigate someone with a minimalist lifestyle?'

Slider had left his side and was talking to Bob Lamont, who had come in person to lift the fingerprints. 'What's it look like?'

'Dabs everywhere. A real mess. She wasn't houseproud,' said Lamont. 'I've done all the usual places – door, light switch and so on.'

'Do the cutlery, wineglasses and bottles in the kitchen, will you,' Slider said. 'Working on the assumption it was the killer she cooked for—'

'You don't want much, do you?' Lamont complained.

'Have you done the CD covers?'

'Just about to.'

'Good. Maybe he put music on to kill by. Oh,' he added, 'and what about the flush-handle on the loo – that's one they often forget.'

'Shall be done.'

Slider's own troops were already starting to sort and bag papers from the areas that had been finished with. Atherton turned as he came back to him. 'I suppose we've got to sort through all this lot to find the next of kin.'

'No, you can ring one of the papers,' Slider said. 'They're bound to have a morgue piece on her.'

'Brilliant, boss.'

'That's me. Try the *Independent* first. Better not start off by suggesting to the *Grauniad* that they know more about the case than you do. And when you've done that, ring the *Ham and Ful* and find out where the downstairs tenant is.'

'He's probably somewhere giving himself an interview,' Atherton said.

Just as Slider was leaving, Lamont came back to him. 'I think we may have something,' he said. 'The cutlery and glasses and so on in the kitchen, and the coffee cups and brandy glasses over there,' he nodded towards the unit, 'have all been wiped clean on the outside. *But* the whisky glasses have both got lip and finger marks on them. Now, assuming one set belongs to the deceased—'

'Nice,' Slider said, brightening. 'They always make one mistake.'

CHAPTER THREE

Three corns on a Fonteyn

WDC Swilley burst into Slider's office. 'Boss?'

'Don't you believe in knocking?' he said sternly.

'No, only constructive criticism,' she said.

'Don't you start. One smartarse in the firm's enough,' he warned. 'I hope you've come to bring me a cup of tea?'

She shook her head. 'Sorry. There's a bloke here from the local paper.'

He frowned. 'Why are you telling me? You know I don't talk to the press.'

'No, boss, but he says he's got information about Phoebe Agnew. His name's Peter Medmenham.'

'That's the man who lives in the basement of her house,' Slider said. 'Concentrate, Norma!'

'Oh, yes. Sorry.' She'd been distracted lately. Her long-standing engagement to the mysterious Tony was at last nearing fruition: at the Christmas party (which, typically, Tony did not attend) she had announced the date for the wedding.

The announcement had set the department seething, because nobody had ever met Tony, and the uncharitable had claimed he didn't exist. Norma was tall, leggy, blonde and glamorous, so the idea that she was a saddo who had to invent a love-interest ought to have been ludicrous; but policewomen who reject the advances of their colleagues have to take what gets dished out. Those she had scorned most cruelly had labelled her a lesbian (and probably fantasised about her in studded leather wielding a whip). Now the same thickheads were saying she was getting married because she was in pod: spite and wounded pride took no account of logic, of course. But even Slider had to admit to a curiosity about what sort of magnificent demigod Tony must be to have captured his firm's own warrior princess.

'So, d'you want to see him?' Norma asked. 'He's downstairs, in interview room one.'

'Eh?' Slider said, startled.

'This Meddlingham bloke.'

'Oh! Yes, I suppose I'd better. Is he alone? He hasn't got a photographer with him?'

She grinned. 'You're safe. He's not even sporting a notepad.'

Peter Medmenham was not at all what Slider had expected. A reporter for a local paper he would have expected to be young and poor; and the name somehow suggested tall and handsome, in the manner of a model in a men's knitwear catalogue. But what he found in the interview room was a short, plump person of indeterminate age, wearing cord trousers in a silvery-olive shade with a lovat-green lambswool sweater. A tweed overcoat, of the venerable wonderfulness that put it in the loved-family-retainer class, hung from his shoulders. His soft face sported a tan which, in the unforgiving fluorescent light, looked fake, and his pale blue eyes were rimmed with lashes so dark they must surely have been helped, especially as the sparse, carefully tended hair was white – or, to be absolutely frank, pale blue. As Slider paused in the doorway, Medmenham opened his eyes wide and made a little theatrical movement of his hands, first out and then to his chest.

'Oh, don't!' he cried in a surprisingly deep, cigarette-husky voice. 'I know! You're looking at *this*!' He touched his head. 'It's a *disaster*! Just *enhance* the white, I said – because when all you've got is a few poor little bits and pieces like mine, you've got to make the most of them – and, lo and behold, out I come, looking like the Blue Fairy in *Pinocchio*! Believe me, this is nothing to what it was like when she first did it. Kylie – that's the girl's name, don't ask me why – said it would wash out, and it *is* doing but, my God! Serves me right for going to a unisex salon, I suppose. *That's* a bad joke, and so was the salon.'

'Mr Medmenham?' Slider asked mildly.

'Yes, and listen to me running on! It's nerves, that's all. Do you mind if I sit down? My poor feet are killing me. What I suffer with them is nobody's business! Of course, these shoes don't help – but you can't argue with vanity, can you?' He had a refined accent, and behind the mascara, his eyes were alert and intelligent. 'You're Inspector Slider, are you?'

'Yes, that's right. And this is Detective Constable Swilley.'

Medmenham sat gracefully, slipping the coat off over the back of the chair in the same movement, and flashed a very white smile at Norma. 'How d'you do? My goodness, you look much too glamorous to be a policewoman! Did you ever think of going on the boards, dear? You really should, you've got the legs for it. Mind you, your feet wouldn't thank me. I used to dance, as well, though you wouldn't think it to look at me now. No Fred Astaire, but I was a decent hoofer in my time. It's all I can do to take three steps now. My trouble always was, my feet were too small for my weight. Put too much strain on them. If I were to show you, it would make you weep, I give you my word.'

Slider sat opposite him and tried to fix his attention. 'I understand you've got something to tell me about Phoebe Agnew.'

'Well, not exactly, but I thought you'd be sure to want to speak to me, as we were so close, so I came straight here as soon as I heard about it.' The blue eyes wavered swimmingly. 'I suppose it *is* true? There's no mistake?'

'I'm afraid not. How did you hear about it?' Slider asked.

'I picked up a *Standard* at the station, and there it was – just a paragraph at the bottom of the front page. It didn't give her name, just said a well-known journalist had been found dead in a flat in West London, but, call me Mystic Meg, I just had an awful *premonition* about it. So I went straight to the nearest telephone and called the *Ham and Ful* news desk, and of course they knew all about it. One of our own had been first on the scene. My God, what a way to find out! I thought I was going to faint, right there in the railway station. I'm still not feeling quite myself.'

'It must have been a shock,' Slider said kindly. The unnatural-looking tan, he had discovered, was make-up after all. Medmenham might well be pale under it: he certainly had a look of strain.

'It was,' he said. 'To tell you the truth, that's another reason I came straight here. I didn't want to go home. Is that silly of me?' He gave a little nervous laugh.

'Understandable,' Slider said.

'I'm not sure if I'll ever want to go back there again. She – she isn't *still there*, is she?'

'No. The body's been removed.'

'The body! Oh dear!' His lips began to tremble and his face threatened to collapse, but he said, 'No, I must stay calm. Can't blub in front of the police.' He drew out a handkerchief from his trouser pocket and carefully applied it to his eyes and lips. 'And I want to *help*,' he added, emerging. 'Poor, darling Phoebe! Who could have done such a thing?'

'Your editor said you weren't at work today,' Slider said.

'My editor? You mean Martin? He doesn't edit *me*, love,' Medmenham said with sudden vigour. 'Barely literate, like most of the staff, but then that's the progressive education system for you. Gender awareness and finger-painting, oh yes, but reading and writing – *oubliez le*! And as for grammar—'

'But I understood you were a reporter for the *Ham and Ful*?'

He looked shocked. 'Oh, not a *reporter*! I do the reviews. Books, theatre, TV. And the interviews and articles – everything on the arts side. Not the music scene – that's *very* different. Very cliquey. I don't have the in. But I'm virtually the arts editor, otherwise. I used to be on the stage, of course, so I've got the contacts. I come from a long line of theatricals. My parents were in variety. I first went on as a Babe in the Wood at the age of six. Golden curls I had then, if you'll believe me! I've done a bit of everything. From panto to musicals, Shakespeare to Whitehall farce. But I went over to the writing side when my feet let me down. It's not only that I can't dance any more, I just couldn't stand on stage for three hours every night. You wouldn't believe how it takes it out on the feet, acting. It's not a thing anyone talks about, really.'

'Tell me how you first met Phoebe Agnew,' Slider said.

'Ooh, that would be – let me think – thirteen, fourteen years ago. Nineteen eighty-five, was it? Back when dinosaurs ruled the earth! My lord, doesn't the *tempus* fuge when you take your eye off it? Time flies like an arrow – but fruit flies like a banana, as they say! Anyway, I met Phoebe at a Labour fund-raiser. Well, there's always been a lot of interplay between politics and the theatre. The luvvie connection. I think a lot of politicians are actors *manqué*, don't you? Especially our present lords and masters – but never mind, that's another story. I could tell you some things but I won't. And the other way round, of course – a lot of actors fancy themselves politicians. I could name names, but nobody loves a gossip.' He pursed his lips and turned an imaginary key over them.

'So how did you come to live in the same house?' Slider pursued.

'Well, when I met her at this do, she was looking for somewhere, and the flat upstairs happened to be empty. She and I took to each other first minute, we were like brother and sister, so I jumped at the chance of having a soul mate upstairs and she jumped at the chance of a nice let that was cheap *and* central.' He sighed. 'If we'd known then what property prices were going to do! We had the chance to buy, and at a price that would make you laugh if I told you it now, but the rent was so reasonable, and neither of us had any dependents, so it hardly seemed worth it. We were quite happy to go on renting. But we were sitting on a gold-mine, if we had but known it. Of course, Sborski would love to get us out now, he could get a fortune selling the flats, but I've been there so long I'm a protected tenant, and it wasn't worth selling the top flat alone. I suppose,' he added starkly, his verve dissipating for a moment, 'now Phoebe's gone, he might sell the rest of the house and just leave me all alone in my basement. Oh, poor me!'

'You're not married?'

'No, I always look like this! Jokette,' he explained, looking round with a pleased smile. 'No, seriously, I should have thought it was obvious I'm not the marrying kind.'

'I don't like to assume anything,' Slider said solemnly. 'So you and Phoebe were close, were you?'

'She was my best, best friend. She was a wonderful person. She *lived* her principles, and there's not many you can say that about. Most people just talk about issues, but she got up and *did* something about it. Mind you, we didn't always agree. I mean, there is such a thing as being *too* liberal. Everything's so upfront and in-your-face these days. I've never made any secret about what I am – where'd be the point? You've only got to look at me – but my generation didn't make a song and dance about it. We kept ourselves to ourselves – and the Brigade of Guards. No, naughty! I didn't say that!' He twinkled. 'But nowadays everybody seems to want to tell everybody everything, whether they want to know it or not. And then, some of Phoebe's lame ducks weren't as lame as they made out, if you ask me. I know a thing or two about persecution, believe you me, and if they were victims I'm the Queen of Sheba's left tittie! Those two awful men she got let off, who murdered those kiddies. Oh, there might have been some doubt about the evidence, but they did it all right, and as far as I was concerned they were in the right place. Well, we argued about that a few times, I can tell you. But you couldn't fault her in the intentions department. She was all heart, Phoebe. When they made her they broke the mould.' His eyes swam again, and he reapplied the handkerchief, sniffing delicately.

Slider nodded sympathetically. 'Have you any idea who might have wanted to hurt her?'

He shook his head gravely. 'No, not at all. She didn't have any personal enemies. She was too good and kind. I suppose some people in authority mightn't have liked her – she did rather stir up things that *some* might have preferred unstirred – but you don't murder someone for that, do you? Well, not in this country. No, I can only think it was one of those random attacks. I mean, there are so many drug addicts and nutters on the loose nowadays, aren't there? Why they ever shut the bins and threw the poor things out on the street I'll never know! Call me an old softie, but they were much better off locked up inside, being looked after.'

Slider thought Medmenham had got into his stride and was playing to his audience, hearing himself and enjoying the flow of words. It was time to bring him down a bit.

'So, tell me, why weren't you at work today?'

'Oh,' he said, almost as if he'd been slapped. 'Well, that's a straight question if ever I heard one! I had the day off, as it happens. I went to see my mother. She's not been very well recently.'

'And where does she live?'

'In Danbury. It's near Chelmsford.'

'Yes, I know where it is,' Slider said.

'You do?' Peter Medmenham seemed very interested in that.

Slider said merely, 'I'm an Essex boy myself. You went down this morning?'

There was a very slight hesitation. 'No, last night.'

'By car? You drove down?'

'No, I don't drive, actually. Never got round to learning – well, I've always lived in London, so there didn't seem much point. I took the train. Stayed overnight. Took the Aged Mum out to lunch today, bless her – she loves eating out – and got the train back straight afterwards. I had to hurry to catch it, so I didn't see a paper until I got to Liverpool Street. That's when I saw the bit about Phoebe, and I came straight here.'

'What time did you go out last night?' Slider asked.

He seemed put out by the question. 'Me? Last night? Why do you want to know?'

'Have you some reason not to tell me?' Slider countered pleasantly.

'No, of course not. Why should I? Well, if it's important to you, I left at eight. I wanted to catch the 9.02 from Liverpool Street, and I always leave myself plenty of time to catch trains. With my blessed feet, I can't afford to have to run for one.' He looked enquiringly at Slider as if for a quid pro quo.

Slider said, 'It seems that Phoebe Agnew had a visitor yesterday. I don't suppose you saw them arrive or leave, did you?'

Medmenham chose to take that as the reason for the previous question, and his face cleared. 'Oh, I see! Well, I didn't see him, but I know who it was. It was Josh Prentiss.'

He said the name as though it ought to mean something, and when Slider continued to look politely enquiring, he went on, 'Goodness, you must have heard of him! He's the set designer who won the BAFTA award for *Bess and Robin*. Wonderful sets – very dark and moody – and then the Coronation scenes, very sheesh! *Please* don't tell me you've never heard of *Bess and Robin* because, frankly, dear, I shan't believe you!'

'I've heard of the film,' Slider acknowledged. Everyone said it was going to sweep the Oscars board this year, and it was being heralded as the harbinger of a new Hollywood love affair with the British film – something that seemed to be harbinged every couple of years with hopeful regularity but never arrived. And these days everyone was supposed to be so interested in the cinema that they not only knew the names of actors, but everyone else involved as well – smart people could discuss the merits of different directors, scriptwriters, producers, even cameramen. Slider felt like a caveman. 'I hardly ever get to the cinema. No time.'

'Poor you!' said Medmenham kindly. 'Well, Josh is an architect by training and has his own company – very successful, makes oodles of money – but he's *famous* for his sets. Hollywood's *mad* to get hold of him, he could name his price, but he doesn't need the money, so of course he can pick and choose, happy man!'

'Was he a friend, or did he visit Phoebe on business?'

'Oh, he and Phoebe are old friends. They go way back. And his wife Noni, too. She was Anona Regan – have you heard of her?' Slider shook his head. 'She was an actress, but she never really made it big time. She was in that sitcom a couple of years ago, *Des Res* – you know, about the estate agents?'

'I don't think I ever saw it. I don't get to see much television, either.' Unless he could bring the conversation round to real ale or the Police and Criminal Evidence Act, Slider feared he was going to end up with *nul points*.

'Oh, my dear, you didn't miss anything! It was a spectacular disaster. Flopperissimo! Poor Noni was the best thing in it, and it was a complete kiss of death to her, poor lamb. She was just trying to revive her career, and after that no-one would touch her *avec le* bargepole. Well, she'd never really made a name for herself, but she was a real trouper, and one can't help feeling sorry for her. Not that she needs the money, of course – Josh has loads – but that's never why one does it. One lives for one's art – well, most of the time!' He smiled again and almost batted his eyelashes.

Slider grabbed the tail of the straying subject. 'So, if you didn't see Josh Prentiss, how did you know it was him visiting yesterday?'

'I saw his car. You see, I knew she had a visitor, because I went and knocked on her door at about a quarter to seven, to see if she was coming down later to watch the serial. You know, *Red Slayer*? The past couple of weeks we've been watching it together over a bite of supper in my place. But when she answered the door she said she had someone with her and she couldn't come.'

'Did you see him?'

'No, she didn't open the door right up, and she stood in the gap so I couldn't see past her. So I said, all right, I'd tape it and we could watch it some other time.'

'And what time was the programme on?'

'Eight till nine.'

'But you were leaving at eight to catch your train,' Slider pointed out.

He turned just a little pink, for some reason. 'Well, that's when I decided to go up yesterday instead of today. If I was going to tape the serial there was no point in staying in, so I thought I might as well go to Chelmsford. And it was when I left for the station', he hurried on, 'that I saw Josh's car. It was parked further down, and I passed it on my way to the tube.'

'You know his car?'

'I've seen him arrive in it enough times. It's a Jaguar – one of those sleek, sporty-looking ones.'

'An XJS?'

Medmenham smiled charmingly. 'If you say so. I wouldn't know. It's dark blue, and the registration letters are FRN, which I remember because they always make me think of the word "fornicator" – heaven knows why!'

'Is Prentiss a fornicator?' Slider asked.

'Oh, good heavens, it's not for me to say!' Medmenham cried. 'Though if he were, one shouldn't be surprised. I mean, he's an architect. What's that old rhyme? *Roads and bridges, docks and piers, that's the stuff for engineers. Wine and women, drugs and sex, that's the stuff for architects.*'

'You seem to be trying to suggest', Slider said, 'that Prentiss was Phoebe Agnew's lover.'

'Do I? Oh dear, I'm sure it wasn't intentional,' Medmenham said with artificial blankness.

'Did he often visit?'

'I believe so. She often talked about him and I'd seen him in there from time to time. As I said, they were old friends. She'd known him even longer than me.'

'Did he always visit alone, or did his wife come too?'

'I never saw Noni there, but of course I didn't watch her door every hour. But Phoebe went to their house too, so she saw Noni there. It was all above board. For all I know, they met for lunch every day.'

The blue eyes were round and expressionless and the lips were pursed like a doll's. It was hard to know what he was trying to suggest or not suggest.

'Did Phoebe have lovers, that you knew of?'

'I wouldn't be surprised,' he said. 'I don't know of anyone specifically, but I mean she was a gorgeous woman, with that lovely hair, and skin like a newborn babe, though she never really bothered much about glamour, knocked about in a pair of old leggings and a floppy jumper. I said to her many a time, you've got legs most women would die for, darling, yet you never, ever show them – and between you and me,' he added confidentially to Swilley, 'she was one of those lucky creatures who never even had to shave them. But she wore trousers *all the time*,' he tutted. 'Still, she never had any shortage of men admiring her. And not only for her intellect, fabulous though it was.' Again, the bland stare. 'I'm sure she had all the affairs she wanted. Not that I knew anything about them. She was always discreet. No names, no pack drill. I certainly never heard her mention any man's name, or heard her name coupled with anyone else's in that context, by anyone.'

On their way back upstairs, Norma said to Slider, 'Was he for real, do you think, boss? Bit of a Tragedy Jill, wasn't he?'

Slider frowned thoughtfully. 'There was something going on underneath his words – or at least, he wanted us to think there was. That's the trouble with actors, I suppose – you can never tell when they're acting.'

'He's only an ex-actor,' Norma pointed out.

'That might very well be the worst kind. What did you make of him.'

'He struck me as possessive. Phoebe was *his* best friend, and she oughtn't to be anyone else's.'

'Hmm. What a life she led, with Lorraine upstairs and Medmenham downstairs, both knocking at her door at all hours, yearning to unbosom themselves.'

'It was her choice,' Norma said unkindly. 'What was she doing living there anyway? I see her as leeching off them as much as vice versa – surrounding herself with sad acts who made her feel important.'

He dropped behind her as they met people coming down. 'But surely she was a big enough name already, without that?'

'No-one's ever important enough in their own eyes,' Norma said. 'We're all insecure. It's only a matter of degree.' She climbed faster than him, and her wonderful athletic bottom bounced just ahead at eye-level, leading him ever upwards. Better than a banner with a strange device. She stopped on the landing and waited for him. 'I couldn't get my head round his kit. Those trousers and that sweater were smart and expensive, but then he tops it off with that whiskery old weasel.'

'Harris tweed,' said Slider, glad for once to be sartorially better informed than one of his minions. 'It lasts for ever, but it costs a small mortgage in the beginning. So it's of a piece with the rest.'

'Oh,' said Swilley. They pushed through the swing doors. 'Maybe that's what he spends his money on, then. If he's a protected tenant, he won't be paying much rent. He'd be a fool to move out of that flat. It makes you feel quite sorry for the Sborski character.'

'Hmm. You know, there's something not quite right about Medmenham. Something he's not being straight about.'

Norma raised her eyebrows. 'I should have thought almost everything.'

'Seriously. There's something wrong about his story.'

'Yes, he didn't seem convinced by it,' Norma agreed. 'And if he was going to see his dear old mum, why not wait till the weekend, instead of taking a day off for it?'

'Why indeed?' Slider said. 'I think I could bear to know whether he did go and see her last night. He's hiding something. Or—' he added with frustration, 'he wants us to think he is.'

'Don't start that,' Norma warned, 'or you'll drive yourself nuts.'

'But even if he is hiding something,' Slider continued, pausing at his door, 'I can't really see him as the murderer. I mean, why would he? And even if he did it, he'd hardly tie her up and rape her, would he?'

Norma looked thoughtful. 'I don't know about that bit. But if it's a motive you want, there's always jealousy.'

'Jealousy?'

'Well, he obviously adored her. She was just the type – a big redhead, a faded star – just the sort they go for. And if she preferred butch men to the sort of sensitive love he could offer – well, that type of jealousy can be worse than the other sort.'

'Interesting,' Slider said.

CHAPTER FOUR

De mortuis nihil nisi bunkum

Phoebe Agnew's parents, it seemed, were both dead, and her next of kin was her only sister, Chloe, married to a Nigel Cosworth and living in a village in Rutland.

Atherton was impressed. 'It's quite hard to live in Rutland. Turn over in bed too quickly and you end up in Leicestershire.'

The local police were breaking the news to her. Porson had held off from issuing a press statement until that was done, so the media frenzy had not yet materialised. The paragraph in the *Standard* did not name Agnew, only said that a well-known journalist had been found dead at her home in West London and that the police were treating the death as suspicious. The late editions of the tabloids were still running the ongoing search for two teenage girls who'd run away with some ponies that were going to be slaughtered ('The story that has everything,' Slider said), while the broadsheets were obsessed with another Government minister sex scandal and the Balkan crisis in about equal proportions.

'I suppose the *Grauniad* will run the obituary tomorrow,' Atherton said. 'After all, she was one of theirs. And I suppose when the details get out they'll all be panting for it. We'll have the Sundays crawling all over us. The rape angle always gets 'em.'

'Her having her hands tied doesn't make it rape,' Norma pointed out. 'She had dinner with this geezer, and they were old mates. It was probably how they liked to do it.'

'Well, said geezer is obviously the next port of call,' Slider said. 'Have you located him?'

'Josh Prentiss? Yes, he's still at work,' said Norma. 'D'you want him brought in?'

'You haven't said anything to alert him?' Slider asked.

'No, boss. I just asked for him, said it was a personal call, and got myself accidentally cut off when they put me through.'

'Good. I'd like to confront him myself. First reactions and so on. Meanwhile, I'd like someone to go over and talk to his wife, get her slant on it before she knows what he's said. Yes, all right, Norma, you can do that. Anyone who's not house-to-housing can make a start on going through her paperwork. You've got it all here now?'

'Sackloads of it,' Anderson said.

'Weeks of work,' said McLaren.

'There's one thing, guv,' Mackay said. 'You know there were two filing cabinets? Well, they were stuffed so full you could hardly get them open, all except for one drawer. In that one the files were hanging quite loosely. The desk drawers were the same – jammed full of papers. It occurs to me that maybe some big file was taken out of that one drawer by chummy.'

'Possible. Any way of knowing which one?' Slider asked. 'Labels on the drawers? Was the stuff alphabetical or anything?'

'You kidding?' Mackay said economically.

'Okay,' said Slider, 'keep that in mind as you go through. Try to classify the stuff and see if there's anything obviously missing. It may not mean anything, though. There were a lot of papers loose on the desk, as I remember, and they might have been what made the space.'

'Anyway,' Anderson said, 'if it was a sex thing, he's not going to go looking through her files, is he?'

'Probably not,' Slider said, 'but it's as well to keep an open mind.'

It hadn't snowed, but the sky had remained lowering, and its unnatural twilight had blended seamlessly with the normal onset of winter dusk. It seemed to have been dark all day, with the lights in shop and office windows making it darker by contrast. 'It's like living in Finland,' said Slider gloomily.

Atherton glanced at him. 'SAD syndrome,' he said. 'Sorry Ageing Detective.'

'Oh, thank you!'

Rush hour was winding itself up. Illuminated buses glided

past like mobile fish tanks; the wet road hissed under commuter tyres, so that, with your eyes closed and a certain amount of good will, you could imagine you were on the piste. Prentiss's office was in a new block in Kensington Church Street – prime real estate these days, especially as it had a car park. Somewhere to leave a car in central London was becoming more valuable than somewhere to lay your weary head. The time would come when it would be cheaper to hire someone to drive your car round and round all day and jump in when it passed you.

When they were finally ushered into Prentiss's large and expensively furnished room, he was standing behind his desk and talking on the phone while he looked out of the large window onto the ribbon of lights, gold and ruby, that wound down to Ken High Street and up to Notting Hill. He gestured them to seats while continuing with his conversation; behaviour that Slider, perhaps unfairly, couldn't help feeling was an executive ploy for impressing them with how busy and important he was.

At last Prentiss slammed the phone down in its cradle and said, 'Sorry about that, gentlemen. What can I do for you?' He didn't sit down, suggesting that whatever they wanted, it wouldn't take him very long to sort it out and be rid of them.

He was a tall man in his fifties, and broad under his pale grey suit, which even Slider could tell was fashionable and expensive. He was not fat, but heavily built and with a certain softness around the jowls and thickness in the lines of his face that was not unattractive, given his age, merely adding to his authority. His beautifully cut hair was fair, turning grey, and brushed back all round to give him a leonine look, which went with his straight, broad nose and wide, lazy hazel eyes. Altogether he seemed a commanding and handsome man, the sort women would fall for badly. A man who could kill? Perhaps, Slider thought, if the reason and circumstances were right. He looked as though he would be single-minded in pursuit of his own ends; and whatever he did, he would prove a formidable opponent. Or at least – Slider amended to himself, wondering if there wasn't a trace of self-indulgence about the mouth and the softness – he'd always make you think he was.

Slider introduced himself and Atherton, and proffered his ID, which Prentiss waved away magnanimously. 'I'd like to speak to you about Phoebe Agnew,' he said.

The gaze sharpened. 'What about her?'

'You are a friend of hers, I understand.'

'Phoebe and I are very old friends,' he said, a faint frown developing between his brows. 'There's no secret about that. I've known her since college days. We've worked on many a fund-raiser together. Why do you ask?'

Defensive, thought Slider. 'Would you mind telling me when you saw her last?'

'I certainly would,' Prentiss said.

Slider raised his eyebrows in his mildest way. 'You have some reason for not telling me?'

'I am not going to answer any of your questions until you tell me why you're asking,' Prentiss said impatiently. 'So either come out with it, or I shall have to ask you to leave. I'm a busy man.'

'You haven't heard, then', said Slider, 'that Miss Agnew is dead?'

Prentiss didn't say anything, but he stared at Slider as if looking alone would suck information out of him.

'I'll take that as a "no",' Slider said.

'Dead?' Prentiss managed at last.

'Murdered,' said Slider.

Slowly Prentiss felt behind him and lowered himself into the high-backed leather executive chair. 'You can't be serious.'

Genuine shock, or an act? Poke him and see. 'No, I go round telling people things like that just to see how they react,' Slider said.

That roused Prentiss. 'What the devil do you mean by coming in here with that attitude? Are you trying to be funny? Do you think this is a game?'

Slider faced him down. 'I most certainly do not. A woman has been murdered, and I never find that in the least amusing. As to attitude, perhaps we can examine yours. I'd like you to answer some simple questions instead of wasting time with ridiculous power-play.'

'How dare you!'

'It's my job to dare. When did you last see Miss Agnew?'

Prentiss seemed taken aback. Perhaps no-one had spoken sharply to him since he outgrew his nanny. 'But I – I don't understand. Phoebe's dead? How? How did it happen?'

'I'd rather not go into that at the moment.'

Prentiss shook his head. 'I can't take it in. It's not possible. And surely you can't be suspecting *me* of anything?'

'I haven't got as far as suspecting anyone yet. You may have been the last person to see Miss Agnew alive. I'd like to know about that.'

'I haven't seen her for weeks!' Prentiss protested.

Slider felt Atherton beside him quiver with pleasure. 'You went to see her yesterday,' he contradicted firmly.

The lion's eyes widened. 'What makes you say that?' he asked with careful neutrality.

Slider only smiled gently. 'You went to see her yesterday,' he repeated. 'Now, would you like to tell me about it, or shall we continue this conversation elsewhere?'

With another stare, Prentiss swung the swivel chair round so that he was facing the window, and left Slider his back to look at for a long moment, while he marshalled his thoughts, perhaps, or reorganised his face. When he swung back, he was in control again, but he looked grave, and suddenly older.

'I don't know what all this is about,' he said. 'Please, tell me the truth. Phoebe was my oldest and dearest friend. Is she really dead? She was really murdered?'

'I'm afraid she was,' said Slider.

'Dear God,' said Prentiss.

Slider pressed him. 'Please answer my question, Mr Prentiss.'

He swallowed and licked his lips a few times, seeming to come to a decision. 'I did go to see her yesterday,' he admitted, 'but I don't know how you knew. It was just a spur-of-the-moment thing – I dropped in on her on my way somewhere else. I was there less than half an hour, and she was fine when I left her. I don't know any more than that.'

'Give me some times,' Slider said.

'I don't know exactly, but it would be about eight o'clock. I mean, I must have got there about eight and left about twenty, twenty-five past.'

'I see,' said Slider in troubled tones. 'You're quite sure about that?'

'I've just said I can't be exact, but that was about the time.'

'The problem is, you see,' Atherton joined in, 'that she told a witness yesterday morning that she was expecting a visitor,

and we have witnesses to the fact that there was someone there
with her between six-thirty and seven. Now you say you called
without warning and not until eight o'clock.'

'That's right.' He paused, frowning with thought. 'It must
have been someone else,' he concluded. 'She must have had
another visitor.'

'Did she say, when you saw her, that she'd had a visitor?'

'No, but – well, if it wasn't me, it must have been someone
else, mustn't it?'

'Where were you for the rest of the day – at work?'

'No, as it happened I was working from home yesterday. I
do that sometimes to get away from the phones.'

'How did Miss Agnew seem to you?' Slider asked. 'Was she
in her normal spirits?'

'I don't know – yes, I suppose so.'

'What did you do?'

'Do? We chatted about this and that. I had—' Something
seemed to strike him.

'You had what?'

'I had a drink,' he said slowly.

Slider smiled inwardly. He's remembered the whisky glass,
he thought. 'Anything else?'

'Phoebe had one as well,' he said in that same distant tone.
And then he snapped back to normal. 'Anyway, that's all I can
tell you. She was perfectly all right when I left her.'

'Where were you on your way to, when you called in?'

He hesitated. 'I was going to a meeting.'

'At that time of night?' Atherton asked.

He looked lofty. 'A ministerial meeting. The business of
government is not nine-to-five. As you probably know, I am
the Government's special advisor in inner city development.'

'Yes, I did know that,' Atherton said. Slider was glad at least
one of them read the newspapers. 'And who were you going
to see?'

'Is it any of your damn business?' Prentiss snapped, getting
some spine back.

Slider took it up. 'Well, yes, I'm afraid it is. You must
see that, as you were with the deceased at such a crucial
time, we have to check your story. I'm sure you wouldn't

expect us to do otherwise, given that Miss Agnew was your friend.'

A pause. 'I went to see Giles Freeman,' he said at last. 'Does that satisfy you? I'm sure', he added with heavy irony, 'you'll accept the word of a Secretary of State, won't you?'

The words *not on a bet* jumped to mind, but Slider went on, 'What was your relationship with Miss Agnew?'

'I've told you, we were old friends.'

'Were you lovers?'

Prentiss burst to his feet. 'Look, I'm tired of your damned impertinent questions! My best friend is dead, don't you understand that? Can't you imagine how I must feel?'

Slider was unmoved. 'Nevertheless, I have to ask you, were you lovers?'

'No, we were not!'

'You were just good friends?'

'Perhaps your imagination is so limited that you can't conceive of a man and a woman being friends, but that's not my problem!'

Slider stood up. 'Thank you for your frankness, Mr Prentiss. I do have to ask you if you will come to the station and let us take your fingerprints and a blood sample for comparison.'

'For comparison with what?' he snapped.

'We need to eliminate any traces you may have left around the flat,' Slider said evenly.

He looked shaken. 'And if I refuse?'

'Then I should wonder whether you had something to hide. I know that if my dearest friend had been murdered, I'd want to do everything I could to help bring the murderer to justice.'

'I don't need you to lecture me on the duties of friendship,' Prentiss said, but after a moment he added, 'When do you want me to come?'

'As soon as possible. Now, if you can. We can give you a lift back with us.'

'No, I'll go in my own car, thank you,' Prentiss said.

'Is that the XJS?' Atherton asked with car-spotting eagerness. 'Dark blue? Reg number something-FRN?'

'Yes,' Prentiss said, slightly puzzled. 'You like Jags?'

'I like all cars,' Atherton said.

'So, Mr Prentiss, are you coming now?' Slider asked.

'I'll follow in five or ten minutes. I've some things to clear up here first.'

When they were out in the car park, Atherton gave a soundless whistle. 'Quite a set up. The rent of that place must really hurt. Then there's the Jag – and he was wearing some serious cash. His suit looked like a Paul Smith.'

'Paul Smith?' Slider queried.

Atherton smiled kindly. 'Like Armani, only more so. Cutting-edge stuff.'

'Thank you,' Slider said humbly. 'So, bank account left aside, what did you think of him?'

'Guilty,' Atherton said. 'Lied straight off about having seen her. Nervous, evasive, falling back on the old lofty arrogance to try and get out of answering awkward questions.'

'He's an architect. Maybe he can't help being arrogant.'

'Still, given she was his best friend, shouldn't he have been more surprised and upset that she was dead?'

'Maybe he is, but doesn't show it,' Slider said.

'Don't be perverse,' said Atherton. 'You're just seeing both sides, as usual. You think he did it.'

'His story may be true. Why shouldn't she have had two visitors?'

'It'll be true just as soon as he's phoned his old friend Giles Freeman to give him the script, which is what he's doing right this minute, by the way.'

'Perhaps. But I can't stop him without arresting him.'

'Ah, yes, and he's not a person to arrest unless you're sure. Too many friends in high places.'

'What is he, a dustman?'

'Laugh it up, guv,' Atherton warned. 'It doesn't stop at Giles Freeman, you know – though that'd be bad enough. Freeman's one of the Coming Men and doesn't like anyone to get in his way. But more than that, the Freeman set has the key to Number Ten. In and out like lambs' tails.'

'You terrify me,' Slider said.

'You're a political ignoramus,' Atherton told him affection-ately. 'How do you manage not to know all these things?'

'I don't get time to read the papers.'

'That's dedication.'

'Apparently Prentiss didn't either – or not the *Standard*, since that's the only place it appeared.'

'Her name wasn't mentioned in that anyway,' Atherton pointed out.

'True. But wouldn't you have thought someone would have phoned him and told him? He must know plenty of journalists, and the word must have got round by now.'

'Maybe they don't like him. All right, what now?'

'Back to the factory. With any luck, Norma will have got something from his wife that we can work with.'

In the car, Atherton said, 'What about the tying up, guv? Do you think it was a sex game that went wrong? Do you see him as the bondage, S&M type?'

'There's no point in wondering until we find out if the finger-marks and semen were his.'

'How much d'you want to bet?' Atherton said.

'I'm not a betting man,' Slider said. He glanced at his colleague sidelong, wanting to ask him about the horse-racing thing, and then deciding it was none of his business. Lots of people gambled. It wasn't a crime.

Campden Hill Square was on a hill rising steeply from the main road, with a public garden in the centre graced by massive plane trees. Fog now draped their bare branches like cobweb, and made fizzy yellow haloes round the street lamps. The steepness and the narrowness of the houses gave it a Hampsteady feel to Swilley. The houses looked unstable, as though they might topple like dominoes and send two hundred years of architecture rumbling out into the Bayswater Road in a lava flow of bricks and slates. And good riddance, in her view. She had as much respect for old London architecture as the Luftwaffe.

The door of Prentiss's house was opened by a small, slender woman. In the gloom of the unlit hall she lifted her eyes to Norma's height with darting apprehension. Her brown eyes, thick dark hair and very white skin reminded Swilley of a lemur.

'Mrs Prentiss? I'm Detective Constable Swilley of Shepherd's Bush CID. May I come in and talk to you?'

She said it in her most pleasant and unthreatening tones, but Mrs Prentiss seemed to be struck breathless and wordless.

She moved her lips and made an uncompleted gesture of her hands towards her chest, as though her lungs had sprung a leak. Swilley, afraid she was going to faint, reached out and held her elbow. 'Hang on, love. Sorry if I startled you. You'd better sit down.'

But Mrs Prentiss shook her off and turned away to lean against the banister of the steep, curving staircase, which was all there was in the hall, apart from a glimpse through an open door of a dining-room. The hall was papered in dark green, a William Morris print Swilley just about remembered from her childhood. It was worn in places, and gave an air of shabby gloom that Swilley had come to associate with a certain sort of wealthy person, as if they felt themselves to be above anything as mundane as refurbishment. It was what she would have expected in a place like Campden Hill, and she had no patience with it.

The impatience now spread to Mrs Prentiss, who she felt was time-wasting, and she said firmly, 'P'raps you could do with a brandy. Tell me where it is and I'll get you one.'

Mrs Prentiss lifted her head. 'No, I'm all right now. Would you like to come upstairs to the drawing-room?' She led the way, walking with a peculiar, rigid gait and holding on to the banister carefully. 'I've put my back out,' she said, evidently feeling some explanation was due.

'Backs are bastards,' Swilley acknowledged with bare sympathy. 'How did you do it?'

'It's an old problem. Comes and goes,' said Mrs Prentiss.

The drawing-room, on the first floor, ran the full depth of the house from front to back, with folded-back doors in the middle. The double room was panelled, had two vast marble fireplaces, and was furnished with large and well-used antique pieces. The panelling had been painted in the dull greyish-green that the National Trust had vouched for as authentic eighteenth century; the drops of the chandelier had that dim lustre, like slightly soapy water, that proved them original; and even Swilley's uninformed and unappreciative glance could tell that the paintings on the walls hadn't been bought or sold in a very, very long time. There was real money here, old-established money, the sort that took no notice of fashion. This room had probably not looked much different in all the years it had existed. Swilley couldn't think how they could bear it.

Mrs Prentiss crossed to a side table on which stood a tray of decanters and glasses. 'I think I will have something. What about you?' she asked with her back to Swilley. Her voice sounded strained.

'No, thanks. Not on duty,' Swilley said.

Mrs Prentiss poured something brown – whisky or brandy – into a glass and threw back half of it, and only then turned to face her. 'Please, won't you sit down? I'm sorry I made such a fool of myself.'

'That's all right,' Swilley said, sitting down. 'I suppose I can look a bit scary.'

Mrs Prentiss lowered herself carefully onto one of the hard settles, opposite her, and sat on the edge of the seat, very upright, nursing the oversized tumbler in her lap. Everything about her seemed neat and complete, from her short-cropped, thick, shining hair to her slender, well-shod feet. Now, with the aid of light, Swilley could see she had the beautiful skin – colourless but glowing, like alabaster – that sometimes went with dark hair. Together with her small, symmetrical features it made her look unnaturally young, though she was obviously in her forties. No, not young so much as un-aged, out of step with the stream of time. A ruined child, Swilley thought unexpectedly: like something out of an old black-and-white film, the beloved but neglected only child, maintaining, in its well-stocked nursery, the exquisite manners that concealed a brooding sorrow. There was a feather of blue shadow under her eyes, as though she were very tired or unhappy.

'It isn't that,' she said. She gave Swilley a searching look. 'I suppose you've come about – about Phoebe?'

'Oh, you've heard?'

'My husband told me. He rang me this morning. I'm just so shocked.'

'You've known her a long time, haven't you?' Swilley asked.

'She was my oldest friend. We were at university together.'

'Oh, really? Which one?'

'University College, London. We were both reading English,' Mrs Prentiss said. 'We took a liking to each other the first day, when we were all milling about wondering where to go and what to do. You know what it's like – if you're lost, you always want to latch on to someone, so that at least there are two of you in the wrong place. Not that Phoebe was, for long. She always knew exactly what she should be doing. I tagged along with her, and after that we always hung around together.' She smiled with an effort. 'We used to sit on the sofa in the corner of the English Common Room in Foster Court all day, and make terrible critical comments about the other students. Phoebe was frightfully left-wing and radical, and they all seemed so conventional: tweedy sixth-formers, Young Conservative types. We thought we were being witty, but it got us a reputation. Some of the others called us *Les Tricoteuses*.' She glanced at Swilley to see if she understood the French. 'We didn't mean any harm. To tell the truth, I barely understood half the comments. But Phoebe led and I followed.'

'And how did your husband meet her?' Swilley asked. 'Through you?'

'No, not really. Josh was at UCL too, reading architecture,' she said. 'We all met through Dramsoc – the Drama Society. I wanted to act – I'd been to stage school – so I joined it straight away, and Phoebe came along just for fun. Josh joined because – well, anyone who was anyone at UCL had to be in Dramsoc.' She smiled with faint self-mockery. 'It was a hotbed of preening student *poseurs*, though of course one only realises that with hindsight. But anyway, that's how we all met. We liked the look of him. He seemed much more sophisticated than the other male students. He had an air about him, of belonging to a larger world. What he saw in us—' She shrugged. 'Phoebe was stunning, of course – that gorgeous red hair and those eyes. Intelligent, too – she was a brilliant student. And so witty – that fabulous stream of words! Everyone was in love with her. I don't know what she saw in me. I was dull and plain beside her.'

If she wanted contradiction, Swilley thought roughly, she'd come to the wrong shop. 'Who knows what friends see in each other? It just happens, doesn't it, friendship?'

'Yes, of course,' Mrs Prentiss said. 'It's a kind of love, and love is unaccountable. At any rate, Phoebe had beauty and brains, though she wasted them, in my opinion. Josh had looks, brains, charisma, *and* a private income – quite the Golden Child. The only talent I ever had was for acting, and even that's proved not to be such a huge talent. I don't suppose you remember me in *Des Res*?'

'I didn't watch it. I think I may have seen a bit of one episode, but it's not really my sort of thing.'

'It wasn't anyone's sort of thing,' Mrs Prentiss said bitterly. 'Yet I suppose in a way it was the high point of my career. High point and death knell. Everyone thinks if you get a sitcom you're made for life, but when it's a stinker like that . . .'

Swilley was not interested in a career post-mortem. 'So at university you went around as a threesome?' she prompted. 'Or was it more two and one?'

'We were a threesome. But when we graduated Phoebe sort of disappeared for a while, and that's when Josh and I started to get close.'

'Disappeared?'

'Oh, I don't mean mysteriously,' Mrs Prentiss said. 'I just mean we lost touch for a while. Three or four years, it must have been. I was in London, trying to get my career moving, and Josh was with a firm of architects, also in London, so we still saw each other. And in the end, of course, it was us who got married. When Phoebe reappeared, we became a threesome again, but with Josh and me the couple within it.'

'Do you know where she was or what she was doing in that time?'

'I imagine she was involved in some protest or other – she was always marching and demonstrating. I don't know where in particular. She didn't live anywhere permanently at that time. When she came back to London it was just the same, just lodgings, and sleeping on other people's floors. She was still a student at heart.'

A touch of disapproval? Swilley wondered. The materialist's contempt for the idealist? 'You didn't agree with her ideas?' she asked.

'Oh, I don't want you to think that,' Mrs Prentiss said hastily. 'Of course Josh and I are *convinced* socialists, always have been. But Phoebe was always much more radical than either of us. I was always willing to sign petitions and make donations, but I never went in for direct action the way she did. I was more interested in my career. And Josh had doubts about some of her pet causes. She was rather hot-headed, and sometimes she didn't examine the issues before jumping in. She was so passionate about things. She and Josh used to fight like cat and dog about some of her ideas – but it never touched their friendship. That goes too deep to be affected by a difference of opinion.'

Swilley nodded encouragingly. 'It sounds marvellous, a friendship like that. So did you see a lot of each other?'

'Oh, you know how it is,' Mrs Prentiss said, looking faintly embarrassed. 'Marriage, children, careers – there never seems to be enough time for getting together with your old friends, does there?'

Swilley declined to party. 'How often did you see her?'

'I suppose – about half a dozen times a year. But we talked on the phone a lot,' she added hastily, as though her dedication had been questioned. 'There was never any sense of being apart, however long it was.'

'When did you last see her, can you remember?'

'She saw the New Year in with us. We had a little dinner party – just family. Our children both made it home, for a wonder. Josh and me, Toby and Emma, Josh's brother Piers, and Phoebe.' She looked at Swilley. 'We counted her as family. The children used to call her Aunty Phoebe when they were little. Toby's twenty-two now and Emma's twenty. They have their own lives, of course, so we don't see so much of them. He's a company analyst for an investment firm. Emma works for a magazine group – followed Phoebe into journalism, you see. Phoebe helped her get the job. She always loved my two as if they were her own children.'

Swilley accepted all this patiently, thanking God she was not the sort of woman who had to define her life by her husband and children. 'At your dinner party, did Phoebe seem in her usual spirits?' she asked.

Mrs Prentiss frowned in thought. 'Oh, yes, I think so. I mean, she always had a lot on her mind, but she didn't talk about anything out of the ordinary. She chatted to the children about their lives, argued with Josh about the Government, had a flaming row with Piers – but that was par for the course.'

'What was that about?'

'Oh, goodness, I can't remember. Something political – the homosexual age of consent, was it? I think it might have been that. They were always arguing – it didn't mean anything. I mean, actually, Phoebe argued with everyone.' She opened her eyes wide. 'I don't want you to think there was any malice in it. It was late in the evening and they'd both had a lot to drink so instead of just debating they started shouting at each other. But Josh told them to shut up because it was nearly midnight, and when Big Ben struck everybody kissed everybody else and it was all forgotten.'

'Did she usually drink a lot?' Swilley asked.

'Well, she *was* a journalist,' Mrs Prentiss said. 'She always was what I'd call a hard drinker, though I've never seen her drunk since our student days. I don't mean she was an alcoholic.'

'But?' Swilley prompted. Mrs Prentiss looked enquiring. 'You sounded as if you were going to say "but".'

'Oh.' A pause. 'It's just that the past few months I've thought she was drinking more than usual. She doesn't get drunk, but once or twice when she's come over we've sat talking and she's just gone on drinking, long after I've had enough and—' she gave a little, nervous laugh, 'frankly, long after I've wanted to get to my bed.'

'Do you think the heavier drinking was to do with some problem she had?'

Again the hesitation. Mrs Prentiss gazed towards the dark window, which showed only a reflection of the lighted room, nothing beyond. 'I wondered whether she had something on her mind that she wasn't telling me about. She's been – less lively and cheerful these past few months. More thoughtful. But then,' she turned the direct, dark eyes on Swilley frankly, 'there's her age to consider. The Change is not easy for anyone.'

Too genteel, Swilley thought impatiently, to use the m-word. 'You must all be about the same age,' she suggested.

'Phoebe and I were just two months apart. My birthday's February the eighth, and hers is April the eighth. Josh was born in June, but the previous year.' She emptied her glass with a sudden movement. 'I'm talking too much, aren't I? I'm forgetting why you're here. You don't want to know all this stuff.'

'It all helps to build up the picture,' Swilley said. 'She never married?'

'No,' said Mrs Prentiss. 'It never seemed to be something

she wanted. Her career and her political interests filled her life. I asked her once, when we were in our thirties, if she wasn't worried about the biological clock ticking away, if she didn't want children before it was too late, and she said, "I can't think of anything I want less than a husband and family."'

'But she had boyfriends, presumably?'

Mrs Prentiss shrugged. 'Men always wanted her – she was so beautiful and exciting. She had affairs from time to time, but they were just casual. Even when we were younger, men were just an add-on in her life. Her career was everything.'

'I'm wondering, you see, who would have had a reason to kill her,' Swilley said. 'Do you know the names of any of her recent affairs?'

'No. I don't think she's had anyone recently,' Mrs Prentiss said. 'The last one I know of was last summer, a man she saw for a couple of months. But she came to a garden party of ours in August alone, and said she'd got fed up with him, and she hasn't mentioned anyone since.' She looked straight into Swilley's eyes; she sat very still, enviably free from the human propensity to fidget, her hands folded together, back straight; revealing her distress at the murder of her friend only by a certain rigidity in her shoulders and face.

'Would she have talked about it more to your husband, perhaps? I understand he dropped in on her at her flat sometimes.'

Mrs Prentiss eyed her tautly. 'Why shouldn't he? It was a three-way friendship. There wasn't anything underhand going on. Josh and Phoebe were friends in just the same way that Phoebe and I were.'

'I wasn't suggesting anything,' Swilley said blandly, 'but it's interesting that you jumped to that conclusion.'

Mrs Prentiss flushed. 'It isn't the first time suggestions have been made. We live in a tabloid world.'

Swilley gave a faint shrug. 'At any rate, your husband was probably the last person to see her alive. He visited her yesterday evening.'

'Who told you that?' Mrs Prentiss asked sharply.

'We have a witness,' was all Swilley would give her.

'Well, your witness is wrong,' Mrs Prentiss said firmly. 'Josh was here all yesterday evening.'

'Then how do you account for his car being parked in her street?'

She didn't even break stride. 'It wasn't there yesterday, I can assure you. Your witness must have seen another Jaguar. They're not exactly rare.'

'You're quite sure your husband was here all evening?'

'All evening and all day as well. He was working from home yesterday. He never left the house at all. Surely', she said, her eyes widening, 'you can't be trying to suggest that Josh had anything to do with it? That would be ludicrous. He loved Phoebe as much as I did. Please don't say anything like that to him: it would break his heart.'

'I'm not suggesting anything,' Swilley said calmly. 'A witness said he was at the flat yesterday and we have to check that statement. You must understand that. There's no need for you to get upset.'

'My best friend is murdered, and there's no need for me to get upset?' Mrs Prentiss cried hotly. 'I suppose it's all in a day's work to you, but you can't expect the rest of us to be so completely callous. And then to accuse my husband of being the killer!' Her voice shook.

'Mrs Prentiss, if he visited her, she might have said something to him that would help us, that's all we were wondering. Nobody's accusing anybody of anything.'

'Well, if that's what you want to know, why don't you ask him?'

'Oh, we will,' said Swilley.

CHAPTER FIVE

Mallard imaginaire

The bitter cold didn't last long. By next day a normal English winter had reasserted itself: mild, overcast, with a fine prickling drizzle from a blank and whitish-grey sky.

Hollis, updating the whiteboard, said, 'You've chosen a right funny time o' year to get married, Norma. You'll want to get the plastic wedding dress and white wellies out.' He was the other detective sergeant on Slider's firm, an odd-looking man with bulging green eyes, a ragged moustache, and a strange, counter-tenor voice with a Mancunian accent. His oddities made him a successful interviewer: people were so mesmerised by his face and voice, he got things out of them without their noticing.

Norma shrugged. 'Least of my problems. I'm just hoping this murder doesn't turn out to be a sticker. I've got enough on my plate without that.'

'Lots of nice overtime to pay for all the booze we're going to drink at the reception,' Mackay pointed out.

'If you think any of you lot are getting invited you've got a screw loose,' Norma said brutally.

'If you think we'll get paid for the overtime, ditto ditto,' Hollis added.

There was a brief and electric silence. Budgetary restraints had curtailed quite a few investigations recently, and much unpaid overtime had been worked, not without grumbling.

Atherton, a folded-open newspaper in his hands, looked up. 'Don't say that, Colin. Please don't say that. I dropped a packet yesterday on Maurice's three-legged pony. Shy Smile!' he said witheringly, with a glare at McLaren.

McLaren shrugged, his mouth full of pastry. 'I never said she'd win,' he bubbled flakily. 'I said she'd walk it.'

'So she did, while the other horses ran gaily past her,' Atherton said bitterly. 'I've got to recoup my losses. Anybody got any tips for Lingfield Park?'

'Never mind the bloody racing,' Mackay said impatiently. 'What about this overtime thing? I can't afford to work for nothing. I haven't paid for Christmas yet.'

'And I've spent a packet on timber,' said Anderson, the DIY fanatic. 'Ever since I gave the wife a nice bit of tongue-and-groove in the kitchen, she wants it all over the house.'

'Must we discuss your sex life first thing in the morning?' Swilley complained.

'Overtime or not,' Hollis said, 'if we don't clear Agnew up in short order, the press'll string us up by the goolies. It's in all the broadsheets today. She wasn't just one of theirs, remember, she was anti-us, so they'll be watching us.'

'Talk about feeding the hand that bites you,' said Atherton.

'We shouldn't have to investigate it at all,' McLaren said resentfully. 'She spent her life slinging mud at us and chumming it up with the slags we put away – serves the cow right if one of 'em turns round and offs her. Why should we care? Good riddance to bad rubbish, I say.'

Norma made fierce shushing gestures at him. Porson had come in, with Slider behind him, and was standing just inside the door, his vast eyebrows drawn down in a frown like hairy venetian blinds. 'Irregardless of who she was,' he announced into the sudden silence, 'I expect my officers to give of their best at all times. Whether the victim is male or female, black, white or tangerine, straight or as crooked as a bottle opener, it's irrevelant to me. In my department everyone goes Club Class. Do I make myself crystal?'

There was a dutiful murmur of agreement, which evidently only went skin deep with some of them. Hollis asked a question that was on everyone's mind.

'Sir, are we going to take this case all the way, or is it going up to AMIP?'

Porson didn't seem to want to be cornered. 'I've been trying to get hold of Peter Judson of AMIP to get that very point straightened into, but he's been proving a bit illusory so far. However, the ball is certainly on our plate for the time being.'

The troops stirred Hollis like a gentle breeze in a wheatfield.

'Only, I can see a scenario, sir, where we do all the work, and then AMIP jump in at the end and claim the credit.'

Porson frowned. 'Yes, well, I don't want to get bogged down on hypotheoretical points—'

'But sir—!'

'Now, you know me, lads,' Porson said firmly, lifting his hands. 'I don't mince my punches. I promise you, Mr Judson will get short shift from me if he tries to prevassilate over this one. In the mean time,' he looked round from under threatening eyebrows, 'let's just get on with the job we're paid to do. It's in the papers this morning, so we'll all be under the telescope from now on.'

'Sir, what about overtime?' said Mackay, his credit card statement writ large all over his face.

The eyebrows went up and down a bit, and then Porson said, 'I shall do everything I can on the renumeration front, I promise you that. But we've got a result to get, and I don't want superfluous attitudes undermining our professional reputation. When push comes to the bottom line, the Job is about service. I think you all know what I'm talking about.'

It made a good exit line, but it left a roomful of muttering complaint. They all knew what he was talking about. He was talking about unpaid overtime again.

'It's like everything in this bloody Job,' Mackay grumbled. 'All the money goes on show, so there's nothing left for getting on with the bloody job.'

Even Hollis, usually silent and loyal, joined in. 'Queen Anne front and a Mary Ann back. We haven't even got enough wheels.'

The troops were slumped in various dispirited attitudes around the room, like marionettes waiting for Slider to pull their strings. 'Right, boys and girls,' he said briskly, 'let's get on with it. In the case of Phoebe Agnew—'

'Slagnew,' McLaren corrected bitterly.

Slider paused. 'Look,' he said, 'I know you're sore about some of the things this woman wrote in life—'

'Like, all of them,' Anderson agreed.

'But she's dead now, and it's our job to find out who did it. So I'll say it again slowly for the hard of thinking: it doesn't matter who she was or what she did, the law is the law for everybody.

Anyone who thinks differently can come and see me afterwards with his P45 in his hot little hand and we'll have a chat about it. Savvy?'

There was an unwilling mutter of agreement.

'Right,' Slider said. 'Let's go. Phoebe Agnew was forty-nine, unmarried, lived alone in a rented flat—'

'Why?' Atherton said. 'She must have been making plenty.'

'Not everyone wants to own property,' Norma argued. 'And we've been told several times that she had a mind above material comforts.'

'I'd like to know, though,' Hollis put in, 'what she did spend her money on. If she didn't have a fancy pad or a lot o' Nicole Farhi suits, it begs the question. I'd like to see a fat savings book.'

'Who wouldn't?' said Mackay.

'Okay,' Slider said, 'that's one thing to look for amongst her papers. But it's probably not important. Robbery from the person or the premises does not seem to have been the motive. She had a visitor, on the evidence of both neighbours – Lorraine Peabody and Peter Medmenham. Medmenham saw Josh Prentiss's car parked nearby at about eight p.m., and Prentiss admits he was there between eight and eight-twenty or thereabouts, but denies having been there earlier.'

'Neither witness actually saw a visitor earlier,' Hollis pointed out. 'Peabody heard music and the street door banging at around seven, and Medmenham says Agnew said the visitor was there at six forty-five and wouldn't let him in; but she might've not wanted Medmenham in the flat for some other reason.'

'True,' Slider allowed. 'But as against that there's the meal. Could Prentiss have eaten a two-course dinner in half an hour?'

'Why not?' said McLaren.

'Not everyone's in your class, Maurice,' Swilley said kindly.

'I don't see the problem,' Anderson said. 'Prentiss admits he was there at eight, and we haven't got an exact time for the murder, so what does it matter whether he was there earlier or not?'

'What matters,' Slider said, 'is finding out what happened. Prentiss lied to us at first about having been there at all. Then he admitted he was there, but only for twenty minutes. He denies having had sex with her—'

'But sex with her was had,' Atherton completed for him.

'And as an added complication, we've got two different versions of where he was on Thursday. He says he was at home until around seven forty-five, at the Agnew flat eight to eight-twenty, and at a meeting with Giles Freeman in Westminster from nine until after midnight. But his wife says he didn't leave home at all that day.'

'We know his wife was lying about some o' that, because we know he *was* at the flat,' Hollis said.

'Also,' said Swilley, 'she said Prentiss told her about the murder yesterday morning—'

'Whereas he put on a good show of not knowing about it when we interviewed him yesterday afternoon,' Atherton finished.

'Well, there's no mystery about why he'd lie,' Hollis said, 'but why would she? To protect him?'

'Obviously. She thinks he did it, throws herself into the breach.'

'Does a wife leap to the conclusion that her husband's a murderer just like that?' Slider queried. 'And if so, why would she defend him?'

'Fear,' Swilley said. 'She might be next.'

'Did she strike you as fearful?'

'Maybe. She didn't seem at ease, anyway.'

Slider moved on. 'How are you getting on with checking Prentiss's movements after he left the flat?' he asked Hollis.

'Not well,' Hollis said. 'I can't get near Giles Freeman. He's got more wrapping round him than an After Eight. The best I've managed is his press officer – and he's cagey as hell. Can't say, no comment, have to check on that. Everyone's going to "get back to me" and no-one ever gets.'

'Keep trying,' Slider said. 'Freeman's got to come across, if he doesn't want a slap for obstruction.'

'Can you slap a Secretary of State?' Atherton asked doubtfully, eyeing his mild-looking boss in his ready-made suit. In the power-dressing league he packed all the force of a digital watch battery.

'I can slap anyone,' he said heroically. 'But this whole Prentiss business is a mess. The trouble is, we know he was there and he admits he was there, but there's no reason why he shouldn't have been there. It doesn't make him the murderer, all his lies notwithstanding.'

'We've got the finger-mark on the whisky glass and the semen,' Hollis said.

'He's covered himself for the finger-mark,' Slider pointed out. 'If the semen comes back his we might have a different picture. But in the meantime, I think we'll have to at least entertain the notion that Prentiss didn't kill her. Give it tea and biscuits, if not a bed for the night. So what else have we got?'

'I'd go for Wordley,' McLaren said. 'Okay, maybe she done him a good turn, but he's got form as long as your arm.'

'He's got no form on sex crime,' Mackay demurred.

'There's always a first time,' McLaren said. 'If you ask me he's an evil psychotic bastard who'd kill anyone without a second thought, just for looking at him sideways.'

Swilley shook her head. 'You're a prat, Maurice. Would an evil psychotic bastard who raped and strangled a woman who'd done him a good turn bother to use a condom, and then throw it tidily down the lav?'

'And not check it had been flushed away properly?' Atherton added.

'Why not?' McLaren defended his brainchild. 'Barmy is barmy. You can't account for nutters.'

'By all means look into him,' Slider said generously. 'Find out where he was and how he felt about Agnew.'

'Maybe he despised her, and hated being done good to,' Atherton said. 'I know I would. But would she have cooked him a nice supper?'

'We don't know the diner was the killer,' Swilley said, and sighed. 'In fact, if Prentiss is telling the truth about seeing her alive at eight, he couldn't have been.'

'Unless the supper was eaten after Prentiss left,' said Atherton. 'People do eat later in the evening in some strata of society,' he informed her kindly. She stuck her tongue out at him.

'Or Prentiss et it,' said McLaren. 'Or there was another visitor we don't know about.'

'The meal is a blasted nuisance,' Hollis said.

'And probably not even important,' Atherton concluded. 'Can chicken be a red herring?'

'Thank you, we won't go down that byway,' Slider said hastily. 'What else?'

'Boss, I'm still not happy about Peter Medmenham,' Swilley

said. 'There's something not right about his story. I think there's something he's not telling us.'

'There's probably a lot he's not telling us. What the average citizen doesn't tell us would make the Internet sag. But follow him up,' Slider said. 'Until we get confirmation on Prentiss one way or the other, there's no need to stop at him. In fact, it seems to me the only way forward is to find out exactly what was going on, that day at the flat and in Agnew's life in general. Let's get some street witness, find out if anyone was seen entering or leaving. Talk to her work colleagues – find out what she was involved in recently. Go through her papers, see if anything shows up missing. And, of course, check the pedigree of everything we've been told so far. Test every statement, follow every lead—'

'You sound like a chorus from *The Sound of Music*,' Atherton complained. 'It's still Prentiss for me.'

'Even if it is,' Slider said, 'I'd like at least to know why he did it.'

Slider came out of the washroom and bumped into Norma.

'Oh – I was just looking for you, boss.'

'Haven't you gone home?'

'Apparently not,' she said gravely. She turned and fell in with him as he walked back towards the office. 'I've managed to get hold of Medmenham's dear old white-haired mum, and guess what?'

'He didn't go down there on Thursday night?'

'In one! And she hasn't been ill – fit as a fiddle, she said. Sounded quite indignant about it. Must have made a mistake, she said. Never had a day's illness in my life, young woman, all that sort of thing. And she wasn't expecting him, either. He turned up about eleven on Friday morning and said he wanted to take her out to lunch. So she drove them both into Chelmsford and they had lunch in a restaurant and she saw him off on the train.'

'That's a long way for him to go just for one meal,' Slider said.

'She said, "He's such a good son, always thinking of little treats for me." Said it before I even asked.'

'Ah! So she thought it was odd, too.'

'I'd guess she did. Also, I checked with the *Ham and Ful* and Martin, the editor, said the notion of having a day off doesn't apply to Medmenham because although he's a regular he's a freelance, so he can choose his own hours.'

'What would we do without bad liars?' Slider smiled. 'So what, I wonder, was he up to on Thursday night? Easiest way to find out is to ask him, I suppose.'

Norma looked serious. 'If he killed Agnew, sir, he's a dangerous man.'

'Is that you worrying about me, WDC Swilley?'

'Somebody's got to, and Jim's gone home.'

'I'm not sure I like that juxtaposition,' Slider said. He walked with her through the CID room, passing her desk on the way to his office. There was a thick file on it. 'What's this?'

She blushed. 'Oh, I was passing the time between phone calls looking at menus. I still haven't sorted the caterers out.'

The file, he saw, was neatly labelled 'Wedding' in Swilley's firm black capitals; and reading no unwillingness in her posture, he opened it and found it full of orderly paperwork, everything from correspondence with the organist over the choice of music to comparative quotations for marquees.

'You're going about it like a military campaign,' he said. For some reason he found that unbearably touching.

'I don't know any other way,' she said, and for a moment her voice was uncertain, and her look as she met Slider's was horribly vulnerable. 'Tony laughs at me, but – you have to be organised about things, don't you?'

'Absolutely,' he said, feeling like Steve Martin. 'It's going to be the end of an era, you know, you getting married.' Expect earthquakes, comets, two-headed calves, he thought; the very globe would gape in wonder – but it didn't seem quite polite to say so. 'So, is it all coming together all right?'

'I wish!' She regained her old ferocity. 'I hate caterers! They start off telling you you can have anything you want, but they've got three standard menus, and you're going to end up with one of them. Whatever you say, there's a problem with it, or it's not advisable and, blow me, there's the standard menu back under your nose. It's like *Alice Through The Looking Glass*. As fast as you walk out the door, you find yourself walking back in through it.'

'So that's why food at weddings always tastes the same,' Slider marvelled. 'Those caterer's prawns, exactly like newborn baby mice. The rubber chicken.'

'I *said* no chicken,' Norma gnashed. 'I said duck. I *swear* we agreed on duck. And when the confirmation arrived, it was down as chicken. What do you do?'

'Keep fighting,' Slider said. 'It's your wedding, not theirs. But shouldn't your parents be doing all this?'

'Don't be silly, at my age? Anyway, my parents are dead.'

'What about Tony's?' She made a face. 'Don't you like them?'

'Oh, they're very nice. All his family are terribly nice – but—'

'Dull?'

'Dull?' It burst from her. 'They're like dead people without the rouge! Boss, d'you think – d'you think I'm doing the right thing?'

Slider spread his hands. 'How can I answer that? Look, you love Tony, don't you? Well, that's the only important thing. Weddings are something you do for the sake of other people. Weddings are hell, but it doesn't mean the marriage isn't right.'

She opened her eyes wide. 'Gosh, that sounded so brill! Did you just think of it?'

'It was pretty good, wasn't it?' Slider said modestly. 'Just hang in there, Norma. We're all behind you.'

'Some of you are more help than others,' Norma said, closing the file with a sigh. 'I asked Jim if he'd help me choose the wines, seeing he's such a wine buff. He said I'd need a Mâcon with the chicken. I was writing it down, when he said, "Yeah, I've watched you, you're a messy eater."'

'Atherton's a pain in the khyber sometimes,' Slider agreed. He patted her shoulder and headed for his office, but she called him back.

'Boss?' He turned, to encounter the unfamiliar vulnerable Norma again, lurking in those usually marble eyes. 'I don't suppose – I mean – are you doing anything on the sixth?'

He turned fully, surprised. 'Are you inviting *me* to your wedding? I thought you didn't want any of us there?'

'I don't want the others. They laugh at me.'

'They don't.'

'All right, not laugh, exactly, but—' She frowned, searching for the words. 'They don't think of me as a real person at all. I'm just old Norma Stits – like a cartoon character.'

Slider knew, uncomfortably, how far this was true. 'They're a bit scared of you, that's all.'

'I didn't ask them to be scared of me,' she said fiercely. 'Why can't they just accept me? I accept them, I don't judge them by their revolting bodies and nasty habits. But to them I'm a freak. Well, I won't have them at my wedding, sneering and sniggering.' Slider couldn't think of anything to say, and in his silence her ferocity drained away. She became diffident. 'Anyway, I know it's short notice and everything, but I wondered if you'd – if you'd give me away?'

He was so surprised he didn't answer at once, and she hurried on, blushing painfully.

'I mean, say no if you think it's a cheek to ask, but my Dad's dead and the nearest thing I've got is a cousin I've never liked, who's got dandruff and BO and terrible teeth. I don't want him. Tony's Dad's offered, but that doesn't seem right to me. It ought to be someone of mine. And you – well – you're practically like family. In a sort of way. I mean . . .'

He had to say something to check this painful embarrassment. 'I always knew there was some reason you never made a pass at me,' he said, smiling slowly. 'I assumed it was respect for my rank, but now I see it's because you thought of me as a different generation.' Now she smiled too, shyly. 'I'd be honoured to do it. Thank you for asking me.'

'Thank you, boss,' she said, and, hugely daring, darted a kiss at his cheek.

'And now you'd better go home,' he said, mock-sternly, because someone had to get them out of this before they both burst into tears.

'Right, boss.' She sat abruptly at her desk and bent her head, shuffling her papers together in a terminal sort of way.

Slider marched himself off into his office.

Mâcon, indeed!

CHAPTER SIX

Things can only get bitter

Peter Medmenham opened the door to Slider and said without
a great deal of surprise, 'Oh, it's you.'

'You know why I'm here?' Slider said sternly.

'Yes. My mother rang me.' He managed to scrape up a
bit of indignation. 'You had no right to call her without my
permission.'

'Don't be silly, of course we did,' Slider said, and Medmenham's
balloon collapsed. 'And we wouldn't have had to bother her if
you hadn't lied to us in the first place.'

Now he only looked miserable. 'You'd better come in,' he
sighed, and stepped back.

Medmenham's flat was a very different affair from either of
the other two. A great deal of money and thought had obviously
gone into it. The narrow passageway beyond the front door
ought, Slider knew from other houses like this, to have been
dark and damp-smelling. In fact it was brightly lit from sunken
halogen lamps in the ceiling and smelled faintly of pot-pourri.
The walls were white, and the single piece of furniture in view
was a delicate mahogany side table of breathtaking simplicity
and elegance – Georgian, Slider thought – on which stood a
narrow glass vase containing a single scarlet gerbera, spiky and
stunning against the white wall.

Medmenham led the way past two closed doors – bedroom
and bathroom, presumably – to the room at the back. This
was the living room, with the kitchen beyond in a new glass-
roofed extension, divided from the sitting-room, American style,
only by a counter. The kitchen was blisteringly modern, all
pale ash and chrome, with a wicker-fronted drawer stack, a
lot of expensive stainless-steel equipment on overhead racks,

and a huge stone jar filled with dried rushes on the floor by the door.

Everything was tidy and put away, except that on the counter stood a large Gordon's bottle and a heavy-bottomed cut-crystal glass, and a small chopping-board with half a lemon and a short knife lying on it.

The sitting-room was decorated in the sort of spare, minimalist style that depended on a very high quality of workmanship to make it succeed. Again the walls were white, and sported a series of black-and-white eighteenth-century political cartoons in huge white mounts and thin gold frames. The polished floorboards were covered in the centre with a large square carpet, very thick and blackberry purple. There was an enormous sofa covered in coarse white material, with lavender-coloured scatter cushions, and a heavy glass coffee table on which stood a single purple orchid in another tall skinny glass. The only other chair was an expensive-looking leather recliner which faced the state-of-the-art television set in the corner. Behind the TV was a cabinet which seemed to have been specially designed to house four video recorders – for his job as reviewer, Slider supposed. Evidently he didn't watch Channel 5 – but then, who did?

'You've really put some work into your flat, haven't you?' Slider said in admiring tones.

Medmenham seemed pleased. 'Do you like it?'

'You obviously have very good taste,' Slider said. 'But I wonder you should do so much when you don't own it. I mean, I suppose you must have had to pay for all the building work yourself?'

'Goodness, you don't think Sborksi would *ever* put his hand in his pocket? I know,' he said, looking round, 'it's probably a bit foolish of me, but the rent is so low, and I'm comfortable here, and my surroundings are so important to me. Things grate, don't you find, if they're not *just so*? And I never intended to move again, so what did it matter?'

'You never intended – does that mean you intend now?'

Medmenham waved him graciously to the sofa, and stood facing him, clasping his hands together as though he were going to recite. 'I don't know. All this business – poor Phoebe – it's so unsettling. I wonder if I'll be able to bear it here now, thinking of her being – you know – up there.' He rolled his eyes at the ceiling. 'And, of course, not having her there to talk to will make such a difference. We always planned to grow old together.'

The lighting in the room came from artfully placed lamps and was designed to be flattering, but even so Slider could see the age and weariness that had come to the plump face. Medmenham had bags under his eyes that even a BA stewardess would have rejected as cabin luggage.

'You were very fond of her?' Slider suggested.

'I thought I'd made *that* clear,' said Medmenham.

'I thought you'd made a lot of things clear, until it turned out you'd been lying,' Slider said sternly.

He made a fluttery movement of his hands. 'Oh, Lord, don't make a big thing of it! I'm not up to it. I can't tell you what a state I've been in these last few days! Look, would you like a snort? Frankly, I'm not going to get through the next half hour without a drinkette. Gin and ton?'

Slider accepted, and having handed him a gin and tonic very nearly large enough to wash in, Medmenham took his own replenished glass and retired to the leather recliner, where he tucked one foot under him girlishly, took a good mouthful, swallowed, and shuddered.

'That's better! Not', he added firmly, 'that I want you to think I'm a boozer. Normally it's moderation in all things, but things aren't normal, are they? And frankly, dear, it's ruinous to the complexion. Oh, I know, don't look! I must look shocking. I've been weeping like a waterfall, and no sleep; but I just haven't had the heart to put any slap on. I've said to Phoebe many a time, you and I just can't go on drinking at our age the way we used to – well, you know what journalists are like, first cousin to a bottomless pit as far as alcohol's concerned; but when you're young you burn it off, don't you? And just lately darling Feeb's been hitting the White Horse a bit hard. I mean, I said, you're not Lester Piggott, darling! But the past few weeks it's been sip, sip, sip like a dowager. So depressing! Not that she can't hold it. Always a perfect gentleman. But you can't punish yourself like that and get away with it for ever.'

This was a promising vein, but Slider had other seams to mine first. 'Let's get back to what you were doing on Thursday evening,' he said.

Medmenham raised his glass to his lips defensively. 'Oh, must we? Look, I know I told a teensy little porkie pie, but, honestly, it's nothing to do with all this – nothing to do with poor darling Feeb. It's purely my personal life, which is so utterly ghastly at the moment I wouldn't trouble anyone with it. I promise you I know nothing about what happened upstairs, other than what I've told you.'

'You have to understand, Mr Medmenham, that I have to verify every statement that's made to me. When people tell me lies I have to assume they've got something to hide. Especially when they can't be accounted for at the time of the crime.'

'Well, you can't suspect me of murder,' he said, almost gaily, and then, looking shocked. 'You don't? No, really, look at me! I'm the human equivalent of a cosy eiderdown. Born a duvet and I'll die a duvet! Even on stage I'd never cut it as First Murderer. *Please* tell me you don't think I'm capable of such a horrible thing!'

'I think you capable of anything you put your mind to,' Slider said seriously, and he saw his words give Medmenham pause. He drank, put his glass down on the counter top and folded his hands together in his lap.

'What do you want to know?' he asked without affectation.

'How much of what you told me yesterday was true? Did you see Miss Agnew at six forty-five? Did she say she had a visitor?'

'Oh, yes, all that was true.'

'But you didn't see the visitor? Or hear his voice?'

'No. There was music playing in the background. Quietly. Vivaldi, I think.'

'So she might have been alone.'

'But then why wouldn't she have asked me in?' Medmenham looked suddenly shrewd. 'Oh, you think I'm a chattering nuisance and she might just want to be rid of me? But I assure you, she was quite capable of telling me she wanted to be alone, and often did. We had a very frank relationship. "Sorry, Peter darling, things to do. Bog off, sweetheart." No, it wasn't that. There was someone else in there: you can *feel*, can't you, when a house is empty? You just *know*. And the way she opened the door only a little bit and stood there in the gap: she didn't want me to see who it was.'

'Why do you suppose she would do that? Was she usually secretive about her visitors?'

'Well—' He thought. 'Not *secretive*. She didn't go into graphic detail about her sex life, and I didn't ask. But she didn't go out of her way to hide the fact when she had visitors.'

'So if it was Josh Prentiss, for instance—'

'Well, why should she try and hide Josh from me?' he said. 'I've known Josh for yonks.'

'It was you who told me that's who was visiting her,' Slider said patiently.

Medmenham put a hand to his cheek. 'You're right! I did say that. Because I saw his car outside. It doesn't make sense, does it?'

'That's what I was thinking.'

He looked at Slider and went a bit pink. 'You think I'm lying? But I'm not! It all happened exactly as I told you, up to that point; and I did see his car in the street. It's only about where I went afterwards that I didn't tell the truth.'

'Well, suppose you tell me the truth now, and we'll see how we get on,' Slider suggested kindly.

'Oh, we can be sarcastic when we try!' Medmenham complained. 'Well, look, I'll tell you, since you make such a thing about it, but it's very painful for me, and I hope you won't repeat it to anyone. Can I trust you to be discreet?'

'If it has nothing to do with the case, I will do my very best,' Slider said.

Medmenham sighed. 'And I suppose that's all I'll get out of you. You're very *hard*, you know. Well, after I'd been up to see Phoebe and she said she wasn't coming down, I came back down here and thought I'd just hole in for the night and watch some television. I'd put the tape in for *Red Slayer*, but I thought I ought to watch that new thing on the Beeb, *Windermere*, though frankly, love, it sounded like the usual old drivel – ess and vee lightly wrapped in panoramic views. So predictable! It would never have got made at all if it hadn't been set in the Lake District. Dear old Auntie's regional promotion plan! I don't know why they don't just give them a Tourist Board grant and be done with it. Well, long story short,' he responded to Slider's look, 'I was just about to change into my kimono and slippers when the phone rang.' He stopped.

'Please,' Slider said, 'the suspense is killing me.'

Medmenham sighed. 'I suppose I've got to tell you. All right, it was Piers.'

'Peers?' With all the Government connections of Josh Prentiss in the background, Slider's mind offered him a section of the House of Lords.

'My *friend*.' He gave it an emphasis to show he was talking about more than friendship. 'And, to be perfectly frank and honest, Josh's brother.'

Slider got the spelling at last. 'Oh, I see! Piers Prentiss?'

'Do you know him?'

'Never met him.'

'I wish I never had. The heartache that little wrecker's given me!'

'How did you know him?'

'Oh, I met him through Phoebe and Josh, of course. I've been to the Prentisses' house to parties and things. Sometimes escorted Phoebe when they wanted the numbers kept even. Always fancied him, but we didn't get together until a couple of months had gone by. Then it was a case of why didn't we do this before? We were made for each other – or at least I thought so. Not that it's been a bed of roses. He's not the easiest man to get on with, let me tell you! But I thought we were settled for life. Then about two months ago, or a bit more, he started acting strangely. Blowing hot and cold. Not phoning. Breaking dates. I thought, hello, I thought – because we've been there before, dear, believe you me! Our life has not been a garden path, by any means. No, I thought, it's got a little something on the side, that's what's going on here! Well, I let it go, because these things happen, and least said, soonest back under the duvet. I thought it would burn itself out and we'd be all right again. That's usually the best way. But then came this phone call. Out of the blue. Not so much as a "brace yourself, love."'

'He was breaking it off?' Slider asked, hoping to move the story on.

'Breaking it off? I'd like to break his off!' Medmenham cried with tiny rage. 'And doing it like that, the little bitch, on the phone! I *had* been expecting to be seeing him, you see. We *were* supposed to've spent Sunday together. But then he phoned me on Wednesday to say he had to go on a collecting trip up north somewhere – a country house sale on Monday, with the viewing on Sunday. He's in the antiques trade, you see. Well, that rang true. Sunday and Monday are the days most antiques shops shut. But he said he was going up on the Saturday night so as to get to the viewing early and leave some bids, and that made me a bit suspicious, because he'd never done that before. Still, I didn't say anything. And then he phones me at seven o'clock on Thursday to say it's all over and he's got someone else and it's the real thing this time. He hadn't been going to go away at all – he planned to spend the weekend with the new one. They'd arranged it Wednesday night – he'd been there, the new one, spent all day Thursday with him, and he'd just gone, so Piers had got straight on to me to tell me it was all over.' He stopped a moment. 'I'm sorry, I'll have to have another drinky. It makes me shake just thinking about it. What about yours?'

Slider declined, and watched as Medmenham got up and mixed himself another G and T. Had it not been Josh Prentiss's brother, he would have been impatient with all this detail, but as it was, he was listening with mind agog. If Piers had done him wrong and it was Phoebe who'd brought them together in the first place and Phoebe was making the beast with two backs with Josh – well, could that add up to enough to make Medmenham snap? Except that the rape still seemed a bit unlikely.

Medmenham returned with his drink, but didn't sit down. He wandered about restlessly, sipping, touching things. Slider prompted him. 'So Piers told you it was all over. What next?'

'Naturally I argued with him. Told him this new thing was a flash in the pan. He says he's known him a while, but it was just ordinary acquaintance before – well, I thought, tell that to the marines! I know the symptoms. I've been dumped on before, believe you me! Anyway, it's obvious that Piers has just been dazzled by a young turk in a Donna Karan suit and Gucci shoes. So different from tweedy old *moi*. He wouldn't say who it was, but he went on and on about how wonderful he was in frankly tedious detail. I said why all the secrecy? Tell me his name. And he said the new one wanted it kept secret, forbade him to tell anyone. I said, love, if he's ashamed of you, but he said no, it was that his career was at a delicate stage. He's going to be frightfully important, and when he is, he'll come out in the open about the relationship.' Medmenham sniffed. 'Piers is such an innocent, he shouldn't be let out alone. One can see why he's gone doo-lally over this power dresser. What *he* sees in Piers is another matter! Seal my lips for *that*, dear, because nobody likes a bitch. But anyway, I wasn't taking it lying down, pardon the pun, because I just *know* it isn't going to work and I'd like to save Piers heartache if I can, despite the way he's treated me, so I said, "Is he with you now?" and Piers said he'd just left. So I said, "Then let me come up and see you. You owe me that, at least, to tell me to my face." Because of course I thought if I could see him I could talk him round. He argued a bit, but I wore him down. I think he was quite glad really, because he was never the slightest use at being on his own, Piers wasn't. I think one should be a world unto oneself. I'm happy as a lark with my own company. But Piers has to be with someone every minute. I suppose that's what the problem was with *us*, because I wasn't there enough of the time. Not that we couldn't have worked that out. Anyway, after a bit he said all right, I could come if I wanted but it wouldn't make any difference. So I went.'

'Went where?' Slider asked.

'To see *Piers*,' Medmenham said irritably, and then, 'Oh, you mean *where*? Well, Chelmsford, of course. He's got the shop there, and a dear little cottage, very *bijou*, stuffed with the most *precious* things. I mean, Chelmsford's Outer Mongolia as far as I'm concerned, anything beyond the Angel Islington just doesn't *exist* for me, but he finds it convenient and it's only forty minutes on the train, and when he wants to stay in London he's got a room at Josh and Noni's, if he's not with me – or someone else, the slut, as I found out to my cost! But don't let's think about that. So anyway, I caught the 9.02, just like I told you – you see, I did tell you the truth, except for some bits that didn't matter – and he met me at the station. We went to a wine bar – what? Oh, Ramblers, it's called. We had a spot of manjare and some drinkie-poos and then we went back to the cottage. I thought everything was all right again, but in the morning, just when I was squeezing the oranges for breakfast, he said as calm as you like that it was still over and that now he'd told me to my face there'd be no call for us to meet again.'

'That must have been upsetting for you,' Slider said mildly. Medmenham seemed to be trembling with rage.

'Upsetting? He'd played me for a complete patsy! I felt like a – well, I felt *used*! I threw the orange juice at him, that's how mad I was – and I'm not a throwing person usually, too conscious of the mess. So it ended up with a flaming row, and I marched out of there and slammed the door. It was dreadful,' he confided, 'because when I'd calmed down a bit I realised I'd have to walk to the station, and with my feet that was no joke! But then I saw a bus coming with Danbury on the front, and I thought of the dear old Aged P, and flagged it down. Quite an adventure, because I never go on buses – well, one doesn't, does one? Normally the Mum collects me from the station and takes me back – she's a marvel, seventy-nine and still driving! She was a bit startled when I turned up, but I said I wanted to take her to lunch, and that way she drove us into Chelmsford and I ended up being dropped at the station, so my poor old feet didn't take the punishment.'

'Didn't she ask you why you'd suddenly appeared?' Slider asked.

'You don't know the Mum. Naturally she suspected I'd flown to her arms from some little *crise* or other, but she'd never ask. Just took it in her stride. She was always wonderful like that. When I first came out to them, my parents, she said she'd always suspected and she loved me anyway, and she talked to Dad like a Dutch uncle to make him accept it – though I don't think he ever really came to terms. Well, fathers don't, do they? Have you got any kiddies, love? I can tell you're married.'

Slider wasn't going to be drawn. 'So you had lunch with your mother and got her to take you to the station?'

He shrugged. 'Like I said. I brooded all the way down on the train, and then when I got to Liverpool Street I picked up the *Standard* and there I saw the para and found out about poor darling Feeb. Well, you can imagine! I was so shocked I thought I'd faint.'

'And when you found out, what was the first thing that went through your head? Who did you think must have done it?'

'Well,' he said, shaking his blue head reluctantly, 'just for a teensy-weensy instant I thought it might have been Josh, because I knew he'd been there – and also, I suppose, because he was Piers's brother and just then I was willing to believe anything bad about a Prentiss. But then I couldn't think of any reason why he'd want to kill her – I mean, they were old, old friends – so I thought it must have been one of those drug addict loonies, like I said to you, breaking in at random. I mean, no-one's safe now, are they?'

'But apart from not being able to think of a motive,' Slider pursued with interest, 'you didn't think Prentiss wasn't capable of such a thing?'

'Oh, I'd think he was capable of it all right,' Medmenham said easily. 'He's a very ruthless man when it comes to getting his own way. I could quite see him murdering someone if they'd become inconvenient, and not thinking twice about it. But he'd do it cleverly and I bet he'd never get caught. But he and Phoebe were very close, so I put it out of my mind.'

'Were they lovers?'

He hesitated. 'D'you know, I don't really know? She never said so one way or the other. Maybe they had been at one time – no, I really couldn't say. It was funny really, they were more like—' He paused, thinking it out. 'I don't know, brothers or something. Or an old married couple. Very close, but almost too close for sex, you know? But then, I've always had my doubts about Josh. He's always played the great butch omi-about-town, but there's just something about him – I wouldn't be surprised if he wasn't a closet queen. Ooh, slap my wrist for gossiping! Still, they say it's in the genes, don't they, and there's Piers to take into consideration.'

Slider thought of the softness he had suspected in Prentiss – a hint of petulance and self-indulgence, it had come across to him. Medmenham seemed to have picked up on the same thing. And it was interesting that he had said that Josh and Phoebe were like brothers, rather than brother and sister.

Well, if Medmenham's story was true, it looked as though he could be ruled out as the murderer, and that was one strand untangled. *If* it was true – and if Prentiss's story was true – and if they weren't in it together. That was enough ifs to make a cult movie.

'I shall have to take steps to verify your story,' he said. 'Which means I shall have to speak to Piers Prentiss.' Medmenham looked dismayed. 'But if he agrees with what you've said, there's no reason why anyone else should know anything about it.'

'Thank you,' Medmenham said a little stiffly. 'The whole

episode was horribly humiliating to me. Of course, we're no stranger to pain of that sort, but, well, one doesn't court it, does one? And then,' he seemed to remember suddenly, and sagged a little, 'the way it ended, with darling Feeb being killed . . . I'd like to put it completely behind me as soon as possible.'

'One more thing,' Slider said, 'you said that she had been drinking heavily just recently. Did you get the impression she was worried about something?'

'Definitely,' he said, sitting up straighter. 'She had something on her mind that was gnawing at her, that's what I thought.'

'Did she tell you what it was? Hint at it in any way?'

'No, not a dickie. I said many a time, tell all, heart face, you'll feel better. Don't bottle it up. But she just laughed and said there was nothing wrong and changed the subject. But she was *brooding*, that's what. Something was preying on her mind, and if she'd *only* trusted her Uncle Peter,' he mourned, 'all might have been well.'

CHAPTER SEVEN

Britannia waives the rules

Slider was in the hall putting on his coat when the flap on the letter-box lifted and vomited a pack of letters onto the floor, like a heron regurgitating fish. He picked them up and shuffled through them. A few minutes later, wondering why he hadn't left, Joanna came out from the kitchen and found him standing there, motionless. The printed heading on the paper held in his hand was IN THE DIVORCE REGISTRY. His head was bent, the thin sunlight coming in through the glass panel of the front door back-lighting his hair in a pre-Raphaelite way. Not for the first time, she wished she could paint.

She leaned gently against him from behind, and he lifted the paper to show her.

'It's the Decree Absolute,' he said.

'So I see.' He said nothing more, only stood there like a sad lamppost, and after a bit she said, 'How do you feel about it?'

'I don't know. Strange.' He hauled a great sigh up from his socks and said, 'It's so bald. The End. Sixteen years of marriage.' He turned to face her and she slipped her arms round him inside his coat. 'I'm a free man,' he said, trying to sound glad about it.

'This is my dangerous moment,' she said lightly. 'Any minute now you'll realise that free means you don't have to settle for me either, and off you'll flit like a butterfly to more exotic flowers.'

'Yes, you should worry,' he advised her. 'I'm such a fickle man.'

'It's all right to be upset,' she mentioned. 'I won't be offended.'

He rested his face against her hair and closed his eyes briefly. It was a gesture that needed no thought. She was his mate now, she was home, and everything he did with her or without her took place in the context of her, automatically, as once it had – though without the same pleasure – in the context of Irene. She was now *selbstverständlich*. And because of that, this piece of paper didn't have the impact it might otherwise have had. He didn't feel upset, he just felt strange. And guilty, of course, but that was endemic. And he couldn't help wondering how Irene would be feeling, receiving her copy of this same document, and opening the envelope in Ernie Newman's house, perhaps in her predecessor's kitchen, waiting for her predecessor's electric kettle to boil.

Joanna squeezed him a little tighter, reading his thoughts effortlessly. 'You ought to ring her, perhaps? It must be a hard moment for her, whatever the circumstances.'

He kissed her gratefully. 'Yes. I will. When I get to work.'

Not here, not from his-and-Joanna's phone. Joanna smiled inwardly. That was male tact. There were so many things he thought she minded, out of some elderly and elaborate code of chivalry he had learned young and never forgotten; and they were hardly ever the things that she really did mind, she who had been breadwinner and decision-maker to herself all her adult life, husband in her own household, without the luxury of a Norman Rockwell aproned wife's sensibilities.

'Yes, do that,' she said in benison. 'I'll see you tonight.'

At the door he turned. 'Have lunch with me?' He knew she was not working.

And she knew he had a murder case. 'Will you have time?'

'For you, always.'

'All right. I'll ring you later and check,' she said, hedging his bets.

The phone was ringing as he reached his desk. It was Freddie Cameron.

'You're up early,' Slider said, switching the receiver from hand to hand as he shed his coat. It was good navy wool, but so old it had gone almost white along the seams. There were men who cared about overcoats and men who didn't, and that was just the way it was.

'I've done your post, old dear.'

'What, this morning? Don't you ever sleep?'

'No, yesterday. *Servissimo*. I'm up to my ears in bodies and I'm going to be in court for the next couple of days, so I thought I'd better put in a bit of overtime. Martha was not amused.'

'I should think not. That way lies divorce and madness.'

'Anyway, I put your report in the mail last night,' Freddie said, with a shrug in the intonation, 'and I've called to give you the edited highlights. Talking of which, I see you've been getting big coverage in the papers.'

'Not me personally.'

'All the broadsheets have had fulsome obits on the Agnew,' Freddie said. 'Career appraisals. Highlights of her campaigns as a mercenary in the justice war. Farewells from journalists and editors. Personal tributes from showbiz personalities and Queen's Counsels – which are much the same thing, of course. An endorsement from Ronnie Biggs—'

'Eh?'

'Just testing if you were listening. They don't seem to have published the fine details of the murder, though, which shows extraordinary restraint.'

'An appeal was made to keep them out,' Slider said, 'but I think they're showing solidarity because she was one of their own, rather than for Mr Porson's sweet sake. But if we don't get home sharpish with the streaky rashers, they'll forget their promises soon enough.'

'Is the case still with you or is AMIP taking it?'

'All AMIP's taking at the moment is aspirin.'

'Ah, the 'flu epidemic.'

'They flew, they have flown. It's down to me and my little chums. So, tell me, was it strangulation?'

'It was indeed. Strangulation with some force. The hyoid was fractured, and there was considerable damage to the thyroid and cricoid cartilages with severe localised bruising and extensive petechiae above the ligature.'

'Any idea what that was?'

'A narrow band of material. Probably a tie, possibly a folded scarf – something of that sort.'

'Pair of stockings?'

Cameron chuckled. 'Tights, dear boy! A good feminist would never wear stockings. And, no, the texture was wrong for tights. The material was smooth. I'd plump for the tie, if you put a gun

to my head. Nicely available, for one thing. Carry it in – and out
– round your neck.'

'If you could get the knot undone,' Slider said.

'There was no knot,' Freddie said. 'The killer relied on strength
and determination. And there were some other points of interest.
The strangulation was carried out from behind, which was not
what you'd expect from the position of the corpse.'

'Are you sure?' Slider said. 'No, silly question, of course
you are.'

'You can see by the comparative depth of the bruising,'
Freddie explained. 'The ligature was placed round the neck,
crossed over at the back and pulled tight. Now, if the ends
had been pulled by someone standing in front of her, the
crossed part would have dug into the neck at the back, but
in fact the pressure is all at the front. So that means . . .' He
paused, inviting comprehension.

'Yes, I see,' said Slider. 'It's pretty difficult to strangle someone
from behind when they're lying on their back on the bed.'

'Ten points,' Freddie awarded him approvingly. 'And when
you add the intriguing little fact that the wrists were tied after
death—'

'What?'

'Dead men don't mark,' said Freddie. 'The ligature round the
wrist was tight, but there was no bruising. However, from the
distribution of hypostasis, she was put into the position we
found her in immediately.'

'So she was strangled somewhere else in the room,' Slider
said, 'and then put on the bed and tied to the bedhead to make
it look like a sexual assault?'

'That's a viable hypothesis,' Cameron said. 'There was, in
fact, semen in the vagina, but there's no bruising or any other
sign of forcible penetration. I've sent a sample off to be typed,
as well as the sample from the condom. Though I doubt we'll
get much from the condom – too dilute.'

'We don't know', Slider said, 'that they are from the same
person.'

'I don't like to contemplate that scenario,' Cameron said. 'But
we have a bonus ball: there was some tissue under the nails of
the left hand. She managed to scratch her assailant: not deeply,
just a surface abrasion, but enough to give us a tiny sample. I've

sent that off to the genetic boys, too. Let's hope it matches one or other semen sample.'

'Let's definitely hope that – and further that it matches Prentiss,' Slider said, 'otherwise it starts getting complicated. Oh – was the sexual penetration post-mortem?'

'No way of telling,' Freddie said. 'Not a nice thought, that.'

'No,' said Slider. 'Not that it would have mattered to her once she was dead.'

'True. Still, at least the condemned woman ate a hearty dinner,' Cameron went on, 'with wine and spirits. I've secured the stomach with contents, in case you want it analysed.'

'I can pretty well tell from the kitchen what she ate,' Slider said. 'There's no reason to think she was poisoned or drugged?'

'Nothing in the pathology, though there are plenty of things that don't show up unless you look for them. So unless you want me to go through the whole pharmacopoeia from Astra to Zeneca—'

'No, not at this point.'

'She seems to have ingested a large quantity of alcohol, which might have made her easier to strangle. D'you want a blood test for the volume?'

'Hold off on that for the moment. I need the semen and tissue typed, and we've got to think about budget.'

'Sooner you than me,' Cameron said. 'Well, I must away. I've two to do at Guy's, before the Old Bailey.'

'Complicated case?'

'That fire in Hendon. Arson stroke murder. Four bodies and a dispute over identity. A pathologist's life is not a nappy one. Let me know if there's anything else you want.'

'A holiday in the sun,' said Slider promptly.

'A holiday? Ah, yes, I had one of those once,' said Freddie.

He heard Swilley's voice in the outer office, saying good morning to Anderson, who was first in. Anderson hardly spared time for a hello before offering yet again to take her wedding photos.

'You don't want to have anything to do with those professionals,' he said earnestly. 'They charge a bloody fortune. A century plus just to turn up, and a tenner a time for the pix. And half of 'em are in league with villains. They give the tip-off about when the house'll be empty, and a gang goes in and cleans out all your wedding presents.'

'Yeah, thanks, Tony, but I really think—'

'Straight up! There's this snout of mine, he used to be in on a shutter scam before he went straight, told me all the wrinkles. He was the fence. Made a fortune. Toasters, microwaves, food mixers—'

'An electric fence, then?'

'You gotta use your loaf, Norm,' Anderson urged. 'I'll do you a real nice job. Did I ever show you my sister's wedding pix? I did this thing off the top of a ladder, with her on the grass and her dress spread out all round her. She looked just like a flower—'

Slider had had enough. He went out to rescue Swilley, and, basking in her look of gratitude, told her about his visit to Medmenham.

'Well, that sounds a bit more like it,' she said.

'Yes, plenty of free-flowing detail to comfort a policeman's doubts. I would still like some confirmation from someone outside the triangle, though. This wine bar they went to – Ramblers. It would be nice if anyone there remembered our couple and could put an approximate time on it. It would be nice to have someone in the case whose word we could trust.'

'Okay, boss, I'll get on to it. D'you want me to chase up Piers Prentiss?'

'No, leave him be. I want Medmenham's story checked first. If it's okay, there's probably no need to touch Prentiss junior.'

Back in his office, he took a moment before he plunged into the rest of the day's work to call Irene. The phone was picked up at the first ring.

'What were you doing, crouching over it?' he asked.

'I was just passing when it rang,' she said. She sounded defensive.

'Are you all right? I got something in the post today.'

'Yes. So did I.'

A silence. 'How do you feel about it?' Slider asked awkwardly.

'How do you think I feel?'

Something in her voice warned him. 'Have you been crying?'

'What if I have? It's a big thing, after all these years. Someone ought to feel something.'

'I'm sorry too,' he said. 'It was never what I . . .' He couldn't say wanted. '. . . anticipated. When I married you, I really thought it was for good. But things change.'

'*People* change,' she said, as though that were something else.

'Yes. We're both different now,' he said carefully. 'I just phoned to see if you were all right.'

'That was nice of you.' He couldn't tell if she was being ironic or not.

'I do care about you, you know,' he said. 'I want you to be happy. And also—' This was more delicate territory. 'Well, I phoned because I wanted to say thanks. That I appreciate all you did for me all those years. I wanted to say – I'm not sorry that we married.'

'Yes,' she said, and the line vibrated with perilous emotions. 'Me, too. Thanks for saying that. We had some good times, didn't we, Bill?'

'We did,' he said, though for the moment he couldn't think what they were. Except the children. They were definitely a good thing. 'Will you tell the children?' he asked.

'I suppose so. When they get back from school. I think they'll take it all right. I mean, they must know it was about due.'

'Do you think', he asked diffidently, 'it would be a good idea if you and I were to take them out somewhere together next weekend? Just the four of us. If I can get the time off.'

'To celebrate?' Irene said, with a twist of lemon.

'Of course not to celebrate,' he said. 'To reassure them. To show we can still be all right together, even though – well, you know. What do you think?'

'It might be nice,' she said cautiously. 'But I won't say anything to them yet, in case you can't get the time. I wouldn't want them to be disappointed.'

If she had learned one thing in the years she had been a policeman's wife, it was not to plan ahead.

Atherton came in, looking as if he had been out on the tiles.

'Late night?' Slider asked casually.

'No, early. Early, early hours.'

His breath had the vinous sting of heavy consumption. Slider thought if he took a breathalyser test right now his drive in to work might take on a whole different complexion.

'Nice to be able to afford debauchery,' Slider said.

'You have yours laid on at home,' said Atherton.

Slider wasn't sure what he meant by that. Had the dog been up to his old tricks? But he didn't feel up to pursuing it. 'I've had Freddie Cameron on the phone,' he said, and passed on Freddie's report.

Atherton's greyness was shed instantly. Alert, eyes wide, he sat on Slider's window-sill and crossed his arms into thinking position. 'Wait a minute, wait a minute, this is weird! He has sex with her, using a condom, because he's a careful boy – or she's a careful girl – and chucks the debris down the lav, presumably as per usual habit; relaxed enough about it anyway not to check that the corpus voluptae is safely off on its journey to the sea. Then he has sex with her again, without precautions. Then gets her drunk, strangles her, and arranges her on the bed to make it look like a stranger-rape, despite the fact that his semen is inside her, ready to finger him as the rapist.'

'It doesn't make sense,' Slider agreed, 'but we don't know what order things happened in. Maybe it was sex with condom, then more drinks, then unprotected sex because they or she were merry enough not to care.'

'Then strangulation,' Atherton acknowledged, 'but why the rape scenario?'

'Not thinking clearly. If he was drunk too . . .'

'But if he was trying to make it look like a random rapist, he ought to have faked a break-in as well. A stranger wouldn't have known that you could slip that lock.'

'He would if he tried,' Slider said.

'Yes, but Prentiss wouldn't know that we'd realise that. If someone's faking something they daren't get that subtle, in case the other side misses it.'

'I'll just sit here and let you argue yourself into a corner,' Slider said. 'There are yet other scenarios.'

'Sell me one,' Atherton invited.

'Sex with condom, drinks, quarrel or whatever, strangulation, and then bondage sex with the corpse, because that's what he really likes, or as an act of revenge – humiliating her when she couldn't fight back.'

'You've got a nasty mind,' Atherton complained. 'But nec-rophilia does at least make more sense than the set-up idea. Anyone who'd do that would be mad enough not to care about leaving the semen behind, and wouldn't need to fake a break-in. But Prentiss didn't have a scratch on his face, did he?'

'It needn't have been the face,' Slider said. 'It could as easily be the neck, or it might be hand or arm, trying to loosen his grip. Or it might have been the bare body while they were bonking. And in any case, Freddie says it's a tiny tissue sample – nothing more than a slight abrasion.'

'I suppose she was too drunk to fight much,' Atherton said. 'I didn't like the woman, but she's gaining my sympathy point by point.'

'But remember, we don't know yet that the semen is Prentiss's, or even that both lots are from the same person. Prentiss may have noshed, made love and left, and the murderer came in afterwards for the rest of the sex. Or someone else might have been responsible for the condom and Prentiss for the rest.'

'And meanwhile we've got an unverifiable alibi for him, and a wife who gives him an alibi he apparently doesn't want.'

Slider smiled faintly. 'Life is fun, isn't it?'

'So what're you going to do, guv?'

'Have a crack at Giles Freeman myself, and get Porson to try and hurry the DNA results. We're stuck without them. Meanwhile, you go and have a bash at Mrs P. Your famous charm and sexual magnetism might get something different out of her.'

'Okay.' He stood to go. 'What's this about you giving the fabulous Norma away at her wedding, by the way?'

'How the hell did that get out?' Slider said, startled.

'Oh, it isn't out. Norma told me. Wanted to crow over me, I think. But I told her you wouldn't go if I wasn't there.'

'And she believed you?'

'Not entirely,' Atherton admitted. 'She called me a lying, weaselling scumbag. So I'm relying on you to get me an invite, guv.'

'Why should I?'

'Could you bear to think of me being humiliated in that

way?' Slider nodded grimly. 'Could you live with yourself after-wards?'

'I could try.'

'You wouldn't enjoy the wedding without me. It'll be nothing but strangers there.'

'My job, of course, doesn't accustom me to meeting stran-gers.'

'Ah, but it's different in a social situation,' Atherton said. 'You need me as a buffer. Look, I'll get your sandwiches every day. I'll be good for ever. Go on, go on, get me an invite, *pleeese!*'

'The furthest I'll go', said Slider, 'is to ask her why she doesn't want you there.'

Atherton shuddered delicately. 'No, no, I'll pass on that. There are some things it's better not to know.'

After a frustrating interval, Slider, too, got as far as Freeman's press secretary, Ben McKenzie.

'I'm sorry, Giles Freeman doesn't talk direct to anyone,' he pronounced.

'What's he got, a mouth at the back of his neck?' Slider asked irritably. 'I don't think you understand, Mr McKenzie, I'm conducting a murder enquiry—'

'No, *you* don't understand,' McKenzie interrupted him firmly. 'We're talking about the Secretary of State, a member of Her Majesty's Government, not some crackhead off the streets.'

'I don't care who he is, he has to answer my questions,' Slider said. 'He must confirm or deny Prentiss's alibi, and make a statement to that effect. I can come myself and interview him, or send one of my officers, or he can come here and do it, but one way or the other it has to be done, and done today.'

'Today? Absolutely out of the question! Giles has got a completely full diary. Even if he were to grant you an interview – which I stress is highly unlikely – I couldn't fit you into his schedule anywhere, not any day this week.'

'Do you want a writ for obstruction slapped on him?'

McKenzie's voice grew rich with irony. 'Perhaps you don't know that Giles Freeman is a *close personal friend* of the Home Secretary. Now are you really telling me you want to blackmail the personal friend of the man who ultimately controls your career?'

Slider smiled happily. 'Are you really telling me that you want the papers to know that the Home Secretary interfered in a high-profile murder case so that his friend could avoid his clear legal and moral duty to help the police?'

There was a beat of silence. 'You'd sink so low as to go to the press?'

'You can always try me and see,' Slider said pleasantly.

'I'll get back to you,' McKenzie said tersely; and then added, as if driven to it, 'I hope you don't live to regret this conversation, Inspector. We don't take kindly to underhand tactics.'

The line went dead.

McLaren came to the door. 'Guv, you got a minute?'

'If I had one of those I'd be a rich man,' said Slider sternly. McLaren was used to his style, and took it as an invitation to come in. Slider looked up. 'What's that on your shirt?'

'Chocolate,' McLaren said, after due consideration.

'You're a health hazard,' Slider said. 'Why can't you eat without spreading devastation in all directions? What d'you want, anyway?'

'It's about Micky Wordley. I've been round his gaff—'

'On your own?'

'It was just a friendly visit,' McLaren protested. 'I wasn't looking for trouble.'

'You might have got it just the same. For Chrissake, McLaren, you're not in this job to get your head blown off!'

McLaren spread his hands. 'Wordley's not that much of a head-banger. He's not going to blow me away just for asking questions, is he? Anyway,' he hurried on before Slider could answer, 'I didn't get to see him. He's done a runner.'

'Gone?'

'Had it away beautiful. Kelly – his girlfriend – says she's not seen him since Wednesday night.'

'Oh?'

'Yeah, some bloke come round about half nine on Wednesday night and they went off together, and he's not been back since.'

'Some bloke?'

'She says she doesn't know him, but I'm working on that,'

McLaren said. 'You could see she was scared stiff. Anyway, a snout of mine says he's heard Wordley's mixed up in something big.' He cocked his head hopefully like a pigeon waiting for bread.

'Something big could be anything,' Slider said.

'That's right,' McLaren said, taking it for confirmation. 'Kelly knows he's up to something with this other geezer, and I reckon if I work on her I can get it out of her. She's got a soft spot for me.'

Slider blinked. 'Well, I suppose a lot of women are fond of animals. But look, if there's any truth in it, that's he's mixed up in something big, it's far more likely that he's planning another robbery, given his form, and given this mysterious other bloke. He's not likely to take a chum along with him when he goes a-murdering.'

'It could be a robbery,' McLaren said, with an air of stretching a point about as far as it would go. 'But if that was it, why would he stay away? Kelly says he's never done that before. He likes his home comforts. The only times he's stopped out like that was when he's been on one of his benders.'

'So what's your point?'

'He's gone out on the piss with this bloke. Next day, still under the influence, he's gone round Agnew's place and offed her in a fit of temper.'

Slider thought a moment. 'And tied her up afterwards to fake a rape?'

'It didn't have to be a fake, did it, guv?' McLaren said intelligently. 'The sex could've been post-mortem. He's the kind of nutter that'd enjoy something like that.'

'Is that what his girlfriend says?'

He shrugged. 'He's got some very funny ideas, according to Kelly. And he likes a bit of bondage. Anyway, she's like a cat on hot bricks – she definitely knows something. If I just lean on her a bit—?' He made it into a question.

'All right, you can follow it up,' Slider said. 'We ought to keep an open mind that it might not be Prentiss. And if Wordley's disappeared we may as well know why.'

'Thanks, guv.'

'But be careful,' Slider added as McLaren retreated. 'Wordley's a dangerous bastard, and he won't like you messing about with his girlfriend's head. Don't go sticking your face into a hornet's nest.'

'I'm not scared of him,' McLaren said.

'If you had any brains you'd be scared,' said Slider.

CHAPTER EIGHT

Lies, damned lies and ballistics

Mrs Prentiss was a long time answering the door, and Atherton was ringing for the third time, purely in the cause of being thorough, when it opened.

'Mrs Prentiss? I'm Detective Sergeant Atherton of Shepherd's Bush CID.' He showed his ID.

'My husband isn't home,' she said.

'I know. It's you I want to speak to.'

'I've already told another detective – a woman – everything I know.'

'WDC Swilley. Yes, but there've been further developments, and I'm afraid I really do need to ask you some more questions. May I come in?'

She stared at him for a long moment, and then sighed and stepped back. 'All right. Do you mind if we talk in the dining-room? I'm not too good at stairs yet. That's why I was so long answering the door.'

She walked ahead of him with the stiff and too-upright gait of the back sufferer.

'Oh, yes, you hurt your back, didn't you?' Atherton said. 'My colleague told me.'

'It's an old trouble that comes and goes,' she said. 'I hurt it in a fall years ago.'

'Horse-riding? Skiing?' Atherton asked conversationally.

'Ballet. I used to be a dancer.' In the dining-room – green silk Regency-stripe wallpaper, dark Edwardian furniture, and a lot of heavy silver that needed cleaning – she pulled out a chair and sat carefully, letting her trousered knees relax outwards in the approved Alexander method.

Atherton sat catty-corner to her and laid his large, smooth

hands on the table, and she looked at them in the way that people in a railway carriage will automatically look at a dog or a child: a way not to meet strangers' eyes. In the dark room, the sidelong light from the window pooled in the patina of the old mahogany, showing up an even film of dust, like pollen on the surface of a pond. There was a faint fragrance of past pot-pourri and dusty carpet, underlined with damp and a hint of candlewax. A bit like a church, Atherton thought: hassocks, cassocks, incense and rot.

Mrs Prentiss looked haggard. Swilley had said she appeared younger than her age, but the shadowed eyes and drawn face before Atherton now had all their years on show. She was suffering; and she was apprehensive. The liar flees when no man pursueth. But even apart from that, if your husband has murdered your best friend, you are entitled to look a bit on the seedy side – particularly when he hasn't been locked up yet.

'I suppose you know what I want to talk to you about?' he invited gently.

'The murder, obviously. I don't know what more I can say to help you.'

'Well, you see, we've got to get one or two things sorted out, haven't we? Because you told us that your husband was at home on Thursday evening, and that wasn't true, was it?'

'Wasn't it?'

Atherton smiled. 'Come on, Mrs Prentiss, you and your husband must have talked about this since we first interviewed you. You must know his story and yours didn't tally. He doesn't even pretend he was here all evening. Why did you say he was?'

She put her hands to her face as though her cheeks were hot. 'Oh, I don't know! I was confused. Upset. A detective came to my door completely out of the blue and told me my best friend had been murdered. Was I supposed to be calm and collected?'

'But you said that your husband had already told you that Miss Agnew was dead.'

'Did I? Well, that doesn't stop it being a shock. And I'm not accustomed to dealing with the police. It frightened me to have that woman suddenly appear on my doorstep.'

'Hmm,' said Atherton, with a kindly, trying-to-understand tilt of his head. 'So because you were startled and upset by the news, you immediately jumped to the conclusion that your husband was the murderer and needed an alibi?'

'No, of course not! It wasn't like that,' she cried indignantly.

'Well, what was it like, then?'

'Oh, I don't know. I wasn't really thinking clearly. I was confused.'

'I don't think you were confused. I think you were defending him. It's a natural instinct in a wife, isn't it?' She didn't answer. 'But what were you defending him against, if you didn't think he did it?'

'Getting mixed up in it, I suppose,' she said, as if goaded into answering the unanswerable. 'I wanted to protect him from trouble – scandal – the newspapers. Anything like that could damage his career. I just wanted your colleague to know that Josh couldn't possibly have had anything to do with it. I wanted her to go away and leave us alone.'

'Yes, well, telling lies isn't the best way to stop us coming back, is it?'

She met his eyes at last, and hers were anxious, guarded. 'I suppose not. But as I said, I wasn't thinking clearly.'

He tried a shift of direction. 'Did you know your husband had gone to see Phoebe Agnew on Thursday?'

She hesitated, and there was something there in the dark depths, he thought, something cautious. It was the look a suspect gave you when they didn't know what it was safe to say, how much you knew. His heart lifted, as it always did at the scent of guilt.

'No,' she said after a substantial think. 'But why shouldn't he? They were good friends. All three of us were good friends.'

'Did he often visit her without you?'

'I don't know how often he visited her, but there was no reason he shouldn't, or that he should tell me when he did. There was nothing going on between them, if that's what you're suggesting. Of course, that's bound to be the conclusion everyone will leap to, that they were having an affair behind my back, especially given the way she was found. But that's precisely the reason I wanted to protect him. Once the press gets hold of it, they'll turn a decent friendship into something sordid and underhand.' Her voice rose a little in agitation. 'Something commonplace and disgusting and deceitful!'

'I'm afraid we can't be responsible for what the newspapers print,' Atherton said soothingly. 'I wish we could. Do you know where your husband went afterwards – when he left her flat?'

'To see Giles Freeman, on Government business,' she said promptly.

'He told you that, did he?'

'Yes.'

'I wonder, then, why you didn't tell us?'

She looked away nervously. 'I didn't know at the time that that's where he'd gone. He told me on Friday night, after he'd spoken to you.'

'So what you're saying is that he went out on Thursday evening without giving you any indication of where he was going? Was that usual?'

'I'm not his gaoler,' she snapped.

'Quite so. But married couples usually say, "I'm off to such and such a place, darling" when they get up and leave, don't they?'

'I don't know what other married couples do,' she said stubbornly.

'But weren't you a bit curious? Husband gets up and leaves the house without a word? And when you hear later that your best friend has been murdered you assume that's where he went and tell a lie to protect him?' She didn't answer. 'Mrs Prentiss, I have to press you on this point. Can't you see how odd your behaviour looks? I must know the truth. Did your husband say on Thursday night where he was going?'

She put her hands between her knees and squeezed them, hunching her shoulders. She looked like a cold bird on a winter branch, thin and vulnerable. 'I don't remember. It's all so confused. I was so upset about Phoebe it's driven everything out of my head. I expect he did say. He probably said he was going out on business, or going to a meeting. In fact, yes, I'm sure that's what he did say. He said he was going to a meeting at the Ministry, and that he might call in on Phoebe on the way. Yes, and I remember now, he said had I any message for her, and I said just give her my love.'

All this was less than convincing, Atherton thought; and why was she so nervous? Had Prentiss threatened her? Well, perhaps he wouldn't need to. Just being married to a man who had murdered your best friend must make you eager to please him. 'And what time did he go out?' he asked.

'I don't know. About half past seven, a quarter to eight maybe. I didn't notice particularly.'

'He was with you all morning and afternoon, was he? Did he go out anywhere else before that?'

'No, he was here.'

'What did he do all day?'

'He read some papers, did some writing. We had a late lunch. I don't remember in detail.'

'Where did he do those things? Was he in the same room as you all the time?'

'I don't understand.'

'If he wasn't actually in the same room as you all the time, he might have left the house without your knowing.'

'Of course he didn't leave the house,' she said robustly. 'I'd have known. Anyway, he didn't leave the room for long enough to go anywhere.'

'And what time did he come home on Thursday night?'

'I don't know exactly. It was very late, after I'd gone to bed. After midnight – nearer one o'clock I think. But that was usual, when he was on Government business. They often have late meetings when the House is sitting.'

'Did he ring you at all that evening?'

'No.'

'You were in all evening?'

She looked startled. 'Of course I was. What do you mean?'

'I mean, were you in all evening? Did you go out? If you were out, you wouldn't know if he'd phoned.'

'We have an answering machine. But I was in all evening. And he didn't phone. Why should he?'

Atherton was silent, letting her stew, letting her relax. Then he said, 'A little while ago, when you were talking about the trouble the newspapers would make for your husband over his relationship with Phoebe Agnew, you said, "Especially given the way she was found". What did you mean by that?'

A stillness came over her. 'I don't understand.'

'Well, how *was* she found? What aspect of the way she was found made you think it would cause trouble for your husband?'

'I don't know what you mean. I don't remember what I said. But it's obvious the papers will make trouble for him when they know he visited her that night, won't they? Everyone always assumes the worst.'

Joanna phoned. 'About that lunch—'

'Oh, Lord, I'd forgotten. I think it's going to be out of the question,' Slider began.

'It certainly is. I'm cancelling,' said Joanna. 'Some work's come in. The Grossman Ensemble. A concert in Woburn. Rehearsal three-thirty to five-thirty, so I'd have to leave around one at the latest.'

'Leave earlier and don't rush,' Slider advised.

'I did think of it,' she admitted. 'Some of the others are meeting at the Sow and Pigs for lunch on the way.' This was a pub at Toddington, just off the M1, handy for musicians on their way to dates in the north. Slider had learned that there were 'musicians' pubs' which everyone in the business knew and frequented – places with good food, real ale and an accommodating landlord.

'Have lunch with my blessing,' he said. 'Just promise to think of me when you're enjoying yourself.'

'Well, I think I should stop off,' she said, 'because the guy who gave me the date, Gerhard Wolf, will be there, and I'd like to buy him a pint to thank him.'

'Do I know him?' Slider asked. She had pronounced the surname the German way, but wolf was as wolf did in any language.

'I don't think you've met him. Tall, skinny guy, foxy eyes, long blond hair and an earring?'

'I know so many who fit that description,' Slider said. Fox and wolf? This was getting worse. He forced himself to be noble. 'If you chum up to him, maybe he'll get you some more work.'

'Oddly enough,' she said, 'that had occurred to me. How's the case going?'

'With the speed of evolution.'

'So fast?'

'That's how long it takes to get a DNA report back.'

'You know what DNA stands for, don't you?' Joanna said.

'Eh?'

'The National Dyslexics' Association.'

'Go away, Marshall. Go and play some music or something.' As he put the phone down, Atherton came in, rubbing his hands. 'You look pleased. How did it go?'

'Loyal little wifie is dropping him in it as fast as she tries to bail him out.' He recounted his interview with Mrs Prentiss. 'First she says one thing then another. She didn't know where he went and then she did. Obviously he's come home after talking to us and given her a rocket for giving him the wrong alibi. Now she's so confused she can't remember what story they're going with.'

'We don't know that,' said Slider.

'Oh, Mr Caution! All right, but she has been lying, and she was obviously trying to protect him, and what would she need to do that for if he wasn't guilty?'

'Did she admit she was trying to protect him?'

'Yes, she did, as it happens. And here's something odd,' Atherton added. 'She said she wanted to protect him from getting involved because the media would assume he and Agnew had been having an affair—'

'Makes sense.'

'Yes, but listen, then she added, "especially given the way she was found" – the way Agnew was found.'

'Oh?' said Slider.

'Later on I asked her what she meant by that, and she waffled and said she didn't remember saying it; but it must surely have been a reference to the fact that Agnew was found half naked and tied to the bedstead, *à la* sexual games. And that's a detail that hasn't appeared in the newspapers yet. So how did she know, unless Prentiss told her?'

Slider made an expressive face. 'You think he boasted to her about the way he did the murder? The two women were friends, remember.'

'Would you put it past him?'

'She might not have meant anything in particular by it,' Slider demurred. 'It's amazing how little people manage to mean by anything for ninety per cent of their lives. Still, it does look like another piece of evidence against Prentiss.'

'Together with the fact that he told her on Friday morning about Agnew's death and pretended to us that he didn't know. Have you managed to penetrate the Freeman barrier yet?'

'Not yet,' said Slider.

'They stick together, these types,' said Atherton. 'That'll be why Prentiss has got the missus to go with the Freeman alibi – he's betting we won't be able to check it one way or the other.'

'But what puzzles me most is why Prentiss should think a meeting with Freeman constitutes an alibi anyway,' said Slider. 'He could just as easily have killed Agnew first. We don't have an exact time of death.'

'He probably doesn't know that. The general public mostly think we can pinpoint the time of death to within minutes,' Atherton pointed out. 'Still, he'd have done better from the beginning to say he was at home all evening. I wonder why he didn't? He didn't know we were interviewing his wife at the same moment. In fact, if he'd called her earlier on Friday to tell her about Agnew's death, as she says he did, he could have fixed the alibi then.'

'If he'd been anything of a gentleman he'd have left her out of it altogether.'

Atherton looked amused. 'I should have thought, my dear old guv'nor, that murdering Phoebe Agnew pretty well ruled him out of the gentleman stakes. I'm sure they said something about that on my first day at Eton.'

'You were never at Eton,' Slider objected.

'Josh Prentiss was,' Atherton said soberly.

Porson paced back and forth across his room, his face looking older and more ghastly by courtesy of the fluorescent strip light that was needed to augment the thin winter sunlight. He must have been scratching his head in agitation, for his toupee was askew, and the line of natural hair revealed seemed greyer than it had been yesterday.

'You've really opened up a kettle of worms now,' he said, giving Slider a harried look. 'I've had Commander Wetherspoon on the phone, literally bursting a blood vessel. It seems Giles Freeman's evoked the Home Secretary's support and the Home Secretary's got straight on to the Commissioner. He was incrudescent with rage, I can tell you. You can't go around issuing threats to a member of HMG, Slider, not if you value your pension. What were you thinking of?'

'I was thinking of the case, sir.' Slider remained sturdily unrepentant. In the first place he knew he was right; and in the second place, Porson was one of the old school, and no actor into the bargain. 'Does the Home Secretary believe Cabinet Ministers are above the law?'

'No-one's above the law,' Porson said.

'Except the editor of a tabloid newspaper?' Slider amended.

'I'm glad you think it's funny,' Porson snapped. 'Why the hell didn't you come to me when this Freeman type wouldn't come across? I could have passed it up to Mr Wetherspoon to get the Commissioner to tell the Home Secretary to put official pressure on him. It's being side-passed makes Mr Wetherspoon go ballistic, and between you, me and the bedpost it's him we've more to fear from than the Commissioner in all his glory. He's in the best position to retaliate. He can make our lives a mockery just by lifting his little finger; and it's no secret he doesn't like you.'

'That's a cross I'll have to bear, sir,' said Slider. 'And if I'd gone the long way round, via the official channels, would I have got a result so soon?'

Porson's crest went down, and he sighed and scratched his poll. 'No, you wouldn't, and that's an indispensable fact. Well, I've done my bit by reprimanding you. In fact, I told Mr Wetherspoon I was on your side. It gets on my goat, this attitude that you have to pussyfoot round people just because they've got themselves installed somewhere up the higher arky. We shouldn't have to ask permission to talk to someone in the pursuit of duty, no matter who they are. As it happens,' he added confidentially, 'the Commissioner doesn't like being leaned on any more than Giles Freeman, and especially not by a portentious little shit like McKenzie. He backed you all the way.'

Slider couldn't conceal his surprise. 'The Commissioner did?'

'Oh, yes. He told the Home Secretary that Freeman's got to come across or he'll be prosecuted just like you, me or Rosie O'Grady. And come across he has.'

'I'm glad, sir.'

'But you've certainly stirred up a mare's nest in Government circles,' Porson went on, shaking his head sadly. 'The fact of the matter is that Freeman has categorically denied that Prentiss was with him that evening. Blown his story sky high. And Prentiss, in case you didn't know, is a special advisor to the Government. A chum. A member of the inner sanction.'

'I did know it,' Slider said.

'Well, you see what you've done. One spoke on the wheel of power has placed another spoke in a very embarrassing position. Involved him in potential scandal. You've forced them to decide between Freeman and Prentiss, and they don't like it.'

'*I've* forced them? It's Prentiss's fault for lying.'

'In the real world, yes,' Porson said. 'But the Government likes people to sing from the same hymn sheet. And Prentiss is valuable to them and they don't want to lose him. They already had their heads to the grindstone trying to work out a way round the problem, when you shoved your size nines in and brought it to a crisis. Now too many people know about it, and they'll have to drop Prentiss, which pisses them off more than somewhat. You're a marked man, Slider.'

'I'll try hard to care, sir,' Slider promised.

'Yes, well,' Porson said. He cleared his throat, looking at Slider reflectively. 'You're not interested in politics, I take it?'

Slider shook his head. 'I've never had the time.'

'The higher you go, the more it matters,' Porson said. 'But times have changed, and none of us can afford to ignore the political aspic of the Job any more. It affects all of us, right down the line to the coalface. So next time there's a problem of this sort, bring it to me first. Do you savvy?'

'Yes, sir,' said Slider. 'What's happening about Freeman? Is he going to make a statement?'

'It's on its way. You can take it as read that Prentiss didn't visit him that evening and precede on that assumption.'

'Good. I can't say I'm completely surprised. But it gives me some ammunition against Prentiss. If we could just get the DNA profile back quickly—' He looked hopefully at his boss.

'I'm on to that,' Porson barked, 'so you needn't give me the Battersea Dogs' Home treatment. Given who Prentiss is, and the press interest, I think it's important enough to justify some positive budgetary outlay. I'm prepared to pay the lab the extra for the quick result. As soon as we get the confirmation we can jump on him, before he finds any other political trees to hide behind. Meanwhile, there's no harm in keeping some pressure on about his lies. If he's talking to us, he can't be talking to anyone else, can he?'

'Right, sir.'

Porson nodded dismissal. Slider, on his way out, paused to say, 'Sir? Thanks for backing me up.'

'You're at the sharp end. You shouldn't have to worry about politics,' Porson said. 'That's what you've got me for.'

He looked old that morning, but, for all his oddities, impressive. A totem carved in enduring granite; a giant in a world of pygmies.

CHAPTER NINE

The food, the cad and the bubbly

The result on the semen was waiting on the desk when Slider got in the next day. He took it through to the office.

'How'd you do it, boss?' asked Swilley. 'Only yesterday they were pretending they'd never heard of us.'

'Undue influence and bundles of used fivers,' Atherton suggested.

'Mr Porson flashed his legs and suddenly we were first in the queue,' said Slider.

'So what's the score?' said Mackay.

'They couldn't get anything from the condom – the sample was too dilute,' Slider said. 'But the semen from the vagina matches Prentiss's blood sample.'

'I always knew he was lying,' Swilley said with satisfaction. 'What about the tissue under the nails? Did that come from him too?'

'The result of that test hasn't come back yet,' Slider said. 'Bit of administrative confusion. Mr Porson asked for the semen result and they evidently separated that out.'

'Still, if the semen's Prentiss's, we've nailed him in that lie,' Swilley said.

'And of course you all know now, don't you,' Slider said, looking round and gathering attentions, 'that Giles Freeman has made a statement that he didn't see Prentiss that evening, and that there never was a meeting scheduled. In fact the House was sitting and there was an important division, so there is no doubt Prentiss made it up.'

'Ah, what it is to have friends!' said Atherton.

'But look here,' Slider said, 'the fact that Prentiss has been proved lying about these things doesn't make him the murderer.

He admitted all along that he had been at the flat—'

'Not quite all along,' Atherton said. 'Only after we told him his car had been seen.'

'All right, almost all along,' said Slider. 'Of course this new evidence makes it look more likely that he did it – he certainly behaves as though he's got something to hide – but let's keep an open mind. I want you all to go on with searching her papers and talking to the neighbours and her colleagues. Anyone got anything to report on those fronts yet?'

They went through the most useful so far. 'Early days yet, guv,' Hollis summed it up.

Slider looked round, frowning. 'Where's McLaren?' Nobody answered. 'Has he said anything more about Wordley's where-abouts?'

'Not to me,' said Hollis, 'but I know he was going to talk to that Kelly again, Wordley's girlfriend, last night.'

'Well, keep me posted. It certainly won't hurt to know what Wordley's up to, even if it isn't anything to do with the case.'

'What're you going to do now, boss?' Swilley asked.

'Talk to Prentiss again,' said Slider. 'And this time we'll do it here, on our territory, just to concentrate his mind.'

Josh Prentiss looked every inch a man whose entire life was swirling down the kermit before his very eyes. Sex, power and charisma had abandoned his fleshy face with the suddenness of seaside bathers at a shark alert. Now the face looked merely baggy, and the eyes were pouched and exhausted. His expensive clothes seemed to sit sadly on him, as if they'd sooner be anywhere else. In the institutional drabness of the interview room, where the smell of guilt, mindless crime and cheap trainers had soaked into the distemper, his designer chic looked as out of place as an orchid in a beer bottle.

When they arrived at his office, Prentiss was looking sick and a little dazed, but nodded meekly and without hesitation when they asked if he would accompany them to the station to help them with their enquiry. He had not screamed for a solicitor, which was out of character for a man in his various positions, and Atherton had looked sidelong at his boss when Slider gently insisted he ought to have one. Of course, from the police point of view it was always nicer to conduct an interview without the tortured mind of a legal representative hobbling the progress; but what boots it a policeman if he gains the whole confession and loses his case on procedural quibbles?

At the station, Prentiss had accepted the offer of a cup of coffee, but when it was placed before him he only looked at it blankly, as if such a thing had never come his way before. Well, perhaps it hadn't, Slider reflected. In Prentiss's world, coffee was probably a delicious aromatic stimulant made from freshly ground roasted arabica beans. Maybe he'd never been presented with a dingy ecru liquid that smelled of rancid laundry and been expected to swallow it.

When the brief, Philip Ainscough, arrived, Slider and Atherton took their places and faced him and Prentiss across the table that had heard more futile lies and feeble excuses than a regular army sergeant. Prentiss looked up from his stunned contemplation of caterers' revenge, and said abruptly, 'I've been a complete fool. I realise that now. I should have told you the truth from the beginning.'

'It's always a good idea,' Slider said mildly.

'Is it? Always?' Prentiss said with some bitterness. 'Is one always believed? I think not. The press and the public believe what they want to, regardless of the truth.'

'We're not the press or the public,' Slider said. 'And we've got ways of testing whether something's true or not. For instance, let's start with where you were on Thursday evening. You told us that you were at a meeting with Giles Freeman, but that was a lie, wasn't it?'

'Yes, it was a lie,' Prentiss sighed. 'Look, do you mind if I smoke?'

The reply in Slider's mind, 'I don't mind if you burn' was withheld in favour of a *go ahead* gesture of one hand.

Prentiss drew out and lit a cigarette with hands that trembled slightly, but when he spoke, his voice was calm and reasonable. 'I did lie to you about where I was on Thursday night, but I did it to protect someone who has nothing to do with this business. I hoped you wouldn't check up, given who my alibi was. I mean, if you can't trust a Cabinet Minister, who can you trust?' Atherton made a slight choking noise, and Prentiss looked at him and frowned. 'Well, I suppose I should have known better.'

Ainscough spoke. 'You realise that by approaching Giles

Freeman in the way you have done, you've ruined Mr Prentiss's career?'

'I should have thought he did that himself when he killed Phoebe Agnew,' Slider said.

'You'd better be careful what you say,' Ainscough warned impassively. 'You could be looking at a civil action. And if you're not going to conduct this interview in a proper fashion, my client will withdraw his co-operation.'

Slider shrugged slightly and turned to Prentiss. 'Let's clear up this business of where you were first.'

Prentiss took a long suck at his cigarette, blew out a shaky cloud, and then said, 'I went to see a young woman with whom I'm having an affair. That's why I lied about it. I didn't want her dragged into all this. And I didn't want my wife to know.'

Atherton stirred and gave Slider a look. *Not that old chestnut again!* Prentiss caught the look and a spot of colour appeared in his cheek – indignation, or shame?

'What's the young woman's name?' Slider asked.

'Maria Colehern,' Prentiss said. 'She's my secretary. Not at my firm – I mean, my secretary in my capacity as Government special advisor. We've been seeing each other for a few months now. She has a flat in Kensington – one of those service blocks in Phillimore Walk.'

'Write the address down,' Slider said, pushing a pad over to him.

Prentiss obeyed. 'I suppose', he said, looking from Slider to Atherton and back, 'you'll have to check it with her, but I do hope you'll be discreet. Maria's done nothing wrong, and it would be unfair to make her lose her job over this.'

Slider raised an eyebrow. 'I think we've got a bit beyond "unfair" now, haven't we?'

Prentiss stared a moment, and then burst out, 'I didn't kill Phoebe! Why won't you believe me?'

'Because', said Slider, 'we found Phoebe Agnew tied to her bed, naked from the waist down, and with your semen in her vagina. It seems a fair conclusion to me. What would you think?'

'Don't answer that,' Ainscough said quickly. 'You are not to ask my client to indulge in speculation.'

But Prentiss hadn't attempted to answer. He went white and

fumbled the cigarette to his mouth and sucked on it like an asthmatic on an oxygen mask. He drew in so much smoke that when he tried to speak he could only cough, spouting spasmodic clouds like a dragon with hiccups. At last he gasped, 'It's not possible. You must have made a mistake.'

'No mistake,' Slider said. 'You kindly gave us a blood sample, if you remember, and we've run a genetic test on the semen. So unless you've got a twin brother, we've got a match. You had sex with Phoebe Agnew and then killed her, didn't you?'

Get outta that one, sucker, Atherton thought happily.

Prentiss opened his mouth, but Ainscough snapped, 'Don't answer that.' He looked at Prentiss hard and then said, 'I'd like to talk to my client alone for a few minutes.'

Slider and Atherton left them alone. When Ainscough recalled them, he seemed a little puzzled and uneasy. 'My client has agreed to continue with this interview, though against my recommendation,' he said. Prentiss smoked in silence, his face turgid with thought. 'I must warn you again to be very careful of the language you employ. Remember my client is here voluntarily.'

'All right,' said Slider, 'shall we start again? Let's have an account of all your movements on Thursday, starting from when you got up in the morning, and this time, make it complete and true. Remember that we will check everything.'

'There's nothing to check,' Prentiss said at last. His voice sounded faint and hoarse, though that could have been from the heat of the smoke. 'I got up about seven, and did the usual things, showered, dressed, had breakfast, read the papers. Then I did some work—'

'Where?'

'Where?' He looked surprised at the question.

'Where did you do your work?'

'At home. In the drawing-room. It was only reading – some reports on brownfield sites. I read and made some notes, looked at some drawings. We had lunch quite late – about half past three. Then I—'

'What did you have for lunch?'

'Chicken. Why the devil d'you want to know that?'

'You never know what might be important,' Slider said neutrally. 'Go on. After lunch?'

His eyes moved away from direct contact. 'I did some more work. Then I changed and went out. I left at about a quarter to eight. I'd told Maria I'd be there at eight, but when I left the house I decided on an impulse to drop in on Phoebe on the way. I got to Phoebe's at about eight and left again at about twenty past. And I got to Maria's about half past. I had supper with her and eventually left about a quarter to one and was home at one, or just before.'

Slider listened impassively until Prentiss stopped, and then asked, 'When you left home – at a quarter to eight, you say – where did you tell your wife you were going?'

'I said I was going to see Giles Freeman, of course.'

'I thought you were going to tell me the truth?' Slider said sternly.

'It is the truth,' Prentiss said.

Slider made an impatient movement. 'Now *I'll* tell *you* what really happened. You had chicken that day all right, but you had it with Phoebe Agnew. She cooked you supper, chicken casserole and tiramisu, with plenty of wine, and coffee and brandy to follow. Then you had sex with her. Then at some point you quarrelled. The quarrel escalated, and you strangled her. Realising the position you were in, you arranged the body on the bed with the hands tied to make it look like a rape attack, and left. You assumed no-one would know you had ever been there, but unfortunately for you someone identified your car parked nearby.'

'You're crazy! I don't know what you're talking about,' Prentiss said. 'None of that happened. No, it's all right, Phil. It's complete nonsense and they know it.'

'When we came to see you on Friday afternoon,' Slider continued implacably, 'you pretended you didn't know Phoebe Agnew was dead—'

'I didn't know! That was the first I'd heard about it.'

'But your wife meanwhile had stated to another of my officers that you telephoned her on Friday morning and told her the news.'

Prentiss said nothing to that, though his lips rehearsed a few unfinished words.

'We're going to end this interview right now,' Ainscough said.

Slider ignored him. 'You really should have briefed your wife better. First of all she said you were at home all evening. Now she says you went out saying something vague about business. She didn't know anything about the Giles Freeman story until you told her on Friday night that that's what you'd told us. And the most foolish thing of all is that your Giles Freeman story and your present story about your mistress aren't alibis at all, because there's no evidence about what time on Thursday Phoebe Agnew was killed.'

Prentiss looked like a man in deep shock. 'But – but she must have been killed after eight-thirty,' he said faintly.

'Josh,' said Ainscough warningly.

'And what makes you think that?' Slider asked quickly, to get it in while he still could.

'Because she was fine when I left her.'

'That's enough,' Ainscough said. 'Unless you're prepared to charge my client, we're leaving. Don't answer any more questions, Josh.' He put a hand on Prentiss's shoulder and he stood up, still looking blank and shocked.

Slider had one more try. 'Mr Prentiss, you've told us nothing but lies from beginning to end. Can't you understand that we check everything, that your lies will always be found out? You're an intelligent man, you must see that nothing but the truth can help you now. Tell me the truth. What have you got to lose?'

'Nothing,' he said slowly. 'My career's already gone, and my marriage—' He shrugged, and turned to Ainscough. 'It's all right, Phil. I've got nothing to hide, and I want to get it straight with them. Otherwise this thing will drag on and on. I know what I'm doing.' He sat down again and faced Slider. 'Look, you're on the wrong track altogether. Phoebe and I didn't have a sexual relationship. We never did. We really were just friends. To tell you the truth,' he added, 'she wasn't my type. She was too hard and masculine – and far too much of a slob. She was a great friend, though – a great mate, if you like. She and Noni and I have been friends since university days, but it was Noni I married. Noni's the sort of dainty, feminine woman I find attractive. If you knew anything about me you'd know that was the truth. If you're going to check with Maria you'll see what sort of person she is.'

Slider only nodded expressionlessly.

'Noni's my type,' Prentiss went on. 'She's been a wonderful wife. Smart and pretty. Superb cook. Entertains my friends and business colleagues. An absolute mainstay – the sort of wife and home-maker a man in my position needs. Phoebe's never cared for anything like that. She'd scoff at the idea of taking second place to a man or supporting him in his career. Her own career is all she cares about. And she despises domesticity. She lives in a state of chaos, her clothes are always held together with safety pins, and she's never cooked for me or for anyone in her life. She lives on take-aways. The idea of her cooking supper for me is ludicrous – you simply don't know how ludicrous!'

'She cooked for somebody on Thursday, or didn't you notice?' Slider said.

Prentiss looked distracted. 'No, not really. I mean, there were a lot of dirty plates and things in the kitchen, but that was the way it always was. They could have been there for days, for all I knew.'

'You went into the kitchen, then?'

'No, I just saw as I went past the door that there were dishes stacked up. I didn't go in. Why should I? But it was typical of Phoebe, that's what I'm saying. Noni would never tolerate mess like that – and I like an orderly home.'

'Yet,' Slider pursued, 'despite all the perfections of your wife, you still had to have a mistress?'

Prentiss reddened. 'Are you going to sit in judgement on me?'

'I warned you not to go on with this,' said Ainscough.

'I'm trying to find some consistency in Mr Prentiss's story, that's all.'

'It's all right, Phil,' said Prentiss.

'No, it isn't. If you insist on ignoring my advice then I'm of no use to you. Perhaps you'd like to instruct someone else.'

Prentiss thought a moment and then said, 'All right, you can go. I'll do this on my own.'

'I most strongly urge you not to.'

'Your advice is noted. But I'll do this my way.' When Ainscough had left them, Prentiss gave Slider and Atherton a strange look, part angry, part pleading. He appeared to have braced himself for something, but Slider hadn't any hope it was a confession. Prentiss seemed to have regained his confidence since the low point when Slider had told him his alibi was not an alibi. Had he thought of something – some device for getting out of trouble which, significantly, perhaps, he did not want his brief to hear?

'Okay,' he said, 'I didn't want to tell you this before because it's personal, and I didn't see why the intimate details of my life should be pored over by strangers – but, though I love Noni and she's a wonderful wife, we haven't had sex for a long time. Not for a couple of years. She's been depressed ever since her career flopped. She was in a sitcom and it was panned by the critics.' He paused and looked to see if they knew what he was talking about.

'Yes, we heard about that from someone else,' Slider said.

'Right, well, you must understand how hard that was for her. It ought to have been her big break, and in fact she hasn't worked since. Naturally, she's been very low. And she's getting to a difficult age for women.'

Ah, that was it, Slider thought. The inconsistencies in the story were to be laid at the door of Mrs Prentiss's menopausal irrationality.

'Well, I've been as supportive of her as I can,' he went on, 'but it hasn't been easy. My own career takes up a lot of time and energy; and, frankly, I'm a man who needs a sexual outlet.'

He appealed to them, man to man. Slider and Atherton remained unappealed to, and Prentiss was bounced back into his exposition as off a wall.

'Well, I don't apologise for that,' he said. 'I've always been discreet, and never given Noni anything to complain about. And as for Maria, I assure you she knows the score and she's quite happy with the situation. So where's the harm?'

Slider refused to specify. 'What has this to do with your actions on Thursday?' he asked neutrally.

'I'm coming to that,' Prentiss said. He lit another cigarette from the stub of the first, drew on it and coughed a little. 'Look, I don't like telling you this, but I have to, otherwise you won't understand, and you won't believe me. On Thursday, right from the time we had breakfast, Noni seemed to be in a funny mood.'

'In what way, funny?'

'I don't know, she seemed a bit edgy and excited. I couldn't tell what was going on with her. I was trying to read and she kept interrupting, trying to start up conversations. Talking about the news and my Government job. She asked about holidays, and when we were going to have the children over and so on and so on. I did my best to be patient with her but she was making it hard to concentrate. In the end I had to say that this was a working day at home, and I didn't want to be disturbed, and she shut up and went off.'

'Off?'

'Oh, just pottering round, the way women do. I thought maybe she was sulking, but when she called me to say lunch was ready she'd obviously got over it because she seemed quite happy. Almost—' He frowned, seeming to search for the right word. 'Almost flirtatious. She brought me a glass of champagne first. I said, what's the occasion, and she said, nothing, I always used to like a glass of champagne as an aperitif, and had I changed. I said I still had work to do that afternoon and she said, oh you've got a hard enough head to take it. Flattering me, you know?'

'Go on.'

'Well, she'd done a delicious chicken and rice dish for lunch – she really is a super cook – and at that point I thought, what the hell, the poor love probably needs the company, stuck here alone all day with nothing to do, so I gave in and we had an excellent bottle of burgundy with it. She was being as entertaining as she knew how – chatting and laughing. She has immense charm when she wants to use it. Anyway—' He hesitated, and looked down at his hands. 'Anyway, after lunch she – we – we went to bed.' He was silent a moment, and Slider didn't prompt him. 'It was the first time for a couple of years. She said she hadn't been a good wife to me lately and she meant to make it up to me in the future.'

Another silence, and he looked up unhappily. 'It put me in a difficult position. I mean, I'd got used to the way things were, and I was quite happy with my arrangements. The last thing I want to do is to hurt Noni, and I do love her – there couldn't be a better wife – but the fact of the matter is—'

'You don't fancy her,' Atherton suggested.

'It's not that,' he said defensively. 'I want you to understand. Maria and I – I'm deeply involved with her. I can't give her up. But I knew I'd feel bad about it if Noni and I were also – if we were lovers again. And there was her mental state to consider – Noni's. I've told you she's been very depressed. If she was making an effort to come out of it, and I rejected her, or she found out about Maria after I – oh,' he finished, goaded, 'you must *see*!'

Slider nodded. 'So with all these worries about your wife on your mind, you decided the best thing was to pop out and visit a couple of your mistresses.'

Prentiss reddened and half rose. 'Look, I don't have to take this sort of abuse!'

'Oh, I think you do,' Slider said. 'You invite it, it would be rude not to take it.'

Prentiss was so shocked by this response he hardly knew what to say. 'Do you think this is funny?' he said at last, incredulously.

'No,' said Slider, fixing him with a hard stare. 'I've seen the body of Phoebe Agnew. I don't think there's anything remotely funny about it. So please sit down and stop blustering. I'm trying to get at the truth.'

Prentiss subsided, but he looked angry and disconcerted. 'I don't understand you at all. I'm here voluntarily. I'm doing my best to help you, but I can walk out of here right now and leave you to stew in it, and I will do if you don't start showing me a bit of respect and common courtesy. You're a public servant. And you must know I'm a man of influence. Do you want me to make a complaint against you? Don't you value your career?'

'Let's not talk careers, Mr Prentiss,' Slider said. 'Let's remember why we're here, and what I already know. Now, tell me what happened after you made love with your wife.'

He breathed hard, but answered after a moment. 'I fell asleep. When I woke up it was half past six. I was annoyed because I hadn't done all the work I'd planned to do, and I'd told Maria I'd be round at eight. I jumped up to go and shower, and Noni asked where I was going. She said, "You're not going out, are you?" I said I had to, and she got upset. She felt that after what had happened I ought to stay with her. She asked me who I was going to see and said I should cancel it and I got angry and said it was Government business and she ought to know by now what was important, and she said did that mean *she* wasn't important – well, you know how women go on. Before

I knew what was happening I was in the middle of a row. The last thing I wanted to do was quarrel with her, especially—' He hesitated.

'Especially given where you really were going,' Slider suggested. 'She made you feel guilty and that made you angrier.'

He shrugged. 'You know what women are like,' he said again. 'I will say that was one thing about Phoebe. She never behaved that way. She had a mind more like a man's. That's why I went to see her, really. When I was in the car and starting off for Maria's, I decided to call in on Phoebe and ask her advice about the situation. I didn't know what to do about Noni, and I thought Phoebe could give me an impartial view.'

'Did you tell your wife you were going to call on her?' Slider asked.

'No, of course not. I told you, it was spur of the moment. I didn't think of it until I was driving off.'

Atherton spoke. 'But your wife told me today that you said you were going to call in on Phoebe and asked her if she wanted to send any message.'

'That's not true.' Prentiss shook his head in a goaded way, and drew again on the cigarette. It was burning too quickly, and the glowing lump of tobacco at the end detached itself and fell, landing in the untouched and cooling coffee. Prentiss looked down in vague surprise, and then reached for his lighter. 'I don't know why she said that,' he mumbled through the lighting operations.

'I think I do,' Slider said. 'She was trying to protect you as a loyal wife would. Trying to make us believe your relationship with Phoebe Agnew was innocent.'

'But it *was* innocent.'

'Don't forget', Slider said, 'that we know differently.'

CHAPTER TEN

Faurés a jolly good fellow

It was the early hours of the morning when Slider got home. The streets were empty, shiny with incipient frost, the sky black without feature behind the yellow street light. The houses looked two-dimensional and unreal. It was a bleak time of day, and winter sunrise was too far off to inject a ray of hope.

The streets were parked both sides as far as the eye could see: everyone was at home and accounted for. He had to cruise to find a space several streets away, and then walk back. The parked cars seemed to be sleeping too, tucked in snugly at the kerb; he imagined a windscreen eye half-opening as he passed and then drooping closed again.

He turned a corner, into a better-off street. The security conscious owners had fitted intruder lights, and because the front gardens were so short, he set them off from the pavement, like a row of bathchair colonels on the promenade waking one after the other: 'What? What? What?' He yawned as he walked, and yawning made him shiver. Oh, for bed, for the blissful sleeping heat of Joanna's body, for that wonderful moment when you check out of your brain and slip child-naked into the warm black waters of oblivion!

She woke as he came into the bedroom. 'Huh? Wasser time?' she muttered.

'Sshh! Just after four. Go back to sleep.'

'Huhnn,' she said. He pulled off his clothes and slid in under the covers, cold as a stone, hesitating to touch her. But she reached behind her and pulled him against her scorching flesh, draping her legs over his and rubbing his cold feet with her warm ones. Sighing, he sank into her back, and thought that this was probably the most inexpressibly wonderful sensation life could afford.

Five minutes later she said, 'Can't sleep?'

'How could you tell?'

'I can hear you thinking.'

'I'm sorry, I didn't mean to disturb you. Go back to sleep.'

'No, it's all right,' she said. 'I'm awake now.' She rolled over to face him, and he went onto his back, taking her on his shoulder – their talking position. 'You're very late. Is it the case or another woman?'

'What would I do with another woman?'

'Remind me in the morning and I'll draw you a diagram. So what's happened?'

'We brought the prime suspect in for a little chat,' Slider said. 'We've matched the semen in the vagina to his blood type, and his Westminster boss has blown his alibi.'

'Oh, good. You arrested him?'

'No, he was just helping us with our enquiries. It's not always the best idea to arrest them. Once you do that, you're on the clock and all sorts of rules apply.'

He told her of the long interview with Prentiss, in its various stages. 'While we were talking to him I sent Hollis round to see Maria Colehern, and she confirmed that Prentiss had been there on Thursday night at the time he stated. Not that that was any surprise – if your mistress won't back you up, who will? But Hollis liked her. He believed she was telling the truth.'

'But?'

'It doesn't help him,' Slider said. 'He seemed terribly relieved and grateful when she backed him up, but it doesn't help him at all. She can't be his alibi if we don't have a definite time for the murder, and if he's the murderer he ought to know that.'

'Don't you think he's guilty?'

'Yes, I think he's guilty as hell, but I can't make up my mind if he's playing a long game, or just stupid. He doesn't *seem* stupid, but if he wanted an alibi, why didn't he use his wife? She tried to give him one, but her evidence is so compromised now we can't take her word on anything. Why did he say from the beginning he was at Agnew's flat just for the half-hour? If he was going to deny the rest – including having sex with her – why not deny it all?'

'Maybe he knows someone saw him,' Joanna said. 'Or maybe he doesn't know whether she told anyone he was coming, so he's trying to cover all eventualities.'

'Yes,' said Slider, 'you could be right there. And of course it has worked to an extent. It's tied our hands. We know he was there and he admits he was there but that doesn't prove that he murdered her.'

'Even with all his lies?'

'His lies suggest he had something to hide, but that's not enough,' Slider sighed.

'So what does he say he was doing there?' Joanna asked.

Slider told her what Prentiss had said about his visit.

Phoebe Agnew hadn't seemed surprised to see him. 'Phoebe was the sort of person you could just drop in on,' Prentiss explained. 'She never minded. Liked it, in fact. It wasn't as if she was the houseproud sort who needed advance notice so that she could put her best foot forward. Well, you've seen her place. It was always a tip – like a student bedsit. In fact, in some ways she still lived like a student. She never minded what time of the day or night it was, she was always ready for a drink and a chat.'

Phoebe, he said, had got the whisky bottle out straight away, and he'd accepted a glass and told her his problem over Noni and Maria.

'She seemed in a bit of an odd mood, though,' Prentiss said. 'Distant. Distracted, maybe. At times she hardly seemed to be listening to me. To tell you the truth, I think she'd had a lot to drink,' he added, 'and she was putting away the whisky at an alarming rate. She refilled her own glass and offered me a top-up before I'd taken more than a sip or two. And after that I saw her fill up a couple more times.'

'Are you saying she was drunk?' Slider had asked him. A woman sleepy with drink would struggle less when she was strangled, of course.

'Not really. She always could hold her drink like a man,' Prentiss had said, 'but she has been drinking more heavily these last few weeks. I had words with her about it at New Year – asked her if she realised how much she was getting through. She told me to mind my own damn business. Anyway,' he went on, 'on Thursday night when I'd told her my problem she didn't say anything, just sat there sipping at the blasted whisky, so I asked her if she'd been listening to me. I said, "Just say if I'm boring you and I'll go." And she flared up and said, "Oh, stop being such a prima donna! You think the world revolves around your penis!"'

'It was brave of him to tell you that,' Joanna commented.

'I think he was telling us how exasperating Agnew could be,' Slider said, 'and inviting our sympathy for murdering her.'

'Go on,' Joanna said. 'What did he say next?'

'He said it had suddenly occurred to him that maybe Agnew was starting the menopause too, and that that was what was making her irritable and irrational. So he decided to be patient and kind with her, because she couldn't help it, poor cow.'

'Patronising bastard!' Joanna exclaimed. 'What d'you mean, starting the menopause *too*?'

'He'd wondered if his wife's odd moods were partly from the same cause, because she and Agnew were the same age.'

'How you men do harp on about hormones!'

'Never mind the "you men" business,' Slider said sternly. 'Anyway, Prentiss said he asked Agnew very kindly and calmly if there was something bothering her, and she said, "I've got a problem that makes yours pale into insignificance." So naturally Prentiss asked her what it was, and she said, "I wish I could tell you, but I can't." Prentiss pressed her a bit, said surely she could tell him, he was her oldest friend, and hinted that with all his friends in high places he might be able to help her.'

'Sensitive,' Joanna said. 'Doesn't miss an opportunity for self-aggrandisement.'

'Well, he said that Agnew just snapped at him, "You're the last person who could help me with it." So he shrugged and let it go.'

'And what about his own problem? Did he get her advice?'

'No, he said she seemed to think it was trivial and irrelevant. She said, "You get yourself into these things, try thinking how the other people involved feel", which he said annoyed him because that was exactly what he was doing, trying not to hurt either the wife or Maria Colehern.'

'It's a bugger when women don't recognise a compassionate, self-sacrificing man when they see one,' Joanna agreed. 'So did you believe all that?'

'Oh, yes, there was too much detail for him to have made it all up; and his annoyance with Agnew showed through clearly, which is presumably not what he would have wanted. I can see him losing his temper because she didn't understand him and kept claiming her own problems were worse. And I suppose it explains why he persists in denying he had sex with her: he thinks being her lover makes him more likely to kill her than being a detached platonic friend.'

'Well, he's not wrong there, is he?' Joanna said. 'If she were just a platonic friend he'd shrug off her moods and leave her to it. So where do you go from here?'

Slider moved restlessly. 'We've got to find more evidence. We've got the house-to-house still going – if someone saw him coming out in a dishevelled or agitated condition, that might help.'

'What did Maria Colehern say about him when he arrived on Thursday night?' Joanna asked.

'That he seemed normal enough. Perhaps a bit subdued and preoccupied, but no more than she would expect from a man with his business and political commitments.'

'Well, he might have enough self-control to fake normality in front of her, given that he was relying on her for an alibi.'

'But it *wasn't* an alibi,' Slider fretted.

'Maybe you've missed something that was meant to fix the time of death,' Joanna said. 'Think of it: he left some subtle clue that you haven't cottoned on to, and he's being driven mad with frustration, not able to point it out to you without dropping himself in it!'

'A pleasing thought,' Slider said. 'Anything that could make that bastard writhe . . .'

'What else?'

'What else can we do? Find out more about his relationship with Agnew, I suppose. The thing is, I can't quite see him murdering her on what he's told us so far. Getting mad and smacking her, perhaps; but to strangle a big strong woman like that, even if she is drunk, takes enough time for an angry man to think better of it, if he hasn't got a really adequate reason. Especially a man with as much to lose as Prentiss. There must be more cause between them than that; and if we can nail the *why*, and present him with it, we might shock him into confessing.'

'How will you go about that?'

'We've still got all her papers to go through – something might emerge. And meanwhile, there's his and her nearest and dearest to winkle at.'

'Good. You sound better now you've decided what to do.'

'It's relieved my mind to talk, but I'm sorry I've woken you up,' he said. 'D'you want to get a couple of hours now?'

'You're wide awake, aren't you?'

'To tell you the truth, I'm absolutely starving,' he confessed.

'Then it must be breakfast time,' she said, starting to get up.

'But it's only five o'clock!'

'What's an hour or two between friends? Anyway,' she added, suddenly serious, 'I want to talk to you.'

'Uh-oh! What have I done?'

'Let's get some food going first.'

While he made toast and tea, she scrambled eggs and, in deference to his hunger, grilled several rashers of bacon. The smell – surely the best in the world, especially early in the morning – got his juices going so that he was almost frantic by the time they sat in their dressing-gowns at the tiny kitchen table. They ate with cheerful daytime clatter, just as if the accumulated sleep of the rest of London wasn't lapping at the walls of the house like a reproachful tide.

'So, what have you got to tell me?' he asked. 'How was the concert, by the way? I haven't really seen you to talk to since then.'

'It was nice,' she said. 'Fauré and Schumann. Musicians' music.'

'Isn't it all?'

'Not by any means. Some of the things the public like to listen to, we don't like to play. And vice versa. The best music is both. Brahms, for instance. But I digress.'

He reached across the table for her hand. 'I like it when you do that.'

'Stop mucking about, Bill Slider. I've got to talk to you seriously about Gerhard Wolf.'

'Aha! I knew I ought to worry about a man named after a predator. Do you think it's going to lead to more work for you?'

'Nail on head, with a vengeance,' she said. 'The thing is, you know how tough things are at the moment?'

'Yes, you've told me,'

'I haven't told you everything. The orchestra's got virtually nothing until April. Our Government grant is being "discussed" at the highest levels, which means they want to withdraw it, or merge us with one of the other Big Four orchestras. And worst of all, we may be losing the summer opera tour.'

'You didn't tell me that,' said Slider.

'It's so grim to contemplate I didn't even want to think about it until it was certain one way or the other. But the fact is the opera company's losing money, and the only way they can economise is to cut out the big operas, particularly on tour. They're talking about only taking a chamber orchestra this year.'

'But if they take fewer musicians, you'll still be one of them, surely?' Slider pleaded. 'You're number five.'

'No, I don't mean they want to cut us down to chamber orchestra size. They want to drop us completely, in favour of a chamber orchestra. The Academy of St Paul's is the front runner. So you see,' she concluded bleakly, 'if we lose the summer tour, it means we'll only have something like four months' work a year. No-one can live on that.'

'But you do freelance stuff.'

'When I can get it. There's less and less of that around, too, and more and more musicians going after every job. The fact of the matter is, Bill, that I can't earn enough to live on.'

He was silent. He ought to be able to say, never mind, darling, I'll keep you, but that just wasn't true. He could barely afford to keep himself. Once all the deductions were taken out – tax, National Insurance, the maintenance for the kids, pension contributions, life insurance, payments on the car – he only just had enough left for his food and petrol and so on. In fact, because he was living with Joanna in her flat, he didn't even pay a proper share of those expenses. The contents insurance, for instance, and the council tax she paid – and she covered the whole telephone bill, though he gave her half the gas and electricity.

While the children were at school he was never going to have enough to keep Joanna; and as a Detective Inspector he could neither earn overtime nor take on a second job to boost his income. He could see why some officers, often with more than one ex-wife and family to pay for, got into debt and turned desperate.

'So what has this Wolf person got to do with it?' he asked at last. He had an awful apprehension about where this might be going.

She closed her fingers round his in the manner of a nurse about to exhort a patient to be brave. 'He's offered me a job.'

'In the whatsname – the Grossman Ensemble?'

She nodded. 'They've got a fantastic schedule – dates right into next year, regular bookings for festivals all over Europe. Recording contracts too. Wolfie's brought the musical standard up to a level where all the best conductors want to be associated with them; and Adela Pronck, the general manager, is just a total diva when it comes to publicity and getting bookings. She's had enquiries from all over the world in the last few months. You know what it's like – when you're hot, you're hot. Word goes round and before you know where you are, managements are fighting each other to get you.'

'It's a compliment, then, that they want you?' Slider said, trying to sound positive.

'Yes, it is. And I won't even have to audition. Wolfie's an old mate – he knows my playing. That's why he called me to fill in in Leeds. And Adela never interferes with artistic decisions, so if Wolfie says I've got the right sort of sound and flexibility, it's a done deal.'

She stopped abruptly, as if she had suddenly heard her own voice. Slider felt cold through to his bones, despite the bacon and eggs. 'You sound as if you've made up your mind,' he said.

'No, I haven't, not yet,' she said. She bit her lip. 'It's an opportunity I can't afford to miss. But it would mean living abroad. They're based in Amsterdam. Most of the concerts are in Amsterdam and Frankfurt. And the recording sessions. And they tour a lot, mostly in Germany, Holland, Belgium and Switzerland, and there are American and Australian tours coming up, and Hong Kong in October. Sometimes they come to England,' she added on a failing note. 'As you see. But not often.'

'Yes, I see,' he said. There didn't seem anything else to say.

'It's a fabulous opportunity,' she said.

'Yes, I see that.'

'Bill, what am I supposed to do? If I take the job I'll have to live in Amsterdam. There's just no way I could travel back and forth.'

'How long would it be for?' he asked.

She shrugged. 'It's a permanent job. I don't really see myself living in Amsterdam for ever, and if the business picks up over here again of course I'd want to come back. But – well, it'd be a few years. At least.'

'So what happens to us?' he asked at last.

She took a deep breath. 'That's the problem I've been trying to think around ever since Monday night.'

'I thought you had something on your mind.'

'The only solution I can come up with is that you come with me.'

'What?'

'Come with me. Come to Amsterdam. Make a new life with me abroad.' She squeezed his hand again, to stop the negative she saw gathering like snow slipping down a roof. 'You've got nothing in particular to keep you here, have you? Your old house is sold, and now your divorce is through—'

'My children aren't nothing,' he said.

'I didn't mean that, but how often do you see them anyway? Once a month? You could fly back once a month to visit them – once a fortnight if you wanted.'

'But what if anything happened – an emergency? How would Irene get in touch with me?'

'There are telephones,' she pointed out. 'Amsterdam's not the end of the world. You could get back in a few hours—'

'A few hours!'

'You're being unreasonable. Would you refuse to move to Wales because it would take you a few hours to get back in an emergency?'

'Wales would be quite different.'

'Would it? Amsterdam's no further, really. Just because it's a foreign country—'

'That's not the point. Anyway, I wouldn't move to Wales either.'

'Wouldn't you? Not even if it was the only way for us to

be together?' He was silent. 'Please, Bill, don't reject it out of hand. At least think about it.'

'I *am* thinking about it,' he said. 'Amongst other things I'm thinking what the hell could I do in Holland?'

'The same as you do here.'

'Don't be silly. Policing is completely different over there. I could be a policeman in Wales if I could get a post, but I could never learn a whole new system of law in a foreign country – and they'd never take me at my age anyway.'

She saw the truth of that, though reluctantly. 'Well, you could get some other job, then.'

'I don't speak Dutch.'

'You could learn.'

'I'm not qualified for anything else. The only thing I know how to do is what I do. And anyway, I don't want any other job,' he finished on a burst of honesty. 'I like what I do.'

She drew back her hand. 'Why should it be my career that gives way to yours? If a man gets promoted and moves, he expects his wife to go with him. Well, this is a tremendous promotion for me, and it means moving a few hundred miles. Are you going to stand in my way?'

'It's not a matter of that.'

'Well, what is it a matter of?'

'Jo,' he said painfully, 'I just don't see how it can be done.'

'You mean you're prepared to give me up, just like that?'

'I'm not giving you up. But it's an impossible decision to make.'

'It'll have to be made, one way or another,' she said, 'but not now.' She stood up, pulling the empty plates together. 'This is not the time to discuss it. I can see how it will end if we go on now.'

'I don't see—'

'Please. We'll talk later. Just think about it, will you? You can do that much.'

'I am thinking,' he said.

She turned away to dump the plates on the draining board. 'I'm going to take a shower.'

CHAPTER ELEVEN

Braising with fake hams

He got back to work bathed, shaved and clean shirted, but unrefreshed, his mind raw with this new galloping doom that was suddenly bearing down on him. The missing lab report on the tissue sample from under the victim's nails had caught up with reality and was lying on his desk. He opened it one-handed and read it as he sipped the first unsatisfying cup of machine tea of the day.

'Oh Nora,' he whimpered. Bad to worse. The skin sample was not a genetic match with the semen and blood. The person Phoebe Agnew had scratched was not Josh Prentiss. '*Bloody* Nora.'

'Sorry?' said Swilley from the door.

'Nora, not Norma,' he explained. 'Get Atherton in here, will you.'

'He's not in yet.'

Slider looked at his watch. 'Where the hell is he?'

'I don't know, boss. He hasn't phoned in that I know of. D'you want me to ring him at home?'

'Yes, do that. He might be ill.'

She hesitated, and then said, 'If he's not at home, I know where he might be.' Slider raised his eyebrows. 'At least, I know where he was on Sunday night, and he was late in Monday morning.'

'If you want to say something, say it,' Slider suggested.

She looked away. 'You know I don't gossip. But I know how you feel about Jim and Sue. I like Sue myself. And I happen to know Jim was out with Tony Hart on Sunday night because I saw them together.'

'Oh,' said Slider.

Hart was a WDC who had been on loan to his firm a while back, at which time Atherton had seemed to have a thing going with her. He was now in what was supposed to be a steady relationship with Joanna's friend and colleague, Sue Caversham; but Atherton had always been a serial bonker, and nothing had been more surprising than the idea of him settling down with one woman. How Atherton ran his private life was his own concern, of course, but Slider couldn't help knowing that if Sue was made unhappy, it would upset Joanna. Equally, though, he couldn't run his firm on that basis.

'Well, that's none of my business,' he said.

Swilley gave a faint shrug. 'If he's not at home, d'you want me to ring round for him?'

'No, leave it,' Slider said. 'How are you getting on with checking Medmenham's story?'

'It's all right,' she said. 'I sweet-talked the local boys into doing it. That wine bar, Ramblers – they call it Benders. Heart of the Essex gay scene, but fairly up-market. They don't have any trouble there. Anyway, Prentiss and Medmenham are well known, and the staff confirm they were in there on Thursday from about ten right through to closing at half past eleven.' She looked enquiringly at Slider. 'It doesn't rule out one of them going back to London in the early hours but ...'

'But it's unlikely, unless they're involved in a deep plot. At least we can interview Piers Prentiss with a bit more confidence. What's that in your hand?'

'First report on the latents from Agnew's flat,' she said. 'The prints on the whisky glasses belonged to Prentiss and Agnew, but the wineglasses and cutlery and the edges of the plates had all been wiped clean.'

'Yes, Lamont told me that at the flat.'

'Oh. Well, they're still going through the lifts – there were a hell of a lot, as you know – but they've found two lots that don't belong to Agnew, Medmenham, Prentiss or the girl upstairs. One set was on the edge of the unit the hi-fi stands on, left hand, half a palm and four fingers, as if he's leaned on it while he's doing something with his right.'

'Changing the music or pouring coffee?' Slider suggested.

'Could be. Oh, and we've checked with Records and it's not Wordley's either.'

'Well, he's smart enough to wear gloves if he's there for felonious purposes. What else?'

'Fabric smudges on the front door and the lounge door, as if they'd been held by a gloved hand, or through a handkerchief,' Norma said promptly. 'Someone trying to let himself out without leaving a mark. But, boss, if whoever ate dinner with her was trying to cover his tracks, doesn't that rule out Prentiss? He didn't mind leaving his marks on the whisky glass.'

'Maybe he just forgot the whisky glass.'

'Yes, but I mean, he didn't deny he'd been at the flat, so why should he mind if it was him ate the meal?'

Slider frowned in thought. 'I don't know. Unless he didn't want it to be known that he was there earlier – something to do with the time of death, maybe.'

'His wife says he didn't leave home until after half past seven—'

'If we can believe anything she says.'

'But if she was telling the truth,' Norma persisted, 'it fits with him saying he left home at a quarter to eight, and if he got to Colehern's at half past eight, the window he could have been at the flat's too small for him to've eaten the meal. He could still have killed her, but he couldn't have got outside a casserole and trifle job as well as all the rest.'

Slider rubbed his head. 'I wish we could have checked his stomach contents on Thursday. If Prentiss wasn't the one who ate the supper, then he must have come after the eater, because he said the kitchen was stacked up with dirty plates, and the only ones that were in there were the casserole and tiramisu lot. Which means the eater couldn't have been the murderer or Agnew would have been already dead when Prentiss got there. But if the eater wasn't the murderer, why did he try to get rid of his finger-marks?'

'God knows,' Swilley said. 'This is the nuttiest case I ever worked on. But we know *someone* else was there at some point because of the tissue under the nails and now the rogue fingerprints on the unit.'

'But we don't know that that was the murderer, or even that it was the person who ate the supper,' Slider concluded. 'Someone not connected with the meal could have leaned on the unit for some reason. And she could have slightly scratched someone by accident.'

Swilley nodded. 'And also, whose was the condom, if it wasn't Prentiss's? And why does Prentiss still insist he didn't have sex with Agnew?'

'You identify the questions all right,' Slider said. 'I wish you'd identify some answers as well.'

'Well, maybe the murderer had nothing to do with the meal at all. Maybe he came after both the eater and Prentiss had been and gone, and for some reason he fiddled about with the cutlery and things, and then realised what he'd done and went round wiping anything he might have touched.'

'Why would he touch the cutlery?'

'Maybe Agnew asked him to help her clear up. Maybe it was all still on the table. He helped stack it and carry it out to the kitchen, murdered her, and then had to wipe his traces away.'

'Very obliging murderer,' Slider said. 'Why didn't he murder her first and save himself the trouble?'

'Maybe he didn't mean to kill her. He did it on an impulse, and then got in a panic, tried to remember what he might have touched.'

'I suppose that makes more sense. Faking the rape scene looks like panic. But Prentiss said the dishes were already in the kitchen.'

'Well, listen, boss,' Norma said eagerly, 'it could still be Prentiss. Suppose he went round there for a shag. They're having a drink afterwards and he sees all the dirty plates still lying about, and blows her out for being a slut. They clear up the stuff together, but he goes on nagging and the row develops and he loses his rag and murders her. Then he thinks, shit, I've got to cover my tracks. He wipes everything he can remember touching, chucks old Aggers on the bed and ties her wrists, puts his gloves on to let himself out because he's clever enough to think of that. But then, when you come round asking questions, he remembers he didn't wipe the whisky glasses, so he makes the best of a bad job and says yes, he was there, but only for half an hour and a drink – knowing that we'll find that out anyway.' She looked at him hopefully.

'I love it,' he said. 'It explains everything except why he keeps denying the semen.'

She shrugged. 'Denied it to start with because he thought it made him look too tasty. Now he's stuck with it and doesn't know what else to do.'

'And the skin under the nails, and the other fingerprints?'

'You said yourself they might be nothing to do with it. Someone who called earlier, nothing to do with anything. Might not even have been the same day.'

'But if the skin was still there under her nails at the time of death, it would mean that she hadn't washed her hands since. Okay, she lived in a tip, but she didn't strike me as a dirty person.'

He remembered suddenly a witness from another case, one Sandal Palliser, saying there were untidy people who were personally clean, and dirty people who were models of tidiness: that tolerance of one did not necessarily mean tolerance of the other.

'Yeah,' said Norma. 'Well, I dunno.'

Slider caught an echo. 'You said there were two sets of alien finger-marks?'

Norma roused herself from thought. 'Oh, yes. The other set was on the flush handle of the loo – points to you, guv.'

'I have my uses,' Slider said modestly. 'Are they the same as the others?'

'No. It's a right thumb, and Bob Lamont says it's a woman's – very small, anyway.'

Slider frowned. 'This gets worse.'

'So she had a female visitor,' Norma shrugged.

'Yes, but if the thumb-mark isn't overlaid, it means no-one used the loo after that, so it must have been late in the day.'

'You don't think the murderer was a woman?'

'I wouldn't have thought a woman was strong enough to strangle Phoebe Agnew, unless she was a very big woman.'

'And it was a very small thumb.'

Slider shook his head in frustration. 'There must have been a lot of coming and going all within a small space of time.'

'Like a bleedin' French farce,' Norma assented. 'Well, there's a stack of statements about people seen in the street, from the door-to-door and volunteer witnesses. Maybe some of them will come good.'

'We can hope,' Slider said.

'Meanwhile, where do we go from here, boss?'

'I think we go and see Prentiss's brother,' said Slider. 'But first, I've got some phone calls to make, and I'll have to bring Mr Porson up to speed. Do me a favour, will you?' He pushed the plastic cup away from him in distaste. 'Get rid of this and bring me some proper tea from the canteen. I can't think with my tannin levels dropping like an express lift.'

'Cuppa rosy. No prob,' said Norma obligingly.

Atherton was not at home. Slider hesitated, and then rang Sue. As soon as she answered he wished he hadn't called, because if Atherton was out on the pull, there was nothing he could say to her that wouldn't drop him in it.

But while he was agonising, she said easily, 'If you're looking for Jim, he isn't here.'

'Oh, right,' Slider said.

'Hasn't he turned in to work?'

'Well, he's a bit late. I just wondered . . .' Slider said vaguely. 'I expect he's on his way.'

Unexpectedly, she chuckled. 'You're such a rotten actor. It's one of the nice things about you.'

'What do you mean?' he prevaricated.

'He's been off tom-catting somewhere,' Sue said, still in that amused voice. 'You know it and I know it, and you're wondering whether you've got him into trouble, while at the same time feeling sorry for me.'

'It would be a bold man who felt sorry for you.'

'Hmm. Well, I suppose you mean that for a compliment. But you might as well know, Jim and I had a big row on Saturday, so he's punishing me. I did the shopping, you see, and I got the wrong sort of ham and ruined his quiche. It was in a packet instead of on the bone – a heinous crime, apparently.'

'Oh dear,' said Slider.

'He was mad as fire,' Sue said. 'It was quite funny, really.'

Slider worried she wasn't taking her sin seriously enough. We all have our little ways, and a man's vanity can reside in many places. Kick him in it, and you're socking around for a smack in the puss. He said cautiously, 'Well, he can be a bit pernickety, but after all, he is a very good cook.'

'That's praising with faint damns, all right,' Sue said, and

Slider recognised it as an Atherton phrase. Language mutation was one of the signs of a real relationship, and obscurely he felt better about them.

She went on, 'Anyway, the bloody old ham was just the surface excuse. Underneath, it was the same old row rehashed. You know, the one about commitment?'

'Oh,' said Slider cautiously. It was a word no man liked to hear, even applied to someone else. Like 'castration', just the sound of it made you cross your legs and fidget.

'I want us to move on a stage and he's hanging back. So we quarrel. That's what it's really about.'

'He's been on his own a long time,' Slider said.

'So have I. It isn't easy for me, either. Believe me, I understand the problem. But—' She hesitated. 'Seriously, Bill, I am a bit worried about him. I know he's squeamish about the idea of settling down, and we fight a lot, and that's healthy. And we have ways of punishing each other, and a lot of the time it's half in fun. But underneath I think he's under a lot of strain. Have you noticed it at work?'

Slider felt uncomfortable with the direction the conversation was taking. He was only just learning to discuss himself with Joanna; discussing Atherton with Sue was a breast-baring too far. Besides, he was Atherton's boss as well as his friend, and he couldn't discuss his performance at work behind his back. 'Well,' he said, trying to think of a way not to answer.

But Sue answered for him. 'This gambling, for instance. You must have noticed. I think it's a sort of lashing out. He likes wine too much to waste it by getting drunk, and I won't let him upset me with the threat of other women. So what's left? I think the gambling is him saying, look, I'm being bad. He's doing it to spite me.'

'Why should he want to do that?' Slider said robustly. Why did women think everything a man did was because of them?

'Oh, because I'm there. Like Everest.' It was another Atherton expression. 'He's wound up tight as a watch spring and it has to come out somewhere, and I'm just handy. But I really am worried,' she went on. 'He's getting through a lot of money, and now there's this buying a racehorse thing – had he told you about it?'

'He did mention something about it.'

'He's going to put all his spare into it, and I'm sure it's a scam.' She sounded quite different now, not amused, but chilled and anxious. 'I just know he's going to get really burnt, and I don't know how he'll cope. I wish there was something you could do.'

'Look, Sue—'

'Bill, he's your friend. I know men don't like to interfere in each other's lives, and I know you being his boss makes it a bit delicate, but I really think he's close to cracking up, and I can't get near enough to help him. I'm a newcomer in his life, and, anyway, he's made me the enemy over this, so anything I say will only make things worse. If he gets caught and made a fool of, it's really going to hurt him – not just financially, though that's bad enough. Can't you *please* see if you can help him?' She paused a beat, and added almost inaudibly, 'I do love him.'

That she was shy of saying the words aloud touched him. 'I'll try,' he said. 'But I don't know – he's a very private person, you know.'

'Yes, I know that,' she said, and the amusement was back in her voice.

'He may not like me interfering.'

'If anyone can, you can,' she said. Her confidence did not improve his. 'And you've a right to, if it's affecting his work. At the moment I've no right.'

'I wouldn't say that exactly.'

'He would,' Sue said succinctly.

'Right,' said Slider, emerging into the office, 'let's have the latest so that I can report to Mr Porson.'

'Still trying to follow up the various sightings in the street,' Hollis said, gesturing to a tottering heap of reports. 'We've got everyone from Lord Lucan to Shergar. A scruffy man in jeans and a state of agitation running away. That'd be all right if it wasn't Prentiss. Someone standing watching the house – unfortunately, that was a woman. A smart man doing up his tie as he walked along. I quite like him, because he had something under his arm, a briefcase or a paper or something, and if we are missing a file, that could be it. But he sounds too young to be Prentiss. Nothing hotter than that yet.'

'Okay, keep it up. What else?'

'One of the journos from the *Guardian* got in touch to say that Agnew'd been working on a special project recently,' Mackay reported. 'Something of her own – not for the paper. Very secretive about it – wouldn't say what it was, but he says she seemed worried about it. She hinted it was very important stuff and that it would be bad news if it fell into the wrong hands. That's all I could get out of him,' he apologised. 'But if it was that important maybe there *was* a missing file and that's what she was killed for, and it was just coincidence that Prentiss went round there.'

'Maybe,' said Slider. 'Have another go at this bloke, in case he knows more and just isn't telling. And ask around some of her other contacts. Ah, McLaren, how's your Wordley idea getting on? You've been out of the office a lot. What have you got to show for it?'

'Not much, guv,' McLaren admitted. 'I had a couple of goes at Kelly, and she's given me a description of the geezer Wordley went off with. She says he was a big bloke, mid-thirties, a slaphead with an earring in the top of his ear. She still swears she doesn't know his name, and I believe her now. Says she thinks she's seen him somewhere before but can't place where. But she's obviously shit scared of him and Wordley. I don't want to hang around her too much in case it gets back to him and gets her in schtuck.'

Slider nodded. 'Nothing on where Wordley is?'

'No, but I've had info he was drinking in that club, Porky's, in the Shepherd's Bush Road Wednesday night. Well, that's only five minutes from Agnew's flat.'

'It's a long way between Wednesday night and six-forty-five Thursday evening, when she was seen alive by Peter Medmenham.'

'Yes, guv, I'm working on that,' McLaren said. 'Wordley's not an easy bloke to forget, but a lot of people are scared of him, so it takes time to track him.'

'And what about a motive? Or are you sticking with motiveless violence?'

'Well, there's this stuff Andy was just saying about something she was working on that was worrying her. And Medmenham said she was worried and she'd been drinking heavier recently. Suppose it was something to do with Wordley? She got him off that blag, didn't she, but say she'd found some more evidence that said he did it after all? That'd fry her brains all right, wondering whether to come clean and drop him, or hide it and live with her conscience?'

'Supposing she'd got one,' said Swilley.

Slider shifted impatiently. 'What's your point?'

'Point is, guv, it would give Wordley the best motive to off her,' McLaren said.

'It's a lot of supposing,' Slider said.

'It's more motive than we've got for Prentiss, which is none,' McLaren pointed out. 'And Wordley's a slag with a record for violence.'

'Blimey, you sounded almost intelligent then, Maurice,' Swilley said admiringly. 'You've got to hand it to him, boss.'

'All right, you can stay on it, McLaren, but watch your step. Anything else?' Silence. 'Well, if that's the magnificent total, I'd better just take it to Mr Porson, and hope he doesn't throw a fit. I suppose you all saw the papers today? We're on trial on this one. Keep at it.'

When Slider got back from Porson's office, Atherton had arrived. Slider sucked him into his office with a look.

'I'm sorry I'm late, guv,' Atherton pre-empted him.

'Where were you?'

'I had a bit too much last night and overslept,' Atherton said. Slider noticed he didn't say too much what.

'Is that it? That's your excuse?'

Atherton shrugged gracefully. 'What can I say? I could spin you a line—'

'Well, do,' Slider invited. 'At least a good, four-ply, industrial-weave lie would make it look as if you had some respect for me.'

But Atherton wasn't playing. 'I'm sorry,' he said again. 'I know it's not on, and it won't happen again.'

Slider was stumped. There was nothing in that smooth cara-pace he could address. Having been cast in the role of boss, he could not speak as friend. He would have to find a different way in. 'It had better not,' he said. 'Well, now you're here, I want you to come and interview Piers Prentiss with me. I was going to take Swilley—'

'Swilley? It doesn't take much, does it? One little slip – and after I've given you the best years of my life!' Atherton cried dramatically.

It was a crack in the armour. 'Where were you, anyway?' Slider tried. 'You look like hell.'

'Wednesday's my flower arranging class,' Atherton said, papering it over. 'So how come Prentiss junior? Have I missed something?'

'If you'd been here, you'd have known.' Slider brought him up to speed. 'Porson's quite keen on Wordley, but obviously Prentiss is still front runner, so the next step is to try and get some more information on his relationship with Agnew – and, we can hope, what she was working on – from a safe source. Hence Prentiss's brother. I nearly went without you,' he finished.

'Yes, I'm sorry,' Atherton said, and he sounded genuine this time. 'It really won't happen again. I'll buy you lunch as my penance.'

'It will be a penance. We're going to Essex, remember.'

CHAPTER TWELVE

Primrose path

Piers Prentiss's home was called Primrose Cottage. 'And you can't get more *bijou* than that,' Atherton said. It had half submerged beams and little lattice windows, and round the small, low door a rambling rose grew, which would presumably look divine in summer but at the moment merely lurked thornily waiting for someone's eye to put out. To complete the picturesqueness, the ancient roof was as wobbly as an auntie at a wedding, and the chimney leaned perilously out of true.

'I wonder what holds that up?' said Atherton.

'Probably roadworks somewhere,' Slider said vaguely.

The cottage was in what had once been the high street of a village just outside Chelmsford; but the village had been absorbed, stuck to the town by bland blobs of infill – new 'vernacular' housing as tasteless as sticking-paste. Now the row of mediaeval dwellings, some of them with downstairs fronts converted long ago to shops, stood braced at one end by a petrol station, and at the other by a raw-looking supermarket already in the process of being out-evolved by a greenfield superstore just off the A12.

The building next to Primrose Cottage was an antiques shop with 'Prentiss' over the window in tasteful gold lettering on dark green. The window display was of china, glass, old wooden boxes, silver and jewellery, and a couple of porcelain-faced dolls. Beyond were some handsome pieces of furniture and other, more eclectic items: a pair of leather riding boots on wooden trees, a spinning-wheel, a Victorian child's tricycle and, on the wall, framed classic cinema posters.

'Cinema posters are very collectable these days,' Atherton

said, peering in with a hand shading out the light. 'I'm looking for one myself: Sean Connery and Marilyn Monroe in *Gentlemen Prefer Bonds*.'

'Eh?'

'It's the one where she sings *Diamonds Are For Ever*.'

'I know it well,' Slider said. A middle of the road shop, and probably successful, he concluded: everything looked clean and well tended, and there were no depressing boxes of unsaleable junk, the usual hallmark of desperation. There was a 'closed' notice hanging on the door. He looked at his watch. 'Lunch hour. He said on the phone he eats at home. It looks as though he doesn't keep an assistant.'

They rang the doorbell of the cottage, and waited on the narrow pavement while the local traffic pottered by behind their backs in an unhurried but constant stream.

A barking got up from within, and a moment later the door was opened and a pair of small wiry dogs leapt up like clay pigeons being fired. They sprang with all four feet at once, barking with staccato endurance, timing it so that one took off as the other landed, to get the maximum coverage. But they were not showing their teeth, and the blunt end was eagerly a-twitch, so Slider assumed they meant no harm and turned his attention to the human accompanying them.

'Piers Prentiss?' he asked. He held up his brief and introduced them.

'Yes. Hello,' the man replied. 'Down, dogs! Shut up! Don't mind them, they don't bite.'

Piers Prentiss was as tall as his brother, but thin instead of massive, drooping a little at the shoulders, perhaps the reaction to living in Primrose Cottage, where the clearance was less than generous. His face was interestingly gaunt under the same leonine growth of hair, but cut rather longer, brushed back all round, and completely white. It made a startling contrast to the tanned skin and brown eyes, a shade darker than Josh's, and he carried his head self-consciously, as though inviting comment. Slider guessed he had gone grey very young and made capital out of it; now, however, the lines of his face had caught up. He had the same short, broad nose as his brother, but his mouth was wider, thinner and looser, giving his face a downward drag that made him look older than Josh, and somehow more aesthetic.

A mournful and thoughtful lion, not much of a threat to the wildebeest.

His kit was expensively country casual: loose-fitting dark brown corduroy trousers and a forest-green lambswool sweater with an open shirt collar peeking out at the top; a gold signet ring and an expensive-looking gold watch weighted his long, delicate-looking hands. There was nothing in the least fey about his clothes, but they had the effect of making him look precious, perhaps by contrast. He looked as though he was just standing around inside them, and would have been surprised to discover that anyone thought they were his. In the same way, if you had ever seen him at a bus stop, you would have assumed he was looking for a taxi. This was a man you could not imagine on public transport; Josh would take a bus without a second thought if it suited his purposes.

'You want to talk to me about Phoebe,' Piers Prentiss said. Slider assented. 'You'd better come in. I'm just having my lunch – do you mind? I have to open the shop again in half an hour.'

He led the way down the narrow, flagged passage towards the back, and Slider and Atherton followed, with the dogs' heads appearing regularly at their elbows, like people trampolining behind a wall. It was dark inside the cottage and smelled of damp brick and furniture polish, and Slider caught a glimpse through a door of gleaming wood and old chintz, before being led into the low-ceilinged and dog-smelling kitchen at the back. The reedy sunshine outside bounced off the diamond-paned windows, doing nothing much for the illumination inside. The kitchen looked like an advert from a Smallbone catalogue: no expense had been spared to make it look like the real thing, only better. There was a great deal of exposed brick, interspersed with white painted plaster; dark beams across the ceiling, red-brown quarry tiles on the floor; expensive pine units with black iron hinges and handles, and a huge dresser filling one whole wall floor to ceiling.

'Lovely and warm in here,' Slider commented.

'It's the Aga,' Prentiss said, gesturing to where it sat fatly under the long, low inglenook. 'Sadly the chimney isn't up to much, so it's only electric.'

'What you'd call ohm on the range,' Atherton murmured.

Fortunately Prentiss didn't hear him properly. 'Yes, there must have been a range there, but the previous owners removed it. But to me, the space just cried out for an Aga, so I heeded the cries. I mean, if you've got an inglenook, flaunt it, I always say.'

It was plain what Piers had been doing when they arrived. In the middle of the kitchen was an old pine table on which stood a stoneware bowl half full of yellow soup, spoon akimbo; a rustic-looking wholemeal loaf on a bread board; and butter and cheese crocks, next to which lay the folded-open *Guardian*. It looked like a still-life group; or the Smallbone ad again.

'Would you like some?' Piers offered, gesturing vaguely towards it. 'Lentil soup – home-made. There's plenty.'

'No, thanks all the same,' Slider refused for them both. 'But please don't let us stop you.'

'All right, I won't,' said Piers, resuming his seat. 'Make yourselves at home.'

Slider and Atherton pulled out chairs and sat at the table. The dogs had stopped bouncing in favour of a lengthy and committed smelling of their shoes and trousers. They were terriers of some sort; their square faces and grizzled curls reminded Slider disconcertingly of Commander Wetherspoon, especially as they stared at him with the same dispassion. It made him feel he was on trial.

'So, what do you want to know? It's a terrible business about poor Phoebe. There was a big spread about her in the *Guardian* on Monday – was it? – or Tuesday. I hear,' he twinkled gravely at them over his spoon, 'you've been grilling my brother about it. He's thinking of suing you for wrongful arrest.'

'He wasn't arrested. He was—'

'—helping you with your enquiries, yes,' Piers finished for him. 'You can't sue for that: that's what I told him. Poor dear, he was mortified. He was on the phone last night, keening like an Irish peasant for his lost career – his political career, I mean – because the Government can't bear anything that looks the least bit like sleaze, so poor Josh will be out on his ear before you can say floccinaucinihilipilification.' He paused a beat to see if they appreciated his style, and meeting intelligent interest, he seemed to relax a little and expand. 'I said, love, you don't want to work for that bunch of crypto-fascist asses anyway.' He pronounced it *arses*. 'But of course the tragedy is that he *does*. The architectural stage was never big enough for Josh. The *stage* stage wasn't. Well,' he took and swallowed a spoonful of soup demurely, 'I suppose there's always Europe.'

His voice reminded Slider of dried flowers: a faint, odourless ghost of some great past vigour. He moved his hands as he spoke, as though trying to help the failing voice along, but his gestures had the slow, underwater impotence of the running-dream. Still, talking was obviously very much his thing, for which Slider gave inner thanks. All he had to do was to filter out the useful grit from the river of words. He settled himself, exuding ease and not-being-in-a-hurry. Atherton, noting the posture, resigned himself to a long session.

'Your brother was never on the stage, was he?' Slider asked, on the back of Prentiss's last comment.

'Not an act*or*,' Piers said, striking an attitude, 'and yet, surely an actor *manqué*? Always wanted to be centre stage – always *was* centre stage, let's face it – but without the nuisance of learning lines.'

'He joined the Drama Society at university, didn't he?'

'However did you know that? Yes, he did – though of course in any university, joining Dramsoc has everything to do with social popularity and nothing to do with the theatre. But Josh could have been a thespian if only he'd had the self-discipline. He has real talent, you know. He dissipates it.'

He smiled, and his rather lugubrious face was translated: the charm and pulling-power of his brother were there, but diluted, like September rather than July sunshine.

'On the other hand,' he went on, 'if it comes to the parable of the talents, Josh would say I've buried mine under a bush. We were both born with every advantage, and look at our relative positions now.'

'You come from a wealthy family?' Slider slipped the question in as undisturbingly as an otter slipping into water.

'Oh, yes. Family pile in leafy Buckinghamshire – not too many acres, though. Grandpa and Father were both ambassadors, so they preferred their wealth portable.'

'So you must have spent a lot of time abroad?'

'Oh, no, we stayed at home in good old England.'

'Who looked after you?'

'We had nannies and so forth until we went to school. But

we had super holidays with the parents – up until Mummy died. That was when I was eleven. After that we didn't go and stay with Father because there wouldn't have been anyone to supervise us. But there were always relatives around. And Granny lived in the South of France – we stayed with her quite often.'

'You went to Eton, like your brother?' Atherton asked.

He nodded. 'Eton, Oxford and the Guards was the family tradition – until Josh broke it. After Mummy died, he was always getting into rows with Father. First he refused to go to university at all, and then instead of PPE at Balliol he chose architecture and UCL. Father dropped down dead with shock – well, almost.' He made a deprecating gesture. 'It was heart, but in fact he died in May 1972, just when I was about to do my finals. Still, I like to think it was Josh's rebellion that brought it on. Makes the story so much more symmetrical, doesn't it?'

He brooded a moment, crumbling a piece of bread in his fingers. There was some hostility buried here, Slider thought. Simple sibling rivalry?

'So,' Piers said abruptly, coming back, 'brother and I inherited the family fortune between us. As soon as probate was through, Josh used his to buy his own firm and the house in Campden Hill Square. Such foresight! Everything he now has and is stems from that first sensible investment. I, on the other hand,' he went on with an airy gesture, scattering crumbs, 'used my half to allow me to live comfortably without having to take the antiques business too seriously. It's moot whether the shop keeps me or I keep the shop. Now *whose*, I ask you, was the wasted talent?'

'I hope that's a rhetorical question,' Slider said. Worldly success versus elegant living: was that the issue between the brothers? Piers wanted his comment to sound ironic, wanted his audience to conclude from his denigration of his lifestyle that he thought it superior; but underneath, did he really feel that he was a failure, and that Josh had scored on all fronts?

'Oh, goodness, I wouldn't force you to take sides!' Piers said. He seemed to have been distracted from his lunch. The soup was cooling and congealing around the neglected spoon, and all he had done with the bread was to make a mess on the table. Now he pushed his chair back with a final air. 'What about some coffee?' He stood up, and the dogs, who had gone off trouser duty and were curled together on a beanbag in the corner next to the Aga, lifted their heads hopefully. 'You'll have some coffee?'

'I'm afraid we've kept you from eating.'

'Oh, no, don't worry. I never eat much at lunchtime, anyway. Besides,' he looked down at the bowl with sudden dislike, 'I loathe lentil soup. One might as well eat cardboard boxes.'

'I thought it was home-made,' Atherton said, amused.

Piers looked at him. 'Not by *me*. Good Lord, I'm *nothing* of a cook! No, I have an absolute treasure who comes in. My "lady who does". She cleans, cooks, soothes the brow when fevered, and looks after the doggies when I'm away travelling – doesn't she, woofies? Doesn't dear old Aunty Marjie look after my wuffle-buffles, then?' The dogs looked adoring and waggled their bottoms ecstatically. 'The trouble is,' he added in a normal voice, 'that she's *frightfully* keen on wholemeal nourishment and regular bowel movements. Just like an old-fashioned nanny! So, let me whisk away this *abrasive* nourishment—' He swept the soup bowl up, 'and put on some nice, evil, caffeine-loaded coffee. How do you take it? Why don't you two chaps go and make yourselves comfortable in the drawing-room, and I'll bring it in. Too sordid, sitting in the kitchen with the left-overs!'

The change of room was not a change for the better, for the drawing-room was chill and smelled of mushrooms, but at least it was a chance to have a look round.

'This bloke's a babbling brook,' Atherton complained when they were alone. 'We'll be lucky to get out of here before Easter.'

Slider raised his eyebrows. 'In a hurry? Got some major appointment you've been keeping from me?'

'I thought we had a date,' Atherton said. 'You, me and a couple of pints of the amber foaming.' The dogs pattered in and stood just inside the doorway watching them. 'Watch out, guv,' Atherton hissed. 'Two people in dog suits at twelve o' clock. Don't touch the silver.'

Slider was making a round of the framed photographs which decorated almost every surface. Here was a 1950s black and white snapshot of the Prentiss boys aged about ten and six, with, presumably, their mother and father, standing together on a windy clifftop. The children's faces seemed a nice blend of the parents' different features, with Josh perhaps favouring his spectacularly beautiful mother slightly more, and Piers his rather long-faced father. Even at that age Josh was the more physically attractive, and looked straight at the camera with the winning smile of one who had no doubts he would be liked. Piers seemed to be drawing back, pressing against his mother, his eyes sliding uncertainly sideways, his smile required and perfunctory. Always overshadowed by his brother, Slider thought. A slight rearrangement of the same genes, and you had less of everything – good looks, charm, confidence and success. A first-class and a second-class son. There were things to be said, after all, for being an only child.

Josh featured in lots of the photographs. Here was another of the two boys together, this time kneeling with their arms round two Weimaraners; now a formal picture of them, mid teens, standing behind their seated father with a hint of pillars and chandeliers behind them – some embassy or foreign palace? Another, in their late teens and leaning on the rail of a ship. Here was a wedding photograph, Josh in morning suit and Noni thin as a rail and vividly dark in full white fig, Piers with top hat in hand, head turned, looking out to the side of the picture as though he didn't belong to the group.

Those that didn't feature Josh were of Piers – alone, with dogs, or with various men; the various men alone; and the progress of some children who Slider assumed were Josh's son and daughter. He was interested to note that there was no photograph of Phoebe Agnew anywhere – and also none of Peter Medmenham.

He was just working his way round to the piano and the last crop when Piers Prentiss came in with a tray, preceded by the smell of coffee. 'Here we are! Now let's sit down and be comfortable.' He saw Atherton glance at the clock and said, 'I'm not going to worry about opening the shop again. I hardly ever get passing trade on a weekday anyway, and everyone else knows to try here if the shop's shut. So we can take our time.'

'I was just looking at your photographs,' Slider said. 'I hoped you might have one of Phoebe Agnew.'

'There's one on the bookcase,' Piers said. He put down the tray on the coffee table and crossed the room, and then paused, puzzled. 'Well, that's odd. There was one here. It's gone. It was a rather nice one, of Phoebe, Josh and me in Josh's garden. What on earth could have happened to it? I suppose Marjorie must have moved it.' He made a rapid scan of the room, and shrugged. 'I'll have to ask her what she's done with it. I've got lots of others, though, unframed. I'll get the box out if you like. But first – coffee.'

He poured and handed it, and then from a cupboard in the chimney corner produced a bottle of Caol Ila. 'You'll indulge in a little *pousse-café*? Do you care for malt whisky?'

'I'm rather a fan,' Slider said. Atherton refused, on the grounds that he was driving, and Piers poured two large ones, and then took an armchair facing them, with the dogs at his feet. 'I didn't see any photos of Peter Medmenham, either,' Slider said, when they were settled. He sipped his malt, and noticed with mild satisfaction that Piers drank more deeply of his. 'He told me that you had been friends for many years.'

'Oh, poor Peter!' Piers said, but sounded quite detached about it. 'Did he tell you that our ways have parted?'

'He seems to hope they haven't really,' Slider said.

'Yes, that's what Thursday's little visit was all about. I'd spent Wednesday night with Richard, and we'd planned to have the weekend together, and I couldn't risk Peter barging in on us, so I decided it was time to tell him it was over. Then he insisted on coming over on Thursday night to persuade me that my new love was just a fling, a will-o'-the-wisp leading me from the true path.'

'And it isn't?'

'No,' he said, quite serious for once. 'If you'd seen how sorry Richard was to leave me on Thursday morning, you'd know. I'm sorry about Peter, because we've been together a long time, and I hate to hurt anyone, but the thing with Richard is on a different plane altogether. That's why I took down the photos of Peter. Richard didn't like them being there. I explained it to Peter and tried to be nice about it – I even offered him the photos, frames and all, which was generous because they were solid silver and rather nice – but he just got hysterical and started throwing things—'

'The orange juice?'

Piers raised his eyebrows. 'Oh, he told you that, did he? It made an awful mess – orange juice is so sticky! I was furious. And then he just walked out.' He finished his whisky and reached for the bottle. 'Top-up?'

'I'm all right, thanks.'

'But Peter always was too emotional. He says it's the artistic temperament but you can put *that* another way and say it's pure theatrics. He plays to the gallery the whole time. Richard's so different. He's serious. You'd never believe he was only twenty-eight. He's made me see how superficial Peter always was. And if we're talking talent,' he added emphatically, opening his eyes wide, 'Richard's in a whole different class. To have got as far as he has at such an early age—' He stopped. 'This is all confidential, isn't it?'

'Unless there's anything that bears on the case.'

'Oh, well I'm sure it doesn't. But Richard doesn't want anyone to know about him and me, and he made me swear not to tell anyone. And I haven't, until now, but this is different, isn't it? But we have to be discreet, because when I tell you that he's Giles's junior minister – do you know Giles Freeman?'

'Only by name,' Slider said.

'Best way,' Piers snorted. 'He's the most utterly poisonous toad in the whole Government! Career mad, like all of them, but he's ruthless, and wildly jealous of Richard, naturally, since it's obvious to the most meagre intelligence – a category Giles only just manages to scrape into – that Richard has more talent in his little finger than Giles has in his whole repulsive body! So naturally he's afraid that Richard is going to oust him; and there's a certain amount of homophobia involved – Giles makes a point of being Norman Normal. Anyway, he's just longing for Richard to lose his footing. He daren't move against him openly because Richard has the PM's ear, but if there were a scandal . . .' He looked anxiously from one to the other. 'So we have to be discreet. I hope I can trust you?'

Atherton raised an eyebrow. 'I wouldn't have thought that sort of thing was a problem any more,' he said. 'After all, it's not a crime. And there are lots of gay MPs, aren't there – and several in the Cabinet, come to that. Why should Richard Tyler be worried about your relationship?'

Slider felt a surge of gratitude as Atherton slipped the surname in for his benefit. Now at last he knew who they were talking about. He didn't manage to keep up with the intricacies of politics, the way Atherton did, but even he had heard of Richard Tyler, the party's golden boy.

'The relationship isn't the problem,' Piers said sharply, as though he had been very much afraid that it was. 'But any adverse publicity – you know what this Government's like. So we've always been discreet. We make a point of not being seen in public places together. And Richard phoned me on Friday, the moment he heard about Phoebe's death, and said that in view of my connection with her through Josh we must be doubly sure to keep our relationship an absolute secret. The slightest hint of being mixed up in anything undesirable could ruin his career – and Richard's one of the real high-flyers,' he added proudly. 'He'll be in the Cabinet if the next reshuffle goes the way it's expected. And then – well, the sky's the limit, provided he keeps his footing. He could be the youngest ever prime minister.'

Slider recalled that only a few weeks ago a Cabinet Minister had been sacked for what had been called an 'error of judgement' in a Birmingham knocking-shop. It was the same sort of euphemism as a footballer 'bringing the game into disrepute', meaning, when it came down to it, being mentioned in the newspapers in anything but a flattering context. Yes, the need for discretion was obvious, though Slider thought it a touch of paranoia too far to worry about merely knowing the brother of a man who had been questioned by the police about a murder.

But despite having been enjoined to absolute secrecy, Piers was only too eager to talk about his new love, and as he sipped his way down the malt, he grew more expansive and descriptive, hardly needing Slider's little prompting questions to keep him going. He wanted to tell, and Slider saw something of the truth of what Peter Medmenham had told him, that Piers craved company, and was not happy with his own. The opportunity was all the justification he needed to unpocket himself.

In fact, as the story unrolled, Slider began to feel sorry for Piers Prentiss. He had met Richard Tyler through his brother's involvement with the DOE – some political drinkie-do or other – and it was clear that he had been bowled over by the dynamic young man with the friends in high places. What Tyler had seen in Piers was naturally pure conjecture, but Atherton, with more knowledge of the protagonists than Slider, suspected that it had less to do with the heart than the head. Piers was brother to Josh, who, at the time of first meeting, had been very hot in Government circles; Piers knew a great many showbiz personalities, which could be useful to an ambitious politician; Piers was independently wealthy, and political success never came cheaply.

Slider's different knowledge, of the way these affairs went, read between the lines and gathered that Piers had been Peter Medmenham's boy for a long time, and was now enjoying the heady sensation of having a boy of his own. He had been the junior partner and was now the senior, the one flattered and looked up to for his greater knowledge and experience. There was pride in having been chosen by such a demigod; and, it had to be suspected, there was some satisfaction in having swapped Peter's ageing flesh for Richard's young firm stuff.

But Richard was not going to be constant and available as Peter had been. Already the change of partner had left Piers lonely and rather lost, and being sworn to secrecy was depressing him, when he longed to publish his success and be seen arm in arm with Apollo at opening nights and fashionable restaurants. When the time came and the golden boy dropped him, as he had dropped Peter, he was going to be very lonely indeed. The number of times he assured them that the new relationship was the real thing and would last for ever, suggested that Piers knew that time was not far round the corner.

It was all very sad; but apart from confirming Medmenham's alibi, it didn't get them any further forward on the case, so as soon as a pause presented itself, Slider said, 'You were going to show me a photograph of Phoebe Agnew.'

'Oh, Lord, yes – d'you know, I'd completely forgotten what you came here for,' he said lightly. 'Poor Phoebe.'

Poor Phoebe indeed, Slider thought. He hadn't yet met anyone who seemed genuinely devastated by her loss. Perhaps that was her own fault, but his natural bent was to side with the underdog, and he didn't like to think that anyone should leave the fretted globe without some tears shed for them, even if they had made policemen's lives a burden during their tenancy.

CHAPTER THIRTEEN

Half an oaf is better than low bred

Piers Prentiss went away to fetch photographs, and when they were alone, Atherton said, 'Obviously it's bye-bye lunch. I assume you are going somewhere with this?'

'Nice of you to assume that,' Slider said.

'Sorry, I didn't mean it the way it came out.'

'We've got him talking now. You never know what will emerge,' Slider said. 'I just feel that somewhere in the silt at the bottom of the Prentiss pond is the information we need to understand what happened. We can't ask Josh because we can't trust what he tells us, but if we stir Piers's mud—'

'I see,' Atherton said. 'You're draining the moat to catch a mackerel.'

'Exactly: setting a sprat to catch a thief. But actually I'm trawling rather than fishing. I don't know what I want to catch, but I hope I'll know it when I see it.'

'You have been listening to *What's My Metaphor*,' Atherton announced. 'Tune in next week for—'

He broke off as Piers's footsteps sounded outside the door. He came back in with a large cigar box in his hands. 'Here we are.' He glanced from one to the other as if to guess what they had been doing while he was away. 'Can I get you some more coffee before I sit down? Sure? Right, well, let's see what we've got here.'

The box was full of photographs, and Atherton felt a doomed premonition that they were going to have to look at every one; but Piers shuffled through them as if looking for specifics. He handed one across to Slider. 'That was in the spring of '69. On our way to an anti-Vietnam rally. Goodness, we were young!'

Atherton leaned across and Slider held it between them. Both

Prentiss boys, familiar now from other photos, sitting on a wall; Josh in the middle with his arms round the thin, dark Noni on one side, and on the other what must be Phoebe Agnew, with Piers at the end of the row beside Noni, looking as if he wasn't sure how he'd got there. Tagging along, just tolerated – the fate of younger brothers.

All four were wearing jeans, and the boys had girly haircuts like embryo busbies, as was the fashion then. Noni, neat and tidy, with short-cut hair, make-up, and a smart jacket over her jeans, sat with her knees together and her hands in her lap, looking like an office worker rather than a student. Phoebe had a magnificent, if unkempt, mane of curls which seemed to blow in a wind all her own; her many-layered clothes looked shabby and untidy, and Slider would have bet that her fingernails were dirty; but she stared out into the world with the bright-eyed challenge of Xena the Warrior Princess, and the others paled into insignificance beside her – even Josh. While his arm round Noni's shoulders looked possessive and protective, the one round Phoebe's looked as if he was trying to hold down a wild horse with a piece of garden twine.

'They were all in their first year at university. I was still at Eton, of course. Father was furious that they got me involved – I was only sixteen. But of course it was Phoebe's idea first and last – everything always was. She was the political one. Whether it was Vietnam or Chile or nuclear weapons, there she was, protesting. Josh went along for the fun, and because it was the done thing for students – and to annoy Father, which was practically his mission in life in those days. Noni was never really interested in politics at all, but where Phoebe led, she followed.' He brought out another photo. 'Here they are – best friends. I think that must have been at the Notting Hill Carnival.'

The two women with a crowd in the background; Phoebe's arm round Noni's shoulders, bowing her a little as she leaned forward to the camera, her mouth wide open in a shout or exaggerated laughter, the other arm in the air with the fist closed round a can – only Coca-Cola, though. The wild corkscrew curls waved around the vivid face in sharp contrast to the neat dark head and reserved expression of her companion.

'I wonder what brought them together?' Slider said. 'Was it a case of "opposites attract", do you think?'

'Yes, poor Noni, she does look a bit overshadowed, doesn't she?' Piers said, taking the photo back. 'And when you look at what's happened since, Phoebe's always outshone her. Her acting career never really took off, in spite of everything Josh could do. When they were first married, he made a point of courting producers and directors – though between ourselves he enjoyed every minute of it,' he added archly. 'He always loved the luvvies – still does. And of course, they love him – which is why he's got an award for set designing, while Noni's got nothing.'

'When did they marry?'

'April 1970. Straight after graduating, Josh got himself into a firm of architects and started making friends with the world, and Noni got herself into LAMDA, and then they got married. Father was furious. He wanted Josh to marry one of our set: Noni was a suburban nobody. He'd always planned to buy Josh a house when he married, but that was all off when he married Noni. Josh didn't care – he liked showing he could do everything by his own power. So they lived in a dreadful little rented flat in Earl's Court to begin with – not that I thought it dreadful at the time, of course. I'd just started at Oxford and spent my weekends and every hour I could with them. My dear, the glamour of that pair, to a callow, pimply student!'

'What was Phoebe doing?'

'Heaven knows. She was off somewhere, protesting about something,' he said, throwaway. 'None of us saw her for years. She just dropped out of our lives. Meanwhile, Josh shot up the career ladder and Noni got nowhere. I think that was one of the reasons she got pregnant in the end. Having babies gave her an excuse not to be chasing parts and not getting them.'

He looked thoughtful, as if something had occurred to him. Slider waited to see if it would come out, and then said, 'So when did Phoebe reappear in your lives?'

'That must have been in 1973 – the anti-Pinochet protests, was it? She was lobbying MPs when Josh bumped into her and invited her home, and the three of them more or less took up where they left off. Except that Phoebe was still living a sort of nomadic life, going wherever there was a cause, all her belongings in one rucksack, sleeping on people's sofas – just like a student.' He seemed not to approve of this behaviour. 'She didn't get herself a flat until 1985, after the miners' strike collapsed and she decided to settle in London.' He smiled suddenly. 'You see how dear Phoebe's entire life has been shaped by political events?'

'I see,' Slider confirmed. It was like watching one of those 'The Way We Were' movies. 'Go on.'

'Not much more to tell. Toby was born in 1976 and Emma in '78, so Noni had the perfect excuse to stay home until 1983 when Emma started school. Then Phoebe persuaded her to try and restart her career. Josh by that time had quite a lot of influence and she got parts all right, but she never really broke through, poor thing. Then in 1990, Phoebe won the Palgabria, and Noni got pregnant again.'

'You think there may have been some connection?' Atherton put in.

'Mm, well,' said Piers, 'perhaps I shouldn't say it, but I did have a very naughty thought. It did occur to me to wonder whether she hadn't been a teensy bit jealous of Phoebe from time to time. But it's silly, really,' he dismissed the idea with a wave of the hand. 'Noni would have hated the life Phoebe led, and she was never interested in politics. She was just born for wife-and-motherhood. The last pregnancy turned out badly, though. Poor thing, she miscarried, and because she was over forty by then she blamed herself, though I think the quacks said that was nothing to do with it, it was just bad luck. Anyway, she went into a fearful depression: she was just a wreck for years, until Phoebe encouraged her to pull herself out of it. So she tried again with her career, and she seemed to be doing all right in a quiet way, until she did that dreadful sitcom and had a spectacular flop. Then she just gave up – and who can blame her?'

'So, when was she a dancer?' Atherton asked.

'A dancer?'

'She told me she used to be a ballet dancer.'

Piers shook his head. 'No, you must be mistaken.'

'She said she had a fall while dancing and injured her back. The trouble recurs from time to time.'

'Never while I've known her,' Piers said. 'If she's ever had a bad back she's never complained about it. But I think she did ballet lessons when she was a child,' he added on the thought. 'Maybe that's what she meant. She's never danced professionally.'

Slider picked up the thread again. 'Tell me about your brother's relationship with Phoebe Agnew,' he said. 'Were they more than friends?'

'Much, much more,' Piers said promptly. 'But if you're asking me if they were lovers, the answer's no. Phoebe wasn't his type.'

'That's what he said.'

'There you are then,' Piers said triumphantly, starting on his fourth malt. 'No, what you have to understand about Josh is that these ferociously butch types really don't *like* women. They need to have them around as trophies, but at heart they're afraid of them. Noni was just right for him – the sort of fluffy, ineffectual female that he could dominate and protect. If she'd been successful at her career it might have been different – but there was no danger of that,' he added with unconscious cruelty. 'But he could never get the better of Phoebe. She was fully his equal. Of course, once he accepted that, he found her a better friend than any man could ever be to him, because really butch men don't trust other men either, do they? They see them as rivals. Shocking, isn't it?' He twinkled again, with half an eye on Atherton. 'The poor things are so alone. Crushing women and trumpeting at other men, stamping their feet and competing all the time. No wonder they have ulcers and heart attacks. Testosterone is not a happy bedfellow.'

'Perhaps the strain of his career—' Slider began, provoked by God-knew-what consideration into defending Prentiss to his own brother.

'He was never any different,' Piers interrupted briskly. 'Even as a boy his idea of relaxation was to play some madly competitive sport. He was a rugger blue at UCL, did you know?'

'It didn't come up in conversation,' Slider said drily.

'I've often wondered about those rugger buggers.' Piers seemed to have out-drunk any natural reserve. 'I mean, all that sweaty grappling and rolling in the mud – what's in it for them? Aren't they just a teensy bit too fierce in their protestations of manliness? But never mind! I'm talking too much. All I wanted to say was that Prentiss, R. J. was always one of life's ball clangers, right from school upwards.'

'R. J.?' Slider queried.

'Joshua is his second name. He and father had the same name, so he was called Josh to distinguish him. Anyway,' he resumed his plot, 'that's why Phoebe was so good for him. He could talk to her, tell her anything, discuss things with her without worrying that she'd use anything she learned against him. They fought like mad, but it was a healthy sort of quarrelling because it didn't affect their friendship – which it would have if they'd been lovers – and it didn't damage his career – which it would have if she'd been a man. That's why,' he looked full into Slider's eyes, his own now a little too shiny, like those of a stuffed animal, 'that's why you're way off beam if you think Josh had anything to do with her death. If it was *me* you suspected, there'd be more sense in it. When we argued, it could be nasty, as Noni will no doubt tell you.'

'You didn't like her?' Slider suggested.

'I like my women to be women and my men to be men,' he said. 'I don't like these ambivalent people. In the old days you knew where you were. Now all the edges are blurred and everyone's confused and unhappy. I blame co-education: takes away all the mystery.'

'Mrs Prentiss says you had a quarrel with Phoebe at New Year, at a family dinner party. What was that about?'

'You *have* been busy!' he said waspishly. 'It feels like sitting naked in a shop window, having you know all about my private life.'

'I'm sorry,' Slider said. 'I'm groping about in the dark, you see, as far as this case goes, and there's no knowing what may be important. What did you quarrel about?'

'About Richard, as it happened. She wanted me to give him up.'

'Why was that?'

'Oh, I suppose she was worried about Peter's heart being broken – I don't know. I don't think she said why, come to think of it. I was a bit naughty, really – shouldn't have told her. I promised Richard no-one would know. But Phoebe had a way of getting things out of you and – to be absolutely frank and honest, I was longing to tell *some*one. So I just let it slip ever-so-accidentally, and swore Phoebe to secrecy too, but for some reason she seemed really upset about it. I suppose she'd had too much to drink. Anyway, she lit into me and told me what I was doing with Richard was wrong and it must stop. I got annoyed with her and told her to mind her own business – I had quite a load on too – and we had a bit of a shouting match, until Noni got upset and Josh told us to shut up and asked what it was about. Well, we both felt a bit silly because we couldn't say, could we? So we shut up. Afterwards Phoebe apologised for being a buttinski, and I said I forgave her, and that was that.'

The dogs suddenly catapulted out of their semi-coma on the carpet at his feet and hurtled, barking like rapid gunfire, out towards the kitchen. There was the sound of a woman's voice, and Piers said, 'It's Marjorie, my domestic treasure. Coo-ee! Marjie! In here, darling!'

A moment later a woman appeared in the doorway. 'I didn't know you were still here, Piers. Oh, I see you've got company! Am I interrupting? Shall I vamoose?'

She was thin and athletic-looking in tightly fitting Lycra joggers under a heavy-padded ski jacket; perfectly made-up, professionally coiffed, and with a cut-glass County accent.

'No, come in and meet the chaps,' Piers said, getting up. He introduced Slider and Atherton and said, 'This is Marjorie Babbington, my lady who does.'

'How do you do?' The woman extended a beautifully manicured hand, noted Slider's rather blank look and said, 'Is something wrong?'

'No, not at all,' Slider said. 'You're not quite what I'd been imagining, that's all.'

She smiled. 'Did he portray me as old Mrs Mop? You are naughty, Piers! He's always playing pranks.'

Piers raised his hands. 'I just said you were a treasure, which you are – soothing the f.b., making me all those *delicious* soups! Marjie, darling, can you open up the shop for me now, instead of taking the doggy-wogs out? I've got to talk to the chaps about Phoebe.'

'Of course I can. Oh, gosh, wasn't it awful,' she said, turning limpid grey eyes to Slider. 'Poor Phoebe! Have you any idea who did it?'

'They suspected Josh at first,' Piers said before Slider could answer.

'Oh no, poor Josh! He was devoted to Phoebe.'

'So was everyone, darling.'

'I know. She was so kind. Nothing was too much trouble for her. She helped Clive and me – my husband – when our son got into trouble,' she said earnestly. 'He got arrested with a lot of others at a rave in a barn, and Phoebe went to a great deal of trouble to see the right people and make sure he wasn't charged, because it could have ruined his chances of Oxford. I mean, he hadn't done anything, you know,' she added quickly, 'but some of the others had been taking drugs and it was guilt by association. I just don't understand how anyone could hurt someone so very kind. And you were only talking to her on Thursday, too,' she said to Piers. 'It's awful to think of, isn't it?'

Slider felt as if he'd been hit on the head with a woolly sock. He turned to Piers. 'You spoke to her on Thursday? Why didn't you tell me?'

'It didn't occur, that's all,' he said. 'Is it important? I only rang her to talk about Peter coming to see me. I wanted to ask her what sort of mood he was in. I told Marjie about it, didn't I, darling?'

She nodded. 'On Friday, when I was cleaning the kitchen.'

'What time did you ring her?'

'I don't know, really. About eight, half past, I didn't really notice. I'd been pottering about, thinking about Peter coming and wondering if there was going to be a scene, and then I thought he was bound to have talked to Phoebe about it so I gave her a tinkle. But she said she had someone with her and couldn't talk, so I said it didn't matter, and that was that.'

'Did she say who was with her?' Atherton asked. His suppressed emotion showed in his voice, and Marjorie looked at him enquiringly.

'No. She just said, "Look, Piers, I've got someone with me. I can't talk now. Can it wait?" And I said, "Don't worry, it wasn't anything important", and that was that.'

'How did she sound?' Slider asked.

'Well, a bit unwelcoming,' Piers said. '*Not* happy to hear one's dulcet tones. And, if you want the honest, honest truth, a bit drunk maybe. I thought at first when she answered the phone that I'd woken her up, and then I realised it was probably Bacchus rather than Morpheus. She really had become a frightful toper in the past couple of months.'

'Please, think hard,' Slider said. 'Try to pinpoint the time more closely.'

'Oh dear, I can't. I just don't know,' he said, still not seeming to sense the urgency. But Marjorie Babbington's large eyes came round like car headlamps.

'It'll be on his phone bill, won't it? The itemised calls?' She looked at Piers. 'Your bill came yesterday, didn't it? I noticed the envelope when I picked up your mail from the mat.'

'How long were you on the phone?' Slider asked.

'Only a couple of minutes,' Piers said.

'Then it probably won't show,' Slider said. 'But it will have been logged by BT computer. We can find out.'

Now at last the penny dropped. 'But if it had been Josh with her, she'd have said so,' Piers said. 'Oh, my God!' His eyes widened. 'You think it could have been the murderer? Was I actually talking to her while the murderer was there?'

'It's a possibility,' said Slider.

They drove in silence for a while. 'Are you thinking what I'm thinking?' Slider asked at last.

'Were you thinking that there's never been a recording of the Dvořák symphonies to equal the Kertesz-LSO series of the late sixties?' Atherton said.

'No,' said Slider.

'Neither was I,' said Atherton.

Slider looked sideways at him. 'Is it my imagination or are you getting weirder? What I was thinking was if this phone call puts Agnew alive after, say, eight-thirty, it puts Josh Prentiss in the clear.'

'If you believe Maria Colehern. And if she really did notice the time he arrived.'

'Hollis believed her. But we'll lean on her a bit and see if she creaks. And try and get some outside confirmation of what time Prentiss arrived. Someone may have seen him.' There had been no point in wasting manpower on that before, when they had no definite time of death. 'If only this idiot had told us sooner that he spoke to Agnew on Thursday night, we could have done the asking while memories were fresh.'

'He *is* an idiot,' Atherton agreed. 'Stupid enough to invent a phone call that never happened, to get his brother out of trouble.'

Slider shook his head. 'The Marjorie woman agreed that he told her about the phone call on Friday. If he'd made it up to protect his brother, he'd have told us then.'

'He could have been waiting to see if it was needed.'

'Do you really see him as that cunning?'

'No, you're right,' said Atherton. 'He's educated, well-bred, but basically a clot.'

'I think the call will prove to be pukka,' said Slider. 'It remains to be seen what time it was. If it lets Josh out, it also clears Piers – I wish his name didn't rhyme with so much – and Peter Medmenham, since he couldn't have caught the 9.02 at Liverpool Street if he was murdering Agnew after half past eight, unless he has wings under his posh schmutter.'

'So what does that leave us with?' Atherton said restlessly. 'McLaren's pet theory about Michael Wordley?'

'McLaren is as thick as a whale sandwich,' Slider said, 'but maybe he's got a point.'

'He has – it's his head. Why would Wordley kill Agnew, the only person in the world who's ever loved him?' Slider told him about McLaren's missing file motive. 'Oh, that's why you asked Piers if he knew what Agnew was working on.'

'Yes.' Piers hadn't known. Slider sighed. 'I'm not convinced about Wordley. I'm getting less convinced all the time about Prentiss.'

'Despite his indisputable semen?'

'Well, we know he was there, but maybe all the supper-scoffing and sex-having was nothing to do with the murder. Maybe the murderer slipped in after all the other visitors had left.'

'In that case we'll be on this until next Christmas,' Atherton said. 'Couldn't we try and pin it to Giles Freeman? I've never liked him and there is the spare set of finger-marks to account for.'

'I'll let you go and ask for his prints,' Slider said. 'Tell him what you want them for, won't you?'

'Pass,' Atherton said with a shudder. 'No, I think I'm sticking with Josh. Probably the call was while he was still there. Agnew didn't let on to Piers who it was,' he anticipated Slider's question, 'because they'd been bonking and she didn't want anyone to know.'

'And he killed her because—?'

'Pick a reason,' Atherton shrugged. 'He's probably always loathed her. Why not? Oh, all right, if you want me to be logical about it – his political career is just taking off and she's going to get in the way. If she's known him all those years she probably knows something about him he doesn't want to get out. We just have to find out what it was. No, it's still Prentiss for me. He's the only one who makes sense of all the rest of it.'

'Well, we'll see,' said Slider. 'And then we'll know.'

CHAPTER FOURTEEN

Dial M for dilemma

Porson was pacing about, shaving his craggy chin with an elderly electric razor that buzzed feebly, like a fly on its back, as if it was barely up to the challenge.

'Where have you got with Prentiss? I've got to talk to the press and TV for the evening news, and it's going to get a bit hot under the collar if we don't find something positive to tell 'em. I've had Commander Wetherspoon on the dog again, and he didn't make pleasant listening.' He put down the razor and began struggling with the top button of his shirt. 'Wanted to know why we haven't charged Prentiss yet, after all the fuss we've made. He was more or less inferring that heads will roll if we don't come up with a result in short order.'

Slider hated having to do it to him. 'I'm afraid it looks as though Prentiss is out of the frame, sir.'

Porson did a creditable double take, and froze in the act of tightening his tie. 'What?'

'I've had the report from BT about the telephone call Piers Prentiss put through to Agnew on Thursday evening. It was timed from 8.43 to 8.45; Josh Prentiss arrived at Maria Colehern's flat at 8.30.' He saw the question in Porson's eye and added quickly, 'One of her neighbours saw him going in and confirms the time. A good witness. I don't think there's any doubt that when he left Agnew she was still alive.'

'Oh, good grief!' Porson cried. 'I'm not hearing this. I am not hearing this. You mean to tell me that after a week on the case all you've done is clear the prime suspect? You've upset the Home Secretary – and the PM himself – for no reason? What am I going to tell the press conference? What am I going to tell

Mr Wetherspoon? He'll have my balls for garters. And who's going to tell Prentiss?'

He stamped about and raged for a while, and Slider bent his head and bore it patiently. He didn't blame The Syrup. He was up at the sharp end when it came to censure, and would have to explain it all to a hostile news media gathering. Slider wouldn't have liked to be in his shoes and under those lights.

When he calmed down a bit, Porson sat down – unusually for him – behind his desk, and said, 'So where does it leave you? What have you got left to follow up?'

'There's Wordley, sir. McLaren's still looking into him. But we've got nothing on him, except that he's got a record, and that he's been missing since Wednesday night. And there's a mass of reports on people seen in the street and going in and out of houses. We've been working our way through them. Most of them will be nothing to do with the case, as always, but we may still turn up something. There are Agnew's papers, still being sorted. Something may turn up there. And we've got the team going over her major articles and campaigns, trying to find if there was a conflict of some kind that may have come back on her.'

'In other words,' Porson grunted, 'you're back at numero uno.'

'There's still the possibility', Slider said, 'that it was a random killing. Someone just broke in – the lock's easy to slip – and killed her for the hell of it.'

Porson looked at him sharply. 'But you don't think so?'

'It doesn't smell like that to me.'

'Nor to me,' said Porson.

'I mean, why would they tie her up like that afterwards – unless it was a joke?'

'The tying up aspect of the scenario is what puzzles me most,' Porson admitted. 'No record of those extra fingerprints anywhere, I suppose?'

'Nothing.'

Porson sighed. 'You'll just have to plod it out, then.'

'Yes, sir.'

'You realise, don't you, that Prentiss will probably sue us for destroying his career?'

Slider braved it out. 'I was just doing my job, sir.'

Porson shrugged. 'Best thing you can do is get your head down and get a result, double quick time. Meanwhile,' he stood up, the gloom intensifying on his granite crag, 'my unenviable task is to go and face the cerebos of the press.'

It turned out to be a long day. Prentiss – who in reason ought to have been pleased to be cleared – was not a happy bunny when the news was broken to him, and Commander Wetherspoon was not thrilled to have to be the one to break it. Telephone calls, press briefings, urgent conferences and carpetings followed. Slider was glad to have the bulk of Porson to cower behind. He was a funny old duck, but he stood by his men.

Slider was just putting things away, about to go home, when McLaren came in.

'Guv—'

'You still here? There's no overtime tonight, you know.'

'No, I been out talking to my snout,' McLaren said.

'You're a bleeding contortionist, you are.'

McLaren took it phlegmatically. 'He's got a line on the bloke Wordley went off with on Wednesday night. He reckons the description fits a geezer name of Tucker, Sean Tucker. Ex-bouncer. You know the sort, out-of-work Milk Tray man, all muscles and black roll-necks. Used to work down the Nineteen Club in Warwick Road – I busted him a few times when I was at Kensington.'

'He's got previous, then?'

'More form than a Miss World contest. Tasty as they come. Got sacked from the Nineteen for violent affray, and he's into serious naughties now. Nicked over at Notting Hill a while back for conspiracy to murder, but the CPS gave it away. Anyway, word on the street is him and Wordley's mixed up in something big.'

'Planning a robbery?'

'No, guv,' McLaren said with satisfaction. 'My snout says the word is they've done a murder.'

'Any word on who?'

'No, that's all he said, that Tucker and Wordley are mixed up in a murder.' He eyed Slider hopefully.

'It's a lead,' Slider acknowledged, 'but I've got reservations. Why would Wordley involve Tucker? It wasn't a two-man job.'

'Maybe he didn't know that,' McLaren said. 'She was a strong old doris, and gutsy. She could've put up a fight.'

'Faking the rape doesn't look right for Wordley.'

'He's thick enough to think it might help. And Tucker's always been a clever bastard. No, I can see him thinking it up, and laughing while Wordley does it. What about going round Tucker's gaff and giving him a tug? He lives over North End Road. Tucker's a toe-rag, he never minds shopping his oppos to clear himself. If we rough him a bit, he might drop us Wordley.'

'Well, it never hurts to roust them, I suppose,' Slider said. 'And he might at least know where Wordley is. I'll put it to Mr Porson tomorrow.'

'Tomorrow?'

'It's no good pouting at me, I told you there's no overtime tonight. Anyway, Mr Porson's gone home, and my voice is the last one he'll want to hear until he's had a good night's sleep. I'll speak to him in the morning and if he authorises the manpower we'll see about bringing Tucker in.'

'I was just gonna go on my own,' McLaren protested. 'Have a little chat.'

'Haven't you read the new Health and Safety guidelines? A trained officer is an expensive piece of equipment and you can't just chuck it into a situation without assessing the risk. More than any mother, the Metropolitan Police doesn't want your face altered. Tucker could be dangerous, and you're not going to roust him alone, and that's final.'

McLaren subsided into resentful mumbles. 'I go all out to get this red-hot lead—'

'Tucker will keep,' Slider said. 'If Mr Porson rolls for it, and the budget'll stand it, we'll have a go at him tomorrow.'

As a counter-irritant, trying to find a parking space in Chiswick was up there with the greats. Slider's first words as he came through the door were, 'If I have to park much further away, I might as well leave the car and walk to work.'

'Hello,' said Joanna, coming out into the passage. Her woe-begone face reminded him of the situation he had left behind, and that living in Chiswick might soon be a thing of the past anyway. They looked at each other for a moment, and then he held out his arms and she walked into them.

He rested his weary chin on the top of her head and sought for something tender to say. 'What's for supper?'

'Sausage and mash,' she said, in the tone a farmer's wife might use to say, 'The cow's got mastitis, the hens are off lay and the goat's eaten your trousers.'

'I like sausage and mash,' he said, kissing her ear. 'Especially with fried onions.'

'There are onions,' she conceded. He nudged her face round and kissed her mouth. He had only meant to kiss, but he felt that instant arousal at the touch of her that still surprised as much as it delighted him. His love of her was so continuously, satisfyingly physical. He just wanted to be having her all the time. What was it about her, anyway? Why wasn't she followed everywhere by a pack of stumbling, drooling, lust-dazed men? Maybe it wasn't her, maybe it was *them*. The thought pleased him. There was a nice, kismet symmetry to it; a jigsaw-puzzle satisfaction. Slot their two pieces together and, lo, a bit of God's big picture emerged.

As he had continued kissing her while having these thoughts, the matter had now become urgent, so he started walking her backwards towards the bedroom, shedding his coat and jacket as he went.

Some time later he had a long, groaning stretch and said, 'Ah, that's better than sinking into a hot bath when you get back from work.'

'Gee, thanks,' she said, sitting up and pushing the hair out of her eyes. Some of the strain had gone from her face, so evidently it had worked for her as well. 'You can have one of those too, if you like.'

'I'm too hungry to wait that long. A quick shower will do.'

'All right, I'll go and put the potatoes on.' At the door she turned back and said, 'I suppose, man-like, you think that changes everything.'

'It did for me,' he said. 'Altered my profile, anyway.'

She grinned unwillingly. 'Rude,' she said, and disappeared.

When they finally sat at the table in the bay window of her sitting-room, a bottle of Côtes du Rhône had joined them, and was making itself agreeable all round. While they ate, he told her about the day's developments, and she listened in silence, not throwing herself into it as she usually did. When food and conversation both came to an end and they were left with only the last half glass of wine, she said, 'The problem hasn't gone away.'

'I know,' he said.

'I've just been going over and over it all day,' she said, 'and I can't see a way round.' She looked at him anxiously. 'I'm reminded again that now your divorce is through you're a free man.'

He didn't pretend not to understand her. 'After the proofs of love I've just given you?'

'Hot sex, agreeable though it is, doesn't necessarily mean lifelong commitment.'

'I was referring to eating your sausage and mash,' he said. And then, suppressing a self-conscious smirk, 'Was it really hot?'

'The earth', she assured him solemnly, 'outmoved a Travelodge vibrating bed.' And then she tacked off in her disconcerting way. 'It's always struck me as risky, having those things in California. All over the state, people must be missing earthquakes.'

'I've never been to California,' he said. 'Or anywhere in America. I'm just a home-body.'

'Which brings us neatly to the point. How's that for a link?' she said without pleasure. 'Bill, what are we going to do?'

'I love you,' he said. 'I know that's not an answer, but I thought I'd mention it.'

And she looked sad. 'That sounds like the sort of thing people say just before they split up.'

'I would never leave you,' he said.

'Which just throws it back on me. It's not fair. Why should I have to choose between my career and my man?'

'I'm not asking you to.'

'Yes you are. Implicitly.'

'Well, it's what you're asking me,' he said fairly.

'And you won't even consider it.'

How had they got back here so quickly? 'It's not that I won't consider it, it's that I don't see how it's possible.'

'It may be impossible for you to be a policeman in Holland – I have to accept your word for that because I don't know – but you could do something else.'

'Petrol pump attendant? Road sweeper?'

She glared at him, the rage of the trapped animal. 'If I stay, the same fate awaits me – or doesn't that prospect bother you? Probably not. There's a streak of the old-fashioned male in you that thinks a woman's job is less important than a man's. I suppose all men think like that, underneath. It's just the little woman amusing herself – harmless as long as the housework gets done.'

'Did I say that?' he protested, but mildly. He knew the rage was not really directed at him, but at the situation.

'No, but it's there all the same, the attitude. It's what you think even if you're not aware of it.'

'Like institutional racism?'

That made her pause. 'I'm sorry,' she said. 'That was unfair. But, Bill, I'm good at what I do! And what I do is *me*. If I stop playing the fiddle and get a job as a checkout girl—'

'But that isn't the option that's on offer, is it?' he said carefully. 'If you stay, you'll still play. You may have to take another job as well, to make ends meet, but you won't have to give up playing altogether.'

She stared. 'You *have* made up your mind.'

'No, I haven't, but—'

'I *want* this job! It's important. It's a fabulous opportunity for me, don't you understand? It's like – oh, I don't know – you being offered Assistant Commissioner or whatever.'

'But I don't want promotion. I just want to go on doing what I'm doing. I'm good at it. And what I do is me, too.'

She turned her face away miserably, twiddling the stem of her glass. 'I just can't see a way out.'

'I don't want us to part,' he said after a moment. 'The thought of being without you is – well – I don't know. I don't want to face it.' Inside his head the words flowed, powerful and passionate, but, man-like, all he could get out through his tight lips were crude wooden effigies of meaning. 'Don't try and make a decision now. Let's both think and try and find a solution.'

'I can't hold off for long,' she said. 'Wolfie's going to want an answer.'

'All right, but please, let's try and think of a way round it,' he pleaded.

She shrugged, which meant she'd try, but she didn't know

what else there was to think. For that matter, neither did he. The realisation that he could lose her – or rather that they could lose each other – proved to him how strongly he had taken root in her. He felt shaken, loosened, likely to go over in the next strong wind. And yet, what solution was there? His foolish jealousies of the past, when he thought she might run off with another man, would have been a pleasure now, compared with the pain of this real dilemma.

He was disturbed mid-evening by a telephone call.

'That's my mobile,' he said. 'It must be work.'

Joanna, curled in the corner of the big, shabby leather chesterfield, staring at the television, grunted but didn't stir. On the screen a weather girl with straggly hair and wearing one of those Suzanne Charlton over-the-bum jackets (did they draw from a common wardrobe, like nuns?) was saying, '. . . but the watter wather will at least bring some warmer temchers, tickly in the wast.' Come back, Michael Fish, he thought. We forgive you the hurricane for the sake of your diction. Restore some 'e's to our forecasts.

He went out into the hall and stood by the front door, where the signal was better, to answer. The sepulchral tones of Tidy Barnet smote his ear. If a smoked haddock could speak, he'd sound like Tidy.

''Ullo, Mr S. That diction'ry bloke you was asking about, right?'

That would be Michael Wordley. Tidy, one of Slider's best snouts, had a way of avoiding using names. Telephones – particularly mobiles – were not secure, and his life was perilous enough as it was.

'I'm with you,' Slider said.

'You never warned me you 'ad anuvver bloke askin' questions,' Tidy said sourly. 'Tripped over 'im, didn't I?'

That would be McLaren's snout, presumably. 'I didn't know. One of my men had an idea and put the word out.'

'Yeah, I know 'im. The stupid one.'

'I wouldn't say that.'

'Useless as a chocklit fireman. His snout's a useless bastard an' all. Wouldn't know if you was up 'im wiv an armful o'chairs.' Tidy sounded unusually irritable.

'Sorry if it crossed your lines. My man's snout said dictionary man was involved in a murder.'

'Murder? That ain't what I 'eard,' said Tidy. 'Diction'ry went off Wensdy night wiv a certain party, call 'im Little Tommy, right?'

That would be Tucker. At least McLaren's snout got something right. 'Yes, I know who you mean.'

'Well, they're plannin' a bit o' biz between 'em. Goin' to turn over this rich tart's gaff, right? They was doing the clubs and boozers all Wensdy night, went 'ome well pissed Fursdy morning. Little Tommy's telling everyone he meets, the moufy div. Diction'ry's not 'appy wiv 'im. They 'ad a row in Paddy's club in Fulham Palace Road about two o'clock.'

'Went home where?'

'Little Tommy's gaff. He lives wiv his mum down North End Road.'

'When was the job supposed to be done?'

'Fursdy,' said Tidy. 'They must a done it all right, 'cos I 'eard there was a lot o' tom come on the market sudden. More'n that I can't tell you.'

'Well, thanks,' said Slider. 'You've done a great job. If you can get anything on where the job was or what they did before and afterwards, I'd be grateful.'

'Yeah, I'll keep me ear out.'

'That other thing I asked you about?'

Tidy chuckled. 'Yeah, that's a queer one. Well, it ain't my field, but I laid it off on another bloke, and he'll give you a bell when 'e knows, right? Name o' Banks. Harry Banks, but they calls 'im Piggy.'

Slider was shocked. 'You never use names!'

'Yeah, well, 'e ain't in the business, is 'e? Got nothink to fear from Piggy Banks.'

Slider returned to Joanna. 'Trouble?' she asked.

'That was Tidy Barnet,' he said. 'I'm now expecting a call from a man called Piggy Banks.'

'Your life's one long episode of *The Magic Roundabout*, isn't it?' Joanna said.

After the disappointment over Josh Prentiss, Commander Wetherspoon was only too pleased to jump at Tucker, and being of the generation that loved kicking down doors and shouting, 'Go, go, go!' he recommended the Syrup to arrange a visit to the Tucker demesne on Friday. It proved unfruitful. Mrs Tucker, a phlegmatic, respectable but deeply stupid woman, was found in sole possession. She opened the door to them without waiting for them to kick it in, and confirmed quite willingly that Seanie had come home with Micky Wordley in the early hours of last Thursday morning, both of them a bit pickled. Micky had slept on the sofa. They had got up about one o'clock Thursday afternoon and Mrs Tucker had got them breakfast, a big fry-up, which was what Seanie liked when he'd been out drinking the night before. They'd sat about afterwards having a smoke and a chat, and they'd gone off about three o'clock, saying they were going down the club. No, they hadn't said which club, but Seanie liked the Shamrock in Hammersmith now he was banned from the Nineteen. And she hadn't seen them since.

Hadn't she been worried about that?

No, not really. Seanie was a big boy, he could look after himself. He often went off places. He'd come back when he wanted a clean shirt or something.

Did she know what he and Micky were planning to do on Thursday?

No, they never mentioned. She never knew what Seanie was up to. He was a big boy, he could look after himself.

Did she ever wonder where his money came from, given that he didn't have a regular job?

Oh, he was in business, her boy. She didn't know what sort. He bought and sold things, she thought. She didn't understand business. She left all that sort of thing to Seanie. But he was doing all right. And he was a good boy, very good to his mother. Gave her a lovely watch at Christmas. Second-hand it was, but a very good one, solid gold.

After a close search of Tucker's room and the rest of the house, which revealed nothing but a lamentable collection of pornographic magazines in a suitcase under Tucker's bed, they left. McLaren was elated, and shone in the glow of a prophet proved right.

Slider, however, was sceptical. 'Unless everyone's been holding out on us, I'd hardly call Phoebe Agnew a "rich tart" – and there's no evidence that she ever had a lot of jewellery. She was a confirmed dresser-down, from anything we know.'

'But these stories always get exaggerated,' Hollis pointed out, fairly. 'It's possible Wordley went and did her for some other reason, and lifted her watch or something in the process. Villains like him are daft enough to try and flog it afterwards.'

'Yeah, and we've still got my snout saying he'd been mixed up in a murder, *and* he's missing since Thursday,' McLaren pointed out.

'Well, it's all we've got at the moment,' Slider said, 'so you'd better get on with it. You and Anderson can go round the pubs and clubs and try and find out where they went. Ask all your snouts for information; and ask any of the fences who co-operate if there's been any jewellery through their hands in the past week. You could try Larry Pickett. He might come across, since tom isn't his field.'

After a morning poring over case notes and statements, Slider went up to the canteen for a late lunch, and with an air of what-the-hell, ordered the all-day breakfast. Sausage, tomato, bacon, egg and beans. The baked beans had reached that happy state that only canteen beans know, when they had been kept warm for so long that the juice had thickened almost into toffee. He sat down with it at a quiet table and laid the papers he had brought up with him beside the plate.

He hadn't been there long when Atherton appeared beside him with a tray.

'Can I join you?'

Slider grunted consent, and Atherton unloaded tuna salad and a carton of apple juice. Each of them looked at the other's lunch with horror.

'No fried bread?' Atherton asked, sitting down.

'They'd run out of the proper bread. Only had that thin sliced stuff. You might as well fry place mats.' He dipped a stub end of sausage in his egg yolk. 'Where've you been, anyway?'

'I just slipped out for a minute,' Atherton said. 'Personal time.'

To the bookies, Slider wondered? Atherton, too, had brought a folder up with him, and looking at it upside down Slider read the name of the racehorse consortium company, Furlong Stud, with the address near Newmarket.

'You're not really serious about that, are you?' he asked, a little tentatively.

Atherton swallowed. 'Of course. Why not? Look, you think everything to do with racing must be crooked but that's just paranoia. Thousands of people go into racehorse ownership every year.'

'And lose their money.'

'No,' Atherton said with a patient smile. 'It's an accepted medium of investment now. There've been articles in all the money sections of the papers. These people', he tapped the page, 'quote an investment return of twenty-four per cent.'

'Guaranteed?'

'Of course not guaranteed,' Atherton said. 'But it's not a pig in a poke, you know. We're all going down to see the horse tomorrow. You watch it on the gallops, time it against other horses. And the winning times of the various big races are all published, so you can tell if the animal's fast or not. It's all up front.'

'And how much are you putting in?' Slider asked.

'Fifteen each.'

'Fifteen hundred? It's a lot of money.'

'Fifteen thou,' Atherton corrected, faintly self-conscious.

'You're joking!'

'That's just to begin with. Look,' he added impatiently, 'with a return of twenty-four per cent there's no point in messing about with small change. You ought to come in on it with me. Look how much difference it could make to your finances.'

'I haven't got fifteen thousand,' Slider said, bemused.

'Nor'd I. I remortgaged,' Atherton said. 'You've got to help yourself in this life. If you can't make enough to live on one way, you have to try another.'

'Where have I heard those words before?' Slider said. 'No, wait, I read them – in the Bent Copper's Almanac.'

Atherton looked away, compressing his lips. 'There's no point in talking to you. You're prejudiced. Anyway, it's my business what I do with my money.'

'True,' said Slider lightly, to cool things down. But he was dismayed. This had the hallmarks of obsession about it, and looking at his colleague's face as he forked salad into it with rather angry movements, he could see the lines of fatigue and strain. Atherton had always been one of that blest band of coppers who rode the swell and seemed unperturbed at the end of each day; but since his serious wounding during the Gilbert case, he seemed to have joined the mortals.

Atherton had opened his file and was ostentatiously reading, so Slider turned to his own papers and tried to work out what the loose ends were. Prentiss denying having sex with Agnew on Thursday in the face of all evidence to the contrary was the most annoying: but Prentiss was out of it now. Even if he had lied about that, it seemed he had told the truth about the rest. None of the numerous street sightings seemed to have related to him, but the combination of the phone call and the witness at Colehern's flat put him out of Agnew's way before she was killed.

Prentiss said it wasn't him that had eaten the meal, and if he wasn't the murderer there was no reason to doubt his word on that; so who had eaten it, and wiped away his finger-marks afterwards? The same person who left the marks on the unit? In that case it wasn't Wordley. And then, what about the thumb mark on the flush-handle? How many people had there been swanning about that damned house on Thursday anyway?

And then something occurred to him. He shuffled through his papers for Bob Lamont's report. Why hadn't he thought of it before?

'It says here', he said aloud, 'that the thumb mark on the flush-handle of the loo was the only one.' Atherton looked up. 'It was clean apart from that.'

'But that was—'

'A woman's thumb, yes – but not Phoebe Agnew's.'

'Wiped clean?' Atherton said. Slider nodded. 'Who would do that, except for the murderer? But it doesn't make sense – if the murderer had been and gone, why would a woman go and flush the loo? And what woman?'

They looked at each other for a moment. 'I have an idea', Slider said unwillingly, 'that I really don't want to follow. It occurs to me that there's someone else, apart from Prentiss and Medmenham, who's been lying to us from the very beginning.'

'Loyal little wifie?' Atherton said, screwing up his face at the idea.

'She said Prentiss had told her Agnew was dead on Friday morning; but he seemed not to know about it when we spoke to him on Friday afternoon. We assumed he was lying, but if he didn't kill her, he was probably telling the truth. In that case, how did she know Agnew had been murdered?'

'Yes, and what about that business of her referring to the way the body was left?' Atherton said eagerly. 'If Prentiss didn't do it, he couldn't have told her – so how did she know?'

'She might possibly have learned that some other way,' Slider said, being absolutely fair, 'though in that case why shouldn't she have said so? But then why was she so keen to give Prentiss an alibi?'

'Maybe she wasn't. Maybe she was trying to cover herself. If she was his alibi, he would be hers.'

Slider shook his head. 'That doesn't make sense. If Prentiss didn't know he had to cover her, he would tell a different story – as in fact he did.'

'Maybe she hoped she could get to him before we did, to coach him.'

'Still no good. When their stories did finally agree – after they'd had time to collude – it still didn't cover her for the necessary time. He was at Colehern's flat, but where was she? At home and unaccountable.'

'Hmm,' said Atherton. 'But why should she want to kill her best friend? And would that little slip of a thing be strong enough to strangle a big woman like Agnew – especially when she had a bad back?'

'Probably not – unless Agnew was really drunk. I don't know. There's something there, I'm sure, but I don't know what. Mrs Prentiss has been acting strangely from the beginning.'

'Well, both Prentiss and Piers said she'd been depressed. Maybe it's nothing more than that. Unconnected irrationality.'

'Maybe,' said Slider. He got up, picking up his papers. 'I'll see you later,' he said vaguely.

'You haven't finished your sausage,' Atherton protested.

'Hmm?' Slider said.

'Stick it behind your ear for later,' Atherton suggested.

'Okay,' Slider said, evidently too preoccupied to understand what was being said to him.

CHAPTER FIFTEEN

Albie senior

Eltham Road had a Saturday quiet about it, the sleeping cars of the at-home workers lining the kerbs with an air of having their eyes shut tight. Do not disturb. Slider had to park dangerously near the corner, but there wasn't much traffic about. He just hoped no boy-racer in a BMW came round it too quickly.

Atherton was, even now, probably, driving down to view his wonder-horse; Slider was on his own, without his usual sounding-board. The idea that had been growing on him over the past eighteen hours seemed so far out he could have done with a sceptical audience to tell him whether he was cur-dog hunting, or on a scent.

The house opposite Phoebe Agnew's flat was one of the unmodernised ones, shabby and dirty-curtained. The January light was as pale and sticky as aphid's milk, but the man who answered the door of the area flat blinked up at Slider like a purblind pit-pony. He was tiny, collapsed together by age, and wrinkled like a relief map of the Himalayas.

'I'm Detective Inspector Slider from the Shepherd's Bush police,' Slider said carefully and clearly, holding up his ID. 'Can I come in and talk to you?'

It took a while to sink in – you could almost see the *wait* symbol in his eyes as his underpowered computer struggled to boot up – but then he smiled a pleased, shy smile of tea-stained china teeth, and said, 'Oh yes, that's right, come in, thank you very much.'

The door opened straight into the sitting-room. The room smelled of paraffin, and had a superficial, smeary warmth that did not quite mask the cavernous dank chill underneath. There was a variety of grubby rugs covering the floor, a pair of sagging brown armchairs bracketing the fireplace, and a Utility sideboard bearing an ancient radio with a chipped plastic dial. A small television stood on a square plant stand with barley-sugar legs, and there was a gateleg table against the wall with an upright chair on either side of it.

Clutter fouled every surface, heaps of old newspapers mouldered in corners, and on the mantelpiece sheaves of letters and bills spouted from behind a square electric clock whose art-deco face had a peach-mirror frame which dated it to the 1930s. The fabric had worn off its flex, and the bare wires showed through, dangling down the side of the fireplace to the unreconstructed Bakelite plug in the skirting.

The paraffin heater was milk-bar green, chimney-shaped, and stood on the hearthstone. The old man saw Slider looking at it, and said, 'Bit pongy, is it? I don't mind the smell o' parafeen meself. Some do. It's a nice, clean smell, to my mind, like the smell o' tar or queer soap. Any road up, it works out cheaper'n the electric.'

'It takes me back,' Slider said. 'We had them at home when I was a boy.' It hadn't been the smell of the paraffin he had been sniffing warily, but of the old man himself. His grey flannel trousers were much stained, and the various layers of clothes on his upper body – vest and shirt and knitted waistcoat and jumper and cardigan – were all grubby and food-spotted; his thin hair, carefully combed back in a Ronald Coleman, looked as if it hadn't been washed for weeks. He smelled terrible; but he stood alert as a pre-war pageboy, ready to spring into action, clearly pleased with Slider's presence, as though it were a social visit.

'Make you a cuppa tea, sir?' he said next.

Slider didn't want to think what might lurk in the kitchen regions. 'No, thank you. That's very kind, but no,' he said firmly. 'I just want to talk to you about—'

'That lot opposite,' he finished for him smartly. 'Hanythink I can do to 'elp, I'm most willin'. One o' your gentlemen 'as been here already.'

'Yes, I know,' Slider said. He thought the old boy would enjoy a bit of formality to make him feel important, so he took out a notebook and flipped it open. 'It's Mr Singer, isn't it?'

'Singer, that's right, sir, like the sewing-machine. Albert Singer. Won't you sit down, sir?'

The upright chairs looked less lethal, but Mr Singer was gesturing towards one of the fireside models, and Slider resigned himself and sat, keeping to the front edge so as not to have to lean back into its sinister embrace. The old man hovered attentively until Slider was down, then murmured, 'Thank you very much', and placed himself nippily in the other, hitching at his trouser legs as he sat until the pale, spindly shins gleamed above the grey socks and crimson bedroom slippers.

'Now, Mr Singer, concerning Thursday night last week—'

'Yessir, Thursday night, that's right,' he interposed eagerly.

'You mentioned that you saw a woman behaving strangely.'

'That's right,' Mr Singer said, fidgeting with pleasure. 'I mentioned it to the gentleman as come before, only 'e wasn't too int'rested in a woman, wanted to know about a man.'

Slider nodded. That was DC Cook, on loan from Ron Carver's firm, who hadn't had the patience to probe further. *Did you see a man? No? All right. No, we're not interested in a woman.* The resentment of having to work on some other firm's case, plus an old man like a troglodyte living down a smelly hole, had sent him skipping over this piece of evidence like a stone on a pond. Cook's ingrained training, however, had ensured that he made a bare note that Singer had said he saw a woman acting suspiciously, for which Slider could now be thankful.

'I 'ave to say I never pertickly noticed a man,' Mr Singer went on. 'I mean, there's people up and down the street all day, any number of 'em. I couldn't say one way or the other about any pertickler man. But this woman stuck in my mind.'

'I'd like you to tell me about her,' Slider said. 'Do you remember what time of day it was?'

'Course I do! Thursday night it was, about twenty to nine. I 'ad *The Week in Westminster* on, an' I was waitin' for nine o'clock to turn over to the Weld Service. Listen to that a lot, I do, the Weld Service. They talk proper, like the old days on the BBC – not like the modern lot, can't hardly understand a word they're saying. Gabblin' and funny accents. I don't mind a Jock or a Paddy or the rest of 'em,' he added fairly. 'Met a lot of them in the Services, in the war. They're all right. But

not on the BBC, to my mind. Oughta talk proper on the BBC.'
He paused, lost. 'I ferget where I was.'

'It was twenty to nine—'

'Oh, yes. Thank you very much. Well, like I said, I'm waitin''
to turn over for the news hour at nine, see.' He looked anxiously
at Slider. 'This is how I know what time it 'appened, you
understand?'

'Yes, I understand. Please go on,' Slider said.

'Right,' Mr Singer said, reassured. 'Well, I'm not reely listenin''
to *The Week in Westminster*, see, an' I'm standin' at the winder
lookin' out.'

'It would have been dark outside,' Slider said.

The old man nodded approvingly at his quickness. 'That's
right, sir. What I do, sometimes, is I 'ave the curtains closed,
an' I stand atween them an' the winder, see? Cuts off the light.
I can see out, but no-one else can't see me.'

'Why would you do that?'

'Oh, just lookin'. No 'arm, is it? Weld goin' by, sort o' style.'
Slider nodded. 'Anyway, I see this woman. She's standin' by the
pillar at the top o' my steps, leanin' against it, sort of, looking
at the 'ouse across the road.'

'The house where the murder happened?'

'That's right,' Singer nodded. 'Ten minutes, it must o' been
she stood there, just lookin'. Ever so still, she stood. Unusual
that. People fidget about, mostly, when they stand, but she
stood stock still, just like a soldier.' It had plainly impressed
him, for he paused to replay the image in his mind.

'And what happened next?' Slider prompted after a moment.

'Well, something must of 'appened, because she like stiffens,
as if she's seen something; then she moves away from the pillar a
little bit and looks down the road, like she's watching somethink.
She stays lookin' in that direction for a bit. And then she goes
back to watching the 'ouse. An' after about anover five minutes,
she starts across the road.'

'Could you see that from down here?' Slider asked.

'Well, sir,' the old man said, leaning forward and hitching
again at his trousers in his eagerness – they were practically
up to his knees now – 'I can't see the road, that's true, because
of the angle and the cars, but I *can* see the door of the 'ouse
opposite, on account of it's up the steps. And I see her go up

to the door and go in. Try for yourself,' he added on a happy thought.

Slider went to the window. The area wall straight ahead hid the road but, yes, he could see two thirds of Phoebe Agnew's front door. Probably the old man, given his lack of height, would only see half of it, but it would be enough to see the head and shoulders of a person going in.

'Can you say more exactly what time that was?'

'Well, sir, no,' Mr Singer said regretfully. 'Not exactly. But near as I can say it would a' bin between ten to and five to. It wasn't long afore the wireless give the time at nine o'clock, and I 'as to turn over.'

'You didn't see the woman come out?'

'No, sir. I left the winder, see, when I turned over for the news hour, and then I never went back. But she never come out afore nine.'

Slider nodded. 'Well, that's very helpful, Mr Singer, thank you.'

'Thank *you*, sir. Glad to 'elp.'

'Now, can you describe the woman to me?'

He shook his head sadly. 'I couldn't see her face – too far away, and she 'ad 'er back to me most o' the time. But I'd say she was young. Slim. Short 'air—'

'Light or dark?'

'Dark,' he said certainly. 'She 'ad trowsis on, but not them jeans, dark ones. And proper shoes, not them trainers. She looked like a lady,' he added. 'Y'know what I mean? Not one o' these modern girls, all bits an' pieces, hair like a rat's nest an' no manners.'

Slider nodded. 'I think I know what you mean.'

'An' she stood still as a soldier. I'll never forget that.'

'One last thing, Mr Singer – do you live here alone?'

'Yes, I do, sir, since the wife went. Passed on nearly ten year ago. I manage all right but—' He looked round as if suddenly struck by his surroundings, and gave a little, deprecating smile. 'I dunno what she'd think o' the way I keep the place. But it's not in a man's nacher to be tidy, is it, sir? That's what I reckon. Wimmin are nachrally tidy. Looking after us, an' tidyin' up, it's in their make-up. That's why they're no good at inventin' things. There wouldn't be no jet engines nor motor cars nor anythink if it was left to them, 'cos they only see what's in front of their eyes, an' as soon as a man makes a mess, they wanna tidy it up. But you can't make somethink without makin' a mess, now can you? It ain't reasonable. That's why you never get no wimmin inventors.'

'You could be right,' Slider said. He made a firm gesture of leaving. The melancholy chill was creeping into his bones.

'Well, that's what I think, anyway,' Mr Singer said. He saw Slider to the door. 'I 'ope you get him, sir.'

'I hope so too. You've been a great help, thank you,' Slider said.

As he climbed the steps, up out of the Stygian cave and into the sunlit uplands of normal street level, he was followed by a heartfelt and slightly wistful, 'Thank *you* sir, very much.'

He moved away down the street a little, aware that he would be watched as long as he was in sight. He noticed that, as in many streets of this vintage, the street lights were staggered on alternate sides of the road. There was one almost right outside the Agnew house, which meant that across the road, outside Mr Singer's, there was none. Someone standing at the top of Mr Singer's steps would have been in comparative darkness, watching a door in comparative light.

Maria Colehern's flat had an intercom at the street door. When she answered, he asked for Josh Prentiss. 'Is he staying with you, by any chance?'

'If you're the press,' she answered snappily, 'you can go away. I'm giving no more statements.'

'It's not the press, it's the police. I'm Detective Inspector Slider, and I want a quick word with Josh Prentiss. Is he with you? I know he's not at home or in his office.'

There was a long pause, as if consultation was going on, and then her voice came back. 'All right, come up.' The release buzzed violently.

The building was of luxury flats, built in the thirties and now extremely expensive. Either Maria Colehern's job was more important than he had realised, or she was independently wealthy. As he stood outside her glossy door in the cream-painted hall on the thick green carpet, the door to the next flat silently opened four inches and a face inspected him through the gap. When he turned his head towards it, the door closed two of the inches, but the inspection went on. This, presumably, was the neighbour who vouched for Prentiss's arrival.

Maria Colehern opened her door and looked quickly past him, down the corridor. 'Oh, you are alone,' she said. 'I thought it might be a trick.'

She was extremely attractive: slim, with a sharp-featured, high-cheekboned face, and very glossy dark hair in a bouncy bob held off her face with an Alice band. She was wearing a short mulberry skirt over navy opaque tights, and a skin-tight black Lycra top under an enormous mauve mohair sweater with the sleeves turned up. Her legs were superb, her hands long and beautifully manicured, her make-up subtle and perfect. She looked both very feminine and very capable. She also looked very cross.

'I'm sorry to disturb you,' Slider said in his mildest manner, with a smile that would have disarmed an ICBM. 'It won't take long.'

'We've been badgered to death,' she said shortly, and then, turning towards her invisible neighbour, said loudly, 'All right, Mrs Romescu, thank you, there's nothing to see.' The neighbour's door snapped to. 'Come in,' she said to Slider.

Inside it was amazingly spacious, with a huge hall and glimpses through open doors of large airy rooms furnished with antiques. The air was warm and dry, and smelled of furniture polish, cedar, Miss Colehern's perfume (Estée Lauder, he thought) and, at a level almost below detection, that ghost-memory of chicken soup with barley that haunts all pre-war service flats, as though the shades of a hundred Jewish Mammas live in the air-conditioning vents, sighing over modern eating habits.

Maria Colehern led the way into a drawing-room with a parquet floor partly covered with a thick pink and cream Chinese rug and what looked like French Empire furniture. Slider itched to examine the fabulous bronze group on the marble mantelpiece and the watercolours on the walls, but Miss Colehern had turned in the middle of the carpet to face him with the air of one who was not going to ask him to sit down.

'What is it you want?' she asked. 'I'm not sure if he'll speak to you – or even if he should, without a solicitor. I'm sorry to sound inhospitable, but our lives have been turned upside down, and I really don't think—'

'It's all right,' he said. 'It's not more trouble. I just want a piece of information.'

Her lovely lips parted for more objections when Prentiss came in behind Slider. 'Josh, I was just saying I think you ought to have Philip here if—'

'It's all right, I'll talk to him,' Prentiss said. 'It's the quickest way to get rid of him.'

Slider turned. It was a very different Josh Prentiss from the bedchamber ace he had first met: this one had crashed and burned and his propeller was six feet into the tarmac. He was unkempt, deeply haggard, and smelled of last night's drink, which he must have taken in plenty.

Prentiss must have read his own appearance in Slider's eyes because a bitter look came over his face. 'I didn't think you'd have the nerve to turn up again,' he said. 'Haven't you done enough? You've already destroyed my life – what more do you want? My political career's over, my firm's had orders cancelled, my wife's thrown me out, my chances of the Oscar are now zilch, and last night a Hollywood producer turned down a design he was crazy about a week ago. I've become untouchable, and it's all your fault.'

'Your wife's thrown you out?' Slider said, picking the bit that interested him.

'She thinks I'm a murderer,' he sneered. 'I wonder how she got that impression?'

'Did she actually say so – that she thinks you killed Phoebe Agnew?'

'Well, let me see. She looks at me with horror, shrinks away and screams "Don't touch me", and says she can't live under the same roof with me any more. What do you think that means?' Despite his ironic delivery, Slider could see the genuine distress underneath.

'I'm sorry. It's been an upsetting experience for everyone. But there are one or two things I need to confirm with you.' He went on quickly before any more objections could be voiced. 'You told me that Phoebe Agnew seemed to be worried about something that last day. Are you sure she didn't tell you anything about what was on her mind?'

'What's this, a new line you're pursuing? You've really convinced yourself I didn't do it?'

'I don't think you did it,' Slider said patiently. 'And if you'd been completely frank and honest with me from the beginning, I probably never would have. Now please, will you answer the question?'

'No, she didn't tell me. She said she wished she could but she couldn't.'

'I wonder why she couldn't tell you? Was there any area of her life she had previously kept secret from you? Do you remember coming up against a barrier like that at any point in your past friendship?'

'No,' he said. 'We talked about everything – or at least, I thought we did. She wasn't a reticent person. She had no taboos.'

'Have you any idea what she was working on recently? We've had a hint that she had a big project, something important and possibly dangerous.'

He frowned. 'Apart from her regular stuff for the papers, you mean? No, the only thing I knew was that she'd been working on a book.'

'A novel?'

'Of course not. A biography. I don't know whose, but it would be someone political, no doubt. But she'd been writing that for – oh, six months at least. I don't think you could call that important, except to her, and I don't see how it could be dangerous.'

'No,' Slider agreed. 'I know she was never married, but did she ever have a—' Slider fished around for the right words. 'Was there a "one great love of her life", do you know? A major romantic entanglement?'

'No,' Prentiss said. 'Not that I ever heard about. She was the most unsentimental person I ever met. She liked love affairs – the sex part – but they never seemed to touch her emotionally. I never knew her to be "in love" in that way. Certainly she never mentioned anyone. Why do you ask?'

'It's the meal, you see,' Slider said. 'She cooked a two-course meal for someone, and you said it was ludicrous to suppose she would have cooked it for you. So who did she do it for?'

'I can't think of anyone she'd cook for,' he said blankly.

'She'd take a bullet for you if you were her friend, but she hated cooking.'

'Do you have a key to her flat?'

Slider slipped the question in and Prentiss seemed about to answer automatically and in the negative, when he thought of something and paused.

'As a matter of fact,' he said reluctantly, 'I have got one.' He was actually blushing, and Maria Colehern looked at him in concern. 'But I didn't use it that day.'

'Josh, I really think you ought to call Philip,' Miss Colehern began urgently.

Slider shook his head at her. 'It's all right. I really *don't* think he did it. But I can see', he went on, to Prentiss, 'that it might have looked incriminating if you'd mentioned it before.'

'I wasn't hiding the fact,' Prentiss protested. 'I'd just forgotten about it. Phoebe gave it to me ages ago, when she was going abroad for a couple of weeks and I thought I might like to use her flat while she was away.' His eyes pleaded, and Slider understood that he had wanted to take a woman there, which was not a thing to mention in front of Maria. 'But I'd completely forgotten I had it. And I *didn't* use it that day.'

'Where is the key now?'

'At home, I suppose,' he said. 'We've got a key rack in the kitchen behind the door with all the spare keys on it, and I hung it on there. I haven't touched it since.'

'Did your wife know whose key it was?'

'I don't know. She may have. It might have come up in conversation, or Phoebe might have mentioned it. I really don't know. It wouldn't matter, anyway. We have neighbours' keys and friends' keys and the children's. It would have been quite natural to have Phoebe's.'

'Your wife used to be an actress, I know, but was she ever a dancer?' he asked next.

Prentiss seemed puzzled by the new direction. 'She did ballet as a child, but that's all. She was never a professional dancer, if that's what you mean.'

'So, this old injury to her back – where did that come from?'

'Old injury—' he frowned, and then his face cleared. 'Oh, you mean this present trouble she's got? It's just a pulled muscle, that's all. She slipped coming down the stairs and twisted it saving herself.'

'When was that?'

'Friday morning,' Prentiss said.

'Did you see it happen?'

'No, it was while I was at work. Why?'

'So when you went to work on Friday morning she was quite all right? No backache?'

'No. Well,' he added, 'she was still in bed when I left for work, but when I got home on Friday evening she was hobbling around in agony and she told me then that she'd done it that morning. Why are you asking? What's this about?'

Slider shook his head, pushing the question away. 'There is one last thing I want to ask you, and then I'll take myself out of your hair.' He looked up and found Maria Colehern's eyes on him, intent and troubled. She was an intelligent girl, and she seemed to be running somewhat ahead of her seedy old mate with his booze-sodden synapses. Slider realised that he needed to get her out of the way. What Prentiss chose to tell her afterwards would be his affair. 'I'd like to ask you this one question in private, if you don't mind,' he said to Prentiss. 'If Miss Colehern would be so kind as to excuse us?'

She didn't like it, but since Prentiss didn't object, she could only brand him with a searingly significant look, and leave the room. When they were alone, Slider said to Prentiss, 'I have to ask you this again, and I want you to be completely honest with me. I can't impress on you how important it is that you tell me the truth. Did you have sex with Phoebe Agnew that Thursday?'

Prentiss looked annoyed. 'No! How often do I have to say it?'

'We found your semen in her.'

'It wasn't my semen. You made a mistake. I didn't have sex with her.'

'And that's the truth? Please, it's important.'

'She and I didn't have that sort of relationship. I only ever did it with her once, way back when we were students, at a post-finals party. One of those spur-of-the-moment things on a heap of coats in someone's bedroom. I told her the next day how sorry I was, and that I'd never have done it if I hadn't been extremely drunk – though she was no more sober herself. Anyway, that was thirty years ago, and we never did it again. I doubt whether she would even have remembered it – it's certainly not something I ever think about. And that's the truth. It was always Noni and me. How can I convince you?'

'I'm convinced. Thank you,' said Slider unhappily.

Norma was waiting for him outside the station, looking elegant in trousers and heeled boots and one of those loose, wrap-around overcoats that only tall women with good figures can wear. She climbed in beside him, her cold cheeks pink, bringing a whiff of Eau de Givenchy with her, and said, 'Hi! Where are we going?'

'To see Mrs Prentiss,' Slider said. 'Thanks for coming in.'

'Pleasure. I'm only fretting myself to death over the wedding at home. Only a week to go.' She hunched her shoulders. 'So what does Mrs P know?'

'More than she's telling us, that's for sure. I don't understand it all yet.' He remembered a line from a book – he couldn't now remember which one – in which the author described a character as 'standing as still as only a soldier or an actor can'. Slider knew that stillness. It had reminded Albert Singer of a soldier, but, 'She was an actress,' he said aloud. 'It's important to remember that.'

'It is?' said Norma.

Slider didn't hear her. He had doubted Peter Medmenham at first, thinking that you never knew when an actor stopped acting. And Medmenham thought Noni Prentiss a sound actress. 'If I'm right, Mrs Prentiss has been playing a very long game indeed,' he said.

Norma caught the tone of his voice. 'You don't think *she* did it?'

'It's the same old question of who do you believe? She said Josh phoned and told her that Phoebe was dead, but he appeared not to know about it until we interviewed him. We believed her, so we thought he was lying. Then there was her remark about "the way the body was left". If he didn't divulge that little detail to her, how did she know it? And there's the question of her bad back.'

'The old dancing injury?'

'Except that she's never been a dancer – and Josh says she had no old injury. She told him she hurt it slipping down the stairs on Friday. But it occurred to me that most people who hurt their backs do it trying to lift something heavy.'

Swilley was there. 'Oh. But if she hurt it on Friday—?'

'She was still in bed when he went to work on Friday morning. So it could have been already hurting – he wouldn't know.'

'And there's the female finger-mark inside the flat,' she remembered. 'If she says she's never been there, and it proves to be hers . . .'

'Yes,' said Slider. 'And Josh says he really didn't have sex with Phoebe Agnew on Thursday.'

'But—'

'You have to ask yourself, who else had access to his semen apart from him?'

Swilley's face curved in distaste. 'Oh, good God!'

Slider said nothing more, and she did not break the silence. It was too horrible to discuss. If he was right, it was something close to monstrous.

The house was silent. 'No answer,' Swilley said at last, when she had knocked and rung extensively. 'She must be out.'

'She's in there,' Slider said abruptly.

Norma glanced at him, and shrugged. There was no arguing with instinct. She looked up at the house. The landing window was partly open. 'Did you hear that cry of distress, sir?'

Slider followed her gaze. 'Could you get up there?' he said in surprise.

'Drainpipe. Easy.'

'All right. God help us if the neighbours are watching. It seemed like a very loud cry for help,' he said for the record, and added, 'If she's there, be careful. She might be desperate.'

Swilley slid out of her coat, handed it to Slider, and swarmed with light, muscular ease up the drainpipe, which had been thoughtfully placed in a more trusting age nicely adjacent to the window. It was a sash window, and there were a few heart-stopping moments as Swilley struggled to push it up one-handed, and Slider imagined her falling, the drainpipe breaking, or Noni Prentiss appearing like Norman Bates in a wig and stabbing her through the window.

But at last Swilley got it up enough to wriggle in and disappeared. A moment later the front door opened and she let him into the hall. 'No sound anywhere,' she whispered. 'Maybe she's asleep – or out.'

Slider stood a moment, his senses prickling. 'Downstairs,' he said.

He led the way. The narrow, dark stairs bent at the bottom into the subterranean gloom of an eighteenth-century basement kitchen. It had been knocked through into one room, front to back, which gave it a window at each end; but both windows were below ground level and, as the saying goes, twice fuck all is still fuck all.

Swilley shivered, wondering how people could live like this. The kitchen floor was stone-flagged, the cupboards were old pine painted grey-green, and there was a big, battered pine table in the middle, so it probably looked much the same as when it was first built. All very desirable in a certain stratum of society, but Swilley was a Möben girl at heart. It was at least warm, with an Aga in the chimney, where the original range would have stood. She had shivered from distaste, and the suspicion that gloomy basements always meant beetles.

Slider stepped out off the stairs into the kitchen, and at once there was a rush of movement. Noni Prentiss had been pressed against the wall beside the staircase and now flung herself at him. Her right hand was upraised, and even this poor light was enough to glint melodramatically off the blade of the large butcher's knife clenched in her fist as it swept downwards.

CHAPTER SIXTEEN

Origin of the specious

Reaction was instant and instinctive. Slider heard the movement and was side-stepping and turning even as Swilley launched herself from her vantage point one step up, grabbing the wrist of the knife hand as she brought the attacker down. Swilley was tall and strong and Mrs Prentiss small and slight and it was over, there and then. Mrs P disappeared under Swilley's body, Slider was knocked out of the way, and the Kitchen Devil went scooting off across the stone floor and under the table like an electric rat.

Mrs Prentiss had made no sound before Swilley got her; she could make none after, with the breath knocked out of her; but she writhed with the strength of desperation until Slider said, 'Keep still, or you'll hurt yourself. Just stop struggling and we'll let you up.' At the sound of his voice she became still, and when Slider had retrieved the knife and put it out of harm's way, Swilley rose and helped her up, still keeping hold of her wrist.

'You're hurting me,' Noni said. Her face was deathly white, gleaming faintly in the basement gloom like a peeled hard-boiled egg.

Slider nodded to Swilley to let her go, and she rubbed her wrist with the other hand but made no other movement. She was trembling so much it almost beat the air, like wings.

'I'm sorry we startled you,' Slider said.

She looked at him with glazed, unseeing eyes. 'I thought it was him. I thought he'd come back.'

'You mean your husband?' She swayed, as if she was going to faint. Slider pulled a chair out from the table and guided her to it. 'So you were going to kill him too, were you?'

'I thought he'd come to get me,' she said.

'Come to get you? Why? Because you threw him out?' She only stared. Slider pulled out another chair and sat down facing her. 'Why did you throw him out?' She didn't answer. 'Mrs Prentiss, look at me. Why were you trying to kill your husband?'

Swilley had been looking in cupboards, and had found a bottle of Sainsbury's brandy. She poured some into a tumbler and brought it over to show Slider, who nodded. She put it down in front of Mrs Prentiss, carefully closed her icy hand round it and said, 'Drink some of this. It'll make you feel better.'

In a few minutes the bolting terror had subsided in favour of a lower-key mixture of fear and misery. Slider observed her with interest. If Josh was looking haggard, this was a woman who had been all the way to hell and only halfway back. It fitted with his suspicions; now he had to find the best way of getting her story. If she had killed Phoebe Agnew, it must have been in the grip of emotions so powerful they might well rob her of speech, even of reason. Better to come to it indirectly, he thought, and from a long way back. This jump wanted long, wide wings, or the horse would refuse.

'You've had a hard few days,' he said at last. 'You've been living with a terrible secret. But it's over now. The secret's out. I know you were at Phoebe Agnew's flat that Thursday. I know what you did there. Now it's time to tell me everything in your own words, and get it off your chest.' He nudged her hand. 'Have some more of that. That's right. You're not afraid of me, are you?' She shook her head slightly. 'Good. So, then, tell me everything. Begin with you. Tell me all about you.'

It took a little coaxing and some gentle, probing questions before she began. But then it all came out, slowly at first, but with growing fluency: a story of love and of love mistaken, of the shadow that killed it and the crop of bitter jealousy that grew up in its place.

Anona Regan had been an only child, cherished daughter of rather elderly parents. Her mother was thirty-eight when she was born, her father seven years older. He was a cobbler by trade and had his own small shop in a respectable working-class suburb of London. By the time Anona was growing up the business was doing well enough for him to hire an assistant and keep his hands clean attending the counter; a change that conferred the perilous gentility of white-collarhood on him and his family. His wife had never worked. They lived in a neat maisonette which she kept spotless; she made her own and her child's clothes, cooked the plain, unimaginative meals of the fifties, and always put on her hat to go shopping.

Anona grew up a quiet, well-mannered, docile child, bending like sea-grass to the languid tides of the elderly household; the sort of little girl in hair-slides and white socks who never had any difficulty in staying clean, who played nicely on her own and could be relied on at any meal table not to spill or speak with her mouth full. At school she gave no trouble to teachers, and occupied the unexceptional place towards the bottom of the top third.

She had a little girl's passion for ballet, and since it seemed to Mrs Regan a wholly proper, feminine interest, Anona was allowed to begin dance lessons. It proved something for which she had a talent, and though she passed the eleven-plus and could have gone to grammar school, she pleaded in a quiet way to audition for a local well-known stage school, and was allowed. There she did solidly well, though not brilliantly – the hallmark of her life – and since, unlike many of the other pupils, she was also reasonably good at the academic lessons, the headmistress said it would be the sensible thing for her to go to university, just for insurance. With a degree, she would always be able to get a job if the stage failed her.

Anona never resisted the sensible, and her parents were proud and bewildered at the idea of a child at university, something that was becoming more common by 1966, but was still outside their frame of reference. The shop was doing less well – people were throwing away shoes and buying new ones now, instead of having them mended – and there was no longer an assistant; but Mr Regan, sixty-three, said a man with his own business never had to retire. He learned how to work a machine for cutting keys and engraving dog medals, and so managed to scrape up the money to supplement Noni's grant.

Quiet, clean, obedient Noni went to UCL in the October of 1966. Decades always have a time-lag, and the sixties, in the sense that history thinks of them, were just really getting under way. London was finally breaking free of the massive undertow of the war: the last of the bomb-sites were built over, there were goods in the shops and money to buy them, restaurants were opening to serve exotic food a world away from gravy and two veg, and young people were having notice taken of them in a way that was bound to go to their heads.

At UCL Anona Regan met Phoebe Agnew, who was so different from her, and who seemed to represent everything exciting about that magic decade. It was hardly too much to say that Noni fell in love with her. Phoebe was wild and beautiful, with her strange, loose clothes and unkempt mane of red curls. Phoebe smoked, drank, and talked incessantly, said unconventional things, used swear words, understood politics; laughed out loud, spoke to lecturers as if she were their equal, and addressed members of the opposite sex with teasing frankness. She even, Noni suspected, *had* sex. Most of the girl students talked about having it, but like Noni shied away from the awful reality, Phoebe didn't talk about it much – brushing the subject only casually in passing – but that seemed only to confirm the idea that she knew enough about it first hand to take it or leave it.

Phoebe was also brilliant, a top scholar with a real talent for writing, and she knew what she wanted to use her writing for. Other students were reading English because they had been good at it at school and couldn't think of anything else to do. They supposed, vaguely, that they would eventually become teachers. But Phoebe already had a track record in political activism and journalism. Why, that summer of 1966, before even starting at university, she had wangled her way into a trip to Chile, organised by a militant student group, to build a youth centre; and while there she had actually managed to get an interview with Allende, the Marxist leader of the land reform party. The interview appeared in the official Students' Union newspaper, and was subsequently reprinted in the *Socialist Worker* and précised in the *Guardian*. Thus Phoebe proved to her impressed fellow students that she not only knew what she wanted to do, she was getting on with doing it.

It was not to be wondered at that Noni was fascinated by this vivid extrovert. What Phoebe saw in her was less obvious. Perhaps it was the attraction of opposites; or perhaps Phoebe saw that Noni was not quite as much of an opposite as it appeared. For Noni was different from the other students. She too knew what she wanted to do, and she had a talent: that became apparent when they joined Dramsoc. Not everyone who joined wanted to act: it was the fashionable society to belong to, and was therefore a means to meet the most interesting members of the opposite sex. But plays were put on, and members auditioned for parts. Phoebe got one because her intellect dictated that she would succeed at what she undertook; Noni got the lead role because she could *act*. Phoebe's respect for Noni grew; Noni copied Phoebe's style in a quiet way, and the two girls achieved a small local fame together.

Josh did not audition for plays. Josh had joined Dramsoc so that he could have the pick of the women students; and the pick of the Dramsoc members, as far as he was concerned, were Noni and Phoebe.

At first it was an equal relationship. The three of them were drawn together, and took to hanging around and going out as a threesome. 'At least, that's what I believed,' said Mrs Prentiss. So far, she had told her story in a dreamy undertone, as if it were the history of someone quite detached from her. But now a bitterness began to creep in. 'I thought it was the three of us. But I see now it was always Phoebe. Always. Always. Right from the beginning.'

'You mean – her and your husband?' said Slider.

She nodded slowly, the now empty tumbler held in both hands before her face. 'How could I compete with her?'

'Weren't they just friends? He said it was a purely platonic relationship.'

'He told you that? What a *liar* he is! A man can't be "just friends" with a woman. It doesn't happen. I should know – God, I've lived with it all these years! All the Sophies and Stephanies and Carolines – all his secretaries and researchers and whatever else he liked to call them! Well, I put up with it. In a way, it didn't matter, because he didn't care a jot about them, the little sluts. But Phoebe – how could I bear that? It was different with her. He loved her.'

'Have you any evidence that they had a physical relationship?' Slider asked.

'Evidence?' She opened her eyes wide. 'You should have

heard how he talked about her! He praised her to the skies. "Phoebe was so different – Phoebe understood – Phoebe had a real intellect." Not like poor stupid Noni, oh no! And he was always ringing her. They'd talk for hours on the phone. He asked her opinion. They had lunch together. He was always dropping in on her. And you ask me if I had any evidence?'

'It could still have been platonic—'

'Men and women don't have platonic relationships,' she said flatly. 'Not in the real world.'

There seemed no way of arguing with that. 'But she was your friend too,' Slider said.

'We did everything together at college. And afterwards she was always there. She helped me, advised me. I trusted her – she always knew better than me what to do. She had a – a *grasp* of things. I've never been clever like Phoebe, but she said I had something more important, that I had talent.' She rocked a little, mourning her friend. 'She did everything for me, sorted out all my troubles. If it wasn't for her, I wouldn't even have had Toby and Emma. Josh never wanted children – he hated his own father too much. But I wanted them so much. She told me just to stop taking the pill. I would never have dared. But she said he'd love the children once they were there, and of course he did. And when he found out what I'd done, she stopped him being angry with me. Took him away and talked to him and wouldn't let him shout at me. She always loved Toby and Emma; and they loved her. They called her Aunty Phoebe. She used to pretend to tell them off about that, but she loved it really.'

She rocked harder, and the tears began to slip out. Slider kept very still, letting the story come.

'Then when Emma went to school, it was Phoebe persuaded me to take up my career again, and made Josh use his contacts to get me on. He would never have bothered if she hadn't nagged him. He never thought my career was important. But Phoebe believed in me. She said I could be great – and I *was* good, I was!'

She met Slider's eyes in an appeal, and he nodded. 'I know you were.'

She seemed appeased, and went on. 'She always backed me up. When I got pregnant again and Josh wanted me to have an abortion because he said I was too old, she blew him up.

She said I must have the baby. She was always dead against abortion. She fought him tooth and nail and made him change his mind – anyway, made him leave me alone about it,' she amended. 'He was never really persuaded.'

'Maybe he was worried about your health,' Slider suggested.

She shrugged the intervention away. 'She wanted that baby so much, almost as much as I did. When I lost it, it was her that cried. I couldn't cry – it was all locked up inside me. But I couldn't have got through if it wasn't for her.'

She paused and wiped the tears from under her eyes with her fingers and, finding her nose was running too, rubbed it on the back of her hand – an unconscious reversion to the childhood state before appearances mattered, showing how far from her normal poise she had fallen in the crash of what had been her life.

'It sounds as though she really was your friend,' Slider said. 'She must have loved you.'

Noni stared at him. 'Yes, that's what I thought. But I see now it was all an act. It's only in the past few years I've started to realise what was really going on. Now I know what a fool I've been. She was playing me along, while she and Josh carried on behind my back. It was them all the time, the two of them, heads together, laughing at me. I was the outsider.'

'But it was *you* he married,' Slider said.

'Yes, and how he regretted it!' she cried bitterly. 'He only married me because she'd gone away somewhere. The moment she came back he brought her home, and after that they started their game of making a fool of me. *That's* the real reason she made me have the kids – to keep me out of the way. She was jealous and wanted him to herself. I didn't see it at the time, but I see it now.'

'But you said she really loved the children – and they her.'

'Yes. She did. I suppose she couldn't help it. Oh, I don't know! Leave me alone, can't you! She's dead now, and it's all over. It doesn't matter any more. Nothing matters any more.'

She began to cry in earnest, putting her face into her hands. It was plain she was deeply confused about the situation; that she had loved her friend and even now, having convinced herself that there had been an affair going on, didn't want to believe it.

Slider saw how the layers of emotion – of love and admiration,

of hurt and jealousy – had been confounded by a basic lack of
understanding, an inability really to see what Phoebe Agnew had
been about. A woman like her was so different from Noni that
her motives must always have been a mystery. What you don't
understand, you can only interpret according to your own lights.
So, there could be no friendship without sex between a man
and a woman; and an unmarried Phoebe could only have been
jealous of and therefore hostile towards Josh's wife Noni. Add
to that Noni's emotional breakdown following the loss of a child
and the failure of her career, and the comparison of that with
Phoebe's burgeoning success, and you had a seething cauldron
of love and hatred that could easily spill over into action.

Probably it went all the way back to university, when Noni had
wondered what clever Phoebe saw in her, and the seed of doubt
was planted. Perhaps the soil was already fertile: didn't they say
that all actors were insecure? That they became actors to escape
from themselves into personae that they could control? And then
Phoebe had to go on from strength to strength, winning fame
and awards, while Noni never made it to the top, and had only
her marriage to comfort herself with. And even in that one poor
sphere of achievement, all she had to hug to herself, it seemed
Phoebe outshone her. Josh liked Phoebe better, praised her to
his wife. Naturally the wife came to think that a philandering
stud like Prentiss must be having an affair with her. So the
stage had been set for the action in which Anona Regan was
sure she could play the leading role with conviction.

The tears were subsiding now. Swilley had found a box of
tissues on the dresser, which she put down before Mrs Prentiss,
and mopping up was now taking place.

'Tell me what happened on Thursday,' Slider said.

The story came out painfully. Despite Joanna's caustic comments, Josh Prentiss hadn't been wrong about Noni's being at
a difficult age. She had started to have menopausal symptoms
and was feeling unhappy, unloved and unattractive, especially
as she and Josh had fallen into a pattern of hardly noticing each
other. He was busy with his career, and she had nothing much
to do, with the children gone, her own career in ruins, and her
husband away from home more and more of the time.

But on Thursday he had said he would be home all day – he
hadn't mentioned his intention to go out in the evening – and

following the hallowed advice of women's magazines through the ages, she had decided to try to make herself attractive to him. She began by taking an interest in his work and making bright conversation; but when he dismissed her rather testily, she had turned to plan B and concocted a delicious meal for him. It, or the wine that accompanied it, had done the trick, and she had been able to persuade him into bed, where they had engaged in the first sexual congress in many a long moon. So her chagrin and fury had been all the greater when he jumped out of bed and rushed away afterwards with what she thought was a lame excuse. She felt spurned.

Left alone, she had brooded on her wrongs and, as she had done more and more lately, blamed Phoebe for all of them.

'So you went round to her flat. Oh, yes, I know that,' Slider said. 'You were seen going in. There's no point in denying it.'

Mrs Prentiss sighed. 'All right. I went to have it out with her,' she agreed on a downward note.

'You didn't know your husband was going there that evening?'

'He said he was going out on Government business. I knew that was a lie. I knew he was going to see a woman. But I didn't think it was Phoebe. He never tried to hide it when he was going to see Phoebe – he just told me straight out.'

'So what happened?' Slider asked.

'I walked round there, but when I got to the door I could hear voices inside. A man's voice. She wasn't alone.'

'Did you recognise the voice?'

'No, I couldn't really hear well enough. I could just hear it was a man. So I—' She paused for a long time, her eyes fixed on some internal horizon. 'I gave it up and went home,' she concluded feebly.

Slider leaned forward a little. 'That's not true,' he said sternly. 'I thought you were going to tell me the truth?'

'I am,' she said faintly.

'You didn't just go round there to talk to her, did you? You wouldn't have needed the key for that.'

'The key?'

'The key to Phoebe Agnew's flat.'

'I don't know what you're talking about,' she said, but she was looking at him now. She seemed appalled and fascinated at the same time.

'You took the key to her flat, which she had given your husband long ago, and which hung on the rack alongside those to your children's flats. Did that seem like an insult to you? Anyway, you took the key so that you could slip in without her hearing. And what else did you take with you? A pair of tights, was it?'

Noni's lips moved, but no sound came from them.

'Phoebe never wore tights, did she? She *always* wore trousers, so the odds were she didn't even possess a pair. Anyway, you could hardly have taken time out to search for them when you got there, so you took your own. You knew she'd been drinking heavily recently, and you thought that with luck she'd be pretty well out of it by half past eight, so if you let yourself in you could creep up on her and get something round her throat before she knew you were there.'

'I wouldn't really have done it,' Noni whispered, her face drawn with horror. 'You can't, can you? Not how ever angry you are, you can't kill a person – not unless you're mad.'

'But you were mad,' said Slider. 'Mad with jealousy. This woman who had been your friend had outshone you all your life, and now you thought she'd stolen your husband from you. So killing Phoebe Agnew wasn't enough. You wanted to punish your husband as well – your husband who had made love to you that afternoon, and then left you to go to his other woman. You had to kill her, and make it look as though he had done it. You had to make it *absolutely certain* that he would be charged with the murder. When did you hatch your monstrous plot, Mrs Prentiss? And how did you get hold of the condom full of your husband's semen?'

Mrs Prentiss stared at Slider as if he were the hangman approaching with the noose. 'I didn't—'

'And then, when we came to question you, to make absolutely sure we'd suspect him, you told lies about where he was, so that when we found out they were lies we'd think you were trying to protect him. Everything you said to us, that sounded so innocent, was meant to incriminate him. A very long game you've been playing, Mrs Prentiss, and it almost worked. But you were careless. You left your fingerprints behind. We've found your fingerprints – in a flat you say you've never been in.'

She went cheese-coloured and doubled up, and Swilley came

round the table to take hold of her neck and push her head down
between her knees. 'Take it easy. Don't try to sit up. Breathe
slowly and deeply – that's right.'

When she had recovered enough to speak, she said falteringly,
'You're wrong, so wrong—'

'I don't think so. That's how you hurt your back, shifting her
body to the bed. You had no old back injury. And you told your
husband you'd slipped down the stairs.'

'That's true, I did say that. But I didn't kill her! Listen,' she
said desperately, 'and I'll tell you.'

It was like a madness that had taken hold of her, she said.
When Josh got out of bed, saying he was going out, she had
felt as though he had slapped her face. After making love as
they had, she had thought he would spend the evening with her.
She asked where he was going, and he said it was Government
business. She screamed that that was a lie, he was going to
see some woman. He lost his temper and yelled back. Then,
apparently realising that arguing was only slowing him down,
he calmed down and repeated that it was Government business,
and added that the only woman he ever saw apart from her was
her best friend Phoebe. Presumably he thought that would allay
her jealous fears. Instead it had convinced her that Phoebe was
at the bottom of all her troubles.

'He went into the bathroom to shower, and he threw the
used condom into the waste-paper basket in there,' she recited
tonelessly. 'I saw him do it before he shut the door. He never
put them down the lavatory. He said it blocked it up. The basket
has a bin-liner in it. When he'd washed and changed he went
downstairs without a word, and I lay there in bed, looking at
that bin. I could just see it, inside the bathroom door.'

'So you went and got the condom out again.'

She nodded slowly. 'It came to me all at once, the whole
plan. I thought I'd kill her and then put his semen in her so
that there was no way he could deny he'd been with her. I
had a little plastic syringe I'd got from the vet years ago for
giving the cat his medicine. I used that to get the semen out. I
put a pair of tights in my pocket, and took the key and walked
round there.'

'Go on. What time did you get there?'

'About half past eight, I suppose. I don't know exactly. I went to the door first and listened, and heard the voices inside. So I knew he was still there. I went and stood across the road where I could see the house and waited. It was then I started to calm down. I realised I couldn't do it. You can think of killing someone, you can want to, but when you actually face them alive – you can't really, can you? I wanted her dead, but I'm not that ruthless. So I was going to give it up and go home, when the door opened and I saw him come out.'

'Saw who come out?' Slider asked quickly.

'Josh, of course.' Her voice hardened. 'Seeing him come out started it all up again. I imagined them in there together, talking, laughing, making love. I wondered how many other times he must have gone to her without telling me. I could just see them, laughing about me and how easy I was to fool. I *hated* him then.' She stopped abruptly.

'So what did you do?' Slider prompted.

'I waited a long time to make sure he'd really gone, then I went across and let myself in quietly. Crept into the sitting room. And there she was, sitting in the chair, dead. It was so horrible! I can't tell you.'

She stopped for a bit, trembling, leaking tears, while she wound herself up for the rest. Slider waited, patient as nemesis, the awful sympathy that invites confession.

'I realised, you see, that I'd been living with a murderer. I've been living with him ever since. Can you imagine what that's been like? Every day, wondering whether he'd come home and do the same thing to me. I kept seeing her in my mind's eye – her face all swollen, that mark round her neck . . . If he did that to her, what might he do to me? When I heard you coming just now, I thought it was him, come to get me.'

'I see,' Slider said.

'That's why in the end I went through with the rest of the plan. I thought if I just left her like that he'd never be caught. I knew he was clever. He'd get out of it somehow.'

'You could have told us what you knew,' Swilley said.

Noni had forgotten she was there. She looked at her blankly and then said, 'How could I? He'd have found out and killed me. And what if you hadn't believed me? It would be just my word against his. So I did the rest of it, to make sure he got caught. It was horrible, horrible – I can't tell you! And now you've let him go! Why did you arrest him and then let him go?'

'Go on with your story,' Slider said. 'What happened next?'

She hunched her shoulders, pressing her clenched fists against her breastbone in a defensive pose. 'I thought I should die. In that room with her, looking like that. He must have done it with his tie, I suppose. And she was still warm.' She closed her eyes and swallowed, and her throat clicked. 'He'd done it only minutes before. She'd been alive only minutes before, and now she was dead. I'd never seen a dead body before. I think it made me a little bit mad. Otherwise I couldn't have—' She shuddered.

'Tell me,' said Slider.

'I dragged her over to the bed. She was so heavy, I had a terrible job getting her up onto it. That must be when I hurt my back. Then I took her clothes off – just the bottom ones. Tied her arms to the bed rail. And put – put the semen in her with the syringe.' She met Swilley's gaze. 'I had to make sure he was caught – and it didn't matter to her any more. And I threw the condom into the loo. No-one but me would know he didn't do that. I almost flushed it away – reflex reaction – before I stopped myself. Stupid.' She shook her head.

Slider's mind was reeling. 'That's when you left the finger-mark,' he said. All the brain-ache this woman had given them! 'But don't you realise, if he had done it using a condom, there wouldn't be any semen in her?'

She looked blank. 'No,' she said faintly. 'I never even thought of that. Stupid of me.'

'I suppose you didn't do badly for a first attempt,' said a grim Swilley. 'Did you wipe your finger-marks off everything else before you left?'

'I didn't touch anything else. I was very careful. I pulled my sleeve over my hand to open the door on the way out.'

Slider pulled himself together. 'Is this the truth you've told me now?'

'The truth,' she said, out of the blackness where she watched the endless reel of her own private X film: the appalling thing she had found; horror and guilt at what she had been prepared to do; horror and fear at discovering her husband had done it; the week she had spent living with it, with him, and wondering what was going to happen next.

'Do you wear contact lenses, Mrs Prentiss?' Slider asked.

She lifted her eyes to him, faintly surprised. 'No. I have glasses for driving, but I don't wear them otherwise.'

'You're short-sighted, then?'

'Only a little.'

'You were watching the house from across the road, and it was dark, and the street lamps aren't very bright in Eltham Road. You saw a man come out of the house that you thought was your husband, but it wasn't. No, I mean it. By the time you reached the house your husband was some distance away, in someone else's house. We have witnesses.'

'It was him. I saw him.'

'No. Your husband didn't kill Phoebe Agnew. He has an alibi. The person you saw come out of the flat was only someone who looked like him,' said Slider with awful pity.

She was silent a long moment as it sank in. 'Oh, dear God, what have I done?'

'What you've done', Slider said, 'is to interfere with the scene of a crime and seriously impede our investigation, while attempting to incriminate your husband for something he didn't do. Perverting the course of justice is a grave criminal offence for which the maximum penalty is ten years' imprisonment.'

Mrs Prentiss stared as another layer of desperate realisation was uncovered in her mind. 'I was so sure it was him,' she whispered. And then, 'What happens now?'

'You'll have to come with us to the station and make a complete statement. After that we'll decide whether charges will be laid against you,' Slider said. Swilley glanced at him, noting his distracted tone of voice. He was going through the motions here, but his mind was already galloping off, trying to work out the next step. If it wasn't Prentiss and it wasn't Mrs Prentiss, who the hell was it? They weren't just back at square one, they hadn't even got the board out of the toy cupboard yet.

CHAPTER SEVENTEEN

First among equines

'Damn and blast,' said the Syrup, quite mildly, all things considered. 'That's what comes of working weekends.'

'Swilley's taking her statement now,' Slider said. 'As far as charging her's concerned, I think she's pretty near the edge already—'

'Yes, well, that's not your decision to make,' Porson said sharply. 'Perverting the course is a very serious matter indeed, and not something to exercise leniency over. Besides, we've already got the Home Secretary in a right two-and-eight about Josh Prentiss and Giles Freeman. And this is a government that likes to be seen as above repute. Caesar's wife and all that. They don't want any more scandal.'

'I doubt whether charging Prentiss's wife with trying to stick him with the murder will absolutely kill all scandal stone dead, sir.'

'Don't be satirical, Slider. In your position, you can't afford it. We're a week into the investigation and what have we got to show for it? You've gone at Prentiss like a bull at a china gate, and now we're left with egg all over the carpet and a hostile press praying for our blood! We've got off lightly so far, but the Sundays have had all week to sharpen their pens, and they'll have the knives out for us all right. So you'd better have some plan of action up your sleeve, or there's going to be some pretty derisory comments made higher up the echelon, I can tell you.'

Slider tried not to shrug. What else could he have done but follow up the obvious leads? But bosses had to yell at you: they had bigger bosses upon their backs to bite 'em. 'Well, we know that there was someone else there on the Thursday,' he began, 'because of the finger-marks—'

'Oh, thank you very much!' Porson barked. 'An insightive comment, given that we know she didn't strangle herself! Is that what I gave up my afternoon's golf for?'

Porson played golf? Slider stared at him absently, wondering whether he wore a cap, and how he kept the rug on on windy days. Porson, fortunately, did not note the direction of the stare, only that it was blank. 'Yes, well, you look as if you could do with a bit of time off yourself,' he said more kindly. 'You're played out, laddie. When you've finished with Mrs Prentiss, you'd better go home. Give the old grey matter a rest. Have a shit, a shave and a shower and come up with some new lines to follow up.' His eyes followed Slider to the door, and he added, 'We can still hope for something on Wordley. I'd really enjoy nailing that sod.'

'I'll see what I can do, sir,' Slider promised.

Joanna had a rehearsal and concert at Milton Keynes on the Sunday, which was almost just as well, since he had some heavy-duty thinking to do. He was a long way down when the phone rang, and it took him a while to surface and get out to the hall to answer it.

'Bill? Chrise me, laddie, I thought you weren't going to answer. Asleep over the Sundays, were you?'

'Oh, hello, Nutty.' It was Nicholls, the uniform sergeant on duty. 'No, I was thinking, that's all. Took me a while to realise the phone was ringing. What's up?'

'We just had a phone call from Piers Prentiss. He had a bit of information for you. Didn't sound like much, but he seemed nervous as hell, so I thought I'd mebbe pass it on straight away.'

'You never know what might be important,' Slider said. 'What did he have for me?'

'He said he'd just remembered it – though I suspect he'd been a wee while working out whether or not to pass it on. But he said that while he was on the phone to your murder victim on the evil day itself – is this making sense?'

'Yes, go on.'

'Okay. While he was on the phone to her, he heard something in the background – in her flat, d'ye see? It was a pager going off.'

'Is that it?' Slider said after a pause.

'That's it, chum. Any use?'

'I don't know. You say he sounded nervous?'

'Aye, ahuh. Wettin' himself.'

'Well, then, evidently he thought it was important, though I can't quite see why for the moment. Unless he recognised the particular bleep.'

'Or he heard something else he hasn't coughed up yet,' Nicholls suggested.

'Yes. I'll give him a ring and ask. Well, thanks, Nutty. All serene down there?'

'Quiet as a church.'

Slider rang off, went to look up Piers Prentiss's number, and dialled. There was no answer. Slider was a little surprised – he'd have expected an answering machine. He rang Nicholls, and asked him to get Piers to ring him direct on his mobile, should he be in contact again.

As soon as he put the phone down, it rang again. This time it was Irene.

'Oh, God, I'm sorry. I was supposed to arrange something with you and the kids for the weekend,' he remembered.

'It's all right,' she said resignedly. 'I didn't tell them it might be on because I guessed it wouldn't be.'

'I'm really sorry. It's this case—'

'It's always a case. *You're* a case, Bill Slider! I sometimes think the Job is all there is to you. Take it away and you just wouldn't be there at all.'

It was too close to home, this comment. He thought of Joanna going to Amsterdam without him. 'I think you're right. Maybe I should give it up.'

She wasn't used to him agreeing with her. Even now she didn't want to hurt him. 'Oh, no,' she said. 'I didn't mean it. You're a good copper, and it's important work.'

'I don't know,' he said glumly. 'The Job's not like it used to be. And I start wondering whether there isn't more to life than this. I've always given you and the kids a raw deal. You've always come second to it.'

'No,' she said, defending him against himself. 'Maybe it wasn't always a bed of roses, but your job put food on the table, that's what matters.'

He smiled to himself. 'You're a very traditional woman,

aren't you? There are things a husband does and things a wife does.'

'Well, I happen to think men and women were made that way, that's all, and these hard career women cause more trouble than they know. If they stayed home and cooked for their men and their children, the world might be a better place. There might not be so much crime to keep you working weekends.'

That was one very neat link. TV would love her. 'Look, we'll do it next weekend, definitely – all right?'

'If your case is finished by then.'

'If it's not, *I'll* be finished,' he said.

He looked at his watch when he put the phone down. Joanna wouldn't be back for hours yet. He wondered how Atherton's trip to Newmarket had gone. He could do with someone to talk to, he told himself; and if Atherton wanted to exercise his culinary skills on their behalf, he wouldn't object to that, either.

He dialled the number, and a cheery Atherton answered at once. Oh, hi! Yes, he'd had a great day, thanks. Of course, come on round. Had Slider eaten? He was just going to knock something up. Nothing special, just a store-cupboard job. No, it was all right. Well, okay, Slider could bring a bottle, if he liked. Red for preference.

Slider cleared up, left a message for Joanna in case he stayed late, and drove round, calling in at an Oddbins on the way for a bottle of Fleurie that he knew wouldn't make Atherton's eyebrow twitch. He was very tired and looking forward to a bit of comfort, and not prepared to have the door opened to him by WDC Tony Hart, dressed in tight ginger moleskin trousers and a white ribby sweater that left everything to be desired.

''Ullo,' she said cheerfully. 'S'prised to see me?'

'Surprised doesn't begin to cover it,' he said.

Atherton appeared behind her. 'Tony came with me to Newmarket,' he said. 'She's got a good eye for a horse.'

'Spent me formative years down bettin' shops,' she said. 'Me dad liked a flutter.'

'Get him a drink,' Atherton commanded her. 'I've got to get back to my chopping.'

Slider was divested of his coat and installed in an armchair with a glass of wine and Oedipus, the black former tomcat, kneading bread on his knees and purring like a DC10 about to take off. He glanced at the open door to the kitchen, and said quietly to Hart, 'Well?'

'Well what?' she bluffed.

He gave her a stern look. 'What are you doing here?'

She pulled a chair from the dining-table, reversed it and sat astride it, facing Slider. 'Listen,' she said broadly, 'I'm offered it on a plate, I'm gonna take it, ain't I?'

'Are we talking about the same thing?'

'You don't like me goin' out wiv Jim?' she said. 'Well, the way I see it, it's up twim, ennit?'

'He's seeing someone else.'

'All's fair in love an' war. This uvver bint can take care of 'erself – an' so can I.'

Slider shook his head wearily. 'It's none of my business. I just don't want him to get hurt.'

'Yeah, well, s'prisingly enough, I care about that an' all. What jer fink, I'm chasin' 'im for 'is money?'

Slider took the proffered side turning gratefully. His own emotional life was in enough strife not to want to get mixed up in Atherton's. 'Talking of which, what do you think of the racehorse scheme?'

'It looks all right. Dead posh stables an' everything. Nobs wiv nobby voices. Nice-lookin' gee-gees.' She shrugged. 'Personally, I fink he's nuts, puttin' all his dosh into it, but that's none o' my business. If he wants to chuck it about, that's up twim.'

'They told him there'd be a return of twenty-four per cent,' Slider said.

'If there was,' she said with unexpected shrewdness, 'evryone'd be in on it, wouldn't they?'

'Can't you talk him out of it?'

'Like I said, it's not my business.'

'If you really cared about him, it would be.'

The cheery, throw-away air disappeared like a conjuring trick. She looked suddenly upset. ''Course I care about 'im. An' if you ask me he's 'eadin' for a nervous breakdown. So what're *you* doin' about it? Don't dump it on me. *You're* the one who ought to've seen that coming. You're his boss.'

Atherton appeared with a plate of bruschetti. 'You two quarrelling? What about?'

'You,' said Hart, with an edge to her voice. 'Satisfied?'

'Oh, what it is to be loved,' he said, with one of his own. He handed the plate. 'Everyone wants a little piece of me, but there just isn't enough to go round.'

Slider gave Hart a hard look, and asked him conversationally, 'How was your horse?'

'Fantastic,' said Atherton. 'Brilliant. Ran like a hare – well, like a racehorse really. Bloody fast. Beat everything else on the gallop. Clever, too. As it passed us I heard it say to the horse next to it, "I don't know your mane, but your pace is familiar."'

'Seriously,' Slider pleaded.

'I tell you, it's good. Carrington – he's the boss-feller there – timed him while we watched, and the time's up there with the best. Everyone was very impressed.'

'What are the others like – in the syndicate?'

'All businessmen. All successful men in their own field. They wouldn't be going into it if it wasn't pukka. Like I told you, these days it's not a mug's gamble, it's a sound investment.'

'I don't see what "these days" has got to do with it,' Slider said, 'but – anyway, you're going for it?'

'Bloody right I am,' Atherton said. 'Eat all these. I've got mine in the kitchen.'

He departed. Hart looked at Slider. 'Pax?' she suggested. 'I fink he's a plonker parting wiv his akkers, and no-one ever got rich on the ponies, but it's his business, all right?' Her look hardened. 'And so am I.'

Slider remembered how when Hart had first joined them, Joanna had believed she fancied him, Slider. How wrong she had been proved! 'All right,' he said, 'pax it is.'

She crossed her arms on the back of the chair, pushing her bosom up under the sweater to sensational effect. Those ribs were never meant to take that sort of strain. 'So, how's *your* love life?' she asked casually. 'Married what'sername yet, Joanna?'

He didn't stay long at Atherton's flat. With Hart there, he couldn't talk much to him about the case, and no other conversation flowed easily between the three of them, despite Hart's efforts to amuse. They ate a soufflé ham and mushroom omelette with a salad and diced sautéed garlic potatoes – Atherton's scratch, store-cupboard meal – and drank the Fleurie, and then

Slider left them to whatever they were going to do together, which to judge by the way Hart wound herself round Atherton in the doorway probably wasn't a game or two of backgammon followed by the late-night movie and a cup of cocoa.

While he was driving home, his mobile rang, and he pulled over and stopped at the side of the road to answer it.

''Ullo, Mr S.' It was Tidy. 'I got a bit a gen for you.'

'Good man.'

'Turns out your two villains was involved in a murder after all.' Slider's heart jumped, but Tidy went on, 'Trouble is, it wasn't your murder.'

'What?'

'Yeah, well, this is 'ow it was. They done this job Fursdy arternoon, right, this old girl lives in 'olland Park. Your bloke 'ad got info she was gonna be at a weddin', so they could just walk in and out easy as pie. Well, Fursdy night they was out 'itting the 'igh spots, right? Celebratin'. Only Little Tommy, right, he's a moufy git, and he was talkin' it up big about the gear they'd got. So your bloke, Diction'ry, tells 'im to shut it. 'Ad a right ding-dong in this club down Earlsfield—'

'Earlsfield?'

'Well, they'd been travellin' a bit by then. That's where they'd fetched up. Anyway, they goes back to this flat wiv this other bloke they picks up at the club, game o' cards, few drinks, right? Then the row break out again. It all turns nasty. Your bloke's elephants, Little Tommy's a nutter, *'e* winds *'im* up, Little Tommy does 'im wiv a knife.'

'This is still Thursday night?'

'Yeah. Well, early hours o' Friday. They done the job about free o'clock time, an' they've been boozin' ever since. Now it's after midnight. So, anyway, Little Tommy sticks 'im an' as it away on 'is toes, right, so the other bloke, the bloke whose flat they're in, 'e dumps Diction'ry down St George's A & E and scarpers issell.'

'And that's where Dictionary is now?'

'I reckon. You'd better ask 'em. Or the local rozzers. Mr Nidgett, ennit, down Wandsworth nick? He'll tell you.'

Joanna came home shortly after he got back.

'Hello! Where've you been?' she said. 'I called you before I left.'

'At Atherton's. He gave me supper.' He didn't want to have to mention Hart's presence, so he hurried in with Tidy's phone call. 'So a rather tasty suspect has been taken out of the frame. Not that I ever really fancied him, but it would have been nice to clobber a real villain for this one.'

'I love it when you talk dirty,' she said.

'Wordley's in intensive care in St George's,' Slider said, 'and not likely to live, according to Derek Nidgett, the DI over at Wandsworth. They didn't know who he was to begin with – had no ID on him – but one of the porters recognised the bloke who brought him in and they eventually traced him back to his flat. So then he – the other bloke – saw the game was up and started rowing for the shore. Now they're looking for Tucker on an expected murder charge. But the upshot is that Wordley's accounted for from about six o'clock onwards, and we know Phoebe Agnew was still alive at a quarter to nine because that's when Piers Prentiss spoke to her. And in fact, that must have been only minutes before she was killed.'

He went on to tell her about the rest of his day, and Noni Prentiss's part in it.

'So what do you do now?' Joanna asked after a respectful silence.

He shrugged. 'Go back. Look into Agnew's life in more detail – if we can find it. Look for inconsistencies. Find out what she was up to.'

'You've wasted an awful lot of time on these Prentisses of various hues.'

'Yes,' he said feelingly. 'But we had to check out the obvious people first. And at least now we know we aren't looking for someone who faked a rape to cover his tracks. Whoever strangled her left immediately. There was a report of a man with a file or something under his arm, fixing his tie as he walked along the road. That could be something. And there's this business of her telling a colleague she was doing some important work that might be dangerous.'

'Sounds like baloney to me,' Joanna said. 'What was she, working for MI5? I'll tell you', she added, putting the kettle on, 'what seems like an inconsistency to me. That bit about her persuading Mrs Prentiss to have the baby. These radical, feminist, anti-establishment, political types are usually fiercely pro-abortion, but you say Mrs P said she was dead against it. Cup of tea?'

'Yes, please.'

'And how was Jim?' she asked abruptly.

'He went to see his horse. He said it was fast. He's still determined to go through with it.'

'I know. I spoke to Sue a while ago. He'd just phoned her to tell her how wrong she was about it.' She looked at his unhappy face and added, 'Don't worry too much. If he took the trouble to provoke her about it, at least it means he cares about her opinion. He wouldn't bother to try and upset her if she meant nothing to him.'

'I suppose not.'

'It must have been after you left that he phoned her. How did he seem? Did you think he was miserable?'

Slider thought of Atherton bidding him goodbye, standing grinning in his doorway with Hart's elastic limbs wrapped round him, a glass of wine in his hand, and Elgar One on the CD player.

'Yes,' he said.

Swilley came into Slider's room. Atherton was perched on the edge of the window-sill, hands in pockets, legs crossed at the ankle, every inch the elegant, insouciant Englishman – Richard E. Grant, but without the flurried awkwardness. He and Slider had been discussing the case; Slider, sitting behind his desk, seemed gradually to be being walled in by the piles of files, which were growing at the rate of Manhattan skyscrapers.

Swilley had more papers in her hand.

'Ah, here comes the lovely Norma,' Atherton said, 'on lissom, clerical, printless toe. Is that one of Hymen's lists you're entering?'

Swilley never encouraged him. 'Is that a burk I see before me?' she countered. 'Boss—'

'That's me,' Slider said, thinking it was time to get into the conversation.

'You wanted us to look for anomalies. Well, there's this. I don't know if it's anything,' she added apologetically.

'Anything could be anything. Fire away.'

'Well, you know there was a bunch of stuff on one of the chairs under a blanket?'

'Yes. I imagined she'd shoved it there in the course of clearing up.'

'You could be right. There was some recent correspondence and a telephone bill on top, so it could have been lying about waiting to be dealt with when she cleared.'

'And some clean underwear,' Slider added, 'which she hadn't had time to put away yet.'

'That's right,' Swilley said. 'So maybe she was interrupted or ran out of time or whatever, and just shoved it all under the blanket to get rid of it and make the room look tidy.'

'I wish I knew *why* she wanted the room to look tidy,' Slider said fretfully.

'To impress the person she cooked the supper for,' Atherton said.

'That's just the same question moved sideways,' said Slider. 'Anyway, go on. What have you found?'

'It's a letter from a female called Sula Brissan, dated Monday the eighteenth of Jan – so if she sent it first class it would have arrived on the Tuesday or Wednesday, depending what time of day she posted it. She says she encloses a copy invoice for the work done up to the beginning of December and she says, "I hope you won't mind my asking you to settle this outstanding invoice as soon as possible. You know that I was working almost exclusively on your project, and cash is always a bit tight after Christmas. Any time you want me to pick up the research again, I shall be more than willing."'

'And was it an outstanding invoice? Very large, or covered with gold leaf or something?' Atherton asked.

'Couldn't say. It wasn't there,' Swilley said.

'So Agnew was a tardy payer,' Atherton commented. 'Just what I'd have expected. She had a mind above material things.'

'It wasn't that she couldn't afford it,' Swilley said. 'She had plenty in her bank account. But that wasn't my point. The thing is, this letter suggests she's done quite a bit of work for Agnew, but I can't find the invoice or any trace of her – the Brissan woman – amongst the papers. You'd have thought there'd be a letter from her or another invoice or something with her address or handwriting on it, but no, nothing. Well, it just occurs to me that if there *was* a file missing from that filing cabinet, maybe that's where the Brissan stuff went.' She looked at Slider hopefully.

'And in that case, she might be in a position to tell us what Agnew was working on in the last few months,' Slider completed for her. 'Well, it's a thought. Where does she live, this female?'

'It's an address in Fulham.'

'Not too far. Okay, let's see what she's got to say. No, wait, not you,' Slider said to Swilley. 'I'd sooner have you on the files—'

'Who wouldn't?' Atherton murmured.

Swilley turned on him. 'If you've got something to say, say it out loud.'

'He can't tell talk from mutter,' Slider said kindly. 'Don't mind him. I'd like you to keep going through the papers. You', he turned to Atherton, 'can go and interview Miss Brissan.'

'Sounds like a drunken beauty queen,' Atherton said cheerfully. 'Me for that! Giss the address, oh blest police siren. Ta. If I'm not back in two days, send the RCMP.'

Slider translated with an effort. 'The Mounties?'

'No, a really cuddly motherly prostitute,' said Atherton.

Swilley watched him go. 'You shouldn't encourage him, sir, you really shouldn't.'

CHAPTER EIGHTEEN

We shall not all sleep, but we shall all be changed

Atherton had visualised Sula Brissan as tall, sveldt, young, and languid with unfulfilled passion. She turned out to be a brisk woman in her forties with short, thick grey hair; but she did have paralysingly lovely, deep-set blue eyes, and had evidently been sexy for so much of her life that she regarded Atherton with the unmistakable look of a woman who expects to be fancied. Obediently, he fancied her, so they got on well.

'Yes, I read about it, of course. It's terrible,' she said, making tea and loading the washing machine at the same time. To judge by the laundry, Atherton thought, exercising his detective skills, she had teenage children rather than little ones, which might not present such difficulties if she wanted to break out. On the other hand, there was a small baby to hand, in a car seat set on the floor; a steriliser/warmer stood on the window-sill, and a couple of bottles and teats were in the drying-rack. Atherton's signals were confused.

'And you've no idea who did it?' she went on.

'Not at the moment.'

'There was all that speculation in the papers about Josh Prentiss, of course,' she said thoughtfully. 'Poor Josh, it's buggered his career. Not that I like him much, but I'd never have thought he was capable of murder – and in any case, why Phoebe? They were old friends.'

'You know him – Prentiss?'

'I know just about everybody,' she said, without conceit. 'I was a Parliamentary researcher for years, and then I did all the Westminster stuff for IRN, before I went freelance.'

'So tell me, did Agnew and Prentiss make the beast with two backs?' Atherton asked.

'No,' she said with a pitying laugh at his naivety. 'It wasn't like that. Everybody knew they were just friends. It was a famous case – proof that platonic relationships can exist. No, they were like two old schoolfriends, or brother and sister, or something. She was more of a brother to him than his own brother, really.'

'You know Piers Prentiss as well?'

'I've met him,' she said. 'I don't know him well.' She handed him his tea in a mug. The kitchen was large and extended, untidy in the way of a much-used family room, and full of thin sunshine and the companionable noise of the washing machine and, in the background, the unheeded radio tuned to Capital. A fat Cyprian cat sat patiently at the glass-panelled back door, waiting to be let in. Middle-class family life in the nineties. 'So what did you want to know?' she said, leaning against the sink and sipping her tea.

'What was the research you'd been doing for her?'

'It was background for a political biography she was writing.'

'Biography of whom?'

She hesitated a moment. 'Oh well, she's dead now so I don't suppose it matters. But it was a big secret. Nobody knew except me and her. It was Richard Tyler.'

Atherton raised an eyebrow. 'He's a bit young for a biography, isn't he?'

She smiled. 'It's not how old you are but how much you've done. Look at all the biographies of the Beatles that came out as soon as they were famous, and they were even younger. She's been working on Richard for about six months now, ever since he became a junior minister. He's a remarkable person, and due to be remarkabler. Do you know about him?'

'That he's a member of the Freeman set and very in at Number Ten,' Atherton said.

'Oh, you do know your political gossip? I somehow never thought of policemen as being interested in things like that.'

'Most aren't. I'm unusual.'

'So I see.' A flirty look passed between them. Then the baby started crying; just like Jiminy Cricket. 'Well, if you know that much,' she said, putting down her mug and picking up the baby with a practised movement, 'you'll know that Whitehall is seething with factions. Ambition is rife. Richard's one of the young turks and the hottest tip for rapid promotion.' She slung the baby against her shoulder, supporting its bottom with one hand. 'He has a fabulous intellect and a photographic memory. He advises at the highest level, promotes the image, and disses the opposition – and I don't mean the official Opposition either, but the outs in the Party. He's known as a fixer, and he's got a publicity team that spins like Shane Warne on speed. *And* he's good-looking. No wonder the media love him. Well, you've seen all the Sunday supplement guff about him. They've even done his taste in interior decor – "the Tyler look", etcetera, etcetera.'

The baby, which had quietened when she picked it up, began wailing again. 'He needs changing, the little beast. Oh, don't worry, I won't do it in front of you,' she added with a laugh at his expression. 'Grandchild,' she explained. 'I thought I'd done with all this, but Nature kindly arranges a second go. My daughter's what the tabloids call a "working mum".' The baby, expertly jiggled, lowered the gain a notch. 'Where were we?'

'Tyler. You obviously think the world of him,' Atherton said.

She made a face. 'I don't have to like him to know he's hot. My tip is that once the reshuffle's announced he's going to be the biggest media obsession since Princess Di. That's why it all had to be secret, Phoebe's book on him.'

'Why, had she uncovered some terrible secret?'

'No, nothing like that,' she said. 'For commercial reasons. Phoebe was a very prestigious commentator. If anyone had known she was working on it, they'd have tried to get in first and steal her thunder. It's cut-throat, the world of biographies. I can't tell you! The big political ones sell in the hundreds of thousands. I've researched for a few people, and believe me, if you get a good idea for the next subject, you keep it strictly to yourself.'

Atherton looked his disappointment. 'So all her secrecy and dark hints about her latest piece of work were nothing more than commercial prudence?'

'Why, what did you think?'

'Oh, that maybe there was some danger to her from what she was doing.'

'Oh, no,' she said robustly. 'She's not exposing the Mafia, you know! And Richard may be ruthlessly ambitious, but he's perfectly respectable. So are his people. An old political family.

Steeped in it. His father and grandfather were both MPs and his mother was the daughter of a life peer and former Cabinet Minister. Funny how it so often does run in families,' she mused. 'Like actors, really. You have the Redgraves and Masseys and so on, and you have the generations of politicians, too.'

'I suppose in both cases, you get on as much through personal contact as talent,' Atherton suggested.

She grinned. 'In the case of MPs, much more! So what else did you want to know?'

'Who has the papers now – the work you and Phoebe had done so far?'

'She had it all. I don't keep copies of anything once I've sent it off. I suppose', she said regretfully, 'it'll all moulder in some police locker somewhere for ever, and someone else will eventually have the same idea and bring out their inferior Tyler biography.'

'Well, I suppose all the papers will be released to her next of kin sooner or later,' Atherton said. 'Which is her sister, I imagine.'

'I never knew she had a sister,' said Mrs Brissan. 'Maybe I should write to her and see if she'd let me have them.'

'You could try,' Atherton said. 'Tell me, did Richard Tyler know she was doing this biography?'

'I really have no idea. She never said one way or the other.'

'Isn't it usual to get the subject's permission?'

'Depends. There's the authorised biography, if the subject is controversial or powerful – gives it more weight. And if there's any chance of being sued for libel, it's best to get them to read what you've written and okay it. But otherwise you get more punch from launching it on an unsuspecting world – and you can get some brilliant publicity if the subject does object to anything. It's more fun that way if you've got the balls – and Phoebe certainly had them.'

'But she'd have had to have his permission to interview his parents, say, or look at his personal documents.'

'His parents are dead. And the work I did for her only concerned public records. Whether she asked him for anything else – as I say, I've no idea.'

'So you'd been working on this for some months – and then you stopped? Why was that?'

'Well, that was a bit odd,' Mrs Brissan said, frowning. 'She wrote to me in December to say that she didn't want any more work done. Just like that. No reason given. Naturally I rang her to ask what was going on, because I'd got quite involved in it. But she was very offhand, not like her usual self. I mean, we'd known each other for years, but she talked to me as if I was a stranger. She wouldn't say why she was stopping, just repeated that she didn't want any more work on it, and asked me to send anything I had outstanding, including any rough notes. She said she didn't want me to keep anything relating to the topic. I was a bit offended. I said, you don't think I'd pass them to anyone else after you'd paid for them, and she said she was sorry, she didn't mean to offend me, it was just that she had rather a lot on her mind. So anyway, I sent her everything I still had, plus my invoice for the work, and that's the last I ever heard from her. But she didn't pay the invoice, so I sent it again – just before she died. I suppose *that* won't get paid now. Not that it matters beside what happened to her, poor thing.'

'Well, thanks,' Atherton said, feeling they had come to a dead end. 'You've been a great help.' The baby was quiet again, and so that it should not have been a completely wasted journey, he added, 'Would you like to have lunch with me – my way of saying thank you?'

She gave him an infinitely knowing look. 'I'm a married woman.'

'I only offered you lunch,' he protested, lifting his hands.

'No you didn't – and thanks very much. When you're a mother of three, and a grandmother of one, it's nice to know you've still got it.'

'You've got so much you could take on a couple of assistants,' Atherton said, yielding.

She eyed him thoughtfully, and turned away to put the sleeping babe back in its carrier. 'Is there a Mrs Atherton?' she asked, her back to him.

'Not unless you're volunteering.'

'Not for all the tea in Lancashire,' she said. She straightened and turned. 'But you ought to get married. It can be lonely, being an ex-rake.'

Atherton staggered. 'Good God, you don't pull your punches, do you?'

'You and I understand each other,' she said. 'I've been there, done it – just ten years ahead of you. Don't get left behind, that's my advice. Married men live longer, and they're much less likely to commit suicide.'

'Richard Tyler?' Slider said. 'I wonder whether that was why Phoebe Agnew wanted to stop Piers seeing him? That row they had at New Year, you remember?'

'I don't quite see why,' Atherton said. 'I mean, if anything it would be beneficial to her, wouldn't it? Another personal contact with her subject – maybe access to more information. He might tell Piers stuff he wouldn't tell anyone else – and Piers is such a blabbermouth he'd let it all out as soon as she applied the single malt in sufficient quantities.'

'Yes, I suppose you're right. It would make more sense for her to encourage the relationship.'

'Anyway, I don't see that it helps us. Even if there were a file missing, and even if that was it, the only person who knew about it was Mrs Brissan—'

'According to her.'

'Quite. But Agnew hadn't even told her dear old mate Josh who the subject of her biography was, so it seems likely she *did* keep it secret. And why should it provoke anyone to murder her anyway?'

'You're right. In any case, it doesn't look as if that's the thing that was worrying her,' Slider said. 'She said to Josh she had a problem that would make his pale into insignificance, and that he was the last person who could help her with it, and it's hard to see how her research for a biography could fit either of those categories.'

'So what next?' Atherton asked.

Slider leaned back and put his hands behind his neck to stretch it. 'God, I don't know. There ought to be something in her papers, or somebody she knew or worked with ought to have known what this problem was. If she'd been worried and drinking more heavily for the last few weeks, you'd think she'd have told someone.'

'Maybe it was just the menopause after all,' Atherton said. 'All in her mind.'

'And she was murdered by telekinesis?'

'By a random lunatic.'

'Thanks. That's helpful.'

'Lunchtime, guv,' Atherton said. 'Give yourself a break. Feed the brain cells.'

'Yes, you're right. I am hungry, now you come to mention it,' Slider said, shoving his chair back and standing up. 'I fancy a big plateful of—'

Of what, Atherton was never to know – though he suspected chips – for the phone rang.

Slider picked up. It was Detective Inspector Keith Heaveysides of the Essex Constabulary. He was sorry to have to tell Slider that Piers Prentiss had been found dead in his shop this morning, and in view of Slider's recent interest in him, Mr Heaveysides wondered if he'd like to come along and pool information, hopefully to their mutual benefit. Pardon? No, it certainly wasn't natural causes, and there didn't seem to have been any robbery, either from the person or the premises. Yes, certainly. Not at all. They were all on the same side, weren't they? Not a problem. His pleasure entirely.

Slider liked Heaveysides straight away. He was one of those tall, full-fleshed, fair men who go bald right over the top very early in life, but keep a boyish face as if in compensation. He seemed a genuinely nice person, but yet to have survived in the Job with a name like his, he must have had a toughness, or at least an inner serenity, to survive the teasing.

He took Slider and Atherton into his office and gave them coffee (from his personal filter coffee machine, so it was drinkable) and biscuits while he filled them in on the story.

'It was his cleaner who found the body,' he said.

'Marjorie Babbington?' said Slider.

'Oh, you know her, do you?'

'We met her when we interviewed Prentiss at his house. She must be pretty upset.'

'She's holding up well. You know the sort – stiff upper lip. Anyway, she was doing the cleaning in the house this morning when someone comes knocking at the door. It's a local chap, name of Hewitt. He's gone past and seen the lights are on in the shop, tried the door and found it's locked, so he's called at the house in a neighbourly way to say did you know you've left the lights burning.'

'Was the closed sign up?'

'Yes, and he's a regular customer of the shop, so he knows it's usually shut on a Monday. That's why he wonders. So anyway, Babbington answers the door, Hewitt says blah-di-blah-di-blah, she says Prentiss isn't there. He says it's an awful waste of electricity so she says all right I'll get the keys and come and turn 'em off.'

'Where did she expect Prentiss to be?'

'Well, Monday being the closed day, he could be anywhere. She wasn't worried. If he was going away for any long time he always told her so she could look after the dogs, but as it was she thought he'd just popped out. So she gets the spare keys and goes in by the back door, and there's Prentiss lying dead behind the counter.'

'How did he die?'

'It looks as if someone knocked him down from behind with a blunt instrument, and then strangled him,' said Heaveysides. 'The ligature's been removed so we're no wiser about that, but the police surgeon said it was a smooth band, maybe a silk tie. Prentiss must have been groggy from the blow because he hardly struggled – just a couple of broken nails.'

'Break-in?'

'No, both the shop doors, front and back, were locked.'

'You said spare keys. What other sets were there?' Atherton asked.

'I was just coming to that,' said Heaveysides. 'Mr Prentiss had his own set on his own key-ring, which he kept in his pocket, and they were missing. We've had a bit of a search of the house, and immediate environs, but they haven't turned up yet.'

'I doubt if they will,' Slider said. 'And you say there was no sign of any robbery or theft?'

'Nothing as far as we can tell. Of course, in an antiques shop like that you don't know what was there to begin with, but everything looks all right. And Prentiss's money and credit cards were still in his pockets. It's a bugger,' he added feelingly. 'He was a nice old stick. Everybody liked him. You know that in places like this you can get a lot of prejudice and queer-bashing, but it never seemed to touch him. And this is a quiet community. We haven't had any violent crime here in years, leave aside the odd fight outside the pubs of a Saturday night.'

'Yes, it's a miserable business,' Slider said. He remembered his long talk with Piers, the shadow Prentiss, the B-side brother; conjured up the charm of his rare smile, the wry intelligence, the humour. Now it was all stopped, just like that, in an instant, in the twinkling of an eye. His corruptible must put on incorruption: but no-one had asked him if he was ready. His life, stolen from him, just like Phoebe Agnew's – and for what? What was the connection?

Heaveysides raised anxious eyes to Slider's. 'You've got something going on with Prentiss's brother, haven't you? Do you think the cases could be connected?'

'I have a nasty suspicion that they almost certainly are,' Slider said. 'But the brother's been cleared of our murder. It seems likely, on what you've told me, that whoever did this did our job as well. But I'm afraid we haven't a clue yet who that might be.'

'Ah, well, it goes like that sometimes,' Heaveysides said wisely. 'Would you like to talk to Babbington?'

'Thanks, that would be helpful.'

'I've got to get back to my own lads – but you'll let me know if you get anything that'll help me?'

'Absolutely. I'm grateful to you for letting me in on this. There's a lot wouldn't.'

'In my view, we're all on the same team,' Heaveysides said.

'I wish everyone thought like that,' said Slider.

Marjorie Babbington was white, rigid, and red-eyed, but she wasn't giving in.

'I'm sorry to put you through it all over again,' said Slider, 'but I'd be grateful if you would tell me what happened. I've had it from Inspector Heaveysides, but I may hear something slightly different from you, or you may remember a detail you didn't tell him.'

She said, 'I understand. I don't mind how often I tell it, if it helps catch whoever did this awful thing. How could anyone hurt someone like Piers? Do you think', she asked, meeting his eyes bravely, 'it was the same person that killed Phoebe?'

'I think it very likely.'

'Well, I hope you get them,' she said fiercely, 'and I wish we hadn't abolished hanging.'

'So, tell me, when was the last time you saw Piers?'

'Yesterday afternoon, when he was walking the dogs. He went past along the lane, and I waved to him from the kitchen window.'

'What lane is this?'

'The lane that runs behind our houses. You know I live a few doors down from Piers?'

'I do now.'

'Oh. Well, there's a lane that runs along the back of the whole row. Just a narrow mud track, really, too narrow for a car, but it gives access to our backyards. Anyway, he went by about, oh, half past three or thereabouts, walking the dogs. He waved back to me quite cheerfully. And that was the last time I saw him – until—' She couldn't finish it.

'All right,' said Slider soothingly. 'Tell me about this morning. When did you come to the house?'

'It was about half past nine. I came along the lane and let myself in at the back door—'

'Was it open or shut?'

'Oh, it was locked. He used to leave it open in the old days, but we had a spate of burglaries a few years back and I made him get into the habit of locking the house when he went to the shop. But in any case, the shop's closed on a Monday, so when I found the back door locked I knew he must be out. So I let myself in with the key.'

'What keys do you have?'

'Of Piers's? Only the back door. I always come in that way.'

'And what about the shop?'

'I don't have a shop key. Piers gives me the spare set if he wants me to look after it for him.'

'All right, go on. You let yourself in. How did the house seem?'

'Well, just as usual really. I didn't notice anything out of place. Oh,' she remembered, 'except that the dogs seemed unusually hungry.'

'They were in the kitchen?'

'Yes, on their beanbag. They rushed to me and jumped up and down, just as they always do, but then they went to their bowls and barked like mad and pushed them with their noses, the way they do when they want to be fed. Naturally I assumed Piers had fed them before he went out, so I just gave them each a Bonio. It's very wrong to overfeed dogs. Of course, now I think of it, they probably hadn't been fed since last night, poor things, but how was I to know?'

'You weren't, of course. So what happened next?'

'Well, I let them out to do their tiddles, and started my cleaning, as usual. Then Mr Hewitt came to the door and asked for Piers, and when I said he'd gone out, he said he'd left the lights on in the shop. I thanked him for telling me and said I'd go in and turn them off.'

'How come you didn't notice when you came past?'

'There are no windows to the shop at the back. The back door lets onto a sort of lobby with coat hooks and fuse boxes and the cloakroom, so you wouldn't see any light walking past at the back. Anyway, I got the spare set of keys—'

'Where are they kept?'

'In the bureau drawer in the drawing-room. I took them and went out the back way, to the back door of the shop, let myself in, and there was Piers lying behind the counter.' She stopped and drew a shaky breath. 'Of course, he couldn't be seen from the front door, or Mr Hewitt would have raised the alarm.'

'I'm sorry to put you through it, but how was he lying?'

'On his front. His – his face was turned sideways a bit. It. was – swollen – and—' She stopped and put her face in her hands. 'I could see he was dead,' she said, muffled by her fingers.

'How was he dressed?'

She was a long time answering. At last she lowered her hands, in control again. 'Fully dressed. In his cord trousers and tweed jacket,' she said briskly.

'Did he look as if he had struggled? Were his clothes disarranged? Was anything knocked over?'

'No. The rug was rucked up a bit under him, but that was all. If anything had been knocked over, it must have been put straight again. And nothing seemed to be missing – except his keys, so they tell me.' She stared unhappily at her hands. 'I hate to think of him lying there all night like that, while the poor doggies waited and waited for him to come back.'

'Why do you think he was there all night?'

'Well, the police said – said he'd been dead for about twelve hours. And of course there was a light on in the shop last night.'

'Ah, you didn't mention that before,' said Slider. 'How come you saw that?'

'Oh, I didn't. It was Mr Hewitt. He said he'd taken his dog for a walk last thing last night – about half past ten – and he'd passed the shop on the way back and saw the light on then. Naturally he didn't think anything about it – why should he? But when he came by this morning and saw it was still on, he thought he'd better tell Piers he'd forgotten it.'

She looked enquiringly at Slider, who had lapsed into thought. Eventually he roused himself and said, 'You didn't notice anything in the house missing or disturbed?'

'Not really,' she said apologetically. 'I might have if I'd been looking for it, but of course I wasn't.'

'What keys were on the key-ring that Piers kept in his pocket?'

'The shop front and back and the house front and back.'

'So whoever took them could get in and out of the house without leaving a trace.'

'Yes, I suppose so – if the dogs would let them.'

'Are the dogs fierce?'

'Well, quite,' she said. 'If they don't know you. I mean, if Piers is there, or I am, they wouldn't hurt a fly, but if someone broke in – I know they're small, but with two of them they could be a real nuisance to a burglar.'

'And they were in the kitchen, but with the run of the house?'

'Yes, they—' Her eyes widened. 'There, now, you were right, I have remembered something that was different. The kitchen door was closed – the one between the kitchen and the rest of the house. That was always left open, but this morning when I went in it was closed.' She looked apologetic. 'I noticed it and didn't notice it, if you know what I mean. I mean, until you know something's important, you sort of dismiss it from your mind, don't you?'

'Yes, I know exactly what you mean,' Slider said. 'One last

thing, that photograph that went missing, the previous time we came to see Piers – did it ever turn up?'

Her eyes widened. 'No, it didn't, and that was odd, because he thought I'd moved it, but I certainly hadn't. I thought maybe it had fallen down behind something, but I looked when I was cleaning and didn't find it. So where it went is a mystery.'

When they had left her, Atherton said, 'What was that about the photograph? Was it important?'

'I've no idea,' Slider said. 'I'm just punting. Anything could be anything.'

'You don't know what's important until you know what's important,' Atherton agreed. 'So what do you think happened?'

'I suppose the murderer called on him last night and per-suaded him to go over to the shop for some reason. Knocked him down, strangled him, and then went back to the house for something, using the keys from his pocket to let himself in and lock everything up after him. And shoved the dogs in the kitchen and shut the door while he looked for whatever it was.'

'Or maybe', Atherton said, 'he met Piers at the house, and shut the kitchen door before they went to the shop together. That way he could come back in the front without disturb-ing them.'

'It's possible,' Slider said, 'though he'd run more risk of being seen going in that way.'

'But I wonder why he left the shop lights on?'

'Oversight, probably. Or maybe he'd been careful not to touch anything, and didn't want to leave prints on the light switches. He could have let himself out with the key without having to touch the door, you see.'

'But then if he went to the house to rummage round he'd have had to have gloves, wouldn't he?'

'Well, we don't know that he *did* rummage round,' Slider said. 'He might have taken the keys just to let himself out and lock the shop, and the kitchen door being closed was just a fluke and not related to anything. Which way's the incident room, do you suppose?'

'I'd bet that way. Want to thank Mr Heaveysides?'

'That, and to see if they'll let us have a rummage of our own through Piers's papers. Though I doubt whether it will reveal anything. I wish I knew what was going on,' he said sadly. 'This maniac has killed two people now, and it would be nice to know if anyone else is in the firing line before he gets to them.'

CHAPTER NINETEEN

Probably the best laugher in the world

There was the familiar blue-and-white barrier tape boxing off the cottage and antiques shop and the road and pavement in front of them, and a small crowd of the usual sort – shapeless women in C&A macs and headscarves, slovenly unemployed youths in trainers and scrub-headed ten-year-old truants astride mountain bikes of fabulous expense.

As Slider and Atherton were admitted through the barrier and walked towards the front door, Slider was surprised to hear his name called with some urgency.

'Mr Slider! Over here!'

It was Peter Medmenham, gripping the tape and staring at him with the urgency of a pointer. He looked out of place against the grimy background in his neat charcoal grey overcoat and yellow wool muffler. His shiny little feet were set in the gutter of the mud-streaked road, and a coating of fine mist droplets made his blue-white hair look dingy grey.

Slider went over to him. 'How did you get here?'

'The police telephoned Josh, and he called me right away, to let me know,' he said. 'I had to come.' He hadn't put on any make-up, and the cold had brought out the network of fine thread veins, red over the blue of his cheeks. He looked pinched and old. 'I should have been with him,' he said starkly. 'He phoned me yesterday. He's hardly seen anything of his new friend. I think he was lonely. But I wouldn't go. Pride, you see. And now he's—'

'I'm sorry,' Slider said, and he really, really was.

Medmenham shook the sympathy away. 'My own fault. They're saying it was a break-in. Is that right?' His eyes appealed, but for what, Slider didn't know. There was no comfort he could give this man one way or the other.

'I don't know,' he said.

Medmenham swallowed, reaching for words. 'I wonder – if you can ask for me. I can't get anyone to listen. His things – photographs, for instance. Just something of his to keep. If I could go in, just for a moment—?'

'I'm afraid that's not possible. But all his things will be released to his brother eventually. Why don't you ask him? I'm sure he'd let you have something.'

Medmenham shook his head again, as if Slider had said something hopelessly naive. 'It's awful to be kept out like this. Like a stranger. I should have been with him. It wouldn't have happened if I'd been there.'

'I must go,' Slider said. He turned away, and Medmenham's voice, lifted a little, followed him like a sibylline pronouncement on the damp air.

'He'd have left him soon, you know, the new one. Dropped him. It wouldn't have lasted.'

Slider glanced back from the door, and he was standing there at the barrier, as still as only an actor or a soldier can; small and upright, staring into the distance, the bright dab of pure colour at his throat marking him out from the surrounding browns, greys and sludges. He was as unlike as possible the rest of the crowd, the real natives of this place and this event. Some of them were looking at him, with curiosity and faint hostility, like sparrows just about to start pecking an escaped budgerigar.

It was fortunate that Slider was still at the house when the call came through from Shepherd's Bush that a Mr Henry Banks wanted to meet him in a pub in Sudbury, because it was only about twenty-five miles from there, straight through on the A131. If he had started off back to London he'd have been going in the opposite direction.

There was Atherton to deal with, but one of the local boys offered to drop him at the railway station, and the trains from Chelmsford were frequent and fast. Atherton gave him a curious look as he left: it wasn't often that Slider did anything Atherton didn't know about. But Slider said it was a meeting with a snout of his – which was almost the truth – and a man's snout was sacrosanct, so he couldn't very well ask any more.

It was a slow drive, with the afternoon pootling traffic clogging up the roads: elderly Cambridges and Metros driven by old men in hats who could only just see over the wheel; cheap hatchbacks with rusty bumpers and the back door secured with string, driven by red-faced men who looked as if they might well have a pig or a crate of chickens in the passenger seat. They all drove at forty-five miles an hour in the exact centre of the lane and never looked in their rear-view mirrors, so it was impossible to pass them.

There was that melancholy feeling of all comfort ending that you only get towards dusk in the countryside in winter. The sky was pinkish along the horizon, the bare trees looked chilly, and here and there a lone rook flapped slowly home, straight as the crow flies. Loneliness breathed up from the brown furrows and the scattered, crouched houses. The oncoming dark seemed a menace to flee. You felt you had to get indoors as quickly as possible.

He thought of his own childhood home, the dank cottage with its garden full of cabbages and brussels sprouts and the drain in the kitchen that smelled of tea leaves. Suddenly he was ten again, and coming home across the fields, his feet weighted with mud and his cold legs aching so he could hardly get along, and the night mist beginning to be exhaled from the black water in the field drains. But indoors, if he could only get there, would be lights, and the furry, comfortable warmth of paraffin heaters, and Mum in the kitchen, where a mum always ought to be, getting tea. Women and food: how they locked on to your heart, taking it so young that if you had ever been properly loved and nurtured, you could never quite untangle them again. And did you ever, ever get over losing your mum? It seemed absurd after so long, and at his age, to be seized with such a yearning to go home; but she was gone, beyond reach, and a grown man wasn't allowed to feel like this.

The bricks and street lights of Sudbury came as a relief. It had been a pretty town, though like everywhere else now it had its rash of ugly little new houses creeping out over the outlying fields like psoriasis. It was years since he had been here, but he remembered his way about all right, as a pub man does, navigating from inn sign to inn sign. The Rose and Crown was one of those tiny beamed cottages, long and low with diamond-pane windows, sunk slightly below the pavement level, that look as if they've shrunk together with age, like little old women. He pushed open the oak door – probably five hundred years old, and how many unthinking hands had pushed it open in that time? – and stepped into the parlour. It had a red carpet and red velvet banquettes and beams everywhere, a game machine flashing its lights in a corner like someone humming to himself, and at one end a glorious log fire, just getting into its stride. There were two customers sitting on stools at the bar. One was talking to the landlord, who was obviously an old friend; the other was at the far end, near the fire, reading a newspaper.

'Afternoon,' said the landlord pleasantly. 'What can I get you?' His friend looked round as well, and half smiled; the reader didn't look up from his paper.

'Afternoon. A pint of Adnams, please,' Slider said, and drifted, as though of no purpose, down the bar, to station himself between the other two customers, but closer to the newspaper man.

The pint came. The landlord made a remark or two about the weather, looking at Slider keenly with copper's eyes, as though assessing where he came from and what he was doing here, and then politely left him and went back to his friend. Slider turned his back on them casually to look at the fire, leaning his right elbow on the bar. The man with the paper looked up. The paper, Slider could see now, was a sporting one; the man was small, thin, and deeply lined in the face, with an all-weather complexion and hands like wooden clubs.

Slider met his eyes and raised his eyebrows. The man nodded slightly. After a suitable pause, Slider said, 'Might have a bit of snow before the weekend, I shouldn't wonder.'

'C'n do with it,' he said, in a voice faint and hoarse with a lifetime of fags. 'Warm winter don't kill the bugs.' He had a Norfolk accent.

'At least there haven't been too many sporting fixtures cancelled, though.'

'There's always an upside and a downside.' The little man up-ended his pint and Slider took his cue.

'Get you another?'

'Don't mind if I do. Ta very much.'

When the landlord had refilled the glass and the little man had offered and lit a cigarette, they were licensed to talk without drawing suspicion; though Slider had the uncomfortable feeling that the landlord had no illusions about why the stranger in the well-worn suit had suddenly turned up at his pub.

There was nothing in the least porcine about Piggy Banks – it was evidently just one of those inevitable nicknames, like Chalky White and Lofty Short. 'You was wanting to know about Furlong Stud, then?' he asked in due course. Another couple of customers had come in, and the landlord was further off. On his way down the bar he had also turned on the background music, a courtesy Slider could normally have done without, but useful now. Had he done it deliberately?

'Yes,' said Slider. He made a polite gesture towards his wallet pocket. 'I expect you'll have expenses to cover.'

Piggy slid his eyes away modestly. 'Half a cent'ry'll cover it,' he said. 'Tidy's a mate of an old mate of mine who wants to do him a favour. Slip it me after so that lot don't see.' With a jerk of his head towards the rest of the population.

'I don't think there's much the guv'nor doesn't see,' Slider said, feeling he ought to warn Banks that his cover might not be impenetrable.

'He used to be one of your lot. Cozzer from down London. He's all right. I know him and he knows me. Anyway, Furlong. It's a scam, o' course.' He looked to see if Slider knew that.

'I thought it must be. Do you know how?'

'Ever heard of a horse called Hypericum?'

Slider shook his head. 'I'm not a racing man.'

Banks didn't seem to mind that. 'Smashing colt. Got everything – blood, bone, and a heart as big as a house. Unbeaten as a two-year-old, won the Queen Anne Stakes at Ascot and the Prix Morny at three, and the Canadian International. He was a real engine. Second in the Guineas and would've had the Derby, but they over-raced him and he broke down. After that he was never really sound. When he was fit, he could beat anything, but he'd go all right for a while and then break down again.'

He took a drag on his fag and had a long, sustaining cough. 'Anyway,' he began again, breathlessly, 'this codger Bill Carrington used to be Hypericum's trainer. He loved that horse. When they decided to sell it, he couldn't bear to see it go where it might not be well treated, so he bought it himself and left to set up his own place.'

'Where did he get the money?'

'Oh, he had a bit put by. He's not a bad trainer – had a few winners. Bit o' prize money stashed away. And he may have had a backer, I dunno. The new place, I reckon it was all meant to be legit. But it ain't that easy to get on, specially when you're starting up. And Hypericum – they don't call him that now, use his old stable name, Gordon – anyway, he didn't improve. Couldn't race him. So Carrington hit on this scam.'

'Which is?'

'Just a twist on the old ringer dodge,' Banks said, with a shake of the head that it should be so easy. 'A lot of what they do's legit. Breeding, training, racing. But when they get a horse that don't show, looks all right but ain't gonna get in the money, they set it up for the syndicate. Pull in a lot of daft city types with more money than sense, show 'em the horse in stables, and then on the gallop they bring out Hypericum. Dye his coat to look like the other. The mugs see him run, they think they can't lose. Carrington gets ten times the value of the horse, plus all the running expenses for a couple of years before they get fed up and jack it in. And the beauty of it is, the paperwork's all right as rain. Nowadays, with lip tattoos and microchips an' all, you'd have a job putting a ringer in a race. But the mugs, they bought a certain horse, that's what's in the contract, and that's what gets entered in the races. Beautiful.' He sighed over his pint. 'It'll break Carrington's heart when Hypericum gets too old, or breaks down for good. But he'll have had a good run for his money by then.'

'It sounds too simple to be true,' Slider said.

'Like all the best dodges,' Banks said wisely, 'it works on greed. The punter twists himself.'

'Greed, yes. The brochure said the investors could expect a return of twenty-four per cent,' Slider said.

Banks nodded. 'That's a little joke of Bill Carrington's. A while back, last year I think it was, there was a newspaper article about investing in racehorses. Everyone talked about it around the stables. And it said that on average you could only expect to get back a quarter of what you put in. So it's not twenty-four per cent *on* your investment, it's twenty-four per cent *of* your investment.'

Slider didn't know whether to laugh or cry. Banks was looking at him speculatively. 'You going to do anything about it?' he asked.

'What? Oh, no. It's not my field. I just wanted to save a friend of mine from making a fool of himself.'

'Glad of that,' Banks said. 'I done this as a favour, but I wouldn't like it to get about I been talking. Wouldn't do to make meself unpopular.'

'I won't tell anyone. You can trust me. Jockey, are you?'

'I was. National Hunt. Till I broke me hip. Big horse fell on me, going over the fifth at Aintree. Joey Jojo his racing name was, but we called him Socks. Big chestnut, two white legs be'ind like a Clydesdale. Lovely horse. Gor, could he jump! And kind? But he came down on me and broke me hip, and that was the end of me riding career. Still, I was the lucky one.'

'How's that?'

'They mended my hip, but he broke his leg, and they 'ad to shoot him.' He took a long pull at his pint. 'He was a lovely horse.'

Echo of Tennyson, Slider thought. She has a lovely face; God in His mercy send her grace. He slipped Piggy Banks his fifty, drained his pint, and left under the clocking gaze of the landlord, into the whizzing darkness of rush hour.

A little pricking rain had started, and it was cold. Everyone was hurrying home to their tea and telly, and the world seemed too big and dark and hostile. Slider's mind was full of other people's misery – Medmenham's, Noni Prentiss's, even Josh's – for who knew what emptiness his swaggering had been meant to hide? And the unavenged dead haunted him, their sadness the greatest of all, to be over and finished before their time, no more life for them, no more anything. He believed in ghosts – or shades, or furies, or something. When he was very little, they hadn't had electricity at the cottage, and lamplight gave itself to believing in things half seen. His mother had said the dead watched over you and were nothing to be afraid of; but their eyes, whether reproachful or forgiving, were not what you wanted your darkness peopled with.

The other main road out of Sudbury, the A134, went almost through Upper Hawksey, the village of Slider's birth. It was as long as it was broad to go back that way, via Colchester instead of via Chelmsford, he told himself; and if he was passing within a mile of the cottage, he might just as well call in and see Dad.

Bumping carefully down the muddy, rutted track from the road to the cottage, he saw the light up ahead of him, the single square of the kitchen window, hanging flat on the absolute blackness beyond the headlights like a painting on a velvet wall. Pulling onto the parking space at the end, he saw that the square was pale red, light shining through the red gingham curtains drawn across the window. When he cut the engine and got out, there was that absolute silence that went with the absolute blackness, something you never got in Town, and which thrilled down his spine, like the evocative smell – Christmas trees and tangerines, for instance – that takes you straight back to childhood.

The kitchen door opened, spilling light out, and his father stood there in the doorway. He looked frail with the light behind him; his neck rose in cords from the worn collar that had been snug last time Slider had seen him. Slider was aware that he had not been down for some time, and he was seared with a panicky guilt. He would make time to come down more often; he would bring the kids to see Grandad; he would bring Joanna – Dad liked Joanna. He shouldn't let the Job blot out everything else.

'That you, Bill,' said Mr Slider – not a question, but a greeting.

'Hello, Dad. I was passing this way, so I thought I'd call in.'

Silently Mr Slider stepped back from the door to let him in. Not one for wasting words, wasn't Dad. Inside the kitchen was spare and spotless, much as it had been in Mum's day, but not dank any more – central heating had been installed long ago.

'How are you?' Slider asked, as one does.

'I'm not complaining.' Mr Slider regarded his son impassively a moment. 'Cuppa tea?'

'Thanks. I'm sorry I haven't been down for a while.'

'Busy, I expect.' He was wearing grey trousers and a grey lambswool sweater over a brown and beige check Viyella shirt which Slider recognised as one of his own which he had passed on to Dad when the collar got too tight for him. How many years ago? It had to be ten, probably more. The collar was rubbed white along the fold, and the sweater was darned at one elbow with a man's patient clumsiness; but everything about him, and about the house, was spotless, and as he walked past Slider to go to the gas stove, he carried only the clean smell of fabric softener. Slider felt a rush of desperate love. It wasn't necessary, you see, to be like Mr Singer! For all these years his father had kept house, tended his garden, gone out shooting rabbits and wood pigeons, cooked his tiny meals, slowly washed up and put away, and at the end of each day, retired to his neatly made, empty bed; never complained, paid his way, kept up standards, was no trouble to anyone. But what did he think, what did he feel?'

'How do you do it?' Slider asked aloud.

'Do what, then?' Mr Slider asked, putting a match to the gas.

'All this,' Slider said, waving a hand round the kitchen. 'Just keep going on, without her. Doing – things. How do you bear it?'

'You just do,' Mr Slider said. He settled the kettle over the flames, and turned to regard his son with steady, faded blue eyes. 'You have to get on with things, don't you?'

One day, Slider thought, I'll look like that. His father's grey hair grew the same way, made the same shape as his own; they had the same eyes, the same build, except that Dad was now thin with age. He wondered suddenly, vividly, what Joanna would look like when she was old. 'Dad, I'm in trouble,' he said.

Mr Slider nodded. 'Thought it must be something.'

'I'm afraid I'm going to lose Joanna.'

'Ah.' Mr Slider stared thoughtfully a moment longer. 'Have you eaten?'

'No,' Slider discovered. He had been kept from lunch by the phone call, and hadn't eaten since. 'I'm starving.'

'I haven't had mine yet. Beans on toast, I was going to have. Suit you?'

'Fine. Thanks.'

'Sit down then. No, I'll do it. Can't have two women in one kitchen, your mother used to say.'

Slider sat and watched as his father pottered about, assembling the meal, knowing he would not be hurried, that the listening must wait until the meal was before them. Dad would always listen, but he liked to have something to occupy him while he did. Eyes must not be met while personal matters were being aired.

At last the plates were on the table, the knives and forks, the cruet, the cups of tea. 'Tuck in,' said Mr Slider.

And Slider told him about Joanna's job offer.

'How long's it for, this job?' Mr Slider asked when he paused.

'It's a permanent job. Years, anyway. Maybe for good.' He watched his father's hand reach out for the sugar-caster: a brown, old-man's hand, all knuckles, the fingers thickened from a lifetime's hard work. 'It's a wonderful thing for her, for her career. I just don't know what to do.'

'No, I see that,' Mr Slider said, stirring his tea. 'O' course, it's her decision, whether she goes or not.'

'But her decision will be affected by mine, whether to go with her or not.'

'That's right. You can't duck it that way,' his father said approvingly.

'But what could I do over there?'

'Get a job, I suppose. Other people manage somehow.'

'And give up the Job?'

Mr Slider knew enough to recognise the capital-letter distinction. 'Well, that's the other side of it, isn't it.' He looked up, suddenly meeting Slider's eyes, his usual impassivity softened by the hint of a smile. 'It's what you'd call a dilemma.'

Slider said nothing, only applied himself to the last of his beans.

'Thought I'd sort it out for you, did you?' Mr Slider said knowingly. 'Give you a quick answer. Rabbit out of a hat. I can't do that, son. I can only tell you that I like your Joanna, and I think she's good for you. Only time I've ever heard you laugh is when you're with her.'

'What?'

'Oh, yes,' Mr Slider nodded. 'I don't mean you don't smile or have a chuckle, you're not sullen, but it's only with her you really laugh out loud.'

'She makes me laugh,' Slider admitted.

'Your mother did me, too.'

'Really?'

'Oh yes. She was a very funny woman, your mother. In a quiet way.'

'I never knew that,' Slider said. He had loved his mother, but she had never struck him as a comedian.

'Well, you wouldn't,' said Mr Slider, gravely twinkling. 'Kept it for me. When we were in bed.'

Slider asked, a little shyly, 'Do you miss her?'

'Your mother? All the time. Every day.' He looked round the kitchen as if he might see her, having mentioned her. 'Funny, I can't remember what she looked like, now, not really, but there's a hole where she ought to be.' He picked up his cup with both hands and sipped his tea. 'A job's just what you do to stay alive. There's good ones and not so good. But your wife's something else.'

The problem was back. 'But what could I do? The only thing I know is the Job. And there's my pension to think about.'

'Yes, you've got to think about that.' Mr Slider drained his cup and put it down, and began gathering the plates together. 'You stopping a bit? I was going to light the fire. We could have a game of crib and a glass of beer.'

'No, I've got to get back,' Slider said absently, too absorbed in his own thoughts to wonder what the alternative for his father would be.

'Ah, well,' Mr Slider said.

Slider dragged himself up. 'Let me wash up, anyway.'

'No, no, I can do it. Not much here.'

At the door, Slider said, 'Thanks for the tea. I wish you could have told me what to do as well.'

'Your trouble is, you always think too much,' Mr Slider said. 'Ask yourself, what does it say *here*?' He tapped himself on the chest. ''Cos that's what you'll have to live with.'

Slider smiled suddenly at this typical Dad-advice, and put his arms round his father in a quick hug. He felt all bones. They didn't often do this, which made it a bit perilous, but Mr Slider returned the pressure briefly, and gave his back one or two pats, as undemonstrative men do when emotions threaten to assert themselves.

CHAPTER TWENTY

Sense and Sensibility

Slider didn't feel up to telling Atherton about the racehorse business straight away. It would keep for now, he thought. He needed to get home to Joanna. She met him with determined brightness, and he took his lead from her. She cooked for them, and they ate, chatting lightly on neutral subjects, and then spent the evening gamely *not* talking about the problem. But probably neither of them could have said afterwards what they had watched on the television; and when they went to bed, they clung together as if it were their last night on earth.

Atherton was late in again the next morning, and when he did appear he looked more white and strained than ever. Slider eyed him with scant sympathy. 'On the slam again last night?'

Atherton shook his head. 'I've lost Oedipus.'

'Oh,' said Slider. 'What d'you mean, lost?'

'I let him out last night when I got home and he didn't come back. I went round the streets calling and calling for him but I couldn't find him. I went out looking again this morning – that's why I'm late. Sorry.'

'I'm sure he's all right. Cats go on the wander sometimes.'

'Not him. And he *always* comes when I call.'

'Well, he's an old cat, isn't he? They can get a bit contrary. He'll turn up again when he's ready. I expect you'll find him waiting on the doorstep when you get home tonight.'

Atherton shrugged, rejecting the comfort. It didn't seem the right moment to tell him about Furlong Stud and add to his troubles. Anyway, there was the case to consider. Slider called everyone together in the CID room and brought them up to speed on the Piers Prentiss murder.

'The MO looks similar, and there was no robbery of any sort

so we have to assume a personal motive. I don't think it's going too far to suppose the two murders are connected.'

'Yes, but what's the connection?' Swilley said. 'There's Richard Tyler – she was working on his biography, and Piers was his new lover, but why should that make anyone kill either of them?'

'Yes, and if she'd been working on the Tyler biog for six months, why was she only worried and drinking heavily for the last few weeks?' said Atherton.

'Maybe she'd found out something about him – some nasty secret,' Hollis suggested.

'I should have thought that was a biographer's dream,' Atherton pointed out. 'It'd make her happy, not miserable.'

'Yeah, but if the papers are missing – all the stuff she did on Tyler,' Anderson began.

'Well, we don't know they are,' said Swilley fairly. 'We only know we haven't found them. She might have sent them to someone. Or be keeping them somewhere else.'

'Anyway, if a rival biographer had stolen the papers, I don't see why he would have killed her,' said Atherton. 'That's a bit extreme, wouldn't you say? I mean, I know the literary world is cut-throat, but surely not literally.'

'Anyway, she'd apparently stopped work on that,' Swilley said. 'Stopped her researcher, anyway.'

'We do know from several sources that she was deeply worried about something,' Slider said, 'and I think our best bet is that the murder's connected with that. But what was it?'

'It's got to be something in her life, some area we haven't uncovered,' Hollis said. 'Something she was involved in or someone from her past who had a grudge against her.'

'Yes, I can't believe it was just random,' Slider said. 'But it's hard to see what Piers Prentiss had to do with it. There doesn't seem to be any mystery about him.'

'Boss,' said Swilley, 'it seems to me the one big question mark we've got that we haven't gone into is what she was doing during those years after university when she was so-called missing.'

'Not much of a mystery there,' Mackay said. 'She was off protesting, doing the hippie bit.'

'Anyway, it's a hell of a long time ago,' Atherton said. 'Even if you could find out, I doubt if it would have any relevance. Who's going to hold a grudge for thirty years?'

'Well, you just never know, do you?' Swilley said, annoyed.
'And nor will you, unless you can find someone to ask.'

'Don't get snitty, you two,' Slider intervened.

McLaren, who had been scratching a bit of egg yolk off his
tie with his thumb nail, looked up. 'You could ask her sister.
We've not had a go at her yet.'

There was a brief silence, and then Swilley said, 'Maurice,
that's a stroke of genius. All those things I said about you –
I take 'em back.'

'You said he wasn't fit to live with pigs,' Hollis supplied
obligingly.

'Well I was wrong,' said Swilley. 'He *is* fit to live with pigs.'

'Har har,' said McLaren. 'So what about it, guv?'

'Yes, why not,' said Slider. 'But not you. Swilley, you can go
and see her.'

'Why does she get all the trips out, just because she's a bird?'
McLaren said resentfully.

'I want you', Slider told him, 'to re-interview the witness
who saw the man tying his tie. Try and get a more detailed
description from him, and if he thinks he can, get him in to do
an e-fit. Atherton, you're good with women. You can go and
see Noni Prentiss again, try and get a better description of the
man she saw leaving the house. Hollis, we're going to go over
everything we've got so far and look at it from the perspective
of Piers Prentiss, see if anything clicks. And Mackay, get our
notes on Piers Prentiss and Marjorie Babbington over to Keith
Heaveysides at Chelmsford and make sure he keeps us informed
of anything that comes up at their end – especially if it turns
out that anything was missing from the house. Not goods and
chattels, but papers of any kind. Come on, boys and girls, let's
get cracking.'

The tiny county of Rutland had not only laboured under the
disadvantage of being abolished and reinstated by successive
governments, subsumed into Leicestershire and then exhumed
again, but a large part of it had been drowned by the making
of Rutland Water, a vast reservoir. Still, it was pretty country –
quintessentially English shire country, of the green rolling hills,
woods, river valleys, thick hedges and stone walls variety. Good
hunting country – not that Swilley thought of that. She was

a Town girl, and green was not her favourite colour. If she went too far from a tube station for any length of time she got the bends.

Phoebe Agnew's sister, Chloe Cosworth, lived in a new square stone house, slipped in amongst the old square stone houses, in Upper Hambleton, the village on the tongue of land that stuck out like a jetty into Rutland Water. The tongue had once been a steep hill, rising above Middle and Nether Hambletons, which accounted for its survival: its sister villages were deep under the water.

Mrs Cosworth was a tall woman in her fifties, as tall as Swilley herself; slim to the point of gauntness, and plain. She had a long face and bad skin – presumably from childhood acne, for it was pocked, and looked thick and puckered over her cheeks. She wore no make-up, and her lips were thin and grey; but her grey hair, cut short, was expensively layered, and her clothes, though dull, were also expensive, so it wasn't lack of money but by intent that she looked as she did – which was pretty well as different from Phoebe as it was possible to get. Phoebe had been beautiful, wild and untidy; Chloe was plain, conventional and neat.

The inside of the house was just as much of a contrast with Phoebe's flat. Everything seemed new and almost grimly clean and shining: reproduction antique furniture, John Lewis fabrics and plain-coloured, thick Wilton carpets. There was no speck of dust, nothing lying around, no newspaper or discarded shoe. It was like a brand new showhouse. The only personal touch was a surprising collection of china figurines, modern mass-produced ones of the sentimental girls-in-long-dresses sort that you see advertised on the backs of colour supplements. It seemed oddly out of character, for Mrs Cosworth was horsily brisk, and her husband, it quickly transpired, owned a very large engineering firm.

She was perfectly willing to talk, provided Swilley with coffee and a coaster depicting the middle bit of Constable's *The Hay Wain*, and settled down in the immaculate, bare living room to tell whatever Swilley wanted to know, and more.

'I haven't had much to do with Phoebe in recent years,' she said. She had a toneless voice, rather hard, accentless, as though it too had been purged and swept and redecorated like the house to show nothing. 'Our lives have always been very different, as you can probably tell. I never approved of the way she carried on, but blood is thicker than water, and I've always been willing to see her whenever she wanted to visit. But I suppose as we've got older we've got more set in our separate ways. It's not that we've fallen out, it's just that we don't get around to seeing each other.' She paused a moment. 'Well, it's too late now, of course.'

'Do you mind about that – that it's too late?' Swilley asked, curious about this impassivity.

'Of course I mind,' she said. 'Phoebe was all the family I had – apart from Nigel, of course, but you don't count a husband as family, do you?'

Swilley left that one alone. 'There were just the two of you? No other brothers or sisters?'

'Just us. Literally.' She glanced to see if Swilley wanted to know more and, seeing receptiveness, went on to tell, in clipped and unemotional tones, the circumstances. Chloe and Phoebe's father, headmaster of a private boarding school in Leicestershire, had walked out on his wife and family one summer day during the school holidays and was never seen again. It was one of life's great mysteries what had happened to him. Phoebe had always inclined to the theory that his bones were lying undiscovered at the bottom of some quarry or lake; Chloe believed he had simply gone off with another woman and successfully changed his identity – still fairly easy to do in the fifties. What their mother thought, she never divulged. The three of them were left particularly badly off, since until he was declared dead, there could be no question of a widow's pension; and the accommodation had gone with the job.

Mrs Agnew moved with her children back to Oakham, her home town, took rented accommodation and found a job. Phoebe was ten and Chloe twelve at the time. Swilley gathered, with a bit of reading between the lines, that Phoebe was her mother's pet and had also been her father's: she was very pretty, exceptionally intelligent, bright and lively. Chloe had gone to secondary mod, Phoebe to grammar school; Chloe was doing typing, shorthand and housewifery while Phoebe did Latin, philosophy and higher maths; and Phoebe had a gaggle of boys hanging around the school gates for her every afternoon, where Chloe had only one swain, a very dull boy called Barry, who had short legs and wore glasses and was a swot. The other boys called him Barold. She disliked him in a mild way, but since she was not pretty it was assumed, even by Barold, that she'd be grateful for his lordly attentions.

Chloe grew up believing in 'the baby's' superiority in every sense, and that the superiority must be nurtured by the rest of them. When their mother died six years later, probably of overwork and underinterest in life, it seemed natural to Chloe that she should support her sister.

'I'd left school at fifteen. I did a secretarial course and then started work with a local firm. But when Mother died Phoebe was ready to go into the sixth form and then on to university. It would have been a crime to make her leave and get a job. So we stuck together. I got a better job with more money, and Phoebe stayed on at school. Once she got into university, she got the full grant, naturally, so the strain was taken off, but it was a hard couple of years.'

'What did you think of her going off to Chile?' Norma asked, just out of curiosity.

'I never liked her political activities,' Mrs Cosworth said harshly. 'And frankly, they've been an embarrassment sometimes. Nigel never approved. He's very – conventional. He's fifteen years older than me, and his generation has strict ideas about what's right and wrong.'

'How did you meet him?'

'I worked at his firm. I was his secretary, in fact.'

How conventional, thought Norma. It's nice to hear of old traditions being upheld. He must have been attracted by her youth, she supposed, because she didn't seem to have any other charisma.

'We married in 1968, when Phoebe was still at university,' Mrs Cosworth went on. 'He was very good about helping support her, and giving her a home during the vacations. Not that she was home much – always off somewhere, to some peace camp or something.'

I bet she was, thought Swilley. Old Nigel must have been a good incentive to stay away.

'But she worried Nigel dreadfully. He was always terrified she was going to get into the papers or end up in gaol. In the end, of course, it was trouble of a different kind she got into, and that was just as bad in its own way.'

'What trouble was that?' Norma asked, though she had guessed.

'She turned up at our house one day and said, "Chloe I need your help. I'm pregnant." Just like that.'

'When was that?'

'It would be – oh, September 1969. It was tactless even by her standards,' Mrs Cosworth went on, 'because I'd just had a miscarriage.'

'Oh, I'm sorry.'

The eyes moved away. 'It was a bad one,' she said tonelessly. 'And I was never able to have a child afterwards. We didn't know that *then*, of course. Nigel was furious that Phoebe had dumped this thing on us, but I told him I was the only family she had and we had to help. So he offered to pay for her to have an abortion. He said any child of hers was bound to grow up a criminal so that was the best thing.'

My God, thought Swilley, as a world of pity opened up before her. She could see it all. The meek, cowed Chloe, grateful for having been married and still under discipline to her boss; the pompous, stiff-necked man without the slightest sensitivity to his young wife's feelings; the wild, red-haired beauty, full of passionate feelings about everything. Chloe, having lost her own child, was told she had to persuade her sister deliberately to do the same.

'What did Phoebe say to that?'

'She wouldn't do it,' said Mrs Cosworth abruptly, and stopped. Swilley waited. At last she went on, 'Nigel was surprised – he'd thought, being the sort of girl she was, she'd jump at the offer and be grateful. But she went absolutely mad, said it was murder, jumped down poor Nigel's throat. They had terrible arguments about it. Screaming matches. It was dreadful. In the end he said if she wouldn't have the abortion, he washed his hands of the whole business, and she could get out of his house, too.'

So that, thought Swilley, was the origin of the stance against abortion. She could imagine a hot-blooded girl like Phoebe Agnew, an intelligent girl, flying into a rage at the tactlessness of this man, flying to the defence of the sister who had worked to put her through school. 'So what happened?' she asked.

'In the end I persuaded him to let Phoebe stay until after Christmas. It was a dreadful time, though.' Understatement of the year, thought Swilley. She could imagine it. 'Then I helped her get into one of those mother-and-baby homes, in Nottingham. The baby was born in March 1970 and they arranged for it to be adopted.' She stopped again, staring at the illuminated plastic coals of the electric fire in the imitation Adam fireplace. 'She came to see me just after she'd signed the adoption papers. It was in the daytime, when Nigel was at work. She cried and cried and cried. I've never seen anyone cry so much. And then she stopped and blew her nose and said, "Well, that's that." And she started talking about Vietnam.' She shook her head. 'She never spoke about it from that moment onwards, and I don't think she ever cried again, for anything. At least, I never saw her. She just put it out of her head. I never understood how she could do that. And then Nigel came home and she got up and left. Not a word of thanks to him for all he'd done for her. She went off, and we didn't see her for a couple of years.'

'Do you know where she went?'

'To America, to join the anti-Vietnam movement. She was there until her visa ran out. Then it was back to Chile, I think, and then – oh, I forget. She was always off somewhere. She used to phone me sometimes, but that was all. She lived on a commune in Wales for a while, I think. She was such an embarrassment to Nigel. I sometimes half think she did it deliberately to annoy him.'

She said it idly, as if she didn't mean it, but Swilley wondered if she hadn't hit on a truth, or at least a part of it. A life spent not just protesting against man's general inhumanity to man, but against Nigel Cosworth's specific inumanity to the Agnew sisters.

'Eventually, of course, she settled down – or at least, she became a bit more respectable. Once she was established as a proper journalist and started to get famous, Nigel took to her a bit more, and she started visiting us again. Of course, he disapproved of her subject matter a lot of the time. Well, most of the time, if I'm honest. But she was very well thought of in her own circles, and he respected that.'

I bet he did, the nasty snob.

'I can't say they ever liked each other, but they were polite to each other – for my sake, I suppose.' She looked up. 'And now she's dead. Do you know who did it?'

'No,' said Swilley. 'I'm afraid we don't yet.'

Mrs Cosworth sighed. 'Nigel says it must have been one of her hippie friends. That living the way she did, it's only surprising it didn't happen before. He said—' She stopped.

'That it served her right?' Swilley suggested. She had a fair picture of the sort of conversation that went on between the Cosworths regarding the sister-in-law.

Mrs Cosworth didn't answer directly. 'He's a good man,' she said. 'He's just of a different generation. He never understood Phoebe. Well, frankly, neither did I. She was my own sister, but I never understood how she got to be so hard. She never seemed to have any feelings for anyone. She never married, you know, despite being so beautiful. Nigel said she wasn't like a woman at all, so it wasn't surprising no-one would have her; but it's my belief that plenty wanted her, she just didn't want them.'

'What about the father of the baby?' Swilley asked. 'Did she want to marry him?'

'She never said anything about him. I asked, of course, but she wouldn't even tell me his name. I never knew from that day to this who it was. Nigel said', she added, seeming to have lost some of her protective reserve about her husband, 'that she probably didn't know herself.'

Nigel, thought Swilley, was just a total peach.

According to the Nottingham police, the mother-and-baby home had closed down in 1975.

'It's interesting,' Swilley commented to Slider. 'There's just this window of about ten years when hundreds of thousands of babies went for adoption. Before that girls didn't have sex, or the boys married them. After that, they knew about contraception, or they kept the babies themselves.'

It had been a privately run home, but the premises it used were council-owned. In the absence of any other information, it was to be assumed that the records would have gone back to City Hall and stored somewhere there; but it would be a long job, as preliminary enquiries proved, to find anyone who knew where they were precisely, or would even be willing to look. The other way would be through the County Courts, or the Central Register, almost equally time-consuming.

'Does it matter, boss?' Swilley asked, when she came to report failure so far. 'I mean, what's the baby got to do with anything?'

Slider got up and walked to the window, and Atherton shifted over to make room for him. The short afternoon was fading, and the yellow of shop lights made the grey seem greyer. 'It occurred to me, you see,' he said, 'that the weirdest thing about her last day was that supper. This woman who hated cooking and lived a gypsy life in a reconstructed student bedsit. Who would she cook chicken casserole and tiramisu for? She even went out and bought a cookery book for the occasion. Who is the only person in the world who cooks for you, apart from your lover or wife?'

'Your mum,' Atherton said, getting there.

Swilley stared. 'You think she'd somehow traced her kid and invited him round for a nosh?'

'I can't think who else she would go to the trouble for. Lorraine Tucker said she was flushed and excited when she met her with an armful of groceries that day. And she tidied up the flat, which everyone says she never did, not even for a lover. If she wasn't in love, what else could it be?'

Swilley nodded slowly. 'It makes sense, I suppose. But how would she find out?'

Atherton came in. 'She researched. She was used to doing research, she knew how to go about it. And who had she been researching for the past six months?'

'Richard Tyler,' Slider said. 'A junior minister at the amazingly young age of twenty-eight. Which would mean he was born in 1970.'

'If we—'

'I did,' Slider anticipated. 'I phoned Mrs Brissan. March 1970, she said, according to the Parliamentary *Who's Who*.'

'A lot of people must have been born in March 1970,' said Swilley. 'Was he adopted?'

'I don't know. It doesn't say.'

'It would be a large size in coincidences,' Atherton said.

'Maybe not so very large,' Slider said. 'When girls gave up their babies for adoption in those days, they were asked if they had any stipulations about the adoptees – religion or particular interests or whatever. And the stipulations were followed when possible. Phoebe Agnew might well have stipulated that her child must go to politically conscious parents. It was the biggest thing in her life, then as later. And since she was an intelligent white girl, there would have been a lot of competition for her baby, so the agents would have been able to be choosy.'

'Okay so far,' Atherton said cautiously.

'Tyler's father comes from an old Nottinghamshire family, and his parents lived at Stanton-on-the-Wolds, which is less than ten miles from Nottingham. And Richard's the only child. If they couldn't have children of their own, and applied to adopt, they'd have filled Phoebe's requirements perfectly. I know it's all speculation, but it fits.'

Atherton wrinkled his nose. 'You think she started doing the biography as an excuse to find out if he was her son?'

'I don't think so,' Slider said. 'Why should she ever begin to wonder if he was? No, I would suspect it was the other way round. He was her biography choice because he was hot. Then, as she went into his background, she started to have her suspicions.'

'Another long coincidence?'

'Not coincidence – concurrence,' Slider said. 'People with the same interests tend to end up in the same place. Tyler was brought up by a political family, so he went into politics. That's natural. And he had the talent – that might be hereditary. Phoebe Agnew was a political creature and ended up in the same general circle, which is not, after all, such a large one that everyone doesn't know everyone else. And then she picked on Tyler for sound commercial reasons. Not coincidental at all, when you think of it – inevitable, rather.'

'She might also have been attracted to him without knowing why,' Swilley said. 'I read an article that said you are naturally attracted to people who look a bit like you.'

'Explains a lot about incest,' said Atherton. 'Does he look like her?'

'I've never studied him closely enough to find out. That's the thing about recognising people. You have to know what you're looking for before you see it,' Slider said.

'But I don't see how it helps us,' Atherton sighed. 'Why should anyone kill her for being Tyler's mother? And what about Piers? Where does he come into it?'

'Besides, boss,' Swilley said. 'I've just thought – it couldn't have been Tyler she did supper for, because Medmenham said when he spoke to Piers on the Thursday evening, he said his new lover had been with him all day and had only just left.'

'Yes, he did say that,' Slider said. 'But I've looked at the notes on our interview with Piers, and he told us that Tyler left on the Thursday morning. I wonder whether he told Piers to say he was there all day, in case he needed an alibi. But Piers was such a plonker he forgot by the time we came to see him.'

'What would he want an alibi for?' Atherton said. 'We know whoever ate the meal didn't kill her, because Josh Prentiss was there afterwards.'

'He might just not want anyone to know she was his mother. She wasn't exactly an asset, was she?'

'I don't know – eminent, prize winning journalist, all the right political connections—'

'But with a wild past, a scruffy lifestyle, and in any case not as eminent and respectable as his parents. And some people still think there's a stigma about being adopted,' said Slider.

Norma shook her head. 'I can't see her telling, if he didn't want her to. Why would she?'

'Are you kidding?' Atherton said, 'It would be a bombshell for her biography – certain best-sellerdom.'

'Yes, but she wouldn't sacrifice her own kid for money like that.'

Atherton snorted, and Slider intervened calmly. 'Still, he might want to keep any contact between them to a minimum, and it would probably cause comment if it was known he had been at her house. I can see how he might want that kept secret.'

'I suppose clearing up who ate the meal would be a help to us, even if he wasn't the murderer,' Atherton said. 'What are you going to do, guv?'

'Ask him, I suppose,' said Slider. 'If I'm right about this, and it was him she cooked supper for, he might have some other information that would explain the connection between the two murders.'

Atherton boggled. 'You're going to ask Richard Tyler – *the* Richard Tyler – if he's the illegitimate son of Phoebe Agnew?'

'Why not?'

'Lions' den time,' Atherton said. 'Sooner you than me.'

CHAPTER TWENTY-ONE

Red Slayer

It took a long time to get hold of Richard Tyler. Given the difficulties Slider had already caused by his pursuit of Giles Freeman, he felt he ought to clear it through Porson before he tackled him. He told Porson he just wanted to talk to Tyler about Piers Prentiss – background stuff, to see if he said anything that could suggest a connection between the two murders. He said nothing about any of the other possibilities he was pondering. If they were put up front, he'd never get an interview at all.

Everyone else had gone home by the time the phone rang with his permission. Tyler would see him that evening in his private office at the House. Slider received the news without joy. He had spent the waiting time making other enquiries and piecing things together, and for the last half-hour had been sitting alone and thinking, and his thoughts had brought him only darkness. He collected up his papers, shoved them into a folder, and went out. It was getting colder, as forecast. He looked up automatically to see if the sky was clearing, but of course in the middle of Town, with the street lights, you couldn't see the sky at night. Clouds or stars, they were equally hidden. The weather was what happened – you weren't allowed to predict it.

He was shown into Tyler's office at exactly nine-thirty. Tyler was standing behind his desk, talking on the telephone while with the other hand he flicked through a pile of papers. His eyes registered Slider and he nodded, and freed his hand to gesture to the large leather chair on the other side of the desk, without breaking the rhythm of his speech.

Slider had a few moments to study him. The general look of Tyler was familiar to him from newspapers and the television screen, but of course in the flesh people have details to be taken in which make them quite different, close up, from their image. The rather long, smooth, pale face, and the dark brown hair slicked back with gel were what he knew, together with the exquisite suiting and elegantly dashing silk tie. What was new was that he was much taller than Slider had expected, and broad at the chest – Slider had gained an impression of slenderness from the TV, but Tyler was quite well built, and what he had taken to be padding in the shoulders was all him. The television also didn't do justice to the remarkably beautiful, luminous hazel eyes, or the firmness of the wide, narrow-lipped mouth. He had read descriptions of Tyler as 'feline' but that didn't really cover it. Feral, he thought; and ruthless. He was apparently very popular with women, and Slider could see why: he'd provide a safe but exciting ride, and look very, very good to be on the arm of.

Chronologically he might have been twenty-eight, but there was something in this man which had never been young, was as old as ambition itself. Close to, there was a hint of fox in the hair, though it was hard to see under the gel, and a spark of red in the eyebrows; and there were freckles on the backs of the pale hands. Large hands, they were, bony and strong, undecorated except for a thin, old gold ring on the left little finger. The fingers of the right hand drummed a moment impatiently on the desk as he spoke into the telephone, and then snapped a paper over with a sharp sound. Strong fingers, with short-cut, well-kept nails. Very clean.

He put the phone down at last. 'Well, Inspector, what can I do for you?' he asked uninvitingly. He looked at his watch. 'I can't give you long.'

'In that case,' said Slider, rousing himself from the clutches of his thoughts, 'I'll be direct.'

'I wish you would.'

'I'd like to know where you were on Thursday the twenty-first of January. Thursday week past.'

Tyler's eyebrows went up. 'That is not what you are supposed to ask.'

'You agreed to talk about Piers Prentiss,' Slider said, 'so I assumed you wouldn't mind telling me that.'

Tyler seemed to consider. 'Well, if you already know that I was with Piers all day that Thursday—' he began.

Slider interrupted. 'Ah, yes, I know that's what he was supposed to say,' he said apologetically, 'but you know Piers –
or rather, you did. I'm afraid he blurted it all out. About you
leaving on Thursday morning. He managed to remember to
tell Peter Medmenham that you were with him all day, but by
the time I went to talk to him, he'd forgotten your instructions.'

The really scary thing, Slider thought, was how little impact any
of this had on Richard Tyler's expression. His face remained
impassive, his eyes bright and thoughtful. Whatever he would
do, he would do, Slider felt. You might as well try and talk a
lion out of eating you.

'I think you'd better leave,' was what he did eventually say.

'Oh no, don't say that! Because we've got so much to talk
about. Look, to save you trouble, I'll tell you that I know
you were at Phoebe Agnew's flat on Thursday. You left your
fingerprints behind.'

'Impossible!' he said quickly.

Slider leaned forward a little. 'Because you wiped them all
away?'

'Because I wasn't there.'

'Well, I admit you did a very good job,' Slider went on, as
if he hadn't spoken. 'You've got a wonderful intellect and a
photographic memory, as I've been told by several people.
You made a mental note of everything you touched so that
you could wipe it afterwards. You even had the wit not to
wipe the whisky glasses, which you knew you hadn't used, so
that any prints there would incriminate someone else – Josh
Prentiss, as it happens. You know Josh, of course?'

Something did stir in the amber depths then; but Tyler said
calmly, 'You are talking complete drivel. Your statement is
a nonsense for the simple reason that you do not have my
fingerprints to compare with any you might have found at
the flat.'

'You're right, of course. I'm just assuming the rogue set –
the set that doesn't belong to anyone else – is yours. And you
won't refuse to give me your prints for comparison, will you?'

'Certainly I refuse.'

'Oh. That makes things difficult. I can, of course, bring
pressure to bear on you, but I wouldn't like to do that. It's
much better if you do the thing voluntarily. Much better for

your reputation as an MP to be seen to be helping the forces of law and order. And, after all, why shouldn't you have supper at Phoebe Agnew's flat? Nothing wrong with that, is there? She was your mother, after all.'

'I don't know what you're talking about,' Tyler said, but he sat down, rather slowly, behind his desk, and Slider felt a tired surge of triumph. If he really didn't know, he'd have thrown Slider out. But he wanted to hear – to know what Slider knew.

'Your date of birth and that of Phoebe Agnew's illegitimate child are the same. She gave her son to be adopted and the order went through the Nottingham County Court. Your parents lived in Nottinghamshire, and you were their adopted child. That's as far as I've got at the moment, but tomorrow I shall get a reply from the County Court records office and the two ends will be brought together, so it would be a waste of time for you to deny it. And why should you? She was a mother to be proud of, wasn't she? A very fine journalist and a woman of intellect.'

'Go on,' said Tyler, without emphasis.

'Oh – well, all right. I suppose she discovered your identity in the course of researching for her biography of you – did you know about that, by the way?'

'No. I had no idea she was intending to write one.'

'I suppose she told you about it when she invited you to supper?' No answer. 'We have your finger-marks, you remember. On the unit in her sitting-room, the one under the window that the hi-fi sits on. I suppose you must have leaned on it when you poured coffee or something.' He demonstrated on the edge of the desk with his hand. 'Palm and four fingers.'

Behind the bright eyes a reel was being replayed. Slider's information was tested against memory. Tyler sighed, just faintly, and said, 'Since you seem to know so much, I will admit that she telephoned me at the office to invite me to supper. I refused, naturally, and then she said she had some important information that she had uncovered while researching my biography. Given her reputation as a journalist, I was inclined to give her credence, but I told her she must tell me what it was about there and then. She was unwilling at first, but when I threatened to put the phone down, she told me the same story that she seems to have sold to you, about her being my real mother – which is absolutely not true, by the way.' So, Slider thought, he's going to play the end game. 'I'm afraid the poor woman was demented. I don't know what was wrong with her, but I do seem to have an extreme effect on some women. She was obviously obsessed with me, but I think there was already some mental instability, and I've heard she drank very heavily. At any rate, I told her she was mistaken and put the phone down very firmly. And that's all I know.'

Slider shook his head slightly. 'I'm afraid that's not true.'

Tyler continued impatiently, 'It is a matter of public record that I was in the House on Thursday night. There was an important division at seven-thirty and the whips were out. You will find my name entered amongst the Ayes. I think that must be conclusive enough evidence even for you.'

'Yes, I know you voted. I've checked that,' Slider said. 'Of course you left her alive. You dashed up to Westminster for the division, to make sure you were known to be at the House. But you weren't there earlier. It's an easy place to dodge around and not be seen in, so that even if no-one could swear to having seen you, no-one could swear you weren't there. You were in the division lobby at seven-forty, as everybody knows. And then you went back to Phoebe Agnew's flat.'

'Absolute rubbish. I'm not going to listen to any more of this,' Tyler said, but he didn't move. His shining eyes were fixed on Slider, and for all his experience, Slider couldn't tell what he was thinking or feeling. Perhaps all it was was vanity, the desire to hear himself talked about.

'You were there at the flat with Phoebe at a quarter to nine when Piers telephoned her. Piers told me all about it.'

'Piers couldn't possibly have known—'

'That you were with her? Why, because she didn't mention your name?'

'No, because I wasn't there,' he said calmly.

'While he was on the phone to Phoebe, he heard your pager go off in the background.'

'One pager is exactly like another,' Tyler said.

'Not quite. Each type has a different bleep. Obviously there are lots like yours, but the bleep he heard was that sort. He recognised it. He'd heard it before when he was with you. It troubled him so much when he finally remembered hearing it, because he couldn't think what you were doing there. Did he ask you on Sunday – this last Sunday, I mean? Did he put his worries to you?'

'Be careful what you say,' Tyler said. 'Be very careful.'

'Oh, I'll be careful. And there are no witnesses to this meeting, so it doesn't matter anyway, does it? But I have checked with your office, and they did call you on the pager at a quarter to nine that evening. Because no-one knew where you were – they thought you were in the House, but they couldn't find you. It's all making sense, isn't it?'

'Not the slightest. So what was I doing at the flat on this extraneous second visit, in your fevered imagination?'

'Phoebe Agnew had told you on your first visit what she wanted you to know – the thing that was troubling her so desperately for the last few weeks of her life. You had to dash off for the division, because there was a three-line whip, as you've agreed. But you couldn't leave it there. All the way up to Westminster you must have been thinking about the implications of what she said, and realising that if it ever got out, your career would be over. So you went back and killed her.'

Tyler gave a shout of laughter. 'What? Oh, this is very entertaining. I'm glad I granted you this interview. Go on. When you've finished, I'm going to have you removed, and I think you'll find your career is pretty well over, but I'd like to know how far your imagination stretches.'

'You were careful,' Slider said. 'You telephoned her to make sure she was alone – I've checked the records of your mobile, and the call is there. Afterwards you wiped away all your finger-marks – you even remembered to wipe the flush-handle of the loo, which was pretty smart of you, because that's one that's usually forgotten. There was just the one on the unit you missed, but no-one's perfect, are they? And you collected all the paperwork on yourself, which you'd got her to show you on the first visit – I suppose that's why you stayed to supper, wasn't it, to give you time to make sure you found out everything she had on you.'

'More,' said Tyler, leaning back in his chair. 'This is fascinating.'

'Unfortunately for you, you were seen leaving the second

time. By two people. One of them saw you walking down the street re-tying your tie – the one you used to strangle her. He said you had a file or newspaper or something under your arm – the missing file, I suppose. Destroyed now, I imagine?'

'Imagine is right.'

'The other person saw you actually coming out of the house. Interestingly, she mistook you for Josh. And she was the one that moved the body, by the way. It must have been a terrible shock to you when you read the details of how the body was found.'

Something glinted in the depths of the golden eyes. 'Go on,' he said, but he wasn't laughing now.

'There's not much more,' Slider said, dully. He was very tired now. 'The next day, as soon as the news broke, you telephoned Piers to tell him to keep your relationship secret, just in case anyone put two and two together. But in the end you decided you couldn't afford to take the risk. If it got out, it would be the end of you. And Piers had confided his inconvenient worries to you. So Piers had to go as well.'

'Why on earth should I worry about my relationship with Piers being known?' Tyler said loftily. 'I am quite comfortable with my sexual orientation, and so, I can assure you, is the Party.'

'Yes, I know that,' Slider said. 'But they wouldn't be so happy about incest, would they? That's almost the last taboo, really, when you think of it,' he added conversationally. 'That, and possibly necrophilia.'

Tyler sat very still, staring at him, not in fear or anxiety, but it seemed in deep thought.

Into his silence, Slider went on. 'There were one or two little clues that put me on to it. Small things. Josh Prentiss's first name is actually Richard. He was called Josh to distinguish him from his father, another Richard. He and Phoebe Agnew had one sexual encounter, when they were both the worse for drink, at a post-finals party in June 1969 – that was when you were conceived. But afterwards Josh was quick to repudiate the encounter, and he was already attached to Anona Regan, Phoebe's best friend. So she didn't tell him. She never told him, in fact, just went away quietly, had the baby, and gave it up for adoption.

'I don't know whether she harboured a secret love for Josh

all her life, or if she was just chastened by the experience. But after that she never let herself get attached to anyone. She concentrated on her career, and had casual affairs. But I imagine parting with her child was a deep vein of hurt. Then in the course of researching your biography, she discovered the truth about who you were. That was enough to make her thoughtful, but not deeply unhappy – after all, you were doing well in your chosen career, and she must have been glad to know how you had turned out. But then the unthinkable happened. You started an affair with Piers – he blurted it out to her at Christmas, even though you had impressed on him it was to be kept secret. Ironic, isn't it, that the only person he told was the one who really mattered.'

'Ironic,' Tyler said tonelessly.

'Though I dare say she would only have been the first of many – not the world's most discreet man. Anyway, it was from that time that she became more and more anxious, started drinking heavily, obviously wondering whether it would be worse to tell you or not tell you. At a dinner party at New Year, she tried to persuade Piers to give you up, but he was deeply smitten, and wouldn't hear of it.'

'Piers was very attached to me – and I to him,' Tyler said, with a creditable attempt at a little break in the voice.

'Yes, I can believe that,' Slider said. 'A colleague of mine remarked that people are often attracted most to the people who resemble them. And really, now I come to examine you, you do look more like your uncle Piers than your father Josh. That's often the way, isn't it – that children resemble their parents' siblings more than their parents. Same genes, different mix.'

Tyler wasn't looking at him. He sat very still, staring past Slider's head at the silk-covered wall.

'Finally, when it seemed that the relationship between you and Piers was not going to go away, she decided to break the silence of a lifetime and tell you. She thought if she told you the awful truth, you would simply break things off with Piers. But she couldn't resist having you to herself for a little while first. Doing for you what mothers do for their children, what she had never done for anyone – cook. She was so happy that day – a perilous sort of happiness, but still. I'm glad you gave her that, at any rate.'

Tyler's lips quirked and he made a curious gesture – almost a 'don't mention it' of the hand.

'You had to hurry away for the division, and while you were away you started to think of the danger to your career if ever any of this got out. You're a rising star, with everything before you. Someone even said to me you could be the youngest ever prime minister. You could kiss all that goodbye if ever the story were known. You could kiss your job goodbye, come to that – this is a government that won't stand for any scandal, as you of all people must know. Phoebe said she'd never tell, but could you trust her? And what would she write in that damned biography of hers? You realised then that there'd be no peace for you while she lived.'

A clock on the bookshelf struck tinklingly. Tyler had been slumped in thought. Now he looked up. 'Division,' he said.

'I've nearly finished,' Slider said. 'There's only Piers left now. The how of that's easy. He was always ready to see you, any time. And he would be easy enough to persuade to go over to the shop. I suppose you didn't want to be killing him with the dogs around. Did you take the opportunity to look round the house for any incriminating letters or documents? Was that why you shut the dogs in the kitchen? Oh,' he remembered, 'by the way, it was you that took the photograph of Phoebe with Piers and Josh from his sitting-room on the Thursday, wasn't it? To study her features, was it, to see if there was any likeness?'

'I have to go,' said Tyler.

'Piers was unlucky, really – there'd have been no need to kill him if he hadn't been your lover. Were you sickened by the thought that he was your uncle, and what you'd done with him? Once he was dead and gone, the fact that you'd ever slept with him could be forgotten, couldn't it? But I wonder if he would have been the last. What about Josh? Phoebe swore he never knew, but could you rely on that? And who else might have known? A secret has so many threads, trying to eradicate it is like trying to root out ground elder. You could have been embarking on a lifetime of murder.'

Tyler stood up. It seemed an effort; but once he was on his feet, he took control. His shoulders seemed to square, his face to firm. Ruthlessness did not come and go. You either had it, or you didn't.

'You are absolutely insane,' he said, 'and while it's been an experience to listen to you, I must warn you that to repeat any of this will bring the full force of the law down on your head. You have absolutely no evidence whatsoever for any of this nonsense.'

Slider looked up at him. 'She scratched you while you were strangling her. Such a slight scratch you might not even have noticed it, but we got enough tissue from under her nails for a DNA sample. I take it you wouldn't object to giving us a blood sample for comparison?'

Tyler's lips parted, but he said nothing.

'And you see, now we know who we're looking at, we'll get more evidence. You can't come and go around London without being seen. And the investigation into Piers's death is only just beginning. They'll find traces of you there.'

'You're mad,' Tyler said at last.

'No. I wish I were. On my way here, I thought perhaps I was, but now I've seen you, I know. If I was wrong, you'd have thrown me out long ago. But you had to hear me out, didn't you? Not only to find out what I knew, but because you love being the centre of attention.'

'You'll never make a case of this,' Tyler said, with absolute certainty.

'Won't I?' Slider stood up. 'Well, maybe I won't. But the main thing is, you know that I know. So if you should have any more thoughts about eliminating people who might know your secret, you'll put them aside quietly, won't you – the thoughts, I mean, not the people?'

And suddenly, shockingly, Tyler laughed; a big, ringing laugh like a golden bell. From a man who was invincible, who could fly. 'But you would be number one on that list, wouldn't you?' he said.

Slider only shook his head slightly, and turned away. There were a few seconds as he crossed the room to the door when his back was to Tyler, and the hairs on the back of his neck stood on end, wondering if there would be a silent rush of catlike feet behind him, and a soft, deadly blow, or two big white hands round his throat. But he made himself plod on without flinching, and then the doorknob was in his hand, and he was out and free.

And he told himself not to be silly, of course the man wouldn't kill him right there in his office. Or, indeed, at all. His fear was just the effect of mighty charisma on the mediocre man, that was all.

Porson was inclined to agree with Richard Tyler, that Slider had no evidence, that he was raving mad, and that it would never stick together into a case.

'The fact that he heard me out,' Slider said, swaying with weariness and emotional reaction, 'and the fact that he hasn't blown the Department sky high, point to his guilt. He ought to be screaming writs by now. The Home Secretary should be threading tiny cubes of me onto a skewer for kebabs. But he's said nothing.'

'He probably hadn't found a calculator with enough digits to work out the damages he's going to get,' Porson said. 'Don't count your chickens! When he gets a moment to spare he's going to hang your balls out to dry on the biggest, longest washing line in the world. And,' he added before Slider could speak, 'when he's finished, I'm going to have my turn in the laundromat. What the hell came over you? How could you go in there like that with this cockatoo story without checking it with me first? How long have you been in the Job? Have you forgotten everything you ever learned about proper procedure?'

'I didn't see how I could get any further with procedure,' Slider said. 'So I just had to face him with it to see if I was right. And I was thinking of Josh Prentiss. I couldn't be sure he wouldn't be next. This man is totally ruthless.'

Porson shook his head, lost for words.

'We'll get other evidence, sir. The DNA. The finger-marks. The street sightings. His phone records. He has no alibi. And we can prove that the relationship existed.'

'I don't think you understand,' Porson said, with a patience that was more unnerving than his rage. 'Whatever you can prove about his relationship with the deceased or anybody else, or even his presence in the flat, you can't prove he killed her. It may be very heavily suggested by the circumstantials, but this is one case above all that the CPS won't take on without a cast-iron confession-plus-evidence. Even if you had a video of him actually in the act, I doubt if they'd touch it.'

'You mean, some people are above the law?' Slider said resentfully.

'No, just that sometimes you can't punish them in the normal way.' He eyed Slider a moment, thoughtfully. 'If you can convince me and I can convince the Commander, action will be taken. His career will be over, I promise you that. And that'll be as much punishment to a bloke like him as being banged up in the pokey.'

Unfortunate choice of words, Slider thought, with a tired surge of humour. But the old boy perhaps wasn't far wrong. And at the moment it was hard to care. Porson saw the heaviness of his eyes, and said, 'Go on, get off home now. And don't dilly-dally on the way.'

Slider hadn't a dilly or a dally left in him. He turned without a word and went.

The lights were still on downstairs in Atherton's *bijou* residence. Slider had remembered he still had to tell him about Furlong Stud and thought he might as well get all the pain over at once. When the door was finally answered, and Atherton stood there, framed by the light, Slider got it out quickly in a blurt.

'Look, I'm sorry to have to tell you this, but I've had some research done on your racehorse thing, and it turns out it's a scam.'

He got that far before he realised that Atherton wasn't listening – that there was, indeed, something far wrong with his friend. Was he drunk? Ill?

'Are you all right?' he asked.

Atherton didn't speak, only stepped back and sideways to let him in, shutting the door behind him. Everything in the little sitting room looked the same – no immediate evidence of doom or calamity. Slider turned again. 'What's up? You look funny.'

'It's Oedipus,' Atherton said.

'Still not come back? Well, don't worry too much. I'm sure he'll turn up.'

Atherton shook his head. 'I found him in the garden. Under the ceanothus.'

'Found him?' Slider registered the passive nature of the verb.

Atherton nodded. His mouth, shut tight, seemed to be a

strange shape; and then Slider saw with rippling horror that he was crying.

'He just – he just – crept away and died,' Atherton gasped, and then he sat down in the nearest seat and buried his face in his hands.

Slider sat, too, and waited a long time. The pain of seeing Atherton cry was very bad. It was the end, he realised, of something that had begun a long time ago, at the point of Gilbert's knife, or perhaps even before. Who knew how any of them paid the debt? It had to come out somewhere, the cost of the Job.

When the crying had eased a bit, he laid a hand on Atherton's rigid shoulder, and pushed a handkerchief into his fingers, and then went into the kitchen and took his time finding a couple of glasses and pouring some whisky, to give him time to mop up.

When he came back, Atherton looked pale and exhausted. He took the glass without a word and drank half of it.

Slider said, 'Where is he? Do you want me to deal with it for you?'

Atherton shook his head. 'Thanks. But, no, I have to do it. He was my—' He couldn't quite manage the end of the sentence.

'What will you do?' Slider asked after a bit. Atherton's back garden was tiny.

'I'll dig up the ceanothus and put it back afterwards. It was where he liked to sit.'

Slider nodded, and they drank in silence for a little while.

At last Atherton roused himself. 'You sorted it.'

'The case?'

'Nicholls phoned me.'

'Oh. Well, I don't know. It's not really sorted.' He was too tired to go into it now. He waved a hand. 'I'll tell you tomorrow.'

'Yeah. You'd better get home.'

'Do you want me to help you with—?'

'No. I have to do it. I'll do it tomorrow. Thanks, though.'

Slider eyed him. 'I don't like leaving you. Are you going to be all right?'

'Christ, it's only a cat,' he said roughly.

'No, it isn't,' said Slider. 'You should have someone with you.'

Atherton looked away. 'D'you think – if
would come?'

ged not to smile. 'She never goes to bed very
she?' he said seriously. 'Give her a ring.'

I will,' Atherton said.

ng into his car Slider thought, there are just some times
en what a boy really needs is his mum.

anna was asleep when he got in, for which he was grateful.
He didn't think he could bear another word, question or even
sidelong look. He cleaned his teeth with a minimum of fanfare
and slipped delicately into bed beside her, and she turned with
a warm, woolly murmur into his arms but didn't wake.

But despite his tiredness, sleep didn't come to him. He lay in
the tide of Joanna's breathing, feeling the world turn with him,
big and slow, easing round the dark side; and thought of the
people whose lives he had stumbled into, and whose pains and
faults clung to him like sticky cobweb. He had achieved nothing,
solved nothing, saved nothing; and that it had all been done for
worldly ambition, without pity or humanity, exhausted him, as
evil always had the capacity to do. It was Phoebe Agnew who
came back again and again, and he wished he had not seen
her face, discoloured and suffused. He was glad he hadn't seen
Piers dead – at least he'd been spared that.

The Greeks thought patricide the worst sin. Well, let's hear it
for matricide! For Phoebe Agnew, a woman he had never met.
Her life had stopped when she parted with her baby: having
declined motherhood she could not properly enter adulthood,
but was doomed to go on repeating the same few lines over
and over again, the ultimate perpetual student; growing older
but never really up, until the day came when she met him again,
and the circle was closed.

Josh Prentiss, a vain man, in love with his own youth, might
well find the student irresistible; and if they hadn't actually had
sex together all those years, well, that was the least of it. Noni
had grieved that it had always been Phoebe, and perhaps she
wasn't far wrong after all. Did Josh know, really, even if only
subconsciously, how Phoebe felt? That he was the one man
she had ever loved? Ha!

But he wished he didn't have an image of her, flushed and

excited with her bagful of shopping, wa
to supper, her lost child. What had she ev
save his life? And so he took hers. If you listen
you can hear the gods laughing.

He fell at last into an exhausted sleep, too dead fo
and woke with a start to find it was daylight. Wrong,
his head shouted. He must have slept in.

'I let you sleep in,' said Joanna. 'You were dead to
world.'

He struggled up to sitting position. She was standing by the
bed, in her dressing-gown, holding a mug from which a snippet
of steam arose, like the irresistible wisp that used to drag the
Bisto kids along to the haven of kitchen, mum and gravy. Oh,
bugger, he had to stop thinking about that.

'Tea,' she said.

He took the mug and thanked her with a croak. She sat down
on the edge of the bed with a serious look, and the functioning
bit of his brain shouted *Uh-o, trouble! Bad talk coming!*

'Bill,' she said, 'I've been thinking. About this job offer of
mine. No, wait,' she lifted a hand. 'Don't say anything. The
fact of the matter is, I realise I haven't really been fair on you.
Whether I take the job or not is absolutely my decision, and it
was unfair of me to expect you to take responsibility for it. You
can't make up your mind about the situation until I've made up
mine, otherwise it's like me asking you to decide for me. So I've
thought and thought, and I've taken the plunge.'

'Uh?' was all he managed to get out from his matted brain
via his matted mouth.

She smiled a tense smile, as of one who has screwed herself
up to the sticking point. 'I've decided what I'm going to do,'
she said.